PUBLISHERS' PREFACE.

For thirty-one years, this book has met popular favor, and a sale of *one hundred and sixty thousand copies*. Its sale now is steadily increasing, notwithstanding the worn condition of the plates.

This 35th edition, now printed from new plates, is offered, believing it will outlive its fifty-six years of copyright.

But few works of fiction are accredited with such favor, or with such extensive circulation.

THE

WHITE ROSE

OF

MEMPHIS:

𝔄 𝔑𝔬𝔳𝔢𝔩.

BY

W. C. FALKNER.

"Stone walls do not a prison make,
Nor iron bars a cage ;
Minds innocent and quiet take
That for an hermitage ;
If I have freedom in my love,
And in my soul am free,
Angels alone that soar above,
Enjoy such liberty."

Richard Lovelace.

M. A. DONOHUE & COMPANY

CHICAGO   NEW YORK

Windham Press is committed to bringing the lost cultural heritage of ages past into the 21st century through high-quality reproductions of original, classic printed works at affordable prices.

This book has been carefully crafted to utilize the original images of antique books rather than error-prone OCR text. This also preserves the work of the original typesetters of these classics, unknown craftsmen who laid out the text, often by hand, of each and every page you will read. Their subtle art involving judgment and interaction with the text is in many ways superior and more human than the mechanical methods utilized today, and gave each book a unique, hand-crafted feel in its text that connected the reader organically to the art of bindery and book-making.

We think these benefits are worth the occasional imperfection resulting from the age of these books at the time of scanning, and their vintage feel provides a connection to the past that goes beyond the mere words of the text.

As bibliophiles, we are always seeking perfection in our work, so please notify us of any errors in this book by emailing us at corrections@windhampress.com. Our team is motivated to correct errors quickly so future customers are better served. Our mission is to raise the bar of quality for reprinted works by a focus on detail and quality over mass production. To peruse our catalog of carefully curated classic works, please visit our online store at www.windhampress.com.

WINDHAM PRESS
CLASSIC REPRINTS

THE WHITE ROSE

OF

MEMPHIS.

CHAPTER I.

"SPEAK it out, captain; I know by your looks you have something to say, and I am full of curiosity to hear it."

"Very true, my dear fellow; I have at last hit on a scheme which I think will prove very profitable, and will be glad to take you in as an equal partner."

"Glad to hear it; I am ready for anything to make an honest living."

"I have chartered the best boat on the river, and mean to put her to work on the line between here and New Orleans, and shall of course be her commander, and would be glad to have you take charge of the office, and we will divide profits."

"I am truly grateful, captain, for the manifestation of confidence contained in your offer, and will gladly undertake the business."

"Very good; then we may consider it settled so far. The next thing to be done is to get up a handsome advertisement, and meantime the boat must be re-painted, re-furnished and overhauled generally."

"Give the necessary instructions as to these things, captain, and draw on me for my share of the expenses. By the by, what boat have you chartered?"

"The 'Star of the West;' but I will have her name changed, as I do not like that one. What shall her new name be?"

(7)

"I leave that to you, and trust you will select a pretty name; there is nothing like having a pretty name for a pretty boat. Shakespeare was decidedly mistaken when he thought that there was nothing in a name."

"I agree with you there, Sam, and insist that you shall select the name."

"No, no; but I'll tell you what we will do: you write down three names, and I'll write three; we'll put them in a hat, and the first one drawn shall be her name."

"All right."

The names were written, placed in the captain's hat, and Sam was requested to draw out one.

"What have you got, Sam?" said the captain.

"The prettiest name that ever was seen on a wheel-house. You might have given me a month to think about it, and I never should have thought of such a sweet-sounding name."

"Well, what is it?"

"The White Rose of Memphis."

"I am truly glad to know that you think it a pretty name, and we will have the letters made in gold."

"When can we be ready to start, captain?"

"It will take six weeks to get everything ready. We must manage to make a grand display when we start on our first trip."

"You had better prepare the advertisement, then, and let it appear at once. Suppose we give a grand masquerade ball on board just before we start."

"Capital idea, Sam; we'll make the first trip one of pleasure, so as to attract the attention of the public. I'll prepare the advertisement at once."

The foregoing conversation was carried on between Captain Oliver Quitman and Samuel Brazzleman, two well-known and very popular steam-boat men of Memphis, whose experience in that business had won for them an established reputation for reliability and integrity.

The following advertisement appeared in one of the morning papers a few days after the conversation above related:

The new and splendid passenger boat, "White Rose of Memphis," has been purchased by Captain Oliver Quitman, and will be put on the line between Memphis and New Orleans. She will start on her first trip at 9 A. M., on May 1st, for the Crescent City, under the immediate command of her owner. Samuel Brazzleman will officiate at the clerk's desk, and Dave Halliman, at the wheel. The old reliable river man, Thomas Henderson, has agreed to take charge of the engine. Professor Frazzlebrains's splendid string band has been employed to make music for the amusement of the passengers. A grand masquerade ball will be given on board the "White Rose" on the evening of the 30th inst., and arrangements will be made to continue the amusement every night during the round trip. The grand saloon is eminently suited for dancing parties, and has been gorgeously furnished with everything necessary to make the passengers comfortable. It is the intention of the captain to make the first trip one of pleasure and amusement. Reduced rates will be given to excursion parties who may apply for them for the round trip.

This advertisement (as might be expected) created quite a sensation among the fair sex of Memphis, and added very greatly to the cash receipts of silk merchants and milliner shops; while it caused a corresponding shrinkage in the money bags of doting parents of marriageable daughters. Memphis was then, and is now, famous for the beauty of her women, and the muddiness of her streets. Cotton bales and pretty women seem to be a spontaneous production in and about Memphis, and, in spite of bad government and yellow fever epidemics, she is handsome and lively still.

"Well, Sam, old fellow, what do you think of the prospect?"

"Splendid! we have made a ten strike this time—every room has been engaged, and still they come."

"Is she not a beauty, Sam?"

"Never saw her match in my life. What's the time, captain?"

"Eight thirty, and time for the maskers to begin to arrive; by the by, here they come now. Has the music arrived?"

"Long, long ago, captain; everything is ready."

"Good, Sam; we must put our best foot foremost tonight; much depends on first impressions. Have you got plenty of wines and ice?"

"Oceans, oceans of all kinds."

This conversation occurred on board of the "White Rose," between Captain Quitman and Samuel Brazzleman, who were both rejoicing at the prospect of a remunerative trip, which was to begin on the next morning. Before nine o'clock the dazzling lights in the long saloon were streaming down on the vast crowd of maskers as they glided along through the mazes of the·dance; while soft, sweet sounds floated out on the night air. Fantastic costumes, sparkling jewels, white, blue and red plumes, rustling silk, shining satin, soft velvet, sparkling diamonds, high-heeled boots, splendid music, the popping of champagne bottles, the hum of many voices, the merry laughter, the brisk and graceful movement of charming women, were all contributing to the dazzling show. All kinds of costumes were to be seen, old-fashioned and new, gaudy and plain. Mary, Queen of Scots, with her rich, royal costume of Scotland, all bedecked with sparkling diamonds, was dancing with Ingomar, the Barbarian Chief, with his savage beard reaching to his waist, and his top-boots all shaded with gold. The knight of Ivanhoe, with his glittering armor on, was dancing with the first maid of honor, who wore blue silk, and yellow mask. Don Quixote, the Knight of Salamanca, dressed in shabby but quaint armor, was jumping high and awkwardly, as he danced with the second maid of honor, who was a graceful dancer, dressed in orange-colored silk with pink mask. Henry of Navarre, with his black plume waving high above the throng, was marching up and down the saloon with the queen of Sheba leaning on his arm. Sancho Panza, with his clownish costume, was playing the clown to perfection, to the great amusement of the children. The Duke of Wellington and Napoleon were taking a mint julep at the bar, while George III. was quarreling with Sam Brazzleman because he wouldn't tell him the name of the lady who represented the Queen of Scots.

"Positively against our rules to divulge the names of parties in mask, without their consent," says Sam.

"Well, does she reside in Memphis?"

"Can't answer; I tell you it is contrary to orders."

"Is she going to New Orleans on this boat?"

"Yes."

"Good! I'll find out who she is, if I follow her to the other side of the world!" and the imitator of the defunct tyrant made his way to where the mysterious queen stood conversing with her Barbarian Chief.

"Who is that lady dancing with Ingomar?" inquired George III. of Ivanhoe.

"Do not know; wish I did."

"I'll give a hundred dollars to know who she is."

"I'll go you halves," says Ivanhoe.

George III. and Ivanhoe were not the only ones who wanted to know who was personating the Scottish queen. It seemed to be a general desire among the male maskers to know who she was. It is hard to say what caused this general wish to know who she was. It might have been caused by a combination of circumstances. There appeared to be a desire on the part of the gentlemen to get near her. Was it the soft, sweet melody of her voice, or was it the queen-like grace of her movements? Perhaps it was the profusion of golden hair that fell, unconfined, beneath the quaint crown of sparkling jewels that graced her brow; or it may have been the little provoking, pretty foot that now and then made its appearance as she floated like a fairy over the floor. When she took her seat at the piano, and began to sing, while the rich, sweet voice rose until the saloon seemed to be filled with soul-stirring music, curiosity went up to fever heat, and George III. would have given his kingdom to know who she was. Ingomar, the Barbarian Chief, with his long, shaggy whiskers, stood near the queen, turning the music sheets as the song progressed, and occasionally stooping to whisper something in her ear, which she answered with a nod and a smile. As soon as the song was ended the knight of Ivanhoe requested Ingomar to present him to the queen. Ingomar in a low whisper asked her permission to present the knight of Ivanhoe, which was promptly granted.

"I have the honor, your Majesty, to present my distinguished and honorable friend, Sir Knight of Ivanhoe." A graceful bow and the queen held out her little white hand, which Ivanhoe pressed to his lips.

"Sir Knight, we are delighted to know you. Shall we have the pleasure of your presence during our excursion to New Orleans?"

"I am profoundly grateful for your Majesty's condescension, and shall be overjoyed at the privilege of making one of the party."

"To-morrow being the first day of May, our festivities will commence, and it is our royal pleasure, sir knight, that you shall attach yourself to our court during the trip."

"I cannot find language, my dear madame, to express my gratitude for the distinguished honor you confer upon me."

"Partners for a quadrille," rang through the saloon as the band struck up a lively tune. George III., the Duke of Wellington and Napoleon all made a dash toward the queen at once, each one anxious to secure her as a partner, but with a low bow and a sweet smile she turned to Ivanhoe, took his arm, and was soon gliding through the dance. The British King appeared to take his discomfiture rather hard, while Wellington looked somewhat chop-fallen; but Napoleon proposed that their sorrow should all be drowned in a bowl of punch, which was agreed to, and the trio marched to the bar to commence the drowning process.

"Devilish provoking," muttered George III.

"What's provoking?" says Wellington.

"That mysterious piece of humanity styling herself queen of Scots. I shall always hate masquerade balls after this. I don't think they are respectable at all."

"Come, come, your royal highness, you should not surrender at the first repulse; Ivanhoe has only gained a temporary triumph, and if you will come to the charge again with a brave heart, you may yet compel victory to perch on your banner."

"Ingomar had a monopoly until Ivanhoe leaped into the arena and carried off the prize, and I advise you to show a bold front. Strategy won't win in battles of love. If you expect to win, don't attempt to make a flank movement, but come boldly up to the front. Remember that 'faint heart never won fair lady.'"

"I don't want to win a fair lady, or any other kind of lady, until I know who she is."

"I guess you will find that out to-morrow, for she is going to New Orleans."

"True, but I learn that she means to make the entire trip incog."

"Impossible, sir, impossible; how can she remain on this

boat two or three weeks without being recognized by some one?"

"That's the question to be settled hereafter; she will have to play the game very cautiously, if she prevents me from finding out who she is. By the by, do you know who that savage-looking fellow is who personates Ingomar?"

"No, but you may be sure the queen knows him; did you notice how affectionately she leans on his arm, and how close she puts her mouth to his ear when she speaks to him?"

"Yes, to be sure I did; but she is now playing the same game on Ivanhoe."

"Who the deuce is Ivanhoe?"

"I don't know that either, and without meaning any discourtesy to you, I beg to say that I don't care a copper to know who he is."

"I hear that it is the intention of Ingomar and Ivanhoe to imitate the example of the queen by making the trip incog."

"By all means let them do it; and I suggest that we three do the same, and keep our names concealed from them, and we shall have rare sport. Don't you know that the ladies will die of curiosity if we conceal our names? Let us form a combination against them, look and talk mysteriously, and my word for it, propositions will be made for a treaty looking to a general disclosure of names and the discarding of masks."

"Capital idea, my lord, and you may depend upon my hearty co-operation. As soon as the boat leaves the wharf to-morrow let the war begin."

"Perhaps the captain will object to passengers going in disguise all the time."

"No; he told me that the queen intended to make the entire trip in mask, and that the same privilege would be extended to all who desired to avail themselves of it."

"Very good, very good; then the alliance, offensive and defensive, may be considered as ratified and confirmed."

"Charge, Chester, charge! and on, Stanley on!" said Wellington, as he drew the cork from a fresh bottle of champagne.

"Screw your courage up to the sticking point, my gallant king, and with the emperor and duke at your back, move on the enemy, unfurl your banner, cry 'havoc,' and let slip the dogs of war. Confusion and discomfiture shall overwhelm our foes."

"We must win the queen of Sheba to our side at all hazards, as I learn that she and her two maids of honor are going on the excursion."

"That shall be your task, then—to secure her co-operation. See her at once, and if she will join us, we will have an easy victory."

"You may depend on me for that," said the counterfeit king, as he started on his recruiting expedition. "I'll be back in a moment, and report progress. Meantime you and Napoleon mature the plan of the campaign during my absence."

George III. soon returned with a favorable report: "Her Majesty presents her compliments to the emperor, and my lord the duke of Wellington, and will be much gratified to have them enrolled as permanent members of her festive court, which will be convened on the hurricane deck at eleven o'clock A. M. to-morrow."

"Now you have her message *verbatim*," said the king, as he dove both hands into his pockets, with a self-satisfied look. "Won't we have rare sport? won't we make the enemy die of curiosity? We must organize thoroughly, and make a systematic siege, and if we don't capture the entire party before three days, take my hat and hang it on the tallest wave that rises behind the 'White Rose of Memphis.' We must seem to ignore the other party entirely—look and talk as if no such party were aboard; drop mysterious hints—about things that never were heard of, speak of love-making that we could tell more about if we would. Let all these hints be carelessly dropped in the hearing of some one of the other party, and you may be sure that they will sue for peace and union before we reach New Orleans. Should any one of the other party ask questions (which they will be sure to do) shake your head, look mysterious, shrug your shoulders, and heave a mournful sigh. Do you think the world ever produced a woman that could stand that? Would you believe it, the queen of Scots' first maid of honor is now half dead to know who I am? Can't I see how she has been watching me for the last hour?

I'll capture her the first thing to-morrow and employ her as a spy in the enemies' camp."

At last the ball ended, the guests departed, save those who had engaged passage for the grand excursion, and they had retired for the night, to dream of the sport to be enjoyed on the morrow, while Captain Quitman paced proudly on the hurricane deck, with heart swelling with satisfaction at the pecuniary prospects before him.

CHAPTER II.

The eventful and long-looked-for day on which the "White Rose of Memphis" was to start on her first trip had come at last, and a mighty stir, indeed, did that day produce on and under the tall, romantic bluff in front of Memphis. The morning was delightful, the atmosphere pure and invigorating, the sweet odor of fresh spring flowers was on the breeze, mingling with the soft notes of music produced by the band from the hurricane deck. The stars and stripes floated gracefully from the flag-staff, dark clouds of black smoke rose from the chimneys, a white cloud of steam struggled up through the black smoke and disappeared far above, innumerable drays rattled along the pavement, carriages thundered over the rocky road, carriage drivers swore at dray drivers, dray drivers returned the compliment with interest, in language not of a religious nature, deck hands sung "Dixie," cabin boys danced juber, chamber-maids darted hither and thither, apparently anxious to perform their duty, without the slightest conception of what that duty was. A villainous urchin, in the arms of his nurse, was making a heart-rending noise with a tin horn, and a passenger muttered something not taught at Sunday-school.

"Them's my sentiments to a T," said another man who had been annoyed with the tin horn.

As the hour drew near when the boat was to start the confusion increased. The pilot was at his wheel, the engineer was at his engine; Captain Quitman stood on the upper deck in front of the pilot house, looking happy, and feeling vastly important. Hundreds of men, women and children in holiday costumes stood on the bluff, shouting and waving white handkerchiefs to their friends on the boat. A mocking-bird in a cage on the boiler deck imitated every imaginable sound with his wonderful voice, while a parrot, perched on a pole near the clerk's office, kept crying, "Let her rip! let her rip, Sam!"

"How much steam have you got, Tom?" cried the pilot through his speaking-tube.

"One sixty, sir, and still rising."

"All right; blow off the mud valves and keep a good head; we must make a good run at the start."

"Time's up, Dave; let her go," said the captain. "Run her up to the mouth of Wolf, make a turn to the left, and then let her come down with her best speed."

"Let go the head line," cried the mate.

"Draw in the stage," says the captain.

"Go ahead on the larboard, and back on the starboard," cried the pilot to the engineer.

"Go ahead on the steward, and back on the cook-house," cries a mischievous little negro, who is dancing a jig in front of the pilot house.

The boat moves slowly up stream until a point opposite the mouth of Wolf river is reached, then makes a graceful curve to the left, and comes flying past the city with a speed never equaled by any other boat on that river. As the "White Rose" passed the last crowd on the bluff a tremendous shout rose from a thousand voices, which was answered by the throng of passengers who lined the deck of the boat. As the golden rays of the morning sun glanced down against the side of the boat, and played and danced with the painted glass of her cabin, a thousand dazzling streaks of light flashed back, presenting a sight of indescribable beauty. It was but a few moments until the boat passed round the bend below President's Island, and shut off from view the tall domes of the bluff city; but the fresh green foliage with which the tall trees were clothed presented a scene of beauty on which the beholders gazed with delight. As might have been expected, quite a sensation was created among the large crowd of passengers when a dozen or more men and women appeared on deck disguised with as many different and curious costumes. A murmur of dissatisfaction rose among some of the passengers, which threatened to produce trouble; but finally it subsided when the clerk announced the fact that all the maskers were well known to him, and that they were respectable people.

"How is your royal highness this morning?" said the Duke of Wellington, as he shook hands with George III.

"First rate, first rate, my lord. How is it with you?"

"Fine, fine, sir! Splendid day this! By the by, where is the emperor?"

"Here he is. Now let us commence the siege at once. I see her Majesty, the queen of Sheba, and her attendants, are waiting for us. The Scottish queen has marshaled her forces on the hurricane deck."

"How is that?" demanded the emperor.

"They have all taken seats in a circle, and seem determined to continue the selfish plan. Now we will take seats at a respectable distance from them—just so as to be in hearing distance, and begin the battle according to our original plan. Our object is to so rouse their curiosity as to force them to come to our side, or in other words, to induce them to come and mingle with us. A little skillful maneuvering on our part, and the victory is ours."

"Lead, lead, my gallant king! You shall be our commander in this fight. Take the queen of Sheba to the field, and the emperor and I will bring up the maids of honor, and then let the skirmishing begin."

A canvas had been put up above the hurricane deck and seats arranged under it, in order to afford passengers an opportunity to view the grand scenery without being exposed to the rays of the sun; and this spot had been selected as the field of action. The queen of Scots and her party were seated in a circle, near the stern of the boat, wholly unconscious of the hostile preparations which were being made by the queen of Sheba and her adherents. Ingomar was entertaining the queen and the ladies of her court with an eloquent description of the burning of the steam-boat "Bulletin," and the heart-rending scenes that were witnessed on that occasion. The queen of Sheba with her party was located about twenty feet from the spot occupied by the queen of Scots.

"Now," said George III., making a low bow to the queen

of Sheba, "what is your Majesty's pleasure? What is to be the fun to-day?"

"Social conversation and enjoying the beautiful scenery will occupy us till luncheon, and when we have had enough of that, we will then form our plans for the future."

"By the by," said Wellington with a loud voice, evidently intended to attract the attention of the Scottish queen's party, "have you heard the strange news?"

"No, no; what is it?"

"There are two detectives aboard in mask, on the look-out for the perpetrator of a diabolical murder that was committed near Collierville day before yesterday. They have tracked the man to this boat, and have satisfied themselves that he is aboard, and are prepared to arrest him. They have got a man spotted, and are going to take him off at Vicksburg."

"That's the best shot that ever was fired," whispered Napoleon.

"See," said the queen, "the shot has taken effect. They are all looking this way, and intently listening. They are dying to hear more. Give them another shot."

"What were the circumstances of the murder?" inquired Napoleon, as he raised his voice and winked at Wellington.

"Oh, it was a most horrible and cruel murder—it was a love affair. The deceased was a young and pretty girl; she had loved not wisely, but too well. Poison was the means used to produce death."

"There, there, Wellington," whispered Napoleon; "let 'em rest on that a while. They have all been gradually moving this way. They can't hold out much longer."

"Let me throw one more shell into their camp," whispered Wellington.

"All right; go ahead."

"There is a skillful pickpocket aboard of this boat, and those who have money had better be on their guard. One passenger has been relieved of a purse containing five hundred dollars. The pocket was cut clean off, and so skillfully done that the owner knew nothing about it until his attention was called to it by a friend. I fear that our amusements will all be interfered with, and that we shall be compelled to lay aside our disguises, because, whoever he is, you may be assured he is in mask."

"Good, good, Wellington!" said George III., in a whisper; "stop; you have got them completely demoralized, and we may safely wait for the result."

"Oh, mercy on us!" exclaimed one of Queen Mary's maids of honor, "we are in the midst of thieves and murderers! Didn't you hear that gentleman say that a bloody murder had been committed, and that a gentleman had been robbed, and that both criminals were aboard of this boat? Who knows but what we shall all be murdered and robbed!"

"Don't look toward them," said Wellington; "the last shot has mortally wounded the last one of the party." This sentence was whispered, so as not to be heard by the opposition.

Ivanhoe drew near Wellington and said: "Pardon me, sir, but I beg to inquire about this dreadful murder of which I heard you speak just now."

Wellington shrugged his shoulders, and gave a deep sigh. "Horrible! horrible; must cruel! unprecedented! but that's all I know about it." And with a knowing wink at George III., Wellington observed: "Look at that beautiful little island there. See what delightful foliage. How splendid it would be to have a picnic on that nice green turf under such a cool-looking shade!"

"Oh, wouldn't that be delightful!" said the queen of Sheba.

"We'll have a picnic to-morrow," said Napoleon. "The boat is going to take on a large lot of cotton just below Helena; and we will order the steward to prepare a picnic dinner, and we will have a dance, as well as a dinner."

Ivanhoe bit his lip with vexation as he returned to his party no wiser than when he left it.

"Hold your hand over my mouth, else I shall be compelled to laugh out," said the queen to her first maid of honor.

"Pray, don't laugh," cried the young lady; "it would cause them to suspect something."

"What did you learn about the murder?" inquired the queen of Scots, as Ivanhoe returned to his seat.

"Nothing," was the solemn reply. "They all seem to be an ill-mannered, ungenteel crew, and, for my part, I am inclined to think they have been making sport of us."

"I see through it all," said Ingomar gravely. "They are offended because we did not invite them to mingle with us. For my part, I am unwilling to notice such silly conduct. I like amusement well enough, but it must be such as sensible people may engage in. Allow me to suggest that we move to another place and inaugurate a regular systematic plan to while away our idle moments."

The suggestion was unanimously concurred in, and the entire party went to the front end of the boat, and soon were seated, leaving the other party overwhelmed with mortification.

"That is too bad!" exclaimed Napoleon; "we had won the victory, and lost it by all grinning at once. They have evidently seen our hand, and we have lost the game."

"Suppose we invite the other party to join us," said Ingomar. "If we expect to enjoy our trip, it would be advisable to dispense with the rigid rules of decorum and become acquainted with each other."

"Your sentiments are generous and noble, sir, and are heartily approved; and with your permission I will invite the other party to join us."

"Have I your permission, madame, to deliver the invitation?"

"Yes, and I trust it will be accepted."

Ingomar approached the spot where the queen of Sheba and her party were seated, and with a dignified bow said: "I am requested by my royal mistress, the queen of Scots, to present her highest regards to your Majesty, and request the pleasure of your company at her royal court. She further requests me to beg you to bring all the ladies and gentlemen of your party with you, in order that a friendly union may be entered into, for the better enjoyment of such festivities and pleasures as may be jointly considered worthy of well-bred and intelligent people."

"Right noble and worthy chief, most eloquently hast thou delivered the message of thy royal mistress, and it would be extreme rudeness for us to refuse to accept it. Therefore, we request you to convey to her Majesty our most distinguished regards, and inform her that her generous offer is accepted, and that it will be our pleasure to visit her festive dominions."

"My royal mistress will be delighted with the news." And as he said this he raised the queen's hand to his lips, then turned and delivered his message to the queen of Scots.

"I am going to laugh," said the first maid.

"Laugh as much as you please, now; it can do no harm; we are forever disgraced; we are beaten, overcome, captured!" said Wellington, as he clinched his fists with vexation.

"Is this the victory that we have been fighting for?"

"I call it a complete victory," said the queen. "Was it not the object of our plan to force them to invite us to join them, and have they not yielded? You may be sure they would never have given us the invitation had it not been for the bait which we threw out to them."

"I agree with your Majesty there," said George III. "We have accomplished the object for which we contended, and now let us join their party, and make ourselves agreeable."

"Be it so, then," replied Wellington, as he offered his arm to the queen and led her to where the other party were seated.

The two queens seemed to enter into a contest as to which should be considered most polite. The graceful bowing, the gentle hand-shaking, the sweet smiling, the high compliments, and general bearing, were such as might have been witnessed between Queen Victoria and the Empress Eugenie when they first met.

"Now," said Ingomar, addressing the two queens, "as I understand the object of this excursion to be one of pleasure and amusement, permit me to suggest that we organize ourselves into a sort of committee of the whole, and agree on some plan by which each hour of the day shall be furnished with some kind of innocent sport."

"We think the idea a good one, sir," replied Queen Mary, "and we appoint you and Ivanhoe as a select committee, whose duty it shall be to draft a set of rules or by-laws for the government of our court. We allow you one hour for the performance of that duty; meantime we will amuse ourselves by a promenade in the saloon."

Promptly at the expiration of the hour the queen ordered her court to convene on deck in order to hear the by-laws read.

"We are now ready to hear what you have written," said the queen, speaking to Ingomar.

"We have the honor to inform your royal highness that we have performed the duty assigned to us, and are now ready to report."

"Read the report, my noble chief."

Ingomar read as follows: "Whereas certain ladies and gentlemen of the good city of Memphis, State of Tennessee, have embarked on an expedition of pleasure, on board of the steam-boat known as the 'White Rose of Memphis,' and whereas the aforesaid ladies and gentlemen are desirous of contributing as much as they can to the happiness and pleasure of their comrades thereby, and by means whereof they expect to obtain innocent enjoyment for themselves and their associates, therefore be it remembered that on this, the first day of May, the following rules and regulations have been adopted, and the honor of each member pledged that said rules and regulations shall in all respects be complied with and faithfully obeyed, and that any one who shall be guilty of a willful violation of any one of the rules shall be considered disgraced and unworthy to be a member of this association, and shall be excluded therefrom:

"RULE 1st. Her Royal Highness, the queen of Scots, shall reign as the grand sovereign of this association.

"RULE 2d. It shall be the duty of the reigning sovereign to determine what shall be the plan of amusement for the day, and give orders accordingly.

"RULE 3d. No disrespectful language to be used by any member of this association.

"RULE 4th. The right of each member of this association to remain in disguise is recognized, and no one shall be questioned as to his or her real name without his or her consent.

"RULE 5th. None but harmless sport shall be proposed or indulged in."

"We think the rules very good," said the queen, "and we now propose their adoption. All who favor the rules make it known by saying aye. It is unnecessary to call for the nays, as the vote is unanimous in the affirmative—and the rules are adopted."

"Well," said Ingomar, "your Majesty will issue your commands for the day. What shall be the programme?"

"It is our royal pleasure that each member of the association shall be required to relate a story consisting of events, the truth of which are to be vouched for by the narrator. I dare say that each one will be able to tell something that will be both amusing and instructive. Love stories would be preferable; but no one shall be restricted as to that. Personal reminiscences of the party who may tell the story would be listened to, doubtless, with attention and pleasure. Therefore, it is our royal command that the Barbarian Chief, Ingomar, shall now proceed to relate a story."

"Ingomar! Ingomar! Ingomar! a story by Ingomar!" cried every one.

"It would have been more to my liking to have listened to others, may it pleasure your Majesty, but as it would be rank treason to disobey your command, I shall endeavor to comply, by relating the history of transactions, many of which came under my own observation in and near the city of Memphis. The substance of the story would no doubt be very interesting were it well told, but I greatly fear I shall bore you all by my awkward manner of telling it. But there will be a consolation in knowing that if you should become wearied of it, you can command me to stop, which order I beg to assure you I would more gladly obey than any other you could give."

"If your manner of telling the story is as modest and well spoken as the apology, we shall be very much delighted, I assure you. Therefore we command you to proceed."

"As the occurrences which I am about to describe all have an intimate connection with the city of Memphis, and as many of the persons who played prominent parts in the story are now residing there, I think it proper to inform my audience that the names used are fictitious. I could not for a moment think of parading the real names of the actors before the public without their consent."

"The idea is commendable, sir, and only serves to increase our anxiety to hear the story. Therefore we again command you to proceed."

"There's the gong for luncheon," cried Napoleon as he sprang to his feet. "Postpone the story until after refreshments."

"That's a splendid idea!" said Ingomar. "It will give me time to collect my ideas."

"Very well," said the queen. "We will assemble here immediately after lunch, to listen to Ingomar's story."

Ingomar led the queen of Scots to the saloon, while Wellington offered his arm to the queen of Sheba, and the party went down to lunch.

CHAPTER III.

THE arrangements which Captain Quitman had made for the accommodation of the large party of excursionists were of the most costly and liberal character, showing that neither labor nor money had been stingily expended. The spacious saloon had been gorgeously decorated by an experienced artist, while innumerable historical incidents and poetical scenes had been painted on the snow-white surface of the wall in front of each state-room. Three scenes in "Mazeppa" appeared first on the left as you entered from the front. The first picture represented the beautiful wild steed in the act of making a plunge forward, while Mazeppa is being bound to his back. The second scene represented the foaming steed as he bounded through the forest, with the large gang of wolves in pursuit; and the last showed the dying steed stretched on the ground, while a flock of vultures covered the surrounding space, ready to begin the work of destruction. The artist had executed the work so skillfully that one might almost imagine that he could hear the horse's hoofs as they thundered against the earth, and distinguish the hideous howl of the savage wolves. The next painting represented Achilles driving his chariot round the walls of Troy, dragging the helpless body of Hector by the heels, while the beauteous wife of the dead hero stood weeping on a distant tower, as she witnessed the horrible cruelty. Then a little farther down on the same side, we see Cleopatra seated in her magnificent gondola, gorgeously clad in her royal robes, surrounded by her officers and slaves, while she sails over the glittering surface of the water, where she goes to conquer a mighty warrior with her irresistible charms. We come next to a ludicrous scene representing Gulliver on the island of Lilliput, standing erect with his legs placed far apart, while twenty thousand Lilliputian cavalry, with the king and queen at their head, are marching between his huge legs. A beautiful representation of the burial of De Soto in the Mississippi river appeared farther on. Many other thrilling scenes appeared which we cannot spare time to describe.

So the guests marched into the spacious saloon. Professor Scatterbrains's band played a national air, the soft, sweet sounds filling the room with a delightful harmony. The gorgeous display of costly table-ware that adorned the festive board was such as one might expect to behold at a king's palace. Massive goblets of solid silver, tureens, pitchers, castors and fruit stands of shining gold, large china vases, filled with fragrant flowers, arranged in pairs from one end of the table to the other, while gilded china imported from the East, of various colors, green, yellow and blue, wrought in quaint but beautiful patterns, covered the snow-white cloth. Two beautiful thrones for the especial use of the two queens had been erected at the head of the table, one on the left, the other on the right, handsomely decorated with pink velvet cushions and canopied with blue cloth, richly studded with stars of silver and gold. The charming picture that met the eyes of the delighted guests caused an exclamation of delight to escape from the lips of many a beautiful belle, as they filed into the saloon.

As soon as all the passengers were seated, the captain, waving his hand toward the vast crowd by way of commanding silence, said:

"My young friends, if you wish to please me, and enjoy this excursion, I hope you will lay aside all feelings of restraint, become acquainted with each other, and engage in such innocent sport as is calculated to amuse and instruct. Julius Cæsar said:

> " 'Let me have men about me that are fat,
> Sleek-headed men who sleep o' nights.
> Yon'd Cassius has a lean and hungry look.
> He thinks too much; such men are dangerous.'

"Now, my young friends, the sequel proved that Cæsar was right in his dislike of the lean and hungry Cassius; give me friends who laugh and grow fat—men and women who can throw off the dull cares of life, and condescend to be pleasant and happy on occasions like this. There are times when man should be serious, but there are also times when he should be social and sportive. I have spent money and labor freely in order to complete the arrangements for the comfort and pleasure of my guests, and it will gratify me greatly to know that I have not made a failure. I was gratified when I heard of the admirable plans which your Majesty has adopted in order to amuse and entertain your loving subjects. Indeed, sir, I am delighted to know that our little scheme meets with your approbation; we thought it would afford innocent amusement, as well as profitable food for thought. The Barbarian Chief has kindly consented to entertain our party by the relation of a story which is to be the first of a series to be told during our trip."

"I hope," said Scottie, "that the noble Barbarian Chief will tell us all about Parthenia, the beauteous little captive whose irresistible charm subdued and tamed Ingomar, and led him with the rosy chain of love from the barbarian camp to the walks of civilization, converting a heartless savage into a fond and gentle lover. Oh, how I should like to capture such a hero! it would be such fun to tease him until he began to rave, and then to soothe him with sweet whispers from the soul. I would make him gather flowers for me, and then talk to him about 'Two souls with but a single thought, two hearts that beat as one;' and I would enjoy such sport so much!"

"For my part," said the queen of Sheba, "I would much prefer to listen to a patriotic story, such as the 'Scottish Chiefs,' or 'Thaddæus of Warsaw;' I admire those noble-hearted heroes who are always willing to die for their country, but manage somehow not to do it. The heroic Thaddæus of Warsaw was very anxious to sacrifice himself for his country, but finally took a more sensible view of it, and fled to England, and married Mary Buford, the great heiress."

"I prefer love stories," replied Scottie; "give us something like 'Henrietta Temple,' 'Alonzo and Melissa,' 'Foul Play,' or 'Little Dorrit.' "

"I prefer 'Gulliver' or 'Crusoe,' " said George III. "I do not think I could command sufficient patience to listen to such a love story as 'Henrietta Temple.' "

"Give me something like the 'Talisman,' or the 'Heart of Midlothian,' and you may count on securing my undivided attention," said Ivanhoe.

"Permit me to make a suggestion to my young friends," observed Captain Quitman, "which I have no doubt will contribute greatly to your pleasure. We have a young gentleman aboard whom I consider an excellent Shakespearean reader. I had the exquisite pleasure of hearing his rendition of 'Hamlet' one evening at a social gathering in Memphis, and I have no doubt he would consent to gratify his friends by repeating it to-night."

"We would be more than delighted if you could prevail on him to give us an entertainment of that sort this evening," rejoined Queen Mary.

"If we can be so fortunate as to organize a troupe of poetical readers," observed the Duke of Wellington, "it would instruct as well as amuse our friends. If such a scheme should be desirable (and I am pleased to think it would), I can produce a young lady who can repeat 'Lalla Rookh' from memory; and I have no doubt that there are many others aboard who could give us some excellent readings of poetry."

"We commission the duke and Captain Quitman as our agents to organize a troupe," rejoined Queen Mary; "and our programme will be to listen to Ingomar's story this evening, and, at night, to assemble in the saloon and hear the recitations."

"I shall not be able to complete the relation of my story this evening," said Ingomar.

"That will make no difference," replied the queen; "we

will be entertained by our Barbarian Chief during the day, and the poetical readings during the night."

"That will be a most excellent plan," said Captain Quitman; "variety is the spice of life you know."

"Yes, and I beg to remind your Majesty," exclaimed the duke, "that the opportunity to shake the fantastic toe must be provided for."

"Of course," ejaculated Captain Quitman; "that is a consummation devoutly to be wished. We can find plenty of time for that. Dancing hours will be from seven till nine, and the literary exercises will commence at nine, and continue until Morpheus takes command."

"I wonder what kind of a story the Barbarian Chief is going to dish out to us," said George III. "Will it treat of war, love, or politics; will it tell of battles, and blood, or will it describe sweet birds, sweet flowers, and sweet love?"

"It would be better, perhaps, to tell the story first, and answer your questions afterward," replied Ingomar. "I shall tell it under protest. The materials which are at my disposal, if skillfully handled, would construct an interesting novel; but I am not vain enough to imagine that I can weave them into anything like a good story. My life has been crowded with many thrilling incidents—I have tasted the bitterest dregs in fortune's cup, and I have sailed on the smooth ocean of pleasure; and as her Majesty has commanded me to entertain her guests with a story, I shall confine myself to a truthful history of scenes in which I have been an actor. In order to save time, I shall group the most prominent incidents, and set them down in the city of Memphis and vicinity, taking the liberty to change the venue of an important criminal case from New York to the Bluff City. If you should ask me by what authority I venture to change the venue from one State to another, I would answer by referring you to the numerous instances where the United States Courts have exercised the arbitrary power to do such things. Shall I, as a champion story teller, regularly commissioned by a mighty and beauteous queen, be denied the privileges claimed by a little United States Court? I say the venue is changed to Memphis, and when I begin to describe the interesting trial, I trust no one will be so inquisitive as to examine the records, with a view to contradicting my truthful history. If I choose to introduce my *dramatis personæ* under *nom de plumes,* I hope my friends will raise no objections, because, while I claim that the acts of public men constitute public property, I am afraid to take too much liberty in that respect, lest I should endanger my valuable person."

"We command you to cease your continuous talk about preliminaries," observed Queen Mary, as she waved her hand impatiently toward Ingomar; "no one shall be compelled to listen to the tale. Tell the story, and let us judge for ourselves as to its merits."

"I obey your Majesty's commands," replied Ingomar.

"Perhaps," said Captain Quitman, as a quizzical smile played on his handsome countenance, "our friend Sancho Panza would contribute something of an intellectual character to our programme to-night."

"Maybe he will do us the honor to become a member of our literary club," said Scottie, as she courtesied to him.

"I beg to assure you, madame, that you honor me too highly, but at the same time permit me to say that I have no doubt I shall be able to render some assistance. If, as I understand, it is to be intellectual amusement you seek, I flatter myself with the opinion that my contribution will be invaluable."

"What shall it be, Sancho?" inquired George III.

"I will repeat the multiplication table from beginning to end, and whistle 'Yankee Doodle.'"

A perfect roar of laughter was produced by Sancho's thrust, but the young people became convinced that nothing was to be made by poking wit at him. A couple of politicians, who occupied seats near the lower end of the table, were engaged in an animated discussion which was attracting considerable attention.

"For my part," said General Camphollower, "I think that our Government dealt too leniently with rebels after the war."

"I believe," replied Colonel Confed, "that the views you express were those held by men who never smelled burned powder, or heard the whistle of a hostile bullet; but all brave soldiers who fought in the Union army, from General Grant down to the humblest private, were opposed to any harsh measures."

"I perceive," replied General Camphollower, "that you are not being much reconstructed."

"Gentlemen," said Captain Quitman, "pardon me for interrupting your conversation, but I would beg to suggest the propriety of eschewing politics while on this, excursion. Let the past bury the past—let us cultivate a feeling of friendship between the North and South. Both parties committed errors —let both parties get back to the right track. Let us try to profit by our sad experience—let us teach forgiveness and patriotism, and look forward to the time when the cruel war shall be forgotten. We have a great and glorious nation, of which we are very proud, and we will make it greater by our love and support. It was a family quarrel, and the family has settled it, and woe be to the outsider who shall dare to interfere!"

"Hurrah! hurrah for Uncle Sam!" was unanimously shouted by all the passengers.

"Uncle Sam shall live forever, and those unpatriotic politicians who have crippled him shall be driven into obscurity. Let peace and good will, brotherly love and good faith, exist between the North and South, and let Satan take those who wave the bloody shirt."

"Good! good! hear! hear!" was shouted long and loud by all the guests, while the two politicians shook hands across the table, and bumped their glasses together.

By this time the table was cleared, and the waiters began to uncork innumerable bottles of champagne.

"Ladies and gentlemen," said Captain Quitman as his tall, handsome form rose high above the crowd, "fill your glasses and hear my toast." Some little confusion then ensued while each guest was having his glass filled, and then the captain's voice rang out as he spoke: "Here is to the Union as it was in the days of its purity." General Camphollower responded in an eloquent speech, and took his seat amid thundering applause. Then, reaching his hand across the table toward Colonel Confed, he exclaimed: "Here is my hand, colonel—let us shake across the table, and consider it the bloody chasm."

George III. whispered to the duke: "Do you know that lady yonder in the black silk domino?"

"Indeed I do not; in fact, I had not noticed her."

"There is a mystery about that woman, as sure as we stand here; just look at her, will you—she is weeping. I have been watching her for the last half hour, and there is a strangeness in all her movements hard to understand, and harder still to describe."

"Come, come, my lord," exclaimed the duke, as he laid his hand on the shoulder of the king, "you cannot deceive me—you are endeavoring to imitate Romeo; he fell in love with Juliet at a masquerade."

"Upon honor, I have not said a word to that lady, and I have no intention or desire to do so; but I would like very much to know who she is. What can be the matter with the poor lady, I wonder; don't you see how she is weeping?"

"I dare say that the song the queen sang a while ago has called up unpleasant reminiscences. She may have sung that song to a lover who was afterward killed in the late war. This unfortunate land is full of aching hearts and crushed hopes. Thousands of mothers, sisters and sweethearts are weeping and wailing for dear ones who silently sleep in bloody graves."

"That is all very true; but that lady is distressed about something that has happened on this boat, because she was weeping before the queen sang the sweet song. She did not go to the table at lunch, and she has been continually passing among all the passengers and apparently searching for somebody."

"Well, I hope she will succeed in finding the individual she is looking for, if, as you think, she is really shadowing some one."

"My lord," said the queen, as she approached the duke, "if you will be so good as to collect our friends on the hurricane deck, we will order the Barbarian Chief to commence the relation of his little story." The duke courtesied to the queen and immediately began to execute her commands; and it was but a few minutes until the entire party were seated on the upper deck.

The party having arranged themselves in a circle, in the center of which sat the queen in a large arm-chair, Mary bowed to Ingomar, and requested him to commence his story.

Ingomar took his seat facing the queen, in a comfortable low chair which had been provided for his especial use, and began to relate the following story:

INGOMAR'S STORY.

"I was born in Nashville, Tennessee, and was six years old when my mother died. I was her only child, and, as a matter of course, was much petted and greatly beloved by her. The memory of my dear mother is as indelibly fixed on my mind as the inscription on a marble monument, though I trust that my poor heart does not in any manner resemble the cold, unfeeling marble. My father was, at the time of my mother's death, a prosperous merchant, but from that date he began to neglect his business, and, I regret to say, commenced to spend his time at hotels and liquor saloons. I was left at home, alone with the house-maid and another servant, except what time I spent at school. I was too young to understand or realize how rapidly my father was traveling the downward road, but I soon began to notice that he was unsteady in his walk, and that he was becoming cross, and hard to please. I did not know then that he was growing fond of brandy, nor did I imagine that one whom I loved so dearly could do anything wrong. But alas, how soon was this blissful ignorance displaced by a knowledge of the awful truth! My father had been born and bred a gentleman, and, when not under the influence of brandy, was as kind and tender with me as heart could wish. The exact amount of his fortune at the date of my mother's death I never knew, though I have since learned that it was no insignificant sum; but, as a natural result of his neglect of business, the firm became involved more and more every year, until it finally collapsed at the end of the second year after my mother's death. When I was eight years old the servants began to talk of leaving, on account of the bad treatment which my father gave them—complaining of a neglect on his part to pay them their wages. I also frequently heard them hint of a second marriage which my father was contemplating, which, as may be imagined, gave me great uneasiness, for I had imbibed the usual prejudice felt by children against step-mothers. But if I had known then what I do now, I should have entertained very different views. If there ever was an angel on earth, my step-mother was one. I shall never forget my feelings when the house-maid informed me that my new mother would be brought home that evening. My heart felt as if it would break, and my eyes were filled with tears, as I let my young mind wander back to the happy days when I had been fondly held to my own dear mother's bosom. While I was dreaming of the happy days that were forever gone, and occasionally shudder-ing at the prospect before me, my step-mother, accompanied by her two children, entered the room where I was, and with-out ceremony caught me in her arms and kissed me. I have never ceased to love her from that moment. She was a frail, delicate, darling little woman, with dark brown hair and ex-pressive blue eyes, and a voice as sweet as the. music of the cooing dove; and her two children were very much like her as to beauty and gentleness of disposition. Harry Walling-ford, her son, was one year younger than I, and his sister, Charlotte, was one year younger than her brother. She was the very image of her mother, having the same kind of deep blue eyes, only somewhat larger, and her hair, of a bright golden hue, floated in pretty curls about her well-shaped neck and shoulders. Her skin I thought was too white, as it had rather a bloodless appearance, amounting to transparency. The eye-lashes were long, the brows likewise, which gave to the countenance something of a dreamy, thoughtful appear-ance. I may have been rather extravagant in making my judgment as to her personal appearance, but I thought then, and I think now, that she was the most charming little crea-ture that I had ever beheld. Harry was a spare-built, and as I thought, rather effeminate boy, but a more manly fellow than he proved to be I never knew. He and I became bosom friends from the start, and we were both in love with Lottie. He loved her as a brother, and I worshipped her, because I could not help it, and to be candid, I never tried to help it. How was it possible for any one to associate daily with such a darling child and not love her with all his heart? Lottie seemed to permit me to love her, as if such devotion was no more than her just dues, and without making any demonstra-tions of affection for me. I am at a loss to know how to begin to describe Harry Wallingford, for I must say that I

never had met any one before or since who possessed such a
combination of peculiar traits of character as he did. Sometimes you would think he was the most cold-natured, passion-
less boy that ever was created, and then, when anything happened to rouse him, he would show such signs of passion as
to almost frighten me, or when any cause of real sorrow
would come upon him, his heart would begin to melt at once,
and he would weep like a woman. There was no such feeling
as jealousy between Harry and me on account of my love for
his sister; being then mere children, and all intensely in love
with each other. We were all sent to the same school, situated about a mile from our home. We were kept at the same
school for four years, and oh, what happy years were they to
me! Not a ripple of sorrow ever crossed the smooth surface
of our sea of pleasure, save when my father would come home
intoxicated, and then, for a time, we would collect in the garden and speak in whispers, lest he should find us. He was
very kind to us when sober, but when his reason was clouded
with brandy, he seemed to be jealous of the love which our
mother manifested toward us, and often gave way to his passion, and abused her in a most shocking manner. Poverty
began at length to make its unwelcome presence at our home,
but we were too young to realize or feel its influences as our
poor mother did. The servants had all left us, because my
father had no money to pay their wages, and our mother was
compelled to do her own work; but Lottie was as industrious
as a honey bee, and assisted her mother all she could, while
Harry and I did all we could to make her work light. We
cultivated the garden, made the fires, and assisted Lottie to
milk the cow. In fact, we made ourselves useful in every
way we could, and in spite of our poverty we were very happy.
I don't think my step-mother would have married my father
if she had known of his bad habits; but after the fatal step
had been taken, she seemed to have made up her mind to
make the best of her bad bargain. No matter how thick
and heavy were the troubles that crowded on her, she always
met us on our return from school with a pleasant smile; and
the same love and tenderness which she bestowed on her own
children were at all times extended to me. When our wardrobe began to grow scant, and our garments to become seedy

and sometimes full of rents, our dear mother would work till midnight, with Lottie by her side, mending them. I would often drop my book and gaze at Lottie as she sat by the dim lamp, the golden curls falling about her shoulders, while her little fingers made the needle bob up and down with lightning speed, as she mended a rent in my old coat, and wonder if the angels' in Heaven were like her. My father spent but little of his time at home, which circumstance enabled us to snatch happiness from the very bottom pit of poverty. I was deeply grieved to notice that my mother's health was gradually declining, but I did not know then that it was the result of overwork and scanty food, coupled with the cruel treatment from my father. Neither Harry nor I had a suspicion of the true state of affairs, else we would have quit school, and gone to work in order to help support the family. When our little basket would be filled with provisions every morning by our mother before we started for school, we did not know that she was left frequently to work hard all day without a morsel for dinner. I would have worked night and day as a slave to have made her comfortable, and so would Harry; but the secret of her real condition was concealed from us until we had been at school four years, when we began to realize the situation. We at once left the school and began to seek employment, but in this attempt we were often doomed to disappointment, because we were too young to expect to get situations as clerks, and not strong enough to do much at manual labor. Harry was one of those persevering, tenacious kind of boys that never abandon anything they undertake, and, although he was younger than I, he was the leader in all our enterprises. He was self-reliant, energetic and hopeful. I was the reverse of that, and I could not accomplish anything except when I was encouraged and led by him. I therefore submitted to his leadership, and followed him from place to place seeking employment. Sometimes we would manage to secure several little profitable jobs during the day, and every cent we got was handed over to our mother. Then some days we would traverse the streets from early morning until night without finding any work to do, and when this would happen our scanty supply of provisions would grow more scant, until we found the wolf at our very door. I do

not know how my father managed to obtain his meals, for he
scarcely ever came home, and when he did come he was so
much overcome with brandy that he would fall down on a bed
and sleep for many hours, then rise and go straight to the
nearest whisky shop. It was about six months after we were
compelled to quit school that a strange-looking man, with red
nose, and bloated face, and very shabbily dressed, staggered
into our house, and informed my mother that her husband
had fallen from a second-story window and broken his neck.
I learned that my father had been carousing with a gang of
disreputable men in the second story of a drinking and
gambling house, and had staggered through the window,
falling head-foremost on the stone pavement below. His
neck was dislocated, his head and face mangled, and he was
quite dead when his drunken companions went to him.
This dreadful ending of my poor father's life gave my
mother such a shock that she was compelled to take to her
bed, from which she never rose again. It was not quite a
month after my father's remains were deposited in the grave
when my darling step-mother's gentle spirit went to its
eternal home. The last days of her life were not days of
suffering, as is usual in such cases, for she informed her weeping children that she was perfectly free from pain.

" 'Come here, my son, and sit near me,' she said to Harry
one day a short time before her death. 'I wish to speak to
you about what you shall do when I am gone.'

"Poor boy! he was weeping as if his heart would break.
No one ever loved a darling mother more than Harry loved
his; and no mother ever had a more noble, dutiful son than
Harry.

" 'You must not grieve about me after I am taken from you,
my darling boy; but you will live such a life as will enable
you to come to meet me when it is ended. I need not advise
you to be good, noble, honorable, all through life, because I
feel assured that you will be all that. But few mothers have
been blessed with such children as I have, and therefore I can
depart from them with a loving faith and hope of meeting
them again. One promise I shall ask you to make, though, and
that is that you will devote your life to the protection of your
sister, Lottie. The pitfalls and dangers which lie in the path

of human life are much more numerous and much greater in the road of a young girl than are to be found in the one of a young man.'

" 'Dear mother,' said I, as I knelt by the bedside and seized her little pale hand, 'I now solemnly promise to join Harry in this sacred duty. I will follow him through life to aid in protecting my darling sister; for I love her with all my heart, and do here now swear to devote my life to her service!'

" 'God bless you, Edward!' she said as she placed her hand on my head; 'this is very good in you, and will be remembered to your credit where good and bad deeds are recorded.'

"Harry was unable to make a promise of any kind, being so overcome with grief that he could not utter a word, but had fallen on the bed by his mother's side, clinging to her neck, and pressing his lips to her pale brow. He appeared to lose control of his feelings—an unusual thing for him to do, for he was generally more self-possessed than other boys. His mother whispered to me, directing me to take him away. I lifted him in my arms and carried him to another room and laid him on the bed, and remained with him until he became somewhat calm.

" 'Oh, Edward,' said he, while his eyes were full of tears, 'how can we live without her? Shall that darling, sweet face be forever hidden from us? What will become of poor Lottie when our mother is gone?'

" 'Can we not work for her? Can we not take care of her? I will help you, Harry. I will never forsake you and Lottie. I will go with you to the end of the world, to help work for Lottie. You are my brother, she is my sister, and nothing shall ever part us but death.'

" 'Thank you, Eddie, you are very good; and we shall stay together.'

"Lottie was soundly sleeping, unconscious of the fact that she was soon to be motherless. We had so far kept her in ignorance of the situation, but I afterward was convinced of the great error we committed in doing so, for when the time came in which concealment was no longer possible, she was wholly unprepared for the blow. She had not suspected that her mother was on her death-bed, but had been continually chatting cheerfully about the new blooming flowers, telling her mother how pretty they would be by the time she should be able to walk in the garden. Every morning she placed a fresh bouquet of fragrant flowers on a little table by her mother's bedside, and would sit for hours talking to her, while she was busy mending garments for Harry and me.

"It was a beautiful day in early spring when the gentle spirit of our darling mother took its leave of this world. The sweet songs of many little birds loaded the air with their delightful music. The fresh, cool breeze came stealing through the open windows, sweetened with the fragrance of spring flowers, and all nature seemed to exert her energies to make our mother's last moments happy.

"'When I am gone,' she said to Harry, 'you will take Lottie to my brother who resides in Memphis. He will give her a home, and you and Edward can find employment there. I leave you in the hands of Him who promised to be a father to the orphan. "Blessed are they that mourn, for they shall be comforted." "Blessed are the pure in heart, for they shall see God."'

"These were her last words, and without a struggle or symptom of suffering, she fell asleep in the arms of death like one dropping off in usual slumber. Her arms, which had been twined about Harry's neck, were gently removed, and he was carried away in a swoon, while poor Lottie sank down on the lifeless body, totally prostrated with her great sorrow."

CHAPTER IV.

THE description of the death-bed scene was given by Ingomar in a low, tremulous voice, which showed that he was struggling hard to smother his grief, while Queen Mary was seen to brush a tear from her cheek quickly, as if she were trying to appear unmoved. A long silence ensued, and the maskers sat motionless and anxious to hear more of the story. Why the queen should be so deeply moved by the story was a mystery to many of the listeners. Who is she, anyway?

was the question that many of the maskers mentally asked themselves.

"Please to proceed with your story," said the queen, bowing to Ingomar.

Bending low in acknowledgment of her courtesy, Ingomar proceeded as follows:

"The county undertaker was sent for by some of our neighbors, and was about to take charge of our dead mother's remains, in order to give it a pauper's interment, and we never, perhaps, would have understood the deep degradation, but when the plain, pine-board coffin was brought to the house I saw Harry gaze at it for a moment; and such a strange look, too, it was. A deathly paleness overspread his face, as he directed the man to carry the rough box away; and although he spoke low and gently, there was a firmness in his tone that convinced the man that he had better obey.

"'Come with me, Eddie,' he said, as he gently plucked at my sleeve. 'She sha'n't be buried in such a box as that.'

"I, of course, followed him to the nearest undertaker's shop. No words passed between us as we walked side by side, but I noticed that he had ceased to weep, and that there was an expression on his features evincing indescribable suffering. His face still retained its extreme paleness, while his thin lips were firmly compressed.

"'My mother is dead, sir,' said he to a middle-aged gentleman of benevolent appearance, who met us at the door of the shop. 'I want her remains put away in a nice rosewood case. I want her buried in a nice grassy lot in the north-east corner of the cemetery. I have no money to give you, sir, but we have some household furniture, some of which is very valuable; there are some beds and bedclothing, a cow and calf; give my dear mother's remains a decent burial. Take all we have, and let me know what is lacking to compensate you, and I give you my word of honor that you shall never be the loser thereby.'

"The kind-hearted gentleman fixed his gaze on Harry's pale face, and continued to stare at him for several seconds, as if he were trying to pierce him through with the fierceness of the look; then, abruptly turning on his heel, he went behind the counter, placed both elbows on it, resting his cheeks on his hands, then commenced a renewal of the strange gaze. Harry never for a moment turned his eyes from the man's face. At last the man rose up and struck the counter a heavy blow with his fist, as if he were endeavoring to murder some enemy.

" 'You'll do! I'll take your word of honor; there's no falsehood hidden behind that face—your mother shall have the most cozy spot in the cemetery, and the finest rosewood coffin in the house; there, now, go home, and I'll attend to everything.'

"Right well indeed did the generous man keep his word, for I don't think I ever saw a prettier burial case, and the grave was dug in a green shady spot where the turf was very thick and fresh.

" 'What shall we do now, Harry?' said I.

" 'Do as we promised our dying mother, of course. You know she made us promise to take Lottie to our uncle at Memphis; we must prepare to go at once. You stay here with Lottie, while I go to see Mr. Fogg, the undertaker, and arrange with him about the furniture.'

"He soon returned and informed me that the business had been settled, and that Mr. Fogg would take possession of the effects on the next day. We at once began to make arrangements for commencing our journey to Memphis, as soon as Mr. Fogg should take possession of the furniture. That gentleman kindly offered to let us keep the furniture, and allow us to pay him the funeral expenses when fortune should be disposed to deal more kindly with us. But when Harry informed him that in pursuance of his mother's wishes we were going to Memphis, he agreed to take the furniture, saying that it would amply suffice to pay the debt which we owed him. Accordingly, early the next morning the keys were delivered to Mr. Fogg, and we set out on the road toward Memphis. We had not the most remote idea as to the nature of the journey that lay before us. We were as ignorant regarding the distance as we were about the means necessary to take us there. We had often heard and read about Memphis as a young and thriving city on the banks of the great river, and when I now look back to that time, I can scarcely realize the extreme simplicity of our minds, and the extravagant ideas we had as to our ability to accomplish the journey. We were too deeply plunged in sorrow to ever think of making inquiries as to the distance or the best route to travel. We might have saved money enough by the sale of our effects to pay the funeral expenses, and then had enough left to pay our fare on a boat to Memphis. But we considered nothing—thought of nothing but misery. Kind people there were plenty, who would have gladly aided or advised us, but we sought no aid, nor did we speak of our intentions to any one. The greatest trouble that presented itself to our young and thoughtless minds was the sad leave-taking of the poor but dear home where so many happy days had been spent. There was the little garden, with its neat beds of new flowers that had flourished under the constant care bestowed on them by Lottie; there were the jolly little birds, singing so sweetly in the blooming apple-tree near the window; a thousand things of a trifling sort, but dear to the memory, were now to be looked at for the last time. How could it be expected that under the circumstances we should make the necessary preparations for such a journey? How could we think of bread and meat, clothes or cash, when our poor hearts were melting with the very bitterness of sorrow? The wonder is that we should have started with anything at all. We hastily packed a few extra garments into a couple of sacks, snatched up a few articles of food, and with eyes swimming in tears, bade adieu to our home forever. Harry moved on in front, Lottie and I following. Not a word was spoken; no one bade us good-by; no one consoled us in our desolation; and we neither asked nor sought it. As we passed through the streets, a strange look would occasionally be cast on us by the pedestrians as we passed them. We saw but little, and were moving on in silence, when I perceived that Harry had turned his course and was going toward the cemetery. I knew his object, and was pleased to know that we should once more be near our dear mother. We entered the city of the dead, approached the sacred spot in silence, and fell upon the little mound of fresh earth that rose above our mother, and moistened it with our tears. Harry had brought a little basket of fresh flowers which I had not noticed until I saw him placing it on the grave. Mr. Fogg had promised to have a

plain marble slab erected with the proper inscription, to mark
the spot where our mother rested. He complied with his
promise. But a beautiful monument now rises high over the
grave which we afterward had erected. We remained nearly
an hour bathing the cold earth with our tears. No words
were spoken, no passionate outbursts of grief were heard; but
in solemn silence we knelt side by side and paid the last trib-
ute of love to the memory of the dead one who slept below.
At length Harry turned away; I took Lottie by the hand
and followed him, and soon we were moving along the road
outside of the city limits. We traveled about ten miles the
first day, and I was surprised to see that Lottie had not appeared to be fatigued at all. She had walked by my side all
the time, her beautiful eyes fixed on the ground, and I noticed ever and anon a fresh shower of tears would fall from
her eyes. She was a heroine in the strongest sense of the
term—never complaining, unselfish, confiding, hopeful, and
when not thinking of her great loss, she always smiled sweetly
when speaking to Harry and me.

"'Are you tired, Lottie?' inquired Harry after we had
marched about five miles from the city. 'If you are, we will
stop and rest awhile.'

"With her usual smile lighting up her sweet face, she answered in the negative, shaking her head till the golden curls
danced about her shoulders. 'Go on, brother, pray don't
mind me; I am not the least tired.'

"As the sun began to disappear behind the steep hill that
rose on the west side of the road, and the shadows of the tall
trees on the hill-top were growing very long, we began to
think of the manner in which we should pass the night.

"'Shall we stop at a way-side inn?' said Harry; 'or shall
we camp in the woods?'

"'We had better camp out,' I replied; 'because we will
soon be out of money if we undertake to secure lodging at a
way-side inn.'

"This was the first time that the money question had been
mentioned or thought of by either of us. Harry and I both
instinctively commenced to examine our pockets to see how
much money we could command, and found that the sum to-

tal, when put together, amounted to two dollars and seventy-five cents.

" 'I have got twenty-five cents,' exclaimed Lottie, as she produced the shining coin from her pocket, and handed it to Harry, looking as if she thought it sufficient for all expenses.

"Harry was unanimously chosen cashier, and the funds all handed over to him, the grand total amounting to three dollars; and this little sum was all we had to depend on for our subsistence. Harry sighed as he held the money in his hand, evidently beginning to reflect seriously now (when it was too late) as to the folly of undertaking such a journey with so small a sum of money. This was perhaps the first time that either of us had given a thought to the question of finance, and those who are inclined to sneer at our ignorance must not lose sight of the fact that we had a double excuse for it. In the first place we were mere children—I being then in my thirteenth year, Harry in his twelfth, and Lottie not quite eleven. Besides this, we had been so suddenly deprived of both our parents that our great sorrow absorbed all our thoughts; but now, when the situation began to be disclosed, it was too late to mend the matter.

" 'We will not stop in a house,' observed Harry sadly. 'We can't afford to incur the expense. We must economize in every way we can.'

"So it was agreed that we would depend on grass and leaves for a bed, and the blue sky for our shelter. As the sun finally disappeared we came to a halt near a bubbling spring that gushed from a little bluff near the edge of a thick patch of timber, depositing our little effects at the root of a beech tree, whose branches were thickly covered with leaves, which would protect us from the falling dew; and soon a blazing fire shot its cheerful flames forth, as the blue smoke curled gracefully up among the branches of the tree. Our household and kitchen furniture (if I may be permitted to use a facetious remark), including table-ware and all, consisted of three little tin cups, three pure silver tea-spoons, and one little tin coffee-pot; while our stock of provisions consisted of one pound of pulverized coffee, four pounds of salt pork, three pounds of raw ham, and six pounds of baker's bread, one box of matches, and one pound of brown sugar. With her sleeves rolled up above her elbows, her round white arms looking very pretty, a clean white apron tied with a pink ribbon about her waist, Lottie was busy broiling some slices of ham on the coals, while Harry was trying to make the water in the coffee-pot boil. As I sat on the turf leaning against the tree, watching the operation with intense interest, my eyes followed Lottie in all her movements; and I am not now ashamed to confess it—I mentally asked myself, whose wife will she be when she becomes a grown lady? 'Mine, mine!' The last words seemed to force themselves from my lips in much louder tones than was intended, for Harry asked me whom I was speaking to?

" 'Is the water boiling yet?' I asked, by way of hiding my confusion.

" 'I think it is,' was the reply.

"It is a true maxim that necessity is the mother of invention,' which was practically demonstrated on that occasion by Lottie's ingenuity in arranging our supper table. She went to the edge of a little brook near by, selected a smooth, flat rock some fifteen inches square, washed it very clean, and placed it on the turf; then she went back, selected three other rocks of the same kind, only not so large; and, after she had scrubbed them till they were very clean, she placed them on the ground near the large rock; then with a little forked stick she lifted the slices of ham, and placed them on what she was pleased to call a table. When the broiled ham had been placed on the table, she sliced the bread and placed it by the ham, then arranging the three little tin cups in a row on the table, she poured out the strong, black coffee.

" 'Supper is ready now,' she said with as much dignity as if she had been inviitng us to a costly banquet. We accordingly gathered round the table, seating ourselves on the grass and Lottie held a spoonful of sugar toward me.

" 'Have sugar in your coffee, Eddie?' she said softly as I held my cup toward her to receive it.

" 'You are a capital cook, Lottie, and a real genius in the way of inventive faculties,' said I.

" 'I am truly glad you are pleased with my cooking; but you know I have had but little chance to show you what I can do. I shall improve very much too when I have a chance.'

" 'I dare say you will, and I mean to see that you shall have a fair chance one of these days.'

"I can truly say that I enjoyed that meal as much as any one I ever ate. Notwithstanding its lack of variety, it was enough for me to know that it was prepared by the one I loved so dearly. Supper being over, I began to erect an edifice to be used as a sleeping apartment by Lottie; and having watched the display of inventive genius which she had exhibited in procuring table furniture, I felt it to be my duty to exert all my mechanical skill in the erection of a sleeping chamber for her. I stuck four little forked sticks in the ground, then laid several small straight sticks across the top, and covered the building with branches cut from the green trees. I put them on so thick that it would have kept out the rain. Then I took a great number of the same kind of branches and set them round the sides, leaving a little opening at the end next to the fire; then I gathered up a large quantity of dry leaves and spread them on the turf, in this quaint little house, took my coat, spread it on the leaves, placed my little sack of clothes at the back end for her pillow, and crossing my hands behind my back, inspected the entire building, and was satisfied.

" 'There it is, Lottie,' said I. 'When you wish to retire your bed-chamber is ready.'

" 'You are very kind, Eddie, and I thank you very much; but where will you and Harry sleep?'

" 'O, never mind about that; we'll make us a nice bed of leaves on the other side of the fire.'

" 'You had better lie down, Lottie,' said Harry. 'I dare say you are very tired, and then, you know, we must go a long way to-morrow.'

"Lottie took a little Testament from her satchel, and read a chapter as she stooped near the fire so as to get the benefit of the light, replaced the book in the satchel, then went into her cozy little bedroom. Harry and I sat gazing silently at the fire, watching the columns of smoke as they went winding up through the green leaves above our heads. A mocking-bird every now and then would make the night air ring with a song, as he sat on the top of the tree. The gentle murmur of the little brook, as its sparkling waters went dancing among the rocks, had a soothing effect on my mind. No words were spoken by either of us. We were not asleep, but both were dreaming. My body was still, but my mind was at work. The architectural skill of my mind was being taxed to its utmost capacity. The castle which I was preparing to build was one of indescribable beauty and symmetry; the foundation had been laid, materials for the edifice collected, and the magnificent structure began to assume a finished appearance. But, alas, just as I was rounding off the beautiful dome and giving it a finishing touch, the whole building came tumbling topsy-turvy down.

" 'I'll die first!' Those words came gushing forth, and I was as much startled by them as Harry was.

" 'What are you talking about?' said he.

" 'Nothing,' was the reply, for I was ashamed to have been caught muttering to myself. I had fallen into a habit of muttering to myself, especially when my mind was very busy with some sort of castle building, which was by no means seldom. The materials out of which my castle had been built were very good, and the workmanship not at all inferior, but the main part of the foundation had been laid on sand, which proved to be too weak or soft to support such a weight; hence the destruction of one of the most beautiful castles ever built. The materials used in the building were composed of pure love. The dome was made of sweet prospects of a cottage in a shady grove near Memphis, with Lottie as my wife. The magnificent fluted columns that were to adorn the portico of my castle were made of long years of true service, which I had vowed to devote to Lottie's happiness. The polished cornice, that was to make such a charming finish to the four fronts, was made of an imagination, or golden dreams of a long and happy life to be spent with dear Lottie as my wife. But suppose she should fall in love with and marry some other fellow. This supposition was the sand that brought my castle down. As the castle came crumbling down, it was the fall that startled me, and I exclaimed in my bitter anguish: 'I'll die first.' If I had uttered the entire sentence aloud, it would have read thus: 'No other man shall ever be

Lottie's husband. No, never! I'll die first!' Let it not be inferred that I was at all disposed to abandon my occupation of castle building, for I set about the work again with a more determined resolution to finish the grand enterprise; but before I got it finished my eyelids began to feel very heavy and I soon was compelled to lay aside my tools for that time, and was directly sleeping soundly on my bed of leaves by the side of my dear brother. I imagine that I must have slept very soundly during the night, for if I was at all disturbed by dreams, they could not have been of an unpleasant kind, else I should have remembered them when I awoke. Only one dream came to interfere with my repose, and that occurred after sunrise next morning. I dreamed that Lottie and I were on the banks of a beautiful little river, whose deep blue water glided smoothly along, filled with innumerable tiny fishes, and that I was holding my hook in the water to catch them. Just as a beautiful little trout began to nibble at my hook, and when I was expecting to fasten him, a huge mosquito, with long, sharp bill, alighted on my nose and began to partake of his breakfast. I struck at the impudent intruder, and hit Lottie's hand, who was tickling my nose with a blade of grass.

" 'Get up, brother sluggard, breakfast is ready,' said she, as she pointed toward the smoking ham which she proceeded to place on the table.

" 'How did you rest last night, Lottie?'

" 'O, very well, indeed; thanks for the nice, comfortable bed you made for me.'

" 'Did you not get cold during the night?'

" 'No, I don't think I did, for I slept very soundly, and probably should have been sleeping yet, but brother Harry called me at daylight to help him get breakfast. I feel so much refreshed that I shall be able to walk a long way to-day.'

"We arranged ourselves round the table, and soon dispatched our breakfast, and began to prepare for a renewal of our journey. Harry and I carried all the household and kitchen furniture in the two little sacks which swung on our shoulders; while Lottie was not permitted to carry anything but her little satchel. The road we traveled on the second day of our journey traversed a part of the country that was thickly inhabited by thrifty farmers; rich green clover fields spread out on our left, while large numbers of fat cattle were grazing on the rich pasturage. Many beautiful residences, with well-cultivated gardens in front of them, appeared on each side of the road. Happy children frolicked on the green turf, honey bees sucked the sweet clover blossoms, busily collecting their winter store of food. Hundreds of little birds made charming music among the green trees that lined the roadside. The scenery was altogether delightful, but we stopped not to enjoy it, but moved steadily on, with minds bent on the accomplishment of the task before us I marched as usual by Lottie, Harry moving steadily in the lead. I would occasionally drop behind, for no other purpose than to watch Lottie's pretty little feet as they rose and fell with fairy-like tread, making such nice little tracks in the dust. Notwithstanding the many eventful years that have passed since then, I remember well how I almost worshipped the dust that kissed her feet. Toward noon I noticed from her movements that she was becoming very tired, but in answer to my questions on that subject, she tried to make me believe differently. I whispered to Harry, calling his attention to the fact, and suggested that we had better stop to let her rest. We halted near a running stream, and selecting a cool shady spot, we threw ourselves on the grass. We had traveled about eight miles, and I began to feel somewhat fatigued myself, and when I was comfortably stretched on the ground I soon fell asleep. We rested about three hours, eating a cold snack of bread and ham, and then resumed our journey, moving steadily on until the sun went down, when we halted, having marched about fifteen miles in all that day. And I was deeply pained to see that Lottie began to limp with her left foot, which I learned was caused by a painful blister which appeared on her instep. I took my knife and cut a little hole in the shoe, so that the blister would not be rubbed by the leather, and the grateful look that she cast on me would have been compensation for any amount of trouble. A description of our second encampment is unnecessary, as it was nearly similar to the first, the only difference being the lack of cold spring water, which we of course regretted; but we managed to make out with the water from a clear running brook near by. Having finished our frugal repast, I set about preparing Lottie's sleeping apartment, which I soon completed, pretty much on the same plan as the one I had made for her the night before, though I think I made a much better job of it this time. We had finished our preparations for the night, and were seated near the fire, when a strange, hungry-looking dog came up, deliberately seating himself by Lottie, and began to whine and lick her hand. He would in all probability have wagged his tail, but he had none; and it seemed that his misfortunes had not stopped with the loss of his tail, for he had only one eye and one and a half ears, the half of his left ear being painfully missing. Lottie was a little startled and perhaps frightened at first, but when she saw how anxious the poor dog was to make friends with her, she held out her hand and patted his back. The mournful expression of his countenance, and the dilapidated condition of his body, at once enlisted her sympathies, and she gathered up all the scraps of bread and meat and gave them to him, which he devoured quickly, and like Oliver Twist, 'wanted more.' When Lottie went to bed the poor tailless old dog laid himself down at her feet with dignity and composure, doubtless thinking that he had found a friend at last. I watched the dignified movements of the strange animal with some degree of interest. He paid no attention to Harry and me, but appeared to consider it his duty to guard Lottie. It was a clear case to my mind of love at first sight. How could the poor dog help loving her? Birds, dogs and men all loved her. The fact is, it seemed that she was made to be worshipped by men, animals and birds. I suppose that with his one eye the old dog could see her kind, beautiful face, and that he knew she was good. Judging from appearances, one might safely conclude that the dog had been an inhabitant of the earth for a great number of years, and that he could form a correct opinion as to the character of those whom he chose to serve. When we started on our journey next morning old Bob (as we had named the dog—the name being suggested to our minds by his lack of a tail), began to walk with strange dignity by the side of Lottie. He was the first dog I ever saw that couldn't trot; but his principal gait was a walk, though he could strike a gallop when occasion required, and was often seen pacing. Trouble began to crowd on us the third day of our journey—our little stock of provisions was exhausted. Lottie, though she would not complain, was beginning to fail; her feet were covered with blisters, and it was distressing to see her struggling to conceal her sufferings. She took off her shoes and attempted to walk barefooted, but the road was covered with innumerable flinty rocks, the sharp points lacerating her tender feet in a shocking manner. It made my heart ache to see the stones stained with the blood from the wounds on her feet, and I told Harry that we would be forced to stop, as it was cruel to keep her on the road in the condition that she was. I saw the tears trembling in his eyes when he examined his sister's feet. We came to a little creek, and I took Lottie down to the water's edge and bathed her feet in the cold water, and wiped them with my handkerchief. I then procured some slippery-elm bark, and made a kind of soft plaster of it and covered her feet with it, then bound cloth over the salve, and was gratified to hear her say that the pain was greatly relieved. It was but a few moments after I had completed my doctoring operations, when a farmer came along the road driving a team of four horses; he invited us to get in his wagon, as he was going on our road as much as ten miles. This invitation was of course gladly accepted, and we were soon seated in the wagon, moving on leisurely, but much faster than we had been in the habit of traveling. I enjoyed the ride more on Lottie's account than on any other, knowing as I did that it was giving her a chance to rest."

"There's the gong sounding for supper," cried Scottie; "let Lottie ride in the wagon till we eat."

The party rose and went down to the table.

CHAPTER V.

QUEEN MARY took Ingomar's arm, and Ivanhoe offered his to Scottie, and as they went toward the saloon, Scottie said to Ingomar, "Do pray tell us what became of Lottie. I am dying with curiosity to know whether you married her or not."

"You had better allow me to tell the story in my own way," he replied dryly.

"I think so, too," observed the queen. "It would spoil the story to skip from one part to another. Let us re-assemble after supper and hear more of it."

"I think the queen has had something to do with the story," whispered Scottie to Ivanhoe. "She has been constantly wiping the tears from her eyes, and she always turned her face another way, endeavoring to conceal her emotion; and I could see her hand tremble distinctly."

"Very true; I noticed it, and I dare say that she knows more of the story than she is willing to tell. By the by, have you noticed those two seedy-looking men who have been watching us all the time?"

"No; pray tell me about it."

"I have a suspicion that they are detectives, looking for some one who has committed some great crime. I accidentally overheard a part of their conversation this morning. One of them pointed at one of our party and said, 'He is the man.'"

"Which one of our party did he point at?"

"Ingomar."

"What further did you hear?"

"The other man replied that there was no doubt about it."

"Are you sure they were speaking about Ingomar?"

"They pointed at him, and I therefore concluded that the conversation referred to him. I fear that our amusements will be broken up ere long."

"I hope they will not interfere with Ingomar until he finishes his story."

"Yes, it would be vexatious to have it cut short by his arrest. It may be a false alarm, but something strange is going on. The movements of the queen have excited my curiosity more than anything else. Look here; those are the men I was telling you about. See how they are eying Ingomar. Don't let them see you looking at them. I mean to try to unravel the mystery."

"I can't think that Ingomar is a criminal; he speaks so kindly to every one, and then he is so eloquent when telling his story."

After supper the party re-assembled on deck, and after a few moments spent in conversation, the queen ascended her throne (the large arm-chair being used for that purpose), and commanded Ingomar to proceed with his story. In obedience to the queen's command, he proceeded as follows:

"It was near night when we reached the point where the farmer informed us that we must get out of the wagon, as he was not going any farther on our road. There was an old, dilapidated, vacant house near the point where we parted with the farmer, which would protect us from a thunder-storm, that was then threatening to burst on us. Lottie's feet were so much swollen and so badly lacerated that she was unable to walk at all, and I lifted her from the wagon and carried her into the old house. I was grieved beyond measure to witness her sufferings; for, in addition to the pain she was suffering on account of her wounded feet, I noticed that she had some fever. Our condition was by no means pleasant; in fact, it was becoming serious. Our provisions were exhausted, Lottie about to fall ill, the weather prospects gloomy, only forty miles of our journey completed, and only three dollars in our purse; the prospects were of a nature to make my heart sink within me. While I was making a fire, Harry went to a farm-house hard by to purchase provisions. He bought a chicken and a few pounds of bread from a widow lady for twenty-five cents. He also bought a little tea for Lottie. It devolved on Harry to prepare supper, which he commenced as soon as he had returned with the provisions. I was busily engaged in making a bed for Lottie, working very fast, so as to get it finished, before the rain should begin to fall. The lady who resided at the farm-house permitted me to take some dry straw from a pen near by, which I spread out on the floor near the fire, placing my coat on the straw, and requested Lottie to lie down and rest until we could make her some tea. I took the bandages from her feet, bathed them in cold water, then replaced the bandages, and was greatly pleased to hear her say that she was much better, and felt as if she could sleep very comfortably.

" 'You must not go to sleep,' said Harry, 'before your tea is ready. We shall soon have some nice broiled chicken and good tea ready for you.'

"'I shall try to keep awake, but my eyelids begin to feel very heavy, I assure you.'

"It did not take Harry many minutes to cook supper, and it made me very happy to notice that Lottie partook of it with a good relish.

"'Well,' said she, 'brother Harry, you must permit me to thank you for making such good tea. I am going to sleep now, and I bid you and Eddie good-night;' and it was but a short time till she was sound asleep.

"Dark, angry-looking clouds began to collect overhead; the ominous sounds of distant thunder gave warning of the approaching storm; heavy drops of rain began to rattle on the dry boards on the house-top, increasing rapidly until it fell in torrents. The wind dashed with great force against the tottering walls, and whistled mournfully among the trees, while Harry and I sat gazing vacantly into the fire, our minds busy, as usual, castle building. Old Bob had managed to make a pretty fair supper off the bones of the chicken and such other scraps as he could find, and was licking his nose with apparent satisfaction, as he coiled himself down by Lottie's feet. It was after midnight; the rain continued to fall steadily, the wind blew more violently, the fire had ceased to blaze, and darkness pervaded the room. Harry had been asleep several hours, and I was dozing near the hearth, when I was startled by a loud, shrill scream, uttered by Lottie. In an instant Harry and I were by her side. Scream followed scream, while old Bob was leaping and jumping about the room in every direction. Such confusion as appeared was beyond my comprehension. A most singular noise rang through the darkness—slap, slap, crack, crack, and old Bob seemed to be in a deadly struggle with something. What it was we knew not. Lottie kept on screaming, and I knew that something awful had happened, because she was no coward. On the contrary, she was a real heroine.

"'For Heaven's sake make a light,' said I to Harry, as I took Lottie in my arms. He obeyed me at once, and it was but a few minutes till the fire began to blaze so as to light up the room, though it seemed to me it was a very long time.

"'What in Heaven's name has happened?' cried Harry,

while he was throwing fuel on the fire, and trying to make it blaze.

"I made no answer, of course, for I was busy with Lottie, and knew as little of the cause of the confusion as he did. I was endeavoring to compose Lottie, who was trembling like one with an ague fit. Every now and then I felt some strange substance slap against my legs, while Bob threw himself first one way, then another, struggling as if he was fighting for life.

" 'What is it, darling?' said I. 'Tell me what has happened?'

"No answer, but I felt her head drop heavily on my shoulder as the weight of her body came against my breast, and I knew she had either fainted or was dead.

" 'Be quick, Harry, she is dead! do pray make a light!'

"It is a well-known fact that when one gets in a very great hurry to accomplish anything the anxiety to do it quickly very often prevents him from doing it at all, or operates greatly to delay its accomplishment. I was conjecturing a thousand kinds of awful things that had happened, and, as usual in such cases, never hit near the real one. The first thing that suggested itself to my mind was that some savage wild animal had come into the room, and had frightened Lottie. There were at that time many bears, and some few panthers, and large numbers of wolves, existing in that part of the State, and I thought one of those animals had ventured in the house. I heard the continuous snapping of teeth, and the strangest sounds—not like anything I had ever heard before. I spoke sharply to Harry, and accused him of a want of feeling for his sister, for which I was very sorry as soon as the words had passed my lips; he was so frightened that he hardly knew what he was doing. At last the fire blazed up, casting a bright light over the floor, when I was almost paralyzed with horror at the spectacle before me. One large rattlesnake lay dead at my feet, while old Bob was shaking the life out of another of equal size. It was the noise made by the rattles on the tails of the snakes that had sounded so strangely. I had never seen a rattlesnake until that moment, and therefore did not know what was making such a singular noise. Lottie lay in my arms as pale as death, and I saw that she had been

bitten on the wrist by one of the snakes. There were two
small holes made through the skin, and two little drops of
blood had come out through the wounds. The flesh had
already begun to turn a yellowish color. The poisonous
fangs had been driven deep into the flesh and the deadly
venom was beginning to take effect. I suppose the snakes
had come up through the crack in the floor, and had perhaps
coiled themselves in the straw near Lottie; and that, in her
restless slumbers, she had struck the serpent with her arm,
and thus provoked it to strike, because the rattlesnake never
bites unless provoked in some way. I have heard it said, too,
that they always go in pairs, and I had also heard experienced
persons say that the safest remedy for snake bites was to cut
out the flesh in which the fangs had struck, and then for some
one to suck the wound with the lips so as to extract the
poison as soon as possible. Fortunately I happened to have
in my pocket a knife with a very sharp blade. Without a
moment's reflection or hesitation I seized the flesh of the
wrist between my finger and thumb and cut out a piece large
enough to include the entire wounds made by the poisonous
fangs of the serpent, then placed my lips over the wound and
began to suck with all my strength. The wound bled freely,
and I continued to suck it for over an hour. Lottie had immediately regained consciousness after the cutting of her
wrist, and held her wound to my mouth, while the grateful
glance which she cast on me was ample compensation for the
risk I was taking. We could not then tell whether she was
suffering much or not, for one of her peculiar traits was never
to complain of anything; but she declared in most positive
terms that the only pain she experienced was the slight suffering caused by the wound I had made with my knife on her
wrist. After sucking the wound for an hour, I began to feel
deathly sick—a strange dizziness seized upon me—the house
appeared to be turning round with great rapidity, and a blindness fixed itself on my eyes; I gasped for breath, and felt as
if I was being smothered. My blood seemed to be boiling
hot in my veins; I sank insensible on the floor; and when I
regained consciousness I was on a clean nice bed, in a cozy
little room, with Lottie's golden curls dangling about my face,
for she was kissing me when I came to my senses, and my

face was moist with the tears that had fallen from her dear eyes.

" 'Where am I? What has happened?' were the questions I put to her.

" 'Hush, Eddie dear, you must not talk; you have been dangerously ill; and oh! how I hate myself for being the cause of your illness. Why did you not let me suffer from the poison, instead of trying to kill yourself?'

"Then a dim recollection of what had happened began to come to me. 'How long have I been ill?'

" 'Five days, and oh! such long, miserable days were they, too! We thought you were going to die, and that made us so very unhappy; but when the doctor left here this morning he said that all danger was over; and then I knew that God had answered my prayers; because I have prayed constantly and fervently to Him, asking Him not to let you die. If you had died, I should have looked upon myself as your murderer. I never should have seen another happy day. There now, don't talk.' And she placed her hand on my mouth just as I was going to ask more questions.

"I noticed that she had her hand in a sling, and was about to question her about it when she covered my mouth with her hand. I afterward ascertained that she had not been entirely relieved from pain, that her wrist and arm had been very much swollen, and had caused intense suffering, but that she had watched by my bedside day and night, never sleeping any, except such short naps as she could take by leaning her head on the edge of my bed. If I had loved her before this, and I assert that I did, what do you imagine my feelings toward her were then? It would require a more expressive term to describe them than I am able to command.

" 'Tell me, Lottie, all that has happened; it appears like a dream.'

" 'I will, if you promise to lie still, and keep quiet.'

"I made the promise reluctantly.

" 'When you fell insensible on the floor, from the effects of the poison which you had sucked from my wrist, I began to scream so loud that Mrs. Holly heard it, and she and her son came to see what the matter was. I thought that you were dead, and I, of course, couldn't help screaming. We had you brought to this house, and Harry went after Dr. Dodson, who lives five miles away. When he came he made you drunk with strong brandy, then gave you an emetic, then made you drunk again, then gave you another emetic. He kept on repeating this treatment until he thought all the poison had been thrown off. Then he bled you until you fainted; then he gave you more brandy, mixed with opiates, and you slept a long time; but you kept talking all the time in your sleep about me and the snakes. The good doctor remained with you all that day, and all the next night; then he went away, telling us that all danger was past, and that you would be sure to get well, which of course made us very happy, because we had all been so frightened when we thought you were going to die. Doctor Dodson said that there was a slight cut or wound on your lip, and that when sucking my wrist the poison managed to make its way through that little wound and got into your blood, thereby causing all the trouble. There would have been no danger, he said, but for the wound on your lip. He said you were the greatest little hero he had ever heard of; those were his very words, because he said that I would have died in ten minutes from the poison if you had not sucked it out of my veins. Harry, poor fellow, has been working all the time in the field to pay Mrs. Holly for our board, and when we get done paying her, and you get well, we are going to go over to Doctor Dodson's and work for him, to pay him for saving your dear life; and when we have finished paying the doctor, we will then start on our journey to Memphis. There, now, I have told you everything; take this beautiful bouquet in your hand, and lie perfectly quiet, while I go and make your soup.'

"My eyes followed the lovely form till she disappeared through the door. Then I began to count the minutes by the stroke of the old clock on the mantel, and the wheels of time seemed to stop while she was away from me. She returned at last.

" 'Here is a nice bowl of soup, and you must drink it, for you have eaten scarcely anything since you have been ill.'

"I had no appetite at all, but I drank the soup to please her; and I dare say it did me much good, for I was very weak.

"On the morning of the eighth day of my illness I was able
to leave my bed, and, with Lottie's assistance, could walk
across the room. Then the next morning she took me into
the flower garden, while I leaned on her shoulder for support.
I was very much gratified to see that all the wounds on Lottie's feet had disappeared, and that she could wear her shoes
again without pain; and I determined to invent some plan to
protect her feet when we should again begin our journey. I
procured some strong cloth and made a pair of shoes, sewing
leather soles on the bottom, so as to prevent the stones from
cutting her feet. The cloth uppers would keep her feet from
blistering, while the thick leather soles would protect them
from the gravel. She watched me intently while the work
progressed, and when it was finished she expressed great
wonder at my skill. The truth is, it was a very clumsy job,
and the shoes were ugly, but they answered the purpose for
which they were intended, for she never was troubled any
more with blisters or sore feet. We had been at Mrs. Holly's
two weeks, when I entirely recovered; then we went to work
for Doctor Dodson, to pay his bill. He was very kind to us;
his bill was moderate; in fact, he was willing to let us go without paying anything, but Harry would not hear to it. He
vowed he never would leave until the last cent was paid. I
always thought he had very strange views on such subjects.
He was too sensitive, I imagined, because he abhorred the
idea of accepting anything like charity. I do believe he
would have starved rather than to eat bread for which he was
unable to pay. We remained with the doctor ten days, during which time Harry and I plowed a large field of corn,
and cleaned out all the grass. Lottie insisted on being permitted to help us, but Harry would not allow it; therefore
she went to work in the garden, and I mean what I say,
when I assert that it is my candid opinion that garden never
before had been in such a splendid fix. She destroyed every
weed and blade of grass—cultivated the vegetables, trimmed
the shrubbery, transplanted the flowers; in fact, she made an
Eden out of a wilderness. When the work was finished the
kind-hearted old doctor was profuse in his praise.

" 'I declare,' said he, as he gently stroked Lottie's hair, 'I
have been amply rewarded for my attendance on your brother,

by your services, to say nothing of the valuable work done on my farm by Harry and Edward. I wish all my patients would pay me as well as I have been paid in this instance; if they did, I should soon grow very rich. I will not allow you to work another lick, and when you wish to start on your journey, you shall have as much provisions as your two brothers can carry.'

"The morning after this conversation we parted from our kind host, and set out on our journey toward Memphis, loaded down with nicely cooked provisions.

CHAPTER VI.

"It was on a Friday morning that we parted from Doctor Dodson; the weather was getting to be uncomfortably warm, and we were compelled to travel very slowly, lest Lottie should be prostrated by the heat. Ten miles a day was the average distance which we marched. We usually started at sunrise, walked five miles, then rested in the shade until four o'clock, and marched the other five miles by dark. As we had determined not to travel on the Sabbath, we began early in the day on Saturday to look for a cool, shady spot where we might rest comfortably until Monday morning. Shade and pure water were two articles that must be found adjacent to each other, before we could expect to pass the time pleasantly. We, however, had the good luck to come to a spring where many large trees stood, all overgrown with grape-vines, making a covering not only sufficient to keep off the hot rays of the sun, but a shelter that would have protected us from a heavy shower of rain. It proved to be an unfortunate spot for us, as an occurrence happened there that gave us a great deal of trouble. The place where we halted was only one mile from the county-site, and it was from this village that the source of our troubles came. It was Sunday evening; we had finished our humble supper, and were all engaged in singing an old favorite song. I suppose that it was our singing that attracted the attention of some rude boys from the village. There were three boys in the gang that came up to where we

were seated; the leader, a lad whom I supposed to be about
fifteen years of age, whose features exhibited unmistakable
signs of dissipation and brutality; the other two were much
younger and appeared more genteel. The leader, whose name
I afterward learned was Benjamin Bowles, in a domineering
tone said:

" 'Is this a singing-school, or a Gipsy camp?'

" 'Neither, sir,' Harry replied.

" 'Is it a Sunday-school, or a camp-meeting then?'

" 'No, sir, it is neither a Sunday-school nor a camp-
meeting.'

" 'Then what in the deuce is it?'

" 'It is no business of yours, sir, and we would be much
obliged if you would let us alone.'

" 'Oh, would you, now? See here, little sweetheart, I'll
give you a dollar for one of those pretty curls.' And he
reached out his hand to take hold of Lottie's hair. She
blushed and moved to Harry's side. I felt the blood in my
veins begin to boil, and the demon to rise within my heart.

" 'You had better go away and leave us alone,' said Harry,
as he made a movement toward the boy.

" 'Now, do you really think so?' said he sneeringly. 'What
a polite nice boy you are!'

"I thought Harry was going to strike him, but Lottie laid
her hand on his shoulder.

" 'Don't have any difficulty with him, brother, he will go
away directly,' she said softly.

" 'Now that's a daisy, my little queen,' he said; 'let us be
social.'

"The other two boys seemed to be disgusted with the rude
conduct of their comrade, and began to persuade him to go
with them back to the village; and when he peremptorily refused, they went away and left him.

" 'Let us drink and be friends,' said he, as he drew a flask
of brandy from his pocket and presented it to Harry, who of
course refused; then offering it to me—'You'll drink with me
I know, won't you, old boy?'

" 'No.'

" 'Well, indeed, I must say that I never met such uncivil
fellows in my life. If you won't drink, suppose we have a

dance.' Then he began to caper about like a madman. 'If
you won't drink nor dance, suppose we have a boxing match.'
Then he threw himself in an attitude supposed to be that of
an experienced pugilist.

"'Give me a drink of water then,' he said, 'and I will leave
you.'

"I went immediately to the spring to fetch him some water
in order to get rid of him. The spring was over a hundred
yards from our camp. I had arrived at the spring and had
stooped to dip up the water, when I heard Lottie calling
me.

"'Come quick, Eddie,' she screamed, 'he is killing Harry!'

"I got there as soon as I could. The boy was gone, and
the blood was streaming over Harry's face from a wound on
his head. The boy had evidently sent me off after water on
purpose to have a chance to abuse Harry; because as soon as
I was gone he seized Lottie by the wrist and attempted to
kiss her, when Harry struck him on the head with a small
stick; then he threw Harry down (being much larger and
stronger than he was), and began to beat him, when old Bob
seized Bowles by the leg, tearing the flesh to the bone. Then
the boy quickly released Harry and scampered off, vowing
that he would have revenge. Harry was not seriously hurt,
and very soon we were all asleep. We had scarcely finished
breakfast next morning when the town marshal came out and
arrested all of us, saying that Bowles had caused a warrant to
be issued against Harry for an assault and battery committed
on him. We were required to go with the marshal to the
mayor's office, where we were ordered to wait until that individual should finish his morning nap. We had been there
about two hours when his honor came bustling in. Falstaff
would have appeared lean by the side of this moving mountain of fat. He was the largest man I ever saw; the greasy
rolls of flesh under his chin lay in waves on his breast; his
jaws bulged out like the jaws of a fat hog, and a couple of
teeth in the corners of his mouth stuck out over his lips like
the tusks of a wild boar. Two little bunches of hair on the
sides of his head were all he had; the red skin on top of his
head was sleek, and glistened like polished metal.

"'What have you got for me this morning, Mr. Marshal?'

he inquired as he seated himself by a table and began to adjust his spectacles on his large nose.

" 'We have two cases for trial this morning, sir,' said a foppish young man. 'One criminal case and one civil suit.'

" 'Ah, good! We'll try the civil suit first.'

"The plaintiff in the civil suit was a pale-faced, poorly-dressed woman, with a forlorn, forsaken, half-starved appearance, who sat on a bench with a sickly-looking infant in her arms. When she stood up to be sworn as a witness she was compelled to lean on the table to keep from falling.

" 'What is your complaint, madame, against Judge Bosh?' demanded the mayor gruffly, as he stared savagely at the poor woman. In a low, tremulous tone she stated her case:

" 'I contracted with Judge Bosh to work for him three months, for six dollars per month; I worked for him for two months and three-quarters, then fell ill, so that I was unable to work any more. He refused to pay me because I was unable to work the other quarter of a month. As soon as I got able to walk I went back and offered to work out my contract, but he said that it was too late—that he had made other arrangements. We are out of provisions at home, sir, and I hope you will make the judge pay me for the work I have done for him.'

" 'No doubt you do, no doubt you do,' growled the fountain of justice, as he told the plaintiff to stand aside. 'What has the defendant got to say?' and he smiled blandly on Judge Bosh as that distinguished individual stepped forward and laid his hand on the Bible. 'It is unnecessary to swear you; please make your statement.'

" 'That woman contracted to serve me three months. She failed to comply with her contract. As to her reasons, I know nothing about them, neither do I wish to know. A contract is a contract, and it binds both parties. She violated it, and I demand judgment.'

" 'Certainly, certainly, judge; most assuredly you are clearly entitled to it. Judgment against plaintiff for cost,' he muttered as he wrote down the entry on his docket.

"The poor woman staggered out of the room, and fell fainting on the pavement.

" 'What's next, Mr. Marshal?'

"'A charge of assault and battery against Harry Walling-. ford.'

"Is that the little scamp who tried to murder our esteemed young friend, Bowles? He looks like a first-class rascal. I'll teach him a lesson that he'll not forget soon. O, Lord, how wicked this world is getting to be!' And he attempted to sigh, but it was a savage growl.

"Bowles was sworn as a witness; he took the stand, and commenced uttering falsehoods from the start; I was almost struck dumb with astonishment at his total disregard of the solemn oath he had made to tell the truth, the whole truth, and nothing but the truth. He wore a bandage on his 'head, and pretended to be suffering intense pain from the wound on it, while he had his leg in a sling. He stated that he 'had been attracted to the camp by the singing, and that as soon as he arrived there he was insulted and abused in a most rude and vulgar manner by the two boys, the girl joining in with them. He said that while his back was turned toward the defendant he was knocked down with a club, and the savage dog set on him, lacerating the flesh of his leg; that as soon as he was able to regain his feet he had made his way home, completely prostrated from loss of blood.'

"'Shocking, shocking!' growled the mayor savagely, as he began to open and shut his mouth rapidly. 'I wish I had the power to send all of them to the Penitentiary; they are traveling thieves, no doubt.'

"'We are no thieves, sir,' exclaimed Harry, springing to his feet; 'the insinuation is false!'

"'Silence, sir! How dare you insult this honorable court? I guess I'll put you where you won't have a chance to murder anybody soon. Any other witnesses, Mr. Bowles?'

"'No, sir,' said Bowles meekly, 'that's all.'

"'Have you any witnesses, sir?' he said to Harry.

"'My sister was present, sir, and knows all about it.'

"'Of course, of course, she was present; and I suppose you expect me to believe what she has to say, ha?'

"'She will tell you the truth, sir, and nothing but the truth, and I hope no insinuation will be made to the contrary.'

"'Ah, no doubt; come here, gal, and be sworn; and be sure you confine yourself to the facts. What are you shaking that way for? Nobody wants to eat you. Put your hand on this Bible.'

"Lottie was very much frightened, and was trembling like an aspen leaf. Tears were streaming down her cheeks and I stepped to her side to re-assure her.

" 'Take your seat, sir, and let her tell her own story,' said the mayor, as he thrust his huge finger at my nose.

"I obeyed reluctantly, and Lottie began to tell her version of the matter. A large crowd of spectators had come in to witness the proceedings, and I perceived that the eloquent manner in which she was delivering her evidence was winning the sympathies of the crowd. I saw several of the spectators wiping tears from their eyes while she was describing the death of her mother, and telling how she and her brothers were trying to get to their uncle at Memphis. Her extreme beauty and modesty, the sweet melody of her voice, and the simplicity of her pleading, to some extent softened the marble heart of the mayor. She began to regain her self-possession as the story of her sufferings came from her lips. The brutal old official leaned back in his chair, with his mouth wide open, gazing with wonder at the angelic creature before him. Lottie seemed to have lost sight of the case before the court; but she began to plead for her brother with such persuasive eloquence that every man in the house was moved to tears. She gave a graphic description of her adventure with the rattlesnakes; showed her wounded wrist to the court, which had been nearly healed up when it was badly hurt again by the violence of Benjamin Bowles, who had insulted her and hurt her wounded arm at the same time.

" 'Cowardly villain was he, to insult my darling little flower queen!' exclaimed Doctor Dodson, as he hurriedly caught Lottie in his arms and pressed a kiss on her brow. 'Where is the cowardly wretch who has dared to insult this poor orphan child? Let me see his face. I'll venture the assertion that it is more like a beast's than a man's face.'

"Bowles limped out of the room, being careful to keep behind the crowd as he passed out, looking as if he had important business that required his immediate attention at some other place.

" 'Why, my dear doctor, how do you come on? I declare

I'm delighted to see you!' exclaimed the mayor, seizing the doctor's hand and making an obsequious bow. 'I am glad to see that you know this little lady; I dare say you will be able to throw some light on the matter now before the court.'

" 'I should say I did know that darling little orphan child. I know she is the sweetest little lady in the land; and who dares to say otherwise? Yes, and I know those two boys there (pointing to Harry and me); any one who has aught to say against them let him say it now in my presence !'

"The good old doctor was very much excited as he continued to defend our side of the case. Having exhausted himself, he dropped into a chair, and began to wipe the large drops of perspiration from his brow; and, as he blew his nose, he gave a snort that startled every man in the room.

"The mayor seemed to be at a loss how to proceed; for he was afraid to offend Doctor Dodson, who had been his family physician for many years; besides this, he was largely indebted to the doctor; and it was not exactly convenient for him to pay the debt just then. On the other hand, Benjamin Bowles was the son of a merchant to whom he was owing a very considerable sum, and he was anxious to decide the case so as not to offend him. The idea of deciding the case according to the rules of law and justice from the evidence never for a moment came into his mind.

" 'My dear doctor,' said the mayor, as he scrambled up from his seat, 'let me consult with you a moment privately.'

"The doctor followed him into a private room, when the mayor said: 'Doctor, what do you know about those three children ?'

" 'I know enough to convince me that the boys are heroes, and that the girl is a lovely little heroine. I know that they are friendless orphans, which should entitle them to the sympathies of all good men. I know that any one who would oppress or wrong them ought to go to the——'

" 'Yes, yes, I know, doctor; I'll discharge them at once.'

" 'You should never have molested them at first. What business had that Bowles boy at their camp, I should like to know? You knew that he was the meanest, most unprincipled boy in this county, and I am surprised that you should so far have forgotten yourself as to have those poor helpless children dragged into court as if they were thieves. Now that's what I think of the whole business. You go in there and discharge those children immediately, else we are enemies for life.'

" 'Oh, my dear doctor, I beseech you, don't for a moment imagine that I would oppress the orphans, or deal harshly with the helpless. I was going to discharge them anyway. I was merely investigating the case for form's sake. You know one has to appear stern and unbending sometimes, while his heart is melting with pity.'

" 'Yes, I know how it is. I have long been acquainted with the secret goodness of your heart; I wonder how you could keep it smothered so well.'

" 'Ah! doc, one in my position has much to contend with. It's a difficult thing to hold the scales of justice so as to be impartial. I am not fit to be in office—my heart is too tender; I can't keep from sympathizing with the weak and helpless, even when they have violated the law. I think I shall resign.'

" 'I would if I were you; your heart is too tender for the place; but let us go in and have the children discharged.'

"The mayor resumed his seat, adjusted his spectacles, and deliberately surveyed the crowd.

"My young friend Wallingford, we have had some difficulty in arriving at a correct conclusion respecting our duty in this case. We have patiently listened to the evidence, pro and con, and find in many respects a great conflict; that is to say, somewhat of a contradiction between the statements made by Mr. Bowles and the evidence given by Miss Wallingford. But I am pleased to be able to say that it is the opinion of the court that no willful perjury has been committed in this case; but the apparent conflict grew out of the confusion caused by the interference of that savage old dog in the little unpleasantness. The court very much regrets that it has no power to imprison dogs, or to impose fines upon them. This is more especially to be regretted in this case, as it is the opinion of the court that the dog is the only MAN to blame in the matter. That being true, and as there is no lawful authority given me to punish the dog as he deserves, I am consequently compelled to dismiss Master Wallingford from custody and tax the corporation with the cost. I would admonish my young friend to endeavor to teach his dog better manners in future, lest he might involve his master in some serious trouble. Adjourn court, Mr. Marshal; and don't fail to collect the cost in the case of Mrs. Bonds against Judge Bosh.'

"Now let the curtain fall, for the farce is finished. It was a lucky thing for us that Doctor Dodson came to town that day, for Harry would have been sent to prison but for his timely arrival. Lottie threw her arms round the old gentleman's neck and kissed him fervently, and I saw the tears trembling in his eyes as he pressed her to his heart.

" 'Heaven bless you, my child!' said he. 'I had a daughter about your age, but she is dead. Poor thing, she was very much like you; and should you ever need a home, come to me and you'll find one.'

" 'I thank you so very much—much more than words can express, and I hope God will reward you!'

" 'There, there, child, hush, or you'll make a fool of me!' and he left the room with the brim of his hat pulled down over his eyes to hide his tears.

"Once more we were permitted to renew our march on the road to Memphis; and during the next three days nothing occurred worthy of mention. We were happy because Lottie kept up so well—she was so cheerful, and never complained; the cloth shoes I had made for her proved a great success; no more blisters appeared on her feet; the weather, though quite warm during the day, was pleasant mornings and evenings, while the nights were delightful. We continued our gipsy plan of camping out nights, and traveled leisurely during the day, so as not to fatigue Lottie.

"But as I hear the music in the saloon, which is the signal for the dance to commence, I shall break off the thread here, and promise to take it up again when her Majesty shall be pleased to command me."

"I had rather listen to the story than to dance," said Scottie.

"So would I," said the queen.

But just then the band struck up a lively air, and the temptation of the dance proved irresistible, for the majority of the maskers hastened to the cabin, and the others had nothing to do but to follow.

CHAPTER VII.

IT required no summons to be issued by the queen next morning in order to assemble her followers. They were on deck immediately after breakfast, long before the queen made her appearance, anxiously waiting to hear more of the tale. Therefore, when her Majesty made her appearance, Ingomar was at once requested to proceed, which he did without preliminaries.

"Incidents apparently trifling oftentimes shape our destiny. But in making this statement I do not mean to convey the impression that I am about to describe a trifling incident, but the insignificant circumstances which caused the incident are what I refer to. Had it not been for an old bob-tailed, one-eyed, stray dog that happened to take a fancy to Lottie, and concluded to cast his destiny with her, there would have been no use telling this story. Old Bob was fond of chasing rabbits. One day he started one; the rabbit ran for life; Bob ran for the rabbit. The rabbit ran in a certain direction; Bob ran in the same direction; he followed the rabbit, and we followed him; while doing so we came to a gravel pit, which gravel pit I am sure we never would have seen had Bob not started the rabbit; but as he did start it, thereby causing us to go to the gravel pit, I shall proceed to tell what followed. A large number of men were shoveling the gravel onto flat cars, to be hauled on the line of the railroad for ballasting the track. The rabbit took refuge in a hollow tree near where the men were at work; they came and cut the tree down and caught the rabbit. We sat down near the gravel pit to rest; the foreman invited us to ride on the gravel train to the next station, which was directly on our road. We were delighted at the prospect of a ten-mile ride on the cars, and what made it most desirable was the fact that it would put us ten miles nearer Memphis in a few minutes, whereas it would be a good day's walk if we had to foot it. We thanked the foreman heartily and accepted his kind offer.

" 'Hurry up, my men,' said the foreman, as he looked at

his watch, 'throw in lively; we have no time to spare, for we must get to the station before the passenger train.'

"The men threw the gravel on the cars with great rapidity, and very soon the flats were loaded and the train began to move. Lottie and I took seats on the car next to the engine, while Harry went forward to ride on the pilot.

" 'My little man,' said the engineer to Harry, 'it is very dangerous to ride on the pilot. You had better not attempt it, as we are compelled to run very rapidly so as to reach the station before the passenger train.'

"I was astonished to see that Harry paid no attention to the warning; it was so different from his usual way of doing things. It was I who had been considered reckless, while Harry was looked upon as the embodiment of prudence and wisdom. Lottie called to her brother, begging him to come back and ride with her; but he sat immovable and silent, without turning his head to notice her. Harry afterward informed me that a strange, unaccountable desire to ride on the pilot of the engine seized upon him, and he could not resist it.

" 'It may be imagination, merely,' said he, 'but I thought something whispered to my mind, positively directing me to ride there. I had the inclination to heed the warning of the engineer, but a most mysterious influence seemed to rivet me down to the spot, so I could not move. I have heard that notice of approaching events was often conveyed to the human mind through the medium of dreams, but in my case the notice came while I was wide awake, and in a manner to me incomprehensible and most mysterious. Call it superstition if you will; call it nonsense if you choose; I care not; I state facts, and you may draw your own conclusions.'

"I did not argue the question with him, for I perceived that he was deeply in earnest, and his manner was so serious that I thought best to say nothing against his strange theory.

" 'Let her run, Dan,' said the conductor to the engineer, as he held his watch in his hand; 'only ten minutes till number four is due at the station, and eight miles to run.'

"The engineer, who had a frank, open countenance and keen, intelligent eyes and iron-gray hair, seized the lever and gave a backward pull, and the engine dashed forward like a ball discharged from a siege gun. Fences, trees and houses all seemed to be flying; the wind whistled about Harry's face, and played with his dark-brown hair as it floated straight out behind his head. He held his hat in his hand, while his face was all aglow with excitement.

" 'You had better order that boy away from the pilot,' said the engineer to the conductor, as he opened the throttle to let on more steam; 'he might get hurt where he is; we are taking great risk anyway; the track, you know, is very crooked from here to the station; if a cow, or hog, or anything should be on the track, he would be killed.'

" 'You had better not ride there, my little man,' said the conductor, 'it is very dangerous.'

"Harry sat immovable, as if he had been fastened there with bolts of steel, while the train flew onward at the extraordinary speed of a mile per minute. It is very probable that Harry did not hear the warning given by the conductor, as the noise made by the engine as it thundered on may have prevented it. At all events, he did not move; he was rapidly approaching his destiny; whether that destiny was for weal or woe will be a matter for after consideration. Harry always contended that it was a supernatural influence that compelled him to take his seat on the pilot of that particular engine at that particular time. He said that the influence, or whatever it was, came upon him with such unmistakable distinctness that he would have resisted any attempt to force him away. The more I ridiculed the idea, the more firmly did he stick to it.

" 'It was Providence,' said he, 'that is certain.'

" 'I wonder if Providence made old Bob start the rabbit, merely to guide us to the gravel pit?' said I.

" 'No doubt of it,' was his reply.

" 'I didn't know before now that you were so full of superstition.'

" 'If it is superstition to believe that Providence prompted me to ride on the engine that day, then I am overflowed with it.'

"The brave old engineer stood with his hand on the lever, his sleeves rolled above his elbows, his face blackened with smut and smoke, his gray locks pushed back and streaming in the wind. Undaunted courage was stamped on every feature; his lips were firmly closed, and the picture he presented reminded me of the description of Vulcan which I had read in Homer.

" 'Will she make it, Dan?' inquired the conductor.

" 'Yes, I think so,' replied the engineer; 'but it will be a close race—two miles to run; two minutes and a quarter to make it in.'

" 'We're safe then,' said the conductor. 'They can hear us coming and will wait for us.'

"Within one mile of the station there was a sharp curve in the track where it swung round the base of a tall ridge, then lay out on the top of a very high embankment, thence across a bridge, with a straight run from there to the station. The train was coming round the curve with unusual speed, as it was running down grade. Harry sat on the pilot with his eyes fixed in front, and just as the train came round the last spur of the ridge, he saw a little girl sitting on the gravel in the center of the track, with her apron filled with wild flowers, which she was busily weaving into festoons. The train was within one hundred yards of her before she was discovered. She was on the part of the track that lay on the top of the high embankment, the sides of which were very steep, and it was full thirty feet to the ground from where the little girl sat. The engineer immediately blew the signal for down brakes, then reversed his engine (a very dangerous operation to perform while running rapidly down grade); all the brakes were put on, and the brakeman seemed to strain every nerve to hold them as much down as possible. The engineer kept his whistle shrieking and screaming in order to warn the child of her danger. She rose and started to run toward the bridge, then hesitated a moment, and made a move as if she were going to jump over the embankment. An Irish woman who was the child's nurse had imprudently left her on the track while she was gathering the flowers some distance from it. When the nurse discovered the danger to which the little girl was exposed she hallooed to the child, telling her to leap down the side of the embankment. She made a movement as if she were going to do it, then evidently became frightened at the great distance to the ground. Meantime the train was

rapidly approaching the spot where the child was, notwithstanding the fact that all the brakes were down and the engine reversed. The momentum was so great, and the grade
being downward, the train continued to move forward. The
noise made by the whistle, added to the thundering sounds
made by the approaching train, only served to increase the
child's confusion. The second time she started to run across
the bridge, and again she ran back a few paces; then became so paralyzed with fright that she stopped, unable to
move. The train was within a few feet of the little girl, and
it now became certain that the engine could not be stopped
before it reached the bridge, although it was running quite
slowly, not faster than a man could run; but what did that
signify? Wouldn't the child be crushed to death unless the
engine could be stopped before she was reached? It was plain
to be seen that the little girl had lost her self-possession, and
she stood gazing at the approaching train in despair. She
had very long hair, which floated loose down her back, while
the flowers lay scattered on the ground where she stood. The
picture she presented then was pretty, 'tis true, but the situation was awful. My heart grew sick at the sight. I noticed
Harry getting down on the very front of the iron frame commonly called the cow-catcher; but what good could he do by
that? The engine was within ten feet of the little girl when
I saw the old engineer turn his face away and throw both
hands to his eyes, as if he were trying to shut out the shocking
scene that was about to be witnessed.

"'Oh! great God have mercy on us,' he exclaimed, as he
turned away.

"Harry placed his foot on the outer end of the longest bar
of iron, then made a desperate leap forward, seized the child
by the arm, and both went rolling down the steep side of the
embankment. He made the leap when the engine was only
about six feet from the child, and he must have made his cal-
culations very accurately, for he only let one foot strike the
ground between the rails, while the other struck the ground
outside of the rails. The slightest miscalculation or the least
mistake, would have been fatal to him as well as her for whom
he made the gallant leap. At the base of the embankment
there was a pond of muddy water, bordered with briars and

broken rocks. Harry and the little girl landed in the middle
of the pond, bruised and bleeding from many wounds. The
engine came to a halt as soon as it struck the bridge, and the
engineer leaped down to where Harry lay in the water and
lifted him up in his arms. It was an affecting sight to see
the man of iron nerve weeping like a child.

" 'My brave little hero,' he exclaimed, as he pressed Harry's
brow to his lips, 'are you hurt?'

" 'Not much sir, I believe, though my leg is broken,' said
Harry.

"Poor fellow! he fainted in the arms of the strong
man who carried him up the embankment and placed him on
the train. The little girl had a severe contusion on her
temple, caused by falling against a sharp-cornered rock at the
base of the embankment. She was also placed on the train,
and then it was put in motion, and soon was at the station,
and a surgeon sent for, while the wounded children were removed to a hotel near the depot. The mother of the little
girl (a pale-faced, delicate little woman of great beauty)
swooned and fell to the ground when she saw the bleeding
child in my arms. The father of the child took her from
me.

" 'In Heaven's name pray tell me what has happened!' said
he, as he took his daughter from me.

" 'She is not seriously hurt, sir,' said I, and then I told him
what had occurred.

"Harry had regained consciousness before we reached the
station, and when he saw how Lottie was weeping as she held
his head in her lap, he smiled pleasantly. 'Don't be alarmed,
Lottie dear, I am not seriously hurt—just one leg broken,
that's all. Wasn't it lucky that I happened to be on the
front of that engine? Is the little girl much hurt?'

" 'No, I think not,' said the conductor, 'she got a slight
cut on the temple.'

" 'Wasn't she a pretty little darling?' continued Harry; 'I
fell in love with her as we rolled down the embankment together; and when I get to be a man, if she is willing, we'll
go down the path of life together.'

" 'His mind is wandering,' whispered the conductor.

"Harry overheard him.

" 'Perhaps it is,' said he, 'but let it wander as much as it likes, so long as it happens to stray in that direction. Hush crying, Lottie dear, I tell you I am not much hurt; I shall be well again in three weeks.'

"The old surgeon arrived, threw off his coat, rolled up his sleeves, and went to work like a man who knew what he was about; and I was struck with admiration for the man when I saw the skill with which he reset the broken bones and placed the splints.

" 'There now, we're all right, my brave little hero,' he said, smiling as he finished pinning the bandage. 'Keep it moist with cold water to prevent inflammation, and in three weeks this leg will be as good as the other one. By the by, what's your name, little man?'

" 'Harry Wallingford, sir.'

" 'Ah, ha! a very nice name, too, it is. And the pretty little girl whose life you saved is the sweetest little angel that ever touched the earth!'

" 'Who is she?' Harry inquired.

" 'Viola Bramlett is her name. She is the daughter of Mr. Bolivar Bramlett, of New York City, who is traveling in the South for the benefit of his wife's health. They have been stopping at this hotel some three or four weeks, and being called in to see Mrs. Bramlett professionally, I have had a chance to become well acquainted with the family; therefore, you see, I speak advisedly when I say that little Viola is an angel.'

" 'I hope,' said Harry, 'that she is not badly hurt.'

" 'Oh, no; she is not hurt much at all—a slight contusion on the temple, and a few scratches from the briars—that's all. Her father will be in to see you directly; he is overwhelmed with gratitude to you; and little Viola (Heaven bless her!), won't talk about anything except the pretty little brave boy who kept her from being killed. She insisted on coming to see you now, but I persuaded her to wait till your wounds were dressed. So you see that you may expect soon to be overflowed with thanks and kisses from the sweetest little darling that the world ever saw. Ah, you're a lucky lad, anyway. Good morning; I'll see you again this evening; don't move the wounded leg; keep it perfectly still, and talk as much as you please to the little angel when she comes to see you.'

"Then the old surgeon bustled out of the room, and went to visit his other patients. It was but a little while after Harry's wounds had been dressed when Viola came bounding into the room, threw her arms round his neck, kissing his lips at least a dozen times in rapid succession. Then she said, with a voice which I thought very sweet and musical: 'Oh, you don't know how much I thank you for saving my life! Papa says that I should have been crushed to death but for your bravery. He says you are a real hero, and he is going to divide all his money with you. My papa has great heaps of money, and he is going to give you half of it, and I am to have the other half. Now, won't that be nice?'

"I watched her movements with intense interest, and concluded that the old surgeon's description of her charms had not been exaggerated. Harry gazed at her with such a look of admiration that I was convinced that he concurred in the opinion expressed by the surgeon in regard to her exceeding great beauty. Mr. Bramlett then made his appearance, and was very enthusiastic and profuse in his thanks to Harry for saving his little darling, as he called Viola.

" 'She is all we have, sir, and if she had been taken from us, it would have been a fatal blow to our happiness. Words cannot express the gratitude we feel toward you; and, as soon as you get well, we shall talk more about it. I am a man of business, and not a man of many words; therefore, you shall hear from me again when you get well;' then, bending down, he gathered Viola to his heart, and as he kissed her fervently, said: 'Go now, my darling, and get some choice flowers for the little brave hero who risked his life to save you. You must be his nurse, you know, and must keep him well supplied with flowers and iced lemonade, etc., etc;' and before the sentence was finished Viola had skipped off to collect the flowers.

"Very soon she came in with her apron full of roses, pinks and geraniums, and deposited them in great heaps on Harry's bed, filling the chamber with their sweet odor.

" 'Now, Mr. Harry,' she said, 'there's your nice flowers; and, while you are enjoying their fragrance, I must go and

fetch you some lemonade and ice. Papa is máking the lemonade for you, and he told me to give you the flowers, and then
to come for the lemonade.'

"She was gone but a moment, when she returned with a
little tray, on which sat three goblets full of lemonade and ice;
giving the first goblet to Harry, she then gave the other two
to Lottie and me. When she went out Harry said: 'Eddie,
isn't she the sweetest little thing you ever saw?'

" 'Yes, with one exception, undoubtedly,' I replied, casting
a side glance at Lottie. She understood my meaning, and
blushed crimson as she turned her face away.

" 'Of course you think Lottie is the prettiest, and I sha'n't
quarrel with you about that.'

"I was delighted to see Harry so cheerful under his sufferings, because it was plain that his wound was paining him.
His leg was broken about three inches above the ankle joint;
but thanks to the skillful old surgeon, no lameness or deform-
ity resulted from it, and in less than four weeks he was able
to walk without crutches. The railroad men from far and
near came to see Harry, and they almost worshiped him.
The old engineer came every day to inquire how he was getting on, calling Harry his brave little hero. Mrs. Bramlett
was unremitting in her attention to Harry, overwhelming him
with grateful thanks. She said that her husband had concluded to go with us to Memphis, and never to part from us
until he saw us safely landed with Harry's uncle. The days
of Harry's convalescence were days of unalloyed happiness to
me; for I had nothing to do but to saunter among the flowers
with Lottie, while Harry was with Viola all the time."

The queen requested Ingomar to suspend a while. Then
the party began to promenade the deck.

CHAPTER VIII.

SCOTTIE was leaning on the arm of Ivanhoe, as they promenaded the deck, conversing in subdued tones.

"Have you noticed that lady with black silk domino and
yellow mask?"

"No; what about her?"

"That's she leaning on the arm of the old gentleman with long, white whiskers. I suppose he is her father. Her movements have a mystery about them that excited my curiosity. She has been listening to Ingomar attentively all the time, yet she never speaks a word to any one, except the old gentleman, nor does she mingle with our party; yet she follows Ingomar wherever he goes, as though she was a spy on his track."

"Indeed! that is strange; and to add to the mystery, I see that those two seedy men have kept close to Ingomar all the time, and appear to be in earnest conversation, which is always carried on in whispers. I think something unusual will develop itself soon."

"So do I; but I hope it will be nothing against Ingomar; I believe he is a perfect gentleman."

"I hope you may be right there; but it won't do to judge by appearances."

"Look, look! see that woman in the black domino! she is pointing at Ingomar now, and whispering to the old gentleman. I heard her say in a whisper to the same person last night that the suspense was killing her; now, what could that mean?"

"You are too much for me there; but we must wait patiently for further developments; meantime, let us get our party together and hear more of Ingomar's story."

"Yes, yes; I am anxious to hear more; go see the queen, and ask her to order the tale continued."

"About five weeks after Harry had been hurt Mr. Bramlett came into his room, and after talking for a few minutes on general topics, he handed him a roll of bank bills, containing one thousand dollars.

" 'Take this, my brave little hero,' said he, as a present from Viola; and if ever the time comes when you should need a friend, just write to me, and I promise you that I will respond.'

" 'You are very, very kind, sir,' said Harry, as he bit his lips, and it was plain to be seen that he was deeply offended, on handing the money back; 'I hope you won't think me rude, sir, but I can't take your money.'

"I was greatly vexed at Harry's conduct; here was money enough to answer all our demands; it seemed to me that no one but a crazy person would refuse such a sum.

" 'Why, my little friend,' said Mr. Bramlett, 'you must allow me to show my gratitude in some way; and how could I do it any better than by helping you with ready money? You must think of your little sister; she must be taken care of; and how can you do it unless you have money to pay her board and buy her clothes?'

" 'I can work for her, sir, and so can Eddie; we shall both work for her; I should feel like a beggar, sir, if I were to take your money.'

" 'All a mistake, I assure you; I have an ample fortune; you saved the life of my darling Viola, and you must allow me to do something to show my gratitude.'

" 'I was not thinking of money, sir, when I saved your daughter; I was thinking of her.'

" 'No doubt, no doubt you were; but you have suffered much on account of the gallant deed, and I shall be deeply mortified if you refuse to allow me a chance to show how much I feel the obligation.'

" 'I am very sorry, sir, to hear you say that; but really, I cannot take any money.'

" 'Suppose then, we make a trade. Let me loan you three thousand dollars at five per cent. interest, taking your note, with Edward as security, on condition that you use the money in completing the education of yourself, your sister and Edward; then you study law, and when you begin to make money at your profession, you shall pay my money back with interest. What say you to that?'

" 'That would be worse; it would be receiving the money under false pretenses; I can readily understand the kindness that prompts you to make the offer, but as I never should be able to pay your money back, it would not be right for me to take it.'

"Mr. Bramlett left the room rather abruptly; he was vexed at Harry's obstinacy, and when he went into his wife's room he said: 'That foolish boy refuses to accept any aid from me; I declare it is too bad; it is a shame to see them start eut afoot again; he is the most high-strung chap I ever saw; I'll resort to strategy; I'll employ some agent to look after those children.'

" 'Allow me to make a suggestion,' said Mrs. Bramlett to her husband; 'as we are going to Memphis, anyway, you might procure a situation for the boys with some of your business friends in Memphis, and then you could place money with your agent and have it paid to them in such sums as they need, making them believe all the while that they are earning it; that would keep them from feeling that they are objects of charity, for to tell you the truth, I rather admire their high-strung notions, as you call them. Of course they are too young to be of much service to anybody, but it would encourage them if they could be made to think that they were earning their support.'

" 'Thank you, dear, for the suggestion; it is the very thing. We will go to Memphis to-morrow, and the matter shall be arranged.'

"Of course, we were ignorant of this arrangement, and did not find it out for many years afterward. I was at that time unable to support Harry's independent views, and tried to argue the question with him, but it was a failure on my part.

" 'I should despise myself,' said he, 'if I were to take the kind gentleman's money, knowing that I never should be able to pay it back. Then, perhaps, it would displease our uncle if he knew we had accepted money in the way of charity.'

"He went so far as to refuse to take the train with Mr. Bramlett until that gentleman promised to furnish him employment as soon as we should reach Memphis, by which we could re-imburse him for the money advanced to pay our fare; and I don't believe he would have done that but for the influence brought to bear on him by Viola, who threw her arms about his neck and declared that she would cry her eyes out unless he went with her to Memphis.

"When we arrived at Memphis, Mr. Bramlett took us to the Worsham House, promising to inquire for our uncle on the next day; and when he came back, after having gone out for that purpose, and informed us that our uncle had gone to California, with a view of making it his permanent home, we began to realize the fact that we were now left all alone and must think and act for ourselves.

" 'What are we to do now, Harry?' I inquired.

" 'We must seek employment at once,' said he, 'and we must lose no time about it either. You stay with Lottie, and I'll go out and see what we can get to do.'

"Harry returned after three hours' absence, and the look of disappointment that appeared on his face convinced me of his failure before he told it.

" 'No one seems to want us,' he said gloomily, as he dropped exhausted on a chair. 'I have met nothing but disappointment at every point; but I will try again, when I get rested.'

"Lottie wiped the perspiration from his brow with her handkerchief, and ran her fingers through his hair.

" 'You must get some work for me to do, too, Harry; you know how nicely I can sew, and how neatly I can cut and fit a lady's dress. I shall make a great deal of money, if you'll only get the work for me to do.'

" 'I know you would, Lottie, but no one will give us work. I fear, because we are strangers here, and people don't like to trust strangers, you know.'

" 'Papa has gone out to hunt work for you to do, Harry,' said Viola, as she pushed Lottie gently away from her brother; 'you go and stay with Eddie there, Miss Lottie, and leave me to look after Harry. I shall be jealous, you know, if you pay so much attention to my hero. Speaking of work, I heard papa say to mamma that he would find a good place for you to live at before he left the city; then we are going to New Orleans, and then we are going to Havana, and then we are going to come back here to see you; and then won't we have lots of fun?' And stooping down with her mouth to Harry's ear she said: 'I've got something nice for you, but you must come with me to my room before I show it to you, because Eddie and Lottie are not to see it at all, so come along now.'

"Of course Harry went, and he was not prepared for the surprise which she gave him, for she held up a large golden locket swinging to a heavy gold chain. 'There it is; isn't it pretty? Papa gave seventy-five dollars for it, and you must accept it as a present from me. You see it has got my picture in it. I thought maybe you would like my picture to look at when I am gone; for I'm sure I should like very much to have yours to look at when I am so far away from you.'

" 'I shall wear this pretty picture next to my heart as long as I live, and I shall always love the darling who gave it to me.'

" 'You must get your picture made, and give it to me before I go away, won't you?'

"Harry did not know what answer to make, for he knew that it required money to have a picture made, and money was not his.

" 'Maybe so,' he said sadly.

" 'O! don't say that; you must not by any means refuse me your picture.'

" 'You shall have it as soon as I can earn the money to pay for it.'

" 'Never mind the money, I'll get that from papa; he always gives me money when I ask him.'

" 'I should rather pay for it with my own money; then it would be a present from me.'

"I persuaded Harry to remain at the hotel until I should make a tour through the city to try my luck in seeking employment. I went from house to house, from one end of Main street to the other, asking at all places for work; and then I went on Front row, and tried every business house for employment, willing to do anything to make an honest living. I offered to drive a dray, or to roll barrels, or any sort of work that anybody might want done; but no one seemed to care to employ me. I suppose it was my green and seedy appearance that went against me, and I was returning to the hotel, completely overcome with fatigue and disappointment, when I heard a familiar voice call my name.

" 'Ah, ha! here we are again, Eddie, old fellow; you are the very chap I was looking for. Ah, ha! Eddie, what good luck?'

"I was seized by both hands, and looking up, saw the kind

eyes of old Doctor Dodson bent on me. No one will ever
know how my sad heart leaped for joy when I heard his kind
words.

"'Yes, yes. Ah, ha! You were the very lad I wished to
see. I have just come to Memphis with a view of making it
my home; I have bought a drug-store, and mean to practice
my profession here, and sell drugs also, and I mean to put
you in the store as my clerk, etc., etc. Ah, ha! Eddie; yes,
yes; you see it all now, don't you?'

"I was so overjoyed with the news that I was unable to
answer then; but as soon as I could collect my ideas I
thanked him and promised to accept his kind offer. It was
agreed that I should commence business with the doctor on
the next morning.

"'Ah, ha! Eddie, all settled, you see; that's business. I
mean to make a great doctor out of you one of these days.
You've got a splendid head for a doctor. Ah, ha! that you
have, my boy. There now, you may go until to-morrow, and
then to business, you know.'

"I hastened to the hotel to impart the good news to Harry
and Lottie, and I must say that I had risen at least one hundred per cent, in my own estimation. Wouldn't I now be
able to support Lottie, and Harry, too? I imagined that I
should be able to support them with all ease; but that, of
course, was one of the childish dreams which often found
lodgment in my simple brain. When I returned to the hotel
and imparted the good news to Harry and Lottie, it made me
very happy to see how much pleasure it gave them. Meantime Mr. Bramlett had been arranging his plans, or rather
executing the plans he had determined on previously. He
was seated in the office of Mr. Rockland, an eminent lawyer,
who had for many years been his agent and adviser.

"'Mr. Rockland,' said Mr. Bramlett, this is a delicate
matter, and I trust you with its management; and I may as
well tell you now that it will require some strategy, and much
skill, to make the plan work smoothly. I have never met with
three such children. They are as proud as Lucifer, and as
independent as if they had the wealth of the Rothchilds; and
if they ever should suspect that the money comes from me,
the whole business goes overboard certain.'

" 'I see,' said the lawyer. 'I think I shall be able to manage the business so as to accomplish what you wish. If I understand you correctly, Mr. Bramlett, you want those children properly educated, and then you want the boys to be put to the law as soon as their education shall have been completed.'

" 'Just so, Mr. Rockland; you understand me correctly. I feel under great obligations to young Mr. Wallingford, and have offered to show it by aiding him, but he rejects my offer merely through pride; therefore I mean to help him in this secret manner. I beg you not to stand back on account of money—draw on me for all that may be necessary, and the cash will come.'

" 'The description you have given of those children convinces me that my task will be rather an agreeable one; because pride and independence are by no means evil qualities, unless possessed by ignorant people; and they are far from being ignorant, judging from what you have told me. Mrs. Rockland will be glad to receive them, as we have no children of our own; consequently, she leads rather a lonely existence; so you may consider the matter settled.'

" 'Here is a card for Harry Wallingford,' said a bell-boy, as he dipped his head in the door.

"Harry read as follows:

" 'HARRY WALLINGFORD:
" 'SIR—Please call at my office immediately. I wish to see you on important business. Respectfully, N. ROCKLAND.'

"Harry went to the office without delay, while his mind was crowded with conjectures as to what kind of business was to be discussed. He found Mr. Rockland seated near a table covered with a huge mass of papers, busily engaged looking over them, and when Harry entered the office the old lawyer fixed his eyes on him for a moment as if measuring his worth.

" 'Take a seat, little man; I suppose you are Harry Wallingford?'

" 'Yes, sir.'

" 'Mr. Bramlett was speaking to me about you, and, by the by, he has given you a very favorable recommendation, and I have concluded to offer you employment, if we can agree on

terms. I want a boy to help me in my office, and you shall
have the place, if you think it will suit you.'

" 'I shall be glad, sir, to get the place, and shall try to
please you.'

" 'Very good; I shall not be able to offer you very large
wages.'

" 'I could not expect it, sir.'

" 'Then to come to the point, I propose to board and clothe
you and your sister for the work you and she can do. She
can be a sort of companion to Mrs. Rockland. You see we
have no children, therefore your sister will no doubt be able
to help Mrs. Rockland in many ways; meantime she can go to
school; so can you; but then you will have to work very hard,
because I shall require you to work mornings and evenings,
and sometimes late at night. This, you know, must be understood before we close the contract. If I board, clothe and
educate you and your sister, you see it will require all the
money that you and she could earn.'

" 'I am afraid, sir, we shall not be able to earn enough to
pay for all that.'

" 'I'll risk that; but you'll find I shall keep you very busy.
And then I must find a situation for your step-brother.'

" 'He has found a situation with Doctor Dodson, sir.'

" 'Oh! has he? That's lucky; then we are all right; is it
a bargain between us?'

" 'Yes, sir; and I am very thankful. When do you wish
me to commence?'

" 'Stay with Mr. Bramlett until he starts to New Orleans,
then bring your sister to my house, and we shall go to work.'

"When Harry came back his handsome face was beaming
with pleasure; and while relating what had occurred, he did
not fail to congratulate Lottie on the chances which she would
have of securing an accomplished education. Fortune seemed
to have made up her mind on this occasion to shower her
brightest smiles on us all at once. Had she not provided us
with good homes, kind friends and all we could expect or
wish for? And right here I feel it to be my duty to express
my thanks to old bob-tail Robert; for it was all brought about
by him. What a slice of good luck it was that caused him to
take a fancy to Lottie on that eventful night when he came to

our camp and began to lick her hand! I suppose Madame
Fortune had prompted him to do it. We never knew who
was old Bob's master before he concluded to cast his lot with
us, but from his 'lean and hungry look' we inferred that he
had been serving a cruel master, and that he was out on a
foraging expedition when he happened to come upon our
camp. The night was dark, and I suppose he came near
enough to see Lottie's sweet face, as she sat gazing into the
fire, and here is the substance of what I imagine passed
through old Bob's mind as he peered into Lottie's face with
his one eye:

"'I am very hungry; the fact is, I am about to perish
for food; my master is unkind and cruel; instead of giving me food, he gives me nothing but blows and curses, and
I believe I shall run away from him, and seek me another
master. That little girl has a beautiful countenance, and I
expect she has a kind heart, and I think she would have
compassion on a poor old hungry dog like me; I believe
I'll venture up to her, and lick her hand, and maybe she
will give me a bone to gnaw on. Oh! how I wish I had
a beautiful tail to wag, in order to make her pity me. I am
afraid my ugliness will frighten her, and if it does, I shall be
driven off, and then shall get no bone; but my poor stomach
is so empty, and my mouth waters so, that I shall venture up
at all hazards. If she drives me away it can't make matters
worse, and if she is kind and gives me a bone, I'll follow
her, for her sweet face leads me to think she'll do to tie
to.'

"Immediately after having the unuttered conversation with
himself, old Bob ventured up and licked Lottie's hand; the
result was he got a medium supper, and found that the favorable opinion he had formed as to the kindness of her heart
was by no means too extravagant. We know what followed
—at least we know that Bob followed Lottie, and we further
know that his fondness for rabbits led us to the gravel pit,
which led us to the gravel train which carried Harry to the
embankment, where he saved the life of Viola, whose father
caused Mr. Rockland to give us good homes, and this proves
that it is better to give a poor dog kindness than kicks. Now
who knows what might have happened to us if old Bob had

not trusted to Lottie's kind face that night, or if she had
taken a stick and beaten him? I dare say we should have
been wandering about the streets of Memphis, friendless,
houseless, and penniless; working for our daily bread, and
sleeping in some filthy, sickly den, while dear Lottie would
have been dressed in rags. But now, through her kindness to
poor old one-eyed, tailless Bob, she has got a splendid home,
good friends, fine clothes, and bright prospects unfolding
themselves for the future. Who will venture to deny, that
old Bob was possessed of good judgment? Who will say that
he did not make a good selection, when he concluded to take
Lottie for his mistress and protector?

" 'Well, here we are. Ah, ha! Eddie,' said Doctor Dodson
next morning, when he met me at the door of his new drug-
store. I suppose you are ready for business? Ah, ha!'

" 'Yes, sir.'

" 'Good, my boy, good!'

"Then he began to instruct me as to the duties I was to
perform, and teaching me the names of the various kinds of
drugs. I went to work with the determination to succeed, and
to please my kind-hearted employer. It was but a few
months before I knew the names of all the drugs, and could
make up the prescriptions with skill and safety; I was very
proud to find that the doctor was pleased with me. The doctor's wife was as kind to me as if she had been my own
mother, and, all things considered, I had a happy home, and
was contented.

"Harry and Lottie were delighted with their new situations; but I did not see them as often as I wished, though I
went with Lottie to church occasionally, and sat in the same
pew with her, and read my prayers in her book, and then
mixed drugs and built air castles the remainder of the week.
But I am getting tired of talking about children, and I expect
my hearers are tired of it, too, and I shall therefore say but
little more about it. If I have bored you with too much talk
of dogs and children, I beg pardon, and promise to make
a long leap over the space of seven years. They were years
of happiness to me—so were they to Lottie and Harry.
Lottie is eighteen, and more beautiful than ever. The large
dreamy eyes are the same, but the tall, queenly form has filled

out, presenting a model that an artist would delight to paint from. The stamp of intellect was sparkling on her white brow, and she was (as I thought then, and think now) the most charming girl that my eyes had ever looked upon. Harry had made rapid progress in his legal studies, and would be ready to enter on his professional career by the time he was twenty-one; while I was an overgrown, awkward young man, rather shy, and sneaky when in the presence of strangers; though I had studied closely, and Doctor Dodson said I would some day be a great physician. It was arranged that I should attend the lectures in Philadelphia, and I thought it best to have an understanding with Lottie before I left. I had never asked her to be my wife. I became jealous and unhappy because Lottie was surrounded by devoted admirers, many of whom were men of wealth and high social standing; and I was alarmed lest I should after all lose the great prize. But let us rest a while, and I'll tell more about it in the next chapter."

CHAPTER IX.

"LOTTIE had been at the Bards Town School in Kentucky for four years; but she usually spent the summer vacation at home. She graduated with the highest honors, having won the first prize in Greek, Latin and French, and triumphantly carried off the costly gold cup offered for the best original poem. There were two things combined which contributed to her success. In the first place, she possessed the active brain, and the ambition; and in the second place, she had been trained and taught much of the time by Mr. Rockland before she went to the Kentucky school. The iron lawyer would often take her into his library and make her recite lesson after lesson, when he would lecture her on the different branches of her studies. Then he would stray away into ancient and modern history, poetry and politics, spending hours in expounding them to the mind that was so able and willing to grasp the meaning. He would often make Lottie draw up bills in chancery—write pleas and declarations

under his direction. Then he would explain all the legal
points in some important case, and request her to look up the
law and arrange his brief. It was a remarkable fact that Mr.
Rockland would neglect his best paying clients in order to
cram his solid ideas into Lottie's grasping mind.

"'Ed, she will be home to-morrow,' said Harry Wallingford as he ran his hand under my arm and walked down the
street by my side. 'I have just received a telegram from her;
she left Bards Town this morning, and is now in Louisville.
Mr. Rockland is going to give a grand ball in honor of her
great triumph as the champion prize-taker at Bards Town.
I suppose you have heard about her wonderful victory?'

"'Yes.'

"'See here, old fellow, is that all you have to say in
praise of this wonderful sister of mine? What is the matter
with you, anyway? You look as if you wanted to murder
somebody.'

"'There is nothing wrong with me at all, and I am glad
to hear of Lottie's grand achievements,' I replied rather
dryly, because I had begun to discuss with my mind on the
probabilities of losing Lottie. I knew full well that many a
gallant knight would be ready to leap into the arena as a
contestant for the charming prize—ready to battle to the
death to win the hand and heart of the most lovely, the most
beautiful and the most talented girl in Tennessee. When I
weighed my chances well I was forced to the conclusion that
they were too light to go into the balances against many other
young men who I knew were going to enter the lists. Lottie
had always manifested a partiality for me, but I was afraid
that it was more a feeling of sisterly love than anything else.
During our childhood days we had often talked of the feelings
of true love which we had for each other; but Lottie was
now a woman, and I did not want her to love me as a brother.
I had no money, and but little education—was green and
awkward, timid and ugly, and had no confidence in myself;
but I was determined to break many a lance before a rival
should carry off the great prize.

"Mr. Rockland was so deeply in love with Lottie that it
amounted to idolatry, and it was generally believed, and
publicly expressed, that he would settle his large fortune on

her. He was extravagant in the expenditure of money for her comfort; in fact, he poured it out like water to gratify her slightest wish, though she was rather inclined to be economical and prudent. She seemed to think more of her books and music than she did of dress and display.

" 'Ed, old boy,' exclaimed Wallingford, after a long pause, 'did you know that I was very proud of my sister?'

" 'Yes.'

" 'Ah, yes, I tell you what it is, she is ahead of any girl in Memphis, so far as intelligence and goodness are concerned. Mrs. Rockland says that she is going to set Lottie out when the ball comes off.'

" 'How set her out?'

" 'Pshaw! don't you know what they mean by setting a girl out? Of course you do. When a girl is ready to receive matrimonial propositions they set her out; that is, they hang out the sign. As the gamblers say, they spread their lay-out, don't you see? Well, Mrs. Rockland is going to rig Lottie up and throw her at the heads of the male community, as it were. Now, Ed, let me tell you one thing: I mean to have something to say in that little skirmish, and the man who marries my sister must be the reliable sort. If any sap-head bumpkin begins to caper around Lottie, I'll just give him unlimited leave of absence; and if he don't take it, I'll wring off his head.'

" 'Do you intend to marry her to a rich man; or shall she marry for love?'

" 'Of course she shall marry the man of her choice, provided he is of the right stamp. I don't care about the length of his purse, but he must have brains, and a heart of the right sort, and he must have an established reputation for honor and integrity. If any man were to marry my sister and be unkind to her, don't you know I would kill him?'

" 'I should be inclined to do such a man some great bodily harm myself.'

" 'Thank you, Ed, I believe you would; and well you might, because, you know, Lottie always loved you as a brother.'

"I felt my heart make a sudden leap and drive the blood to my cheeks when he spoke of brotherly love. I wanted none of that sort. I felt miserable, and was unable to conceal my feelings.

" 'By-by, old boy,' said Wallingford, as he turned into the street that led to his office. 'You must call and see us when Lottie gets home.'

"I bowed stiffly, said nothing, and hurried on to my home by no means satisfied with the prospects. 'They are going to set her out, are they?' I said mentally. 'Good! I'll be there when the show begins, and though my chance is slim, yet I'll die hard, if die I must.' I made a draw on Doctor Dodson for cash to pay for a first-class ball dress, and felt profoundly thankful to my tailor for the skill he displayed in the make-up. I did not call to see Lottie when she arrived , because I wanted to appear at the ball in my splendid new costume, so as to take a fair start in the matrimonial tilt I knew the other young men would make.

"Grand indeed were the preparations that were being made for the great ball , and the young people who had been so fortunate as to receive an invitation were looking forward impatiently to the eventful day; and no one thought about it more anxiously than I did. I was very full of apprehension and doubt in regard to Lottie's feelings toward me, and I propounded a thousand questions to my own mind about it. 'Will she look down from the high circle where fortune has placed her to the humble sphere in which I am doomed to dwell? or will she forget the poor awkward boy who, in the happy days of old, was glad to kiss the dust that had felt the touch of her little feet? Why should she stoop so low as to even think of me? What right have I, a poor half-educated clerk, to expect such a brilliant, beautiful heiress to lavish her favors on me, when men of wealth and high position are ready to lay their honors and wealth at her feet? What right have I to aspire so high?'. 'None—none—none!' was thundered in my ear by Common Sense, as the answer to my mental questions. 'Miss Charlotte Wallingford is not for your sort,' said Reason 'She is fit for the wife of a king!' 'Yes, but I saved her life,' said my Mind, 'and she is under obligations to me.' 'True enough,' Reason replies, 'but it does not follow that she must marry you. Women's lives are often saved by their servants, yet they do not marry them.' 'But

it will kill me if Miss Wallingford marries any other man.'
'No matter if it does—why should she care? the world will
never feel the loss—the sun will shine as bright, the flowers
grow as sweet, and the seasons will come and go after you
are dead just as they did when you were alive.' With such
unpleasant reflections as these I had managed to work my
mind up to an unusual degree of excitement. I became
gloomy and unhappy to such an extent as to attract the attention of my good mother (as I called Mrs. Dodson), and she
begged me to tell her the cause of my misery. I evaded her
questions, and sought solitude, where I could give vent to my
sorrow unmolested. She cast many an imploring look at me
when I would leave my food untasted. My cheeks grew pale
and my appetite failed, and I hugged my misery to my breast,
and told my secret to none. I was proud, and felt offended,
but had no reasons to give for it. No one had been unkind to,
or in any manner maltreated me, yet I was querulous, melancholy and despairing.

"'Ah, ha! here we come, my boy,' said Doctor Dodson one
morning as he came into the store. 'What's the matter,
what's the matter, Ed, my boy? speak it out, speak it out,
let it come; what makes you look like a ghost, my boy?
Pshaw! don't tell me such a tale as that, my boy, ah, ha!
don't you do it, I say; indigestion! did you ever know a
Russian bear to have bad digestion? No, no, Ed, my boy
you needn't try to fool me—you can't do it. The discuss is
in your mind, ah, ha! don't you see? Yes, yes, that's what's
the matter. Something has gone wrong. I'd say it was a
love scrape, if it was any other boy; but my old booby has
too much sense for anything of that sort; ah, ha! don't you
see how it is, my boy?'

"I soon became convinced that the good old doctor would
pry the secret out of me unless I resorted to falsehood, which
I resolved not to do; therefore I begged him to let me alone,
promising to tell him everything at the end of ten days.

"'Ah, ha! very good, my boy; I won't press you further
just now, but I mean to hold you down to your promise, don't
you see? I won't let you go to Philadelphia while you are
looking like a defunct specimen of humanity, ah, ha! don't
you see? You look more like a fit subject for a grave-yard

than a medical school, ah, ha! yes, that you do, my boy.
There now, go to work, and quit this moping about as if you
wanted to sneak into a tomb.'

"I was glad when the doctor was called to see one of his
patients.

"At last the time for the grand ball arrived, and I had
arranged my toilet with unusual care. My good mother
had been persuading me to send my card to Miss Ella Will-
chester, a charming young lady residing just across the street
from our house, but it would have required the strength of a
forty horse-power engine to make me escort any other girl to
Lottie's ball. I thought it would be treason to her if I offered
any favors to any other girl. The fact is, I could not think
of anybody else but Lottie; her image was floating before my
eyes by day, and swimming in my mind when I was asleep.
I did not make my appearance at the ball until after ten
o'clock, for I wanted to slip in quietly, unobserved, in order
that I might see whether Lottie had even so much as thought
about me. I must acknowledge that I felt rather sheepish
when I was going round so as to come in at the side entrance,
hoping to get in unnoticed. The band commenced playing a
lively waltz as I stepped on the veranda at the end of the
ball-room, and a dozen couples went whirling round and
floating gracefully through the hall. I took a seat on a chair
near a window, where I could peep between the folds of the
rich lace curtains and watch the movements of the guests
within. I noticed a half dozen young men crowd round a
young lady whose back was toward me. They were struggling
with, and jostling each other, all apparently eager to get a
word with the young lady. Who was the fair one that
attracted such attention? was the question that came up in my
mind. I could see the tall, queen-like form, but could not get
a view of her face. The square shoulders and straight body,
the beautiful arms and bright golden hair were visible, but my
mind was full of curiosity to know who she was. I thought
it might be Lottie, but then she was too tall—or at least I
concluded that after a moment's reflection. It was Lottie,
nevertheless, and I had lost sight of the fact that it had been
nearly a year since I had seen her. She abruptly left the
crowd of admirers.

"'Excuse me a moment, please,' I heard her say as she
went to her brother, who occupied a seat just inside the room,
and within six feet of where I was. 'Brother, has Eddie
come yet?' I heard the question distinctly.

"'No; I don't think he has,' was the reply.

"'I am afraid he is ill, else he would have been here long
ago.'

"'Pshaw! sister, never mind Ed; he isn't the sort that gets
sick.'

"'Oh, I am so sorry he is not here!'

"I could bear it no longer; my heart was again in my
throat, and I thrust my hand in between the curtains, and
said: 'I did not expect you would have time to spare a
thought about me on such an occasion as this.'

"She uttered a smothered scream, sprang through the door,
and seized both of my hands and began to jerk them up and
down. Never had my eyes beheld such a lovely object as the
one then before me, such radiant beauty, such lofty, dazzling
charms, such large, liquid blue eyes and bright golden hair,
such round, pretty arms, such a tall, stately form! Nothing
could match this angelic creature! I was stunned—surprised, and almost paralyzed, as I stood staring with open
mouth at the wonderful beauty before me. 'Is this Lottie?
Can this be the same little blue-eyed thing who tramped so
many miles by my side long, long ago?' That was the question that naturally forced itself on my mind. I could not
realize the fact that this radiant model of perfection and the
little sore-footed tramp were one and the same person.

"'I am going to give you a real good scolding, Eddie,' she
said as she still held both of my hands tightly clasped in hers.
'Why have you not come to see me before now; and what
made you come so late to-night; and what made you slip in
here and hide as if you had been doing a mean thing?'

"All I could do was to stand like an idiot, staring at the
indescribable beauty before me, unable to utter a word. I
then and there concluded that she never would be mine. No
such woman could ever come down low enough to be the wife
of a half-educated pill-maker.

"'What is the matter, Eddie?' she exclaimed in an anxious tone, as she cast a look of surprise at me. 'You are

ill—your hands are very cold, and your face is as pale
as death.'

" 'No, I am very well, I thank you,' I managed with a
struggle to say.

" 'You are trying to deceive me, but you cannot do it; you
have been ill?'

" 'Partners for a quadrille!' exclaimed the leader of the
band, and three young men made a dash toward Lottie, each
one claiming her as a partner. She took the arm of Mr.
Heartsell, after some little controversy as to whose turn it was
to dance with her, and soon was floating through the waltz
with him.

" 'By Jupiter! She is a stunner, ain't she, Sam?' exclaimed a dandyfied youth as Heartsell led her away.

" 'Your head's level, and don't you forget it!' replied the
one addressed, who was a little, hook-nosed law student
with but a small amount of brains and lots of brass.

"Wherever I went I could hear groups of young men
lavishing their extravagant praises on the wonderful young
beauty who had so suddenly blazed down among them like a
newly discovered planet.

"As soon as Lottie was released from Heartsell she came
back to me. 'Eddie,' said she, 'I want you to enjoy yourself
here to-night, and you must let me introduce you to some of
these charming young ladies. I heard one expressing an anxiety to be introduced to that tall, handsome young gentleman with the shaggy whiskers. I think she is smitten with
both you and your whiskers; come, let me introduce you!'

" 'No, you must excuse me—Lottie, I will not dance to-
night, unless it is with you.'

" 'Indeed, you do me great honor, and I'll put you down for
the third set, as I am engaged for the next two, and would
have been for every other one but I declined the honor. You
must excuse me now—I am acting hostess to-night, as mother
is not very well.'

"I waited for my turn with no small degree of impatience,
as I sat like a picture against the wall watching Lottie as she
glided like a fairy through the mazes of the dance. She was
dressed in white satin, trimmed with lace of the most exquisite
and costly pattern, with close and smooth-fitting body, which

set off her round, straight form to great advantage. A cluster of sparkling diamonds fastened both ends of a pearl necklace which met on her bosom, while a large white rose was pinned at her throat with a little golden arrow; and a broad band of gold encircled each wrist, while a large amethyst set glittered from each one of the bracelets. Her long, golden hair was coiled up in two plaited rolls, and pinned on the back of her head with a pair of Cupid-darts set in diamonds. I never had seen Lottie so exquisitely dressed before, although she was always very particular and neat in her toilet. Mr. Rockland had ordered her set of diamonds from New York especially for that occasion.

"At last the time arrived when I was to waltz with her, and I would have been glad to offer an excuse, because I was trembling like one in an ague fit, and felt as if I were going to make a botch of it. I knew I was clumsy, awkward, and a novice at the business, and just as I was about to stammer out an excuse, the band struck up a lively waltz, and Lottie seized me without ceremony and almost dragged me to the middle of the floor. I imagined that the eyes of every one in the room were gazing at me, and I was about half right, for my tall, gawky form loomed up above all the other men, which attracted the attention of the spectators. When we began to whirl round the room Lottie let her cheek rest on my shoulder; and I felt her cool sweet breath fanning my face, while her beautiful eyes gazed up into mine with an expression of unmixed delight. I had not failed to notice how differently she acted when waltzing with me from what she did with other men. Her fair cheek had never touched another man's shoulder on that night, and no one had been able to keep her on the floor as long as I did. I soon became warmed up, and my blood boiled with the intoxicating influence of the music, and the love for the girl whose cheek rested on my shoulder. I forgot everything but the dear idol who was so near my heart, and would have kept whirling round until my limbs gave way under me, but the music ceased, and I led Lottie to a seat; but I did not get a chance to enjoy her company many moments before she was surrounded by a crowd of young men, who insisted on leading her to the piano. The musicians had laid down their instruments, and were enjoying a smoke on the veranda, and Lottie was urged to sing. I drew as near as I could, and took my stand on her left. She ran her fingers rapidly over the keys and then asked me what she should sing.

" 'Give us something to remind us of olden times!'

" 'Very well, here is one of my own invention:

" 'In the happy days of yore
A hero loved me then.
Let my tears of sorrow pour,
My happy days are o'er,
For he loves me now no more—
He loved me truly then.

" 'Oh, what bliss it is to know
A hero loved me then!
His young heart was all aglow,
And as pure as driven snow;
I must let my hero go.
He loved me truly then.

" 'All the happy days are past—
A hero loved me then.
This poor heart is o'ercast
With sorrow's consuming blast,
My hero broke it at last,
He loved me truly then.

" 'I remember every vow—
A hero loved me then.
It crowds my memory now,
For he kissed me on the brow,
Then he sweetly told me how
He loved me truly then.'

"Every time she lingered on the words 'A hero loved me then,' her eyes were raised to mine for a moment and I thought I saw an appealing look in them, and a glance of inquiry. When she came to the last three lines her voice trembled slightly, and when she fixed her beautiful eyes on me I saw that they were moist, though no tears fell from them. She repeated the last three lines in a low, plaintive tone.

"For a few seconds after the last sweet sound had ceased not a word was spoken. Lottie declined to sing any more, notwithstanding she was urged to do so by the entire audience, but she rose from the piano and made her way to me, and running her arm under mine, said:

" 'Come, Eddie, take me out where we can get a little fresh air—I am smothering in here.'

"The proposition suited me admirably, for I was anxious to be alone with her, and went out on the portico and began to walk up and down the floor, while Lottie leaned on my arm, with her face turned up toward mine. I was too happy to talk; my heart thrilled with delight, and I remained silent. After making a few rounds on the portico without speaking, we took seats on a low wooden bench, where a thick cluster of honeysuckle vines formed a canopy that would conceal us from the prying eyes of Mr. Heartsell and two other young men who were apparently watching us.

" 'Now, Edward,' said Lottie, 'I want you to tell me what is the matter with you? Come now, don't try to deceive me, for you know you cannot do it.˙ I have not seen you smile to-night. You don't look or act as you did in the happy days of old. You were always cheerful and pleasant then, but you look pale and serious now.'

" 'Lottie, I know I could not deceive you if I were to try; but I have no wish to do anything of the sort. I am unhappy, but I do not know that I could give any good reason for it. One thing, however, I will say, and that is I think we shall never see any more such happy days as we have spent together. I see a great gulf beginning to flow in between you and me, which sooner or later will drive us apart forever!'

" 'Pshaw! Edward, you ought not to talk that way—it pains me deeply to hear it. No gulf could be made wide enough to separate me from such a dear, good, noble *brother* as you have been to me; but what do you mean when you speak of a gulf coming between us?'

" 'You have an accomplished education, a superior mind, as well as very great beauty, and are to be a great heiress. Mr. Rockland is proud and wealthy, and is very fond of you, he will expect you to marry some distinguished man of his own choosing. I may be mistaken, but I don't think he would be pleased to have me as a frequent visitor at his house. He did not speak to me to-night, but cast on me a cold, contemptuous look, and bowed stiffly.'

" 'Now see here, Edward, in the first place, I think you are very much mistaken in supposing Mr. Rockland dislikes you.

He is naturally a very stern, sad man, but he has a warm, tender heart, and I believe he loves me dearly; but I tell you now plainly that the man who hates my dear, noble brother must hate me too. And when it comes to the question of matrimony, I guess I will have something to say about that. In the first place, I do not want to marry at all, and in the next place, I shall be very certain never to marry any man unless I love him with all my heart!'

"While she was uttering the words just mentioned she made the heels of her little boots clatter against the floor rapidly, and I could see by the sparkle of her eyes that she meant what she said. I was partially pleased, and partially vexed—pleased to hear her say that she never would marry any man unless she loved him; vexed to hear her speak of her love toward me as a dear *brother*—I wanted a different sort of love. She now took the beautiful white rôse from her throat and put it in the button-hole of my coat, and while she was doing so her lovely face was within three inches of mine, and I felt her cool breath gently touching my cheek. When she finished the job, over which I thought she lingered a long time, she gave me a gentle slap on the cheek and said:

" 'There, now, that is very nice; and I want you to drive away that ugly frown from your brow, and go in and help me to entertain my guests. Will you do it?'

"Yes, Lottie, you know I will do anything to please you; but stop a moment—I want to know what you meant by composing such a song as the one you sang a moment ago? Who is it that loved you truly then, and loves you now no more?'

" 'Ask me no questions, and I will tell you no falsehoods, but I guess you could answer that question better than I could. But come along now—we must go in, for I heard some one inquiring for me; give me your arm, and don't forget the ugly frown.'

" 'Trust me now, Lottie, and I'll be as polite to your guests as a French dancing master.'

" 'Good enough, Edward! so come along.'

"We returned to the ball-room, when Mr. Heartsell came up to engage Lottie as his partner for the next set.

" 'I beg you to excuse me, Mr. Heartsell—I am going to dance with Mr. Demar in this set.'

"Now here was unmistakable evidence of partiality on Lottie's part toward me, for I had not asked her to dance with me; in fact, I had not intended to dance any more that night.

"My self-conceit went up to a premium, my heart swelled with indescribable delight, and I began to think that after all I was not to be laid entirely on the shelf. I knew that Heartsell was going to be a suitor for Lottie's hand, and I considered him my most dangerous rival, as I was aware of the fact that he was Mr. Rockland's favorite. He bit his lip with vexation as I led Lottie off to begin the waltz, while a feeling of triumph swelled up in my bosom. When the waltz was ended, Lottie parted from me as she whispered:

" 'Now, Eddie, remember my guests, and try to help to entertain them.'

"As she left me, Heartsell drew up in front of me, and stared at me for a moment, while I thought that I perceived something like a sneer of contempt play for a second on his face. 'Hullo, Demar!' he exclaimed, 'where did you get that beautiful white rose?'

" 'That, sir, was fastened here by the prettiest girl in this room,' I replied, haughtily, as I drew myself up and walked away. I saw his cheeks grow purple with anger as he went toward Lottie, who was talking with a middle-aged lady near by.

" 'Miss Wallingford,' he said as he bowed low before her, 'will you honor me with a short interview?'

"Without uttering a word, Lottie took his arm and was led out through a side door which opened on the corridor. They came round on the outside of the room and stopped within six feet of the seat where I was, and immediately opposite a window, the sash of which was up, but the curtains were down. I knew from the tone of Mr. Heartsell's voice that he was angry with Lottie about something.

" 'You seem to be enjoying yourself better than usual to-night.'

" 'Why should I not enjoy myself when I am among so many good kind friends?'

" 'I am truly glad to see you enjoying the society of your very good *friend*.'

" 'Why do you choose to use the singular number?'

" 'Because if you have any more than one friend (and I am happy to believe you have), you have been very careful to avoid letting them know that you recognized them.'

" 'Why, Mr. Heartsell, how can you be so unjust as to say that?'

" 'How many times have you danced with me to-night?'

" 'Once.'

" 'How many times with Mr. Campston?'

" 'I have not danced with him at all.'

" 'Did he ask you?'

" 'Yes.'

" 'How many sets have you danced with Demar?'

" 'Two.'

" ' "Now, in the name of all the gods at once, upon what meat doth this our Cæsar feed that he is grown so great? Why, *man,* he doth bestride the narrow world like a Colossus, and we petty men walk under his huge legs and peep about to find ourselves dishonorable graves." '

" 'If your sarcasm is intended for Mr. Demar, I beg permission to say that you might find a dishonorable grave without peeping about his legs to find it.'

" 'Oh, I crave your pardon, Miss Wallingford, I assure you I meant no offense; but candidly, I should be glad to know what Demar has done to entitle him to such distinguished privileges? How is it that this great Cæsar can monopolize the beauteous belle of the ball, while we petty men must peep about among common people to find ourselves partners?'

" 'Mr. Heartsell, it is not agreeable for me to listen to wit of this nature, because Mr. Demar has been to me a devoted friend, a true, noble, unselfish brother. Look at that scar on my wrist, if you please.'

" 'Well, I see it; what about that?'

" 'That scar was made by the poisonous fangs of a rattle-snake, and I would have died in ten minutes but that this generous, heroic brother drew the poison from my veins with his lips, and came very near losing his own life by the brave deed. Well may you compare him with Cæsar, because, while you do it in jest, I will do it in earnest, for his courage entitles him to all the honors that an inexperienced girl like me can bestow. If it should be my pleasure to grant him more favors than I do to other gentlemen, I trust I can do so without giving offense to them.'

" 'Ah, Miss Wallingford, you are an eloquent orator, and if Cæsar did have his friend Marcus Antonius to defend him, Demar has a more eloquent defender in you. I envy him, and would make any sacrifice to win such favors as fall to his share. I dare say you are quite lucky to have two such brave, good brothers as Demar and Wallingford.'

" 'Indeed, I think so, and am happy in the thought, too.'

" 'By the by, Miss Wallingford, you have lost that beautiful white rose that I saw on your throat a while ago.'

" 'You are mistaken, sir, I did not lose it.'

" 'Ah, indeed! I asked you to give it to me, and you refused; you certainly did not present it to another gentleman?'

" 'And why should I not give it to whom I pleased; was it not mine?'

" 'Hem! yes, I cannot deny that, but such partiality as that would clip an insult very close, and I am loth to believe such a charming lady as Miss Wallingford would offer an indignity to one who loves and who esteems her so highly as I do.'

" 'Now, Mr. Heartsell, I should be very unhappy if I thought I had given you any just cause for offense, but in this instance I must say it appears to me that you are manufacturing a mountain out of a mole-hill. If you desire it, I will present you with a basketful of roses this instant.'

" 'No, no; you shall do nothing of the sort. It was not the rose itself that I cared for, but it was the emblem which would have come with it. May I know who was the lucky donee?'

" 'Certainly you may, for I assure you there is no secret connected with it. I had the *honor* (she put the accent heavy on the honor) to present the rose to my noble, heroic brother, Edward Demar.'

"Now we should never use extravagant language, and we should worship no living being except God; but on that particular occasion I confess I committed such a sin; though if the recording angel sets it down against me, I believe he will credit me with a partial justification, at least. How could I sit there and hear the most charming woman in America boasting of the *honor* she had done herself by presenting a rose to me, and not feel an inclination to fall down and worship her? How could I hear her dear voice sounding eloquently in praise of me, without thinking extravagant thoughts? The fact is, I was so much excited that they might have heard the loud throbbings of my heart, if they had listened. I determined, however, to put an end to Mr. Heartsell's little *tete-a-tete,* because I knew it would please her. I went round on the north side and passed across, coming up to where they stood, and coughed as I approached, in order to notify Lottie of my arrival.

"'Your friends will be curious to know what has become of their fair hostess, Miss Wallingford,' I observed, as I halted by her side.

"'Ah, thank you, *brother,* for reminding me of my duty,' she replied, as she took my arm and bowed stiffly to Heartsell. 'We will finish our little quarrel at another time, sir.'

"'No, no; the victory is yours, and I make an unconditional surrender. Render unto Cæsar that which is his, but don't crowd things on him that don't belong to him.'

"'That fellow Heartsell is an impertinent scamp, and I mean to tell him so.'

"'If you do you will displease me beyond measure, for I think he is a perfect gentleman; I am ashamed to say that I have treated him rather unkindly to-night, and I mean to apologize as soon as I have an opportunity.'

"'Oh! very well, if you love him, you should let him know it by all means!'

"'See here, Edward, I must request you not to mention Mr. Heartsell's name in my presence any more to-night; and I will also ask you to excuse me now, as I must really mingle among my guests, and give them some attention.'

"Then she left me, and soon was surrounded by a crowd of young men. I did not have a chance to talk with her any more that night, and when I went home my mind was full of strange conjectures and conflicting emotions. One question appeared to be pretty well settled, and that was a perfect knowledge on my part that all my hopes of happiness would be destroyed if Lottie should refuse to marry me. Love is a strange passion, and no one knows how it can upset a man's equanimity, unless he has learned it by actual experience. It

is a passion that produces indescribable happiness to those
who are loved in return, but of all the distressing pains and
horrible torture that mortal man ever felt, that which he suf-
fers when his mind is racked with doubt on that subject is the
greatest. I had resolved a hundred times to have that question settled, but when in Lottie's presence my tongue was paralyzed and my brain refused to lay out a sensible idea. I had
ordered a jeweler to make an exquisite gold ring, with a beautiful diamond set, and had Lottie's and my name engraved
on the inside. This I had carried in my pocket for two weeks,
intending to ask her to accept it as an engagement ring, but
for reasons already stated I failed to do it. I had written out
and memorized what I supposed to be an eloquent speech,
which I intended to deliver with the ring, but my courage
oozed out the very moment those large, beautiful blue eyes
set their sight on me. Lottie had a strange habit of looking
me square in the face, which never failed to set my limbs to
trembling and my heart to thumping. I was considered a
privileged guest at Mr. Rockland's house, not by him, but by
Lottie, and I visited there often, and was frequently so unlucky as to meet Mr. Heartsell there, and sometimes other
young men who had entered the lists. I watched Lottie very
closely, but I could not tell whether she loved any one of her
suitors or not. So far as I was able to judge, she treated all
alike.

"I spent at least three days of each week strolling about by
Lottie's side, half crazy with love for her, sometimes buoyed
up with hope, at others struggling with suspense and despair.
Summer was about to step out, and autumn was ready to walk
in. The weather was hot and dry, while dust and heat hung
about over all things. Vegetation was parched and withered
by the long drought, while gloom and dust combined to make
me very miserable, except when I was lingering with Lottie
in her beautiful flower garden, which, owing to her industry,
was always delightful and cool, for she had everything thoroughly watered every evening. The east side of her garden
was thickly shaded with young magnolias, whose broad green
leaves protected the thick velvety turf that covered the ground
beneath. The west side was set apart for flowers alone, and
notwithstanding the protracted drought that had prevailed,

they looked as fresh and vigorous as they did in May and
June. Old Uncle Zack, as Lottie called the old negro gardener, was always anxious to please his pretty nightingale (a
pet name he had given Lottie). During her attendance at the
Kentucky school, Uncle Zack had been the manager of her
garden and her birds, and on her return she found that the
duty had been faithfully performed. A charming summer-
house stood near the east boundary of the garden, all covered over with clustering vines and blooming roses. It was
at this delightful spot that I had spent so many happy hours
with Lottie. A large wooden table sat in the center of the
summer house, and low willow chairs were ranged around the
sides, and when the weather was fine the table was covered
with books, maps, sheet music, drawing materials, magazines
and a guitar. Lottie called this her study, for that was the delightful spot where she practiced music and drawing and re-
viewed her studies generally.

"The time when I was to start to Philadelphia for the purpose of attending the medical lectures was near at hand, and
still I had not been able to muster up the courage to make
my love known to her. Doctor Dodson was anxious for me
to start immediately, because he was uneasy about my health,
which was on the decline, but he had no suspicions as to the
cause. He thought that a trip to the sea-coast would be ben-
eficial; then he had some business at New York and Boston
which he wanted me to transact for him. I could have told
him that no journey would restore my health. There was one
thing, and only one, that could ever bring health and happiness back to me. I knew that could I be assured of Lottie's
love, all would be well with me; but if that was denied, I
never would know health or happiness any more.

"One sultry evening near the end of August, when the sun
was about to disappear in the West, after having scorched and
burned the earth for twelve consecutive hours, I found myself
lingering in the summer-house by Lottie, where I had been
for a long time trying to collect the necessary courage to tell
her of my love.

" 'Sing one more song for me, Lottie, before I go, please,'
said I, as I drew my chair closer to hers.

" 'What shall it be?' she inquired, as she picked up her guitar and began to run her fingers over the strings.

" 'I would like to hear the one you sang the night of the ball—I do not know its name. It says something about a hero who loved you in the happy days of old, who loves you now no more.'

" 'Oh, yes; I never will forget that song, for it is one of my favorites, and my own composition. Do you like it, Edward?'

" 'I like to hear you sing it, but I do not think I like the sentiment, for I am sure no one ever loved you in the days of old who does not love you now.'

"I saw a crimson tinge steal over her cheeks, as her beautiful eyes were for a moment fixed on me.

" 'A hero did love me, long ago, anyway, though I don't know so well about it now; but let that pass—we poor, foolish women should never complain about anything.'

"She then began to tune the instrument, which was suspended by a broad blue ribbon that passed over her left shoulder and was tied to a little brass hook in each end of the guitar.

"Lottie's voice seemed to be in excellent tune, and in all respects under her control, though it was low and tremulous; and when she came to the line that said, 'He loves me now no more,' she looked me full in the face, and repeated the line in a pathetic tone that brought the tears to my eyes. Every vein in my body was full of hot blood. When Lottie came to the last three lines her voice sank to a mere whisper, and I could see that some unusual emotion was at work in her bosom. She paused a moment as the sweet echo of her voice gradually died away, and then she turned round, and fixing her eyes upon me, repeated the last verse:

> " 'I remember every vow—
> A hero loved me then.
> It crowds my memory now,
> For he kissed me on the brow,
> Then he sweetly told me how
> He loved me truly then.'

"She laid the guitar down and turned her face another way, and as I leaned forward slightly, I saw something like a drop of dew trembling on her cheek. That little trembling tear settled my fate. An unaccountable boldness came upon me, and all my timidity disappeared, and I was rash, impetuous, and I might say rude, because I seized her hand and pressed it to my lips a dozen times in rapid succession. My impetuosity seemed to astonish and frighten her, and she began to move away.

" 'It is time I was in the house, Edward,' said she as she moved away; 'mother will be calling me if I don't go.'

" 'No, no, Lottie!' I exclaimed as I moved toward her; 'don't go now; remember I am going away next week, to stay a long, long time, and we never may meet again. The fact of the business is, I think I never shall come back to Memphis any more.'

"Her beautiful face grew a shade paler, but she soon regained composure: 'Come along then, and let me show you my pretty birds,' she said as she moved toward a little latticed house that stood about fifty feet from the summer-house. I imagined she was endeavoring to get my mind fixed on other subjects than the one on which my thoughts were bent. I followed her, and when we entered the cozy little house, the old parrot began to laugh and chatter away.

" 'Lottie! Lottie! Lottie!' he screamed, as he leaped down on her shoulder. 'Ah, ha! here we come. Lottie! Lottie! Lottie! ah, ha! here we come!'

" 'How did he learn to imitate Doctor Dodson so perfectly?' I asked.

" 'The doctor frequently comes to see me, and old Roderick has heard him so often that he has caught his expressions.'

"A mocking-bird was singing in a cage that sat on the joist, and a dozen canaries were making sweet music in their little silver-mounted houses, while an old jackdaw was muttering to himself in a wire cage. Each bird seemed to be making music for his own amusement, and on his own hook. It was a combination of discordant sounds, which might have been good music if they could have been induced to sing one at a time. It was a shrewd maneuver of Lottie to decoy me to that place, for no man could talk loud enough to be heard amid such an ear-splitting clatter as was made by these birds.

"I concluded that she had resorted to this strategic maneuver in order to avoid the disagreeable revelation which she
had guessed I was about to make. Then I became angry,
and that increased my courage and made me quite reckless,
and I was determined to know my fate before I left. I
believed she could read my inmost thoughts, for I had never
seen her more embarrassed than she was then. The sun had
entirely disappeared, and a dark purple bank began to loom
up in the East, indicating the approach of twilight; while the
face of the moon every now and then peeped down through
a column of white clouds that flew across the horizon. As
the dew began to dampen the flowers around us, a delicious
fragrance arose and filled all the air with its ravishing
sweetness. I took Lottie's hand, and placing it under my
arm, led her back to the summer-house, and took a seat by
her side. Old Bob came up and laid his head on my knee
and began to whine, and tried to wag his tail, but it was too
short. Notwithstanding the poor old dog was stone blind, it
was plain that he recognized me.

"'Lottie,' said I, 'this faithful old friend remembers me,
and I am glad to know that there is one living thing in this
cold world that cares for me. I want you to take good care
of him for my sake when I am gone, for I guess I will not
see him any more. I never shall forget those happy days
when we were poor, homeless tramps—penniless, friendless.
and simple, but hopeful and cheerful.'

"Her face was turned away—her eyes were bent on the
ground, and she was busy plucking the tender leaves from a
bunch of roses, and scattering them at her feet. I knew from
the rise and fall of her bosom that some strong emotion was
at work in her breast; but I thought it was caused by an
unwillingness to listen to my melancholy expressions.

"Taking her left hand, I enclosed it in both of mine, and
after holding it a moment, I ventured to raise it to my lips
and stamp it with many fervent kisses; then I pressed it over
my loud throbbing heart, while her face was still turned away
from me.

"'I wonder if any other man ever will press this little hand
against his heart, and call it his?'

"She instantly withdrew it with a sudden jerk, as if an

insect had stung her, and then fixing her expressive eyes on
me with a reproachful look, said:

" 'I declare, we must go to the house now; mother does
not like to keep tea waiting for any one.'

" 'She will excuse you when you inform her that I was
making my farewell visit; who knows that we ever shall meet
again in this world?'

"Once more she turned her face away and gazed on the
ground.

" 'Lottie, here is a beautiful diamond ring I want you to
wear; it will prevent you from entirely forgetting the one
who has always loved you.'

"As I uttered those words in a trembling tone, I took her
hand and slipped the ring on her finger, which she did not
resist, nor did she give any signs of assent; in fact, she did
not seem to notice what I was saying or doing; but I could
see that she was deeply moved with excitement, as her body
was trembling violently.

" 'Lottie, will you write me a letter occasionally when I am
far away from the one I love so dearly?'

" 'Yes, Edward, I will answer all your letters.'

"After I had placed the ring on her finger, I again pressed
her trembling hand against my heart.

" 'Lottie, it will be a long time ere we meet again, and I
suppose you will be married to some distinguished man before
my return?'

"A gentle shake of the head, and a slight jerk of the hand,
was her only answer.

" 'Will you ever think of the boyish tramp who long ago
claimed you as his little wife, after I am gone?'

" 'Yes, Edward, I never shall forget the halcyon days of
old, for although we were poor, homeless wanderers, we were
not unhappy.'

" 'Lottie, I loved that pretty little tramp devotedly then,
and time has increased that holy passion, until it has filled my
heart, my mind, my soul, my brain, my body, my thoughts,
my dreams and my blood! Fortune has not lavished her
favors on me, but that is not my fault. I know I am ignorant,
green, poor and uneducated, doomed to occupy an humble
sphere in life, while the blind goddess has been more liberal

in the bestowal of her favors on you. Your beauty and your talent alone would have placed you on a plane far above my lowly valley; but when it is known that you are to be a great heiress, I feel as if it would be too presumptuous on my part to ask you to be mine. I know that I have a rough, ugly and awkward appearance—that I am not such a person as fine ladies love to look on; but I possess a large, fond heart, that holds an ocean of pure love for you. Lottie, why do you not say something; why do you turn your face away from me? Have I offended you by my presumption? If I have dared to talk of love to you, it does not necessarily follow that you are bound to give a favorable answer; in fact, I have no right to expect you to make such a one. If you cannot love me, say so, and I promise never to annoy you any more with my suit, but will endeavor to promote your happiness in every way I can. I profess to be a man of honor, and believe I possess a remarkable amount of pride—too much to annoy any lady about my love who cannot return my honorable passion.'

"Her body now began to tremble more violently than ever, shaking like a leaf stirred by the storm, but she still remained silent, and kept her face averted.

" 'Why do you not speak to me, Lottie? Am I to understand that the refusal is caused by the scorn you feel for my presumption, or is it because you hate to pronounce the doom which you know will consign me to a life of misery? In the name of those happy days of old—in the name of our dear, dead mother—in the name of the great ocean of love which this poor heart holds for you, I implore you to speak to me now!'

"A tear then fell from my eyes, and dropped on her hand, which I still held against my heart; that caused her to start up suddenly, and snatch her hand away. Then she gazed down at the tear which still glistened on her hand, and I saw another tear start from her left eye and roll slowly down her cheek—it trembled on her chin a second, and then fell right on the one that still sparkled on her hand. The two tears mingled into one, and as they did so her head suddenly fell against my heart, and then I knew that the great prize was mine. Looking up into my face with a gaze of unutterable sweetness, while tears were streaming from her beautiful eyes, she whispered:

"'Eddie, I have always loved you more than language can express, or mind can imagine, and I was sure you knew it all the time. I have never thought of loving any one else; and I do not mean to allow you to slander yourself any more in my presence as you have done here this evening, for I think you noble-hearted, generous, intelligent and brave, and I know you are very handsome!'

"I was too full of joy to speak; and the man who never kissed the lips of a pure woman with a knowledge that her virtuous heart was all his own, cannot understand the indescribable bliss that was mine.

"'Edward,' she whispered, while her large, liquid blue eyes were rooted on me, 'have you ever read "Romeo and Juliet?"'

"'Yes, darling, very often; but why do you ask the question?'

"'My love for you is like that which Juliet felt for Romeo. I gave you my heart long, long ago, and if I had it back again then I would borrow her sweet words which she employs in speaking to Romeo:

> "'But to be frank and give it thee again,
> And yet I wish but for the thing I have.
> My bounty is as boundless as the sea,
> My love as deep: the more I give to thee
> The more I have: for both are infinite.'

"'The sentiment is very sweet, and the language appropriate and expressive, but I trust that our love will not end so sadly as did that of Romeo and Juliet.'

"In the midst of my great joy I did not forget to return my sincere thanks to the great Creator, for bestowing on me such a precious gem.

"'Lottie, dear, I believe if you would try you could compose a sweet song suited to this occasion, and I hope you will do so, and sing it here every evening while I am far away. Make the effort, and I dare say you will compose one with sentiments as sweet as ever poet wrote; then fix an hour at which you will come to this very spot and sing it, and I will at the same hour steal away and commune with you in spirit, while I gaze on yonder bright star, and listen with my imagination to the sweet music my darling is making here for me.'

" 'Edward, I promise to make the attempt, and if I succeed, I will sing it here at this lovely spot every evening at precisely nine o'clock, when the sky is cloudless; and I will think of you while singing it.'

" 'And will my darling promise to be mine when I return, thereby making me the happiest man that ever walked on the earth?'

" 'If papa gives his consent, and if brother Harry is willing, and if you do not fall in love with, and marry, some beauteous Philadelphia belle, and if I do not die of loneliness while you are so far away from me, and if you do not withdraw the proposition, and if, upon reflection, you are willing to take me with all my imperfections, why, then, I reckon so.'

" 'Now there are a great many if's contained in that answer, but let it rain if's until I return, and I will surmount them all. If my path was sown thick with dragons' teeth, and at every step producing armed men to oppose me, I would march on to secure my great prize!'

" 'Edward, can you not postpone the time set for you to start to Philadelphia for a few weeks?'

" 'Yes, and will gladly do so, for I must settle the question of the if's before I go. I must know Mr. Rockland's mind, as well as Harry's in regard to our betrothal, before I leave Memphis.' "

CHAPTER X.

"WELL," said Ivanhoe to Scottie, "what was it you wished to say to me?"

"Oh, I was dying of curiosity, you see, and I thought maybe you could save my life by telling me something. I declare, something strange is going to happen; and you must tell me what it is."

"It would be an easy task to tell you all about it, if I knew anything about it myself; but as I happen to know nothing, how can I tell you anything?"

"Pshaw! You are no true knight, Sir Ivanhoe, else you would not let a lady die of sheer curiosity, without an effort to save her. You are not like the brave knight of Ivanhoe of Sir Walter Scott's creation."

"Show me an enemy who fights with steel, face to face, and then you'll have cause to change your mind. By the by, what discoveries have you made about the black domino?"

"Very little, I assure you—just enough to keep me on the rack. But have you really unearthed no secret respecting the two seedy men?"

"Just enough to keep me on the rack, too."

"Well, aren't you going to tell me what it is?"

"I have been setting Greek against Greek, and you know what Byron says will happen when Greek meets Greek."

"Oh, bother Byron and his Greeks; tell me what you know?"

"I bribed the chamber-maid and set her on the track of the seedy men."

"And, pray, what's the result?"

"They are sure-enough detectives; that much I have discovered through my spy."

"Good! What else?"

"They are shadowing some one on this boat."

"They are doing what to some one on this boat?"

"Shadowing him."

"Oh, is that all? You mean that they are keeping some one out of the sunshine."

"No, no! I mean to tell you that they have spotted their man."

"Spotted their man! Poor fellow! what color were the spots they put on him?"

"Ah, Scottie, I perceive that you are not posted in regard to the peculiar language usually employed by the police department; when a detective officer sees a man who he thinks is the one he wishes to catch, he begins to follow and watch him, and this is called shadowing him."

"Ah, indeed! then what is meant by spotting their man?"

"The same thing."

"Yes, yeq, I see now; but who have they been spotting or shadowing?"

"Ingomar."

"Goodness gracious! Is it possible?"

"It is not only possible, but it is absolutely so."

"I declare, that is too bad! If I were a man I'd pitch 'em both overboard, so I would. They look like a brace of sneak thieves anyhow. What can they want with Ingomar?"

"That I don't know; but you may be sure I'll find out ere long, for I have got a clever detective on their track; in other words, I have got them spotted."

"If a hundred witnesses were to swear that Ingomar was a criminal, I wouldn't believe it."

"Don't believe anything unless you want to, but what would you think if it should turn out after all that Ingomar has murdered his rival in love?"

"Oh, horrible! Don't speak so, I beseech you!"

"Such things have happened, and why not happen again?"

"Yes, but Ingomar is not a man of that sort; I'd risk my life on it."

"Well, now, I have told you all I know, let's hear about the black domino."

"I have found out scarcely anything, except the fact that she is very sad, and is often found weeping in her state-room. I have been watching her closely, though she seems to avoid me as much as she can. I think the old gentleman with the white beard is her uncle, and I heard her say to him this morning that she could not endure it much longer."

"Endure what much longer?"

"That was all I heard; but she was weeping as if her heart would break, and the old gentleman tried to comfort her, and I heard him say that the matter should be settled in some way soon."

"What matter did he say should be settled?"

"How should I know? I have told you all I heard."

"I'll put my detectives on her track, too, and I'll unravel this business, if it takes all the money I possess. See here,

Scottie, did you know that I am dying with curiosity to know your real name?"

"Indeed, I did not."

"Well it's so; and why not relieve me?"

"Because the queen would be offended if I were to do it."

"Tell me your real name, and the queen shall never know of it."

"You shall know me when I know you, and not before."

"Very well; that is fair, at all events, and I am content. But I see the queen beckoning us to come to our seats to listen to Ingomar's story."

As soon as the maskers were seated the queen ordered Ingomar to resume.

"The next morning after Lottie had promised to be my wife, I mentioned the subject to Doctor Dodson, as I considered it my duty to do so.

" 'I am going to be married, sir,' said I, 'as soon as I get my diploma.'

" 'Ah, ha, indeed! and pray who's to be the unlucky woman that you have resolved to render miserable for life?'

" 'I don't intend to make any woman miserable, neither do I expect to marry any woman.' I said this rather sharply, as I felt a little ruffled.

" 'Ah, ha! and you don't mean to marry a woman, yet you say you are going to be married. I suppose you expect to marry a wood-nymph or a fairy. I guess you do not aspire to an angel.'

" 'That's exactly the state of my case; it's an angel sure enough.'

" 'When did she light on this part of the globe?'

" 'Seven years ago.'

" 'Ah, ha! here we come, you sly old rascal! I see how it is now. I have suspected you of villainous designs against Lottie for some time, and I see I was not mistaken; but look here, my boy, that dear girl is too good for you; she's worth a thousand such bundles of humanity as you; and right here let me say a few words with the bark on them. If ever you speak a cross word to that dear girl, or give her an unkind look, the fact is, if you ever give her cause to regret her choice, I'll—I'll, yes, I'll, ah, ha! I'll give you a dose of

strychnine, which is considered by the profession the most
polite way of getting rid of mean dogs; ah, ha! don't you
see, my boy?'

"He gave me a punch under the arm with his thumb.
'Yes, ah, ha! I'll poison you as I would a rat or a dog, if ever
you dare to cause my little queen a moment's pain.'

" 'I promise to swallow all the strychnine in the drug-stores
if ever I do an act willingly to give dear Lottie pain.'

" 'There! there! ah, ha! spoken like a man. Here we
come; take my hand, and my blessing with it, you rascal!
Ah, ha! what a lucky scamp you are! What on earth possessed the girl, to make her fall in love with such an overgrown mushroom. Well, well, well! I can scarcely believe
that Lottie is in earnest; she has agreed to marry you out of
pure pity, you good-for-nothing scamp. Well, if Lottie is fool
enough to marry you, I'll be fool enough to give her all my
property in order to enable her to support you; ah, ha! you
see how it is, don't you, my boy?'

"I was very glad to see that the good old doctor was really
delighted with the news of my engagement.

" 'Ah, ha! Eddie, here we come, my boy! go to work, go
to work; you are going to be the head of a family, you know,
therefore you must have something to support a family with.'

" 'What do you wish me to do, sir?' I inquired.

" 'Take an inventory of these drugs, of course; ah, ha! my
boy, take stock, take stock; find out how the business stands.
See how the business stands; see what's on hand, and mind
that you don't lose too much time thinking about Lottie. Ah,
ha! my boy, you see how it is yourself, don't you? Take
stock, find out everything. How can a man support a family
without something to do it with? Ah, ha! my boy, tell me
how it can be done? Can't tell? of course you can't ; neither
can I—impossible!—family can't be supported on air, or gas
—must have bread—bread, of course. Well, how are you
going to buy bread when you have nothing to buy it with?
Lottie must have bread—you know; therefore go to work, take
stock, take an inventory, then the business is half yours; ah,
ha! you see now, don't you, Eddie, my boy? Full partner
signboard: Dodson & Demar, Druggists and physicians, etc.,
etc., etc. Ah, ha! do you see, Eddie, my boy? Lottie's a

lady, you know; must have nice clothes; must have bread; money buys bread, money buys clothes, money buys nice home; where does the money come from? Drug-store, of course—full partner. Ah, ha! Eddie, my boy, here we come, Dodson & Demar; now go to work, fix things lively, let me see balance sheet with nice figures; have everything done up in apple-pie order; think of Lottie as much as you please, but mind you don't take a dose of dog poison by mistake. Do you know the reason why I like you, Eddie, my boy? Ah, ha! of course you do; 'tis because you don't play billiards. You can't play whist; you can't play poker; you can't play chess; you're a booby, that's what you are, Eddie, my boy, ah, ha! therefore I like you. I admire boobies, who can't play billiards nor poker. I'm a booby myself, you see, consequently I like 'em. Lottie likes boobies—that accounts for her foolish love for you; she learned that from me; shows her good sense. I told her that boobies were the best in the long run; billiard players, poker players, chess players, perfumed pretty boys are splendid fellows in a short race, but when it comes to long heats, they are always left behind.'

"Doctor Dodson had the utmost contempt for idle young men, and usually expressed his opinion in language by no means complimentary to that class. I was highly pleased to know that I was to be admitted into the firm as an equal partner—it would enable me to support my Lottie as a lady in that station of life to which her accomplishments and beauty entitled her. It was my duty to make known my engagement to Mr. Rockland, and to ask his consent to our marriage; and this was a task which I dreaded exceedingly; because I was not so sure that he would sanction the union. Mr. Rockland was a first-class lawyer who had accumulated a splendid fortune by his profession, and he was one of those austere, cold-natured kind of men whose ambition had usurped many of his good qualities; yet he loved Lottie with all his heart, and so did his wife; but I had a strong suspicion that they were inclined to encourage Mr. Heartsell in his suit for Lottie's hand. The more I thought the matter over, the more I dreaded to mention it to Mr. Rockland; I had a high regard for him because he loved Lottie. He had given her a home, a real happy home, where she had been surrounded with all the comforts and luxuries that money could procure; he had given her a first-class education—nay, more than that, he had educated Harry, who was now preparing to enter the legal profession with brilliant prospects. Mr. Rockland was always busy—in fact, he was injuring his health by incessant labor, and I knew he would be annoyed if I should attempt to seek an interview with him during business hours; I therefore watched for an opportunity to speak to him when he should be passing from his office to his residence. One evening, about three days after Lottie had promised to marry me, I saw Mr. Rockland walking toward his residence, with a large bundle of papers under his arm. He was looking very pale and sad, and I felt my knees trembling as I approached him for the purpose of speaking to him about Lottie.

" 'Are you in a great hurry, Mr. Rockland?' I inquired timidly.

" 'Yes, Edward,' was the solemn answer, 'I am always in a hurry; but why do you ask the question?'

" 'I was wanting to speak to you about a matter of great moment; but if you are busy, I can wait.'

" 'Will it occupy much time, Edward?'

" 'No, sir.'

" 'Then walk with me to my residence, and I'll hear what you have to say.'

"I walked in silence by his side as he led the way to his home. Lottie met us at the gate, and greeted Mr. Rockland with a kiss, then took my arm.

" 'What is the matter with you, Eddie? you look as if you had been ill.'

" 'You must be mistaken, Lottie, for I never was in better health in my life.'

" 'Come then with me into the garden; I wish to show you my new pet—it is the prettiest one of all.'

" 'I beg you will excuse me just now; I have come to see Mr. Rockland on a matter of importance; and he has kindly granted me an interview; when that is attended to, I shall be more than pleased to see your pets.'

"She looked inquiringly up into my face: 'Oh, very well, I will excuse you on that plea. You know you men are always thinking of business.'

"I don't think she had any idea of the nature of the business I had come to attend to. She walked by my side till we arrived at the house; then placing her mouth to my ear, she whispered:

" 'Don't be long about the business—I am dying to be with you.'

" 'What's that you are whispering to Edward about, Lottie?' said Mr. Rockland, with his low, solemn voice.

" 'Oh, never mind, papa! you go in and attend to your business, and don't be inquisitive; you are so much accustomed to cross-examining witnesses in court that you wish to practice on me to keep from getting rusted. You can't pump me as you do other witnesses; so there now, go along about your business.' And as she finished the sentence she threw her arms about his neck and gave him two or three kisses. 'Now go, you dear old darling you!' Then she went capering off toward the garden, while Mr. Rockland's eyes followed her with an eager look of intense love.

" 'Ah, Mr. Demar,' said he, as he stood and gazed at Lottie, 'she is the sweetest darling in the world; do you know that I love her just as much as I could if she were my own child? She is the most extraordinary girl I ever saw, sir; the most charming disposition; sings like a nightingale. I have employed an eminent music teacher, and mean to bring out her great genius. She has been taught music, but it was by ordinary teachers; the one I have secured lately is of a different sort. The fact of the business is, Mr. Demar, that girl has so wound herself about my heart that it would kill me to lose her. My wife loves her dearly; but, sir, the feeling I have for her goes beyond mere love—it is something like idolatry—soul worship; something which one may feel, but which he can't describe. I mean to will all my property to Lottie; and I may be permitted to say to you, Mr. Demar, confidentially, that it will be no inconsiderable sum. She will be ahead of any girl in Memphis, so far as wealth is concerned, and far beyond them in the way of accomplishments. Be seated, Mr. Demar,' said Mr. Rockland, at the same time taking his seat at the table opposite to me. 'I'll hear you now.'

"I gasped for breath, and felt like one choking; I strug-

gled desperately to regain self-possession, and succeeded
sooner than I thought I should. The fact is, I became very
angry at seeing the cold, unfeeling expression that settled
on Mr. Rockland's face; and I began to reason with myself:
'Why should I tremble in this man's presence? Why should
I be afraid of him? What right had he acquired that he
should be able to hold my fate in the hollow of his hand?
What if he did love Lottie—didn't I love her more than he
did? Why should I be compelled to come as an humble sup-
pliant to him, begging him to give Lottie to me? What right
had he to give her to anybody? How came she to be his
property? Who should dare dispute my superior claim to
her?'

" 'Mr. Rockland,' said I, 'Lottie has promised to be my
wife, and I thought perhaps it was proper to tell you of it.'
I did not ask his consent, which it was really my duty to do;
but, as I have said, I was angry at the austerity and coldness
of his manner, and tried to assume an independence which
I now think was wrong. Mr. Rockland made a grab at a
chancery bill that lay near him, and commenced turning over
the pages as if he were looking in it for an answer to my
words. I thought I saw a slight tremulousness in his hand as
he held the paper, while his face turned a shade paler.

" 'It was very imprudent in Lottie, to say the least of it,
and I must say, Mr. Demar, that common courtesy should
have induced you to mention the matter to me before saying
anything to Lottie. She is young and inexperienced—much
too young to think of matrimony.'

" 'I will wait, sir, until she is old enough,' said I.

"Mr. Rockland patted the floor with his boot-heel, and
tapped the table with the chancery bill, and I thought he was
viewing me with contempt. The blood burned in my cheeks,
and doubtless made them very red; he remained silent for
some time, as if undecided as to what he should say next; at
length he struck the table a sharp blow with the bill and
said:

" 'Lottie is not my daughter, Mr. Demar; but she has been
placed under my protection, and I consider it to be my duty
to act in this matter as if she were my own child. Doubtless
she imagines that she is in love with you; young girls of her

age always act foolishly, no doubt; but I suppose it to be a mere childish fancy, and not, as you imagine, a real love affair. Therefore, you will pardon me for suggesting the propriety of canceling what you are pleased to call an engagement, leaving her free to act as her best judgment may dictate when she arrives at an age that will enable her to view things from a more matured standpoint.'

" 'If Lottie wishes to cancel the engagement, Mr. Rockland, it may be done. But, sir, I think you are mistaken when you conclude that her love for me is a mere girlish fancy. We have loved each other for many years, and I assure you it is no common love either.'

" 'No doubt you think so, Mr. Demar; and your confidence in that respect may help us to arrive at a proper understanding. If (as you think) she really loves you with such a true devotion, you certainly will not object to allowing the engagement to be canceled, with the understanding that it may be remade when Lottie shall arrive at the age of twenty-one, provided she then may wish it.'

" 'I can only repeat what I have said before, Mr. Rockland; if Lottie wishes to be released, by all means let it be done; otherwise, I must beg you to let the engagement remain undisturbed. But, sir, I am willing that the marriage may be postponed until I shall have obtained my diploma, and settled down to work in my profession; meantime understand me, sir; if at any time Lottie shall intimate a wish to be released from her engagement, I promise to raise no objections.'

" 'Very well, sir; if such is your decision I must acquiesce, of course; therefore, you must promise not to mention the matter to Lottie any more until I shall have interviewed her on the subject.'

" 'Certainly, I give you the promise most cheerfully.'

" 'You must promise further than that, Mr. Demar; you must pledge your honor not to speak to Lottie at all until I have had a talk with her. She is in the garden now. You will return to your place of business, and allow me to make your excuse for leaving without seeing her.'

"I hesitated, because my suspicions were roused. I did not like the cold, iron look that appeared on his face, nor the evasive expression of his piercing dark eyes. I was afraid he intended to make Lottie believe it was my wish that the marriage engagement should be broken off—else why was he so anxious for me to go away without seeing her? Noticing my hesitation, he evidently divined the cause, for he said:

" 'Oh, you need not fear to make the promise, Mr. Demar; I will do everything openly and above board. I shall, of course, endeavor to convince Lottie of the great error she has committed. No dishonorable means shall be resorted to. I shall say nothing to her behind your back that I would not say to your face; but I only wish to have a talk with her alone, when she is not influenced by your presence; that's all, I assure you, Mr. Demar.'

" 'You will not try to make her believe that I wish the engagement broken?'

" 'Certainly not; how could I do that when I know you don't wish anything of the sort?'

"His frank, candid manner re-assured me, and I made the promise, and immediately took my leave. As I passed out through the gate Lottie saw me, and called me to come to her. I shook my head and passed on. Notwithstanding the distance that lay between us, I could plainly see the look of astonishment that overspread her beautiful face. She had started to meet me, almost in a run, but when she perceived that I was avoiding her she came to a sudden halt, and the little basket she held in her hand instantly fell to the ground, scattering the flowers round her feet, while she appeared to be struck dumb with wonder. What could I do? Had I not given my most solemn promise not to speak to her until Mr. Rockland could have an interview with her? When I saw the painful expression of her dear face I wheeled round and started toward her; then recollecting the promise I had made, I hastened away. I began to snuff danger in the breeze.

"Mr. Rockland was an honorable man—so were Cæsar's assassins all honorable men. Mr. Rockland thought it was his duty to prevent the marriage between Lottie and me—the lean and hungry Cassius thought it was his duty to kill Cæsar. Mr. Rockland did not think of this poor heart of mine, or

care how it would wither and die if he took Lottie from me—
Brutus did not think or care for the heart of his friend, as he
plucked away the bloody blade from Cæsar's heart. If Mr.
Rockland thought it was his duty to have the engagement
broken off, I felt certain that he would leave no means un-
used which would tend to accomplish it. I thought then, and
think yet, he was really an honest, conscientious man; but
what will a man not do in order to gain his object, when he
feels that in doing it he is performing his duty? More
cruelties have been committed by men while doing what they
believed to be their duty than ever were committed wantonly.
I suppose that Jeffries, the bloody tool of a tyrant, thought
he was performing his duty as an impartial judge when he
was making all the air of England shriek with the cries of
dying victims.

"I left Mr. Rockland in his library. He rang a little bell,
which was answered by a servant.

" 'Tell Lottie I wish to see her in my library immediately.'

"In a few moments she came in with an inquiring look on
her face.

" 'What is it, papa? Tell me quick—I am in a great hurry.'
She had come up behind his chair, and was running her
fingers through his gray hair, every now and then pressing a
kiss on his brow.

" 'Oh, you dear old darling! why don't you commence?
can't you see I am all attention? What made you let Eddie
run off like a thief? Don't you think when I called him back
he shook his shaggy head and refused to come! Now, papa
dear, what have you been doing to my Eddie?'

" 'How came he to be your Eddie?'

" 'Because he loves me, and I love him; now the cat's out
of the bag.'

" 'Nonsense, child! I implore you not to talk so foolishly.'

" 'No nonsense about it at all; pray where does the foolish
part come in? Is it wrong, papa, to love such a dear fellow
as my Eddie?'

" 'It was wrong for a girl of your age to enter into an
engagement without consulting any one; and that was what I
wished to speak to you about.'

" 'Oh, indeed! was it? Now, you dear old darling, you aren't going to scold me about it, are you? No, of course you won't; if you do, I'll make your tea as weak as water, and I'll put pepper in your toast till it shall burn you up, indeed I will!'

" 'I couldn't have the heart to scold my darling!'

"As Mr. Rockland said this he threw his arms round her waist and drew her to his heart, covering her brow with a kiss. Mr. Rockland was vanquished; her charms were irresistible; and the great lawyer, with nerves of steel and an iron will, who could brow-beat witnesses, intimidate judges and over-ride facts, found himself confounded, vanquished and helpless—all done by a pretty face and two large, dreamy blue eyes. The truth of the matter is, Mr. Rockland loved Lottie so devotedly that he was unable to withstand her displeasure.

" 'Take a seat, Lottie,' he said, 'and let us come to an understanding in this business at once; sit down, and we will talk the matter over dispassionately, like sensible people.'

"Lottie took a chair on the opposite side of the table, and fixing her beautiful eyes on him, said:

" 'I'll hear what you have to say, papa.'

"The man of iron returned the gaze with a cold, calm look. After a long silence he said:

" 'Lottie, my dear child, you know I love you as I love life. The only aim I have is to promote your happiness; and I demand of you permission to cancel this foolish engagement which you have so imprudently entered into with Edward Demar. Have I your permission to cancel it?'

" 'Only on condition that Eddie wishes it to be canceled.'

" 'Mr. Demar did not say he wished the engagement canceled; but he agreed that it should be done if you were willing, and authorized me to say as much to you.'

"The blood left her cheeks for a moment, then came back with a tremendous rush, yet she managed to keep calm.

" 'Send for Eddie now, papa, and let me hear him say he is willing to annul our engagement.'

" 'That is unnecessary, Lottie; you have my word that such is his wish, and you know me too well to suspect me of pre-

varication; again I command you to break off this most
absurd and imprudent engagement; will you, or will you not,
do it? I demand an answer, yes or no?'

"Lottie's bosom rose and fell with unusual emotion, while
her eyes were fixed on Mr. Rockland.

" 'Yes or no, Lottie?' again demanded the man of iron.

" 'Dear, dear papa, for Heaven's sake don't ask me to be
false to the man I love! I'll not marry him until he returns
from Philadelphia; by that time I will be better able to make
you a sensible answer, but I beseech you not to press me so
now; you know how I love you—you know how much I
appreciate your kindness to me; listen, therefore, to my
entreaty—grant me time for reflection.'

" 'Not another moment will I give you to make an answer
to such a sensible request; any girl whose judgment was not
choked with a foolish infatuation would be able to answer
such a reasonable demand without a moment's reflection. Do
you wish to tie yourself to a man who is anxious to get rid of
you?'

" 'No, no! a thousand times, no, papa; and no one knows
this better than you.'

" 'Then, Lottie, for the last time, I demand authority from
you to cancel this foolish engagement; will you, or will you
not, give it?'

" 'Not unless Eddie wishes it,' was the calm reply.

" At last the man of iron lost his temper:

" 'Then, Miss Wallingford, you will oblige me by seeking
a home elsewhere.'

" 'Oh, papa, dear, darling papa! please unsay those cruel
words! I am not afraid of hardships; neither am I afraid of
poverty, but it is your displeasure that I dread more than all.
I love you truly, earnestly, devotedly, as much as any child
ever loved a parent. Oh, papa, revoke those cruel words!'

" 'Leave me, leave me!' thundered the lawyer, as he pushed
Lottie away from him rather roughly. She retreated to the
farther end of the room and stared at Mr. Rockland with
astonishment, while a mysterious change came over her. She
approached the table, took a seat, and hastily penned a note
to Edward Demar:

" 'DEAR EDDIE—Come to me as quickly as you can. I wish to consult you on important business. Yours,

" 'LOTTIE.'

"Then she touched a little silver bell that lay on the table and a man-servant bowed himself in at the door.

" 'Did you ring, miss?' inquired the servant.

" 'Take this note to Mr. Edward Demar without delay; you'll find him at Doctor Dodson's drug-store. Tell Burley to come to me instantly.'

" "The man servant had scarcely passed the veranda when Burley, a mulatto woman, appeared at the door.

" 'Did you send for me, miss?'

" 'Pack my clothes in the large trunk, Burley; then get Archie to help you bring it down; set the trunk on the front portico; tell Archie to put my parrot in his cage, and to bring all my pets and place them by my trunk. Tell him to tie a string round old Bob's neck, so I can lead the poor blind friend along while I am seeking a new home. Old Bob and I have been tramps many days together, and we'll not part now.'

" 'Oh, Lottie, my darling, come to your old cruel papa's arms! I give up—I surrender—I take back all I have said. Marry Eddie if you will, but don't leave me—I can't live without you; you shall have your own way in everything.'

"Lottie, of course, went into Mr. Rockland's arms, and covered his brow with kisses. That was what I call a triumph of woman's rights. Here was a lawyer who commanded money, influenced courts, directed banks, intimidated witnesses, cleared guilty clients, compelled judges to bow to his great talent; and then in comes a weak little girl and rules him, the same as a raw recruit is ruled, by the commanding general. She bids him go, and he goes—she commands him to come, and he comes. Talk about woman's rights! What on earth do women want with any more rights than they have? They have complete control of the world—because they control man, and through him the world."

"There is the gong for lunch," observed the queen, "and you may suspend until it is over. It is our wish, though, that our friends re-assemble here immediately after luncheon, to hear more of the story."

CHAPTER XI.

"Suppose you and I don't go down to luncheon," said Scottie to Ivanhoe; "I am not a bit hungry, and would very much prefer remaining up here; how is it with you?"

"That's my fix, exactly; I'm glad you mentioned it. Take my arm, and let us have a walk and a talk both."

"Agreed; now what did your spy report, a moment ago, about the two detectives?"

"I shall find out everything that is going on. It is such rare sport, too, to be tracking detectives who imagine themselves to be so clever!"

"Oh, bother the clever detectives! tell me what you know."

"Now, Scottie, don't you begin to lose your temper; you know I have made a confidante of you."

"I think you and I ought to be very good friends."

"So do I."

"I think we ought to know more about each other."

"So do I."

"When do you intend to tell me who you are, Scottie?"

"As soon as the queen gives her consent."

"What has the queen got to do with it, I should like to know?"

"No doubt you would; but I have given my solemn promise not to reveal her name nor my own to any person without her permission; and she has promised that as soon as Ingomar's story is finished all secrecy may be discarded. But now I want to hear what you have discovered about the two seedy men."

"They are going to arrest Ingomar, and take him off at Vicksburg; he is charged with a bloody murder (so the seedy men say). They state that he committed the crime somewhere in Mississippi, and while in jail awaiting trial managed to make his escape. The friends of the murdered man offered a large reward for the capture of the perpetrator, and then the State added another large sum to that offered by the friends of the deceased, and those two seedy men are officers from Mississippi who have got Ingomar spotted."

"Does Ingomar know they are watching him?"

"No, I think not."

"Then why not warn him of the danger?"

"That would be wrong, because if he is guilty he ought to suffer; if he is innocent he is in no danger."

"Do you believe he is guilty?"

"I can't say that I do, for I know nothing about it. I shall therefore accept the legal theory, which regards every man innocent until the contrary is established by competent proof."

"It would require a pile of evidence as high as Pike's Peak to make me believe that Ingomar is a murderer."

"So it would to convince me."

"What have you discovered about the mysterious lady in the black domino?"

"Ah, my spy has met her match there! With all her cleverness, the black domino is too much for her. One circumstance, however, has been brought to the surface; the black domino is shadowing Ingomar too, and the strangest thing about it is, that she is not in any manner working with the seedy men—it's a separate game."

"Goodness gracious! what on earth can it all mean?"

"I'm sure I don't know; I wish I did."

"Perhaps she is the wife of the murdered man; or she may be his sister, or his sweetheart, who is watching him."

"Can't say as to that; but it is certain that she is shadowing him. One circumstance connected with her, however, tends to prove your theory about it. The lady in the black domino seems to be unusually melancholy all the time—has often been seen weeping, and never speaks to any one. That goes to prove that she has lost a dear friend or relative; and it may be, as you say, that she was related to the man who was murdered."

"The truth is, I can't stand this suspense much longer; I shall die of mere curiosity if things don't change soon."

"I beg you not to make a die of it, Scottie, before I get a look at your face."

"And pray why should you wish to see my face?"

"I am sure I should like it."

"Suppose you did like it—what would that signify?"

"It might bring about a coincidence, you know."

"Look, look! there comes the black domino; see how she follows Ingomar! I saw her pointing at him just now, and whispering something in her uncle's ear. The whirlwind is going to burst on us ere long; don't you think so?"

"Indeed I do! There is a strange game being played on this boat—it may end in a tragedy."

"Pray don't talk that way—you frighten me. I think I had better mention the matter to the queen, and have this nonsense ended at once."

"No, no! don't do that, by any means, I beseech you. Our best plan is to remain silent and wait for the denouement."

"Be it so, then, sir knight. You shall be my champion when the war begins."

"I shall be proud of the honor—I'll emblazon my banner with the name of Scottie, in letters of gold, and fight the world in arms in defense of my lady-love. Then I'll imitate the brave Spanish king, when he met Sir Roderick Dhu on Clanalpine's lofty height. You know he threw himself against a rock—which I'll do when the fight opens."

"But there are no rocks here, you see."

"Oh, never mind that; I'll make the pilot-house answer for the rock. I'll just throw myself against it while you can hide inside, and then hear me cry:

> "'Come one, come all! this rock shall fly
> From its firm base as soon as I.'"

"Brave, bravo! my gallant knight. I'll swap my domino for a laurel crown, to deck the brow of my brave champion."

"There, there, Scottie, I cry enough! Come, let us join our friends—they are waiting for us yonder. Don't you see the queen is beckoning to you?"

"When I received Lottie's note requesting me to come to her immediately, you may guess how my heart fluttered—for I thought something serious had surely occurred, and but very few moments elapsed before I was at the gate in front of

Mr. Rockland's residence. It was a considerable walk from the drug-store to his residence, and I was compelled to halt in order to rest a moment before entering, as I wished to appear composed. While I was leaning against a tree wiping the perspiration from my face and panting with fatigue, I saw Lottie coming rapidly toward me. She had been watching for me.

" 'Oh, Eddie, it's all settled!' she exclaimed, as she caught both my hands in hers. I made a move as if I were going to take her in my arms. She gently pushed me back. 'Don't be quite so familiar, Eddie—can't you see papa looking at us? Oh, such a storm as we have had here to-day! Papa ordered me to go away from his home because I wouldn't let him tell you that I wanted our engagement broken off."

" 'Well, why didn't you take him at his word? you knew where you could find another home.'

" 'I did, but the good, dear old darling relented before I could pack my things, and fell to hugging and kissing me, and wouldn't let me go.'

" 'Lottie, Mr. Rockland is really a good man, and I respect him very much—mainly because he loves you.'

" 'Indeed he is! and my heart was most broken when he ordered me to go away; but did you wish to have our engagement broken off?'

" 'No, you know I did not! What could have put such an idea as that into your mind? Mr. Rockland did not tell you I wished it ended, did he?'

" 'He didn't say that you said so, but he said you were willing to cancel it if I would consent to it.'

" 'Ah, I see now how it is: Mr. Rockland put the case very strong in favor of his side. That was a good stroke of policy, you see, Lottie; you didn't believe for a moment that I wanted to have the engagement canceled?'

" 'No, I did not.'

" 'I declare, Lottie, I never saw you look so pretty before.'

" 'I am truly glad that you think so; it makes me very happy to please you.'

" 'Ah! how could I be otherwise than well pleased when I know Lottie loves me? I feel like a new man since I found it out. Will my Lottie always love me?'

" 'Yes, of course I will; I am so very, very happy when you are with me, and so miserable when you are away from me. What shall become of poor me when my Eddie goes away to Philadelphia?'

" 'Let us look forward to the happy day that brings me back to my love. Let us keep our minds on the bright future, when we shall be always together.'

" 'I wish I could do that, but I cannot; I shall all the time be thinking you are ill, or that something has gone wrong with you. I should die if you were to fall ill among strangers!'

" 'I'll take good care of myself for your sake; I'll be prudent in all things, and let you know if anything goes wrong; but you must do the same.'

" 'Let us go in; I see Mr. Rockland waiting for you—he is going to talk to you about our engagement, and you must be careful not to offend him.'

" 'Fear nothing on that score; I think we will now come to an understanding entirely satisfactory to all parties concerned.'

"Mr. Rockland met me on the portico with his cold, placid smile, and directed me to follow him into the library. He also asked Lottie to go with us. Pointing to a seat, he requested me to take it; Lottie stood calmly by my chair, while Mr. Rockland took his usual seat on the opposite side of the table.

" 'Mr. Demar,' he began, with his austere tone of voice, 'I have had an interview with Lottie on the subject about which we were speaking a short while ago.'

" 'So Lottie told me, Mr. Rockland.'

" 'Her views and mine differed somewhat; but we have managed to reconcile them to some extent; and we may therefore reasonably hope to have all things amicably settled.'

" 'I am truly glad to hear it, Mr. Rockland.'

" 'Thank you, Edward; are you willing to promise me that the marriage shall be deferred until the end of two years from this date?'

" 'Indeed, Mr. Rockland, I should like very much to be able to comply with your request, but why not let the marriage be solemnized when I return from Philadelphia in the spring?'

" 'Lottie would be too young to marry then.'

" 'Grant papa's request, Eddie,' said Lottie; 'I am very willing to put it off indefinitely, if you can be with me often.'

"That settled the question; so it was agreed that Lottie should be my wife at the end of two years.

" 'Come,' said Lottie, as she took my arm, and looking up at me, her sweet little mouth puckered up in a comical shape; 'we'll go to the study now, as everything has been settled between you and papa; I want to show you some new flowers that I have secured; oh, they are such nice ones! They flourish better in the fall season than they do in the spring.'

"She led me through her flower garden, stopping occasionally to point out the different plants, giving a graphic description of their nature and the manner of their culture; and when we came near the summer-house the old parrot began to chatter:

" 'Ah, ha! Lottie! here we come—here we come!'

" 'Can't he say anything but that, Lottie?' I inquired.

" 'Oh, yes, he can talk a great deal when he takes a notion. Did you know I had a letter from Viola, Eddie?'

" 'No, have you?'

" 'Yes; let me read it to you; she writes such a nice, smooth hand, and her letter is so friendly; but here it is:

" 'New York, Aug. 16.

" 'DEAR LOTTIE—I must first offer an apology to you for neglecting to answer your last letter. You must not for a moment think that the delay was caused by a lack of love for you on my part. When your letter came I had not returned from my boarding school, but as soon as I came home and found your darling letter I lost no time in answering it. Oh, Lottie, I am so happy just now that I cannot find words to tell you as I should like to do. Papa has consented to let me spend the winter in Memphis, and you may look for me by the last of September. Oh, isn't that delightful? Won't we have lots of fun? I often think of you and your heroic little brother—but I ought not to speak of him as your little brother now, I suppose, because he must be a man by this time. I have his picture, you know, Lottie, and oh, how much I do think of it! I keep it next to my heart all the time. All the gold in California could not buy it from me. I expect Harry has changed very much since we parted—you know I was only a little child then, but now I am a great, overgrown mushroom—and as green as a half-grown gourd. Dear papa says I am pretty, but you know evidence of that kind is unreliable; still I

confess I should like to know it was true. You may tell **Harry**
—I suppose I ought to say Mr. Wallingford—that I have not forgotten him, and I don't think I ever shall. I was so glad to
hear that he was going to make a great lawyer of himself. Mr.
Rockland says, in his letters to papa, that Mr. Wallingford, possesses great talent, and will be sure to distinguish himself some
day. Would you believe it, I shed lots of joyful tears when papa
read the letter to me? I envy you; how happy you must be! how
proud of such a brave, heroic, talented brother! You see, I am
well posted in everything that concerns you and your noble
brother. I often wonder if he ever thinks of the little foolish
girl he kept from being crushed to death by the engine? I wonder if he has forgotten how he and I went rolling and tumbling
down the embankment together! I was so much delighted at your
description of your flower garden; I know I shall enjoy it very
much. You people of the dear sunny South have great advantages over us in that respect. I think I should like to live in the
South all the time. I suppose you knew I had a darling little
brother—yes, I know you did, because I remember now that I
told you of it in my other letters. Poor little fellow, he is not a
healthy child at all; he is now nearly five years old, and looks
like a mere baby, though papa says he will come out all right
after a while. Did I ever tell you what his name was? I don't
think I did. Well, you see mamma and papa couldn't agree on a
name for him, and, to keep peace in the family, it was agreed
that I should have the honor of selecting his name. What do
you think I did? I named him after your heroic brother. We
call him Wallie. That, you know, is an abbreviation of Wallingford. He was baptized as "Harry Wallingford Bramlett," and
papa and mamma were both delighted with the good selection I
made. But I must close now, because I fear I have made this
letter too long, anyway. Present my highest regards to your
brother, and accept my best, truest love for yourself, and write
soon to

" 'Your true friend,

" 'VIOLA.'

" 'That's a splendid letter, Lottie, for a girl of sixteen to
write,' said I, when it was read through.

" 'She is not quite sixteen yet, either,' said Lottie.

" 'That document conveys the best news, my darling, that
I have heard since you told me you would be mine.'

" 'To what part of it do you refer?'

" 'That wherein she says she is going to spend the winter
with you. It will be a great consolation for me to know,
when I am so far from you, that you will have such a sweet
friend for a companion. I was thinking of the long, dreary
winter days and nights that you would be compelled to pass

through all alone, but now how could you be lonely with such a lively little cricket as Viola?'

" 'I dare say she will prove a great comfort to me, yet she cannot fill the aching void that will be caused by your absence.'

"As she said this her large dreamy eyes were glancing up at me, while a tear trembled in each, and I drew her head against my breast, too happy to speak. I led her to a seat, letting her fair cheek remain resting on my heart, while my mind went straying into the future. A thousand thoughts of various kinds intruded on me—some pleasant, others very different. What if Mr. Rockland should resort to strategy, during my absence, to entrap my Lottie into a marriage with Heartsell? What if he should throw his great intellect, with his vast wealth and influence into the balance against me? Would my Lottie be able to withstand it? Would she be able to do battle successfully against such odds? These unwelcome questions forced themselves upon me, causing a shudder to dart through my body. Lottie felt the shock, and exclaimed:

" 'What's the matter? why do you tremble so? I declare, your heart made a violent jump just now, then began to flutter and knock against your breast; what does it mean?'

" 'I was thinking how I should feel if you were to cease loving me, when I went away, and should marry Mr. Heartsell!'

"She started up, looking at me reproachfully: 'How can you talk so; didn't you know I had rejected Mr. Heartsell's offer?'

" 'Indeed I did not; I was not aware of the fact that he had made it, though I knew he intended to do so.'

" 'Well, he has done it, and you may be easy now.'

" 'Tell me what he said, and what you said.'

" 'Mr. Heartsell, I think, is a very nice, good man, and worthy of a true woman's love; but I had no heart for him, because you, like a good old thief, went and stole it. I felt highly honored by Mr. Heartsell's partiality, and told him so; but I thought it my duty to tell him the truth at once, which I did. I told him my hand and heart belonged to another. Poor fellow! he wept when I told him I loved another, and could not love him. He said he would not give me up, but would wait until I should think better of him; and he seemed to think that I would change my mind and love him after all; but don't you know that I can never change?'

" 'I can't express my admiration, Lottie, for your extraordinary prudence; not one girl in a hundred would have taken the proper view in such an emergency. Of course you did right to tell Mr. Heartsell the whole truth; most girls under similar circumstances would have evaded the truth, and left the man a reasonable hope.'

" 'By the by, have you ever mentioned our engagement to brother Harry?'

" 'Oh, yes, I named it to him before I did to any one else.'

" 'And what did he think of it?'

" 'He was glad of it—said it was just what he expected and desired—congratulated me heartily—said I was a lucky fellow to be the winner of such a heart—said he knew you loved me, all the time—told me that if ever I caused you trouble he would kill me—and, to tell you the truth, Lottie, I believe he would kill any one who would bring trouble on you.'

" 'Oh, he is such a noble, generous, heroic brother! Viola loves him, and I hope they will make a match of it.'

" 'Ah, Lottie, that will never happen.'

" 'May I know the reason why you think so?'

" 'Viola is a great heiress, and you know how proud Harry is; no matter how much he might love her, he would never tell her of it. Do you know that I think the only fault Harry has is his unprecedented pride? I have been acquainted with many proud men, but there is something in Harry's pride that places it beyond anything I ever have witnessed in other people. No, Lottie, let me advise you not to build your pyramid of hopes on a foundation of that sort.'

" 'Is Mr. Bramlett very wealthy?'

" 'Mr. Rockland tells me that he is a millionaire, and you know he has only two children.'

" 'Then I must confess that I don't think Harry would be doing exactly right were he to seek Viola's hand in marriage. If that's what you refer to when you speak of his pride, I am fully prepared to indorse it.'

"The dreadful day for my departure had come at last; the

awful moment in which I was to part from Lottie had come and gone. The parting words had been uttered—the bitter tears had been shed, the farewell kiss given; the long, loving embrace was over. I had handed dear Lottie, fainting, into Mrs. Rockland's arms, and was on my way to Philadelphia."

CHAPTER XII.

"I ARRIVED in New York City in due time, and set about the work which Doctor Dodson had charged me with. When I reached Philadelphia I found a long letter from Lottie. Here it is:

" 'DEAR EDDIE—Your letter was received yesterday, and if you knew how happy it made me you would write me one every day. I have read it through at least a dozen times, and every dear expression is engraved on my heart. I beseech you to take good care of yourself, and you must be sure to tell me if you ever feel the least ill. But lest I should bore you with so much talk about love matters, I will tell you something about Viola. She has been with me nearly three weeks, and is the sweetest, prettiest little cricket that any one ever looked upon—not so little, however, as you might think, for she is as tall as I am. She has a most charming disposition—as gentle as a dove—and can sing, oh, so sweetly! it would make you weep to hear her play on the guitar, while singing one of her plaintive songs. She is complete mistress of the piano and guitar. I had been flattering myself that I was a pretty good musician, but when I heard Viola play my conceit oozed out. She is in love with Harry, but, just as I expected, he is too proud to let her know how he loves her. He maintains a dignified stiffness of manner, when with her, that chills me to the heart and frightens her. I wonder if this hateful money of Mr. Bramlett's is going to break these two young, loving hearts? Viola has Harry's picture—wears it in her bosom all the time; I saw her kissing it the other day and crying over it, when she thought no one was near. What a darling little wife she would make for Harry, if he would only ask her! I wish I had a gold mine, so I could give it to him, and make his fortune equal to hers. I believe he loves her fervently, and would tell her so, but for the hateful gulf that Mr. Bramlett's gold has placed between them. I fear that much sorrow is in store for both of them; but let us hope for the best. Viola and I are rooming together; poor old Bob dozes on the hearth in my room all the time since the weather got too cold for him to stay in his house. He has quit quarreling with old Roderick, and they have become

very good friends now. The parrot comes up to my room every
night, and takes his snooze in the closet. He has learned to
speak several new words since you went away. It would amuse
you to hear him try to say Philadelphia; but he can't do it—the
word is too big for him. I was trying to teach him to tell where
you were living, and when he failed to say Philadelphia we com-
promised on New York, because he can say that as plainly as I
can.

"'Mr. Heartsell has called on me several times since you left.
Poor fellow, he looks so sad! He treats me with such tender
consideration—never mentions the subject; I suppose he has
given up all hope in that direction. I can't help having the very
highest respect for him; but do not become jealous, for I don't
love him the least bit. How could I love any one else when my
Eddie has taken my heart away with him?

"'I think poor old Bob will die before you come home—he is
very old, you know; I never let him want for anything—how
could I, as I think of the time when we were poor homeless
tramps? Do you ever let your mind wander back to those old
days when we were all tramps? Have you forgotten the cloth
shoes you made for me while you were convalescing at Mrs.
Holly's farmhouse? I have got those old shoes yet; I am pre-
serving them as relics of the happy days of old.

"'Papa says that he will have to mortgage his estate to buy
postage stamps if I don't quit writing so many long letters to
you. I don't care if he does—I mean to write a long letter every
day.

"'The autumn weather has been delightful, and you may guess
Viola and I have made good use of it. She is the liveliest girl I
ever saw—always mirthful and happy, except when Harry gets
on his high horse of pride; then a shade of melancholy chases
away the jolly look. Alas! what misery will ensue if Harry does
not conquer this strange, mysterious passion called pride. Poor
girl! she does not know that it is the hateful money that keeps
Harry and her so far apart. Harry is not happy, as he was before Viola came, and I begin to see a cloud of sorrow rising in
the distance which is sure to burst over their heads, unless something intervenes to prevent it. Oh, love, love, love! what a wonderful thing thou art! How much happiness canst thou give
when circumstances are favorable, and what misery when unfavorable! When I think of what exquisite delight your love has
given me I can't realize the fact that the same kind of passion
has caused so much misery to others. I am so selfish in my love,
yet so happy; but then, when I think of the many long, dreary
days that must elapse before I shall see you, I am in despair. I
sometimes imagine that I should like to fall into a trance, and
not wake up till you return. The old clock on the mantel goes
on ticking away deliberately, while an age seems to intervene between the strokes. Oh, how can I wait so long before I shall look

again in those dear eyes? Your eyes always looked so tenderly down into mine; I could read your thoughts when gazing in your eyes. You were always so tender and gentle with me, in the good old days; when my feet were bleeding from their many wounds, I remember you lifted me in your arms—when I was unable to walk—and carried me to the banks of the little brook and bathed my feet so tenderly! Do you never let your mind recall those happy days? I call them happy days, though they were not unmixed with sadness—but those were the days in which you won my heart. Do you remember the evening when old Bob came to our camp looking so poor and miserable? What a lucky thing it was he happened to take it into his head to follow me! But you will be laughing at me when you read this nonsense. Well, do you know, darling, I don't care how much you laugh at me? I rather like it, when I know you love me so well. Viola is looking over my shoulder just now, telling me to give you her highest regards; and I imagine it makes her sad to know that my love is returned, while she thinks hers for Harry is not. Harry says he wishes to be kindly remembered by you; he thinks you are the best fellow in the world—shows his good sense, don't it, darling? Well, I suppose when you read this long letter you will be tired; but I could write all day to you and never tire. I could write a volume about love, and then not have space sufficient to describe all I feel for my darling; but I reckon I had better halt here. Good-by, and don't forget the kisses I have sent in this letter. Your faithful, loving

" 'LOTTIE.'

"I often think that men who never loved are not capable of understanding the wonderful mystery, because they are often heard to speak of it as simple nonsense—a foolish weakness, only known to weak minds. I have been told that many a man has lived a long life, and died without ever having felt the charming influence of true love; if they did, they died in ignorance of what real happiness was. To say that I read Lottie's sweet letter a thousand times would, perhaps, be an exaggeration—to say I only read it once would be short of the mark; I read it a great many times. But I must hasten on, and not consume your time with too much talk about my dear Lottie, as I shall have many thrilling events to describe —events that occurred after I had finished my attendance at the lectures. I will, however, ask permission to read one of my letters to Lottie, after which I promise to hasten on to the stirring events which really constitute the gist of this story.

" 'DEAR LOTTIE—Your highly appreciated letter was here when I arrived, and were I to exhaust Webster's unabridged, I am sure I could find no words adequate to describe the pleasure I felt while perusing it. You inquired if I ever let my mind wander back to the old days, when we were homeless tramps. Ah, yes, Lottie! my mind has traveled a thousand times over every path where your dear feet have trod. I can call to mind every little trifling circumstance that was in any manner connected with you. I have seen nothing in the shape of a woman that can begin to compare with my Lottie.

" 'I am stopping at the Girard House, on Chestnut street— have comfortable quarters on the second floor, fronting the street. That is one of the most beautiful streets in the city. Every evening it is crowded with splendid equipages and handsome ladies, but none so beautiful as my Lottie. Independence Hall is situated on this street; I spent one whole day looking at the quaint old relics that are to be seen there. The old bell, whose brazen tongue proclaimed the birth of a new nation nearly a hundred years ago, is there still. The heavy old carved chairs that were used by the members of the Continental Congress may be seen in the very places where they stood when occupied by those heroic old patriots. A life-size portrait of George III. hangs on the wall. His youthful features have no expression that would indicate the tyrant. The old flint-lock pistols used by Lafayette during the war of independence are great curiosities in themselves. Washington's camp-chest may be seen, with the cooking utensils used while commanding the American army; all put together would scarcely weigh fifty pounds. A common lieutenant of the present day would tender his resignation, if he were required to reduce the bulk of his camp equipage to that used by the Commander-in-Chief in 1776. This is a fast age, you know, and ideas have changed since the honest days of old. Strange reflections crowded on my mind as I gazed on those dear old relics. Where are all those brave old soldiers now? Where are all the heroic men and beautiful women who inhabited this continent then? All dead, all gone; perhaps not a living soul can now be found on the earth who heard the old bell proclaim the notes of liberty to the people in 1776.

" 'Philadelphia is a beautiful city—so clean, so quiet, so charming; everything so systematic. I think I should like to live here, but for the severely cold winters. I visited Girard College the other day, and would you believe it, Lottie, a man at the gate asked me if I was a preacher. Now, don't I look like a preacher? Have you ever imagined that I, in any manner, resembled one? Of course not, yet he did ask me the strange question. I, of course, answered promptly, No! and then he allowed me to go in. My curiosity was roused, and I didn't stop till I learned the reasons why the question was put to me. Mr. Girard inserted a clause in his will that no minister of the gospel should ever be permitted to enter the inclosure.

"There are many things to amuse and instruct one in this sober old city, and I mean to give you a more elaborate history of them in my next letter. I don't think I ever shall make a very great surgeon, because the dissecting room is a very unpleasant place to me. When engaged in it I can't for the life of me keep my mind on the business before me, but, in spite of me, it will go straying off into the realms of philosophy. The first time I entered the dissecting room I felt unusually sad; the subject was a young man of powerful frame, well-shaped limbs, brawny chest and handsome face, whom I supposed to be about my own age. A feeling of horror thrilled through my whole frame as I saw the sharp, glittering steel inserted in his white flesh. I then and there became convinced that I never should master the science of surgery, if that was the only way it could be done. When the dead man's brain and heart were taken out, I took the heart in my left hand and the brain in the other, seated myself as far away as I could without leaving the room, and began to philosophize in a most singular manner. What is this little dark red lump of flesh that I hold in my left hand? Answer—The human heart, the supposed seat of life, the little governor that regulates the quantity of blood that each tiny vein is entitled to as its share. This little lump of flesh puts all the small pumps in motion that move the red life through the human body. This little insignificant thing is the great throne where love holds his court; where all the passions assemble round to pay homage to the king of love. In what corner of this little ball does love hold his court? Where is the identical spot? How is it we can feel it, and not see it? How can so much delicious joy find room in this little bulk? How can it produce such heavenly joys, such ecstatic bliss, as I feel in my love for my Lottie? Then again, how can so small a bulk suffer such untold, indescribable torture as we endure when we love some beautiful object who returns scorn for true love? As I held the heart in my hand, I thought of Shakespeare's wonderful creations of beauty, and asked myself the question, Was his great heart like this? How could a man possessing a little heart like this, compose such soul-inspiring poetry? Then I thought perhaps it was the brain where all those beautiful things originated, and I turned my attention to it. What was it? Nothing but a few ounces of soft, fatty substance. Is this the great spring from whence such brilliant ideas flow? Was the great Bard of Avon's brain like this? How could such an insignificant mess of fat give life to such soul-stirring sentiment, such heaven-born inspiration? Was this little gob of fat all that Napoleon had to depend on to enable him to overturn kingdoms and to make kings out of peasants? Did Alexander and Cæsar have brains like this? Did Byron's base of thought depend on such a slender foundation as this? The more questions I propounded to myself on the subject the more I became bewildered. Scientists assert that the brain is the dome of thought; but if it is so, I must say that the dome of thought is a very insignificant dome.

No, it is the soul that dwells in the head, sitting back on its throne, that directs and moves everything. It is not dependent on this little lump of fat for its existence, nor is it in any manner indebted to it for the thoughts that man produces. The soul sits on a throne in a man's hand, and issues orders, like a king from his earthly throne; all parts of the body are moved by orders from the soul; just as great armies are moved by orders of the king. When the body falls into decay the soul steps out uninjured, and reports to its Creator for duty. Who made this incomprehensible thing called a soul? God. Who made——? Stop right here and seek to know no more; trust everything to that mysterious Power who created this admirable machine called man.

" ' "What are you doing, Mr. Demar?" inquired the professor; "you have been looking at those little organs a long time—what have you discovered?"

" ' "Enough to convince me that man is a poor, helpless, ignorant thing, unable to tell anything about his own creation."

" 'I then took a sharp knife and began to dissect the heart. I cut it into a hundred little slices, looking with all the eyes I had to see where love resided, but my search was in vain. Was my Lottie's heart like this? Was my own heart like it? If so, why could I find nothing that would indicate the part where love dwelt? I knew from the feelings of my own heart that love dwelt there; but with all my surgery I could not find it. I was so nervous I did not sleep a wink that night, and I think I shall not attempt to pry into the secrets of nature any more. When I know that my Lottie loves me dearly, and that I adore her beyond everything on earth, that is enough for me, and I shall not again attempt to investigate secrets which God never intended weak mortals to know. I am happy, oh, so very happy! no matter how or wherefore; I am happy, and that's sufficient.

" 'I was exceedingly sorry to hear that Harry still clings to his absurd notions of pride; it will kill all pleasure, destroy all hopes of happiness, unless he discards it. Why should he reject the love of such a charming woman, when it would make him the happiest man in Memphis if he would lay aside his foolish pride? I fully concur with you in the idea that his conduct is going to produce unspeakable sorrow. I knew that Viola loved him when she was a mere child, and she is worthy of any man's love. Use all your powers of persuasion, my dear Lottie, on him; see if you cannot convince him of his error. I know he loves you dearly, and has a high opinion of your judgment, and I trust you may be able to induce him to change his mind. I am sorry to be compelled, however, to tell you that the reports you have heard regarding Mr. Bramlett's wealth have not been at all exaggerated. His estate is estimated at ten to fifteen hundred thousand dollars. I was invited to dine with him during my stay in New York. I accepted the invitation, and was delighted with the entertainment. The dinner party consisted of a dozen invited guests besides the family—all persons of distinction, except myself, of course. One ex-Governor, one United States Senator, one Brigadier-General, and two railway presidents; the others were newspaper men, and bankers, and two literary ladies. Mrs. Bramlett, knowing how green I was in such matters, took charge of me at the start, and piloted me through so skillfully that I was not at all embarrassed. To describe the grand display of wealth that met my eyes would be, indeed, a difficult task. Mrs. Bramlett made a great many inquiries about Harry; so did Mr. Bramlett. They both seem to think a great deal of him, and, no doubt, would readily consent for Viola to marry him. Mr. Bramlett is by no means a gold worshiper; he has made his fortune by energetic work and close attention to business, is very liberal with his money, and exceedingly popular with the business men of New York. Mrs. Bramlett is a confirmed invalid, though she is one of the best little women I ever knew. But, dear Lottie, I must not undertake to tell everything in one letter, but will reserve something to be said in my next. Having kissed this paper a hundred times for you, I now bid my darling angel good night. Yours, forever and ever,

" 'EDDIE.'

"I had been in Philadelphia but a short time when the news of Mr. Bramlett's death reached me—and Lottie informed me, by letter, that Viola was overwhelmed with grief at the loss of her father, and that she had immediately started home, accompanied by Harry. I was glad to learn that Harry had gone home with her, for I still clung to the idea that Viola would yet be his wife. I was satisfied that she soon would be left all alone, for her mother's health was wretched, and it was certain she would not long survive her husband. I received a letter from Harry, soon after his arrival in New York, and as it has an intimate connection with this narrative, I think I had better read it now:

" 'DEAR EDWARD—I presume you have heard of the death of Mr. Bramlett, as sister Lottie promised to give you the information. His death has cast a cloud over Viola's young life; she loved her father devotedly, and is plunged in despair at his sudden death. Misfortunes, it seems, never visit us singly, but most always come crowding on us in platoons. Mrs. Bramlett is dying now—we don't think she will last more than twenty-four hours longer. Poor Viola! I pity her from the bottom of my heart. I am so glad I consented to accompany her home, and that I can be with her during this awful affliction! She is the most amiable, charming girl I ever knew; the sweetest disposition, the gentlest manners—and I believe I might say the most beautiful, too. I will tell you a great secret, if you will keep it to yourself—I am desperately in love with Viola—nay, to tell you the whole truth, I adore her—and my love is returned without discount; I might say with a good interest; but alas! I can never marry her, you know. There is an impassable gulf that separates us. I should despise myself if I thought that I was a sneaking fortune-hunter. I would look upon myself as a disgraced, unworthy, mean fellow, and so would everybody else, were I to take advantage of that poor girl's situation.

"'Mr. Bramlett made a will placing all his property in the hands of trustees, to be divided equally between Viola and her brother, Harry W., both to have control of their respective shares on arriving at the age of twenty-one years. Mrs. Bramlett was amply provided for under the will, but she will not live to enjoy the benefits of her husband's generosity. Stanley Ragland, a half-brother of Mr. Bramlett's, is named in the will as guardian to Viola and her brother. Mr. Ragland resides in Memphis—a lawyer, though I don't think he is engaged in the practice of his profession now. I am glad to know that Viola is to reside permanently in Memphis; it will be a consolation to see her now and then, even if she is to be some other man's wife. I never shall see another happy moment after the day that Viola is wedded, and, as a matter of course, she will not remain single long. Memphis will swarm with unscrupulous fortune-hunters as soon as Viola arrives, and it becomes known that she is an heiress to a great fortune. I shall remain here until after Mrs. Bramlett's funeral, for the purpose of accompanying Viola and her brother to Memphis. As I have already said, the poor woman cannot possibly survive more than two days longer. Viola's grief is crushing her young heart, and I think it best to take her away from here as soon as possible. Her brother is a handsome, well-disposed boy, and I think I shall like him very much; he is a bright, lively little fellow, and has become very much attached to me. I am proud to have such a boy named after me; that, you know, was done by Viola—which, you perceive, is another evidence of her affection for me.

"'I shall be glad to hear from you as soon as I get home, and shall expect you to write often. Poor Lottie! she hated so much to part with Viola; they had become true friends—loved each other fervently; she will be quite lonely until we get home. I have extended this communication much longer than I intended, and must apologize to you for it. With many wishes for your good health and happiness, I am,

"'Yours most truly,
"'HARRY WALLINGFORD.'

CHAPTER XIII.

"THREE days after Harry's first letter reached me I received another announcing the death of Mrs. Bramlett, and informing me that he would start for Memphis, in company with the two orphans, on the following Monday, with a view of placing them with their guardian. About two months after Viola had arrived at her new home, with Mr. Ragland's family, I received another long letter from Harry, the perusal of which caused me much pain; and, as I think it would assist me on with this history, I will read it now:

" 'DEAR EDDIE—It is with a heavy heart that I write this communication, because things are not going on well here by any means; and I would not distress you with a history of our troubles, but I know you must learn of them sooner or later. Viola has changed very much since she arrived here two months ago. She is by no means like the same girl she was when she came here last fall. There is a breach between her and me that grows wider every day—since she became aware of my determination not to place myself in a situation where the world would be justified in applying the dishonorable name of fortune-hunter to me. I was alone with Viola one day in Lottie's flower garden, happy to be near one I loved so devotedly. I think I must have lost control of myself—I was so completely overcome with my passion that I scarcely knew what I was doing. I think she concluded that I was about to make a declaration of my love for her, and to make her an offer of marriage. I am sure I do not know exactly what I did say; but I will try to tell you the substance of what occurred. She was pinning a rose on my breast, while her sweet lips were near mine, and I seized her hand and kissed it.

" ' "Miss Bramlett," said I, "how beautiful you look to-day. Do you know that I think you are the most charming girl in the world?"

" ' "How should I know your thoughts, Mr. Wallingford, about anything, when you are so cold and formal with me? You always talk to me as if I were a mere stranger, whom you had never met before."

" ' "Don't call me Mr. Wallingford, I beseech you; speaking of coldness, that makes me shiver."

" ' "It is a poor rule that won't work both ways; you made it, and should not now complain of my adopting it."

" ' "The retort is just, and I have no right to complain; but we are both getting to be quite formal of late; nevertheless, I may be permitted to think and speak of your great beauty, I hope, without offending you."

" ' "Oh, no offense, I assure you, Mr. Wallingford—I am used to flattery, and it does not make me vain at all."

" ' "No doubt you are often annoyed with compliments, but I was only speaking the honest truth when I said I thought you were the most beautiful creature I ever saw."

" ' "Indeed, I am much gratified to know that you don't think me ugly. I never saw but one gentleman whom I thought was extra handsome; but, alas! he has a heart as cold as an iceberg, and is too proud to be happy."

" 'I knew in an instant to whom she alluded, and I felt my heart begin to melt at once.

" ' "May I know the name of this wonderful paragon?' I inquired, as I gazed eagerly into her expressive eyes.

" ' "Oh, never mind his name—he is a particular friend of mine, anyway."

" ' "Is he nothing more than a friend, Miss Bramlett?"

" ' "If he is, he is too proud to say so. Like Achilles, he wraps himself up with his cloak of selfishness, and smiles at other people's woes."

" 'I still held her little hand in mine, every now and then pressing it to my lips.

" ' "Viola, how can you be so cruel, when you know how miserable I am?"

" ' "I had no idea that you were miserable; pray what has caused it?"

" ' "I love one whose high position places her so far above my humble sphere that I know she never can be mine."

" ' "We are all equals in the eyes of God, and the accidents of birth or fortune should make no difference with us—the worth of the man should be measured according to his deeds."

" ' "No doubt your theory is altogether correct, but you know that the world takes a different view of it."

" ' "A man who strives to please the world in all things may expect to please himself in none. For my part, I think the world's a humbug, and society a tyrant; and the man who worships either will make himself miserable. I believe it was Mr. Pope, in his 'Essay on Man,' who said,

> " ' " 'Honor and shame from no condition rise,
> Act well your part, there all the honor lies;
> Worth makes the man, and want of it the fellow;
> The rest is all but leather and prunella.' "

" ' "Viola, don't you know that I have been loving you devotedly ever since we first met?"

" 'Her head sank down, and she turned her face from me to hide the tears that were streaming from her eyes. I was crazy

with passion; my brain was on fire. I forgot my pride, I lost
my self-possession; I was, for the time being, raving mad with
love; I took her in my arms and held her against by heart—
her head resting on my shoulder. I would be willing to suffer a
long life of pain for an hour of such joy! but, alas! it could never
be. Suddenly I recollected what I had done—I saw the folly of
it—nay, I began to see the meanness of it, and my cheeks burned
with shame. I felt like a cowardly sneak; I sprang away from
Viola.

" ' "Pardon my presumption, Miss Bramlett; upon my honor, I
was joking; I beg you to forgive and forget me; I did not think
of the impropriety of my conduct. Let us be good friends; that
is all I ask, nothing more. I shall go to California. I—I—could
have loved you, Miss Bramlett, under different circumstances;
but, as it is, I must try to forget you; good-by—let us part as
friends."

" 'I took her hand in mine—it was as cold as ice, and her face
was deadly pale; I started to leave her. I had gone about twenty
paces from her, when I heard a groan—such a groan of despair
as never before broke on my ear! It was not loud. but sounded
like the knell of death to me. I hastened back, and found Viola
lying on the ground, apparently dead, her temple stained with
blood, that came from a severe wound which she had received
from falling against a corner of the bench. For a moment I was
paralyzed with horror, the first thought that occurred to my
mind being that she had committed suicide. But Lottie had
heard the groan, and came running to ascertain the cause. She
sat down and placed Viola's head on her lap, and began to wipe
the blood from her temple.

" ' "Bring water—quick, Harry!" said Lottie.

" 'I hastened to the house, seized a bucket of water, and was
back in a moment. Lottie sprinkled Viola's face and bathed her
temples, and in a short time signs of returning life were appear-
ing. I was gratified to find that the wound was not serious, and
that all danger was over. I lifted Viola in my arms and carried
her to the house, having my bosom stained with her precious
blood. She did not open her eyes at all while I was carrying her
to the house; but I saw tears falling rapidly from them. I whispered a few words to Lottie, by way of directing her what course
to pursue, as I placed Viola on a sofa, and fled like a coward
from the premises. I know you will condemn my conduct, and I
know I deserve it; but, as God in Heaven is my judge, I meant
to do nothing wrong. My reason was overthrown by my intense
passion. You have been in love yourself, and can readily understand how love can steal away one's reason. Who can love as I
love Viola, and then be discreet? Who can retain his senses
when his blood is boiling in his veins and his brain on fire? I
confess my conduct was shameful, disgraceful and cowardly. I
should never have placed myself under the influence of her
charms—I should have kept my love for her a secret, but in her

presence I could not do it. I have sworn a solemn oath that I would never ask her to marry me while I am penniless and she so rich. I thought I was right then, and I have never changed my mind. Having made that resolve, it was criminal in me to act as I did. I think I shall go to California soon, because I cannot endure the torture that will be mine if I remain near her. I am foolish enough—call it vanity, if you please—to think that if I were in California I might make a fortune in a few years; then I could claim Viola's hand without feeling degraded in my own estimation. I never, until lately, cared to be rich, but now I would make any sacrifice, endure any hardship, to accumulate wealth.

" 'Viola left our house the next morning after the affair in the garden, and has never been back any more. The occurrence mentioned happened two weeks ago, and I must say I have never seen such a change in any one as has come over Viola. The beautiful rosy tint has left her fair cheeks, and her disposition seems to have undergone an unaccountable change. Her conduct is causing her friends great pain and uneasiness. She treats Lottie with a strange coldness, and passes me with a dignified bow. She has become perfectly reckless with her money—seems to be determined to get rid of it; she does not use it in showy dress or costly jewelry, but is giving it away to the poor as fast as she can. Her guardian endeavors to restrain her, but she heeds not his counsel or his commands. She appears only to study the best and fastest way to get rid of her money. She says she hates the very name of money, and that she means to give it all to the poor as soon as it comes into her hands. Mr. Ragland says her income is very great, but that within two weeks just passed she has given away one whole year's income, and is borrowing more. Of course she can borrow as much as she pleases, and seems to be determined to use her credit. What is to be the result of this strange freak God only knows. I wish you were here, for she might be influenced by you—she always appeared to like you. Her guardian is greatly distressed at her conduct; he says it is inexplicable to him. I fear that something awful is going to happen. You would not think it possible for any one to undergo such a radical change as she has. Come home as quickly as you can; you may be able to do something with her. Lottie is overwhelmed with grief; we are all in despair—her guardian has given up all hope! Start immediately. I shall leave for California as soon as you arrive. My uncle has made a great fortune there; he offers to aid me if I will come, and I shall accept his offer at once. I must get away from here at all hazards as soon as possible. Probably Viola would recover her former gay and lively feelings if I were away. If her entire fortune were now under her control she would give it away in a month. She is annoyed with many suitors, but she gives none of them any encouragement; in fact, they complain that she does not even treat them respectfully.

" 'Lottie joins me in love to you, and also in the hope that you
will come home soon after this letter reaches you. Dear Lottie
is quite low spirited since Viola has quit visiting us, and nothing
but your presence here can revive her. It is useless to tell you
how much Lottie loves you, because you have known that all the
time. She is a dear, darling sister. God bless her, she will make
you a good wife.

" 'Hoping to see you at home very soon, I am,
" 'Yours truly,
" 'HARRY WALLINGFORD.'

"Within twenty-four hours after the receipt of that letter I
was on my way home, and although I was being hurried on
at the rate of forty miles an hour, I felt as if I were going at
a snail's pace. When I arrived at home I of course went to
see Lottie before talking with any one else. I found my
darling all that heart could wish. She was more beautiful,
more charming in my eyes than ever. The large, dreamy
blue eyes were swimming in tears of joy as I held her to my
glad heart, and I saw a look of love that satisfied me that I
was the possessor of a treasure of great value. I lingered by
my darling's side until late at night. Every little trifling incident was described—the days of old were alluded to and
discussed, while the present and future came in for a full
share. Harry's case was adverted to, and plans suggested by
which we hoped to be able to bring about a reconciliation between Viola and him. Old Bob was dead, and had been
honored with a grave in Lottie's flower garden. Old Roderick was alive, and in splendid humor for talking when Lottie
and I called to see him at his headquarters.

" 'Ah, ha! here we are, Lottie! Eddie's in New York!'
screamed the old parrot, as he jumped down on Lottie's
shoulders.

" 'Ah, ha! here we come, my boy!' exclaimed Dr. Dodson,
as he met me at the door and gathered me by both shoulders,
holding me square before him, and gazing into my face with
his kind, keen eyes, first drawing me close to him, then pushing me back, as if inspecting some article he intended to purchase. 'Ah, ha! here we are, my boy, all right! You've
come out wonderfully; much taller, much better looking;
don't look so green—more polish—not such a booby now, are
you, my boy?'

"I did not have time to answer his questions; he pitched them in so thickly and rapidly that I could not have put a word in edge-wise.

" 'Glad to see you home again, my boy! plenty of work to do, lots of patients on hand; you can dive in, you see, right away. Been to see Lottie? Yes, of course you have! had to see her before you came to me. Oh, you sly rascal! had to go to her first, eh? Well, well, well, such is life, you know! I was a fool once myself, when I was young! We are all fools when in love! I was in love with Dolly when she was young; Heaven bless her! I think I am in love with her yet! There, go in, my boy, and see her; she is crazy to see you. Ah, ha! my boy, here we go!'

"Then he shoved me in the house, calling at the top of his voice:

" 'Here, Dolly, our old boy has come at last! hug him first, then scold him roundly for going to see Lottie before coming to see us. Ah, ha! yes he did, a good-for-nothing rascal! Lottie is making a fool of him! Fact is, she is making a fool of herself, also! Well, well, old woman, we were young once, ourselves! you know how it is, yourself!'

"The next morning I sought an interview with Harry, and was deeply pained to see the change that had taken place in his appearance. His face was very pale, his cheeks appeared to be sunken, and his general appearance indicated great mental anguish. The lively smile that used to light up his handsome face in the days of old was absent now. He greeted me kindly, but the tone of his voice made me shiver; it was so melancholy that it startled me.

" 'How is she now?' I inquired, alluding, of course, to Viola.

" 'Worse all the time—growing more reckless,' said he, with a mournful shake of the head. 'For Heaven's sake, go see her at once.'

" '.Why not go yourself?' I asked; 'you could have more influence with her than all the men in the world.'

" 'No, no! I dare not go near her. My senses always forsake me when I am in her presence; I must go away from Memphis immediately.'

" 'Nonsense! why must you go away? Why not discard this foolish pride, and marry her and be happy?'

" 'If that is the only advice you have to offer, we will let the subject drop; my mind is settled on that question, and it must not be mentioned any more.'

" 'The money is mine,' Viola would reply to Mr. Ragland's remonstrances regarding the reckless manner in which she was squandering it, 'and why should I not do with it as I please? Who has any right to say when and how I shall use it? Who has any right to dictate to me on that subject? This hateful fortune has been my bane, and I mean to rid myself of it as soon as possible! Are there not thousands of poor people in this city who need money? Are there not thousands who toil the livelong day and then go to bed at night hungry? Yes, yes, you know it! Well, I mean to give all my money to them, and hire myself out to work as a governess, if I can; and if I can't do that, I'll wash or sew; nay, I'll serve as chamber-maid at a hotel, before I'll keep this hateful money! Has it not already ruined my hopes of happiness forever? Has it not surrounded me with false friends? Has it not overflowed me with a brigade of brainless fortune-hunters whose silly twaddle about love makes me sick? This accursed gold drives true friends from me, and attracts about me a host of senseless flatterers, whose very presence is hateful to me.'

"There was no boisterous bluster about her manner—no outburst of passion—but a quiet, determined expression was indelibly impressed on her features. It did not require a Solomon to tell me that Harry was responsible for all this; it was as plain as the sun at noontide. What should I do next? was the question that naturally presented itself to me. Should I sit down, fold my hands and quietly wait for the grand smash-up which would be sure to come unless something was done to prevent it; or should I put forth all my energies to save two young hearts from utter ruin? I was deeply impressed with the magnitude of the situation, yet at a loss to know what course to pursue in order to change it. Having pondered over the matter until I was half sick and badly puzzled, in a spirit of desperation I broached the subject to Viola.

" 'Harry is going to California,' I said to her; 'we are all greatly distressed about it, and you might prevent it if you would try.'

" 'And pray, Mr. Demar, tell me what I have to do with the movements of Mr. Wallingford?'

" 'I thought you might not wish him to go,' I said, timidly.

" 'Indeed, Mr. Demar! let me assure you that Mr. Wallingford's plans are in no respect of interest to me. He may go to Jerusalem—if he thinks it will promote his happiness—or to California, or to Hindostan, or to the North Pole, or anywhere else; what is it to me? I am just now engaged in attending to my own business, and I imagine that Mr. Wallingford is pursuing the same line of policy; I am sure I wish him success in all his undertakings.'

" 'Don't you know that pride is drawing both of you apart? Stop, I beseech you, before it is too late! Send a message to Harry by me—let me tell him you wish to see him.'

" 'I have no message to send him; why should I wish to see him? Achilles must occupy his lofty tent and let Greece bleed at every vein. When Patroclus is dead, then he may condescend to take the field!'

"As she uttered those words she was pacing the floor rapidly, back and forth while a strange fire flashed from her pretty eyes. She moved like a queen, and I saw the signs of intense passion disturbing her bosom. The truth is, she was hard pressed for courage to keep from exposing her love for Harry.

" 'Give me that rose you have on your throat,' I said, 'and let me tell Harry you sent it to him.'

" 'No, no! I might offend this proud Greek! Let him enjoy his god-like pride! Why should he be disturbed by others' woes? Do you remember the first lines of the "Iliad"?

"Achilles' wrath to Greece, the direful spring
Of woes unnumbered, heavenly goddess sing."

I am no goddess, but I mean to write a song, and sing the proud man's praise until his great deeds done in the heart-crushing business shall resound throughout the land. You had better marry Lottie, Mr. Demar, without delay; she is his sister, you know, and might catch the inspiration, and learn to despise common people.'

" 'Miss Bramlett, for Heaven's sake don't talk that way! You know how Lottie loves you—she would go any length to serve you. Harry worships you, and all will go well if you will only give him a little kind message.'

" 'I can only repeat what I have already said. I have no message for Mr. Wallingford.'

"I left her with heavy feelings weighing on my mind. Time rolled on, we all rolled on too—or rather drifted on toward our fate. At the end of six months matters were not improved, but had continued to grow worse. Lottie was as true to me as the needle to the pole; not a wave of misunderstanding ever crossed the calm sea of our happiness; all my spare moments were spent by her side. We were too happy to look into the dim future, but we drank in the sweet pleasure of the present, little dreaming of the great cloud of woe that was gathering over our heads, soon to burst on us with all its fury. Shortly after the misunderstanding between Harry and Viola he had fallen ill, and for six weeks his life seemed to be ebbing away slowly; but, thanks to Doctor Dodson's skill and Lottie's nursing, the vital spark was kept in the body until nature came to the rescue. His illness caused him to postpone his trip to California at least until fall, and we were encouraged to hope that we should be able to get him to abandon the trip entirely. I still clung to the idea that he and Viola would not drift apart forever.

"Viola never visited Lottie after the trouble with Harry. I saw her about four weeks after Harry was taken ill. I was not prepared to look for or expect such a change as was visible in her appearance; she presented a perfect picture of despair—her beautiful eyes had a languid, listless look in them that told plainly how she was suffering. Was this the beautiful, gay little girl that I had heard Lottie call the lively little cricket? Was it possible that one could change in that way in so short a time? I could scarcely believe the evidence of my own eyes. When I informed her that Harry was very ill, and that we all thought he was going to die, she started, gazed wildly at me for a moment, then burst into tears.

" 'I was in hopes I would go first,' she said, 'but I can follow him soon; there will be no money up there to keep us apart.'

"When I repeated her very words to him he was deeply affected, which increased my hopes of a reconciliation. He was greatly changed in many respects, and I thought the prospects of an understanding were brightening. The time was near at hand when I was to go to Philadelphia again to take my last course before receiving my diploma. Mr. Rockland had at last consented that Lottie and I should be married when I returned. During the summer Viola contracted a large number of debts, after having exhausted her cash income. Her guardian was very greatly annoyed and embarrassed by the demands of the creditors, and was threatening to resign his office as guardian. The trustees in New York were complaining of the continuous calls made on them for money, and had promptly refused to encourage such extravagance. I must, however, do Viola the justice to say that she did not squander the money where it would do no good, but was distributing it among the worthy poor people of the city. I was invited, one day, to go with her on a visit among the suffering people who were the recipients of her bounty, and, before I had finished the visit, I had occasion to change the unfavorable opinion I had formed in regard to her conduct. She went about the matter in a business-like manner; interrogated a family, ascertained what was needed to make them comfortable, gave an order on a merchant for the articles, and passed on to the next family, repeating the same good work there. I saw large numbers of ragged children clinging to her skirts and pressing kisses on her hands, while sickly mothers were praying for Heaven's richest blessings to fall on the dear angel who had kept their children from starving. As I witnessed those affecting scenes, I was more inclined to indorse Viola's course than I was to condemn it.

"The first of October found me again in Philadelphia, hard at work and full of bright hopes as to the future—reading Lottie's sweet letters of love, and thinking of the happy day that was soon to make her my wife.

CHAPTER XIV.

"ONE morning some three months after my arrival in Philadelphia, I was seated at the breakfast table of the Girard Hotel, when a servant laid a letter on my plate. I saw from the postmark that it was from Memphis, and I recognized the handwriting as Harry's; I lost no time, of course, in opening it. Before I had read it half through I was perfectly paralyzed with horror, and made an effort to rise from my seat with a view of going immediately to my room. I staggered like a man intoxicated, and would have fallen to the floor, but that the steward caught me and kindly led me from the room.

" 'Your letter brings you bad news, I fear, Mr. Demar!' You seem to be quite overcome; shall I get you a glass of wine, sir?'

" 'No, thank you,' I groaned, rather than spoke; 'help me to my room—I wish to be alone.'

"Several of my friends, seeing that something serious had happened, surrounded me, insisting that I should tell them what the matter was, but I begged them to leave me, as I wished to be alone.

" 'It is nothing, my friends,' said I, 'in which you can be of any assistance to me. I have received awful news from home, and shall take the first train to go there. I implore you leave me alone; I must think, I must act, and that immediately.'

"My request was complied with, and the steward kindly assisted me to my room, and left me alone. My hands trembled so I scarcely could hold the letter still long enough to finish reading it; and when I read it to you—which I mean to do—you will not be surprised at the manner in which its contents shook my nerves. It is true that I had been anticipating evil, but never had dreamed of such an awful thing as was described in Harry's letter; my mind was not prepared for such dreadful news. I turned the paper on which the fatal news was written over and over; read and re-read the lines, endeavoring to find something that would raise a doubt as to the handwriting; but no, it was Harry's hand beyond all question—the awful tidings were too true. I fell on a sofa, buried my face in my hands, and endeavored to collect my scattered thoughts, in order that I might take such action as the nature of the case demanded. How long I remained in that position I am unable to say, but it was a great while before I could regain composure sufficient to write. As soon as I could command my nerves I hastily penned the following note:

" 'DR. VANNESSE:

" 'Dear Sir—I would esteem it a very great favor if you would visit me at my room at the Girard Hotel without delay, as I wish to consult you about a matter of the gravest importance. News of a most distressing character has just reached me from my home in Memphis, Tennessee, which makes it necessary for me to go there immediately. I would have gone to your quarters, but the shock caused by the awful news has almost prostrated me; hence I must implore you to come to me.

" 'Respectfully,

" 'EDWARD DEMAR.'

"I rang the bell; it was answered by a little boy.

" 'Take this note to Doctor Vannesse, at his rooms, over at the Continental Hotel, as quickly as you can; tell the porter to come up after my baggage at one o'clock, and have it checked to Memphis; and tell the clerk to prepare my bill—I wish to settle it,' were the orders I gave to the bell boy.

"Then I began to pack my trunks and arrange everything for my journey southward, while the only consoling thought that came to my relief was that I should soon see Lottie, at all events. The bell boy had been gone with my note but a very few moments when Doctor Vannesse came dashing into my room, his handsome features blazing with excitement.

" 'Demar, what on earth has happened? You look like a corpse! tell me, quick, I beseech you! It must be something dreadful to make you look so pale!'

" 'Indeed it is dreadful! nay, it is horrible! I never have heard of such a thing before, in all the days of my life.'

" 'No doubt, no doubt whatever; but why do you not tell me what it is?'

" 'Be seated, doctor,' said I, 'and you shall know; but first let me ask you to furnish me the name of the best and most experienced detective officer in Philadelphia. I want one to go with me to Memphis. We have splendid officers there, but I am requested to bring one from here, so that we can have the services of both departments. There is a strange case to be worked up; great skill and experience will be required, as I think, and I sent for you to get your advice about the employment of some one here whose reputation is his recommendation.'

" 'Dabbs, Zip Dabbs is the man you want; if he can't work up your case, it is not workable. He can pump all the secrets out of a man, while he makes the fellow think he is receiving, instead of giving, information. I guess you have heard of Zip Dabbs—everybody knows him by reputation—he is the very man you want; I'll go with you to see him; it is doubtful whether you can induce him to go with you so far from his usual field of action; then it might cost you more than you are willing to pay—he charges very high for his services.'

" 'I care not for his charges,' was my reply; 'he shall be weighted down with money, if he wants it; money is no object with us in this case.'

" 'Then I advise you to go and see Zip at once, for he worships money, and will go with you to the end of the world if you will pay him well. You have, of course, heard the old maxim, "set a thief to catch a thief;" well, that applies to Zip Dabbs, with double compound force; he is well acquainted with the inside walls of many prisons, and has spent a great part of his life therein; but he has discovered a great secret, and that is, that he can make more money by putting other men in the penitentiary than he can by going there himself. He can change from a well-dressed politician to a dray driver in five minutes; and the change is so radical that no one can detect him. I have seen him spading a garden, in an old red flannel shirt, the hottest day of the summer season, and at night, dressed with exquisite taste, making the most melodious music on a piano. He is a splendid musician—sings and plays as well as anybody. He is as industrious as a honey bee, a splendid piano tuner, and, by this means, often gains admission to high circles where he wishes to obtain secrets that are locked safely from ordinary people. He is the most extraordinary man I ever saw; plays political demagogue to

perfection; makes a splendid speech when he sets his head to
the business; can change from a green, bashful back-woods
Hoosier to a polished man of the world in ten minutes. He
has reduced the art of disguising to a perfect science, and
can make his way through locks without keys. I hope you
will be able to engage him; he is the very man you want.
But, by the by, old fellow, you have not informed me what
has happened that causes you to want a detective.'

" 'Please let us go and see this man first. I wish to leave
on the 2:30 train this afternoon; he may want time to get
ready—we had better see him first. I can talk with you more
at leisure after we have conferred with Mr. Dabbs. If you
will accompany me I shall be under many obligations,
and then I will detail to you the unfortunate intelligence
which has made it necessary for me to employ a sharp
detective.'

" 'Ah, yes! yes, you are right, Mr. Demar; I see you understand how to economize time; that's quite a gift; time,
you know, rolls on, whether we roll or not. It is a great
thing to know how to roll on so as never to be behind time.
We can go and find Mr. Dabbs first, and confer with him;
then, while we talk matters over, he can make his arrangements so as to be ready to go with you.'

" 'Come along then, Demar; we'll go to Dabbs' quarters
now. He holds forth on Chestnut street, just below Independence Hall; you may have noticed his sign sticking on a
shabby panel at the foot of the stairs, on the right as you
go down the street, beyond the hall. Queer man is Dabbs;
you had better let me do the talking, as I know better how to
manage him, perhaps, than a mere stranger would. I hope
we shall find him disengaged, though it would be the merest
accident if we did, for he is nearly always busy; he does more
work than all the other detectives in the city. By the by,
here's his headquarters now; shabby quarters, aren't they?
Seems to me if I could coin money as he does, I'd rent more
comfortable rooms. Just look at the dirt on that floor! don't
think it has been swept since the Declaration of Independence.
I declare, I can't see how people can stand so much dirt.
Phew! what an infernal stench comes up through that hole!
I must call the attention of the sanitary board to it; I declare,

it is abominable, detestable! But come along, and let us get away from this place as soon as we can.'

"'Where is Dabbs?' inquired Doctor Vannesse of a little squint-eyed man with a very sharp nose, the end of which seemed to be making a desperate effort to get into his mouth.

"'Gone out, sir,' was the answer, made in a voice that sounded like the grunt of a hog.

"'I guessed he was out, sir, as it is very plain that he is not in!' said the doctor, angrily.

"I confess that the man's very looks was an insult, and his voice was worse than assault and battery. He was smoking a cheap cigar, his shirt-front all stained with tobacco juice; his little round head was covered with a profusion of coarse black hair, standing out like porcupine quills, and I thought he was drunk as soon as I saw him.

"'When will Dabbs be in?' asked the doctor.

"'Dunno,' was the grunt.

"'Where can he be found?'

"'Dunno.'

"'What do you know about Dabbs?'

"'Nuthin'.'

"'Come along, Demar—that fellow's drunk. Maybe we can find some one on the next floor who can give us some information.'

"We had not reached the door when I heard some one behind me call Doctor Vannesse in a most pleasant voice, and turning round, we discovered the sharp-nosed man laughing as if he would shake himself to pieces.

"'Ha, ha, ha! didn't know me, did you, doc? thought I was drunk, too, ha, ha, ha! Come back and take seats; what can I do for you?'

"I was filled with astonishment; he was the very man we were looking for, so completely disguised that Doctor Vannesse, who had seen him a thousand times, did not recognize him. I never heard a more pleasant tone of voice, and his manners were those of a well-bred gentleman.

"'By Jove, Dabbs!' exclaimed the doctor. 'I came very near knocking you down with a chair; who would have thought it was you? What's up, Dabbs, that makes you look like old Nick's engineer?'

" 'Some of old Nick's agents have been out on an excursion, but I've got 'em jugged; had just finished up the job five minutes before you came in. It's a case of poisoning—always very difficult to work up, you know—but I peeled the peach at last. They had the wrong man arrested, as is usual in such cases, but I unearthed the guilty one, and he's' sure to get a through ticket.'

" 'Well, Dabbs, Mr. Demar here, who is a friend of mine, has a job on hand which he wishes you to work up; he wants you to go with him to Memphis; money is no object in this case—the pay will be liberal. Can you go?'

" 'I guess so, unless the boss has something on hand, just wait here a moment—I'll go and see him. Nothing would suit me better than a trip down in Dixie.'

"Thus saying, he disappeared through a back door, leaving the doctor and me alone.

" 'Deuced sharp fellow, I assure you, Demar—works like a beaver, and hangs on like a badger; never fails to bring the truth to the surface; I hope you will secure him.'

" 'I shall consider myself lucky, indeed, if I can take him with me to Memphis. The case he has been telling us about is somewhat similar to the one I have on hand.'

" 'Ah, indeed! then he will be the better prepared to work it up; by the way, here he comes now. How is it, Dabbs, can you go?'

" 'Yes, it is all right; when do you wish me to start, Mr. Demar?'

" 'On the 2:30 train this afternoon—Pittsburg line; can you be ready by that time?'

" 'Oh, yes, I'm always ready; let me know the nature of the case you wish me to investigate. It may be necessary to send a telegram immediately; nothing like getting an early start in affairs of this kind; a warm track is much easier to follow than a cold one. I happen to have an old partner in Memphis, which I consider quite a lucky thing in this instance; I'll send a dispatch directing him what to do until I arrive. Mr. Tadpoddle will be of invaluable service to me, for he has worked in Memphis, in my line, for many years. Give me your case at once, Mr. Demar, and then I'll telegraph Mr. Tadpoddle what to do.'

" 'This will lead you into the light of the matter, Mr. Dabbs,' I said, handing him the letter I had received from Harry.

"When he had read the letter he handed it back to me, saying:

" 'Bad job, Mr. Demar; these kind of cases are very difficult to manage; but Tadpoddle and I can do it if it can be done. I have just finished up a case similar to this one, and I must say that crimes of that kind are increasing fearfully; and the worst of it is the suspicion, in a majority of such cases, falls on the wrong man; I trust it will prove so in this one. If it should, however, turn out that they have arrested the right one, I must say it is a most horrible affair. I am glad that your friend Wallingford acted so promptly in having the premises placed in charge of an officer—it will facilitate our work very much; then it prevents any smuggling, or putting out of tracks by accomplices, which is often done by partners in crime. You may go now, Mr. Demar; I'll meet you at the depot in time for the 2:30 train; I have nothing to do but pack up my traps, which won't take many minutes.'

" 'Well, Demar,' said Doctor Vannesse, 'let us go to your room now, and then I will hear a history of this case of yours.'

"I went by the telegraph office and sent a dispatch to Harry, informing him that I would start immediately, accompanied by the best detective officer in the city. 'Guard the premises closely—life and death may depend on that,' were the closing words of my dispatch. Arriving at my room, I handed Harry's letter to Doctor Vannesse, and while he was reading I sat and watched the changes in his countenance wrought by the dreadful news it contained.

" 'By Jove! Demar, this is most horrible! It beats anything I ever heard of; do you think she is guilty?'

" 'If she committed the murder she was insane—she never did it while in her proper mind; she was more like an angel than a murderess. The idea that she committed murder for money is absurd; she hated money, and was scattering her fortune promiscuously among the poor and needy. There has been a strangeness in her conduct for the last eight months which has greatly puzzled her friends, and it may be

possible that her mind was not right. She had had a misunderstanding with a young gentleman to whom she was very
much attached.'

" 'Ah, yes! I see how it is; she has been laboring under
temporary insanity,' said the doctor; 'but I fear that will not
avail her in this case. The pleas of insanity are becoming so
frequent that all courts view them with suspicion; I most
earnestly hope you will be able to establish her innocence.
Write to me, Demar, often, and keep me posted as to the
progress of this case; I shall not be able to discard it from my
mind until I know the final result. Good-by, old fellow, I
must leave you now; success to you. My respects to that
charming girl you are always talking about; I'd give a
quarter's salary to see her. If she is half so pretty as you
say she is, it would delight me to look at her; Lottie, yes,
Lottie—that's the name, I believe—by the by, a very pretty
name for a pretty girl; adieu.'

"When the doctor closed the door behind him as he passed
out I began to arrange my baggage, while Lottie's dear image
floated before my mind; and my heart fluttered with excitement when I thought of the great pleasure it would afford me
to be with her once more. I was at the depot twenty minutes
ahead of time, and impatient and nervous; so much excited
that I could not sit five minutes in one place. I think my
pulse must have counted at least ninety to the minute; I
snatched up a newspaper and tried to read, but couldn't do
it; looked at my watch a dozen times—compared it with the
railway clock as often—then began to notice the crowd of
travelers as they came hurrying in, hoping to see Dabbs
among them, but he did not arrive until the conductor cried
'All aboard!' when I saw him elbowing his way through the
crowd.

" 'I was afraid you would be left, Mr. Dabbs,' I said, as he
came up.

" 'Never was left in my life, sir; don't think of me at all;
I'm one of those kind of fellows that ain't left; I know the
value of time, sir; have been dispatching instructions to
Tadpoddle; he's got 'em before now—good, we're off.'

"I found it a great relief to my restless mind to be with
Dabbs, for he was an incessant talker, well posted on general

subjects, and appeared to be willing to impart what he knew without any questions from me. He gave me an interesting history of many notorious criminals whose dark deeds had been brought to light by him as a detective officer. I would interest you with a repetition of them here, but my business is to describe occurrences more directly connected with my story. I will, therefore, read you Harry's letter, as I think it will throw more light on the matter now in hand than anything I could say. Here it is:

"'DEAR ED—Come home as quickly. as you can; we are all in the deepest distress; a great misfortune has fallen on us, and we need you here to help us. Poor Lottie is in great sorrow, and your presence may help to console her. I beseech you not to lose a moment in coming. Viola is in jail, charged with the murder of her little brother. Oh, it is horrible! To think that poor girl should be thrust into a dungeon—like a common murderer—when she is as innocent as a lamb! the very thought makes the blood run cold in my veins. My conscience tells me that I am responsible, to some extent, for this terrible calamity, though not intentionally. The bare idea that Viola would commit such a foul, cruel murder, is preposterous! If every man, woman and child in the city of Memphis were to swear she is guilty, I would believe they were mistaken. Some awful mystery, some deep-laid scheme of villainy, has mixed itself up with the whole affair. and I mean to devote my life to the task of unearthing it. I have registered a solemn vow in Heaven never to seek rest until the perpetrator of this horrible crime is brought to justice. That the poor child has been cruelly murdered by some treacherous, cowardly villain, is a fact beyond all dispute; but the perpetrator has covered up his tracks so effectually that I fear we shall have no little difficulty in catching him. I love Viola; and since this trouble has come upon her I love her more than ever. I hate to use extravagant language, but the circumstances will justify it; I pray God to give me courage, strength and prudence, until I shall have unraveled this strange mystery. I must confess that the evidence points directly to Viola as the perpetrator of this unnatural murder; and there is where the mystery comes in. I happen to know that she loved her little brother devotedly, and instead of killing him, I believe she would have given up her own life to save his. She is an angel in gentleness, as pure as Diana, and I would stake my life, and all my hopes of salvation, on her innocence; yet many people believe her guilty. The poor child was murdered by poison, administered in his medicine. The post-mortem examination developed this fact, so as to place it beyond question, large quantities of strychnine being found in the stomach. I was led to hope that the evidence would establish the fact that the poison had been administered by mistake;

but that hope was extinguished when Doctor Dodson made his statement. The child had been suffering with chills and fever for several days, and Doctor Dodson was called in to take charge of the case; he left five small doses of quinine with Viola, directing her to administer one dose every two hours, commencing at four o'clock P. M. The quinine was wrapped in small slips of blue paper, and the bottle out of which the doctor took it was found setting on the mantel, where he had placed it when he measured out the quantity to be given the patient; and after the child was dead two of the doses of quinine which the doctor had made up were found on the table by the bedside, which, upon examination, were found to be unmixed with any poison; that, of course, destroyed the theory that strychnine had been administered by mistake. Viola says that she gave the child three doses of the medicine, commencing promptly at four o'clock, as instructed by the doctor, and that soon after she gave him the third dose he began to complain of a burning in his stomach, which continued to grow worse until she became alarmed and called a servant to go after Doctor Dodson. The servant was gone a long time, and, when he returned, said that he had been unable to find the doctor; that he had been called to see a patient, and no one could tell when he would be back. By this time the child was in convulsions; Mr. Ragland and his wife were at the theatre, and no other persons were on the premises except the servants, one of whom was dispatched with instructions to bring the first physician he could find, while another was sent to the theatre after Mr. Ragland. The servant who had been sent for a doctor returned in about an hour, accompanied by Doctor Plaxico. It was ten minutes after ten when the doctor arrived, and he found the child in a dying condition. Mr. Ragland and his wife reached home a few minutes before the doctor. The child expired at 11.45 P. M. He had been dead twenty minutes when Doctor Dodson came in, completely overwhelmed with astonishment at finding his patient dead. Doctor Plaxico requested Doctor Dodson to grant him a private interview, and they went into another room, when Doctor Plaxico closed the door, turned the key in the lock, and made a cautious survey of the room to assure himself that they were alone; then approaching Doctor Dodson, he spoke in a low, cautious tone, as if measuring every word he uttered:

" ' "The poor child has been murdered, as sure as God is on His throne."

" ' "Merciful Heavens! Doctor Plaxico, don't tell me that!" exclaimed Doctor Dodson, as he staggered to a sofa.

" ' "I tell you the truth, and nothing but what I know to be truth! Would to Heaven it were not so, but the evidence is overwhelming. That boy died from the effects of poison administered to him by some one in this very house, this very night; I know what I say, and mean what I assert."

" ' "Stop, Plaxico! stop, I implore you; you don't know what you are saying; you have been taking over-much wine."

" ' "No, you are wrong there! not a drop have I tasted within the last twenty-four hours; my brain was never more clear than it is this moment; and again I tell you the child has been murdered!"

" ' "Don't say *murder!* it takes malice to constitute murder; who could bear malice against an innocent little boy like him?"

" ' "Does the highwayman bear malice against the poor traveler when he kills him for his money?"

" ' "But who gets any money by the death of this poor child?"

" ' "The very one who administered the death-dealing drug."

" ' " 'Tis untrue! and who utters it is an idiot!"

" ' "Keep calm, Doctor Dodson, I beseech you; I can forgive your strong language, knowing, as I do, that you will soon be sorry for having used it; but you will be of my opinion as to this case before long. We must make an autopsy, and then you will doubtless be convinced that the child has been dosed to death with poison."

" 'Doctor Dodson leaned back on the sofa, buried his face in his hands and groaned. After remaining silent for a long time, endeavoring to collect his thoughts, he said:

" ' "What evidence have you that causes you to conclude the child has been poisoned?"

" ' "Having seen several persons die from its effects, and seeing the boy die from it this very night. I knew it was poison as soon as I arrived, and might have saved him if I had been here an hour sooner; but it was too late when I came."

" ' "Is that all your evidence?"

" ' "No, no! not by any means; I have found something which I guess will startle you when you see it; look at that and tell me if you know what it is?"

" ' "Of course—that is a small phial of strychnine; but what does that signify; will you please tell me?'

" ' "I found this in a little drawer of a bureau in Miss Bramlett's room. Her brother died from the effects of poison, and she was ordered by you to administer quinine to her brother, but she administered something else. Do I speak sufficiently plain? Do you understand me? Shall I say anything more by way of explaining what I mean?"

" ' "Hush, hush! for Heaven's sake, stop! give me time to think. How many papers of the quinine had been given to the child when you arrived?"

" ' "Miss Bramlett said that she administered three doses, and that the last one made her brother sick!"

" ' "Did you find the doses that had not been given to the patient?"

" ' "I found two papers on the table near the bed containing quinine, and have them here now."

" ' "Have you examined them to see whether they contain quinine or something else?"

" ' "Yes, their contents is pure, unadulterated quinine."

" ' "You don't mean to say that you think Miss Bramlett has intentionally killed her brother!"

" ' "But I do mean to say that very thing; who else could have done it? How could it have been a mistake? Didn't she administer the medicine? Hasn't the boy died from poison? Doesn't she make a large fortune by his death? Wasn't she alone with him all the time? What was she doing with this bottle of strychnine in her bureau? All the lawyers in Tennessee can't save her neck!"

" ' "Plaxico, you are crazy as a March hare! You don't know what you are talking about! I knew that girl when she was a mere child—have known her ever since—and I tell you she is one of the most amiable, sweet, gentle, pure girls in the world. She doted on her little brother, and it is absurd to say that she has murdered him. As for money, she despises it, and has been squandering it by thousands, among the worthy poor of the city. I think the best policy for you to pursue is to keep your absurd opinions to yourself. The poor girl has plenty of sorrow to endure, without your help to increase it."

" 'Doctor Plaxico began to pace the floor rapidly; after a few minutes spent in that way he squared himself in front of Doctor Dodson, and, looking him earnestly in the face for several seconds in silence, he said:

" ' "Dodson, I have many faults, I know—faults of which I am heartily ashamed—I have a weakness, when it comes to wine and other stimulants; but I profess to be an honest, Christian gentleman—a God-fearing man, if you please—and I cannot get the consent of my conscience to let this matter drop here. As I am a living man, I believe that child has been murdered—most cruelly deprived of his young life by his unnatural, heartless sister! Oh, sir! my heart grows faint when I think of it. She, whose duty it was to love and guard that young life, has slipped in instead like a thief and stolen it. Of all the crimes that ever were committed, this one appears to me to be the blackest, the most cowardly and damnable!"

" ' "Is it not possible that you may be mistaken, after all, as to the cause of the child's death?"

" ' "Not at all; the symptoms were unmistakable and certain."

" ' "What course do you mean to pursue in regard to the case?"

" ' "Notify the coroner, of course, have an inquest, make an autopsy, lay the evidence before the civil authorities, and then let the law take its course."

" ' "Be it so, then, and I pray God to give that poor girl strength to endure this great calamity, for of her purity and innocence I have no doubt whatever; and you will some day regret the share you had in bringing this suspicion down on her."

" ' "I never shall regret doing what is my plain duty; though I shall be more than delighted if it can appear that she is innocent; but I beg to say that I think you do me injustice when you speak of my bringing the suspicion down on her. It rather seems to me that the circumstances are responsible for doing that, and not me."

" ' "One question I forgot to ask—have you said anything to Miss Bramlett about the phial of strychnine which you say you found in her bureau drawer?"

" ' "No, I did not; nor have I mentioned it to any one but you. Mr. and Mrs. Ragland know nothing whatever about my suspicions."

" ' "Wouldn't it be advisable not to mention your suspicions until after the autopsy?"

" ' "Probably it would; if you advise that course, I shall gladly concur."

" ' "Be it so, then; let the coroner be notified at once."

" 'I was soundly sleeping in my bed when a messenger from Doctor Dodson came thundering at my door, demanding admittance. Before I was fully awake he informed me that the doctor wanted to see me as soon as I could come to his office. The messenger said that something serious must have happened, for he never had seen the doctor looking so nervous and unhappy. As soon as I could dress myself I hastened to the office; the night was very dark, the streets swimming in mud, the dim lamps at the corners cast a pale, sickly light over the pavement, my boot-heels made a loud, lonely sound as they struck the hard stones, while the messenger walked quietly behind me. My mind was in a fit condition to anticipate coming evil. And strange as you may think it, I felt sure that something awful had happened, and that Viola was in some way mixed up with it. The messenger had by no means exaggerated in his description of Doctor Dodson's excitement. I never had seen him in such a state of agitation as I found him when I reached his office. He hurriedly gave me the details of what had occurred, in substance as I have given them to you, and I was astonished at the coolness with which I listened to the horrible narrative, but I believe I have become callous, and perhaps it is best for me to be so, as it will enable me to do the work before me with the deliberation that is so necessary. Doctor Dodson, Heaven bless him! agrees with me in the opinion that Viola is innocent, and will aid me in establishing it before the world. The first thing I did was to inform Lottie of what had happened, and send her to stay with Viola, in order to sustain her, as much as possible, under this great affliction. Lottie is in great distress, but is a perfect little heroine, and has been with Viola ever since the troubles commenced, indefatigable in her efforts to comfort and encourage her. The next step was to see the newspaper managers and induce them not to mention the matter in the papers. I had a double object in view, in that respect; in the first place, I wanted to keep Viola's name out of public print; my next motive was to keep everything as private as possible, in order to let the detectives have a better chance to work up the case. Doctor Dodson went to see the coroner—who is a good friend of his—and that officer agreed that the inquest might be held privately. Doctors Dodson and Plaxico made a post-mortem examination, when the evidences of poison were unmistakable. The inquest was held in Mr. Ragland's house, and only a few witnesses were examined. The verdict of the jury would have been different, no doubt, but for the phial of strychnine found in Viola's bureau drawer, and what is most singular and unaccountable to me, is that Viola acknowledges she purchased the strychnine, but refuses to tell for what purpose. That circumstance alone caused the jury to render a verdict implicating her. Here is the exact wording of the verdict, after going on with the ordinary formalities and recitations as to dates, venue, etc.:

" ' "We, the jury, do find that Harry W. Bramlett, whose body now lies before us, died from the effects of poison administered to him by Miss Viola Bramlett."

" 'I was present when the verdict was rendered, and I did not faint; in fact, you would have been surprised to see how calmly I received the awful news that I knew would consign Viola to the walls of a dungeon. I could not account for my calmness, unless it was produced by hopeless despair; yet I am by no means hopeless, for I tell you, Eddie, as certain as there is a God, Viola is innocent, and I mean to prove it. She knows something more than she is willing to tell, but I will yet influence her to tell all. She has sustained herself remarkably well through the trying ordeal; but there appears to be a callousness in her manner that frightens me. She seems to be indifferent as to her fate—says she don't wish to live, but I hope she will be better as soon as the excitement passes off. Bring with you one of the most experienced detectives you can find in Philadelphia; don't mind the cost; I have but little money myself, but my friends will aid me. Come without a moment's delay. I have taken the precaution to have the premises closely guarded, in order to let the detectives have a fair chance to investigate the case. Everything in the two rooms occupied by Viola and her brother remains just as it was when the child died, and I have no doubt that a skillful detective will be able to unearth something that will explain the whole matter. I think I could put my finger on the guilty party in ten minutes, but what good would that do unless I could prove it? If my suspicions prove to be well founded, I shall raise a whirlwind here that will startle some people who feel very secure now. I will not breathe my suspicions to any one until I am able to confirm them. I believe I am becoming superstitious; for there seems to be an invisible influence at work upon me. It is the same feeling that told me to ride on the pilot of the engine when I saved Viola's life. That same something tells me that I will again save her, and that she will be my wife. But this letter is too long, anyway, and I will sign the name of

" 'Yours truly,
" 'HARRY.'

CHAPTER XV.

"When I arrived at Memphis I of course meant to see Lottie before any one else, but in going to Mrs. Rockland's residence I had to pass Harry's office. I hurried in to see him a moment, and to inquire about the dear one I was so anxious to see.

" 'How is Lottie?' were the first words I uttered.

" 'She is well,' said Harry, 'but of course anxious to see you.'

" 'Where will I find her?'

" 'She is at the jail with Viola, where she spends most of the time; the truth of it is, Lottie has got more sense than all of us put together. She has exhibited more true courage and prudence in this late trouble than any one of us. Who is this gentleman with you?'

" 'Oh, yes, I beg pardon, Harry; I forgot to introduce Mr. Dabbs. Mr. Wallingford, Mr. Dabbs; he belongs to the detective service, and has come to assist us in this unfortunate business.'

" 'I am glad to see you here, Mr. Dabbs,' said Harry, offering him a seat; this is a most distressing affair, and I hope you will go to work at once. As to money, I beg you to understand that it is no object in this case; you shall have what you want. I hope you will be able to unravel this most singular mystery.'

" 'I shall endeavor to do so, sir; and I must request you not to let any one know that you have engaged my services. We must act with great caution; these kind of cases are often found rather complicated and difficult to manage. I have an old friend here who has been for many years engaged in the detective service—perhaps you may know him—Mr. Tadpoddle?'

" 'No, I am not acquainted with him.'

" 'Well, he's a sharp fellow. I'll go look him up, and we'll commence business at once. It will be necessary, Mr. Wallingford, for us to meet occasionally; where shall I find you when I want to communicate with you?'

" 'Here at my office; you can come in the back way, and enter the inner room, where no one will disturb us.'

" 'All right, then, you shall hear from me soon; good morning, sir,' and Mr. Dabbs went out.

" 'What a strange-looking man he is, Eddie!'

" 'Yes, but they say he is the most skillful detective that ever operated in Philadelphia.'

" 'Well, if that is so, I must say he belies his looks.'

" 'Come, Harry, I must see Lottie; I cannot stop to talk now.'

" 'Wait a moment till I close the office, and I will go with you.'

" 'Don't walk so fast, Ed,' said Harry when we started toward the jail, 'I can't keep up with you; I know you want to see Lottie, but you need not go like a whirlwind.'

"I was compelled to slacken my pace, much against my will, for I wanted to fly to her who was more dear to me than all the world contained.

" 'Have you made any new discoveries about the poisoning since you wrote me?'

" 'Nothing definite, but we think we will be able to strike a track soon; there have been strange doings at Mr. Ragland's house.'

" 'How does Viola bear her trouble?'

" 'Ah! Ed, there is the thing that puzzles me; she acts so strangely in the matter. I can't understand her. She knows something about this business that she will not tell, though she has promised to explain all when her mind gets more composed.'

" 'Is your confidence in her innocence still unshaken?'

"I was truly sorry I had asked the question when Harry's eyes met mine.

" 'How can you ask me such a question when you are so well aware of the confidence I have in that dear girl? Don't you know how I love her? Don't you know I would as soon suspect an angel from Heaven as Viola?'

"I was not surprised at the extravagant language used, because I was in love myself, and knew how Harry felt. I had not walked more than three steps on the jail floor when I heard Lottie's well-known voice exclaim:

" 'That's Eddie,—I know his walk!' and in a moment her darling head was on my shoulder, while her tears of joy fell on my breast. 'Eddie, I am so glad you have come back to help us out of our great troubles; we have been looking for you anxiously, and the moment I heard your step I knew whose it was.'

"My heart was so full of joy that I could not speak for some moments.

" 'Come, Ed,' said Harry, 'you are making a simpleton of yourself about Lottie; leave her and come with me; we must go to Viola; how is she to-day, sister?'

" 'Improving some little, I think, though she can't shed tears. If she could only have a good hearty cry, and shed some tears, I believe it would do her a great deal of good. There is a settled look of hopeless despair on her face that frightens me.'

" 'Does she talk much?'

" 'No; she scarcely ever says a word, except to answer questions. I have tried every way I could think of to lead her into conversation, but without success. She eats scarcely enough to sustain life, though she ate more at breakfast this morning than at any one time since she has been here.'

" 'Go in, Lottie, and ask her if she will receive a visit from Edward and me.'

"Lottie returned in a few moments and informed us that Viola would receive us.

" 'When I told her that you and Eddie wanted to come in to see her I was delighted to see her face brighten up, and she spoke so quickly and said she would be delighted to see you; I think it is a favorable sign; it is the first time she has manifested the least interest about anything since she has been here.'

"I was prepared to see a great change in Viola's appearance, but not for such a one as it was. Her face was as white as marble, and I never had seen such a look of anguish as was fixed on her countenance. She rose, as we entered, and offered me her hand—it was as cold as a lump of ice.

" 'How is your health, Miss Bramlett?' I inquired.

" 'Very good, I thank you,' was the faint reply.

"I never was so embarrassed in my life, and Harry, poor fellow, stood like a statue, unable to aid me; he was more confused than I was. Lottie, however, came to my assistance promptly.

" 'Sit down, Eddie; sit down, brother, and let us talk over old times, while Viola and I are at work. Here, Viola, hold the hank while I wind the thread on this ball.'

"Viola moved her seat so as to face Lottie, and held out her little white hands to receive the hank.

" 'There, now; Eddie, you sit on this side, so I can look at you while I work; you have been away so long I have almost forgotten how you look. I declare, you look much better than you did when you went away; don't you think he does, Viola?'

" 'Yes,' she replied sadly.

"I was delighted at Lottie's skill in maneuvering to divert Viola and lead her into conversation; it was a clever piece of strategy, and, to some extent, succeeded. The jailer was an old school-mate of Harry's, and this proved to be a fortunate circumstance, as it enabled us to secure for Viola a large room, well lighted and ventilated. Harry had caused the floor to be covered with a costly carpet of the most exquisite texture, and heavy damask curtains hung over the windows; then over the damask were hung others of snow-white lace. A bureau, wash-stand, wardrobe and bedstead of polished rosewood gave the room a cozy appearance, while a sofa with red silk cushions seemed to invite the weary body to lie down and rest. On the bureau sat two large china vases, both filled with choice flowers. One rocking-chair, with soft velvet cushions, and two common cane bottom chairs constituted the furniture that Harry had caused to be put in the room. He had even had a costly curtain hung over the heavy iron door, in order to hide from Viola's sight everything calculated to remind her that she was a prisoner. There was nothing to be seen on the inside of the room that looked like the walls of a prison, but it was more like a sleeping apartment. Lottie had been no less thoughtful than her brother of Viola's comfort, for she had brought old Roderick to the jail, and that chatty bird usually made things lively wherever he went. A pair of canaries occasionally enlivened the room with a song, from the little silver-mounted cage that sat on the top of the wardrobe. All these pets had been brought there by Lottie.

" 'Harry,' said Lottie, 'you come and finish winding this thread while I go and see about dinner; we are going to have a real old-fashioned dinner to-day; mind you don't tangle my thread; Viola, as soon as you get through with that hank you'll find three more in my basket; I want you to hold them while Harry winds them off; will you, dear?'

" 'Yes, Lottie,' was the soft reply.

" 'Lottie loves Ed! Lottie loves Ed! here we come, Lottie!' screamed old Roderick, who was peeping down from the top of the wardrobe.

" 'Hush up, you old tattler! you needn't tell all my secrets before company,' said Lottie; and, taking me by the arm: 'Come, you must go and help me get dinner; we don't uphold any idleness here.'

"I divined her object, and followed her from the room, as it was evident she wanted to leave Harry and Viola alone.

" 'You are the sweetest darling in the whole world, Lottie!' said I; 'you can think of so many ways to make people comfortable and happy.'

" 'I am truly glad you think so; I am always happy when you are pleased with me.'

" 'You will always be happy, then, for I am always pleased with you.'

" 'Do you think Harry and Viola will ever make matters up, and be as they were in the good old days?'

" 'Yes, certainly I do; Harry's pride has undergone considerable shrinkage since Viola's troubles commenced, and I think he will be glad to come down from his lofty hobby.'

" 'You must put your wits to work, Eddie, so as to help me bring them to an understanding. I am going to have dinner served in Viola's room, and you must assist in keeping up the conversation, and not sit there looking as if you had a blister-plaster over your mouth, as you did a while ago, but try to invent something to talk about. Now come along, and I'll put you to work,' and she led me to the steward's headquarters.

" 'Mr. Toddleburg,' said Lottie, 'I want you to help me get a good dinner to-day, to be served in Miss Bramlett's room; will you do it?'

" 'How could anybody refuse to do anything when requested by Miss Wallingford?'

" 'Thank you, thank you, Mr. Toddleburg; you are very kind.'

"As Lottie passed on and entered the cook-room, the little man said to me:

" 'That is the prettiest young lady I ever saw, sir, and she is as good as she is pretty. I'll do anything to please her.'

" 'Why don't you come along, Eddie? I mean to put you to work; you shall not be idle here. Take those eggs and break them in that bowl, and beat them well, while I get some flour and sugar; I am going to teach you how to make a real nice pudding.'

"I broke the eggs as she directed, and began to beat them very awkwardly, while I watched her beautiful form moving about like a fairy, her sleeves rolled up, exposing to view the prettiest pair of round, plump, white arms that any man ever saw. By the time I had finished beating the eggs she was measuring the flour into a tray.

" 'There now,' said I, 'my job is finished, Lottie; I think I have earned a kiss, and I demand payment.'

" 'I'll have to give it to you, I reckon; I suppose I must be kind to my old thief, as he has been away so long.'

"Then she approached me, with her hands covered with flour, and held up her pretty lips to receive my kiss.

" 'There, now, go and grind some spice; be in a hurry— I shall need it soon.'

"I obeyed orders and ground the spice.

" 'Now go and tell the steward to have a small table carried to Viola's room, and a nice white cloth spread on it; get four plates, four napkins, four goblets, and everything necessary for four distinguished guests.'

"I went to the steward, and he assisted in arranging the dinner table as Lottie had directed. This was the first time I had helped her to prepare a dinner since the old days of our tramphood, and it naturally caused my mind to stray

back to those happy hours, making me forget the great
troubles by which we then were surrounded. As soon as I
had finished executing Lottie's orders, I re-appeared in the
cook-house, where I found her very busy with the preparation
of the dinner.

" 'How are they getting on, Eddie?'

" 'How is who getting on?'

" 'Why, Harry and Viola, of course.'

" 'Oh, they are getting on splendidly, I judge from the
appearance of things; the hanks were terribly tousled, the
balls all scattered about on the floor, and Viola's cheeks
showed a little crimson tinge; in fact, she blushed perceptibly
as I entered the room. Would you not say that was a favorable omen?'

" 'The very best in the world.'

" 'That was a skillful maneuver, Lottie, to put them to
winding yarn; nothing could have been better.'

" 'I thought so; because if we can get them to talking
freely all will come right.'

" 'They were conversing when I went in, and Viola dropped
the yarn on the floor.'

" 'Ah! if we can just control Harry we shall all be happy
once more. If Viola would only tell what she knows about
the death of her brother, Harry would be able to establish her
innocence and take her out of prison. She, of course, can
never be happy while this dreadful suspicion hangs over her.'

" 'What is it that you think she knows and refuses to tell?'

" 'Oh, don't ask me to tell you what I know. I am somewhat of a detective myself, and I'll have you know that I can
see into a mill-stone as deeply as anybody. You shall hear
from me at the proper time; the murderer of that poor little
boy is not in this jail by a long way.'

" 'What on earth do you mean? Do you know who is the
guilty party?'

" 'I would stake my life on it.'

" 'If you know who committed that cruel murder why do
you allow this poor girl to remain in jail?'

" 'Ah! there's the rub; we must be able to make the proof
before we flush the covey.'

" 'Have you mentioned to Harry anything on this subject?'

" 'Not a word; he was so much excited I was afraid he would commit some foolish blunder and spoil everything.'

" 'Lottie, do you know I think you are the most sensible, prudent girl that ever lived? I wish Harry had half the prudence you have; he has plenty of good sense, but he is so impetuous, so proud and unyielding!'

" 'He never was that way until Viola came from New York to spend the winter with me. He loved her devotedly, and thought it would be dishonorable to marry her while she was so rich and he so poor. If we can get them reconciled, and induce him to propose to her, then we shall soon be able to extricate her from this unpleasant situation. Did you know I have been afraid that Viola contemplated suicide?'

" 'No; I had no idea of such a thing.'

" 'Well, I have been afraid of it ever since Harry was so ill; and if he had died, it is my opinion that she would not have survived him an hour.'

" 'What circumstance led you to believe that?'

" 'Oh, don't be so inquisitive; I am not going to tell you all my secrets. Go on about your business now; I am done with you until dinner is served.'

"I reluctantly obeyed, and returned to Viola's room, where I was overjoyed to find Harry and her engaged in earnest conversation, in an undertone. I was a little sorry, however, when I saw that I had unfortunately interrupted a conversation in which they both seemed to be deeply interested, and I gathered up a few stray flowers that were scattered about the bureau top, and immediately left the room—making it appear that I had merely come in after the flowers.

" 'They are all right,' said I to Lottie, as I entered the cook-room; 'I surprised them in the midst of an earnest conversation, and they were both very much flurried; but I hastened to pick up these flowers and leave the room.'

" 'Did you learn what they were talking about?'

" 'I heard Harry tell one truth, if he never tells another.'

" 'What was it?'

" 'He said, "Viola, I know I have acted the fool; and I pray you to forgive me!" '

" 'And what did she say in reply?'

" 'I entered the room just then, but I saw from her looks that she was going to forgive him.'

" 'How unfortunate it was that you happened in at such a moment.'

" 'Well, didn't you order me to go? and don't you know I obeyed with reluctance?'

" 'Oh, bother your obedience! you are mighty good to obey orders when you want to; but I suppose I must forgive you, and let you stay here, though you shall not be idle. Set that pan on the stove there, and fill it with water; then take the other one off and wipe it dry with a napkin and put it back; don't spill water on the other things; I think I shall make an excellent cook of you one of these days.'

" 'You can make anything of me, because you are such a darling teacher.'

" 'I couldn't make a flatterer of you: nature has taken the job off my hands.'

" 'I wish nature had furnished me with some strong language so I could tell my Lottie how dearly I love her.'

" 'Look at you now! you are dropping the water in that bowl!'

" 'Oh, I ask pardon—I didn't see it.'

"We delayed dinner until late in the afternoon in order to afford Harry and Viola an opportunity to come to an understanding; and we had reason to believe that what we so much desired had taken place. Lottie and I brought the dinner in, and when it was ready she managed to seat Viola and Harry on the same side of the table, and she and I sat at the other.

" 'Now, Viola,' said Lottie, 'I have made you some of your favorite soup; I know you will like it, and I am sure it will do you good, and shall be glad if you will try it.'

"Viola smiled faintly; it was the first thing like a smile that had lighted up her pale face since her brother's death.

" 'You are very kind, Lottie,' she said, 'and I know I shall like the soup; I have no appetite, however, but will try some of it to please you.'

" 'Here are three bottles of home-made wine—real grape juice—take some, Viola, you'll find it excellent. It is the best appetizer in the world—the very thing you need,' she continued.

"Viola took a small glass of the wine and drank it.

" 'What do you think of it?'

" 'It is very good, and I think it will help me to regain my appetite.'

"We spent a couple of hours pleasantly at dinner; I assisted Lottie in clearing the table, and then Harry and I took leave of the young ladies, promising to visit them early next morning.

" 'Well, Harry,' said I, as soon as we were out of the jail, 'how stand matters between you and Viola?'

" 'Oh, we are all right now, I hope.'

" 'Tell me all about it.'

" 'Ah! Eddie, I have been very foolish, and I mean to make all the reparation in my power. Poor Viola! I have caused her much grief, but I thought I was acting right in what I did! · She has promised to marry me when the proof of her innocence can be established.'

" 'Did she tell you for what purpose she had purchased the phial of strychnine?'

" 'No, she positively refuses to do so; and I consider that very unfortunate, because that is the strongest point against her. I have by no means abandoned the hope of yet persuading her to reveal everything she knows about the matter. Her mind is now in a very unsettled condition; and whose mind would be otherwise, with so much to endure! The only wonder is that she has been able to bear it at all.'

" 'When is her case to be tried?'

" 'It is my opinion that she never will be tried; we waived the preliminary examination which, according to our laws, would have brought her into a magistrate's court,—and consented to let her be remanded to jail until the grand jury investigates the case. I took this course to prevent publicity, and to save Viola the pain of being compelled to appear at the bar as a common criminal. Of course she will have to be tried in open court, unless we can untangle the mystery in time to convince the grand jury of her innocence, which I mean to make a desperate effort to do. Viola is in possession of secrets connected with this matter which she refuses to reveal, but I am inclined to hope that as soon as her mind becomes more composed she will consent to tell me everything.'

" 'Did you know that Lottie is also in possession of some strange secret bearing on this case?'

" 'Indeed I did not; pray, what is it?'

" 'She refuses to tell me, but says she will do so at the proper time.'

" 'I declare, there is no accounting for a woman's freaks! If this is not a proper time to tell what they know, I should like to be informed when it would be.'

" 'I think you are wrong there. Lottie, you know, is a sensible girl, possessed of great prudence, and you may rest assured she will aid us at the right moment. She says she knows who it is that committed the murder, and that it is a person who never has been suspected.'

" 'Why does she refuse to tell us who it is, then?'

" 'Because the proof is wanting to establish the fact. By the by, Harry, have you no suspicions on your mind as to who perpetrated the murder?'

" 'I have, but am unable to offer any good reason for it; therefore, I could not think of naming the person on whom my suspicions rest.'

" 'Then it appears to me that there is but very little difference between the position you occupy and the one held by Lottie.'

" 'I must say that I cannot see it in that light; for I understand you to say Lottie informed you that she knew who committed the murder, while I say I only have a mere suspicion as to the perpetrator.'

" 'Well, it amounts to the same thing, after all, because Lottie, I guess, does not really know, positively, who is the guilty party; but we must all get together, some day soon, and have a plain talk and a better understanding. We must tell each other exactly what we know and what we think; then put our shoulders to the wheel and see if we can't make things move in the right direction.'

" 'I agree with you there, Eddie; because if we fail in this business I am a ruined man.'

" 'We are not going to fail; have no fears on that score.

But tell me how it was that you and Viola happened to make things up.'

" 'Well, I don't mind telling you everything; because you are in love yourself, you know.'

" 'I should think I did know it.'

" 'Very good, then, I'll tell you all about it. I wouldn't tell it to you if you were not head and ears in love; because people who don't love don't understand such things. They sneer at the idea of a true and holy affection—call it nonsense, and all that; but you know how it is yourself, don't you?'

" 'Oh, go on! I think I do.'

" 'Well, in the first place, you know my views in regard to unprincipled fortune-hunters, and that I had registered a solemn vow that I never would place myself in a position where such an imputation could be laid upon me. As to that, my mind is unchanged, but circumstances have materially changed. My uncle, who went to California about the time we came to Memphis, has made a large fortune, and I have received several letters from him, and I reckon I had better show you the last one, which came only ten days ago: here it is:

" 'DEAR HARRY—I received a long letter the other day from Mr. Rockland, who speaks in the highest praise of you. He said you would soon be prepared to enter the profession of law with brilliant prospects—spoke of your moral character as being first-class, and seems to be very proud of you. The history he gave of Lottie was such as to increase my curiosity to see her; he thinks she is far superior to other young ladies, and his praise of her beauty and gentle manners was most extravagant. You cannot imagine the pleasure it gave me to hear such a favorable report from my dear deceased sister's children. I presume you know I am a bachelor—such is the case, whether you know it or not—and am living a sad and lonely life here. I have been very fortunate in the mining business—have accumulated a large fortune; have no children to inherit it; no brothers or sisters—in fact, no one to give it to except you and your charming sister. This being the case, you may easily understand why Mr. Rockland's favorable report gave me such satisfaction. When one works hard to make a fortune he don't like to leave it to be squandered by unworthy relatives. It is a source of much gratification, therefore, to know that I shall leave mine in the hands of two such worthy children as you and Lottie. I am getting old now, and would like very much to have you and Lottie with me, and should have sent for you some time ago, but it is my intention to wind up my affairs here and return to Memphis. If I succeed in this, I shall of course expect you and your charming sister to live with me. Mr. Rockland says that Lottie is engaged to be married to a very worthy young physician.'

" 'I am much obliged to Mr. Rockland for his good opinion.'

" 'Hold on until I finish the letter.'

" 'I cannot,' the letter continued, 'express the gratitude I feel toward Mr. Rockland for his kindness to my nephew and niece. I own a large interest in a very rich mine here, and if I can sell it for what I think it is worth, I shall soon be ready to make my home permanently in 'Memphis. You will present to Mr. Rockland my warmest thanks; and tell my charming niece that I am looking forward with anxiety to the time when I shall hold her in my old arms.

" 'Yours most truly,
" 'OLIVER STANLEY.'

" 'Ah! Harry, what a lucky fellow you are!'

" 'Does not the good luck strike you, too? Doesn't Lottie get half? And don't you get Lottie, and her money, too?'

" 'Oh, bother the money! my Lottie is worth a hundred thousand such gold mines!'

" 'Yes, but in my case, you see, it is different; I don't care so much for the money, you know, but it makes honors easy between Viola and me.'

" 'Very good; now, go on and tell me how you succeeded with Viola.'

" 'I shall do so cheerfully; because I like to talk with you about such things, for you are in a condition to appreciate my narrative. Well, you see, when Lottie put Viola and me to winding thread, it afforded a topic of conversation; that was very thoughtful in Lottie, wasn't it?'

" 'I think it was; but go on with your story.'

" 'You see when the thread would get tangled we had to help each other fix it.'

" ' "Run the ball through here, Mr. Wallingford," said Viola, "no, not that way, but the other—just here between my hands; there, that's right; no, I beg pardon, it was all my fault, for you were doing it right before I spoke; you'll have to run the ball back the same way between my hands."

" 'Now, Ed, you must understand that while all this was going on I was not looking at the hank of thread, but was gazing intently at the beautiful darling before me. As a natural result, instead of untangling the thread, we kept making it worse. I shall hereafter recommend all bashful young people to wind yarn when they wish to make love—there's nothing equal to it, as an entering-wedge to conversation.

" ' "Stop, Viola," said I, as I took hold of her little hand, "you have got this thread in a desperate fix; let me hold this end on your wrist while you untangle the other."

" 'This gave me an excuse to hold her hand, which I assure you I did.

" ' "How pale your hand looks, Viola !" I said, as I let the hank fall, and took her hand with both of mine.

" ' "Yes, my hand is pale, I believe."

" ' "You have a very small hand, too."

" ' "Yes, I believe it is quite small; but we had better finish the work that Lottie gave us to do."

" ' "No, let us talk a while; we'll have plenty of time to do the work. I think this is quite a pretty little hand."

" ' "Do you ?"

" ' "Yes, indeed I do; and I think the owner of this hand is very pretty, too."

" ' "I declare, we must finish this thread !"

" 'She then made a grab at the ball and missed it, and it went rolling to the other side of the room. She went after it, —two of the hanks had fallen to the floor—and in crossing the room her feet became entangled in the thread, so that when she picked up the ball and started back she tripped and fell plump into my arms. Of course I could do no less than catch her, else she would have fallen to the floor.

" ' "Dear Viola," I exclaimed, "I love you with all my heart ! Dare I hope that you ever will be mine ? Speak, darling, I implore you ! No man ever loved as I love you ! Give me one little word of encouragement, I beseech you !"

" ' "Do you believe me innocent of the awful crime of which I am charged ?" she asked.

" ' "Believe you innocent, my loved one ? I would as soon suspect an angel from Heaven as you ! Nay, I would risk my soul's salvation on your innocence ! If I had a hundred thousand lives, I'd risk them all on your honor! If a legion of witnesses were to swear you are guilty, I would not believe it! Viola, can you forgive the past? Will you allow me to hope that you ever will love me? I cannot endure this miserable torture."

" ' "Harry, would you be willing to accept my hand while this dark cloud of disgrace is hovering over me?"

" ' "Yes, yes, darling! ten thousand times yes!"

" 'She nestled her face into my bosom and burst into tears; then, Ed, I knew she was mine, and my joy was unutterable. I suppose, however, you know all about such feelings. When she become composed she promised to marry me when her innocence should be made manifest to the world. Now you know all, and can readily appreciate my feelings.'

CHAPTER XVI.

"It was on the morning of the fourth day after my return from Philadelphia that I went to Harry's office for the purpose of holding a consultation with him in regard to Miss Bramlett's case. I was anxious to know what progress had been made by the detectives in their investigations. I had been devoting all my time to the business, and was more mystified at the end of four days than I was at the beginning. I had spent some time in making a survey of the buildings and premises where the murder had been committed; this I had been advised to do by Mr. Rockland, who had manifested considerable interest in the case. I had great confidence in the cool judgment of Mr. Rockland, as well as unlimited faith in him as a skillful criminal lawyer; and he told me that a thorough investigation of the house and its contents was a matter that ought by no means to be neglected; therefore I had undertaken that job as my part of the work. I had taken great pains to make a correct diagram of the house and grounds—including the kitchen, servants' rooms, stables, garden, with all the entrances by which persons could get into the inclosure. I was very much gratified when I presented my diagram to Mr. Rockland, for he examined it carefully, and then observed, 'that the work was satisfactory, and had been very skillfully executed.'

" 'If I am not very much mistaken, Mr. Demar,' he said, 'you will find that this map will be of invaluable service to you before this affair is finally disposed of. If it should turn out, as you seem to think, that the crime has been the work of some other person, you may expect to find secret entrances to the grounds—but I regret to say that I fear you will find no little difficulty in establishing Miss Bramlett's innocence. I have no hesitation, understand me, in asserting that I have always regarded Miss Bramlett as a pure, honest young lady; but, judging from the reports that have reached me in regard to her strange conduct, I am led to believe that her mind has not been altogether right. If it comes to the worst, I shall advise the plea of insanity to be filed. I am well aware of the fact that pleas of that sort are becoming quite common of late, and that the courts are inclined to view them with suspicion, yet in this case I have no doubt that the evidence will be so full as to overcome all doubt. You may depend on me, Mr. Demar, so far as my humble ability may be concerned, because I deeply sympathize with this unfortunate young lady; and then her father was my true friend, and I should be an ungrateful wretch if I did not put forth all my energy and influence in behalf of his daughter.'

"It was indeed with a sorrowful heart beating in my bosom that I separated from Mr. Rockland at the close of the inter·view just related. I had watched Miss Bramlett closely during the frequent visits I had made to the jail, and my observations convinced me that, notwithstanding her mind was sad and unsettled, she had complete control of her reason. Then, in the second place, I knew that if we succeeded in proving her insane, it would be a fatal blow to Harry's happiness. The room in which young Harry Bramlett died was a small square bedroom on the second floor, in the south-west corner of Mr. Ragland's house, and adjacent to the one that had been occupied by Miss Bramlett. There was a partition door in the wall that separated the two rooms. Miss Bramlett's room was a larger one than that occupied by her young brother, and had two windows and one door besides the door that was in the partition wall. One of the windows was in

the front overlooking the street—the other in the side overlooking a small flower garden that lay on the south side of the
building. The furniture of Miss Bramlett's room, which remained just as it was when her brother died, consisted of a
marble-top bureau, a small mahogany bedstead, with canopy
hung with pink silk, a large rosewood wardrobe, a marble-top
wash-stand, a low sofa with green cushions, an easy-chair with
red plush cushions, a cane bottom rocking-chair, three large
trunks and four common cane bottom chairs. A life-size portrait of Mr. Bramlett swung by a red twisted cord against
the south wall of the room, while Mrs. Bramlett's picture, in
a large gold frame, hung just above the bed. A photograph
of Miss Bramlett and her little brother, both in the same
frame, hung near the partition door. As I gazed on Miss
Bramlett's picture, with one hand clasped in that of her
little brother, I was then and there convinced that she never
had murdered him. Such an expression of purity beamed
forth from the beautiful face as to prove to my mind that no
secret thoughts of murder ever had lurked in her breast. I
was informed that not an article in the rooms had been moved
since the night when the little boy died—no one had been
permitted to enter either one of the rooms after the corpse
had been removed, until Mr. Dabbs had arrived. A guard
had been placed at the entrance, with positive orders not to
allow any one to enter the rooms; this had been done at
Harry's request.

˚ "When I arrived at Harry's office I found him alone; but
while he and I were engaged in examining my diagram Dabbs
and Tadpoddle came into the inner room from the back entrance, and informed us that they had important facts to
communicate. This was the first time that I ever had laid
my eyes on Mr. Tadpoddle, and if it had not been for the
seriousness of the business in which we were engaged, I
should have laughed outright as soon as I saw him. The
comical expression of his features—the peculiar shape of his
nose, the fantastic style of his dress, and the singular dispro-
portion which the length of his legs bore to the size of his
body, all combined to produce a ridiculous object. To undertake to describe him would be a failure. He was neither
man, beast, fowl nor fish, but in some respects resembled all.

His right ear was near the back of his beard. The place where his nose should have been looked like a toad-stool on a sapling. His left eye was large and very white, the other small and three-cornered; the little one seemed to be afraid of the big one—they were continually playing hide and seek with each other, and at no time were both on duty at the same moment. When the big one was awake, the little one was asleep. I noticed that when the big one would retire from duty, the little one would come to the front cautiously and gaze over to see if the other had certainly gone; and if any movement was made by the big one, the little one would dart back into his hole. It was clear to my mind that nature did not intend to make a man when Tadpoddle was commenced; but the whole concern seemed to convey the idea that nature intended him for a huge joke.

" 'If you will close that door, Mr. Wallingford,' said Mr. Dabbs, 'so that we will be free from interruption, I have an important report to make.'

"Harry closed the door, and requested him to proceed.

" 'Have you found out who committed the murder?' Harry inquired, as he fixed his eyes on Mr. Dabbs' face with a look of intense anxiety.

" 'Mr. Wallingford, you have learned the lawyer's habit early, I perceive—you have commenced a sort of cross-examination before the examination in chief has been gone through with. You lawyers have a way of setting your pumps to work on a fellow so as to draw out information which in some instances ought not to be exposed so soon—but in this particular case, I trust you will not consider me rude or discourteous if I decline to be cross-examined. It is our business to examine people, and not to suffer ourselves to be examined by them; you need not trouble yourself to put questions to me; I'll furnish you with such information as I think you ought to have, and withhold such as ought to be withheld.'

"Harry bit his lips with vexation.

" 'I suppose, Mr. Dabbs, I ought to submit to such conditions as you may choose to propose; and I shall do it very cheerfully if it will aid in unearthing this mystery.'

" 'So far as mystery is concerned, Mr. Wallingford, I must

at once undeceive you; I have as yet encountered no mystery at all—on the contrary, I think the case unusually plain—don't you, Mr. Tadpoddle?'

" 'Unquestionably, unquestionably, Mr. Dabbs; I never saw a plainer case in my life—evidence ample to convict; never saw a better chain of circumstantial evidence; overwhelming, overwhelming, sir—no use to hesitate; no mistake here. My sister's statement settles the question beyond doubt. I presume, Mr. Wallingford, you know my sister, Miss Jemima Tadpoddle?'

" 'No,' said Harry, his face reddening with impatience, 'I am sorry to say I have not had the honor to know Miss Tadpoddle.'

" 'Indeed, sir! that's unfortunate; I must avail myself of the pleasure to introduce you to my sister; a most remarkable woman, sir—rather masculine in her views, but sensible and prudent. We are indebted to her for our success in this case. The fact is, Mr. Wallingford, I am indebted to my remarkable sister for my success in life generally. She would be delighted to know you, and I dare say you would be much pleased with her. She would be able to advise you in this business, no doubt, as her judgment may be relied on; but let that pass for the present. What was it you were about to observe, Mr. Wallingford?'

" 'I was about to ask a question; but then I remembered that you and Mr. Dabbs had intimated a wish not to be questioned.'

" 'Oh, not at all, sir; you misunderstand us entirely. We don't prohibit questions—we only decline to be examined like an ordinary witness in court. Ask as many questions as you please—we'll only answer such as we choose.'

"Then Mr. Tadpoddle threw himself back in his chair, put the small eye on duty, and waited for the question.

" 'If you have any communication to make in regard to the discoveries you have made, I should like to hear them now!'

" 'Just so, Mr. Wallingford, no doubt you would; and that is what brought us here to-day. I am well aware of the interest you feel in Miss Bramlett's case, and so told my remarkable sister, and she also appreciated the situation very

much. By the by, Dabbs, don't you think we had better tell
Mr. Wallingford what my remarkable sister knows about the
case ?'

" 'I think we had, Mr. Tadpoddle; but let them be told
after the other facts have been related—nothing like beginning
at the right end, you know. There are two ways to tell
anything—one right way, and one wrong way; always commence a story at the right end, you see. What your sister
knows comes last, in order to make the chain of evidence
complete.'

" 'Ah, yes, Dabbs, I perceive now that you are right.
Well, you tell Mr Wallingford about the other things, and
when it comes to my sister's part, then let me in.'

"I was losing my self-possession, and felt as if I must do
something rash very soon; I think I should have hurled a
lump of coal at Mr. Tadpoddle's little gourd head, but my
attention was diverted to Mr. Dabbs, who began to take something from his pocket-book.

" 'This little parcel, Mr. Wallingford, is a dose of strychnine similar to the one that killed Miss Bramlett's little
brother. Well, what of that? is the question that naturally
would come up in your mind. You'll observe, Mr. Wallingford, that I am only drawing an inference as to ideas, etc.,
which would be likely to present themselves. Well, what if
that is strychnine? you say. Very good! I reply, The deceased was murdered with strychnine. Some one administered the poison. Who? ah! that's the question. I answer
without hesitation: Miss Bramlett.'

" 'Tis false!' exclaimed Harry, as he made at the detective
with eyes flashing with rage. 'I'll choke the breath from the
villain's lungs who dares to accuse Miss Bramlett.'

"I quiekly placed myself before Harry, and prevented him
from choking Mr. Dabbs, and endeavored to keep him quiet,
though I thought a little pressure on Dabbs' wind-pipe would
have been justifiable. I succeeded in getting Harry to resume
his seat, then requested Mr. Dabbs to proceed.

" 'If Mr. Wallingford is unwilling to hear facts,' said
Dabbs, 'we had better let the interview terminate here. It
is our duty, as officers of the law, to close our eyes to consequences, and bring facts to light. We can't consider the

feelings and wishes of individuals, in our searches after truth; if we did, we should accomplish nothing. We do not make evidence, we only bring to light that which is made by circumstances and concealed by fraud. If the evidence that we have discovered does not please Mr. Wallingford, we will not thrust it on his hearing, but will deliver it to the officers of the law, whose duty it is to use it in punishing the guilty, and protecting the innocent.'

" 'You are right, Mr. Dabbs, and I was wrong,' said Harry, as he leaned his head down on the window-sill and sighed sadly. 'Tell us the worst at once.'

" 'Well this dose of strychnine was found in Miss Bramlett's room, concealed in the pocket of a blue silk dress which belonged to her.'

"Mr. Dabbs paused, and looked at Tadpoddle. Tadpoddle put the big eye on duty, while the little one made a precipitate retreat. Harry groaned like one whose heart was crushed. I wanted to commit some kind of mischief, but did not exactly know what it was. At length Dabbs spoke again, after he had sufficiently enjoyed the misery inflicted on us by the first revelation:

" 'The mere naked fact that Miss Bramlett had a dose of strychnine in one of her dress pockets does not signify much, but when viewed in connection with other circumstances, the case is different. To sum up the ideas, we must be very cautious to sift things so as to separate the wheat from the chaff; however, we don't always find it prudent even to throw away the chaff; because it will sometimes show us which way the wind blows. Now in this case I think we can see which way the wind is blowing without the use of the chaff. The fact is, the breeze seems to be all the time blowing in the same direction. We found three small scraps of blue paper; two upon chemical examination were found to contain small quantities of quinine, while the other one contained unmistakable evidence of having been filled with strychnine. We found a little package of quinine in the fire-place; now it is very plain that this was emptied out of one of the papers left by Doctor Dodson, and that the strychnine was put in the same paper instead of the quinine. That goes to show beyond doubt that the poison was administered intentionally; but by

whom? you would of course be inclined to ask. Very good;
let us proceed to make the inquiry further.'

" 'Now,' said Tadpoddle, 'I think is the time to tell Mr.
Wallingford what valuable evidence has been discovered by
my remarkable sister.'

"Mr. Tadpoddle's little eye then went back to its hole, and
the big one came to the front.

" 'No, not yet, Mr. Tadpoddle,' said Dabbs, as he bit the
corner off of a plug of tobacco and began to chew it with
great energy; 'there are other matters to be mentioned before
we disclose your sister's evidence. There is the secret gate,
you must remember; that will furnish a very strong link in
our chain—a link which I consider of great importance. So
far, so good. Now, Mr. Tadpoddle, allow me to call your
attention to a certain letter or note—some people, I believe,
would call it a billet-doux; no matter what they call it—
nothing in a name, you know; at least, Mr. Shakespeare so
testified in favor of that idea. Be so kind as to hand me that
billet-doux, Mr. Tadpoddle. I believe I gave it to you?'

"Tadpoddle's big eye retired slowly, and the little one came
out and then darted back; then came out again—a game of
hide and seek being commenced between them. The big eye
seemed to be hesitating, as if undecided about the propriety
of giving the field to the little one. But the little one appeared to have scraped up courage, and made a bold charge
to the front, when the large eye gave up the contest at last,
and hid in its den. Tadpoddle seemed to be waiting to know
which eye he would have to depend on, while looking for
the note, but as soon as the matter was settled, he drew from
his breast pocket an old pocket-book, and began to take out
a great number of old dirty papers, carefully scrutinizing each
one as he took it out.

" 'Ah, here it is, Mr. Dabbs; by Jove, it's a clincher, ain't
it?'

"Dabbs did not reply to Tadpoddle's question, but turning
his attention to Harry, said:

" 'Mr. Wallingford, you will pardon me, sir, but duty is
duty, you know, and at the risk of incurring your displeasure,
I must perform my duty. You will doubtless be surprised to

learn that Miss Bramlett has been holding clandestine meetings with a low-down gambler for many months.'

"Harry would have knocked him down, but I anticipated the movement, and held him in his seat.

"'Edward,' said he, 'must I sit here and listen to this? Am I a contemptible coward? Shall I let them kill that poor girl, and then blacken her fair name? Is this Harry Wallingford who sits here, quietly listening to such a foul slander on the name of his affianced bride! Would you have me to whine and smile and fawn on the base wretch who utters such language?'

"'If ever there was a time when it was necessary for you to control your temper, that time is now. The awful situation in which Miss Bramlett is placed should convince you that nothing can be done for her unless cool judgment and common sense shall take the place of passion and rashness. Mr. Dabbs may be mistaken in his conclusions, and I think he is, yet he believes he is performing his duty, therefore, I beseech you to hear all he has to say. Then, after we have heard it all, we will advise with Mr. Rockland on the subject—I have great confidence in his sound judgment, and I know his sympathies are with us. Give us a promise, now, Harry, that you will endeavor to control yourself—you have committed some great errors, and it behooves you to repair them. You can command your passion if you will determine to do it.'

"'Edward,' said he, 'you are right. I have been very indiscreet, and to some extent inexcusable; I promise to do as you wish. Let Mr. Dabbs proceed. I'll hear all he has to say.'

"I then requested Mr. Dabbs to proceed.

"'I am exceedingly sorry,' said he, 'that Mr. Wallingford should be disposed to censure me for stating facts, when he must know that the discovery of these facts did not afford any pleasure to me; I may say I was pained to find that circumstances were continually pointing to Miss Bramlett as the guilty one. I had hoped to find evidence of her innocence, and such a result would have given me ten-fold more pleasure than anything we could find against her. It is clear to my mind that the poor young lady has been the victim of some heartless villain—or that she has been laboring under temporary insanity. Whether or not I am correct in that opinion it is not my business just now to inquire. That is a question for the courts and lawyers to settle when she is put on trial; my business is to show what has been done, and nothing shall cause me to shrink from the performance of that duty. There is a young man keeping a gambling hell in this city; a young man of handsome face and fascinating manners, though a shrewd, sly scoundrel, who had something to do with this business; and I flatter myself that I shall be able to expose him before I get through with this affair. I have been shadowing him—he often gets drunk, and I never failed to manage his sort. He talks freely when drinking, and I will pump the secret out of him before I quit. I played poker with him the other night; he beat me out of forty dollars— the rascal! but I shall let him win, and give him rope to hang himself with. I'll catch up with the villain yet. His apartments are furnished like the palace of a king. Where did the money come from to pay for it? I dare say he wheedled Miss Bramlett out of it. That unfortunate young girl has been so imprudent as to make frequent visits to these apartments during the dark hours of night.'

" 'Oh, Heavens! Eddie,' exclaimed Harry, as he seized me by the arm, 'have I got to hear such as this, and say nothing? It's more than humanity can bear; it will kill me; for Heaven's sake let this interview terminate—else I shall lose my reason!'

" 'Be quiet, I pray you, Harry,' I said, though I felt the demon rising in my own breast, and needed all the prudence I could command in order to keep me from knocking the man down myself.

"My attempt to soothe and quiet Harry, however, served to aid me in keeping cool, and after the lapse of a few moments, I directed Mr. Dabbs to proceed.

" 'I was about to observe, a moment ago, that Miss Bramlett has been exceedingly imprudent, if not criminal, in her intrigue with Ben Bowles.'

" 'With whom did you say?' groaned Harry.

" 'Why, with Ben Bowles, that unprincipled gambler.'

" 'He must be the same fellow you knocked on the head at our camp,' I said to Harry.

" 'I should not be surprised,' he replied. Then turning to Dabbs, I requested him to give me a description of Bowles.

" 'He is very handsome; has dark-brown hair, very black eyes, is about five and twenty years old, very tall—I should say not less than six feet—dresses magnificently, drinks to excess, has a deep bass voice, and a slight scar on his left temple, close to the eyebrow.'

" 'That is the very man!' said I, as I again requested Mr. Dabbs to go on with his history.

" 'Well,' he began, 'as I was saying just now, I cannot account for the strange conduct of Miss Bramlett, except upon the theory that she has become fascinated with that good-looking scoundrel, and was contemplating a secret marriage with him; at all events, she has been frequently seen to enter his apartments through a private door that opens on an alley in the rear of the house.'

" 'I shall go mad!' said Harry, as his head fell on my shoulder. I could hear his heart throb and jump against his breast, as if in great commotion. 'Can this horrible story be true? Can the devil take the shape of an angel, in order to drag the soul down to hell?'

" 'Hush, hush! Harry, there is some strange mistake connected with the affair, and I'll risk my life on Viola's honor.'

" 'Thank you, a thousand times, from the very bottom of my heart! but where is the cowardly villain who originated this damnable falsehood? Oh, if I could only get my hand on his accursed throat!'

" 'Let us first find out who is working these secret wires,' said I, 'and then we may be able to contend with the enemy with hopes of success. If Miss Bramlett ever has visited that place, she has been inveigled into it by foul and fraudulent means. She was continually searching for worthy objects of charity, and some false, sneaking scoundrel may have entrapped her into that house. How easily might she have been induced to believe that some unfortunate creature was dying in that house for want of food. I know that she would have gone there, or anywhere else, to render assistance where

suffering humanity needed help. No, if this is the worst that
can be said of Viola, you have reason to rejoice; for you
may rest assured she will be able to explain it satisfac-
torily.'

" 'I believe you, and shall hear all that can be said.'

" 'No, indeed, Mr. Wallingford,' said Dabbs, 'far be it from
me to report anything in this case except the naked truth. I
have no bias for or against any one, I assure you. It is the
duty of one in my position to be careful to keep his mind
clear of prejudice, and to look only to the detection of crime;
and if Miss Bramlett shall be able to offer a satisfactory explanation of her conduct in this instance, it will be a source
of gratification to me. My mind tells me that this man
Bowles had something to do with the death of young Bramlett; and if he had, I shall not stop until I can prove it. The
fact that Miss Bramlett has frequently met Bowles under suspicious circumstances has been ascertained to a certainty;
but after all it may, as you have suggested, be easily explained
by her. A lady of Miss Bramlett's tender age, having but
little experience in the wicked ways of the world, would be a
lamb in the power of such a wolf as Bowles. He is frequently out of money; and when such unprincipled scamps
want funds, they would commit murder; or any other crime
to get it. He is extravagant beyond measure, loves wine and
women, keeps four fast trotters at Burton's, bets high at the
gaming table, and occasionally dines his friends extravagantly.
Now all this costs money; and it is my opinion that Miss
Bramlett's money has largely contributed to that establishment. You know that she has within the last twelve months
squandered over ten thousand dollars in cash, besides incurring
debts equal to the cash spent. By her father's will she had
the right to spend the income of her inheritance—but could
not touch the principal. She went through with the income,
and, from all accounts, would have speedily wasted the principal, but the trustees positively refused to allow it. Her
little brother did not draw any of his income at all; and when
he died, his sister, of course, became the owner of his share,
not only of the income, but of the entire estate. People do
not commit murder without a motive. Did Miss Bramlett
have a motive to murder her brother? Of course we answer

unhesitatingly, Yes. What motive? what did she gain by the
death of her brother? Answer—Ten thousand dollars ready
cash in hand, and two hundred thousand dollars added to
her inheritance. If that did not constitute a motive, I would
like some one to inform me what would. Bowles was in great
stress for want of money at that time, as I happen to know.
The wolf may have used the lamb as his agent to get the
funds he wanted. He wrote a note to Miss Bramlett in which
he implored her to let him have five hundred dollars. That
note was found in her dress pocket. It is the document we
mentioned a moment ago, and here it is:

" 'DEAR V.—Don't fail me to-night. Come at eight o'clock. I
will be alone. I am dying to see you. For Heaven's sake let me
have the five hundred dollars, as I am in a tight place just now.
I found your note under the seat in the summer house. I knew
where to look for it. Of course I pressed it to my lips before
I read it. When I see you we will discuss our plans more fully.
If you can accomplish the business with a brave heart we shall
yet be happy. I know that you have the courage to do it, if you
set your mind on it. Detection would be impossible if you adopt
my plan—though we will talk the matter over when I have you in
my arms.
                         " 'Yours and yours only,
                                        " 'B. B.'

" 'Catch Mr. Wallingford there—he has fainted!' exclaimed
Dabbs, as he sprang forward and attempted to prevent Harry
from falling; but he was too late—for Harry was lying on
the floor before Dabbs got to him. I was unable to render
any assistance, being completely overcome with horror at
hearing the contents of the letter. Most of my hopes of
Viola's innocence vanished when the note was read; Mr.
Dabbs lifted Harry up and laid him on a sofa, while Tadpoddle sprinkled his face with water and took off his cravat,
unbuttoning his collar—then Harry began to breathe faintly;
but such a look of despair as settled on his face I never beheld there before. I was unable to offer consolation, for I
was in need of it myself—the blood seemed to be freezing in
my veins. It was plain that Bowles' letter referred to the
plan which had for its object the murder of Viola's brother.
The bare thought that such was the fact made my heart stand
still.

" 'Have we all been deceived by this beautiful girl? Is she, after all, a cruel, calculating murderess, and the mistress of a villain? Could it be possible that one so beautiful possessed the heart of a murderess? Could it be that she who looked like the very embodiment of purity was the horrible thing that I blush to think of? Questions of that nature came pouring in on my mind; and if I had been compelled to answer, I should have been forced to admit that the evidence was overwhelming against Viola. It was plain to my mind that it would not do to depend on Harry any longer—he was more like a raving maniac than anything else. I began to fear that he would seek a quarrel with Bowles—a thing which above all others I thought should be avoided, as it would prevent the detectives from getting at the bottom of the case. If Harry should attack Bowles I knew that one or the other would be killed; and how to prevent it was the question uppermost in my mind just then. I knew all about Harry's ungovernable temper and his lack of fear, and imagined from his looks that he had resolved on something rash —his face was pale as death. I at once divined the thoughts that were passing through his mind, and was endeavoring to invent some plan to prevent a meeting between him and Bowles, when he addressed me in a tone so low that it was not much above a whisper: ·

" 'Eddie, it is all over with me—I am a ruined man; there is but one course left for me to pursue—Bowles must answer for the ruin he has wrought. Poor girl! I pity her, and before Heaven I swear to be her avenger. She is a helpless orphan, and it is my duty to defend her, notwithstanding she has forfeited all right to my love.'

"I grew impatient. I was becoming tired of Harry's imprudence, and could not forget the fact that his selfish pride has caused all this trouble.

" 'I think,' said I, endeavoring to keep down my rising temper, 'that I heard you say if every man, woman and child in Memphis were to swear Viola was guilty, you would believe they were mistaken; and now, at the first intimation of her guilt, without any proof whatever, you are the very one to condemn her. Is this the confidence you have in your affianced bride? Indeed, I congratulate Miss Bramlett in the possession of such a true lover!'

" 'Stop, Edward,' he said, as he rose from his seat and began to walk the floor, 'I know I have said many foolish things, and committed numerous blunders in this business, but it can't mend matters for you to be throwing it up to me. I admit that in some instances my conduct was inexcusable; but I was trying to repair the damage caused by it—it is too late now. Nothing that any one could say would have any effect on me, after what I have heard to-day. My heart has turned to stone, and I don't think it could feel anything at all. Perhaps it is best that it should be so. I have a duty to perform now that will require coolness, and I feel that I could see blood run from the heart of Viola's betrayer without compunction. I have a double account to settle with him; and it shall be settled in a manner that will be final.'

" 'If you would listen to the advice of your friends, you never would let Bowles know that you have obtained a clew to his villainy until you have secured enough proof to convict him in open court. It is very clear that if he is the author of that letter, he has been the prime mover in the murder of Miss Bramlett's brother; and it is also very plain that other letters have been written—for he mentions the place where letters were deposited and received. Now, if you make a row you put him on his guard, and thereby give him a chance to escape; but if you keep quiet and let Dabbs work on him, I think it would enable us to trap him. Above all things let us give Dabbs an opportunity to work up the case, so far as Bowles is concerned. A man must learn to control himself before he can expect to control other people; and when you make up your mind to act with your friends, and not against them, I am prepared to proceed further in this business. If, on the other hand, you mean to seek a quarrel with Bowles, and destroy all hopes of securing proof of his guilt, I beg to say that I wash my hands of the whole affair.'

" 'I will promise to wait until Mr. Dabbs shall have a chance to do what he can; but, remember, I only promise to postpone his punishment.'

" 'Very well; I accept the promise, and we can discuss his punishment at another time. We must see Lottie at once, and prevail on her to tell what she knows. I am sure she could furnish us some important information, if she would. While I am ready to admit that my confidence in Viola's honor has been somewhat shaken, I must be permitted to say that I have not lost all hopes; hence my anxiety to know the truth has been increased very much by what I have just heard.'

" 'Have you anything further to communicate?' said I, addressing Mr. Dabbs; 'if you have, we beg you to proceed.'

" 'Ah, hem! yes, Mr. Demar,' replied the detective, as he took the last corner from his plug of tobacco, 'I have something more to say; and, in the first place, allow me to mention the fact that I heartily indorse your idea as to Bowles. We must by all means keep him in the dark as to what we have resurrected against him. He is a sly, shrewd rascal; but I'll capture him if you don't thwart me. In Mr. Ragland's flower garden there is a large summer-house made of lattice-work, and all covered over with vines. It is constructed in an octagonal shape, with wooden benches, arranged round inside. This house has been the meeting place of Miss Bram‧lett and Bowles. Miss Jemima Tadpoddle saw them there one night at a very late hour. She had called to see Mrs. Ragland one evening, and was informed by the house-maid that her mistress had gone out to attend a meeting of some benevolent society, of which she was an active member; but the maid told Miss Tadpoddle that Mrs. Ragland would be in soon, and while waiting in the drawing-room for Mrs. Ragland's return, she saw Miss Bramlett go into the summer-house. Soon after Miss Bramlett went into the place Bowles came in through a secret entrance at the back of the garden, and went into the summer-house where Miss Bramlett was watching for him. After waiting a long time to see Mrs. Ragland, Miss Tadpoddle left without seeing her; and when she went away Bowles and Miss Bramlett were still in the summer-house. How long they remained there she of course did not know. When Miss Tadpoddle gave us this information we made a thorough examination of the premises, in order to find the place where Bowles got into the garden.

We searched for some time without any result, but at last we found his entering place; and I must give him credit for great skill, for the manner in which he had managed it. The garden was inclosed with a common paling fence of pine timber, painted white, the palings being about four feet high, sharpened to a point at the top, and nailed to a horizontal railing. Three of those palings had been so arranged that they could be taken off and replaced, so as to leave no signs of having been removed. The nails that had originally been driven in to hold the palings in their places had been drawn out, small wooden pins put in their stead—so that when anyone wished to enter the garden he had nothing to do but to draw out the wooden pins, take off the palings and walk in; then replace them, and no one could see that the palings had ever been interfered with. I don't think we should have made the discovery had it not been for the signs left on the grass by the feet of the party, who had evidently entered very often. We found that the ground near the place had been hardened by continuous tramping on it; and this led us to examine the palings very closely; the result was we found what I have just mentioned. We made a very extensive search among the blades of tall grass that grew in the vicinity of the entrance, and we found an article which we believe to be a set that has fallen from a finger ring. I should say that it was of considerable value—as it looks like a genuine diamond. This little article may enable us to get our grabbers on Mr. Bowles; because, if it is his, he of course has the ring from which it has been detached. One thing is certain—Mr. Bowles has not only received Miss Bramlett at his apartments very often, but he has been meeting her in the summer-house many a time. I believe this ends what I had to report to-day. Permit me to take my leave now, and you shall hear from us again soon.' "

Queen Mary now expressed a wish that the further hearing of the story should be postponed, in order that the maskers might have a recess.

CHAPTER XVII.

IVANHOE and Scottie were seated in the rear of the pilot house, discussing and dissecting Ingomar's story.

"What do you think of the story now, sir knight?" inquired Scottie. "Do you like it or not?"

"So, so. Some parts I like, and some I don't. There's too much talk of murder in it."

"Do you think from what you have heard of the story that Miss Bramlett committed the murder?"

"There is no room to doubt it, if we are to judge from the evidence that has come up against her. If Ingomar can get her out of the scrape without flatly contradicting himself, he will be entitled to the premium as the champion story-teller."

"I agree with you there; because if I were on a jury and such evidence was brought before me, I should say guilty beyond the possibility of a doubt."

"Well, Scottie, give me your opinion of Lottie."

"Ah, sir knight! that's an overdrawn picture. Angels have long since quit visiting the earth. I don't think I have heard of any being down in this world since Jacob had such a scuffle with them."

"You are wrong there; they have been here frequently since that affair with Jacob. But let that pass, and tell me what you think of Lottie."

"She makes a splendid heroine for a story."

"That may be true; yet it is so pleasant to hear Ingomar talk about her; did you know that somehow or other an idea has got into this head of mine?"

"No, indeed! is that so?"

"Pshaw! You didn't let me finish the sentence. I was about to remark that somehow an idea had got into my head that you are just like Lottie."

"Oh! you are badly lost now, for I am a plain, simple girl—just like other girls, only not so pretty; and then I have an awful temper. Oh! you ought to hear me when I am angry."

"I am truly glad to hear you say so, for I like a high-tempered woman. They make things generally stand round so lively—have the servants walk to a line—keep the floor so clean—set such nice dinners; and then it is so delightful to have a good, jolly quarrel—get up a great row, shed a few tears, and then make friends—then kiss. Oh, that's the girl for me!"

"You draw one side of the picture very nicely."

"You can't frighten me with such an insinuation; but you only increase my anxiety to know more about you. By the by, were you ever in love?"

"Oh, yes! I was dead in love with a fellow once—he was such a darling! and to tell you the truth, I love him yet. He had such a black beard, such black hair, and was so handsome!"

"My hair is black, and so is my beard."

"I dare say it is. What if it should turn out that it was you, after all! Were you ever in love?"

"Indeed, yes! I loved a pretty girl with dark-brown hair and large gray eyes; and would have married her but for a very trivial little circumstance—she wouldn't have me."

"I suppose she didn't like black hair and a black beard."

"Well, we didn't marry, anyway."

"Suppose, sir knight, you entertain me with a history of your love scrape?"

"I will, on condition that you will follow suit with your little episode, when I am through with mine."

"All right—I'll do it."

"Mine is a short story, but very affecting—and, if you have tears, prepare to shed them now."

"Well, hold on then till I get out my handkerchief. Here it is now—go on."

"I was in the city of Jackson, Mississippi, once, attending the Legislature, of which I was a member."

"Wait a moment till I catch this tear—I think I feel one in my left eye."

"What have I said that could have started a tear?"

"That you were a member of the Mississippi Legislature—
that was the reason your girl refused to marry you."

"Well, perhaps it was; though I have repented of that;
and have promised to go and sin no more in that way; but
I am digressing. While I was in Jackson, I was invited by
some friends, to join them in a picnic dinner on the beautiful
banks of Pearl river. Many lovely women were with the
party—one in particular; it was a clear case of love at first
sight on my side, and spontaneous indifference on hers. The
dinner was magnificent. My girl unloaded a basket. It
made my mouth water to watch her pretty little white hands
lifting out the nice cake, the luscious jam, the roast turkey,
the broiled chicken, the snow-white bread, the great yellow
rolls of butter. I fell in love with her and the contents of
her basket—and felt like devouring the whole concern then
and there. It would have done you good to see the sweet
smile she cast on me as she invited me to take a seat by
her side and eat with her. I made up my mind to make her
an offer of marriage at the first opportunity, and I was very
much mortified to learn that three other fellows had determined to do likewise. All three of them had great advantages
over me—they were not members of the Mississippi Legislature, and I was—I had to carry too much dead weight. After
dinner was over the band began to play a lively tune, and
some one proposed a dance; I made a dash toward my girl,
with the view of asking her to be my partner in the dance.
She smiled sweetly on me, but danced with another fellow.
I then took the pouts and refused to dance at all. While
the angry fit was on me I wandered off down the banks of
the river alone—vowing to cripple somebody before night.
When I had fully made up my mind to do it, the next question was, How could I accomplish it without getting crippled
myself? I could not for the life of me think of any plan
that would enable me to get rid of my rivals without endangering myself; therefore I was forced to abandon the
enterprise altogether. But while I was rambling along the
bank of the river meditating dire destruction, a young gray
squirrel ran across my path, and I caught him and carried
him in triumph to the picnic headquarters. My girl cast on
me another one of her sweet smiles, as she begged me to give

her the pretty, darling little squirrel. I of course forgot my angry fit, and gave it to her; it was but a moment after I had given it into her hand when she uttered a loud scream, and let the little squirrel drop on the ground. The entire party took after the squirrel except me and my girl. I saw the blood streaming from her hand, where the little animal had bitten her. I took off her glove and washed the blood from her hand, then tied it up with my handkerchief. I hid her glove in my bosom, where I have worn it ever since. Here it is now, with the stain of her dear blood on it! Why, Scottie, I declare, you are weeping sure enough! What on earth is the matter?—pray what is it." (She was weeping—the tears running down her cheeks in a stream.) "Have I said anything to offend you? I did not intend it, if I did." (It was some time before Scottie became composed—and Ivanhoe was very much astonished at her weeping so.) "I believe I have about finished my narrative. I really did love that girl dearly, but her father did not like me. Now, Scottie, tell me your love affair."

"You have knocked the foundation from under my story, for you have told it yourself—and I must ask you to give me back my glove. It is mine, and here is the scar made by the bite of the squirrel."

"Good Heavens! Have I the honor to again meet Miss Kate Darlington?"

"If you will leave out the honor part, I will answer, Yes! And I have the pleasure to meet Captain Ralleigh Burk, I presume."

"You have guessed my name, at any rate—but was it true, Scottie (pardon me please, but I mean to call you Scottie all the time, for I like it), that you did love me?"

"Oh, you must not ask impertinent questions; you know we were joking when we commenced it."

"No, I don't! for I never was more in earnest in all my life. I have kissed this little glove a thousand times; and the dear image of the Pearl river girl has been indelibly stamped on my heart. It has been two years since I last saw you, and it has seemed an age to me. I was sure that you were going to marry that other fellow with the red hair."

"Oh, no! I detest red hair—and then I never could marry

a man unless I loved him. The fact is, it wouldn't do for me to marry at all, for I have such a temper."

"Oh, bother the temper! I am willing to risk it. Laying all jokes aside, I love you devotedly, and won't you promise to be my wife?"

"If I lose my temper and break your head with the broom handle, you won't beat me?"

"No."

"If I break up the furniture, while in a passion, you'll go and buy more?"

"Yes."

"Very well, I'll take your case under advisement, and give you an answer when we get back home, provided you don't conclude to withdraw the proposition before it is too late."

"See here, Scottie, this is a matter of too much importance to me to be made the subject of a joke; I don't believe you mean to wound my feelings, yet I had rather you would not use so much levity about it. I loved you at first sight, and meant to ask you then to marry me, but your father seemed to dislike me so that I was afraid."

"In the first place, Mr. Burk——"

"Pshaw! Scottie, don't call me Mr. Burk, but call me Ralleigh."

"If it pleases you, then be it so. Well, Ralleigh Burk, in the first place, I am not joking; and in the second place, you were very much mistaken when you concluded that my father disliked you. He had a supreme contempt for what he called stern-wheel politicians."

"Oh, yes, I see; and he set me down in his mind as a stern-wheel politician."

"I don't say that, mind you, but he looked upon you as the villagers did on the old dog Tray, who was found in bad company. You see how it is, don't you?"

"I think I do."

"Well, now, I think my father would forgive you if you could satisfy him that you had quit politics and gone into some legitimate business."

"Do you, indeed? how kind that would be of him! but suppose I had not quit politics, and that I had not gone into

any legitimate business—in fact, suppose it should appear that
I have not gone into anything except debt?"

"I think it would prevent your going into our family."

"Then I suppose he would not object to my going head
foremost into the Mississippi river?"

"Oh, by no means; I think he would rather see you do
that than to see you in the Mississippi Legislature."

"And may I ask which catastrophe would be most to your
liking?"

"The cold water treatment, by long odds."

"Thank you. I must say that I admire your candor, but
not your sentiment."

"Spoken like a man; I glory in your grit. You're on my
platform, for I have sworn never to marry a man unless I
loved him."

"Scottie, you are a little darling, and that's a fact, and I
want you to try to love me if you can; and if you can't, just
tell me so, and I'll either go to the bottom of the river or to
the Mississippi Legislature, and never bother you any more."

"Hold your head down, so I can whisper something in
your ear: I don't think you will have to drown yourself, or
go to the Legislature."

"No? oh, won't that be jolly! You have removed a mountain from my mind. Let us go dance a while, else I'll do
something foolish."

"You talk as if you hadn't been doing that all the evening;
but you will excuse me, for I don't wish to dance. I like to
gaze out on the bright water and see the moonbeams dancing on it. I like to feel the soft, balmy air as it kisses my
cheeks. I like to feel the gentle motion of the boat, and
watch the white waves of steam as they go rolling up from
the pipes. It is so sweet to sit here and listen to the soft
notes of the music as it comes stealing up from the saloon
and mingling with the dull sound of the puffing pipes. I love
to listen to the regular clatter of the wheels—they make such
pleasant music as they strike the water. The fact is, I am
very happy, and could sit here and dream all night, without
going to sleep. Oh, these wide-awake day dreams; how delightful they are! I am in one of those dreamy moods now,
and wouldn't exchange that feeling for anything on earth!"

"All right, Scottie; I think I'll join you in a dream or two but I am so happy I cannot be still."

"But you must be still if you remain here. I have made up my mind to have a dream, and don't mean to be disturbed. There, now, take a seat and let us watch the moon till she passes that cloud yonder."

"Scottie, let the moon alone; it is a fickle planet, anyway, and I am afraid you will learn its bad habits. If you will do me the honor to take my arm, we will have a stroll. We can quarrel as well while walking as we can while sitting here."

"I suppose I will have to do it, as there is no getting rid of you. But I want you to tell me if you have made any new discoveries in regard to the black domino?"

"Nothing of any consequence; only it is certain that she is watching Ingomar in such a way as to convince me that she is shadowing him for some purpose. My spy has been very vigilant, but has encountered many difficulties. The black domino seems to be suspicious of every one who approaches her, and positively refuses to be interviewed. When she retires to her state-room she always locks the door, and don't even let the chamber-maid enter while she is there. This fact alone is enough to convince me that she has a secret. The chamber-maid tells me that she heard the black domino whispering to the old gentleman with the long beard this morning. She was not close enough to hear all that was said, but she heard the woman say that she was determined to end this intolerable suspense very soon. There appeared to be a difference of opinion between the old man and the black domino, and the chamber-maid said she thought that they were quarreling—however, as to that she was not very positive. What do you think it all means, Scottie?"

"Why do you ask me such a question, when you know I am dying of that terrible disease so prevalent among our sex, known as curiosity. What wouldn't I give to know who and what she is? It seems to me that if the chamber-maid were to try she might find out something."

"It does look so, but nevertheless she has not done it—that is to say, she has done comparatively nothing; but we have not abandoned the field yet, by a great deal."

"Anything further from the Mississippi detectives yet?"

"No—only a confirmation of what we have heard heretofore. It is certain that Ingomar is to be arrested as soon as the boat arrives at Vicksburg. I regret to tell you that we shall have to part with him then."

"I hope he will have time to finish his story before he is arrested. The truth of the matter is, I think it is our duty to tell him all we have heard anyway."

"No, no; that would not only be aiding a criminal to escape, but it would be to some extent criminal on our part. No; let us have nothing whatever to do with it. But, Scottie, haven't you told the queen already what you know about Ingomar?"

"No, not a word. I'll have you to know I am no talebearer. Didn't I promise you I would keep the secret? Of course I did; and then how dare you ask me such a question?"

"I beg pardon; I ought to be pitched overboard; don't you think I ought?"

"Certainly I do, and should go about having it done, but it would make all the fish quite ill."

"Perhaps it would; but I have no idea of being pitched into the river. I know I shall have pleasant dreams to-night, while the dear image of some one will float before my mind."

Ivanhoe then bade Scottie good-night and retired to his state-room, while his heart swelled with joy. He had at last found a haven of rest for his heart, which for two years had been worrying itself about the beautiful girl from Pearl river.

CHAPTER XVIII.

IMMEDIATELY after breakfast next morning, Queen Mary and her party re-assembled at the usual place, where Ingomar was ordered to resume his narrative. All of the maskers were in their places, eager to hear the balance of the story; and Ingomar, without loss of time, began as follows:

"As soon as Dabbs and Tadpoddle left the office Harry began to pace the floor rapidly, with his head hanging on his breast, while I could see from the working of the muscles of his face that he was making a desperate effort to get his feelings under control. After walking the floor for some time in silence he abruptly confronted me, and fixed his eyes on me as if to read my thoughts, then said:

" 'She is guilty, and my career is nearly ended. I cannot survive it, and to tell you the truth, I do not wish to, for I never shall have confidence in any woman again. I shall even lose confidence in Lottie.'

" 'Stop, Harry, I pray you; don't talk so; you will be sorry for this one of these days. Let us not abandon all hopes yet. It is possible that this is a mistake, after all.'

" 'No, no; I understand your motive, and appreciate it, but it is useless to dodge the question; Viola is lost—lost forever! Oh, God! have mercy on this poor girl. But for the sin of the thing, I would kill myself now, and be rid of this intolerable suffering. There is a burning fire in my bosom, and I can feel its consuming flames devouring my vitals. Oh, how I did love that girl! how I worshiped her! So beautiful. So enchanting! How could one so lovely be so wicked? My doom is sealed—the blow to me is fatal. I feel it here. Let it come—the sooner the better. Bowles must die, though. It is a mystery to me why such men should be tolerated in a city like this, where they can rob and murder men, and ruin innocent girls with impunity. If a poor wretch whose wife and children are starving steals a side of bacon to keep the dear ones alive, he is hurried off to the penitentiary in double-quick time; but the well-dressed thief who steals his thousands, corrupts youth, ruins young girls, and dines his friends, is permitted to walk the streets as the lion of the day. It is not only so in Memphis, but I am told it is so in many other cities. How such unscrupulous wretches should be permitted to ply their avocations of robbery among people who make pretensions to civilization is a puzzle to me. But I mean to have a settlement with Mr. Bowles. He is the same fellow who, many years ago, insulted Lottie at our camp, then committed perjury when I was on trial. I have that little affair scored against him; but that is nothing compared with the late business.'

" 'Harry, I would advise you not to let Viola know that you think she is guilty, because if you do she certainly will discard you forever. I am sure she never would forgive you

the second time. You have not forgotten what trouble you
had to get her to pardon your first error; and you had better
be very cautious how you act now. She is as proud and
sensitive as you are, and if you offend her again she never will
forgive you.'

" 'I will, under no circumstances, attempt to conceal my
opinions; if she asks me for the truth, you may be assured
she will hear it. I adhere to the doctrine that honesty is the
best policy. I never have told a deliberate falsehood, and
never will.'

" 'Would it not be best, then, for you not to see her until
we know more about the case? for she will be certain to find
out what you think, and then, my word for it, she will discard
you.'

" 'Do you think I would care if she did? You don't
imagine that I expect to marry her, do you?'

" 'But suppose you go and tell her you think she is guilty,
and then afterward, when it is too late, you find out that she
is innocent—don't you see what an awkward predicament you
then would be in?'

" 'Eddie, please don't try to deceive me. You know she
is guilty. Is not the proof overwhelming? Didn't I cling to
the idea of her innocence until the last prop was knocked
away? But I am determined to see her and demand an explanation. It is but fair to give her a chance. She shall
know what we have heard, and she then must tell what she
knows about it.'

" 'Harry, you will live to regret this step, and I want you
to understand that you take it contrary to my advice and
wishes. If you would let the whole matter rest in the hands
of the detectives until the evidence shall be brought out I
think it would be better.'

" 'Let the responsibility rest on me. I must and will see
Viola once more, and then leave her in the hands of Him
who knows the secrets of all hearts. I will go and see her
now; meantime you go and talk to Mr. Rockland, and don't
think about me at all. I must now steer my own canoe. My
mind is made up, and no power on earth can change it.'

"He then abruptly left the office and went toward the jail.
I trembled to see the strange wild look in his eyes as he

passed out. Mischief was brewing, and I could see it as plain as daylight—but how to prevent it I knew not. I remained in my seat for some time, undecided as to the best course to be pursued. I knew that I must act promptly, but what or how to do I could not decide. After Harry had been gone about thirty minutes, it occurred to me that I ought to go and talk to Lottie and let her know the bad news we had heard, and persuade her to keep Harry and Viola apart until something more definite could be ascertained. I knew that if Harry should see Viola while his mind was in its present condition, something serious would be sure to transpire. I hastened to the jail, but was too late to prevent the meeting. Lottie met me at the entrance, and I saw from her looks that she had suspected something.

" 'Oh, Eddie,' she said, as she held out both hands for me to shake, 'what on earth is the matter with Harry? He came here just now, looking for all the world just like a ghost. He was as pale as death, and I thought he was going to fall down and die at my feet. He staggered from one side of the hall to the other like a drunken man, told me he wished to be alone with Viola, and requested me to stay out of the room until he called me. His eyes showed a wild, unsettled expression, such as I have seen mad men have. What does it mean?'

" 'Lottie, something awful has happened; but I can't stop to tell you now. We must look after Harry—get him away from here as soon as possible. Go in; you must persuade him to go home with you.'

" 'Good Heavens! did you hear that groan? That was Viola—come, quick!'

"I followed her into the room, and at a glance perceived that we had come too late—the mischief had been done. That Harry was absolutely crazy for the time being was as plain as could be. Viola was leaning against the bed-post, pale and trembling, while Harry was passing across the room like an angry tiger in its cage. Lottie was by Viola's side in an instant.

" 'What is it?' she inquired, as she took hold of her arm. 'Tell me what has happened, I beseech you!'

" 'Your gallant brother there I think could tell you better

than I could,' replied Viola, as she drew herself up to her full height. She looked like a queen who had received an insult from one of her subjects. Such a look of scorn as she cast upon Harry as she spoke I never had seen flash from a woman's eyes before. Her cheeks were red with anger, and her frame seemed to grow taller. 'Yes, Lottie, your gallant brother can enlighten you as to what has happened.' Then addressing herself to Harry, she said: 'Why, Mr. Wallingford, didn't you tell your sister how you sat quietly in your chair and heard those two penitentiary birds say that I was the mistress of a blackleg gambler, and didn't kill them? You saved my life when I was a child, and I thought you were a brave hero. Every story I read where a hero was described I coupled your name with, and my childish mind pictured you as greater and braver than all of them. I loved you for your courage; I thought of you by day—I dreamed about you at night. My love grew as I grew, until my poor heart was full to overflowing. The followers in Mohammed never had stronger faith in him than I had in you. Your image floated before my young mind as my beau ideal of all that was brave, noble, generous and kind. I studied by day and by night, in order to make myself worthy of such a hero. My love grew into worship, and if every man, woman and child on earth had told me you were not a brave, generous hero, I would not have believed it. I wore your image next to my heart, and no heathen ever worshiped his idol with half the devotion that I worshiped you. My love was my life—it was my happiness—it was my religion—it was my all! You told me you loved me—you took me to your heart and whispered sweet words of love into my ear—you almost killed me with joy. Then you cast me off and declared that you were joking, and that you never could think of marrying me. I was crazed with grief; and as soon as I got so I could bear the awful affliction, you came and renewed the protestations of love. You offered excuses for your former conduct. I believed you. You swore in the most solemn language that you always had loved me. I credited it, and you asked me to be your wife. I yielded because I loved—nay, the word love is too weak a term to be used—I worshiped you—I adored you. I thought my love was returned—I thought you were perfection itself. In view of all these things, how could you sit and hear my name blackened by a pair of penitentiary convicts, and not kill them? You heard them say I was the mistress of a common blackleg gambler, and did not resent it. Is this the brave hero whose picture I have worn on my heart for ten long years? How could I have been so blinded as to worship such an object? And then, to cap the climax, you come here and ask me to explain why I was in the habit of visiting the apartments of Mr. Bowles continually. Leave me and my affairs in the hands of God—to Him I will render an account of my conduct in this business, but to you never! I have no fears as to my fate. Death to me now would be welcome—why should I wish to live where no one will befriend me? Let them hang me high as Haman—let my name be bandied about the streets as the vilest of the vile. Why should I care, since the only one I loved or cared for thinks me guilty? Let them hang me first and then throw my body in a felon's grave. God, who knows the secrets of all hearts, will take care of my soul. You may go now, Mr. Wallingford; I have no more to say, only to demand that you desist from any further interference in my affairs. Make out an account of all expenses you have incurred and present them to my guardian, and I will see that they are paid. You may go, now, as I wish to be left alone.'

"If Harry heard what she had been saying, he paid but little attention to it; but when she ceased, instead of leaving the room as she had ordered him to do, he stood like a statue, gazing vacantly before him.

" 'Mr. Wallingford, again I tell you I wish to be left alone.' As she spoke she pointed toward the door, and her manner was such as to convince me that it would be better for Harry to leave. Acting upon that conclusion, I led him from the room, and went with him to his office. He spoke not, nor did he make any objections to being taken away—in fact, I didn't think he exactly comprehended what had been said, though he afterward spoke of it as if it were a painful dream. I had often seen him under the influence of excitement, but I had never beheld him in such a state as he was then, and I was afraid to leave him alone, for I imagined that he would seek Bowles immediately. Mr. Rockland came into the office soon after we arrived, and I sought a private interview with him, and in as few words as possible informed him what had happened, and requested him to try to get Harry home as soon as he could. Mr. Rockland was deeply moved when he began to realize the situation. He loved Harry devotedly, and was as much alarmed at his condition as I was; he at once requested him to accompany him home. Harry followed Mr. Rockland without objection, and I went back to the jail at once to see Lottie. I wanted to have a talk with her about the new turn matters were taking, for I had more confidence in her cool judgment than all the rest. She was the only one of us who could look at both sides of a case with an impartial eye. The fact is, she had more sound, practical judgment than Harry and I put together. Nothing could throw her temper off its guard, and I knew that I must look to her for help, because Harry was no longer to be depended on. As soon as I entered the gate in front of the jail, Lottie came out of Viola's room and beckoned me to her side.

" 'Don't go in there—I wish to have a private chat with you. Viola is asleep now; I had to send for Doctor Dodson soon after you and Harry left. The doctor was obliged to give her an opiate before he could get her to sleep. He fears there is danger of brain fever, but thinks it may be avoided by proper treatment. Why did you let Harry come here to-day when you knew what a condition his mind was in?'

" 'I did my very best to keep him away, but he wouldn't listen to me. I think he is mad. I told him above all things not to tell Viola what he had heard.'

" 'But what is it you have heard? You must remember that I am totally ignorant as to the cause of all this trouble.'

"I then gave her a full statement of the facts as detailed to us by Dabbs and Tadpoddle. I saw a strange light flash from her beautiful eyes, and her cheeks flushed instantly with a rush of red blood to them. Her pretty little mouth was at once drawn down at both corners.

" 'And you and brother Harry swallowed this magnificent story as a child of five years would the hobgoblin story told by its nurse—that is, you believed it, of course.'

" 'Lottie, how could we help believing it, when the proof

was so plain? What was Viola doing with Bowles' letter in
her dress pocket? What was she visiting his apartments at
the dark hours of night for? Were they not planning schemes
of murder? Does not the letter prove this beyond all question? What is the use of clinging to an idea that has no
foundation to rest on? If I owned all the money in the
world I would give it to know Viola was not guilty.'

" 'Eddie, I love you too much—I wish I didn't, for I had
made up my mind to give you a real good scolding; but how
can I have the heart to abuse my old booby when I love him
so? But let me tell you one thing now, and be very sure
you don't forget it—if ever you hint or insinuate in my presence again that you think Viola Bramlett is anything but a
pure, honest, virtuous, persecuted orphan girl, I'll make such
a rattling storm in your ears as you never have heard in all
the days of your life.'

" 'If I were to see her murder a brigade, I'd never say so
before you.'

" 'Very good; you had better try to remember that, for I
tell you, Mr. Booby, I know her to be innocent; and that is
not all, by a long jump—I know exactly who is guilty. You
and Harry imagine yourselves to be exceedingly clever. You
bring penitentiary birds from Philadelphia, and pay them
large rewards to blacken the name of a pure, honest girl. I
declare, you ought to congratulate yourselves on the success
of your enterprise!'

" 'Lottie, for Heaven's sake, if you know who committed
that cruel murder, why do you let Viola remain in jail? Why
don't you expose the guilty one, and let the innocent one go
free?'

" 'I shall do that at the proper time. I have got a net set,
and the guilty one is partially entangled in it now; but the
time has not yet come to make the final drag. You and
Harry have been on the wrong trail all the time, and so have
your clever detectives.'

" 'Why don't you tell Harry and me all about the case, so
we can help you?'

" 'I mean to make you help me without telling you anything, because I think it is best to keep my secrets from you;
and as to brother Harry, he never had the starch taken out

of him until to-day. His ungovernable pride has caused all
this trouble, but I think he will not ride such a tall horse any
more. He is a dear, noble-hearted brother, but he never has
put the curb on his temper—in fact, he never has tried to
control his passions; and you know as well as I do that no
one can be happy who can't manage his passions.'

" 'Lottie, where did you manage to pick up such a store
of good sense; it sounds like inspiration. I know it can't be
my love for you that makes me think like that—it is simply
because it is so.'

" 'Not at all; I am nothing but a simple girl, but I have
always tried to command my mind, and through it control
my bad passions, and, to some extent, have succeeded; that's
all there is of it.'

" 'Will you tell me whether Bowles committed the murder
or not?'

" 'He did not, though he is as guilty as the one who did,
and I will have the proof on him when the trial comes off. I
want the grand jury to find a bill against Viola, because her
name has been stained with the charge, and these slanderous
reports have been whispered about the streets against her;
and she shall be vindicated in open court, and I assure you
her fair name will shine so brightly that no spot will be left
on it. The more I know of her the better I love her, and I
know her to be as pure as the falling snow. She concurs in
my views as regards a public trial, and will not shrink
when the time comes. She is a greater heroine than any one
would suppose who is not acquainted with her private character.'

" 'Who is assisting you to look up the evidence in the
case?'

" 'That's one of my secrets which I don't mean to tell you
just now; but it is one who can beat your Philadelphia
detective very badly.'

" 'Why not tell Harry that you know Viola to be innocent?
Don't you know the idea that she is guilty is killing him?
I am afraid that he will seek a quarrel with Bowles; and
either kill him or get killed himself.'

" 'I did tell him that I knew she was not guilty; and I
told you the same thing, yet both of you were ready to credit

the first thing you heard against her. I would have revealed
everything to him, but I could not depend on his judgment
when he is so flustered. I was afraid he would act too hastily,
and thereby overthrow the plans we had set on foot to entrap
the guilty parties. I yet fear that he will commit some rash
act which will frighten the real murderers, and prevent us
from securing the proof necessary to convict. Our uncle has
written him to come to California, and I think we had better
get him to go at once. Uncle Stanley's health has failed, and
he wants Harry to go there to help him wind up his business,
so he can come here to live. He urges Harry to come without
delay, and the best thing we can do is to persuade him to go
at once. He could get back in six months, and by that time
Viola's innocence will be established, and then we will all be
happy once more. You had better see Mr. Rockland on the
subject, and ask him to aid you in persuading Harry to go at
once. In the first place, it is his duty to go and help our
uncle while he is unable to look after his own business; and
in the next place, it will furnish brother something to employ
his mind and keep it from the subject that is destroying his
happiness. If he stays here he will be sure to do something
rash; therefore you must not lose a moment until you get him
started.'

" 'Do you think Viola ever will forgive Harry?'

" 'What a dear old Booby you are! Did you ever hear of
a woman's forsaking a man, when she once loved him truly?
It shows how little you know about a woman's heart. I
suppose men judge women by their own hearts; but let me
tell you that the heart of a woman is no more like that of a
man than day is like night. Man's heart is as fickle and
unreliable as the moon, and will change as often; but once
let a woman give her heart away to a man, and he has it
always. He may drag her down to the lowest precincts of
misery and degradation, and she will cling to and love him
still. He may beat her—he may starve her—he may disgrace
her; but she will never cease to love him. She will go with
him to a loathsome dungeon—she will follow him to the
gallows; and when his neck is broken by the law, for crimes
committed, she will weep over his dead body, and bury her

broken heart in a felon's grave with the unworthy man she loves. How is it with a man? Let the slightest breath of suspicion blow upon the woman he loves, and he forsakes her at once.'

" 'Lottie, do you think that anything ever could happen. that would make me forsake you?'

" 'Yes; a hundred things could happen that would make you hate me, though I think you are the best sample of the lot; and if you should beat and starve me, I should be fool enough to go on loving you just the same.'

" 'Lottie, darling, if ever I do anything intentionally to cause you pain, I shall expect Satan to get my unworthy soul and roast it in his hottest blazes. But candidly tell me, Lottie dear, do you really think Viola ever will become reconciled with Harry? You know she is as proud as he is, and I never saw her in such a rage as she was to-day.'

" 'That's all you know about it. Why, sir, in five minutes after Harry left her she broke completely down—fell on the bed and wept like a child; if he had come back then, he might have taken her in his arms with impunity. She would have nestled her head on his bosom and begged him to forgive her, instead of expecting him to beg her pardon. The truth of it is she is crazy about him, and would die if he were to abandon her. She is too good for this wicked world, anyway.'

" 'I must say that they are both very different from other people; they puzzle and perplex me. Sometimes they are as gentle and submissive as young lambs; then again they remind me of a tornado, sweeping everything to destruction as it goes. Sometimes they resemble the smooth, calm bosom of a lake; then they appear again like the boisterous billows of the ocean when lashed into fury by the storm.'

" 'True enough, Eddie, but it is because they love each other so much. If they did not love so strongly they would be less boisterous.'

" 'Why is it that you and I are getting along so smoothly and nicely?'

" 'That is owing to the fact that no trouble has come across our path. But suppose I were in jail, charged with murder, and you were to tell me to my face that you thought me guilty—don't you think you would start a pretty extensive whirlwind?'

" 'If I were to do such a cowardly thing it ought to be a first-class tornado—one that would blow my worthless carcass out of the world.'

" 'Don't make so many rash remarks; you know it is generally understood that the course of true love never runs smooth. We may have stormy weather yet before the voyage is ended; happiness like ours is too great to last, I'm afraid. But enough of this now—you must go to Harry and remain with him until you get him off to California; then come back to me—I wish to send you on a short journey on business of vast moment.'

" 'Tell me where it is you wish me to go, and what you want me to go for, so that I can have something to think about. It is so pleasant to be thinking of some way to serve you.'

" 'As soon as we can get Harry started, I shall send you to Vicksburg, Mississippi, on business connected with Viola's case. You see, as I have already informed you, I am playing lawyer and detective both. There is certain evidence at Vicksburg that is essential in this affair, and you must go there to secure it. I think I may safely trust you thus far.'

" 'You may trust me implicitly in everything, Lottie, darling, and I'll prove worthy of the trust. But have you any objections to telling me now the nature of the evidence you expect me to secure?'

" 'There is a certain woman in this city who formerly resided at or near Vicksburg, whose antecedents I wish to know something about.'

" 'Then you think it was a woman who poisoned young Bramlett?'

" 'What are you talking about? I said nothing of the sort. You must obey orders and not be so inquisitive—a good soldier, you know, always obeys orders without inquiring the reason of their issuance.'

" 'Very good! You issue orders and leave the rest to me, and I'll bring up my part of the job all right. But what is the name of the person whose history you want?'

"'She has so many names that you will find the greatest difficulty arises from that fact, though you must find out her real name, at all hazards. In order to do this, you must discover who are her parents; and it may be necessary to go to other places besides Vicksburg before you accomplish that. She came from Vicksburg to Memphis—how long she had been residing there I do'not know, but suppose you are detective enough to find out who she is and where she was born and raised. But you must mind and not let any one know your business, because everything must be worked secretly. This woman claims to be a native of Mississippi, and was known by the name of Helen Herndon when she came to this city—that is, she was traveling under that name while coming here, but she dropped it and took another when she arrived here. Now, you will probably find that Helen Herndon is not her real name, but it is very likely that she has resided in Vicksburg under that name. This will aid you to determine who she really is. The main point to be gained is to find her parents and get the full history of her childhood. I suppose her age now is not over thirty, and she has been here five years. She must have covered up her tracks well, else you will be table to trace her back to her parents. You must not let any one know where you are going, nor what your business is. You must find out where she was educated (and, by the by, she has been well educated), and learn everything you can about her school-girl history. I must have some of her manuscript, and this, of course, you can get, if you can find her parents. You must put on your studying-cap, and try to be wise.'

"'I'll try, of course, but do you think I can succeed?'

"'Doubtful.'

"'Ha, ha, dearest, you have the right to make sport of me as much as you please, and I rather think I like it.'

"I built several magnificent castles as I passed along the street from the jail to Mr. Rockland's house. I can't say that I absolutely completed any one of those splendid buildings, because my mind would become confused when I was about to put on the cornice, or the dome, or hoist the columns, and I would find that something was lacking to make the exact finish. A crack in the wall would appear, or a defect in the foundation, a column would tipple down, the dome would lean over to one side, turrets were too flat, the windows too short— something was sure to happen to prevent me from making an absolute finish of my great work. When I went to Mr. Rockland, I found him in his library, busy, as usual, with great heaps of papers before him, which he was examining, one by one. I made known to him the object of my visit, told him Lottie's views, and requested his advice and assistance to get Harry off to California as soon as possible.

" 'That is another proof of Lottie's good sense, Mr. Demar. The fact is, sir, that girl is a mystery, anyway. I can't understand where she managed to gather up so much good, sound, practical common sense. It is true she reads a great deal, and has always been very industrious; but, sir, I believe she is the most talented woman I ever knew. Why, sir, would you believe it, she has made out many a brief for me, hunted up the law applicable to the case, and arranged everything as well as I could do it myself! For instance, look at that brief there, will you? She did that, and she did it as quickly as any lawyer could have done it. She copies all my papers, keeps my books and clerks for me generally. Demar, I don't like to let you have her, at all, and if I thought you would take her away from me, I should be tempted to break off the match.''

" 'It pleases me beyond measure to hear you praise Lottie so, for she deserves it; but I shall never part her from you, if you prefer that we should stay here. I know that she could not be happy if she thought you were miserable.'

" 'I am very much obliged to you, Demar, for making that promise, because I don't see how we could bear to part with our darling. I know I shall miss her valuable services as my amanuensis.'

" 'It is not my intention, Mr. Rockland, to deprive you of her services, so long as it may be agreeable to her to aid you. My aim will be to make her happy, and I dare say she would prefer to continue to help you. I think that this is the place where she managed to gather so much useful knowledge of the law, as well as a great store of general information. She has been with you so much, and heard you expound the law

to others so often, that she has got her mind well stored with
its mysteries.'

" 'Probably that is true to some extent, but she possesses
an extraordinary mind. Mr. Demar, you have been quite
lucky to win the heart of such a woman, indeed you have, sir.
You have achieved a great victory. She is a valuable prize,
I assure you.'

" 'I am sensible of the fact, sir, and shall endeavor to make
her life a happy one. I feel thankful to Providence for
bestowing such a blessing on me, humble and unworthy as I
am; but if a life of devotion to her can make her happy, she
shall certainly be so.'

" 'Enough of this, Mr. Demar; I could talk about Lottie
all day, but we must not neglect other business. You were
about to mention some newly discovered evidence that had
been brought to light in Miss Bramlett's case. I shall be glad
to hear anything in her favor.'

" 'I am very sorry to be compelled to say that this newly
found evidence is anything but favorable to her—to the
contrary, if it is true, it establishes her guilt beyond doubt.'

" 'Poor girl, I am distressed to hear it! but let me know all
at once.'

"I then proceeded to tell him everything that had been
related to Harry and me by Dabbs and Tadpoddle.

" 'That proof will convict her beyond question, unless it
can be overthrown by other proof, and it would have to be
unquestionable evidence to do that. We shall be driven to the
plea of insanity—this is the *dernier ressort,* and is rather a
shaky foundation to build hopes upon. It is most unfortunate
that Harry should have fallen in love with Miss Bramlett;
poor fellow, it is a heavy blow to him, and I agree with you
as to the propriety of getting him off to California as soon as
possible. It is truly his duty to go to his uncle without delay,
and I shall mention the subject to him as soon as his mind
gets composed. He is in an unsettled condition just now.'

" 'Do you think he will go, Mr. Rockland?'

" 'Oh, yes, he will do anything I request him to. He has
been a kind, obedient son to me, and my wishes have always
been law with him. Ah, me! I love the dear boy, and it is

causing me great pain to see him suffering so. He seems to
be perfectly reckless since Miss Bramlett's troubles began—
neglects his duties, stares wildly at space for hours at a time
in silence, eats scarcely anything and is as pale as a ghost.
His mother is in despair about it, and a general gloom per-
vades the premises. Something must be done, and that
without delay. He shall start to California next Monday.
That will rouse him and take his mind off of this painful
subject.'

"Having finished my business with Mr. Rockland, I went
back to the jail to report progress to Lottie.

CHAPTER XIX.

"MONDAY had come and gone, and Harry was on his way to
California. Viola was quite ill, Lottie in distress, and my
mind by no means free of trouble.

"'Here we come, Eddie, my boy,' said Doctor Dodson, as
he came bustling into the drug-store one morning soon after
breakfast. 'Ah, ha! my boy, things are all wrong, all wrong,
sir. That's always the case; one thing goes wrong, everything must follow suit, you know—ah, ha! don't you see how
it is, my boy? Miss Bramlett, poor thing, very ill—threatened with brain fever.—killing herself with grief about Wallingford—Lottie wearing herself out with continual watching—breaking her heart about other people's troubles—don't
sleep enough—eats not enough to support life in a snow-bird.
Ah, ha! my boy, don't you see how it is? Then, to cap the
climax of errors, here's Dabbs and Tadpoddle nosing round
and stirring up slander, and those two hateful old maids
are retailing it out where they think it will do the most
harm. Ah, ha! my boy, do you know those two detestable
old hags? No, of course you don't; I allude to Miss Jemima
Tadpoddle and Jerusha Clattermouth. Ah, ha! Eddie, my
boy, old Nick ought to have them both. Clatter, clatter go
their tongues all day, slandering everybody and everything.
They both have been to the jail, pretending to feel an interest in Miss Bramlett, and they have well-nigh killed the

poor girl with their infernal tongues. Ah, ha! Eddie, my
boy, don't you see how it is? I wish their tongues were cut
out and nailed on the jail door, as a warning to meddlesome
gossips—that's what I wish. Ah, ha! Eddie, my boy, Miss
Tadpoddle is ill. Thank Heaven! I hope the town will
have a little breathing spell while she is sick. The hateful
hag has sent for me to visit her professionally. Ah, ha!
my boy, I mean to send you in my place. She is the very
sort for a young quack to practice on. No harm done if he
kills her, don't you see? Get yourself ready to go, my boy—
give her something to silence her tongue, if you can. You'll
find a charming patient, my boy. Clattermouth is sure to be
there—they are always together—birds of a feather—you
know how it is yourself. Ah, ha! Eddie, my boy, be off now
—stuff her full of medicine—pour in the calomel till you
salivate her—that's as nigh salvation as she will ever get. Go,
my boy; cram her with emetics, then shovel in your purga-
tives. Don't kill her, but prostrate her—stop her devilish
tongue. Ah, ha! my boy, don't you see? Go, go!'

"Of course I went, and when I entered Mr. Tadpoddle's
house I was immediately ushered into Miss Jemima's room.
I stood in the door a moment, while my eyes were busy taking
a survey of the room and its contents. Miss Jemima Tadpoddle was propped up in bed with a dozen pillows, while
Miss Jerusha Clattermouth was bathing her temples with eau-
de-Cologne, and the sick woman's mother was holding a
smelling bottle to her nose. It is my deliberate opinion that
if Shakespeare had seen those three women before he wrote
'Macbeth,' he would have made a better job of it, especially
in the witch department.

"A feeling of disgust crept through me as I approached the
bed where she was, and it cost me an effort to conceal my
feelings. Her neck was not quite so long as that of a sand-
hill crane, but I can honestly say it was the longest neck I
ever saw under a woman's head, and it appeared to be entirely constructed of little round cords. Her skin was as
white as snow, and if she had any veins in her body, they
were not visible to the naked eye.

"Miss Clattermouth was by no means like Miss Tadpoddle
—in fact, I never saw two people less alike than they were.

Miss Clattermouth was a little, dark-skinned woman, with a pug nose, a very small mouth, no teeth, either natural or artificial, and the thin lips appeared to be at a loss to know what to do with themselves. The mouth was entirely too small for the lips, hence they were forced to double themselves up, or rather to roll into little folds, so as to have more room.

"As soon as I was able to get in a word, I inquired of Miss Tadpoddle the nature of her complaint.

"'Oh, doctor! I am so glad you came to see me. I declare, I thought I should die before you got here. You don't know how delighted I am to see you. I never exaggerate. I despise exaggeration—it is my character to despise it. I never flatter—it is my character to hate flattery. You may rely on anything I say, doctor, for I never use extravagant language—it is my character not to use it. I feel so much better since you came—your cheerful smile has almost cured me. I'm sure I soon shall get well. The pleasure it gives me to look at your happy face is much better than medicine. Sit down near me, where I can see you plainly. Feel my pulse. It is much more regular than when you came. I have heard so much about you, Doctor Demar. They told me you were handsome, though they didn't do you justice; but I never flatter—it is my character not to flatter—yet I never saw such expressive eyes as yours. My brother told me about them. But never mind me; you know a woman must talk. Oh! you look so strong and healthy; how I envy you! You are so tall and handsome! Pardon my enthusiasm, I beg you, but I mean what I say. You wish to know what is the matter with me? Yes, of course you do. Well, I mean to tell you. Oh! I have suffered ten thousand deaths since yesterday. Such torture no poor mortal ever suffered before. How I survived it is a mystery—but I must try to describe my sufferings. I never expected to see another day. I had a horrible pain in the back of my head; both temples ached and throbbed all day and all night. My back felt as if it was broken in the middle—my teeth were all aching at once; a kind of smothering about my heart, with darting pains continually going like a knife through my breast. My stomach seemed to be on fire, while my extremities were freezing. My throat was perfectly raw, and the skin has all peeled off my tongue. Every bone in my body seemed mashed into powder. My eyeballs felt as if they were going to jump out of my head. I had the ear-ache in both ears; a most horrid retching about the stomach. I had neuralgia in my left jaw, and a burning sensation in my nostrils, and to tell you the truth, I was quite unlike myself. Do, pray, give me something to relieve me. I'll die, I know I will, if you don't hurry.'

"That interesting female then fell back on the mountain of pillows, closed her eyes and heaved a deep sigh, like one who was about to bid the world a final farewell. I want it to be distinctly understood that I did not intend to commit murder, but I had the necessary malice in me. Miss Tadpoddle had maligned Miss Bramlett, and she had slandered everybody else in Memphis. She had offended Lottie by her malicious reports concerning Viola. I was angry because Lottie was displeased, and here is the soliloquy that I had with myself on that occasion, as nigh as I can remember it:

" 'Very well, my charming Miss Tadpoddle; I have got you in my power now, and I guess I'll get even with you before I quit you. You want medicine, do you? Very good—you shall have it with a vengeance; I'll keep your tongue' silent for a week or two, if there is any virtue in blisters. I'll physic you until you are satisfied!'

"This was the first patient I ever had, and I meant to test the qualities of my drugs. I had brought my case of medicines with me, and was prepared, not only to prescribe, but to administer the drugs. I covered her up with blisters; I gave her an emetic; I put red-hot bricks to her feet; I cupped her temples—the fact is, I made a prescription for each separate pain of which she complained; and with the aid of Miss Clattermouth, I managed to have it all administered. Then I sat down and waited for the result.

" 'Old lady,' I observed to myself mentally, 'I guess you'll remain quiet for a few days, now. You won't trouble Miss Bramlett soon, at all events. Your tongue won't wag quite so glibly as it has been in the habit of doing. You'll wake up directly, if I am not mistaken.'

"Well, sure enough, she did wake up, and it was no half-

way business, either—it was what you call a wide-awake sensation. The mustard began to heat her up, the emetic commenced business, the hot bricks got up steam—in fact, the
skirmish commenced all along the line; but when the pill
brigade made the charge, the engagement became general—
the contest was hot and loud, and the drugs won the victory,
and Miss Tadpoddle was saved—so completely cured that she
never has been very ill since. My reputation as a first-class
physician was then permanently established, because Miss
Tadpoddle's tongue was a better advertising medium than the
New York *Herald.* She was president of the Tramp Reform
Association; then she was a working member of many other
benevolent associations. , She made it her daily business to
speak of my vigorous style of practice. I was certainly well
prepared to treat any disease, because the experiments I had
made on Miss Tadpoddle had enabled me to test the qualities
of all the drugs known to the profession.

"It was somewhere about ten days after my treatment of
Miss Tadpoddle's case when she again sent for me. I found
her in bed—and when I say in bed, I mean it. She was not
propped up with pillows, as she was when I first visited her,
but she was flat on the bed. The truth is, I had so completely
taken the starch out of her that she couldn't sit up.

" 'How do you feel this morning, Miss Tadpoddle?' I inquired, pretending to be interested about her case.

" 'Oh, I am so weak, doctor; but for that, I would be very
well. I did not send for you with a view of taking more medicine—no, no, indeed! I don't think I ever shall need any
more as long as I live. I merely wished to speak with you
about Miss Bramlett's case. I presume that my brother has
told you of the valuable assistance I have rendered him?
Very well; I have something more to say to you on that
subject. I fear you will find that Miss Bramlett is a very
bad woman. I confess I never had much faith in her at first.
She was too proud, too cold-hearted—made too much display
with her money. She was parading the streets continually,
pretending to be assisting the poor, but evidently trying to
create a sensation. One day I met her at the Widow Spratt's
house, and would you believe it, sir, she was dressed within an
inch of her life! She had on a blue silk dress, with real lace

trimmings—and, by the by, that was the identical dress she
wore that night when I saw her go into Ben Bowles' apartments, through the private entrance that opens from the alley.
But I am going too fast.—I was telling you about meeting
Miss Bramlett at Widow Spratt's. Well, sir, she was sitting
on a low truckle-bed, feeding the baby with condensed milk.
It was the dirtiest, sickliest-looking thing I ever laid eyes on;
and the other five children were cramming themselves with
cold bread and turkey that Miss Bramlett had given them;
and they were covered with dirty rags, just like the baby.
Mrs. Spratt is the poorest manager I ever saw. Her children
are half naked and starved. I was really vexed at Miss Bramlett for throwing away her money on such worthless people.
Old Spratt was always drunk, and wouldn't work. He fell
overboard from a steam-boat and was drowned; it was a great
pity he didn't die ten years ago. His children are lazy, good-
for-nothing brats, and ought to starve. Miss Bramlett has
been supporting the whole family since old Spratt died. Mrs.
Spratt, she lies in bed the live-long day, pretending to be sick,
but it is pure laziness; and if Miss Bramlett would let her
alone, she would have to get up and work, or starve. Well,
there are many other families in this city depending on Miss
Bramlett's money for support. It's a scandal and a shame
that such laziness should be encouraged. Let 'em work, or
starve, is my motto. I asked Mrs. Spratt to subscribe something to our Tramp Reform Association, and she wouldn't
give a cent. I begged Miss Bramlett to help us, and she
turned up her nose and absolutely sneered in my face—a
hateful hussy! but I ought not to talk so, because I never
bear malice against my neighbors; it is my character not to
nurse ill-will—"Forgive those who trespass against us," is
my motto—this is what our Saviour taught us. There is
Lottie Wallingford, who thinks the world and all of Miss
Bramlett. I wonder how she will feel when she sees her
friend hung for murder? Her brother was engaged to be
married to Miss Bramlett when the murder was committed;
but they say he has run away to California and left his affianced bride here to be hung, while he goes to get his uncle's
great fortune. Of course that will make honors easy—he
loses his sweetheart, but wins a fortune. That ought to con-

sole him, at any rate. They say you are taking on about
Lottie Wallingford. Doctor, she would no doubt make you
a good wife, if she wasn't so much like old Rockland—always
talking about books and book-learning. She knows too much;
I don't like so much genius. I like business. It is my character to despise poetry. I hate these dreamy, sentimental
women who can memorize a whole book and then repeat it in
public. I hate these silly women who sing nothing but sentimental songs. They are always talking about sweet flowers,
sweet poetry, sweet birds, sweet scenery, sweet music—everything is sweet with them. I hate sweet things; it is my
character to hate sweet things. She and Miss Bramlett have
converted the jail into a picture gallery, concert hall and
book library. For my part, I don't see how the jailer puts up
with such doings. The idea that a murderess in jail, awaiting her trial, should be painting pictures, reading poetry and
playing the guitar surpasses my comprehension. She had
better be reading her Bible or prayer-book, and making preparations to meet her God, for she is certain to be hung. I
know enough myself to hang her, and I mean to tell it. I saw
her with my own eyes when she went into the apartments of
that gambler, at the dark hour of night. You see I had my
suspicions about her, anyway, and when I saw her meet
Bowles in the garden that night I concluded that some deviltry was going on, and determined to watch her. I have the
advantage you see, doctor, over other women—it is no trouble
for me to disguise myself. I am very tall, you perceive, and
my brother's clothes fit me to a T. I made it my business
to waylay Mr. Ragland's premises every night until I succeeded in accomplishing my object. One night about eight
o'clock I saw Miss Bramlett go out of the house by the back
way and walk cautiously toward the rear side of the garden.
I was concealed among the shrubbery, and saw her coming
directly toward the spot where I was. She, however, turned
to the left, passing within ten paces of me. She appeared to
be looking for some one, for she stopped near me and waited
for several minutes; then she turnd square off to the right
and entered the summer-house by the back door. I think she
stayed in the summer-house about ten minutes; at any rate,
she remained in it until I began to grow restless, and was

thinking of trying to slip around to the front door, so as to enable me to see whether or not she was alone. I noticed that she had her face covered with a veil, but I knew her by the dress and shawl she wore—the same she had on the time I met her at the Widow Spratt's. When she came out of the summer-house, she went in the direction of the carriage-house, which you know is east of the former, and about forty yards from it. She passed on without halting, until she reached the extreme back part of the garden. She paused and looked around in every direction, as if trying to ascertain whether or not any one was watching her. But she did not see me; I was too sharp to be caught that way. I am not one of those sap-heads that you have heard so much about. In fact, I hate sap-headed women—it is my character to hate 'em; and as to sap-headed men, they ought not to be permitted to live. But here I am again straggling off from the subject. I beg you to excuse me, doctor; you know I am quite weak yet—indeed I am. It is astonishing to me that I am able to utter a word. Your medicine cured my complaints, it is true, but left me completely prostrated. I don't think I ever shall need any more drugs. But I declare, I must quit wandering off that way. I wouldn't do it, I know, but I am afraid the strong medicine has, to some extent, weakened my mind. Everything seems like a dream. Do you ever dream, doctor? No? Ah, then, you don't appreciate them. Where one's dreams are pleasant, one enjoys the sensation very much; but when the stomach's out of order, one is sure to have unpleasant dreams. Oh! I had such a nice dream last night! I thought that I was—but what do you care about my dreams? I suppose you want me to finish my narrative about Miss Bramlett's movements.'

" 'Miss Tadpoddle,' said I, 'you must, by all means, take another dose of medicine; the color of your skin is not as good as it should be, and I don't like the looks of your tongue.'

"If I could have induced her to take another dose of my drugs then, she would have remembered it to her dying day.

" 'No, no, doctor, please hush talking about your hateful drugs and let me go on with my story. It makes one feel so nervous to have to wait and wait for anything which ought to be told without stopping. There is Miss Clattermouth— oh, it would do you good to hear her relate a story. She can talk all day and never make a hobble. You ought to hear her deliver one of her lectures on the rights of women. She is our champion on that question, and you must not fail to hear her lecture next time. She is the business manager of our Tramp Reform Association, and is one of our best financial agents. You ought to join our Tramp Reform Association, doctor. We have achieved wonders in that society. We have reformed as many as a dozen tramps during the last year.'

" 'In what way did you reform them, Miss Tadpoddle?' I inquired.

" 'Oh, we furnish them board and lodgings for a month, by way of trial, and give them a good suit of clothes. Miss Clattermouth lectures them twice a week, and I give them Bible lessons three times a week. If, at the end of a month, one shows evidences of repentance and reformation, we then furnish him with another suit of clothes, a Testament, five dollars in cash and a certificate of good behavior, and discharge him with our blessing.'

" 'If he doesn't furnish the necessary evidence at the end of the first month, what course do you pursue then?'

" 'We keep him another month, and if he proves incorrigible, we dismiss him without our certificate or blessing.'

" 'The punishment, I must say, Miss Tadpoddle, is indeed very severe. What is to be the fate of the poor tramp who is thus turned loose on the cold charities of the world with no certificate and without your blessing? May I inquire what percentage prove incorrigible and are driven out without the certificate and blessing?'

" 'I should say about ninety per cent. It is a source of regret to know that so many prove unworthy, yet it is a consolation to us to save as much as ten per cent. of the unfortunate class.'

" 'If I understand you correctly, any one can secure two months' board and lodging by representing himself as a tramp.'

" 'Oh, no, by no means; we always appoint a committee

to investigate each applicant and ascertain whether or not he is really a tramp. We have to be very strict in that respect, because we have detected several of our own citizens in the attempt to palm themselves off on us as tramps. You see the rules of our association don't allow us to receive any citizen of the State, but we only take in those unfortunate men who are known as tramps. But enough about that subject. I must finish telling you about Miss Bramlett. I fear I shall fatigue myself too much, anyway, being so very feeble, as you are aware. By the by, doctor, do you remember where I was when we got off of the subject?'

" 'I believe you were telling me about seeing Miss Bramlett go to the extreme back part of the garden, one starlight night, and that she had on a heavy veil.'

" 'Yes, yes, I remember now. I saw Miss Bramlett. Her movements were so mysterious that I became very much excited and curious to know what she was up to. When she got to the back part of the garden I, of course, expected to see her turn and go back to the house, but not so, as you shall hear as we proceed. It never had occurred to me that she was going to pay a clandestine visit at such an hour as that; but you may imagine how great was my astonishment when I saw her removing the palings from the fence. My brother is a most remarkable man. He is like me in one respect—he never exaggerates—that is his character. He is just like me—I hate exaggeration. Well, as I was about to observe—what was it I was going to say? Oh, yes, I remember now. I was on the eve of telling you how Miss Bramlett's mysterious conduct excited my curiosity. Curiosity is characteristic of our sex, you know, and I confess to a weakness on that score. You see I will tell the truth though the Heavens fall. I hate falsehood—it is my character to despise it. Honesty is the best policy—you remember the saying; by the by, it is an excellent motto. But I must be brief, for I begin to feel quite fatigued now—one in my feeble condition ought not to talk much, though when I am strong and well I don't mind talking; it does not tire me at all— but it is different with me now. Just listen to me now; here I am again talking nonsense, instead of letting you know what I saw with my own eyes. Miss Bramlett disappeared through the palings exactly as a ghost would have done. Don't understand me to say or hint that I am a believer in ghosts—no, I never thought of such a thing. Anyway, she went through, and for a moment I lost sight of her, but I was not to be outdone in that way. I hastened to the spot where I had seen her last; but could see nothing of her. I lost no time in leaping over the palings. I suppose you are astonished to hear me say so, but it is no exaggeration, I assure you. Very well, then; I did leap over the palings. Then I was in the street, all right. You see I am very tall, not much short of six feet, and if I do say it myself, I am very active, for a young girl. But let that pass, for I know it does not interest you. Miss Bramlett was walking rapidly down the street when I got over the palings, some fifty or sixty yards from me. I soon shortened the distance between us, being careful to avoid the faint light from the lamp on the opposite side of the street. The lamp-posts were very far apart, and the streets were deserted. The lamps appeared quite feeble, and the light did not interfere with my movements. When Miss Bramlett reached the next block she disappeared round the corner, and I was afraid she had escaped me entirely; but I hastened to the corner, and was delighted to see her within twenty paces of me. The first alley she reached she turned into and again disappeared, but I soon caught sight of her again, and kept close behind her until she came to the private entrance of Ben Bowles' gambling hell. She stood before it a moment, then went in, and the door closed behind her. Now, Doctor Demar, what do you think of such doings as that? Can't you see that she is a very wicked woman, It is no use to say that she is innocent—for I tell you she is guilty, and ought to be hung. All the lawyers in the world can't save her neck. Oh, it makes the cold chills run up my back to think of that girl's wickedness!'

"'Miss Clattermouth made me promise not to talk much, and I must keep my promise—it is my character to keep my word. I despise people who disregard the advice of friends. Miss Clattermouth has been a true friend to me—indeed, she has! I admire such friends. Did you ever see the darling poodle she gave me, Oh, he is such a sweet little fellow!

I must show him to you by all means. I think he is asleep under the sofa there. I hate to disturb him, though—because he always frets so when his naps are broken; but I guess he has got his nap nearly out by this time. Here, Tottie! here, Tottie! Come along and let the doctor see you.' The individual alluded to came crawling ⸱out from under the sofa. I suppose he would have weighed at least eight ounces avoirdupois. He was covered with wool as white as snow. 'Come along, darling; don't be bashful; let the doctor see you.'

"He started toward the bed where his mistress was, but came to a broom handle that unfortunately had been left on the floor,—he couldn't jump over it, and didn't have sense enough to go round it; but he began to scream with great vigor, and I had to help him over it. I sat him on the bed by his mistress, and I am not ashamed to say that I gave him such a squeeze that he was unable to yell any more for some time.

" 'Oh, doctor, ain't he a sweet little darling? How could I help loving Miss Clattermouth, when she gave me such a nice present? But I suppose you don't love dogs, and would prefer to hear what further I have to say about Miss Bramlett. Very well, you shall hear it. I got quite impatient while I was waiting to see her come out of Bowles' den. but I made up my mind to see the end of it, and when I make up my mind to do anything, it is as good as done. I never give up an undertaking, once I resolve to go into it—it is my character never to back down. I hate people who undertake anything and don't do it. I am one of those hanging-on sort that don't do things by halves. I cling on like a badger—I believe that is the name of the little animal that has such a reputation for hanging on with so much tenacity; anyway, I am that kind of a woman. The weather was quite cold that night, and I suffered very much from it, but I didn't mind that at all. I think I should have stood my ground if it had rained lumps of ice as big as my head.

" 'Well, as I was about to observe, I suffered from the cold weather, but I was rewarded at last, for I saw Miss Bramlett come out of the house by the same door through which she had entered; though she was not alone this time—Bowles was with her. I cannot state exactly how long she

had remained inside of the house, but if I was on my oath in
a court-house, I should say it was not a minute less than
three hours. When she came out of the house, she was leaning on Bowles' arm, and they were conversing in an under-
tone. I could not hear all that was said, because I was compelled to remain some distance from them, so as to keep them
from seeing me; but I heard enough (Heaven knows!) to
hang Miss Bramlett as high as Haman. I don't exactly remember how high it was that Haman was hung, though it
was about fifty cubits. Now that must have been a pretty
lofty gallows! A cubit is either eighteen inches or eighteen
feet—I don't remember which. I like that way of executing
criminals—hang 'em high, so everybody can see 'em. I hope
Viola Bramlett will be hung where we can all see the fun.
But I was about to tell you what she said to Bowles. She
was leaning on his arm, with her mouth close to his ear.
You know Bowles, of course. Yes, I am glad you do—he is
such a nice gentleman, so handsome, dresses so exquisite—
then he is so liberal with his money! He aids us in all our
benevolent enterprises. Oh, he is such a darling, clever gentleman! What a pity it is that such a handsome gentleman
should be led astray by that scheming hypocrite, Viola Bramlett! It is very clear that she had him completely under her
thumb; and I am afraid he has been duped by her beauty
and her hypocritical smiles. I heard her calling him "my
dear, darling Ben" at least half a dozen times. Just think of
that, will you? I declare, it makes me sick to think of it.
She was evidently talking to him about the murder of her
brother, for I heard her ask Bowles if he thought there was
any danger of detection. I also heard her ask him if a doctor could tell when any one had died from poison, and how
much strychnine it would take to produce death. Oh, doctor,
it made the blood freeze in my veins to hear her discussing
the murder of her brother. But, mind you, I had no idea
then that she intended to murder her own brother. I followed her and Bowles back to Mr. Ragland's residence. They
halted at the end of the garden, and talked, for a long time,
in an under-tone; at last Bowles took her in his arms and
kissed her. Then she went into the house, while he retraced
his steps to his head-quarters. I immediately returned home

and jotted down in my diary the things I had seen, just as I have related them to you. Now, how can the lawyers keep that wicked woman from hanging? I should like you to tell me if you can.'

"You may imagine what my feelings were when Miss Tadpoddle had finished her remarkable story; but I shall not try to describe them. That Viola Bramlett was lost, beyond all question, seemed to be a fixed fact, and that it would nearly kill Lottie I knew full well. I tried to argue Miss Bramlett's case to myself so as to bring her out unstained; but the proof rose, like huge Olympus, before me. Everything seemed to point unmistakably to her as the guilty party; and if she was guilty at all, it was clear that she had sunk so far down in the pit of infamy as to render it necessary for me to separate her and Lottie.

CHAPTER XX.

"TIME was gliding on unusually slow—it always does when we want it to go fast, and never fails to gallop when we want it to walk. A fortnight had stolen by since my last interview with the interesting Miss Tadpoddle. Dabbs and Tadpoddle were still working like beavers, but accomplishing nothing that anybody wanted them to do. Everything they did seemed to add new links to the strong chain of evidence against Miss Bramlett. Public sentiment, which at first had been strong in favor of her innocence, had undergone a radical change, and was now as strong against her as it had been in her favor. I hate public sentiment—I detest it, for it is a heartless tyrant, anyway, as often wrong as right, and always on extremes. Miss Tadpoddle and Miss Clattermouth were, to a great extent, responsible for the sudden change in public sentiment. Their busy tongues had never been idle for a moment.

" 'I declare,' said Miss Clattermouth, 'the meanest thing Miss Bramlett did was to attempt to involve Mr. Bowles in her scheme of murder. He is a thoughtless, jolly, good-hearted young man, unsuspicious by nature. and the very kind of a man to be deceived by such a honey-tongued hussy as Viola Bramlett.'

" 'Indeed,' observed Miss Tadpoddle, 'I agree with you there. He is one of those confiding, unsuspicious sort of men, easily played on by such an adventuress. My brother was inclined to censure him but you know the simplicity of the good soul—he does not draw the proper distinctions in such cases. He is one of the best officers in the secret service, but he owes most of his success to my judgment. I often make the rounds with him, and as to Miss Bramlett's case, I think I may say without exaggeration (for I never exaggerate) that but for my valuable aid, he never would have secured the proof necessary to convict her. And then, he was inclined to think that Mr. Bowles was as much to blame as Miss Bramlett; but I defended Bowles—I thought it was my duty to do it. I convinced him that it was his duty to let Bowles alone. The truth is, he was about to have him arrested, but I made him consent to use Mr. Bowles as a witness against Miss Bramlett, as I thought his evidence would be indispensable on the trial.'

" 'Oh! I am so delighted to hear it,' replied Miss Clattermouth; 'do you know, Jemima, that I think you are the dearest creature on earth? How could we manage our affairs without you? Bowles is a dear, good fellow—a little wild, I admit, but all young men, you know, must sow their crop of wild oats. I mean to tell him how you have been serving him. He comes to see me quite often, and he should know what a good friend he has in you. I am sure he will make a liberal donation to our Tramp Reform Association as soon as he is advised of your friendly intercession in his behalf. He handles lots of money, and we must get him to take an interest in our affairs.'

" 'Yes, I dare say he will make us a liberal donation if you will explain the case to him. If Viola Bramlett was fool enough to give her money to him, that's no reason why we should not have a share of it. We will get the inns on Bowles, and if we are wise we will make good use of our advantage, but I shall depend on your cleverness to manage the money matter. By the way, what do you think of Charlotte Wallingford?'

" 'She is very pretty, and possesses good talent, but is ruining her character by her friendship for Viola Bramlett. She has no right to thrust herself among respectable people after staying in jail with that unnatural and cruel murderess. She pretends to think that Miss Bramlett is innocent, and for my part, she is welcome to her opinion, if it will do her any good, though she will get a lofty fall when the trial comes off. I am told that they have made a concert room of the jail, and are continually thumping away on an old guitar, and singing sentimental songs. I hate such romantic, pretty doll-babies, anyway, and I know it would make me sick to witness their doings.'

" 'But, speaking of Lottie Wallingford, I don't think she ever will marry Ed Demar. He thinks she loves him, but it is my opinion that she is merely playing with him. I can't believe she loves anybody but herself. She likes to be different from other women. That is the reason she sticks to Viola Bramlett—it is because everybody else has forsaken her. She imagines it will create quite a sensation. She likes to make herself conspicuous, talks with lawyers and politicians, makes a display of learning, holds herself above our Tramp Reform Association, quotes poetry, plays the guitar, and sings love-sick songs. Oh, I despise such women! It is my character to hate 'em. No, no! she ain't going to marry Ed Demar—he is too sober and practical to fill her bill. She will set her cap for a poet or a politician, or some such worthless trash. Demar knows Viola Bramlett is guilty, and would leave her to her fate but for Charlotte Wallingford; he has been tied to her apron string. As for her, I expect if the whole truth were known, she is no better than Viola Bramlett.'

"For me to tell all the tales of slimy slander that were put in circulation by Miss Tadpoddle and her friends, would occupy too much time and would bore my audience. Suffice it to say that Lottie' spotless name came out unscathed. It was impossible to keep her in ignorance of the reports that were being circulated by those malicious old hags, though I had done my best to do it. They always managed somehow to let the parties slandered know of the fact. At any rate, such was the case in this instance; but to my utter astonishment, Lottie seemed to be unmoved by it. No evidence of anger or annoyance was exhibited by her, and she smiled derisively, remarking that if it afforded Miss Tadpoddle pleasure to wag her tongue she had no objections to urge against it.

"One bright, sunny evening, when the atmosphere was soft and invigorating,—I think it was about three weeks after Harry had started for California—I was strolling alone in Doctor Dodson's flower garden, busily occupied in castle building. I did not like the state of affairs, and I wanted to steal away and be alone, so as to sum up things and see if I could make a sure guess as to the future. The painful situation in which Lottie was placed was a source of great uneasiness to me, and I began to think it was my duty to extricate her if possible. I had mentioned the subject to Mr. Rockland, and he promised to endeavor to persuade Lottie to cease her sojourn at the jail, for he agreed with me that the proof fixed Viola's guilt beyond question. But when he mentioned the subject to Lottie she peremptorily refused to abandon Miss Bramlett, vowing that she was innocent, and that she never would forsake her. I had another interview with Dabbs and Tadpoddle, who had discovered a new batch of evidence that appeared to settle the question as to Viola's guilt so completely that it was useless to make any further fight in her behalf. The truth is, I had lost all hopes at last, and the main question to be considered now was how to get Lottie away from the jail. I was well aware of the fact that I was treading on dangerous ground when I ventured to talk to her about Viola's guilt. I took a seat on a low wooden bench in the arbor, and gave the rein to my thoughts. They strayed back to my boyhood days, when I was tramping along the road with Lottie by my side; then they dashed off to California and endeavored to interview Harry. My fancy next snatched up Lottie's lovely image and placed it before me—then my heart grew light. I tried to fasten my thoughts on that dear image, but couldn't do it; for in spite of me, they would wander off to unpleasant subjects. A dozen little birds gave me a serenade with their delightful melody, as they perched among the vines over the top of the arbor, and I tried to induce my mind to interview the sweet little songsters, but it refused. The fact was, my thoughts seemed bent on mischief, that is to say they appeared to be determined to make me miserable, because instead of dwelling on Lottie and the birds, they went off after Miss Tadpoddle and Miss Clattermouth and came lugging them back to my arbor.

"I began to watch the sun as it was going down among the trees on the Arkansas side of the river, looking like a huge ball of fire, and my thoughts must have gone down with the sun, for I stretched myself out on the bench and soon was sound asleep. I dreamed that I was in Heaven, and that a beautiful angel, who had been there long before my arrival, met me at the outer gate, and announced herself as the guide, who had been sent out to escort me in, and to show me the charming beauties of the place. She conducted me along the main street for some distance, where solid blocks of gold constituted the pavement; then she led me through a beautiful landscape thickly studded with green trees, whose foliage gave forth the most delicious perfume. After wandering through those delightful groves for some time, she brought me to the banks of a beautiful river, whose bosom was covered with little boats, gliding over the smooth surface of the water. Each boat contained a band of angels who were singing hymns of praise to the great King of Heaven. My guide conducted me to a lovely spot near the banks of the beautiful river, and instructed me to take a seat on a bench of gold, that was furnished with cushions of exquisite pattern. The spot was covered with strange-looking flowers, whose perfume filled all the air with a sweet scent. My guide then informed me that there was an angel in Heaven who had been watching and waiting for me a long while; that she had been besieging the great Throne with her prayers in my behalf; and she told me to keep my seat and wait a short time, and she would inform the angel of my arrival. She then spread out her golden wings and flew to the northern part of Heaven; then as soon as she disappeared. I was seized with a drowsy feeling, and I lay down on the soft cushions, and soon was asleep. After a while I thought that the flowers overhead began to fall gently down on me. I felt them softly touching my cheek. My guide returned, accompanied by another angel. Oh, she was the most charming creature that I had ever seen! Her beautiful form was robed in spotless white, with long waves of golden hair flowing unconfined about her shoulders. Her large blue eyes gazed down on me, while tears of joy trembled in them. I thought she touched my cheek with the beautiful feathers at the tip of her wing. I shouted for joy and woke myself, and Lottie was standing over me tickling my nose with her handkerchief. There stood the angel exactly as I had seen her in Heaven, only she was dressed in blue silk instead of white, and minus the wings.

" 'Get up, old sluggard,' she said, 'you have slept long enough; I have been waiting over an hour for you to wake, but I think you would have slept here all night if I had not tickled your nose with my handkerchief.'

" 'Oh, Lottie, I have had such a delicious dream; I have been in Heaven; I cannot realize the fact that I am on earth; you were there, too; you were an angel with wings so white and beautiful !'

" 'I hope your dream will come true, when old Time shall settle accounts with us.'

" 'So do I; and I think my dream is a good omen. Sit down, and let me take a good look at you. You appear so fresh and beautiful this evening.'

" 'I notice that you have not forsaken your old inclinations to flatter me.'

" 'No, it is no flattery, I assure you. Pardon me, but I must be permitted to give expression to my happiness in some way, else I could not endure it.'

"She took a seat by my side, while her beautiful eyes looked up into my face; a joyful tear trembled on the long lashes.

" 'How is it, darling,' I at last inquired, as I pressed her hand to my lips, 'that you are looking so fresh and bright, when you have been constantly in attendance at the jail? I was afraid it would make you ill.'

" 'The performance of a duty always gives me health and happiness, no matter how much the labor is.'

" 'How is Miss Bramlett to-day?'

" 'She is quite well physically; but in great mental distress.'

" 'I suppose that is caused by the discovery of the new batch of evidence that was lately made against her.'

" 'What are you talking about? Don't you know that she is grieving herself to death about Harry?'

" 'Indeed, no; and I cannot understand why she should think of him, after having driven him from her presence.'

" 'That only goes to show how little you know about a woman's heart; Viola Bramlett is not thinking of her own situation, but her mind is all the time on Harry.'

" 'Don't you think it is high time she was worried a little about her own condition? The date is near at hand when the grand jury will assemble; and it is certain that they will find a bill, then she will be compelled to stand her trial.'

" 'Indeed, I am glad to know that the day is near at hand when we shall get rid of this business.'

" 'Do you think Miss Bramlett will be ready for the trial when the time arrives?'

" 'Oh, yes; I see no reason why she should not; everything has been arranged except what I was telling you about Helen Herndon, and that I shall intrust to you.'

" 'Do you think it worth while to send me to Vicksburg on a wild goose chase?'

" 'Don't talk that way—you must go at once; I have got some information about her, but not quite all I want. You will find Helen Herndon's mother lives near the city of Vicksburg, and you must go there for the information which I want.'

" 'I'll go anywhere or do anything to please you, but don't give me anything to do that will keep me away very long.'

" 'Oh, no; I could not do that; but you can soon get back, and then we are ready for the trial.'

" 'Are you as hopeful now, Lottie, as to the result of the trial, as you were at first?'

" 'To be candid with you, I must confess that I am not. That Philadelphia detective has managed to excite public sentiment against Viola; it was very unfortunate that Harry should have employed him. He may be a good officer, but he had his mind satisfied that Viola was guilty, and he could not divest himself of it; he was so blinded by his prejudice that he could not see any evidence except such as would operate against her. Some people in this city will be greatly surprised when the trial comes off: things will come to light that will startle some who are now dreaming in fancied safety.'

" 'Does Miss Bramlett know about this late discovery of evidence that was made by Dabbs?'

" 'She knows nothing about anything of a disagreeable nature that my prudence could keep from her., I did my best to stop all those floating rumors from reaching her ears, but in spite of all my efforts, Miss Tadpoddle and Miss Clattermouth will occasionally come to the jail and spout venom worse than that snake which bit me on the wrist; but it was very gratifying to me to see that Viola treated it with scorn. She would be happy if she were reconciled with Harry.'

" 'Lottie, when I was in Heaven a while ago, I did not see any angels that in any respect resembled Miss Tadpoddle—though my guide did not take me to the gossiping department.'

" 'Stop, Eddie! don't use levity now, please—the occasion demands serious thought; let Miss Tadpoddle and her friend, Miss Clattermouth, enjoy their tattling proclivities—they are more to be pitied than condemned. The truth is, I am really sorry for them, because they never knew the pleasures of true love. No one ever gazed down on either of those poor old maids with such a look of love as is now bent on me. We should let the mantle of charity conceal their faults, and look more closely after our own. For my part, I am sincerely sorry for people who have none to love them. What a lonely, unhappy existence must theirs be!'

" 'Lottie, I do honestly believe you have the best heart that ever throbbed in woman's breast.'

" 'You never were more mistaken in all your life, because I have no heart at all—a naughty old thief slipped in and stole it.'

" 'It was only a swap, and you got the worst of the bargain; but such as it is it belongs to you—no one can dispute your title. But really I would give anything for your charitable disposition; I don't think I ever heard you speak ill of any one.'

" 'As to that, I have endeavored to do to others as I would have them do to me. I think it is a good rule not to speak at all about our neighbors unless we can say something in their favor. We all have faults, and we are not so apt to discover our own as we are to detect those of others. Miss Clattermouth and her friend, Miss Tadpoddle, really believe that Viola is a murderess; they think that they are discharging nothing more than a plain duty when they try to convince other people that it is true. But let us change the subject—we must discuss our plans for the future. When can you start for Vicksburg?'

" 'To-morrow morning, if you wish it; you are my commander-in-chief now, and you will find me always obedient.'

" 'Thank you; make it to-morrow then.'

" 'Let me understand exactly what I am going for.'

" 'A few miles from the city of Vicksburg you will find a widow lady residing on a farm—her name is Fanny Totten. This lady had a daughter named Victoria, who eloped with a man of disreputable character many years ago. Now you must find out the name of the man with whom she eloped, and get some one who was acquainted with Victoria Totten to come to Memphis to testify to her identity. You must take plenty of funds with you to defray all expenses; I want you, if possible, to secure one of her pictures and bring it to me; also procure some of her manuscript—anything which will enable an expert to identify her handwriting. You will have to be very cautious or you will arouse the suspicion of Miss Totten's friends. This woman has been traveling under various names, and you must commence at her mother's house and trace her to every place where she has been since she left her mother's roof. I don't think you will find any difficulty in that respect, for she has not covered up her tracks quite as well as she might have done.'

" 'Is she the one you think committed the murder?'

" 'Ask me no questions and I'll tell you no falsehoods. Do what I bid you and wait for the result.'

" 'Lottie, you are a real lawyer, and I hope you will clear your client; but the evidence against Viola rises higher and higher every day, and it will be an up-hill business.'

" 'I dare say you are right in regard to the up-hill part, but as to my being a lawyer, I make no pretensions in that line—I merely wish to serve my friend; but let that pass, and tell me what is this new evidence which you say has been resurrected.'

" 'Have you not heard it?'

" 'Not from a source entitled to much credit. I want to hear it from you.'

" 'Another witness—a respectable gentleman—will swear that he met Miss Bramlett at Ben Bowles' private apartment late at night about ten days before her brother was mur-dered.'

" 'The man who swears that will commit perjury, and shall be punished for it.'

" 'I must be permitted to remind you that Miss Tadpoddle will also swear that Viola was there.'

" 'I never shall believe she will swear it until I hear her do it with my own ears.'

" 'She told me she would, and you may depend on her doing it; and the worst of it is, she will swear that she heard Miss Bramlett ask Bowles how much strychnine it would take to produce death, Oh, Lottie, what will be your fate if Viola should be found guilty? It makes me tremble to think of the awful consequences of such an unfortunate event—it would ruin all of us.'

" 'Eddie, don't be alarmed; remember the old adage, "Sufficient unto the day is the evil thereof." It will be time enough to lament the catastrophe when it occurs.'

" 'True enough, but I should like to see the man who never dreaded approaching evil.'

" 'You must learn a little more philosophy, master a little more patience, and don't give credit to all you hear; but come—you must take me back to the jail. I promised Viola I would return before nine; and she would be disappointed if I failed.'

"I escorted her to the jail, and took my leave to return home and spend the night in sweet dreams about Lottie. What she could want with the private history of Miss Totten was a question that puzzled me. Who was Miss Totten? Who was assisting Lottie in secret was another problem I could not solve. It was evident to my mind that she was working in conjunction with some one behind the scenes. I was inclined to be angry because I had not been told everything. Why should they not confide in me? Wasn't I as anxious to see Miss Bramlett's innocence established as any one could be? Before I reached home I had worked myself into a towering passion, and had resolved to demand an explanation as soon as I should return from Vicksburg. Doctor Dodson met me at the front hall door, and I knew as soon as my eyes met his that he had something to say to me of importance.

" 'Ah, ha! here we come, my boy! glad to see you—walk in. I have something to say to you, my boy—trouble brewing. Ah, ha! real trouble ahead—something must be done—no time to swap horses now, my boy. Lottie's reputation is in danger—she must be saved—no wishy-washy work now. That dear girl is infatuated with Miss Bramlett; she must leave the jail at once, else she is a ruined woman. See to it, my boy—you are the man to do it—don't you see? Ah, ha! you are the one to take her away from the jail. All sorts of scandalous tales afloat about Miss Bramlett; investigation says they are too true. Society will condemn Lottie; her name has already been mentioned unfavorably. Ah, ha! my boy, somebody will be killed before this business is ended.'

" 'Show me the villain who has dared breathe a word of suspicion on the fair name of my Lottie!'

" 'Hush, hush! my boy, that's not the way to talk; let us take the proper steps to save her—she must not be permitted to associate with Miss Bramlett another day. I can't see what Rockland means by allowing her to stay in jail with that unfortunate woman.'

" 'Mr. Rockland has done his best to induce Lottie to return home, but she positively refused to do it. I have been pleading with her also, but it does no good; she vows never to forsake Viola until she gets out of the trouble.'

" 'Pshaw! Ed, it is nonsense to talk about getting Miss Bramlett out of the scrape; she has fallen into a pit of infamy so deep that no power on earth can lift her out of it. Ah, ha! don't you see it, my boy? She has not only committed a most cruel murder, but she has been guilty of other detestable crimes which I would blush to name. While I pity the poor girl, I am unwilling to see Lottie ruined by a foolish friendship for her. Society will not draw the proper dis-

tinctions in such cases. At first I did not believe Miss **Bram-**
lett guilty, but after full investigation I was forced to change
my opinion—all the lawyers in Memphis cannot clear her.
Ragland is very much to blame for this state of affairs; he
has not done his duty as guardian to his brother's daughter.
Ah, ha! my boy, don't you see? The fact of the business is,
Ragland is no account—drinks and gambles all the time,
instead of looking after his business. I can't understand
what induced Bramlett to name Ragland as the guardian of
his children. Anyway, I suppose he was ignorant of his bad
habits. Mrs. Ragland is worse than her husband: thinks of
nothing but self, dresses like an empress, and spends her time
at theatres, balls and on the streets, instead of looking after
her household affairs. How could anything be expected of
Miss Bramlett when left, as she was, a young, giddy girl, in
the hands of such people as Ragland and his wife? That's
the reason I pity the poor girl more than I condemn her. I
mean to petition the Governor to pardon her; he will do it
without hesitation; he was here the other day, and was introduced to Lottie. I heard him say she was the most charming
woman he ever had met; he was delighted with her music, and
says she possesses the brightest mind of any woman he ever
saw. The Governor is a great friend of Rockland, and we
shall have no difficulty in procuring a pardon for Miss Bramlett. Ah, ha! Eddie, my boy, don't you see, poor thing, she
must be pardoned; no use to try to clear her by a jury—
proof too strong. You might as well try to storm Gibraltar
with pop-guns as to get an acquittal in court. But above all
other considerations, we must separate Lottie from Miss
Bramlett.'

"'I don't believe it can be done,' was my reply. 'I think
Lottie never will leave Viola while she is in prison; but if
you will accompany me to the jail early in the morning we
will try what can be done. I am going to start for Vicksburg on the 10:30 train to-morrow, and if we see Lottie it
must be early.'

"'All right, my boy; we will see her in the morning. She
must come away from that jail; but good-night; see if you
can't stir up a sensible dream to-night that will show you
how to manage Lottie in the morning.'

"We were at the jail by seven o'clock on the following morning, for the purpose of trying to induce Lottie to go back to her home. Doctor Dodson stated the object of our visit, at the same time telling Lottie how her reputation was being injured by her association with Miss Bramlett.

"I saw her fair cheeks turn as red as blood, and knew she was angry, though no one would have thought so from her language. She cast an appealing glance at me; I could read her thoughts as plain as print.

" 'Doctor Dodson,' said Lottie, as she laid her hand on his shoulder and looked up into his face, 'would it be charitable, would it be Christian duty, to forsake a friend merely because that friend had been forsaken by the world? It seems to me that that would be the very time when a true friend would stick closer. Now, my dear doctor, you know how much I respect you; you are well aware of the fact that no one has a higher regard for your opinions than I have; nay, you know how much Eddie and I love you—it would make me miserable indeed if I were to incur your displeasure; I believe that when you have looked at both sides of the case with an impartial eye you'll not be angry with me for refusing to forsake my unfortunate friend in this dark hour of her troubles. You say that my reputation has already suffered injury by my association with Viola Bramlett. I regret very much to hear it. I am sorry indeed that my reputation is so feeble as to be crippled by such puny assaults. I have been flattering myself with the idea that an honest woman's reputation could withstand all such assaults and come out unscathed. But if it is true that my character has been damaged by my friendship for Miss Bramlett, it would not repair the damage for me to forsake her now. I must be permitted to have my own way in this matter, and at no distant day you will rejoice with me for having done so.'

"I saw tears trembling in Lottie's eyes as she looked up imploringly into Doctor Dodson's face.

" 'By Jove, child, you shall have your own way!' said the doctor, as he pressed a kiss on her brow; 'you shall do as you like, and I shall cram this fist down the throat of any scamp who dares to speak a word against you, I admire your fidelity to your friend, my child. Ah, ha! that I do.

Miss Bramlett was fortunate in securing such a friend; what does anybody want with a friend except when he is in trouble? Ah, ha! don't you see, Eddie, my boy? We'll go back now. Let Lottie alone; she has got more sense than both of us. Ah, ha! can't you see how it is yourself? Go along and do exactly what she tells you to do. She is pilot of this boat, Eddie, ah, ha! you see it, don't you?"

"I started to Vicksburg at 10:30, and was absent from home a little over three weeks. I, however, succeeded in securing all the information that Lottie wanted, though I had to make a trip to New Orleans before I found it.

CHAPTER XXI.

"There is nothing I detest more than I do a mystery of any sort. Notwithstanding my abhorrence of it, I now found myself, by some unaccountable cause, entangled in a most singular and inexplicable web of mystery. The more I struggled to extricate myself from it the lower down did I plunge, until despite my efforts I found myself inundated and helpless.

"One evening, after I had performed a very hard day's work at the drug-store, I hurried home to seek that rest which the excessive labor of the day caused me to need. It was some time after dark when I lifted the latch of the gate which stood in front of Doctor Dodson's handsome residence and began to walk leisurely along the gravel road leading toward the house. The night was unusually dark, the sky being totally obscured by innumerable black, angry clouds, while ever and anon the sound of distant thunder announced the approaching storm, and an occasional flash of lightning would every now and then cast a bright light around me. I halted a few paces from the gate, leaned against one of the tall poplar trees that stood near the edge of the road, and took off my hat, to let the cool fresh breeze fan my fevered brow. My head was aching severely, my cheeks were hot, and the blood in my veins seemed to be boiling; I concluded that a few moments spent in the open air would relieve me. Soon after I had halted I thought I heard the sound of footsteps approaching the spot where I stood. I knew it was not Doctor Dodson, for he had left town early in the morning to visit a patient in the country, informing me that he would not be home until next day. I became convinced that the grounds had been invaded by some one—perhaps a thief who was waiting for an opportunity to rob the house. I tried to peer through the darkness, hoping to see the intruder, but I was straining my eyes in vain, for I could not distinguish any object at a distance of ten feet, except when the space was momentarily lighted up by the flashes of electricity that often blazed among the clouds. Sometimes I would imagine that I had been deceived; but my doubts were finally set at rest when I distinctly saw the form of a man as he dodged behind a tree just as a bright streak of lightning blazed for a second about me.

" 'Who are you, and what do you want here at this late hour?' I demanded in a loud tone.

" 'Fly for your life, Ed—your hiding-place is discovered; you have no time to spare—the officers are after you—large rewards have been offered for your capture, dead or alive—get away as soon as you can!'

"Those words were uttered in a suppressed tone, while the speaker still remained concealed behind the tree, only exposing his head to my view, which I could plainly see every time the lightning would flash.

" 'Who are you?'

" 'Hush! Ed, for Heaven's sake don't talk so loud, else we will be discovered, for I saw the detective tracking you last night. They will hang you if they catch you! fly immediately, or it will be too late—think of your pretty darling, and for her sake escape while you can.'

" 'Leave these premises this instant, you drunken vagabond!' I angrily exclaimed, 'else I will call a policeman and have you sent to the station-house.'

" 'Hush! I tell you, Ed, this is no time to crack jokes—it is a question of life or death; and if you are determined to throw away your life, you cannot say that I failed to do my duty—I have given you fair warning. You need not be afraid to trust me, for I would die for you if necessary—you may depend on me to fetch your darling to you in any part of the world.'

"I at last arrived at the conclusion that I was in the presence of an escaped lunatic, and that it would be good policy to keep at a respectful distance from him. An unusually bright flash of lightning now played for several seconds among a heavy bank of dark clouds that were hanging very low overhead, spreading a brilliant light over the space around me, which enabled me to get a plain view of the features of this mysterious intruder. The face was that of a young man —rather pale, but very handsome, and I could see that he was well dressed in a close-fitting suit of black cloth, and in the bright light I noticed a heavy watch chain glittering on his vest. Again I inquired of the man his name, and as it was the third time I had made the same demand, I accompanied the inquiry with a threat that I would instantly call a policeman if he refused to give me a definite answer.

" 'Ed, are you crazy?' exclaimed the strange intruder; 'you know well enough who I am; I have encountered serious risk in making my way here in order to warn you of the approaching danger; fly to-night, else you are lost beyond question.'

" 'Why should I fly—who seeks my life? I have injured nobody; if you know of any reason why I should leave my home, say so in plain terms.'

" 'Good-by, Ed,' exclaimed the stranger, as he moved toward the gate; 'my conscience is clear, for I have faithfully discharged my duty, though I may lose my life by the act. They told me you were half mad, but I am now satisfied you are completely so—remember my warning, ere it is too late.'

"By the time he had uttered the last word he passed through the gate, and I could distinctly hear the heels of his boots striking on the brick pavement as he hurried down the street. I called to him to stop and give an explanation; whether he heard me or not I do not know, for he did not answer or halt. I sank down on the turf, buried my face in my hands, and endeavored to call to mind all the events that had transpired around me during that past week. 'What have I done to offend any one?' was the first question I propounded to myself; 'is it possible that I have unwittingly injured any person? have I at any time been deprived of my reason? have I been insane, and while in that condition committed some enormous crime?'

"I remained seated on the turf at least an hour, and perhaps would have stayed longer, but I was aroused from my reverie by the heavy drops of rain that began to fall on my head. I then rose and went to the house, when I was met at the front door by my adopted mother, who had been watching for me a long time.

" 'Come into my room, Edward,' she said, as she took hold of my arm and pressed her lips on my cheek; 'we will take tea there to-night—it is ready, and we have been waiting for you over an hour.'

"I knew by the tone of her voice that something serious was weighing on her mind, and I could tell by the inquiring glance which she frequently cast on me that she wanted to have a talk with me. She rang the bell, and when the servant came to answer it she ordered tea to be served in her room, which she always did when she had any important communications to make to me. I noticed that she kept her large, expressive gray eyes intently fixed on me with a strange look of inquiry. Notwithstanding the facility with which I had been able to divine her thoughts at all times, I was greatly puzzled, as well as embarrassed, on that occasion, by the strangeness of her look. I took a stand in front of a large mirror that hung on the wall, in order to see if there was anything unusual in my personal appearance that caused my mother to stare at me so strangely. While I was looking in the mirror, I noticed that my mother still had her eyes riveted on me, and that she had her hands firmly clasped above her head, which she always did when in trouble. As soon as I turned round she suddenly dropped her hands, took a seat at the little table and commenced pouring out my tea—and I could see that her hand trembled so that she could not hold the cup. She filled the cup as it sat on the table, and when she attempted to pass it to me she let it fall on the floor, breaking it into fragments.

" 'Edward,' she whispered in a tone tremulous from emotion, 'you will have to pour out the tea yourself, for my nerves are somewhat unstrung this evening.'

"I proceeded to help myself in silence, being so much embarrassed by my mother's strange conduct that I was afraid to venture to make a remark.

"Supper over, the servants cleared the table, and my mother took her seat in a large, cushioned arm-chair, and in order to conceal my excitement, I sat down on a low seat and rested my head in her lap. I never before had been so long in her presence without speaking, and the silence was becoming oppressive and painful. When my head fell on her lap, she began to smooth back my hair with her hand, and I felt a tear drop on my cheek that had fallen from her eye.

" 'What is it, mother? what has occurred to distress you so?'

" 'Edward, have you ever committed any crime that would subject you to the penalties of the law?'

"If a powder magazine had exploded beneath my feet, and tossed me onto the top of a house across the street, it could not have given me a greater shock than that question did.

" 'Oh, Edward, my dear son, tell me what has happened? What have you done to cause a reward to be offered for your arrest? I beseech you to tell me everything, and then I will know how to advise you!'

" 'Mother, am I in my proper senses, or am I mad? give me a direct answer to those questions.'

" 'Don't trifle with your mother that way, my son; I implore you to remember that this is no occasion for levity.'

" 'I never was in deeper earnest than I am now, mother, therefore I repeat my question: "Have I gone crazy, or not? have you noticed anything in my conduct, or in my appearance, that would indicate the loss of reason—have I ever been a somnambulist—did you ever know of my leaving the premises after going to bed—have I ever been subject to fits of insanity, or fits of any sort?" Now, mother dear, I earnestly request you to answer each and all of those questions, because my mind is greatly troubled about it.'

" 'Edward, I am afraid that you are not very well to-night, for I am sure you never talked so strangely before. It is hard for me to believe that you could seriously propound such absurd questions to me; but to gratify you, I will give you a candid reply: To every one of those foolish questions I unhesitatingly answer, No; and I will go further, and say that I do not believe the State of Tennessee contains a man who possesses a mind more evenly balanced than yours.'

" 'Very well, my dear mother; tell me why you asked me such a strange question?'

" 'Just before dark, I was walking through the flower garden, inspecting some work that I had ordered the gardener to do, and when I reached the extreme back part, near the fence, I saw a strange woman on the outside who was beckoning to me. She was elegantly dressed, and heavily veiled, so I did not get a chance to see her face. I was considerably frightened at first, because the singularity of her conduct led me to believe that she was crazy, and I started toward the house, when she called my name in a voice I thought I had heard before. I then stopped, and hesitated for a moment, when she said she had an important communication to make which involved the life of some one who was very dear to me. I drew near the spot where she stood, when she made the following statement: "Tell Edward that his place of concealment has been discovered, a large reward having been offered for his capture, and that the law officers are after him. When you deliver this message to Edward he will understand it, and you may tell him that his darling shall be cared for, and conveyed to him as soon as he reaches a place of safety." She then abruptly left me before I had time to ask her name; in fact, I was so completely shocked by the statement she had made that I did not utter a word. Now, Edward, my dear son, tell me what it all means.'

" 'My darling mother, as God is my judge, I declare that it is as much of a mystery to me as it is to you; but of one thing you may rest assured—I never have knowingly committed a crime of any sort that would cause me to conceal myself anywhere. I believe that a combination has been formed against me by some secret enemies, the object of which is to estrange Lottie from me, and to secure her for Heartsell. I do not think they ever will be able to shake Lottie's confidence in me, but there is danger of their winning Mr. Rockland to their side. No, mother dear, you never shall have cause to blush on account of any conduct of mine!'

" 'God bless my noble boy!' she exclaimed, as she again

pressed me to her bosom; 'I believe you, and if you will trust Him who guides the storm, He will carry you through this trouble unscathed.'

"I did not tell my mother about the strange interview I had with the mysterious man on the lawn, as I did not want to increase her troubles. I remained with her until eleven o'clock, then went to my sleeping room, where I was surprised to find a letter lying on my dressing table. I seized the envelope, and with a trembling hand tore it open and read as follows:

"'DEAR ED—Fly for your life—you are discovered. A large reward is offered for your capture. Delay is fatal.
"'Yours truly,
"'TOM.'

"I had scarcely finished reading the letter when a little negro boy—a servant belonging to the household—came in and handed me a note.

"'Here, boss,' he exclaimed, as he shoved the paper in my face, 'dar is de letter what de lady axed me to fetch to you.'

"'What lady are you talking about?'

"'How you 'spect dis nigger to tell de lady's name 'cept he knowed it?'

"'When and where did you see the lady who gave you this letter?'

"'I was gwine to de drug-store to fetch missus some 'scription for dat sick nigger what had de ager, and de lady cotch me by de arm and told me to give de letter into your own hand; den she give dis nigger a whole dollar and went off.'

"'What street were you in when you met the lady?'

"'Squeal street, close to de church.'

"'Beal street you mean.'

"'Yes, boss, dat am hit.'

"'Very well, you may go now.'

"As soon as the little negro left the room I proceeded to open the letter and, lo and behold! here was another document exactly like the one that I had found on my table, except the handwriting, the last one being a very neat, fine hand, while the first one was written in a bold, uneven hand:

" 'Fly for your life—you are discovered. A large reward is offered for your capture. Delay is fatal.'

"This letter had no name signed to it, and no date—it was written on gilt-edged note-paper, and richly perfumed. My hands trembled so violently that I could scarcely hold the letter still enough to read it; and when I did manage to peruse it my vexation surpassed all previous bounds, and I fell back on the sofa and groaned in despair. I remained thus, buried deep in my melancholy reflections, until after midnight—then went to bed, but not to sleep. The old clock on the mantel was ticking regularly, and at every stroke of the pendulum it seemed to say: 'Fly for your life! Fly for your life!' It must have been near daylight when I fell into a troubled slumber, from which I was awakened by the breakfast bell at eight o'clock. My temples were throbbing— my eyes felt like balls of fire, while my blood was feverish. I plunged into a large tank of cold water in the bath-room, which served to cool the fever in my blood.

"Hastily arranging my toilet, I met my mother at the breakfast table with a cheerful smile, which cost me a considerable effort to keep up. She made many anxious inquiries about my health and the manner in which I had rested during the night, all of which I answered truthfully, as far as I could without increasing her anxiety. I took a cup of strong coffee, kissed my mother, and hurried to the drug-store, when a little boy came briskly in and handed me another letter, and darted out at the door before I had time to interrogate him as to who had sent it. I of course supposed it was another one of those detestable notes advising me to 'fly for life,' and being disgusted with documents of that sort, I moved toward the fire, intending to consign the letter to the flames unopened; but glancing at the superscription, I was delighted to discover that it was from Lottie. The contents of the note caused a thrill of delicious joy to dart through my heart. It was like a cold, bubbling spring gushing up in the middle of an African desert before a perishing traveler.

" 'DEAR EDWARD—This is to inform you that I am going to spend the day in my flower garden, for the purpose of superintending the transplanting of some of my flowers, and if it will

not interfere with your professional duties, I should be delighted
to have the benefit of your advice and assistance. Mother and
Mrs. Dodson have very kindly consented to spend the day with
Viola, which enables me to look after my flowers; they, you
know, have been sadly neglected of late.

" 'LOTTIE.'

"When I arrived I found Lottie busily engaged in arranging a fresh bed where she was preparing to plant some tube-
roses.

" 'I am so glad you have come, Edward!' she exclaimed,
as she came to meet me; 'you may make up your mind to do
a good day's work here—just see how the weeds are choking
my pretty jasmines yonder! and there are my geraniums all
dying for lack of attention! I declare, it is too bad, and I
must give Uncle Zack a good scolding for neglecting my
flowers.'

"Notwithstanding her declarations about the lack of attention which her garden had been subjected to, I was filled with
delicious pleasure at the beautiful prospect before me. The
air was loaded with ravishing odors arising from different
kinds of fragrant flowers. A new fountain, with a bronze
statue of Diana standing in the center, had been lately put
up near the summer-house. The goddess held her bow and
arrow in her hand, while a jet of sparkling water came gushing out from the end of the arrow, and fell into a large
marble basin at her feet. A marble Cupid stood on the south
side of the basin, holding a gilded dart pointed toward a
statue of Venus, as she appears rising up out of the water.
Innumerable green turfy walks meandered about among the
charming flowers, while hundreds of beautiful vases in china
and gold, red, blue and green, lined each side, filled with
all kinds of sweet-scented plants. I was so completely intoxicated by the charming sweetness with which the murmuring
breeze was impregnated by fragrant flowers, that I could
scarcely keep from giving expression to my delightful feelings
in shouts of joy. As I stood gazing intently at Lottie as she
moved about among the flowers like a beautiful fairy, I lifted
up my soul in humble thanks to God, for giving me the heart
of such a noble woman.

" 'Why do you stand there all the day idle, Eddie, when

there is so much work to do? why do you not come and help me transplant these flowers?'

"Those questions had the effect of rousing me from my delightful reverie, and I went to work in good earnest and did not stop until the perspiration began to stream from my brow.

" 'There now, Edward, the job is complete, and we will rest under the shade of the magnolias—I am going to give you a nice picnic dinner to-day, to compensate you for assisting me.'

"Then addressing Uncle Zack she said:

" 'Tell Burley to prepare a good dinner for two, and that we will dine in the magnolia grove to-day; send us a small table here, and tell her to be in a hurry, for industrious people are always hungry.

" 'Now, Edward, here is a nice seat for you, and here is one for me,—now we will rest from our labors and have a cozy chat about old times, unless you have got something new to talk about.' Then for the first time since my arrival at the garden, the memory of the mysterious warnings I had received rose up like Banquo's ghost before me. 'What is the matter with you, Edward; are you not well? I declare, your face is very pale!'

" 'I must have exerted myself a little too much while working among the flowers. I guess a little rest in this delightful shade will soon effect a cure.'

" 'See here, Edward,' she exclaimed, as she fixed her beautiful eyes on me, 'you are attempting to do that which you ought to know you cannot accomplish.'

" 'How is that?'

" 'You are endeavoring to deceive me, which it is high time you were learning you cannot do. If you do not immediately proceed to inform me what has happened to distress you, I shall at once conclude that your professions of love for me are nothing more than sounding brass and tinkling cymbals. I knew as soon as I laid my eyes on you this morning that your mind was disturbed about something; and then I must remind you of the fact that I am a first-class mind-reader, and if you refuse to disgorge, I shall at once make a revelation that will startle you.'

"I began to dodge the question by an attempt to change the subject, but she gently placed her hand over my mouth.

"'Not another word shall you utter until you make up your mind to tell me the whole truth—I have a presentiment that our bright sky is about to be obscured by lowering clouds —an invisible influence has been working on my mind, whispering ominous tales of approaching misfortunes. Our smooth sea is soon to be ruffled, and it is high time for us to set about trimming our sails so as to be ready for the storm which I fear is soon to burst upon us.'

"I proceeded to give her a minute history of the mysterious communications which had so disturbed and annoyed me. I noticed that the charming color of the rose that beautified her cheeks gradually disappeared as I imparted the mysterious news to her, and her hand slightly trembled as she attempted to arrange a bouquet from a quantity of flowers which she had gathered. 'Now, Lottie, what do you think it all means?'

"'I will answer you in real Yankee fashion. Do you know of any person who bears malice or ill-will toward you?'

"'No.'

"'Have you had any misunderstanding or quarrel with any man lately?'

"'No.'

"'Have you had any legal entanglements which could cause any one to dislike you?'

"'No.'

"'Then it is a joke that some mischievous person is endeavoring to practice on you in order to have a laugh among his friends at your expense. Let us put our trust in God, and pray to Him for help, and all will be well—let us remember the instructions given by our great Redeemer in regard to prayer. He said: "When thou prayest enter into thy closet, and when thou hast shut thy door, pray to thy Father which is in secret, and thy Father which seeth in secret shall reward thee openly." Now, Edward, I have faith in that precious promise, and if we will pray earnestly in secret, we will come out unscathed in the end—will you do it?'

"'Yes, I promise you I will, Heaven being my helper.'

" 'Very good; then let our unknown adversaries do their worst, we will triumph at last.'

" 'Lottie, you are a real philosopher, and I would give any consideration to be like you.'

" 'Perhaps I am; but I see our dinner coming now, and if you have no objections, we will pay our respects to it, for I am very hungry. Take your seat on the other side of the table, and help me to a plate of soup.'

" 'Lottie, I have a serious question to ask you, and I want you to reflect well and then give me a candid answer; for something tells me that some great misfortune is going to overtake me.'

" 'Let me help your plate to a slice of this venison—it looks very tempting; there, now, be so good as to pass the salad over this way; what were you about to say just now?'

"I could plainly see that she was making an effort to conceal her dreadful apprehensions by keeping up a conversation about one thing while her thoughts were on another.

" 'I was about to propound a very serious question to you, but I guess I had better wait until you finish your dinner, as it is very plain that I shall not have your attention sooner.'

" 'Please hand me the oysters, and then go ahead with your question; and mind you do not turn it into a philosophical lecture.'

" 'Lottie, have you unlimited confidence in my honor?'

" 'Are you fond of stewed squirrel; try some of it—I think it is very nice; as to confidence, I would swear by you if it were not sinful. You know the good book forbids us to swear by anything—hold your goblet over here and let me give you some milk—I think your honor is first-class—won't you have a piece of chicken—as to your integrity, it is good, middling —any other questions you wish to ask?'

" 'See here, Lottie, this may be the last dinner that you and I ever will eat together; in fact, I am afraid that it will, and we must have a serious talk before we part.'

"The goblet which she attempted to hand to me fell on the table and broke into fragments.

" 'There now, Edward, see what I have done—and you are responsible for it, because you have frightened me with your evil prophecies.'

" 'I am truly sorry that I have been so unfortunate as to
disturb your equanimity, but we had better discuss this matter now. I am impressed with the belief that a deep-laid
scheme is on foot, originated and worked by some unknown
enemy of mine, the object of which is to create a breach between you and me. If, therefore, you hear any evil reports
about me, I want you to make a solemn promise that you will
grant me an opportunity to put in my defense before you
venture to condemn me.'

" 'Edward, I have a notion to give you a downright good
scolding—do you think any earthly power could shake my
confidence in you? I would sooner distrust myself.'

" 'Thank you, Lottie, and if ever I give you just cause to
withdraw your confidence from me, may Providence forsake
me, Heaven disown me, and the world despise me!'

" 'I have no apprehensions on that score; I think I am
acquainted with the nobility of your soul—at all events, I am
not afraid to risk my destiny on the accuracy of my judgment.'

" 'Lottie, if it is sinful to worship any mortal being, then I
plead guilty; but while I worship you, it has a tendency to
increase my thankfulness to God.'

" 'Edward, love me as much as you please, but do not forget your obligations to the great Creator—honor and love
Him above all things. There is no real happiness on earth
save that which is sanctioned and purified through God's holy
will. But come, we have rested long enough—let us go to
work, else we will not have time to finish before night.'

"Lottie kept me very busy until the sun went down, and
then taking me by the arm, she led me to a rustic bench in
the magnolia grove.

" 'Now, sir, you may sit down and rest, while I arrange this
bouquet for you; I think you have done a very good day's
work.'

" 'Yes, and I demand my wages—in the first place, here is
a beautiful lock of golden hair that has strayed off from its
companions; and as it looks so lonesome wandering about by
itself, I shall take the liberty to cut it off and put it my
bosom.'

" 'Take it if you wish, and as many more as you want; but how are you going to cut it?'

"I clipped off the pretty straggler with my pocket-knife, and hid it in my bosom, then held her to my heart for a moment, and hurried home, with a soul surcharged with indescribable happiness."

Just as Ingomar finished the sentence, one of the seedy men walked forward, confronting the queen, bowed very low, and taking from his breast pocket a large paper with a huge red seal and a blue ribbon attached to it, gave a grunt and a slight cough, and addressed her as follows:

"I humbly crave your Majesty's pardon, as I fear that I shall be so unfortunate as to interfere with your amusements. The fact is, madame, I am under the necessity of performing an unpleasant duty, but it must be discharged. We officers of the law are very frequently called upon to perform services, in the name of the State, of an unpleasant nature. We have postponed this matter as long as the character of the case will justify. Myself and Mr. Peniwinkle are peace officers, regularly commissioned. We have the honor to hold in our possession a proclamation, or, more properly speaking, a requisition, from the Governor of Mississippi on the Governor of Tennessee, demanding the delivery to us of the body of one escaped murderer. Our papers, as you may see, are all properly authenticated, as the law directs. His Excellency the Governor of Tennessee, has issued his warrant, and we here offer to show it."

Then turning to Ingomar, who appeared perfectly composed, he said:

"Mr. Ingomar, or Demar, or whoever you are, we arrest you in the name of the State of Mississippi, under a warrant we have here now. You will consider yourself as our prisoner."

Then taking a pair of handcuffs from his pocket, he made a move as if to fasten them on Ingomar's wrists.

"Look to the queen," cried Scottie; "she is falling!"

Ingomar caught her in time to prevent the fall, and carried her down to her state-room. He then returned to the deck, where the officers were, and addressed them:

"Now, sir, I am ready to settle this little matter with you. In the first place, you will oblige me by tossing those handcuffs into the river; and you had better be quick about it, else I shall put you in along with them."

The officer was a very small man. Ingomar looked like a huge Colossus as his tall, handsome person towered above the little officer, who began to tremble with fear as he cast an imploring look up into his face.

"My dear sir," began the officer in a tremulous voice, "you don't mean to defy the law, I hope? We are nothing but humble representatives of the law, modestly attempting to discharge a simple duty."

"Will you throw those handcuffs into the river? or would you prefer to go in yourself? I give you two seconds to decide."

The little man threw the irons into the river instantly.

"Now, sir," said Ingomar, "you may consider me your prisoner, if you wish it, and I will accompany you anywhere you may want me to go; but if you have any more irons about you, I advise you to send them after the others without delay."

Mr. Peniwinkle then took another pair of handcuffs from his pocket and tossed them overboard.

"Now, gentlemen, you may take seats here, if you like, and listen to the remainder of a little story which I have been relating for the amusement of my friends. I can finish it by the time we reach Vicksburg; then I will be pleased to go with you to Jackson, Mississippi, to answer any demands which the law may require of me."

Then turning to Ivanhoe, he said:

"Be so kind as to go down and escort the queen up, and inform her that her friends are anxiously awaiting her presence, so that our amusements may be resumed."

Ivanhoe returned in a few moments, with the queen leaning on his arm. She was weeping bitterly, and it was plain to see that the shock had considerably shaken her nerves. Ivanhoe handed her to a seat, when Ingomar said:

"I am exceedingly sorry that your Majesty should have been disturbed by what has just occurred; but I beg to assure you that there is no cause for alarm on the part of my good friends whatever. This affair for which I am now under arrest is by no means new to me, and I don't feel in the least annoyed by it. The only cause of regret is that your Majesty should have been troubled by it; but it need not interrupt the thread of my little story, which I am now ready to take up, as soon as you may signify your pleasure."

The queen was so much distressed by the occurrence just related that she was unable to utter a word. Tears were still falling rapidly from her eyes, while her hand trembled as she made a sign to Ingomar to proceed.

CHAPTER XXII.

THE arrest of Ingomar had the effect to cast a gloom over the entire party, who were beginning to feel deeply interested in his history. All were seated in a circle round the queen, waiting in silence to hear what was to be said next. The queen was making a desperate effort to conceal her emotions, but without effect. The two officers sat staring at each other, evidently very much embarrassed, while Ingomar was the only one who appeared calm and unconcerned. The mysterious lady in the black domino was leaning on the arm of the old gentleman with the long white beard. She seemed to be anxiously watching the two officers and Ingomar, while she stood near the corner of the pilot house, about thirty feet from where the queen and her party were seated. The strange conduct of the lady in the black domino had excited the curiosity of every passenger on the boat, and when Ingomar was arrested under a charge of willful murder it was hard to tell which feeling had the upper hand, curiosity or indignation. If Ingomar had intimated a wish to have the two officers put ashore in a canebrake it would have been done; in fact, Ivanhoe made a proposition to that effect, but Ingomar wouldn't hear to it.

"No, my friends, it is my wish that these two officers should be treated with the utmost courtesy; they are only executing the process which the law has placed in their hands; but I would beg to admonish them that handcuffs are not made for gentlemen. The law considers all men innocent until their guilt is established; and, as I have already stated, this case is by no means unfamiliar to me. It is really a part of the little story which I have been telling; and I promise to tell you all about it before I am done. I guess I can easily conclude the narrative by the time we shall reach Vicksburg; but I must relate circumstances and incidents in the order in which they introduced themselves into my story. About three weeks after I had departed from Vicksburg (where I had gone, as I have heretofore stated, to hunt up certain facts which Lottie thought were necessary,) the grand jury returned into the criminal court a true bill against Viola Bramlett, charging her with willful murder, and the day for the trial was agreed on. Mr. Rockland had made the necessary arrangements with the attorney-general, who was quite a young man, but possessed a high order of intellect. He was a good lawyer, but differed from other prosecuting attorneys in one respect. Nearly all State attorneys imagine that it is their duty to prosecute with a vengeance every unfortunate creature against whom a bill may be found. But attorney-general Quillet was ever ready to enter a *nolle prosequi* when the proof justified it. I was overwhelmed with astonishment one morning to see Harry Wallingford come walking into my office, looking like a corpse. His beard was long and uneven; the hair on his head tangled and unsightly; his clothes were soiled and hung loosely about his body; and his face had no signs of blood in it; his eyes were sunk deep in their sockets, and had a wild, restless stare about them. He held out his thin, bony hand as he dropped into a chair, like one who was very tired.

"'What on earth caused you to return so soon, Harry?' I inquired.

"'My uncle was dead when I reached California, and had willed all his property to his business partner. The will had been presented, proved and probated before I arrived; consequently I had nothing to detain me, so I set out for home; and here I am, as poor as Lazarus, broken down in mind and body, and desperate enough to commit suicide if it was not cowardly to do it. Tell me the news, Ed; though mind you,

I am not prepared for good news—I could not bear it; but if you have anything very unpleasant, please let me hear it.'

" 'I beg you will not talk that way—you horrify me. I have no bad news—at least, nothing worse than you have already heard. The day for the trial is fixed, and Lottie is still hopeful; but you know she is by nature sanguine. So far as my own views are concerned, I am frank to say that I am not at all hopeful. When I talk to Lottie she inspires me with hope; but when I talk with Dabbs and Tadpoddle, they extinguish all. They have both been required to enter into recognizance for their appearance as witnesses against Viola. Mr. Rockland and Doctor Dodson have determined to enter a plea of insanity; and then if she is not acquitted, they are confident that they can induce the Governor to grant a pardon. The Governor was here a few weeks ago and spent the night with Mr. Rockland. When Lottie was introduced to him he was perfectly fascinated with her; and she very adroitly managed to induce the Governor to go with her to the jail next morning. She succeeded in persuading him to be introduced to Miss Bramlett, and he expressed great solicitude for her—praised Lottie very much, and when he left he intimated a wish to see Miss Bramlett come out of her troubles unscathed. I have no doubt that he will pardon Viola if she is found guilty. But, by the by, Harry, how came your uncle to will all his money to his partner, after having promised to give it to you?'

" 'Indeed, I don't know; the fact is, I have quit trying to investigate the causes of things of late. I was not at all surprised when I was told that such a will had been made. The will was made several years ago; and it is possible that my uncle may have contemplated the making of another one in my favor; but his death was very sudden, and wholly unexpected. He had been in declining health, but his condition was considered by no means critical; he was seized with paralysis, and was totally unconscious until death ensued. His fortune was a very large one, supposed to be several hundred thousands, consisting of cash, mining and bank stocks. The will was witnessed by three reputable men, and there was no ground to doubt its proper execution. I took the advice of able lawyers—had them to investigate the case—and they told me that it would be folly to attempt to overthrow the will.'

" 'What a pity it was you did not start there when your uncle first wrote requesting you to come !'

" 'What a pity it was that such a wretch as I was ever born !'

" 'Harry, don't talk so; let us hope for brighter days.'

" 'Hope and I have long since parted company, and Misfortune rules the roost with me now. The goddess of fortune is supposed to be blind, but that is a grand mistake, else how could she throw her darts with such unerring aim at my poor carcass ?'

" 'Harry, you have met with many disappointments, I admit, but you know the sun always shines brighter after a storm; and I believe if you will put your trust in God, do your duty with a brave heart, and command your passions, you will secure happiness yet.'

" 'Don't lecture me, Ed—I can't bear it; I have committed many errors, I confess, but it is too late to mend the matter now. The truth is, I am nothing but a walking bulk of errors anyway, and the sooner I die, the better it will be for the living.'

" 'Dear Harry, you distress me beyond measure by talking so; it shows a lack of courage—a disposition to shrink from trouble when it comes.'

" 'No doubt you think so; it is very easy to philosophize about other people's troubles; but let the whirlwind sweep away all your hopes of happiness and dash you down to the very lowest pit of despair, then you would talk differently. You love Lottie, I know.'

" 'Ah, Harry, I adore her, I worship her—she is the light of my existence—the delight of my soul—my very heart's idol —my angel, my Heaven, my all !'

" 'Very well; suppose she were to betray you, and sink into a slough of infamy as deep as that in which Viola has sunk— could you then lecture so eloquently on patience and hope ?'

" 'I beseech you not to talk that way; it sounds like a sacrilege to me. You don't state a supposable case. My Lottie is as pure as an angel in Heaven.'

" 'So I was foolish enough to think about Viola. I had as much faith in her as you have in Lottie. I loved her as well as it is possible for you to love my sister. I believe God has sent this awful curse upon me for worshiping one of his creatures instead of Him. Don't talk to me about the honesty of women. How could you expect me to have faith in them, since Viola's fall? Ed, I am not a murderer at heart, but that damnable villain, Bowles, must be punished. If he will fight me, he shall have a fair chance; if not, he must take the consequences. You know he first insulted Lottie, and I knocked him down with a stick for it. He then swore he would have revenge, if he took a life-time to get it. And when he found out that I loved Viola, he began to invent schemes to ruin her, and you know the result, alas! too well. He is a shrewd, calculating, cold-hearted villain, and I dare say no girl left like Viola, unprotected, could withstand his devilish plans. I will do Viola the justice to say that I still think she was virtuous; but what can a poor orphan girl do when such a cruel villain as Bowles arrays his plans for her destruction? Druggists will compound medicines for money that will steal away the thinking faculties of the brain, and when that is done, the victory is easily won. How is it that our laws will allow such a villain to march in triumph over the ruined hopes of honest men? But enough of this, Ed. I'll settle with Mr. Bowles.'

" 'Harry, you certainly don't mean to challenge him, do you?'

" 'That is exactly what I mean to do; and if he refuses to fight, then I shall punish him as he deserves.'

" 'Are you willing to violate the laws of the land? Are you not aware of the fact that it is made murder by our laws to kill a man in a duel?'

" 'A curse on the law that protects the villain who destroys the confiding, innocent orphan girl, as Bowles has destroyed poor Viola! A double curse on the law that protects such a sneaking, cowardly villain. No, Ed, it is no use to discuss this matter, because my mind is made up.'

" 'Don't you know that the code of honor, as some men call it, is no longer considered the code of honor?'

" 'I know that Henry Clay fought his duel with John Ran-

dolph, of Roanoke. I know that Commodore Barron killed
Commodore Decatur in a duel. General Jackson killed Dixon
in a duel. Prentiss wounded Foote in a duel. General Sam
Houston shot General White in a duel. I know that General
Albert Sidney Johnson shot his man in a duel. Aaron Burr
killed Alexander Hamilton in a duel. I know that Chambers
killed Lake in a duel. The world did not condemn these
men for fighting duels, and why should it single me out as
an especial object for condemnation?'

" 'Well, Harry, you can't deny making me a solemn promise that you would not seek a quarrel with Bowles until after
Viola's trial.'

" 'I believe I did make such a promise; but I trust you
will release me from it, as things have changed so greatly
since it was made.'

" 'No, you must wait until after the trial, and then I will
withdraw all objections to your management of Bowles.'

" 'On one condition, I will renew the promise.'

" 'What's that?'

" 'You are to agree not to interfere with me and my plans
for a settlement with Bowles after Viola's trial is over.'

" 'I make the promise on those terms. Now you had better
go home, change your dress and seek rest, for you appear
greatly wearied.'

"He left my office then with an unsteady step, and I did
not see him any more that day. Another source of trouble
now began to lower in my pathway. Coming from an unexpected direction, so far as it affected me individually, it was
greater than any I had ever before experienced. Trouble
divested of mystery may be endured, but when it takes us by
surprise, and we feel the blow, but know not who dealt it, it
is somewhat hard to bear. Such was the blow that fell on
me. I could feel it, but couldn't see it. An impenetrable
cloud of mystery began to gather around me, mixing itself
up with all matters in which I was interested. Something
near two hundred yards east of Mr. Rockland's residence,
and on the same side of the street, was a small, two-story
brick dwelling-house, situated in the middle of a small inclosure, containing, I suppose, about a quarter of an acre of
ground. The plot of land was inclosed with pine plank, not

over three and a half feet high. That part of the lot which lay in front of the house, constituting the front yard, was thickly set with short, untrimmed shrubbery, while the other had been used as a vegetable garden. There were only four rooms in the house, two in the lower and two in the upper story, and a narrow hall separated the two lower rooms; a pair of steep stairs commenced on the lower floor near the door and ended on the back side of the house, on the upper floor. The building itself stood in a low, flat place, surrounded with rising ground on all sides, and particularly in the rear, where a tall bluff rose up fully as high as the top of the house. The low, marshy ground where the building was located, and the unsightly surroundings, rendered it very undesirable as a residence; I suppose it was owing to this fact that it was most of the time unoccupied. There were no locks to the doors, and the house had for a long time been uninhabited, save by some lonely tramp who now and then sought a night's lodging in it.

"'I have thought it expedient to give a minute description of this dismal old house, because it has somewhat to do with my history. About the time Harry returned from California, a rumor began to circulate among the negroes (who are by nature very superstitious) to the effect that the house was haunted by ghostly visitors every night. Of course this story was not believed by any except very ignorant persons; but the matter began to attract some attention, nevertheless, because those who did not believe in ghosts were of the opinion that perhaps the house was being used by thieves and counterfeiters. At any rate, it was very certain that one of tne upper rooms was occupied every night by some one, for a dim light was often seen gliding about the apartment. This mysterious circumstance was the usual topic of conversation among Mr. Rockland's servants. The coachman was an old, gray-headed negro named Zack. He was as full of superstitions as he could be crammed, and he vowed that he had seen a ghost, all robed in white, with long, black hair streaming down her back, and a face as white as snow. One evening I met Harry in the street, not very far from the mysterious house; he cast on me an inquiring look, and spoke as if irritated about something.

" 'What woman is that who is staying in that old brick house?'

" 'How should I know?'

" 'I don't ask you how you know, but I demand a sensible answer.'

"I was thunderstruck by his manner, for it was evident that he was very much enraged about something.

" 'Why do you not make me an answer?' he again demanded, his voice still rising with anger.

" 'Really, Harry, upon my word of honor I don't know,' I replied mildly.

" 'I don't believe you, sir,' he exclaimed as he stamped his foot on the ground. 'Be cautious how you attempt to deceive me—I am not in the humor to be fooled with by anybody now.'

" 'Harry, I implore you, tell me what you mean?'

" 'Don't you be uneasy about what I mean; you shall know to your sorrow ere long, or my name is not Harry Wallingford. I am not such a simpleton as you have imagined, as you'll find out one of these days. I am not a coward, nor am I a bully, but under certain circumstances I would kill a man. I am heartily sick of these sentimental hypocrites who pretend to be a man's friend when before his face, but sneak round and stab him in the dark!'

" 'Harry, are you mad?'

" 'No; but I would to Heaven I were; then I could not see and know of the corruption and villainy that boils and bubbles up on every hand. We are in the very middle of a deep sea of treachery and corruption. I thought I had one honest friend; but alas! it was all a mistake, no one will do to trust; they are all hypocrites!'

" 'Harry, you do me grievous wrong to say that; for I swear by everything I hold sacred that never have I, either by word, thought or deed, intentionally injured you. I call upon you in the name of our old friendship—I ask you as a man of honor—I pray you in the name of dear Lottie, whom we both love—I ask in the name of our dead mother—nay, I ask in the name of God, for an explanation of this unmerited insult which you have thrust upon me!'

" 'I warn you now, sir, that I will not permit you to speak

of my dear sister Lottie. She is not for such as you, and the sooner you realize the fact the better it will be for you. It shall be my business to protect her; and you may be sure I am able and willing to do it. If ever I see you in my sister's company again, you will hear it thunder louder than you ever heard it before. I give you fair notice now; and if you value your life, let me advise you not to forget what I am saying. I know you are ready with an explanation, but your oily tongue won't save you in this instance.'

" 'Harry, do you mean what you say? Don't you know that it would kill me to give Lottie up? You would not have our engagement broken off, would you?'

" 'It seems that you are rather dull of comprehension to-day. I thought my language was exceedingly plain. Didn't I tell you that my sister was not for your sort. How could I use language less ambiguous?'

"My ire was now roused to the highest pitch, and I made a desperate struggle to smooth it down. To some extent I succeeded, but not entirely.

" 'I never will surrender my claims to Lottie—never, never! If all the black imps from the infernal regions, with Satan at their head, were here to oppose me, I would not yield my just claim to her hand!'

" 'I am truly glad to hear you talk with so much spirit and determination, because I was afraid that you were cowardly. I know how to manage a brave man, but a coward puzzles me; therefore, we'll see whether you marry my sister or not. There are honest gentlemen in this city, worthy in all respects, who love her, and, when I want her to marry, she can find a husband who won't betray her.'

" 'In Heaven's name, what have I done?'

" 'I have no more business with you just now, sir, You will oblige me by going about yours, if you have any; if, however, you have no business, you had better go, anyway, as I am done with you for the present.'

"Harry waved his hand haughtily for me to leave, and I thought I had to oblige him. I never had seen him in such a terrible passion before. Of all the troubles that I had ever encountered, this was by long odds the greatest. To think that Harry Wallingford, the only brother of my be-

trothed bride, was becoming my deadly enemy, caused my
heart almost to die within my breast. Hadn't we been bosom
friends from early boyhood? Hadn't we endured our sorrows together, and enjoyed our triumphs jointly? Wouldn't
I risk my life, and everything else, to serve him? What
had I done to justify the application of such insults to me?
As I walked toward my office I felt more depressed than I
ever had felt before. Something whispered in my mind a
horrible tale of woes to come. I knew that some sneaking
villain had been at work, but as to who he was or what he
had done, I was totally ignorant. I thought it best to go and
see Lottie at once. I then turned my steps in the direction
of Mr. Rockland's residence, hoping to have an interview
with Lottie before she saw her brother, but I was too late.
Harry had been with her for over an hour before I arrived,
and I did not know what communications he had made to
her until a long time afterward. If I had been advised in
that respect, an ocean of trouble might have been avoided.
Lottie met me at the front gate and led me into her flower
garden. The moment my eyes looked upon her I discovered
that something serious had occurred. It was plain to be seen
she had been weeping.

"'For Heaven's sake, Eddie,' she whispered, as she took
my arm, 'don't go into the house! Harry is there, and in
such a passion as I never witnessed before, and I pray Heaven
I never shall again. What on earth have you done to offend
him?'

"'Nothing whatever, that I am aware of. I met him in
the street a short while ago, and he abused me terribly, swore
that I never should marry his sister, and threatened to kill
me if ever he saw me in your company again.'

"'Oh, Eddie, go quickly; yonder he comes now; he is
crazy with poison; keep out of his way until he is in a condition to listen to reason!'

"I would have obeyed Lottie by leaving at once, but it
was too late; for Harry was within twenty paces of us before
she saw him. He was walking rapidly toward me, while his
eyes glared with anger.

"'I suspected you would disregard the warning I gave

you, though I had no idea you would have the boldness to do it so soon; but this is as good a chance to settle the matter as one could wish. Take that for your impudence, you hypocritical sneak!'

"And before the words were uttered, he slapped me on the mouth with his open hand. I raised my arm to strike him, but Lottie caught me:

" 'Don't strike him, Eddie; he don't know what he is doing!'

"My arm fell harmless by my side; and if he had given me a dozen blows then, I could not have resented it. How could I have the heart to strike my darling's brother when her eloquent tongue was pleading his case? If it had been any other man, I should have pounded him half to death, but he was Lottie's only brother, and she loved him, and that was enough. I resolved then and there that I never would hurt him, no matter what he might do. I could have tied him without an effort, because he was a mere skeleton, anyway.

" 'Oh, brother, has it come to this?' exclaimed Lottie, as she stood trembling and weeping between us. 'How could you have the heart to strike our Eddie? How could you be so cruel as to strike those lips that have uttered so many kind words to you? Have you forgotten the fact that I owe my life to those lips which are now smarting from your cruel blow?'

" 'Lottie,' screamed Harry, as he seized her by the arm and dashed her back roughly against the wall of the summerhouse, 'don't you know that Ed Demar is a deceitful coward who has betrayed you?'

" 'No, no! ten thousand times no!' replied the dear girl, as the tears streamed down her cheeks. 'If God ever created an honest man, it is my Eddie! Don't I know him? Haven't I been with him through sorrow and through joy; and don't I know his honest heart? No, brother Harry, no one can shake my confidence in him—nothing ever shall make me doubt him!'

" 'I tell you, sister, you must and shall cease to receive visits from that deceitful wretch; when I tell you he is a traitor to you, I only say that which I know of my own knowledge, I only inform you of what I beheld with my own eyes. This is no hearsay evidence; this is no report of a detective; but it is a fact I beheld myself.'

" 'Dear brother, I beg you to hush; you are laboring under some unaccountable delusion; your trouble has been so great that it has clouded your judgment. You know that no sister ever loved a dear brother as I love you. I am sure that you would not tell a willful falsehood under any circumstances; but I implore you to let this matter drop for the present. Wait until you have time for reflection. It is so easy to commit irreparable errors—so easy to do things that cannot be undone. Listen to your devoted sister, won't you?'

" 'If you will drive that cowardly sneak from my sight I promise you to let the matter drop for the present; but if he remains here another moment, I cannot answer for the consequences.'

" 'Please leave us now, Eddie,' said Lottie, as she laid her hand on my arm, and cast on me an imploring look. Leave him with me until I can pacify him, and then I will send for you, when he will hear an explanation. You have not betrayed me, have you, Eddie?'

" 'Before high Heaven, I answer, No!'

" 'I believe you, and will always trust you.'

" 'What are you whispering to that hypocrite for? Why don't you order him to leave here as I have directed? You had better not tax my patience too far!'

"I thought it best to leave him with Lottie, hoping that she would be able to keep him quiet until his better judgment should come to his assistance. As I made my way toward my office, I began to ponder over what had occurred, and you may be sure that my thoughts were anything but pleasant. My cheeks burned with indignation when I thought of the blow I had received, and I felt my self-respect leaving me. I began to feel that I had acted cowardly in submitting to such treatment. Who but an arrant coward would have quietly taken such an insult from mortal man? Then on the other hand, I argued the case thus: How could I strike the brother of Lottie, when I know how dearly she loves him? Did she not beg me not to return the blow? How could I do anything against her wish? Then I thought of his feeble health, and the great troubles he had endured, and finally satisfied myself that I had acted right in not punishing him. But the mystery in which the whole affair was clothed puzzled and perplexed me; and the more I discussed the matter in my mind, the greater grew my curiosity. Could it be possible that Harry was laboring under a mental hallucination? or was some enemy of mine at work to undermine me? Could it be that Mr. Heartsell was at work in secret to turn Lottie against me, in order to secure the prize himself? Those questions, and a thousand others of a similar character, came trooping across my mind, until my brain seemed to be on fire. The course that Lottie had pursued had the effect to counterbalance the influence that the other circumstances were producing. She refused to distrust me, and I believed that they never would be able to shake her confidence in me. I felt that I could endure any amount of misery so long as she was my friend and remained true to me.

"I must now tell you of an event that had transpired on the night before the rupture between Harry and myself—a thing about which I was not informed until a long time after it happened. It was not until after the great mischief had been done that I was advised of its cause. If I had been informed at the proper time, irreparable misfortunes could have been prevented. But perhaps I had better proceed to tell what it was that had enraged Harry against me. Early on the morning of the day previous to that on which he had insulted and struck me, Mr. Heartsell called to see him, stating that he had some private communications to make to him. They went into the summer-house and took seats on the wooden bench—the very spot where Lottie first promised to be my wife.

" 'Mr. Wallingford,' began Mr. Heartsell, as soon as they were seated, 'the communication which I propose to make will not be pleasant for you to hear, yet I honestly believe it is my duty to tell you. Of course you are aware of the relations heretofore existing between myself and your charming sister. I loved her very devotedly, and, as you know, asked her to marry me, but she declined, very candidly informing me that she loved Doctor Demar. The frank manner in which she answered my offer of marriage, and the courteous manner in which she treated me, rather increased my affection for her. To be more plain, I still love your sister, and would make any sacrifice to secure her happiness. I had reconciled myself to my fate, and was willing to bear my disappointment with becoming fortitude so long as I had reason to hope that your sister would be happy. But when I became convinced that she was about to marry a man who was unworthy of her —a man who (to say the least) is a hypocritical scoundrel, I determined to make known to you what I had discovered. Edward Demar is either married to another woman, or he is living with her unlawfully.'

" 'Mr. Heartsell, I would not believe such a story if you were to bring a dozen men to swear it! I have known Ed Demar from boyhood to this day, and if he is not an honest man, I must confess that there are none.'

" 'I did not expect you to believe it, for, to be candid with you, I would not have believed it myself had I not seen it with my own eyes. I can readily understand the fact that such confidence as you have placed in Demar is very hard to shake, but you can see for yourself, if you think enough of your sister's happiness to induce you to do it.'

" 'How do you mean that I may see for myself?'

" 'Ed Demar brought a beautiful woman with him from Philadelphia, and as I have already told you, she is either him wife or his mistress—I don't know which. He has her hidden in that old brick house, just over yonder, in that flat. She has lately been moved in that house; he had her concealed in another part of the city, but he has lately moved her to that old building. I think they are making arrangements to elope, as I have overheard some of their conversations. He is to visit her to-night at ten o'clock; and if you wish to satisfy yourself as to the truth of my statements, I will go with you to a spot where you can see with your own eyes.'

" 'Heartsell,' said Harry, as he rose from his seat, his eyes flashing with anger, 'if you have slandered Demar, I will take your life—and if he has betrayed my sister, I'll kill him!'

" 'Very good; you may take my life and welcome, if you

find my statement false. Will you go with me to-night, so as to make the test as to who is to be killed?'

" 'Yes, I will; but I despise to play the spy or eaves-dropper.'

" 'So do I—so does any gentleman; but how can you catch a traitor without doing it?'

" 'True, true! but where shall we meet?'

" 'Here, at this very spot; meet me here at 9:30, and you shall be convinced. By the by, let us compare our time, so as to make no mistake.'

"After the two watches were compared and set with each other, Heartsell took his leave, while Harry sat immovable and silent, with a mind full of gloomy thoughts: Could it be true that Edward Demar was the treacherous hypocrite Heart-sell represented him to be? his heart fluttered with emotions of anger when he thought of the effect such a blow would have on Lottie. Harry loved Lottie with all his heart, and woe to the man who dared to betray her. Harry was at the rendezvous promptly, and had only been there a few moments when he saw Heartsell approaching.

" 'How long have you been here, Wallingford?' inquired Heartsell as he approached.

" 'Only a moment,' was the whispered reply.

" 'Speak low, Heartsell, my sister is in the garden, and I don't want her to know anything about this business.'

" 'Alas, Wallingford, she will hear it soon enough, Heaven knows!'

" 'Yes, and it will be a fearful blow to her, indeed; for she loves Demar devotedly; but I cannot believe he is the treach-erous scoundrel you think he is.'

" 'I did not believe it either until I was forced to; but come, it is time we were going.'

" 'I feel ashamed of myself, Heartsell.'

" 'Why?'

" 'Because this is the first time I ever did anything on the sly; I think we are engaged in a very small business.'

" 'If you love your sister, how can you consider it a small business to take steps to rescue her from the clutches of an unworthy villain?'

" 'Of course not, but these steps ought to be taken openly and not in the dark.'

" 'True enough; but don't they always employ detectives to catch the thief?'

" 'Yes; the best detectives are the shrewdest thieves.'

"While this conversation was progressing, Harry and his companion were walking quietly toward the gloomy old house —their arms locked in each other. The moon was struggling through the clouds that were moving briskly from the south toward the north, every now and then coming out between them and spreading a temporary light over the earth.

" 'This is a most favorable night for our business, Wallingford,' observed Heartsell, as the moon darted out between the two dark clouds, lighting up the road nearly as bright as day.

" 'Why so?'

" 'Because we will be able to see all we wish.'

" 'What do you mean? You talk is if it would afford you pleasure to witness the downfall of Demar.'

" 'Pshaw! Wallingford, you don't know me; I merely meant to say that it was a favorable night to detect this rascal in his treachery. I assure you I should be gratified to find it all a mistake.'

" 'It seems to me impossible for it to be anything else but a mistake; and I feel my cheeks burning with shame—I feel degraded at the underhanded, sneaking course we are pursuing.'

" 'I don't doubt it; I can readily understand the reason— you thought your friend Demar was honest, and that his pretended love for your sister was all reality; but wait a while, and see if you don't change your opinion of him. By the way, here we are—that is the house. We had better turn off to the right, and take up our position back of the building. By standing on the bluff there we can observe what transpires within, for there are several glasses broken out of the rear windows, and this will enable us to get a full view of the interior. Come this way, Wallingford; we'll hide ourselves behind this tree, where we will be on a level with the second story, and in hearing distance of the room. By the way, there she is now, watching for him; speak very low, else she will hear us; she is remarkably pretty; don't you think so?'

" 'Yes, but she looks as pale as death, and appears to be very sad.'

" 'Ah, yes, poor lady, I dare say she has cause to be sad; no doubt she has been betrayed by that scoundrel, and is now beginning to realize her situation. See! she is preparing supper for some one.'

" 'Hush, Heartsell, I hear footsteps coming this way—listen, don't you hear them?'

" 'Yes, and, by the way, that is he, now; stand close behind this tree, or he will see us, for he is coming directly toward us. A plague on the moon! I wish it would get behind that cloud—I fear he will see us. Look! she is coming down to meet him. He is getting over the fence at the corner yonder, and will pass within ten feet of us. Now take a good look at his face as he comes along this way, and tell me who he is.'

" 'That is Ed Demar, beyond all doubt.'

" 'Of course it is; but see, he has stopped, and seems to be watching for some one. Now he is moving this way again. Hark! what noise was that?'

" 'He made it with his cane by tapping on the plank fence. I dare say it was a signal to notify the woman of his arrival, for she is going out to meet him.'

" 'Look, Wallingford, he has taken her in his arms! How does that suit you for a husband for your sister?'

" 'I'll kill him, if they hang me as high as Haman for it!'

" 'Dear Eddie,' exclaimed the woman as she threw herself into the man's arms, 'what made you stay away so long? I have been lonesome and miserable; I cannot endure this suspense much longer—it is killing me. When will you take me away from this horrible place, darling?'

" 'Within two or three days at farthest, my dear,' was the reply, as he pressed her again to his heart.

" 'What would your sister think of this hypocritical scoundrel if she knew what he was?'

" 'Don't mention my sister's name in connection with the double-faced traitor: she shall not be annoyed with him any

more, you may depend on that; but hark! he is speaking
to her; let us listen.'

" 'Has any one been here to-day, Mollie?' said the man as
he led her into the house.

" 'No one has been in the house, but I saw a man standing
on the bluff there yesterday, and thought from his conduct he
was watching the premises.'

" 'I dare say he was, because I begin to suspect that we
are watched; and this makes me the more anxious to get
away from here.'

" 'Come in, dear; I know you are hungry, and I have prepared you a nice supper with my own hands.   I have made
you a cup of strong tea, and broiled you a mutton-chop.'

" 'You are very thoughtful, Mollie, and I consider myself eminently blessed by your love—I feel that I am unworthy
of such good fortune.   I don't think I could endure my
troubles but for the sustaining influence of your love and encouragement.'

" 'Oh, Eddie, if we could escape to some distant land where
no one would know us—where we could feel safe, how happy
we should be!'

" 'Yes, darling, and that is precisely what I mean to do
soon; I would do it now, but there is an unfortunate little
affair that detains me here, though I will get it off my hands
speedily.'

"As soon as the man had dispatched his supper the woman
removed the dishes and returned to where her lover sat, and
began to play with his long, shaggy hair.   It was evident
from her conduct that she loved him devotedly, for she ever
and anon bent over and stamped a kiss on his lips, while her
long, black hair fell unconfined about his face.

" 'Let us leave this place, Heartsell,' whispered Harry; 'I
shall die with disgust; I cannot command my feelings much
longer.   Oh, what a shame it is to see what I have beheld to-
night!   I have often seen my sister kiss that rascal's lips and
shower a thousand endearing expressions on him.   He made
her believe he loved her, and I have heard him swear by
everything sacred that he never cared for any other woman.
I don't believe it would be wrong to shoot him down like a
dog, though I mean to give him a chance for his life.   He or

I must leave the world, and that very soon. Heartsell, Lottie must know of this affair.'

" 'Yes, I think it best to tell her everything. Poor girl! it will nearly kill her; I deeply sympathize with her, and would freely lay down my life to secure her happiness.'

" 'You shall marry her if you want her, because you have saved her. I think she will be guided by my wishes when she finds how she has been deceived in that man.'

" 'Wallingford, if she would love me as she has loved that unworthy scoundrel I would be the happiest man on earth.'

" 'She can't fail to love you when she learns how you have worked to save her; but come, we must go now; we can discuss that matter at another time.'

" 'Wait a moment; they are drawing the curtains down—there, they have put out the light.'

"Heartsell and Harry remained by the tree until after midnight; darkness and silence pervaded the premises, and it was certain that the parties had retired, when they turned and walked back to Mr. Rockland's.

" 'Good-night, Wallingford,' said Heartsell, 'I'll see you again early in the morning.'

" 'Good night, Heartsell, don't fail to come early.'

"Harry went to his room, but found it useless to try to sleep; therefore he spent the night in arranging his plans for the morrow.

CHAPTER XXIII.

"I was in my office early the next morning after I had the difficulty with Harry. I had passed a sleepless night—a miserable, wretched night, and was nervous and irritable when I arrived there. I had not been at the office five minutes when a little negro boy came hurriedly in and handed me a letter. I saw in an instant it was from Lottie; I broke the envelope and read it eagerly:

" 'DEAR EDDIE—For Heaven's sake, keep out of Harry's way today! He is crazy with passion—refuses to listen to reason. I have never known him to exhibit such ungovernable rage before. He makes the most horrible charges against you, and swears he will kill you. What on earth does it all mean? Poor boy! he did not sleep a wink last night, but walked the floor all the time, muttering curses against you. There is some awful secret at the bottom of it all—some strange mystery. I fear some scheming enemy of yours has been planning your destruction. By all means avoid a meeting with Harry until the matter can be investigated. I was on my knees the live-long night, praying for you and my poor brother. My reliance is on God, and let me beg you to trust in Him, too. He will clear the dark clouds from our sky, if we put our faith in Him. Harry is so different from what he used to be—so completely metamorphosed. He used to be so gentle, so kind, always grieving for others' troubles, never thinking of himself—so devoted to you—so loving to me; but, alas! what is he now? All passion—terrible passion—gloomy, irritable, suspicious, jealous and querulous; and, poor boy, I am afraid he is losing his reason. I thought I was brave—I imagined no misfortune could overcome me, but this blow has been too heavy for, me; this awful suspense is more than I can bear. If you see stains on this sheet of paper, you know what made them. My eyes have not been dry since the sad occurrences of yesterday. They have been trying to make me believe my darling is untrue to me, but they never can do that—I am not a bit jealous—I think I know all the goodness of his noble heart, and I never shall believe that he would deceive me. But I must close now, for my time is limited. Again I beseech you not to meet Harry to-day. Your true, faithful

" 'Lottie.'

"I had scarcely finished reading Lottie's letter when Mr. Heartsell walked into the office and, without speaking, handed me a note from Harry. If a bolt of thunder had knocked the roof off of the house over my head, it would have startled me less than the contents of the note; but I have it here now, and will read it to you,

" 'Doctor Edward Demar:

" 'Sir—Circumstances not necessary for me to mention have rendered it expedient for me to inform you that you and I can no longer live in the same city. I will go further, and inform you that the time has come when you must answer for your dishonorable conduct. If you have any sense of honor left, you will readily accord to me the only satisfaction that I require. To be plain, I demand that you name a time and place, without the limits of the State, when and where we can settle the matters of difference between us. My friend, Heartsell, is authorized to arrange preliminaries with you, or any friend you may choose to represent you.

" 'Respectfully,
" 'H. Wallingford.'

" 'Mr. Heartsell,' said I endeavoring to keep control of my feelings, 'am I to understand this as a challenge to fight a duel?'

" 'The language used is very plain, sir, and such was the intention of my friend when he wrote it.'

" 'But I am opposed to the barbarous practice of dueling. The laws of the land prohibit it, public sentiment condemns it, and if I were not opposed to dueling, I could not fight Harry Wallingford. I would not hurt him for everything in the world; and why should he wish to take my life? I never injured him—I love his sister—she is my betrothed bride; and I would as soon think of killing myself as him.'

" 'That, sir, is a matter with which I have nothing to do; but you are mistaken when you say that public sentiment condemns the code of honor. I think the very reverse of that is true; because it is considered disgraceful to back down when challenged. The man who refuses to fight when challenged is branded as a coward, and honorable men shun him as such. Did public sentiment condemn Henry Clay, S. S. Prentiss, Albert S. Johnson, General Jackson and a thousand others I might name?'

" 'Yes, but public sentiment has undergone a great change since then; and our laws did not prohibit dueling then' either.'

" 'Doctor Demar, can you name any one who has ever been punished for fighting a duel?'

" 'I am sorry to be compelled to answer in the negative.'

" 'I dare say you will admit that the reason is owing to public sentiment; but to the point—what answer do you wish me to convey to my friend Wallingford?'

" 'Give me one hour to consider on the matter, and to take the advice of my friends.'

" 'Certainly; but it will be considered dishonorable to mention the matter to more than one friend; and were you to do so, it might cause the civil authorities to get hold of the affair, which you know would serve to widen the breach between you and my friend Wallingford.'

" 'Mr. Heartsell, do you know what has caused Harry Wallingford to become offended with me?'

" 'Oh, yes, Doctor Demar; your little secret is out, and you must face the music.'

" 'What do you mean by my little secret being out?'

" 'Pshaw! Demar, don't undertake to brass it out that way, but never mind, I'll call again at the end of an hour and get your answer. By the way, Demar, you had better accept the challenge, as that might be the shortest road to an adjustment of this business; because if you refuse to meet Wallingford on the field, he will force you to fight him on the streets. If you consent to meet him, a few rounds may satisfy him, when the matter could be settled; but if you decline, I dread to think of the consequences. You know his fiery temper as well as I do; he is very rash and inconsiderate, and is very much enraged against you. Think of these things when you are considering the proper answer to be sent. For the present, good-morning; I'll call again for your answer.'

"For full ten minutes I sat silently gazing at space, and pondering over the situation, perfectly at a loss as to what course would be best for me to pursue. One thing I had made up my mind that I never would, under any consideration, draw one drop of Harry Wallingford's blood. I never would point a loaded pistol at his body—I would as soon think of shooting out my own brains as his. But I knew that something must be done, and that without delay. Who should I go to for advice was the next question to be considered. I first thought of Doctor Dodson; but he was getting old, and was by nature very excitable; I decided that it was best not to mention the matter to him. At last I concluded to submit the matter to General Calloway, a personal friend who had done many acts of kindness for me during my boyhood. I knew he was brave and noble-hearted and had often succeeded in settling affairs of honor without letting the parties resort to arms. General Calloway was a man whose opinions were respected by the community, and he was personally popular with every one who knew him; I was sure that if any one could bring about a reconciliation between Harry and me, he was the man to do it. So I went directly to his quarters and stated the case to him and requested him to assist me.

" 'Let it be understood at the start, general,' said I, 'that

I will, under no circumstances, shoot at Harry Wallingford; but if you think it best for me to stand up and let him shoot me, I will do it. No man knows whether he is a coward or not until he is tried; but I am vain enough to believe that I can stand up and let him shoot at me, if the matter cannot be ádjusted without it.'

" 'What is the cause of the trouble between you and Wallingford?' the general inquired.

" 'I have not the most remote idea; and the strangest part of the matter is, they refuee to tell me. If I have given cause for offense, I am ignorant of it; but Wallingford is so over-mastered with passion that he will not listen to one who demands any explanation.'

" 'Very well, Demar,' said the general, 'leave the matter in my hands, and I'll settle it without resort to arms. Meantime you go across the State line· into Mississippi, and take lodgings near Horn Lake, on the line of the Mississippi and Tennessee railroad. You had better go down there this evening, and I will answer Wallingford's note, in which I shall promise him a meeting to-morrow morning at ten o'clock. I have always found it much easier to bring about an amicable settlement of such cases on the field than in the city; and I never yet have failed to secure an adjustment, where either one of the parties desired it. But when both parties mount their high horses, then we encounter trouble. We will make Mr. Wallingford listen to reason; we will first demand of him a full statement of the grievances of which he complains, and then we will know how to start about making a settlement. Sit down a moment; I'll write the answer to be sent.'

" 'I took a seat until General Calloway wrote the following:

" 'HARRY WALLINGFORD:
" 'DEAR SIR—Your note of this date, demanding of me the designation of a time and place without the limits of this State, for the purpose of discussing certain matters of difference between us, was handed to me by Mr. Heartsell. I have the honor, in reply, to name Horn Lake. Mississippi, as the place, and ten o'clock to-morrow morning as the time; which, I hope, will suit your convenience. Any other preliminaries which you may desire

to have arranged may be done on the part of my friend, General Calloway.

" 'Very respectfully,

" 'EDWARD DEMAR.'

" 'Now, Demar, you go to the livery stable, get a horse and buggy, and go to Horn Lake to-night. Don't lodge in the town, nor don't let any one know your business; in fact, you had better conceal yourself in the country near the village. I will come down early in the morning, when I feel confident we shall have no difficulty in securing a reconciliation between you and Wallingford.'

"As soon as I reached my office I wrote a long letter to Lottie; and when it was finished I sealed and directed it to her, then gave it to our drug-store clerk, and ordered him to give it to Lottie at eight o'clock on the next evening—provided I did not return by that time.

" 'Mr. Todd,' said I, as I handed the letter to him, 'I am going on a short journey, and hope to be back to-morrow evening. If, however, I do not return by eight o'clock, you will deliver this letter to Miss Wallingford with your own hands. You will, under no circumstances, trust it out of your possession, but carry it to her yourself.'

"He stared at me in a suspicious manner for several seconds, and then said:

· " 'Doctor, if any one inquires for you what answer shall I make?'

" 'Oh, anything you choose, as to that. I suppose no one will care to know where I have gone, so they are told when I will return.'

"I then went toward the livery stable, intending to hire a conveyance to take me to Horn Lake, but met one of the railroad employes, who told me that a freight train was going out soon, and I hastened to the depot in time to jump on it as it was moving out. When the train stopped at Horn Lake I stepped off and immediately started to walk rapidly southward. I obtained lodgings for the night at a farm-house about a mile from the village, intending to meet General Calloway, early next morning, according to previous agreement. But Providence had in store for me a different fate, as you shall shortly know.

"It was nearly night when I arrived at the farm-house, and after resting a few moments I took a stroll through a patch of timbered land that lay near the house. I felt that I wanted to be alone, in order to have a reckoning with myself, and to sum up probabilities in regard to the future. I wandered along through the woods, not thinking where I was going or anything about the objects by which I was surrounded, until I found myself on the shore of a beautiful lake. Seating myself at the root of a tree, I took Lottie's picture from my bosom, covered it with kisses and bedewed it with my bitter tears. As I held the darling picture before my tearful eyes, the question whether or not I should ever see her again presented itself to my mind. Would I be forced to fight the duel with Harry on the morrow? Would I be killed and carried back a corpse? These unwelcome queries intruded themselves unbidden on my mind. I will not admit that I was a coward, yet I did not want to die then—I had too much to live for. The scenery by which I was surrounded was surpassingly charming; the smooth, quiet bosom of the lake spread its shining surface before me, and as the slanting rays of the departing sun danced on the still waters, a thousand streaks of variegated lights were reflected against the wall of trees that lined the shore. My eyes were dazzled by the bright beauty of the scene. Large flocks of wild ducks lazily swam about on the calm surface of the water, frequently coming within a rod of where I sat, while thousands of beautiful silver-colored fishes came in droves and began to poke their heads up to the top of the water near me. Great numbers of sweet-singing birds collected on the trees above me, and filled all the air around with a delicious melody. All nature seemed to be making an effort to show me the beauties of the world that I was about to leave forever. She appeared to be arrayed in her richest costume, and soliciting me not to leave her. Why will man be so cruel to his fellow man as to try to push him out of such a beautiful world? Why can we not live as brothers and enjoy the charms of nature, instead of striving to destroy each other? What a happy world would this be if every man would live by the golden rule, 'Do unto others as you would have others do unto you!' Penitentiaries and jails would be unknown; locks and keys would be unnecessary; implements of war would not be manufactured; forts and arsenals would not be built; poorhouses and poverty would be unknown; police officers would be unnecessary, and court-houses would be converted into school-houses; happiness would take the place of misery, plenty would change places with want, and all the world rejoice in the unending millennium. With my mind full of such reflections, I felt humbled in my own estimation, and dropped on my knees, and, for the first time in my life, prayed aloud to God for help in this hour of great trouble. I prayed long and fervently, and whether God answered that prayer or not I shall not undertake to say just now; but leave my kind friends to determine that for themselves after my little story is ended.

"It was some time after dark when I returned to the house and found supper waiting for me; but I declined to eat any —I excused myself, and requested to be shown to a private room. A clean-looking bed stood in one corner, a wash-stand, bureau, and two chairs, constituted the furniture. There were two windows—one in the east side, the other in the south—both covered with clean, snow-white curtains, nicely looped up from the middle. A mocking-bird sat on a tree near the south window, and seemed to be exerting himself to amuse me. I like mocking-birds; but this one was hoarse, and singing out of tune; a half dozen cats were holding a meeting on top of the smoke-house. I might have enjoyed the concert under more favorable circumstances, but the state of my nervous system was such as to deprive me of the pleasure. I needed sleep, and knew that it was my duty to endeavor to get it, so as to enable me to master the situation in which I was placed. The events that were to transpire on the next day were fraught with no little significance, so far as they might result to myself. I threw off my clothes and stretched myself on the bed, first extinguishing the light, and tried to keep my thoughts away from the cat show; but that was a failure. I stood it as long as any man could have done, and would have submitted to the torture perhaps longer, but for my nervousness. I threw a glass tumbler with unerring precision—one cat went to his long home, and the concert closed. But alas! I soon made the discovery that I had

jumped out of the frying-pan into the fire. The cater-
wauling melody was sweet music compared with the noise
made by the frogs in a pond hard by. I am willing to admit
that I had always been of the opinion that a congregation of
cats could make the most soul-scraping noise that ever was
heard; but that night I had cause to change my opinion—I
award the premium to the frog; he can beat a cat to death
and give him an hour's start; a cat has to stop occasionally
to fill his lungs—but not so with the frog; he seems to be all
the time full of wind; at all events, no man ever heard a frog
stop for breath when once he made up his mind not to do it.
The frog pond was not more than fifty yards from my window. I don't know exactly how many there were in that
pond, though it must have been very densely populated, judging from the great noise they made. If frogs were worth a
dollar a head, I am confident that there were enough in that
pond to pay the national debt, not counting the old ones that
had retired from business. I lay and listened to the frogs
until my eyes began to feel heavy; and just as I was about to
fall asleep in spite of the frog convention, a mosquito concluded to make his supper off of my nose. Sometimes I would
actually get into a comfortable doze, when he would light and
begin to put his pumps to work and wake me. I would drive
him away, but he would not take the hint. In order to
get rid of him, I offered a fair compromise: I was willing
that he might pump as much blood out of my feet as he could
chamber, and taking them from under the cover, I held them
out to him; but he rejected my liberal offer with scorn,
and seemed to have made up his mind to fight it out on the
nose line; the result was, after a half hour's contest I killed
him, and then I soon fell asleep. It was but natural to
suppose that my slumbers would be disturbed by unpleasant
dreams. How could anything else be expected, harassed as
my mind was with such unpleasant reflections? I dreamed of
war, blood, duels, and a thousand other things too tedious to
mention; but I must tell you of two of my dreams: I first
fancied that I was a young tadpole, swimming about in the
pond among the frogs. I was very proud of my beautiful
tail, and imagined that all the frogs were dying with envy
because they had lost theirs. It never had occurred to me

that at no distant day I should lose my tail, and be reduced
to an equality with the frogs. I was dashing about among
the frogs, and switching my tail in their faces in a very rude
manner. The fact is, I was tantalizing them for being out of
fashion. I had the misfortune to incur the displeasure of a
celebrated frog who was famous for his courage, and who
possessed an ungovernable temper. I trust that my friends
will not be disposed to censure me for describing such a
ridiculous dream, but I am telling exactly what did occur,
and not what ought to have occurred. In the first place, it
will be well to remember the circumstances by which I was
surrounded. I was about to be forced into a duel with a man
against whom I bore no ill-will, and whom I was determined
not to hurt. Then I was full of perplexity, because I did not
know the cause which had induced him to challenge me.
While my mind was completely unsettled by these unpleasant
reflections, I was trying to steal a little sleep, in order that I
might be in a condition to wrestle with the situation on the
next day. Then it was a natural consequence that I should
dream of duels, Tom-cats, and frogs, especially when it is
remembered that the cats and frogs had conspired to keep me
awake, and when in spite of them I did fall asleep.

"But let me go on with my strange dream. When I had
been so inconsiderate as to flirt my tail against the nose of
the high-tempered frog, I discovered, when it was too late,
that I had involved myself in a serious difficulty; and hoping
to escape the consequences, I sought refuge behind an old
rotten log that lay in the edge of the pond. I was very much
alarmed when I saw a large number of frogs collecting round
the one whose nose I had so imprudently slapped with my
tail. A little timid tadpole swam up close to me, and very
meekly informed me that I was in great danger, as I had
insulted the most important frog in the pond. I was very
much disturbed by this information, and was preparing an
apology to be sent when I received a message from the
insulted frog. To the best of my recollection it was, in substance, as follows:

" 'General Frog presents his compliments to Colonel Tadpole, and begs to say that while bathing in his own precinct
a gross insult was offered him by Colonel Tadpole, who

wantonly flirted his tail in General Frog's face. General
Frog, therefore, has the honor to request Colonel Tadpole to
designate a time and place when and where such satisfaction
can be had as is recognized by the code. General Frog
designates the bearer of this message as his friend, who is
authorized to arrange preliminaries.'

"I am free to confess that I was completely paralyzed with
fear when I received this message, and would have made an
honorable apology, but the bearer refused to listen to reason.
He demanded blood, and swore that if I refused to fight I
was a dead Tadpole certain. I was about to faint from sheer
cowardice when a bold young Tadpole whispered in my ear:

" 'Put on a bold front,' said he; 'General Frog is a humbug
and a bully. Accept his challenge, make him fight with
sticks six inches long and a half inch in diameter; let the
sticks be sharpened at one end. A frog always has his mouth
open, and you can run your stick down his throat and kill
him while he is trying to get a fair lick at your head.'

"I acted on this advice, and being the challenged party,
had the right to choose the weapon. Quite a commotion was
caused when it became known that a duel was to be fought
between General Frog and Colonel Tadpole.

"The weapons were prepared, the space in the water was
measured, and ominous silence pervaded the pond (a thing
that had never happened before) ; we were placed eighteen
inches apart, and when we were ordered to take our places, I
could see plainly that public sentiment was against me among
the frogs, but every tadpole in the pond was on my side.
When the word was given, I made a dash forward and plunged
my stick down General Frog's throat, taking him completely
by surprise. The general's friends carried him off the field,
but he was a dead frog; and when it was announced that the
great General Frog was dead, such a heart-rending wail as
rent the air then never had been heard in the frog kingdom
before.

"The unusual noise awoke me, and I was glad to find it
was all a dream, and that I was not really a tadpole. I got
up, lighted the candle, kissed Lottie's picture a dozen times,
looked at my watch and found that I had only slept an hour.
After pacing the floor for half an hour, I again threw myself

on the bed, and soon was dreaming again. While the second dream was not so full of nonsense as the first one, it was pregnant with unpleasantness. It was what I call a business-like dream—short and to the point. I thought Wallingford and I had failed to reach a reconciliation, and that General Calloway announced to me that I must fight. We fought with pistols at ten paces, and I was killed at the first fire. I suffered all the agonies of death, and as soon as my soul left the body his Satanic Majesty stood ready to take me into custody. I remember exactly how he looked; he had his aid-de-camp with him. They had handcuffs and chains to fasten my limbs. They took me down through a long space of exceeding darkness, when all at once my eyes were blinded by the bright flames that broke on my view. I started up and awoke, and saw two rough-looking men standing over me—while one held a candle, the other had a pair of handcuffs in his hand.

"'Get up, sir, and put on your clothes as soon as you can —we want you to go with us.'

"I did as I was ordered, asking no questions. The first thing that occurred to me was that the civil authority had ordered my arrest, so as to prevent the duel; and to be candid, I was very glad of it. Anything to prevent the duel suited me, for I hated the idea of being shot at merely to gratify a foolish whim of Harry Wallingford. When I finished my toilet, one of the men locked the handcuffs on my wrists, and then commanded me to follow them. Under any other circumstances, I dare say I should have knocked a man down who attempted to manacle me; but I was willing to submit to any indignity and endure any inconvenience that would prevent the duel. I followed the officers submissively and silently, being satisfied that my imprisonment would be only temporary. I would be set at liberty as soon as my friends could arrange to make a bond. The officers put me in a buggy and began to drive rapidly toward Hernando. We arrived there a short time before daybreak, when I was placed on a train and was soon moving rapidly toward Grenada. I was unable to account for this. Why should I be carried out of the country where I had violated the law? A suspicion now began to rise in my mind that it was not the duel which had caused my arrest, and I ventured to ask one of the officers the cause of it. Instead of giving me a civil answer, he broke into a hoarse laugh.

" 'Ha, ha, ha! Tom, just listen to this rascal, will you? He wants to know the cause of his arrest. Now ain't that brassy?'

" 'See here, old fellow,' said the other officer, addressing himself to me, 'that's too thin; now you just sit down there and keep mighty quiet—none of your palaver with me! I've had much to do with your sort lately; they always play ignorant.'

" 'Am I arrested for attempting to fight a duel?' I ventured to inquire.

" 'For what did you say?' demanded the officer, apparently very much surprised.

" 'I thought I was arrested for attempting to fight a duel,' I replied.

" 'Ha, ha, ha! Tom, that fellow is going to try the insane dodge. But look here, old fellow, that game's played out. Your cake is all dough; you are gone up the spout this time certain. It's a pity, though, to hang such a good-looking chap as you, but I reckon it'll have to be done. I guess you won't get another chance to escape; they'll iron you down good this time.'

"My ire was roused as well as my curiosity, and I indignantly demanded to know the cause of my arrest, and where I was being carried.

" 'Come, sir,' said one of the men, 'none of your airs here now. If you know what's good for you, I guess you'll keep your mouth shut, unless you can talk with a little more sense.'

"I leaned back in my seat, and tried to collect my scattered thoughts; but I was so confused that I scarcely could tell whether I was dreaming or not. It was very plain, however, that the duel had nothing to do with my arrest; but what was the cause, was the all-absorbing question now to be settled. They spoke of hanging; what on earth could it mean? They talked about escapes and irons, etc., etc. What had I to do with all this?

"The train rattled on; the lamp cast a faint light through the coach, as the gray streaks of dawn began to steal through the windows. One officer coiled himself up on a seat just in front of me, and began to snore so loud that it could be heard above the rattle of the train. The other one sat by my side with a navy six in his belt, keeping guard while his companion slept. Every now and then he took a drink of whisky from a flask which he carried in his pocket. The train did not stop until we reached Grenada. I was then directed to follow the officers to the hotel dining-room for breakfast. I drank a cup of coffee, but could not eat; my head was aching as if it would burst, and I had a burning fever. We waited at Grenada two hours, when the south-bound train on the Mississippi Central Railroad arrived. I was conducted aboard, and again found myself flying on at the rate of fifty miles an hour. It was late in the evening when I was taken off the train, at a small wayside station, and conducted to a stage-coach that was ready to start toward the east. Myself and the two officers were the only passengers. The driver popped his whip, and we began to move on. Where am I going, and what is to be my fate? was my mental question. What will General Calloway think of me when I fail to make my appearance at Horn Lake? He will think I have fled from mere cowardice. What will Lottie think when they tell her that I have sneaked off and hidden myself to avoid a fight? My letter will be handed to her at eight o'clock this evening, and they will tell her that I have run away. My mental sufferings were very great, while my physical torture continued to increase. The fever was burning me with excessive violence, and I knew that I was going to be seriously ill. My companions were both in a beastly state of intoxication, one of them stretched on the floor of the coach, while the other nodded and snored by my side. The driver was so drunk that he could scarcely keep his seat, and when I begged him to stop and get me a drink of water, he replied with an oath that he 'had no time to fool away.' The road was rough and hilly, and the horses would go up the rise at a snail gallop and then go down at full speed, jolting and tossing me about like a foot-ball. My sufferings were indescribable. It was after midnight when the coach halted in front of a large brick building in the village of P——, and I was ordered to get out. I made an effort to obey, but was so ill that I could not rise from my seat.

" 'You will have to assist me, gentlemen,' said I, 'for I am very ill.'

" 'None of your shamming now,' growled one of the drunken brutes. 'That's too thin—it's too soon to begin that game; out with you, and be quick about it, too!'

" 'I am really very ill, sir; and without help I am not able to stand alone.'

" 'Come along with you, then,—I believe you are trying to play the same old dodge; but we'll fix you this time so you won't get away.'

"As he muttered these words he dragged me from the coach and led me into the house, which proved to be the county jail. They carried me up a pair of stairs and placed me in a dungeon, closed the door, and left me in total darkness. I sank down on the floor completely exhausted, and almost crazed with misery. The blood in my veins seemed to be boiling hot; while the fever continued to increase. My stomach felt as if it were on fire, and I was nearly famished for water. I began to crawl about the floor, hoping to find water; for I had called as loud as I could several times, begging for some to be brought, but no one had answered my cries. After searching about in the dark for some time, I found a stone jug of water that was very warm, but it was better than none. During the search for the water I found a little bundle of straw in one corner of the room, with a blanket spread over it. Throwing myself down on it, I groaned in despair. No mental torture could be greater than I suffered then; the mysterious manner of my arrest, the knowledge that I was on the eve of a dangerous spell of fever, the disgrace that would attach to my name, the opinion that General Calloway would have of me, the sorrow that would fall on my darling Lottie, all combined to drive me down to the lowest depths of despair. While all this mental anguish was conspiring to drive me mad, the burning fever was scorching and parching my blood. I well knew from the symptoms that I was seriously threatened with brain fever; I rolled and tossed myself about on the straw until I

felt my brain grow dizzy. My mind commenced to wander;
I cried aloud for help, but none came. With Lottie's sweet
name on my lips, her picture in my hand, I fell into a state
of unconsciousness. When I regained consciousness I was
a mere skeleton, unable to lift my head from my pillow, and
it was a long time after my reason returned before I could
remember where I was, or what had happened. A little
negro boy came to the door and shoved a dish of provisions
through the bars of iron, then placed a pitcher of water
where I could reach it, and was turning away, when I called
to him in a voice so feeble that I was astonished at the sound
of it. He heard me, however, and returned to the door,
and inquired what I wanted.

" 'How long have I been here?' I whispered.

" 'You bin dar dis trip free weeks; but de udder time,
afore you 'scaped, you was dar two mont's zackly.'

" 'You are mistaken, my boy,' said I, 'because I never saw
this place until this time.'

" 'Oh, yes, boss, you's forgot it; you's bin miglffty sick dis
time; but tudder time you broke de jail and 'scaped. Dis
time you bin so sick—you cryin' all de time—you talk heep
of foolishness—you keep sayin' Lottie! Lottie! sweet Lottie!
all de time when you was sick. You crazy! De doctor sez
you gwine to die, den dey won't hab de fun of hangin' you.'

" 'What are they going to hang me for?'

" 'Oh, yo knows what for; what yo ax dis chap for, when
yo knows all about it? Didn't yo kill mas' Jack Clanton for
nuffin'? But yo is gwine to die shoah, den ob course dey
won't hang you.'

" 'Do they think I am the man who killed Mr. Clanton?'

" 'Of course dey knows it sho' nuff—dey seed yo do it.'

" 'But I tell you I never saw Mr. Clanton in my life, and
I never saw the jail until I was brought here three weeks
ago.'

" 'Oh, boss, yo is crazy yit. Don't dis chap know ye?
Didn't dis nigger tend yo all de time? Didn't yo try to
bribe dis nigger to fetch de file? I 'spect when ye gits better
you'll 'member all 'bout it.'

"Then he went away whistling 'Dixie,' doubtless believing
me still out of my senses, and to tell the truth, I was in-

clined to that opinion myself. It seemed to me to be absolutely certain that I had either gone raving mad myself, or that I had fallen into the hands of a gang of maniacs; but the most plausible argument was in favor of the idea that my mind was wandering. My disease had run its course, and I was free from physical sufferings, except excessive weakness and a general prostration. All the hair had been shaved from my head, and my temples had been scarified all over. The room or dungeon in which I was confined was quite small—not over ten feet square. All the light and air came through a small, square, grated window, about twelve inches wide. However, during the day-time the wooden shutter of the door was left open, which served to aid in ventilating the room; but at night it was closed. Heavy iron bars crossed each other thickly in the door; and a small space was open near the floor through which the little negro usually passed the dishes that contained my food. A short while after the negro boy had left me, a man came and unlocked the door and entered the dungeon, carefully closing it when he had got inside.

"'Well, old fellow,' said the visitor, as he took a seat near me and felt my pulse, 'how do you come on this morning?'

"'Better, I think,' was my reply, 'though I hardly know the nature of my disease. One thing is plain—I am quite feeble—my strength is all gone.'

"'Ah, yes, no doubt you feel very weak; quite natural you should, after such an attack of brain fever. I thought you were going to make a die of it, in spite of my humble efforts to save you; but thanks to a vigorous constitution, which you very fortunately possessed, I have been able to pull you through. You will be all right again in a few days. I have ordered you some beef tea, which you must use freely, and by to-morrow I dare say you will be able to take more solid food. Let me look at your tongue. Ah, that's all right. You won't leave us yet a while.'

"'Doctor,' said I, 'will you be so kind as to inform me if you know why I am imprisoned in this horrible dungeon?'

"'Come, come, my dear fellow! you had better not talk about that unpleasant affair until you get more strength. By no means let your mind run on that subject. By the by, Debar, what lady is this you have been raving about all the time? Lottie! Lottie! Yes, I think that was the name. If you called her name once, you called it fifty thousand times within the last three weeks. The fact is, you talked as if she were present with you all the time.'

" 'She is a charming girl who resides in Memphis, Tennessee, and my betrothed bride.'

" 'Ha! ha! I say, your betrothed bride; but come, come, Debar, you had better keep quiet, I reckon; for I see your mind is not exactly right yet.'

" 'Why do you call me Debar? That is not my name. I am a physician by profession. My name is Edward Demar, and I never saw this jail until the night I came here three weeks ago.'

" 'Pshaw! Debar; I had been hoping that your mind was entirely restored, but I am sorry to find myself disappointed in that hope. Is this the picture of the young lady you call Lottie?'

" 'Yes.'

" 'She must be exceedingly beautiful indeed. That is the sweetest face I ever saw. You have been holding that picture in your hand, and kissing it frequently, while your reason was partially, if not totally, dethroned.'

" 'Oh, sir, if you knew how I worship that dear girl, you would not be surprised at my devotion to her picture!'

" 'I don't think your wife would like to hear you talk that way.'

" 'What in Heaven's name do you mean? I have no wife —nor ever did.'

" 'Look here, Debar, you are either out of your senses, or shamming; for I know a lady who loves you devotedly, and she is your wife, too, and a very true, worthy one at that—a thousand times too good for such a scapegrace as you.'

" 'I tell you my name is not Debar; and I swear I have not been married. I never loved but one woman in my life, and that is Lottie Wallingford, of Memphis.'

" 'Ha! ha! ha! Now this is really interesting—indeed it is! You don't know your own name! Can't remember your pretty wife! Never was here before! Ha! ha! ha! well! well! well! I have often known criminals to try the insane dodge, but I never knew one to deny his own name and repudiate his own wife before. But good-morning, old fellow, I am to blame for letting you talk so much anyway; you just keep very quiet, and drink as much of the beef tea as you can. I will call again in the morning; by that time I guess you will remember your name; and I'll send a messenger after your wife, as I have been told she has got back home. She has been absent a long time; that is the reason she has not called to see you, I suppose. By-by, Debar.'

"Doctor Lamberton was quite a young man, and from our short acquaintance I had formed rather a favorable opinion of him. He was very kind to me, and I learned that he had been unremitting in his attentions to me during my long and serious illness. Doubtless I would have died but for his kindness. When I was left alone, my thoughts went to work more vigorously than they ever had done before.

CHAPTER XXIV.

"AFTER Doctor Lamberton departed I closed my eyes and tried to sum up in my mind all that had occurred since I left Memphis, in order to see if I could make anything tangible out of it. The hours dragged slowly along, a faint light struggled through the small aperture misnamed window, a little mouse stole in and began to nibble at the crumbs of bread on the floor, while I watched him intently. It was a relief to me to see any living thing, no matter what it was; it had the effect of keeping my mind from painful subjects. When the little mouse would finish his repast and leave me alone, I would lie on my filthy straw bed and watch his hole for hours at a time, hoping he would come again to keep me company. A large spider had set his net in one corner of the window, in order to capture unsuspecting flies that were constantly coming in and out through the opening. His net was an ingenious piece of workmanship, and it took him several days to finish it; he could throw his fine-spun thread with as much accuracy as a Mexican Greaser could throw his lariat. After he had completed his net, he built a little neat residence for

himself near it, so he could sit and look through his window
and watch his trap. I noticed that in selecting the location
for his residence, he was very particular to place it so that it
would not be seen by any insect coming in through the window; he erected his apartments inside, and a little in the rear
of the corner of the window-sill, while his net was stretched
across it. The web was woven so very fine that it was
scarcely visible to the naked eye, and many a bold fly lost his
life by being caught in its meshes. Sometimes a vigorous
contest would take place, when a fly would make a desperate
struggle to free himself; but I noticed that the victim seldom
came off victorious. One memorable battle between the
spider and a large bumblebee I think worthy to be described.
As soon as the bumblebee got one of his legs entangled in
the net he commenced to work vigorously to loosen it. The
spider came out and took up his position within two inches
of the captive, and began to throw his lariat at his leg. The
heroic efforts of the bumblebee excited my sympathy, and I
would have gone to his rescue if I had been able, but I was
helpless. I could only lie still and give him my good wishes.
After a while the spider managed to get one leg of his intended victim securely fastened, and I was sorry to think that
the poor bumblebee's fate was to be death; but not so: I
was struck with admiration when I saw the brave fellow amputating his own leg by using his teeth. The spider, however, seemed to realize the situation, for while the bumblebee was engaged in amputating the leg he began to hurl his
lariat at another, and by the time the amputation was done
one more limb was tied fast; but the bumblebee seemed determined to regain his liberty at any cost, so he fell to and
took off the other leg, and did it so quickly that the spider
did not have time to fasten another, and the gallant hero was
free, minus two of his legs. As soon as the bumblebee regained his liberty, instead of retreating, as I expected he
would do, he quietly seated himself on the window-sill and
watched the spider's hall, as if he were not satisfied with
the result of the fight. After a while, however, he .disap-
peared, and I let my sympathies go with him. The spider's
net was completely destroyed, and I was glad of it, but he
set about rebuilding it, which cost him three days' incessant

labor. The little mouse, the spider, and dear Lottie's picture
were my only companions during the long, lonesome days of
my captivity. I would lie on my back for many hours at a
time, with my eyes riveted on Lottie's picture, and ask myself a thousand questions: What is Lottie doing at this moment? I wonder if she is thinking of me! Have they made
her believe that I ran away of my own accord? Perhaps
they have persuaded her to give me up, as one unworthy of
her love. Maybe they have induced her to marry Heartsell!'

" 'Heaven have mercy on me!' I groaned in despair, If
I had known then what was going on at home, I dare say my
anguish would have been greater still; but I presume it was
better as it was, for I might have died if any additional troubles had been thrust upon me, I think that the heroic struggle I had witnessed on the part of the gallant bumblebee to
win his freedom had a good effect on me. I became convinced that a man of courage and strength could accomplish
anything that was necessary, and I then and there resolved
that I would imitate the brave example set by the heroic insect as soon as I recuperated my strength, I would make an
effort to regain my liberty, an effort that should break down
and trample over all opposition. I would not yield like a
base coward, but would be free, or lose my life in the attempt
to accomplish that end.

"It was four days after I had regained consciousness before
I was able to sit up in my bed. Doctor Lamberton visited
me once a day, usually coming early in the morning, and
chatted with me a few moments, gave his instructions and
retired. Then I would be left alone for the remainder of
the day, except when some one would come to bring me food
and drink. Then I would divide my time between the mouse,
the spider and Lottie's picture, giving most of my attention,
though, to the image of my darling. It was so dark in my
cell that I could not read, even if I had had anything in the
shape of a book; and then since the fever had left my brain it
seemed to be lingering in my eyes, and made them sore and
quite sensitive. The doctor brought me a pair of green
glasses to protect my eyes, and told me to wear them all the
time, as my eyes were in very great danger. My recovery was
exceedingly slow.

"As soon as I thought my strength would justify it I wrote a long letter to Lottie, giving in detail all the circumstances that had combined to prevent my return to Memphis. I requested her to see Doctor Dodson, inform him of my situation, and ask him to come to my assistance without a moment's delay. I also requested her to go and see General Calloway and explain to him the cause of my absence from Horn Lake on the day appointed. I informed her of my illness, but did not tell her how serious it had been. I told her the simple truth when I said that her dear picture had been my chief source of happiness during the long, weary days of my solitary confinement. My letter closed thus:

" 'Always trust me, dear Lottie, no matter what you hear about me. I am now, have ever been, and always will be, as true to you as the needle is to the pole.'

" 'I sealed and delivered that letter to the negro boy, who promised to mail it, but I don't think he did it, for no such letter ever was received by Lottie. I waited and hoped for Doctor Dodson to come to my assistance; but, alas! I waited and hoped in vain. As soon as I was able to take a little exercise by walking about the room that small comfort was denied me, for a rough blacksmith came in one day and riveted a heavy chain on my ankle, then fastened the other end to a beam in the floor.

" 'There now,' he exclaimed, when he had finished the job, 'I guess that'll keep you this time! By the way, Debar, how did you manage to get those tools?'

" 'What tools are you talking about?'

" 'Why, of course the tools you used in cutting out when you were in here before.'

" 'I never was here before; and my name is not Debar, either.'

" 'Oh! ah! I see how it is—the insane dodge this time. But look here, old fel', that's too thin—I should advise you to invent something better.'

"I was glad when the uncouth blacksmith took his leave, but sorry to know that he would make another witness to identify me as the real Debar.

"One morning, while I was endeavoring to amuse myself by watching the strange maneuvers of the spider as he was weaving a new wing to his net, the jailer made his appearance at the door, and began to unlock the inner shutter. He was a rough, drunken brute, who scarcely ever came about me, and when he did, he refused to answer any of my questions; I learned afterward that the rough treatment I had been subjected to was owing to the fact that he thought me the man who had made the escape some time previous. When he had finished unlocking the door a lady came rushing into the room and threw her arms round my neck, exclaiming, as she burst into tears:

" 'Oh, Eddie, why did you let them catch you again? I thought you were safe in Mexico by this time!'

"The jailer had immediately slammed the door to and locked it, leaving us alone. I was paralyzed with astonishment, and unable to utter a word for several seconds. As soon, however, as I recovered my self-possession, I pushed her away rather roughly.

" 'Madame,' I exclaimed indignantly, 'you are laboring under a grave mistake. I am not your husband—have not been married—and I never saw you in my life until this moment!'

"She drew back, gazed at me for a moment in a bewildered way, then uttering a most pitiful wail, fell fainting on the floor. I threw some water in her face, and did all I could to revive her, and was gratified to see signs of recovery. She was a very beautiful woman, though her face was quite pale. Her long, black hair came loose and fell in great masses on the floor. Directly she was able to rise, and I saw that she was very much embarrassed. She again fixed her eye intently on me, and appeared to be undecided as to what should be said.

" 'I hope you will pardon me, sir, but you are very like my husband; and then they told me that he was re-arrested, and in this room. I should have known you were not my husband if I had met you in the light, but when I entered this dark cell I could scarcely see my hand before me. I declare, I never have seen two persons so much alike, though you are a little taller than he, I think; and there is a difference in the voice, and perhaps a slight difference in the color of the hair, yours being a shade darker than my husband's. I am

truly sorry, sir, to know that you have been compelled to
suffer so for a crime you did not commit, but I rejoice to find
that my dear husband has not been retaken. He is innocent,
but was unable to prove his innocence. Public sentiment ran
high against him, and he was forced to save his life by
flight.'

" 'My dear madame,' said I, 'you will not hesitate a moment, I hope, in informing the sheriff that he is holding the
wrong man in custody. I have suffered indescribable torture
since my detention here, and I fear that serious consequences
have resulted from my imprisonment.'

" 'Indeed, sir, you shall not remain here another day if
anything I can say or do will secure your release. I will go
immediately to the proper officers and tell them of the great
mistake they have made.'

"She then called the jailer and requested to be allowed to
come out."

"Stop a moment, Dr. Demar," said Mr. Peniwinkle, rising
with his hat in his hand, and bowing low before him and
Queen Mary, "I cannot wait any longer; I most humbly beg
your pardon for the indignity that we have unwittingly offered you. We have been following you for the last ten days,
believing you to be Edward Debar—but I now see what an
unfortunate mistake we have made. While we have been
watching you, we have let the real criminal get away. We
had traced Debar to Memphis, and found where he had his
wife concealed, and have been thrown off his track by the
great resemblance you bear to him. Indeed, the resemblance
must be very striking to have misled us so. We have committed a most unlucky blunder, and have lost our reward.
The real criminal has escaped, and we have been so unfortunate as to offer you an unpardonable insult."

"Not at all, Mr. Peniwinkle," Ingomar replied; "you only
did what you considered right. You thought you were performing your duty as an officer, and I rather feel inclined to
applaud, instead of censuring you. It seems that other officers have fallen into the same error. Be seated, Mr. Peniwinkle, and let the matter drop; I would most willingly
grant pardon, but where no wrong has been committed, of
course there is nothing to pardon."

Mr. Peniwinkle resumed his seat, and Ingomar went on with his story.

"I must now tell you what was transpiring at Memphis while I was in jail, all of which was afterward related to me by eye-witnesses. General Calloway was at Horn Lake very early on the morning that I had promised to meet him there; so were Harry and his friend Heartsell. Ten o'clock, the hour when we had all agreed to meet, arrived, and every one was at his post but me. After waiting for me until eleven o'clock, Harry became impatient, and intimated to Heartsell that it was his opinion that I had fled.

" 'Yes,' replied Heartsell, 'and I'll bet my last cent he has carried that woman off with him.'

" 'Let him go and welcome,' said Harry; 'but I should have been glad to have had one shot at the villain's carcass before he went.'

"General Calloway made inquiries of all the citizens of the little village, hoping to hear from me, but no one had seen me. I of course had managed to get out of the village quietly without being noticed by any of the residents, as that was in accordance with General Calloway's instructions, and I suppose that the two officers who had arrested me had not told any one their business; hence I had been carried off without any one knowing anything about it. When twelve o'clock came, and still no tidings of my whereabouts had been obtained, General Calloway became restless and suspicious. Heartsell approached the general and said:

" 'I suppose it is unnecessary for us to wait here any longer. The time agreed on has passed by two hours ago. I think your friend Demar has concluded that "discretion is the better part of valor;" in plain terms, I think he has run away.'

" 'I cannot believe he has done such a cowardly act as that,' replied General Calloway; 'some serious accident, I fear, has happened to him. He took the freight train at Memphis, and he may have got hurt on the railroad. It is my duty to have this matter thoroughly investigated, and I mean to do it. I have always believed Demar to be a brave, honorable young man, and I shall not condemn him without positive proof. Of course you and your friend Wallingford had better return to Memphis, while I shall take the necessary steps to ascertain the cause of Demar's mysterious disappearance.'

"Harry and Heartsell returned to their homes. As they were leisurely riding back in their carriage, it was agreed that Heartsell should renew his suit for Lottie's hand, and that Harry was to throw the weight of his influénce with his sister to induce her to accept him. Those two rash young men were just like thousands of others who are ignorant as to the material composing a true woman's heart. They imagined that Lottie Wallingford would transfer her heart, with all its pure love, to Mr. Heartsell, and gladly consent to become his wife. But they were building a magnificent castle on a sandy foundation. They had a sad lesson to learn, which it would be well for all men to know. A woman's heart cannot be traded off and bartered round like a bolt of calico or a bale of cotton, but when it is given to a man, it is his! he may bruise it, he may break it, but he cannot transfer it at will. A man's heart is a negotiable instrument, transferable at will; but not so with a woman's. I perhaps should not say that all men's hearts are negotiable, for I know there are exceptions to that rule, but it will apply in a majority of instances.

"It was night when Heartsell and Wallingford arrived at Memphis, and the first thing they did was to go immediately to the old brick house to ascertain whether the woman was gone or not. They found the building empty. They entered and examined the rooms, and after satisfying themselves that the woman was gone, they departed.

" 'Well, Wallingford,' observed Heartsell, as they walked toward Mr. Rockland's house, 'you see I was right after all; she was undoubtedly Demar's wife, and they have fled together.'

" 'Yes, that is true, and I am glad we are rid of them. Demar was a greater rascal than I ever thought he was.'

" 'My dear fellow,' replied Heartsell, 'I never had any faith in him from the start. I always thought he was a consummate hypocrite. He assumed a pious dignity that I know was all a sham. Wasn't it fortunate for your sister that I happened to watch his movements?'

" 'Indeed it was, Heartsell; she owes you a big debt, and I dare say if love can pay it she will be glad to liquidate the obligation.'

" 'Ah! you have cause to be proud of your charming sister. Do you know that I think she is the most talented woman I ever knew?'

" 'My sister is a very sensible girl.'

" 'Indeed she is, Wallingford, and she has an angel's disposition. She is too good for me, but if pure love and devotion can make her happy, be assured she should never know sorrow.'

" 'You have heard of men counting the chickens before they were hatched, haven't you, Heartsell?'

" 'Of course I have; but what has that to do with this matter?'

" 'Suppose Lottie don't choose to see things from our standpoint? Suppose she should still put her faith in Demar?'

" 'Oh! that's not a supposable case; how could she cling to him when she learns his true character?'

" 'Well, you have my good wishes in this new enterprise, and if I can assist you, command me; but here we are at the gate—will you walk in and take tea with me?'

" 'No, not to-night, Wallingford; I'll go home now; but where can I see you early in the morning?'

" 'At my office.'

" 'Very well, I'll call early. Good-night, and pleasant dreams to you.'

"When Heartsell parted with Wallingford he sauntered toward his home whistling 'Mollie Darling,' while visions of triumph floated gaily before his imagination. Since the dreaded enemy had ingloriously fled, he thought as the victor he was entitled to the spoils; in other words, he imagined that since Demar's flight, Lottie would be glad to throw herself into his arms. He was vain enough to believe that she would be ready to thank him for the great service he had rendered and ask his pardon for having once rejected his suit.

"When Wallingford arrived at home he went immediately to his sleeping room to change his toilet before the supper bell rang. Lighting the gas and looking at his watch, he found it only lacked five minutes to eight; he hurriedly began to arrange his dress. Ten minutes had elapsed after he entered the room when he was startled by a loud scream that went ringing through the house; he ran rapidly to Lottie's boudoir.

" 'What is the matter, mother?' exclaimed Wallingford, as he appeared at the door where he saw Lottie lying insensible on a sofa, and Mrs. Rockland standing in the middle of the room wringing her hands, apparently wild with terror. 'Speak, mother! what in Heaven's name has happened?'

" 'Some terrible news must have been brought in that letter, for she still holds it crumpled up in her hand. Doctor Demar's clerk delivered it to her a few moments ago, and when she began to read it she turned deadly pale, then screamed and fainted.'

" 'Demar has eloped with another woman, and she has just now found it out!'

" 'Merciful Providence! my son, is that true?'

" 'It is certainly so; and I trust she will at once discard the hateful villain's memory from her mind.'

"While this conversation was going on Mrs. Rockland was kneeling by the sofa, bathing Lottie's pale face with eau-de-Cologne, and in a few moments evidence of returning consciousness appeared. I had explained everything in the letter, telling Lottie that if I did not return by eight o'clock she might know that I was killed, because I would communicate further news if wounded. It might appear to be an unpardonable imprudence on my part to write such a letter, but it must be remembered that I did not intend her to receive it unless I was killed. I had written my will, bequeathing my little estate to her, which was also inclosed in the letter. Lottie was not one of the sort of hysterical women who faint every time they see a worm or a spider, but she was brave, sensible, self-reliant and strong, both mentally and physically. But notwithstanding all her courage and self-possession, she was instantly overpowered by the contents of the letter. As soon as she was able to sit up, Harry attempted to take hold of her hand, when she drew back with a convulsive shudder, at the same time uttering a suppressed scream. Then she cast on her brother such a gaze as to chill the blood in his veins—it was a mixture of horror, scorn, contempt and pity.

" 'Touch me not, I beg you; that hand is red with a hero's blood, and Cain's mark is on your brow. You have murdered the noblest, the kindest, the best man that ever called you friend! Oh! my unhappy, rash, inconsiderate brother, pray on your knees until the "crack of doom" and maybe God will pardon you. How could you be so cruel as to shed the blood of a noble big heart whose every throb was in friendship for you? Had you lost sight of the fact that I owed my life to the poor victim whose blood you wantonly shed? How could you face our mother in Heaven, with Eddie's blood dripping from your murderous hand? If you were to touch me with that bloody hand of yours, it would kill me in five minutes. Did you hate Edward because he was noble, generous and good? Did you envy his gentle disposition, his even temper and greatness of soul? Oh! blessed Redeemer, have mercy on my unfortunate, rash brother, forgive this awful crime and humble his haughty soul.'

" 'Lottie, I swear by the heavens and all the saints that never have I shed one drop of Ed Demar's blood; he is a hypocritical villain who has betrayed and deceived you; he has eloped with another woman.'

" 'Harry, don't slander the dead, I beseech you; that would aggravate the awful crime you have committed. Shame! shame on you! Why not kill me quickly as you did Edward, instead of torturing me to death? Why not shed my blood while your hand is in? I have no desire to live any longer in this wicked, cruel world. Why should such as I be permitted to live in the world, when you have hurled my Eddie into a bloody grave? Why not kill me, too?'

" 'Sister Lottie, I most solemnly declare by everything sacred that I have not seen Edward Demar since he left the city yesterday; it is true I challenged him, and he agreed to meet me at Horn Lake to-day at ten o'clock, but instead of keeping his appointment, he has run away with a woman that he brought from Philadelphia.'

" 'Edward told me in his letter that you had forced him into a duel, and that he would be here by eight o'clock if he was not killed; and in that letter was his will leaving his estate to me—how then can you tell me he has run away? You and Heartsell have killed him, and in order to conceal your crime you have invented this falsehood! You may go dig my grave, for there is a sweet spirit calling me to Heaven, and I shall soon go to meet the noblest soul that was ever dismissed from the body by the red hand of murder."

" 'I will bring Mr. Heartsell here, sister, who will tell you what I say is true.'

" 'Do not mention that man's name in my presence, for he is more guilty than you, because he has made a dupe of you to destroy Edward. I have tried Edward Demar in adversity, as well as prosperity, and if a legion of such men as Heartsell were to tell me he had proved false, I would not believe it !'

"Lottie then broke completely down, and would have fallen to the floor, but Mrs. Rockland caught her in time to prevent it.

" 'You may put me to bed, mother, I cannot fight it off any longer; I thought I was very strong and brave, but this blow is too much for me. All will soon be over with me, my dear good mother—I feel it very plainly; and when I am dead, I want you to have me buried by the side of Eddie, if his body is ever found. They killed him for loving me, and the blow has killed me, too; poor Viola! tell her I shall expect to meet her in Heaven, where wicked people cannot molest or make us afraid.'

"Mrs. Rockland then attempted to lead Lottie to her bedroom, but was unable to do it, for she fell completely helpless on her mother's bosom. Harry then stepped forward and attempted to take his sister in his arms, when she began to tremble violently, uttering a loud scream.

" 'Oh, mother, please do not let him touch me with those bloody hands; make him go away !'

"Then she hid her face on her mother's bosom, while horrible convulsions shook her body.

" 'Look there, mother.' she exclaimed, as she glared with dilated eyes at her brother, 'do you see that bloody stain on his brow? That is blood from poor Edward's heart; drive the cruel murderer away !'

" 'Leave us for the present, my son,' whispered Mrs. Rockland, 'she is going mad, I do believe !'

"Harry rushed from the room, frantic with grief, and tortured by an accusing conscience, and began to pace hurriedly through the garden, while a horrible fear that he had really driven his sister mad seized upon him.

Mrs. Rockland called in the servants, who assisted her to carry Lottie to her bedroom; then a messenger was sent after Doctor Dodson, who arrived at nine o'clock. When he entered the room he found the patient in a state of total unconsciousness, and a burning fever had set in, while the eyes had a wild, lusterless appearance. Every now and then her body would tremble violently for a moment, and be seized with severe convulsions, lasting from ten to fifteen seconds; then the nerves would relax, and she would remain quiet until another trembling fit would come on. The convulsions continued until after midnight, and when they ceased, the doctor was compelled to resort to strong stimulants in order to revive his patient. The kind-hearted old physician was too well posted in regard to the science of his profession, and the mysterious influence which the mind exercises over the nerves, not to know that Lottie's illness was the result of mental distress.

" 'Ah, ha! here we come, madame,' he exclaimed, as soon as he became convinced that his patient was not going to be tortured by any more convulsions. 'What has happened to Lottie? Ah, ha! yes, what has happened?'

"Mrs. Rockland, with tremulous voice, proceeded to give a detailed history of everything that had occurred, while tears streamed from her eyes.

" 'Ah, ha! I see how it is. Oh, that rash boy! I wonder if he has been so cruel as to hurt Edward?'

"He called on Heaven to witness the truth of his assertion that he had never drawn one drop of Edward's blood; declared that he had not seen him since day before yesterday. I believe he told the truth, for, with all his faults, he would not tell a lie; never has that rash boy uttered a falsehood in my presence, nor has he ever in any manner attempted to deceive me. He affirms that Edward has eloped with a woman that he brought from Philadelphia.'

"'Ah, ha! that is a pretty story indeed! I say, eloped with another woman! ah, ha! when he was heels over head in love with Lottie? Now if Harry Wallingford can snatch the sun from its fiery chariot as it spans the sky and put it in his pocket, and convert light into darkness, then may he expect to make me believe that my boy is a villain. Ah, ha! don't you see? My noble boy was the very soul of honor, the paragon of men, the embodiment of truth, and a stranger to deception. Ah, ha! you see how it is yourself, my dear madame; some intriguing villain is at the bottom of this business, and a horrible suspicion tells me that Harry has been led into a trap. Ah, ha! yes, he has suffered himself to be used as a tool by some scheming rascal who wanted to get rid of my boy! It is Heartsell or Bowles, perhaps both. Ah, ha! don't you see? I will ransack the globe, and plow every sea, and skim every ocean, but I will find my brave, noble boy! If they have killed him, they had better get on the other side of the world without delay, else I will increase the population of hell with their souls. Ah, ha! don't you see?"

"'How is my sister now, doctor?' said Harry, as he met the old physician on the veranda at two o'clock.

"'Bad enough. Ah, ha! bad enough, my boy; brain fever—serious attack—dangerous disease—life in great peril; bad business this—another bright angel added to the Heavenly band. Ah, ha! don't you see how it is, my boy? The world loses, Heaven wins; bright young life foolishly extinguished; had rather die myself; will save her if possible, but don't believe it possible. You hear people talk about broken hearts, ah, ha? that is a mistake—hearts never break; the brain may be broken; then the soul becomes alarmed and deserts the body. Lottie's brain is injured—that affects the nerves; ah, ha! don't you see? Then convulsions ensue, which worries the circulation, and a general collapse of the whole system follows; final result, death or insanity. Ah, ha! yes, death winds up the show in a majority of such cases.

Poor girl! she loved Edward very dearly, and he was devoted to her.'

" 'In that respect,' replied Harry, 'I am sorry to inform you that you are very much mistaken; Edward Demar did not love my sister. The fact that he was a double-faced hypocrite and faithless traitor has been proved beyond the possibility of a doubt. I was foolish enough to believe he was an honorable man who loved my sister truly, but he has betrayed her and eloped with another woman.'

" 'Ah, ha! look up there, my boy,' exclaimed the doctor, as he pointed heavenward; 'do you see that bright star yonder, just to the left of the moon?'

" 'Yes, certainly I do; but what of that?'

" 'Do you notice how near it appears to the branches of that elm tree? it seems to be within three feet of that large limb; ah, ha! do you see it, my boy?'

" 'Yes, very true; it looks as if it were fastened among the branches of that tree.'

" 'Ah, ha! yes, very good, my boy; will you be so kind as to step up on top of that tree, pluck that beautiful bright star from its place in the sky, and bring it to me?'

"Harry began to stare at the doctor with feelings of anger and astonishment.

" 'This is no time to crack jokes, Doctor Dodson, and I am grieved to be compelled to remind you of it.'

" 'Joking, ah, ha! who is joking? I never was in deeper earnest in my life; why do you refuse to do such a trifling favor for me? I want a pretty planet snatched from the heavens, and you will not do it for me.'

" 'Doctor, I confess your language astonishes me; I have ever had a high regard for your opinion, and would make any sacrifice to serve you, but when you ask me to do absurd impossibilities, you can hardly expect a serious answer.'

" 'Ah, ha! you tell me that you cannot snatch that star from the sky, yet you try to make me believe that Edward Demar has eloped with another woman. Whenever I see you take that planet in your hand and lay it down at my feet, then you may try to convince me that my boy was dishonest. Ah, ha! yes, you see how it is yourself, don't you?

Did you ever hear of a certain monkey who raked the chestnuts out of the fire with the paw of an unsuspecting cat? Ah, ha! yes, of course you have; very good, then, you are the unsuspecting cat, and Heartsell is the monkey, and he has been using your paw to rake out his chestnuts. Ah, ha! to be plain, that man wanted to marry your sister; she loved my boy, and therefore Heartsell wants him out of the way; he uses you as his tool to remove his rival; ah, ha! don't you see? Heartsell has practiced a fraud of some sort on you, deceived you, cheated you, and in all probability ruined you, and killed your sister. Ah, ha! don't you see?'

" 'Doctor Dodson,' replied Wallingford, 'I know my faults are numerous; I confess that my unfortunate temper often gets the advantage of my judgment; I may have acted too rashly in this affair, but it was my duty to guard my dear sister's honor; and when I tell you that she has been deceived by Ed Demar, I only tell you that which I know positively. With my own eyes I saw him in the arms of another woman; that woman has disappeared, so has Demar; and that he has fled with her is a fact beyond controversy.'

"At that moment Mrs. Rockland came to the door and requested the doctor to go in to his patient, informing him that she was again in convulsions.

"Harry hurried out of the house and bared his burning brow to the falling dew, while he beat his breast with his clinched fist, hoping to still the gnawing conscience that was torturing his restless soul. All through the night he continued to wander in the garden, half mad with grief, muttering to himself, while the hot blood in his veins seemed to be collecting in his fevered cheeks and heated brow. At early dawn he went in search of Heartsell, and found him sound asleep in his bedroom.

" 'Get up, Heartsell,' he said, as he hurried in, 'I must speak with you.'

" 'What's up now, old fellow; something serious, I guess, else you would not be out so early.'

" 'Ah, Heartsell, I never have passed such a night; I did not go to bed at all. My poor sister is dangerously ill; she thinks that we have murdered Demar, and the doctor is afraid she will die.'

" 'Indeed, Wallingford, that is awful news! Why should she think that we have killed Demar?'

" 'He wrote her a letter telling her all about the contemplated duel, left it with his clerk, to be delivered in the event of his not getting back by eight o'clock. In that letter he told her that if he was not killed, he would be at home at eight, and because he did not come, she concludes that we have killed him. Now, why should he write such a letter if he intended to run away?'

" 'I must confess that it is very strange.'

" 'Has it ever occurred to you that some accident might have happened to him, and that he did not absent himself willingly?'

" 'No; I never had dreamed of such a thing.'

" 'I am afraid we have been too hasty in this business. I love my darling sister as I do my life, and I begin to repent of my rashness in this matter. She refused to let me touch her, shrank from me as if I were a savage wild beast ready to tear her to pieces, cast upon me such a strange, wild look as caused the blood to freeze in my veins, and spoke of my hands being stained with Ed Demar's blood. Then all at once she broke down, and when the doctor came he said that she was threatened with brain fever, and before midnight she was unconscious.'

" 'That is very unfortunate, Wallingford, and as soon as she regains consciousness, I'll go to see her and tell her that you did nôt hurt Demar; she certainly will believe me.'

" 'If you take my advice, you will not let my sister see you, until you can prove Demar to be alive and unhurt. The manner in which she spoke of you was anything but complimentary, I can tell you. She regards you as the cause of all the trouble, accuses you of influencing me; and the truth is, Heartsell, you did persuade me into it. We have been rash and hasty in this matter, and I begin to repent of the part I have played in it. I wish I could be like other men, but my unfortunate temper won't let me. Most people think before they act, but I act first and then do the thinking when it is too late. A most horrible suspicion is crawling over me. I begin to think after all that Demar has not run away. He owns a half-interest in a drug-store here with ten thousand dollars; he made no disposition of it except to will his interest to my sister in the event of his death. He left a sealed paper with his clerk to be delivered to Lottie, and it turns out to be a will. Now, if he had been married to the other woman, why should he will his property to my sister?'

" 'Indeed, that does look a little strange; but what can we do to clear up the mystery?'

" 'Put detectives to work to find out what has become of Demar. Has it ever occurred to you that the woman might have been some relative of Demar?'

" 'No; I have never dreamed of such a thing; but why should he elope with her if she was a relation?'

" 'I don't believe he went away with her, because he took a freight train and started to Horn Lake. I believe he intended to keep his appointment with us, but met with an accident—perhaps has been murdered.'

" 'Wallingford, your language puzzles me; give me time to think.'

" 'Yes, it is very proper we should both do a little serious thinking. It is a pity we didn't do that before. Instead of acting so rashly, we should have demanded an explanation of Demar, and afforded him an opportunity to make it. I can see now the great error we committed. He might have been able to explain it all to our satisfaction, but we did not give him a chance.'

"When Harry left Heartsell, his affection for that gentleman was considerably decreased.

"Time continued to drag along very slowly, or at any rate it seemed so to Harry Wallingford. Lottie's life appeared to be gradually but surely drawing to a close. Her beautiful golden hair had commenced to come out, while the flesh appeared to shrink away. The color had fled from her cheeks, and her eyes gazed listlessly at the ceiling. She would lie immovable from day to day, never complaining, never uttering a word, except occasionally to whisper the name of Eddie. When her reason resumed its throne, she continued to ask for Eddie, and on being told that he never had been heard from, the tears would flow slowly down her cheeks.

" "They have killed Eddie; he is in Heaven, though, and

I am going to see him soon. Give me my darling's picture, mother.'

"When it was given to her she pressed it to her pale lips.

" 'You loved my poor unfortunate brother, and never would do him wrong; yet they killed you.'

"Such language was usually uttered in a low, dove-like tone, and she would continue for hours at a time conversing to the picture. When Harry would enter the room she would turn her face to the wall and shiver, as if she were very cold. When he spoke to her she would hold the corner of a quilt over her ear, as if his voice gave her pain. The doctor finally advised him not to visit his sister until the state of her mind should change.

" 'She thinks you have killed Eddie,' said Doctor Dodson to Harry, 'and so long as she clings to that idea, I think it best for you not to let her see you. Poor girl! she can't last much longer. There is only one remedy that could save her life, and I fear we shall not be able to get that in time.'

" 'What is that, doctor?' exclaimed Harry, as a new hope began to rise in his breast.

" 'If Eddie could be found, she would be all right in a week, but if not, she will be in Heaven before that time.'

" 'Oh, merciful Providence! what shall we do? Doctor Dodson, you are not going to let my darling die, are you?'

" 'Ah, ha! my dear boy, we must bow submissively to the will of God. A physician may patch up the machinery, but he can't make a human heart. That poor girl's heart is desperately wounded, and nothing on earth can cure it except a look at Eddie Demar. Present him before your sister alive and in good health, and I warrant a cure; fail to do it, and you may go dig her grave!'

" 'Oh, doctor, this is horrible; it will kill me, too, if she dies, believing I have murdered Eddie! Can't you quiet her mind with opiates until her physical strength returns?'

" 'Ah, ha! my boy, that's all you know about it; I have given her as much of that sort of medicine as her system will bear, and I tell you again, you had better find my boy, and that without delay, unless you expect to see your sister die. Ah, ha! when that poor girl dies, this world will lose one of its brightest jewels, and Heaven will receive one of the brightest angels that ever went there. Poor Viola will lose her best friend, and we will be left to mourn over crushed hopes. I should like to know what sad fate has overtaken my poor boy. He was the light of my life and the joy of my house. Ah, ha! indeed he was! Some foul play somewhere; ah, ha! my boy; mind you, though, I don't mean to scold you, Harry. ah, ha! you see I couldn't have the heart to do it. Heaven knows you have enough to bear anyway.'

" 'Yes,' replied Harry, 'it is all my fault, but I thought I was acting for the best.'

" 'No doubt you did, ah, ha! my boy, but it has turned out to be a bad job. We are all ruined unless Eddie can be found.'

" 'I'll find him, if he is on the globe, doctor!' exclaimed Wallingford, as he hastened from the room."

"We will take a recess now," said the queen, as she rose from her seat and took Ingomar's arm.

CHAPTER XXV.

IVANHOE and Miss Darlington (nicknamed Scottie) were as usual engaged in an earnest conversation, the topic being a mixture of sentiment and gossip.

"Now, sir knight," observed Miss Darlington, as she led him to a seat, "if you feel inclined to engage in a game of gossip on the old threadbare topic, we will stop here, where we will be free from spies or intruders. The fact of the business is, I believe, that another day of such intolerable suspense will unsettle my mind."

"Perhaps I can furnish you a little scrap of information that will afford temporary relief."

"Tell it then without preliminaries."

"Have you noticed a little, pale-faced lad gliding about like a half-grown ghost?"

"Indeed I have, and there is a peculiar expression on his countenance that attracted my attention; but what about him ?"

"He is the black domino's courier, spy, agent, pilot, general superintendent, or something of that sort."

"By the by, I see that same little ghostly lad yonder leaning over the banisters, just beyond the pilot house."

"Yes, that is he; I happen to know that he is serving the lady in the black domino in some of her mysterious schemes. Knowing, as I did, how much it would relieve you to obtain any clew that would unravel the unpleasant mystery by which we are surrounded, I took the liberty to play the spy myself. If I have been guilty of a mean thing (and to be candid, I think I have), you will have to answer for the sin of it, for I was prompted to it by my anxiety to gratify the curiosity of some one who was very dear to me."

"Indeed I am very grateful; but pray tell me what you have discovered?"

"I heard a conversation between the little, pale-faced boy and the lady in the black domino."

"Well, what did it amount to?"

"The lad pointed toward Napoleon, and said, 'There is your man.'

" 'How do you know that is he?' inquired the black domino impatiently.

" 'I have seen him from where I was hidden under the bed in his state-room!' replied the lad promptly; 'and,' continued the little fellow, 'I can assure you, madame, beyond all question, he is the very man you are after.'

" 'What is the number of his state-room?' inquired the black domino.

"Then the boy made an answer which I did not distinctly hear, as they both began to converse in a low, hurried tone. There is a stack of mattresses on the larboard side, and I was leaning against it, and they were on the other side. After a long, whispered conversation, they began to talk a little louder, and then I heard the boy say:

" 'I have found out all you wish to know about Napoleon, and you had better act promptly.'

" 'No, not yet,' replied the black domino, 'my plans are not ripe yet; but you must keep your eye on him until I am ready.'

" 'You may depend on me to do that,' replied the lad; 'he never shall leave this boat without your consent.'

" 'You are a splendid detective, and shall be abundantly rewarded for your faithful services.'

" 'I have already been rewarded,' said the boy, 'ten times more than I deserve. I would do anything to please you!'

" 'I thank my little friend, and mean to show my gratitude in a tangible shape one of these days. I am going to purchase a nice cottage for your mother if I ever get enough money.'

" 'You are too kind, miss; you have done more for me than I deserve; but I will serve you as long as I live. I hope you will succeed in bringing that bad man to punishment for his wicked crimes.'

"They then went away and I heard nothing more."

"It seems she is shadowing Napoleon."

"Yes, that is certain."

"What does it all mean?"

"Ah! that is the question I should like to have explained."

"Have you ever mentioned the subject to the little boy?"

"No."

"Call him here and let us endeavor to pump the secret out of him."

"Come here a moment, little man, if you please."

The lad promptly approached and fixed his large, restless eyes on Ivanhoe with a look of inquiry.

"What is your name, my little friend?"

"Spratt, sir."

"Where do you reside?"

"I have no home at present, sir."

"Did you get on board this boat at Memphis?"

"No, sir."

"Where did you get on?"

"At Friar's Point, sir."

"Where are you going to get off?"

"I do not know what point I shall stop at—that depends on circumstances."

"What circumstances?"

"If you will excuse me, sir, I had rather not tell that."

"Oh, certainly, my little friend, you need not tell anything unless it suits you. Do you know the lady in the black domino?"

"Yes, sir."

"Would you object to tell me who she is?"

"I could not do it without her consent; I think she does not want her name known just now."

"I will give you this twenty-dollar bill if you will tell me her name."

"I beg you will excuse me, sir."

"I will give you a hundred dollars if you will tell me who she is."

"I could not do it, sir, if you were to offer me a thousand dollars!"

"Does she reside in Memphis?"

"No, sir."

"Where does she reside, then?"

"I had rather not tell you that, sir."

"Do you know the man who personates Napoleon?"

"Yes, sir."

"Will you tell me who he is?"

"That is also a secret which I am not at liberty to reveal."

"Can you tell me whether or not he got on this boat at Memphis?"

"I could tell you, sir, but I must not talk about him. You will soon know all about it."

"What right had you to go into that gentleman's state-room and conceal yourself under his bed?"

"How did you know I did that, sir?"

"I heard you tell the lady in the black domino about it."

"I hope, sir, you did not play the eavesdropper?"

"No; but you and the lady talked about the matter where I could not help hearing it."

"I hope, sir, that you will not say anything about what you heard, because if you do you will be sorry for it when you know what caused me to go into his room."

"You have been watching Napoleon by the lady's directions—is that not the way of it?"

"Since you have made the discovery, it is useless for me to deny it; but, sir, I beg you to say nothing about it."

"How long do you want me to keep the secret?"

"But a very short time, sir. That man who represents the emperor is a very grand villain, and if you were to reveal what you know, it might upset all the plans we have been arranging to capture him."

"Why not capture him now?"

"The lady in the black domino is waiting for something to happen which I am not permitted to tell."

"Very well, my little friend, I promise you I will not reveal your secret."

"I am very much obliged to you, sir, and you shall know all about the matter very soon. I will go now, sir, if you have nothing more to say to me."

As the little fellow bowed politely and moved away, Scottie heaved a sigh and said:

"Heigh ho! was anybody ever so inundated with mystery as we are?"

"If they were, I should pity them."

"I must say that is a very polite, manly little fellow; and that head of his is full of brains."

"Yes, and he has been playing a very deep game, if I am not very much mistaken."

"What in Heaven's name does it all mean?"

"I would give my bottom dollar to be able to answer the question."

"Let us try and pump the secret out of Brazzleman—I dare say he knows all about it."

"I have been trying to get him to tell me who the lady is, but he positively refuses to do it—in fact, I do not believe he, or the captain either, knows who she is."

"Look yonder, will you—that mysterious woman has been watching us all the time. She is going to that boy to find out what we have been saying to him. I declare, this is really provoking; and I am not willing to submit to it any longer!"

"Can you suggest any plan to get rid of the nonsense?"

"Suppose we complain to Captain Quitman?"

"I should not like to do that, after making a promise to the lad to keep his secret."

"How would it do to cross-examine Napoleon on the subject?"

"That would be the most imprudent step we could take, for it appears that the black domino has got him spotted. I think we should not say anything to any one about what we know until something more is developed."

"See yonder; she is leading that boy to her state-room. Mischief is brewing, and a culmination will be reached soon."

"Well, let matters jog along; come down and dance a set—- I hear the music."

"I have no objection—in fact, I am glad you proposed it, as I think the dance will take my mind from this unpleasant subject. I have often heard of people suffering with curiosity, but never till now did I know how one could be so much excited."

Ivanhoe then led Scottie down to the saloon, and soon was gliding round in a lively waltz with her fair cheek resting on his shoulder. George was looking supremely happy, as he waltzed with the queen of Sheba. A dozen other couples were enjoying themselves, while keeping time to the splendid music.

"Come," said Ivanhoe, as soon as the waltz was ended, "let us go back on deck, as I have thought of something else to tell you."

"I hope you are not going to harp on the same string?"

"That is exactly what I am going to do; but I have something new to tell you. Just a moment before we began to waltz, George told me that the whole secret was divulged."

"What secret?"

"The mystery about the black domino."

"Well, what does it amount to?"

"She is a confidence woman—a female pickpocket—an expert thief, and that lad is her pal."

"Now, I do not believe a word of that story, for she has been weeping frequently. Confidence women do not shed tears—pickpockets do not act like that woman."

"I shall venture no opinion, so far as I am concerned. George says that she has stolen a large sum of money from Napoleon, and that the boy helped her do it."

"If that is true, why do they not arrest her at once?"

"They have not got sufficient proof to justify that course yet, though they think they will be able to do it very soon."

"If I live a hundred years, I never will wear another mask, or associate with others who do. I am very sure that we would have enjoyed our excursion much better if we had not appeared in mask."

"I agree with you there—these masquerades are only suited to furnish opportunities for thieves to ply their trades."

"As soon as Ingomar finishes his story (and I hope he will not stop a moment until he is through with it), we will put an end to this nonsense."

"I will go and request the queen to re-assemble her party at once, so that we may hear the remainder of the tale without further delay."

"I wish you would."

Ivanhoe then went to look for the queen, who issued her orders for the party to meet immediately. A majority of the passengers came up with Ingomar and the queen, as they were becoming deeply interested in the story. The maskers all being seated, the queen directed Ingomar to resume.

"I was very much disappointed when Mrs. Debar returned to my cell and informed me that the civil authorities refused to believe her when she informed them that I was not her husband—they thought it was a ruse invented by her to get her husband out of prison; but she was kind enough to bring a lawyer to see me on the subject. Mr. Deediddle was a middle-aged man, with a very red nose and a ponderous stomach, evidently a devout worshiper of Bacchus. I don't think I ever before saw such a red nose on a man's face. He was a perfect talking machine; and I was rather distrustful of him, but he assured me that there would be no difficulty in securing my release.

"'Fact is, Mr. Demar, I'm an old hand at the pump—no cure no pay, is my motto,' said Mr. Deediddle, as he wiped the perspiration from his brow with a red handkerchief of enormous size. 'Fact, Mr. Demar, I have walked in the legal harness for twenty years; what I don't know about law ain't printed yet. Fact, Mr. Demar—never lost half a dozen cases in my life. Fact, sir, and when you get me on a *Habeas Corpus,* I can beat the inventor of the writ. Ah, sir, that's a glorious writ. Fact, sir, it's the paladium of liberty—it's the Alpha and Omega of American freedom. Fact, sir, I'll pry you out of this horrible place, sir, with this great lever of the law—this center pole of the prisoner's castle of hope. Fact is, Judge Flaxback always yields to me—he is very fond of whist, and I always let him win, then he returns the favor when making decisions. Fact, sir, he never decides against me—he always stops with me during court—he loves good wine—I always keep the very best. Fact, sir, I keep him full; but business is business, you know, Mr. Demar—no cure no pay. I believe I told you that was my motto—yes, sure enough I did; but a retainer, you know, is always customary —a small retainer—say fifty dollars. Fact is, Mr. Demar, business is business, you know.'

"I gave him fifty dollars as quickly as I could, and would have given him double that sum, if he had demanded it.

"'For Heaven's sake, Mr. Deediddle,' said I, 'get me out of this miserable place, and you shall be well paid.'

"'Fact is, sir, you shall be out before to-morrow night. Judge Flaxback is to be in town this very day, and I'll have a *Habeas Corpus* served on the sheriff immediately.'

"I was glad when he went away; it was but a short while before he returned, accompanied by the circuit court clerk, who came to administer the oath, that I had to make in order to procure the writ. I made the oath, and again was left alone, when bright rays of hope began to steal in on me. I laid myself down on my hard bed, and began to gaze at Lottie's picture; my mind was so intensely fixed on the dear image that I did not hear the jailer when he opened the door.

"'Thanks be to Heaven, Eddie, I have found you at last!' exclaimed Harry Wallingford, as he sank down by my side and burst into tears. 'I am the vilest wretch that ever disgraced the face of this green earth. I have spread misery and ruin around all who loved me. I have broken Lottie's heart, and she is dying. Doctor Dodson says she cannot live three days longer. Why was I ever created? I dare not ask you to forgive me! If remorse could kill, I would have been dead long ago—there is a flaming fire consuming my vitals— yet it will not kill me. Lottie will die with a curse on her lips against me, for she believes I have murdered you, and it will be too late to undeceive her, for she is failing fast. I have killed the sweetest sister that mortal man ever had. Eddie, I would give the world, if it was all mine, to recall the past—if I could only atone for the crimes that I have committed. Poor Viola has been tried and convicted, while Lottie was too ill to know anything about it. They have kept the awful news from her, but she soon will leave this wicked world.'

"He then sank helplessly on the floor and groaned aloud. I could only stare at the unhappy boy whose rashness had caused all this misery. I felt no enmity toward him. I pitied him from the very bottom of my heart. I remembered how he had loved Viola, and how he must have suffered on her account. Then I thought of his love for Lottie, and knew that the errors he had committed were caused by his love for his sister. As soon as I could sufficiently command my feelings to enable me to talk, I began to do what I could to console him.

" 'There is no reason why you should feel remorse at all; grief comes natural under such circumstances; remorse is the pain produced by a consciousness of guilt; guilt cannot exist where there has been no willful intent. The mistakes you have committed were errors of judgment, not of the heart. It is the intent that constitutes the crime. You were prompted to act by love for your sister, and I feel more inclined to approve than to condemn you. I have always loved you—I love you yet; and if Lottie could live, we would all be happy again. Rise up, I pray you; let us forget the past, and work together to repair the errors committed. I promise you that, so far as my feelings are concerned, no ill-will ever shall find lodgment in my poor heart against you.'

" 'Eddie, you are different from all other men. Your heart is more noble, more generous and more forgiving than others', it is a knowledge of that fact that makes my conscience condemn me. You should have cut my unworthy head off when I gave you that insulting blow. If you knew how my conscience gnaws and burns me for that mean, despicable act, you would indeed pity me!'

" 'You should not feel so about that, because you thought I had betrayed your sister, and it is a brother's duty to protect the honor of his sister. The truth is, I think under the

same circumstances I should have acted as you did. From
what I heard, Mr. Debar resembles me so much that it requires close inspection to tell one from the other. Now,
you saw Debar with his wife in Memphis, and mistook him
for me. You naturally concluded that I had deceived and
betrayed your sister. Believing that to be so, you determined to punish her betrayer. Harry, I admire you for it;
don't ask me to forgive you, for there is nothing to be forgiven.'

"'Yes, but for my rashness, coupled with my unpleasant
temper, all the trouble might have been avoided. You could
have explained everything, but I did not give you a chance.
There is where I committed the unpardonable error that has
ruined all of us.'

"'I hope that things are not so bad as you seem to
think. We must act now, and that promptly. A dispatch
must be sent to Doctor Dodson without delay; and if you
will go and procure a messenger to take it to the nearest
telegraph office, I will write the dispatch while you are getting the messenger ready. See that he is well mounted, on
a good horse, for he must make at least eight miles per hour;
it is twenty-four miles from here to the nearest telegraph
office. Tell the messenger that he shall have as much money
as he wants, if he will make speed. Go quickly—make the
necessary arrangements while I write the dispatch.'

"He hurried from the jail instantly, while I penned the
following message:

"'DOCTOR DODSON—Tell dear Lottie I am well and safe; will
be home day after to-morrow. Harry is with me, and everything
is explained. A man resembling me very much killed Clanton;
he was imprisoned to await his trial—he escaped—I was arrested
and detained, under a mistaken belief that I was the criminal.
It is a mere mistake of personal identity. The real criminal was
in Memphis. Harry saw him there with his wife, and thought
it was I—hence his enmity toward me. It was all a mistake:
everything is now understood. I will be released to-morrow on
habeas corpus. Save dear Lottie's life. Tell her to live for my
sake. Send me a dispatch every ten minutes till I come.'

"By the time the dispatch was ready Harry returned, accompanied by an intelligent looking lad about eighteen years
old, who promised to be at the telegraph office with the dis-

patch inside of three hours. I handed him fifty dollars, and directed him to wait at the office for an answer.

" 'Leave your horse at the station, and procure a fresh one, and when the answer comes, bring it to me immediately. I shall want you to carry another dispatch as soon as you bring the answer to this one. I will pay all the expenses and remunerate you to your entire satisfaction; then I will give you as a present this fine gold watch.'

"The lad's bright black eyes fairly blazed with delight as I held up the pretty prize before him.

" 'You may trust me, sir; I'll deliver this dispatch in two hours and a half from this moment.'

"Before the last word was out of his mouth, he was half way down-stairs, and two seconds afterward I heard the clatter of his horse's hoofs as he dashed down the road. I stood and listened until the sound grew faint, then died away.

" 'Eddie,' said Harry, 'if God only would let dear Lottie live, I would spend the remainder of my life on my knees, pouring out earnest thanks to Him. I would discard pride and self-love, and endeavor to control this unfortunate temper of mine, and devote my days to His service.'

" 'I am so glad to hear you talk that way; maybe God will think of your good resolve, and reward it by saving her life. Somehow, I have a hope that we shall hear favorable news when our messenger returns—I cannot think that I am never again to behold those beautiful blue eyes; I can't realize it. The ways of Providence are full of mystery, but we know they are ever just; and knowing this to be so induces me to cling to the hope that our Lottie will be spared. It is my candid opinion that if she had been well Viola would have been cleared, because she was in possession of strange facts, in connection with the case, which would have produced a different verdict.'

" 'Ah! my poor sister may have believed in Viola's innocence, in fact, I know she did; but that belief was founded on friendship instead of facts. No, the proof was full and complete, and Mr. Rockland told me that during his thirty years' practice he had never known the guilt of a prisoner so fully established. You no doubt imagine that you have suffered much, but your cause of sorrow is very slight when compared with mine. If poor Lottie dies, the loss will be as much mine as yours; for you cannot love her more than I do; and when she leaves us she will go direct to Heaven, where you can go to meet her. But how different is it with Viola; I loved her as well as you loved Lottie; no man ever loved a woman more devotedly than I loved her. I might have borne to see her die, if she was as well prepared to meet God as Lottie is; but when I know that she is forever lost to me, and perhaps her soul is lost, too, I feel and know that I cannot bear it!'

" 'The pardoning power of God is unlimited; Christ did not die for righteous people alone, but to redeem sinners; and if you will have faith in Him, and serve Him with all your heart, you may be permitted to meet Viola in Heaven after all. But here comes Mr. Deediddle to talk about the *habeas corpus.* Let us hear what he has to communicate.'

"Mr. Deediddle came blustering in, and it was with some difficulty that he squeezed his ponderous body through the small door of my cell.

" 'Ah! confound such small doors!' he muttered, as he began to brush the dust off his coat with his red bandana. 'I can't see why people make such small doors, anyway. Well, Demar, I dropped in merely to let you know that we are all right—Judge Flaxback has made the *habeas corpus* returnable at nine o'clock to-morrow morning; he is to spend the night with me. Fact, sir, here's his note accepting my invitation. I'll wine him, dine him, and card him to-night. I'll play whist with him all night, and let him win; that will settle our case all right; fact, sir, trust me to manage his sort.'

" 'But, Mr. Deediddle, I would prefer that no underhand means should be used in my case. I can prove my identity beyond all doubt.'

" 'Oh! no doubt you can, Mr. Demar, but what good will proof do when the mind of the court is against you Fact, sir, you had better let me manage the case in my own way. Fact is, I am an old hand at the pump; been in harness over a quarter of a century; I am the man to pry you out—wine and whist are the great levers to pry with before Flaxback. Fact is, he can't get round 'em.'

"Mr. Deediddle rattled away for nearly an hour, and I was glad when he took his departure. He had been gone but a few minutes when Mrs. Debar came in. Harry gazed at her in great astonishment for several seconds, then said:

" 'Eddie, this is the lady I saw in Memphis, in that old brick house, and I thought I saw you there with her.'

" 'It was my husband, sir, and not Mr. Demar. We were stopping in an old dilapidated brick house; my husband was waiting for some money to be sent to him. He made his escape from this jail and went to Memphis; I followed him, and one night we fled, as we learned that detectives were following us. I have just received a letter from my husband; he is in Matamoras, Mexico, and I am going to meet him as soon as Mr. Demar is released.'

" 'I see through it all now—you and your husband left Memphis on the very night when Demar was arrested at Horn Lake; this unlucky coincidence led me to believe that he had eloped with you, and had been false to my sister. Acting on this belief, I have committed an unpardonable blunder, and caused my sister's death and ruined all my friends.'

"As Mrs. Debar wiped the fast falling tears from her eyes, she said: 'I am truly sorry to hear of your misfortunes, but hope things are not so serious as you seem to think. I, too, have had my share of trouble; my poor husband has been compelled to exile himself from his country when he was innocent. I love him, and I mean to go where he goes; I will share his sorrows, and do my best to make him happy. It is true that my husband killed Mr. Clanton, but he did it in self-defense, and would have been able to prove it, but unfortunately, the only witness who saw the whole transaction died soon after the killing.'

"Mrs. Debar now went away, leaving me alone with Harry. She promised to be present on the next morning at the trial, to give her evidence, which would, of course, be greatly in my favor.

"It was after night, and just six hours from the time my messenger had started with my dispatch, when he came dashing into my cell with an answer. He had made the round trip, a distance of forty-eight miles, in six hours. He informed me that he had to wait at the office just one hour for the answer, so he had done the traveling in five hours.

"My hand trembled when I took the dispatch from the messenger, and well it might, for I knew that little paper would tell a tale that would seal my fate. It would tell me whether or not those charming blue eyes were ever again to gaze on me. It would decide whether or not I was ever to clasp dear Lottie to my heart again. I hesitated, and looked at Harry, but saw no encouragement there. He was as pale as death, and trembling from head to foot, and seemed to have ceased to breathe.

"'Eddie,' he gasped, 'you may be prepared to hear the very worst, for her case was hopeless when I left home. That telegram will either tell you she is dead, or that she is dying.'

"'Heaven have mercy!' I exclaimed, as I glanced over the contents of the dispatch. My worst fears were realized—my darling was dying.

"It is useless for me to try to describe how I felt when I read the fatal news. No one can understand or appreciate it even if I could select words to tell how great was my misery. It was over half an hour before either of us spoke, and there is no telling when the silence would have been broken, had it not been for the messenger.

"'Will you wish to send another dispatch?' inquired the lad, who had been silently witnessing this painful scene. 'If you do, sir, I can be ready to go again as soon as I can eat a bite and procure a fresh horse.'

"'I shall want to send another dispatch at daylight in the morning.'

"My audience will readily understand what cause for grief I had when the dispatch is read. Here it is,

"'DEAR EDDIE—The welcome news of your safety received, would to Heaven it had come a week sooner—it would have saved our dear Lottie's life; but, alas! it came too late. Put your trust in God, my unfortunate boy, and bear your great sorrow as becomes a brave man. Lottie cannot possibly live more than forty-eight hours longer. She is sinking very fast. Her mind is perfectly clear, and when your dispatch was read to her she smiled sweetly as her eyes brightened up, then closing them, the tears began to stream from them. She pressed your picture to her lips, and said:

" ' "Poor Eddie, how glad I would be to see him before I die! Then I wish to see brother Harry, so he can forgive the wrong I have done him. I thought he had killed Eddie, and refused to believe him when he denied it."

" 'She talks of you and Harry all the time. I wish it were so that you could get here before she dies. You might do it, if you get released in time for the up-train to-morrow evening. I will send another dispatch early in the morning.

" 'DODSON.'

"I had sent up so many silent but earnest prayers to God, in which I had implored and begged Him to let my dear Lottie live, that I was loth to believe He would take her from me. I could not realize the fact that her beautiful young person was to be consigned to the grave. When I had seen her last she was the very picture of health and life, her fair cheeks all aglow with vivacity, her large expressive eyes filled with evidences of hope, and her elastic step indicating strength and vigor. Now how was I to realize the fact that all this strength, health and vigor were gone, while that fair form was struggling in the very arms of death? The fact is, I was so bewildered with grief that I was unable to think correctly on the subject.

"Harry spent the night in my cell, and I can assert truthfully that he was more completely subdued by his deep grief than he ever had been before. I think that a great change was wrought in him on that occasion, which has since proved of no little benefit to him. His indomitable pride was partially cured, and his haughty spirit completely humbled; he threw himself prostrate on the floor, calling aloud to God for help. He did not rise from the floor during the night, though he never closed his eyes in sleep; sometimes he would remain silent for several minutes—perhaps he was praying; then again he would seem to be convulsed with his great sorrow. I paced the floor in silence, for I was sunk so deep in despair that I was scarcely able to command my voice. My heart yearned for freedom; my mind flew to Memphis and looked at my darling as she was wrestling with death.

"The first gray streaks of approaching dawn that came

stealing through my small window were indeed a welcome
sight to me. As soon as it was light enough to enable me to
see to write, I penned a message to be immediately sent to
Doctor Dodson. The messenger was promptly on hand at
six o'clock, ready with a fresh horse to start with my dispatch,
and long before the sun began to peep over the eastern hills
he was dashing with great speed toward the telegraph office.
He would be back with fresh news by eleven o'clock, by which
time I had reason to believe I would be restored to liberty,
and then I would fly to my darling. After the messenger
was gone I instructed Harry to go out to the village and secure two of the best horses that could be found, and to have
them ready saddled and hitched in the court-house yard, in
order that we might be off instantly after the trial should be
over. I knew that the trial would not consume much time,
as the proof would be ample and unquestionable, and I
thought maybe we might be able to start by ten o'clock.

"The rough blacksmith who had riveted the irons on my
leg was employed the evening before the trial to cut them off,
and I was enabled to secure a little exercise. In his rough,
uncouth manner, the blacksmith apologized for the unkind-
ness he had shown toward me when fastening the manacles
on my limbs. As I was not in a mood to cherish ill-will, I
accepted the blunt apology and extended my hand to the
honest mechanic, who seized and gave it a hearty shake.

" 'Never saw two peas more alike than you and Debar!
No wonder the officer took you for Debar; I was ready to
swear that you were the identical man. It's lucky they found
out the blunder, ain't it? They might have hung you by
mistake; that would have been rather awkward, wouldn't it?'

"I made no answer to this strange inquiry, for I was
thinking about other things.

"Harry returned soon, and informed me that he had been
so fortunate as to secure two splendid young horses, whose
owner had informed him that they could take us to the
station in two hours and a half, without any danger of hurting them. My dungeon door was now thrown open, and all
restraint on my movements withdrawn.

" 'I thought you were the same scamp who broke jail and
left me with the bag to hold,' said the jailer. 'Everybody

was down on me for letting Debar get away when I couldn't
help it—some rascal furnished him with tools, and I knew
nothing about it until he was gone; therefore, when they
brought you here I thought you were the same man, and I
didn't care to be kind to the man who had acted so badly as
Debar. You are the very image of Debar, and then your
name sounds so much like his. I can detect a slight difference in the color of your hair and that of Debar; then he
had a small scar on his forehead, just above the left eye. It
was very slight, and quite small, not over half an inch long.
I have his photograph here, and if you will look close you
can see the scar very plain.'

"I looked at the picture, and sure enough the scar could be
plainly seen. This circumstance of itself would justify Judge
Flaxback in ordering my release; in fact, the trial would be
a mere form to be complied with, as everybody now admitted
that a mistake had been committed. The villagers discussed
it on the street corners, and laughed over it, cracking their
jokes, little dreaming of the awful consequences that had
resulted to me by the mistake. I dare say that a vastly different feeling would have permeated the breasts of those people if they could have witnessed the dying agonies of poor
Lottie Wallingford. If they had known how my heart was
broken by the sad mistake, they would not have been laughing and joking about the matter as if it were a very funny
coincidence. I could not eat my breakfast—my appetite was
gone, but I drank a cup of warm tea, which the jailer's wife
was kind enough to bring to me. She seemed to sympathize
with me when she found out how deeply I had been wronged.
I looked at my watch every five minutes; I was full of impatience. It seemed that nine o'clock would never come—but
nevertheless it did come at last. The town clock began to
strike, when the jailer said it was time to go."

CHAPTER XXVI.

DURING the short recess the queen had agreed to allow,
which was granted at the request of the Barbarian Chief, the
excursionists assembled in various little groups on different

parts of the boat, while most of them were discussing the merits of Ingomar's story. George and the Duke of Wellington were seated apart from the other passengers, deeply interested in an animated discussion—the subject being the eccentric movements of the black domino and the unusual sadness of the queen.

"My lord," observed the king, "did you notice that the queen fainted when those two men arrested Demar?"

"Of course I did! and that is not all—the lady in the black domino fainted, too, when the Barbarian Chief was arrested."

"Now, I would like very much to know who this Barbarian Chief is, and why both of those women should manage to faint about him. I have never been so fortunate as to have as much as one woman care enough about me to faint for me."

"As to that, I am decidedly of the opinion that you have lost nothing on that score; but, between you and me, there is something mysterious connected with that woman in the black domino. So far as the queen is concerned, I imagine that she is one of those good-hearted, sympathetic women, the kind who have more tears than talent—a sort of Niobe."

"Look at that man yonder leaning against the corner of the Texas, and see if you can discover anything singular about him."

"Why, that is Henry of Navarre; of course there is nothing strange about him. Why do you ask the question?"

"He is not the man who wore that uniform when we started from Memphis."

"Why do you conclude that he is not the one who personated Navarre at the ball?"

"He is not quite so tall, but has a more dignified carriage; and then he does not mingle with us, or participate in any of our amusements, as the real Navarre did. The original Napoleon has also slipped out of his costume, and a counterfeit has slipped in; and the strangest part of the mystery is that no one knows what has become of the parties who originally personated Navarre and Napoleon. Now if this is done in order to enable those men to play a little joke on the ladies, there is no harm in it, but I suspect that some sort of mischief is afloat. I guess it will appear in the wind-up that

these two men, and the black domino, are in some way interested in each other; and you may be sure, if they are, that it
will produce mischief."

"The truth is, we are all engaged in playing a farce, and I
am heartily ashamed of my part of it—it reminds me of
Shakespeare's 'Much Ado About Nothing.'"

"I cannot by any means indorse that idea, for I have been
very much interested in Ingomar's story."

"It is too tedious. Give me something lively—something
to make me laugh—such as 'Bill Arp,' or 'Artemus Ward,'
'Don Quixote,' or 'Mark Twain.'"

"I prefer love stories. I like to read about women who
prefer death to a loveless marriage, and men who are always
getting into scrapes in attempting to protect virtue."

"I guess, then, you like the 'Bride of Lammermoor' and
the 'Talisman'?"

"Yes, and all the other thrilling novels written by Sir
Walter Scott."

Don Quixote now came up and joined the king and duke
in the conversation, which soon drifted back to the lady in
the black domino.

"By the by," exclaimed Don Quixote, "I think that mysterious woman is about to stir up a row between Napoleon
and Navarre. The cauldron is boiling and bubbling furiously, and blood is on the face of the moon."

"How do you know that blood is on the moon, when that
planet is on the other side of the globe?"

"Of course you understand I was speaking metaphorically
as to that; but really, I should not be at all surprised to hear
of a requisition being made for pistols and coffins for two.
To be more explicit, I think a duel is on the tapis."

"Now, sir knight," said the duke, "if you are in possession of any news that will in any manner relieve our minds
about that strange woman, I earnestly beg you to let us hear
it at once; for you know what a deluge of curiosity she has
manufactured on this boat."

"I am very sorry to be unable to furnish any information
on that point of a reliable nature—all is conjecture as far as
the black domino is concerned; she has had a long interview
with the captain. I happened to hear enough of the conver-

sation to convince me that Navarre and Napoleon were the parties discussed; then the captain appeared to be angry, and I distinctly heard him mutter an oath or two, after he parted with the black domino. Colonel Confed informed me that a duel was likely to be fought, and that the lady in the black domino was at the bottom of it, but he refused to mention the names of the parties to the quarrel; though I am convinced from what I have heard that Navarre and Napoleon are to be the combatants."

"I guess it will turn out to be a tempest in a teapot, or a mouse born of a mountain," replied the duke, as he handed the king and Don Quixote a fresh cigar; "I wish," continued the duke, "that Colonel Confed and General Camphollower would cease their continual clamor about politics; they have bored every man on this boat half to death, and each one seems to imagine that the fate of the nation depends on his opinions."

"They have succeeded in bridging the bloody chasm; but they have split on the state rights question; they have generously consented that the war shall be considered at an end."

"Now, that indeed was very kind of them, for I dislike to hear people continually harping on the war; but let that pass, and we will go back to the subject. Did you tell the captain that Napoleon and Navarre were interlopers, intruders, counterfeits, wolves in sheep's clothing?"

"How could I impart information that I did not possess myself? What do you mean by intruders, interlopers, etc., etc.?"

Then the duke imparted to Don Quixote the grounds of his suspicion.

"They are not the same men who personated Navarre and Napoleon at the ball; I would risk anything on the truth of my assertion; and they are both spotting the black domino."

"If that is true," replied Don Quixote, "it is our duty to mention it to the captain without delay; and, gentlemen, I further suggest that we combine our wits, and, if possible, prevent any hostile meeting, if such is contemplated by any of our excursionists. In the first place, I am opposed to the barbarous practice of dueling upon principle; then it is prohibited by the laws of the land, and positively contrary to

God's holy ordinances. In addition to all these objections, we must remember that a duel might put an end to all of our innocent amusements; therefore I wish to know whether you will co-operate with me in the effort to prevent it?"

"We certainly think your views very correct, and will gladly join you in your peaceful mission; but I am of the opinion that it is a false alarm."

It required some ten or fifteen minutes to collect the entire party, for they were scattered about the boat, deeply interested in conversation. Nearly every one of the maskers had been discussing the mysterious woman in the black domino. At length the queen ascended her throne, and, after a moment's pause, ordered Ingomar to proceed.

"When I was conducted into the court-room by the deputy sheriff, his Honor, Judge Flaxback, occupied the judicial bench; fixing his little round eyes on me, he surveyed me like a snake endeavoring to charm a bird. A large crowd of village idlers had assembled in the house, attracted there, no doubt, by the peculiarity of the case. Flaxback reminded me of an Egyptian mummy that I had seen in a museum. He was a little dried-up specimen of decaying humanity, exhibiting in his person and dress unmistakable evidence of dissipation and dilapidation. His nose had evidently been broken with a heavy blow of some sort, for an ugly scar was apparent running horizontally across his face, while his nostrils flared outward, presenting rather an ugly appearance. He rested his chin on a plank in front of his seat, and continued to gaze at me with a lazy, half-asleep sort of a stare that caused my cheeks to burn with indignation. Every man in the room had his eyes riveted on me, staring with open mouth as children do at an elephant, while Flaxback seemed to be waiting for the inspection to be completed before proceeding with the case. When a drop of blood starts from such a man's heart, with a view of making a journey to his extremities to furnish a little life to them, it bids a long adieu to its home, knowing that the chances are ten to one in favor of its freezing to death on the way. I sat and impatiently watched the strange looking judge, wondering why he did not proceed to dispose of my case. He continued to eye me for full thirty seconds, and then in a voice sounding like that made with a file when being used to sharpen a handsaw, he ordered the clerk to read the sheriff's return on the writ of *habeas corpus.*

" 'No return made, sir,' said the clerk, as he began to grab promiscuously about, snatching up every paper in sight, and looking as if he were hunting for a small hole to crawl into.

" 'Where's the sheriff?' demanded the judge, in a voice which was evidently meant to be loud and threatening, but which really did not amount to a respectable whine.

" 'Fact is, may it please your Honor,' said Mr. Deediddle, 'the sheriff has just stepped over to Mr. Dick Sninkle's saloon to get a glass of *water.*'

"A smile might have been seen on the faces of a majority of the spectators—they all knew that water did not agree with the sheriff. The officer soon made his appearance, and the judge asked him why he had neglected to return the writ.

" 'The writ commanded me to bring the body of Edward Demar before the court, and here he is; what else could I do?'

" 'Mr. Clerk,' said Flaxback, 'enter a fine of ten dollars against Mr. Postholder, for failing to return the writ, and unless the return is instantly made, the fine will be doubled.'

"The sheriff was so badly confused that he did not know what he was about; he cast an imploring look at the clerk, made a dash at a pile of papers on the clerk's desk, then looked up at the ceiling, like an old duck listening for thunder when her puddle had gone dry.

"While all this nonsense was being exhibited, I was sitting there suffering indescribable torture; every moment of time seemed to be worth a mint of money to me, yet it was being wasted by those people as if it were valueless. There is no telling when the farce would have ended, but for Harry's thoughtfulness. He took the writ, and in three minutes wrote out the return and requested the sheriff to sign it, which he was very glad to do; he would have signed his own death warrant then without objection. Mr. Deediddle now made a raid to the front, and began to address the court.

" 'Fact is, your Honor, it is unnecessary to enter into an investigation of the circumstances connected with the murder of Mr. Clanton, as this is purely a question of personal iden-

tity. If the prisoner at the bar is not Edward Debar, why of
course he will be discharged—fact, sir—fact.'

"The district attorney consented that the investigation
might be confined to the question of personal identity.

" 'Swear your witness, Mr. Clerk,' growled the judge.

"The clerk began to hunt for the Bible.

" 'Why don't you swear your witnesses, Mr. Clerk?'
screamed the judge impatiently.

"The clerk became more confused; he grabbed up a book
which he thought was the Bible, but when he found out that
it was Mark Twain's 'Innocents Abroad,' he let it fall on the
floor, and began to grab at everything in the shape of a book.

" 'If you don't swear these witnesses, Mr. Clerk, I'll send
you to jail !' screamed Flaxback.

"By this time the clerk could have been passed off as a
first-class maniac; his actions were frightful; he threw out
both hands in every direction, and at last snatched up
George's Digest, and swore the witnesses on it before he discovered his mistake.

" 'Mrs. Debar was put on the stand first. She testified to
the fact that while I was very much like her husband, I was
not the man. The district attorney put her through a rigid
cross-examination—not because he thought she was swearing
falsely, but he had a suspicion that she had aided her husband in making his escape.

" 'Mrs. Debar,' said the district attorney, 'didn't you smug-
gle the tools into the jail to enable your husband to effect his
escape?'

"Harry sprang to his feet in a moment, his eyes flashing
with anger; I trembled, because I was afraid he was going
to commit some imprudent act that might detain us, when I
was so anxious to be flying toward Lottie; but I had cause to
change my mind very soon, for he made a modest, but
eloquent, appeal to the court in behalf of the unfortunate
wife, who was in tears.

" 'I appeal to this honorable court,' said he, 'to protect this
unfortunate lady; her condition is such as to entitle her to
the sympathies of all good men. The law does not require
her to answer questions that would tend to criminate her;
and even if the law did not protect her, the dictates of com-

mon humanity should be a sufficient motive to induce the
honorable attorney for the State to withdraw such a question.
We must remember that we have been taught to admire the
devotion which a wife feels for her husband. A true wife
will not forsake her husband when misfortunes overtake him;
but the greater his troubles are the closer she will cling to
him; and it should prompt every true gentleman to respect
the noble sentiment of love that induces her to do it.'

"When Harry took his seat a murmur of approval was
heard among the spectators, and the district attorney said:

" 'I fully indorse the sentiments so eloquently expressed
by my young friend, and will therefore not press the question
further; I will also say to the court that I am fully satisfied
that Mr. Demar has been unjustly imprisoned. I was well
acquainted with Edward Debar; and I hesitate not to say
that I never saw two men so much alike as he and Mr. Demar; though if they were both present I think a considerable difference might be detected. Debar had a slight scar
over his left eye, which alone would be sufficient to distinguish him from the prisoner now at the bar. I therefore
give my consent, if the court please, that Mr. Demar may be
discharged.'

" 'Let the prisoner be discharged, Mr. Sheriff,' growled
the judge, as he ordered the officer to adjourn court, and the
great farce was ended.

"No doubt the judge and all of his officers imagined that
they had done for me a very great favor in releasing me, for
which it was my duty to feel grateful. Now, I am in favor
of a faithful enforcement of the laws; but the law is often
used by unworthy men as a means of oppression. Judicial
murder has been committed in the State where I was so unjustly punished by imprisonment. The case of young Boynton, mentioned by Mr. Wharton in his treatise on criminal
law, might be cited in proof of this. That poor boy was
hung by the neck until he was dead for a crime he did not
commit. He was a mere lad, only eighteen. He was charged
with the murder of Mr. Ellis; and when he was led out by
the sheriff to be executed, he began to scream and beg the
spectators to save him, declaring before God that he was innocent. He leaped from the scaffold into the arms of the

assembled multitude, imploring them to protect him. Poor boy! he was put to death, and before his body had mingled with the dust the real murderer died, and on his death-bed confessed that he had murdered Mr. Ellis, and that young Boynton was innocent. This scene was enacted in a county adjoining the one where I had been so unjustly held as a prisoner. Who shall be able to repair the injury so wrongfully inflicted on me? Who will ever know the extent of the wrong?

"Three minutes had scarcely elapsed after my release, when Harry and I were mounted on our high-mettled steeds, and dashing down the road at a rapid speed. I knew that if we got to the station in time to meet the north-bound train, we would have to press our horses to their utmost powers. Our steeds were young, vigorous and full of good mettle, and needed no whip or spur to urge them on.

" 'Let them go as fast as you like,' said the owner of the noble animals, as he handed me the reins; 'they have excellent bottom, and will carry you as swift as the wind.'

"We had much uneven ground to pass over, many tall hills to climb and innumerable gullies to leap, but we never halted —on, on we dashed.

"We had placed ten miles of ground between us and the village of P—— when I saw the courier coming at a gallop to meet me; his horse was foaming with perspiration, convincing me that he had been hard pressed. The lad dashed up, and handed me a dispatch.

" 'I had to wait two hours at the office before the answer came,' said the boy, as he placed the envelope in my hand.

"This time I was prepared for the awful news; hence I did not feel such a shock as I had felt when the other dispatch was handed to me, though the news was worse than that contained in the first telegram. But you would probably understand matters better by hearing the telegram read; it is from Doctor Dodson, who remained with Lottie all the time:

" 'DEAR EDDIE—Your second message was received. I deeply regret that I have nothing but the worst news to communicate— our darling Lottie is slowly but surely passing away. She may possibly live twenty-four hours longer, though I think she will die to-night. I would be so glad if you and Harry could get here before she dies, because she expresses such great anxiety to see you. She says she does not feel a particle of pain. God seems to be merciful in that respect. Her mind remains perfectly clear, and she converses rationally, but most of her conversation is about you and Harry. I believe if she could see you it would greatly relieve her mind, and that then she would pass away without a struggle. If you could reach home to-night you might see her before she dies. May God, in His great mercy, give you courage and strength to bear this great loss with becoming fortitude! DODSON.'

"As soon as I finished reading this telegram I handed it to Harry, then told the messenger to go to the village and remain till morning, so as to give his horse the necessary rest, and the next day to go back to the station and get our horses and deliver them to the owner. I presented him my fine gold watch, as a reward for his faithful services, then dashed away as fast as my gallant steed could carry me.

"'When we were within five miles of the station Harry looked at his watch and observed:

"'If we get to the station in time for the up-train we will have a close race indeed; we have only twenty minutes to make the five miles.'

"I did not believe that I was doing wrong on that occasion when I urged my noble horse forward to the very top of his speed. I knew it would distress and press him both for us to make it in time, yet I believed he could do it without endangering his life. My conclusions were correct; for we did dismount at the station as the train dashed into the streets of the little town. We gave our horses in charge of the livery stable keeper, and stepped on the platform just as the train began to move.

"I wish I could convey to my audience a correct idea of my feelings when I began to hope I would reach home in time to see Lottie before death claimed her. I hastily wrote a dispatch with my pencil, intending to have it sent forward from the next office, notifying Doctor Dodson that we were on the train and would reach home that night. Here is the identical telegram—I have been careful to preserve them:

" 'DEAR DOCTOR—We are aboard the train, and will be home to-night. For Heaven's sake don't let my darling die before we come! Send an answer so it will meet us at Grenada. We are

due there at eight o'clock. Tell Lottie that we are begging **God**
to spare her dear life. Cheer her up with hope; I can't bear **the**
thought of losing my darling!'

"This dispatch was handed to the operator at the first office
we reached, who promised to forward it without delay. Then
I dropped down on my seat and spent every moment in earnest prayer.

"It was fifteen minutes past eight when the train arrived
at Grenada, and I believe that city is just one hundred miles
from Memphis. That is the place where the Mississippi and
Tennessee Railroad connects with the New Orleans, St. Louis
and Chicago Railroad, and we would have to take the Mississippi and Tennessee road to go to Memphis. As soon as the
train halted I hastened to the telegraph office to inquire for
news, as I was expecting an answer to my last message. I
was well acquainted with the young man who had charge of
the office at Grenada—he had formerly resided in Memphis.
He was about my own age, and we had been bosom
friends for many years. I rushed into his presence and
hurriedly inquired if there was a dispatch in the office
for me.

" 'Take a seat, Demar,' said the operator, 'you look very
ill; can I do anything for you?'

" 'Any telegram here for me?' I exclaimed, disregarding
his kind offer.

" 'Yes,' he hesitatingly answered, 'but you had better take
a seat and compose yourself before you read it. The news it
brings is very bad, though I infer that you have been expecting it.'

"The objects in the room seemed to be running round, a
blindness began to close over my eyes, and I felt a smothering sensation in my throat and lungs. The operator very fortunately happened to think of a bottle of spirits of camphor
that he had bought from the drug-store that day—he seized
it and sprinkled my face and moistened my beard with the
liquid, which I believe prevented me from fainting. After a
few minutes had elapsed I requested him to give me the dispatch.

" 'You may give it to me now,' I said, 'because I am prepared for the very worst.'

"He handed the envelope to me and I read the following words:

" 'MY DEAR BOY—Trust in God—He alone can comfort you now—our darling is dying. Death began to lay his cold hands on her dear body at four o'clock. She may linger four or five hours longer, but I think all will be over before that time. She expressed so much anxiety to see Viola that the sheriff very kindly consented to bring her here, and when they met it was the most affecting scene I ever witnessed. I fear we committed an error in allowing Viola to come, because as soon as the sheriff started away with his prisoner Lottie became worse, and is still rapidly failing. But how could I have the heart to refuse to let her see Viola, when she insisted so earnestly to have her sent for? Lottie leaves many messages of love with us to be delivered to you when you come, provided you do not arrive in time to receive them from her own lips.

" 'I beseech you, my dear boy, to bow submissively to the will of God—and remember you can meet Lottie in Heaven if you try. You will also understand that you are not the only one who grieves for this great affliction.   DODSON.'

" 'When does the train start for Memphis?'

" 'Seven o'clock in the morning,' replied the agent.

" 'Alas! that would be too late; all will be over before then,' was my reply.

" 'I believe,' said the agent, 'that under the circumstances the superintendent would let you have an extra train for a reasonable compensation. I will ask him by telegraph, if you wish it.'

" 'You are very kind, sir, and I thank you; please make the request without delay. Tell the superintendent that money is no object—the value of the engine and coach is offered, and will be promptly paid if required. I beg you, sir, not to lose a moment. If you only knew how precious time is to me now, you would be in a hurry!'

"While I was urging the agent to send the message, the clicking of the instrument under his thumb and finger indicated the fact that the electric fluid was dashing the request into the office at Memphis. The dispatch was gone in three minutes. A short conversation was then commenced between the superintendent at Memphis and the agent at Grenada. As the clicking of the instrument carried the words to the ear of the operator, he conveyed them to my ear by word of mouth.'

" 'Is number seven there?' inquired the superintendent.

" 'Yes,' was the operator's reply.

" 'Is she in good running order?'

" 'I will ascertain in a moment.'

" 'Go ask Mr. Steelbrim to come here quickly,' said the operator to a little negro who was dozing near the door.

"The little fellow rose up, shook himself, rubbed his eyes with his sleeve, gaped, and staggered up against the wall and said:

" 'Sir!'

"The order was quickly repeated, and the boy walked leisurely away. It was but a few minutes until a little dark-haired man, with long black whiskers and large expressive eyes, entered the office. His garments were covered with grease and smut, and his hands were thrust deep down in his pockets, and a don't-care sort of expression was visible on his face.

" 'Is number seven in good running order, Mr. Steelbrim?' inquired the operator.

" 'Apple-pie, hunkadory, O. K.—no mistake. Never nothing wrong with that old gal when under my command, you bet!' was replied by the greasy little man as he limped across the floor, for his left leg was shorter by two inches than the other.

" 'How long before you can heat her up and be ready to make a quick run to Memphis, Mr. Steelbrim?'

" 'Do it in less than no time, sir; the old gal's pretty hot now—just began to cool her off. She hain't been in more'n ten minits; but what's up?'

" 'An extra train to Memphis; a quick run—very important—no time to be lost—get ready immediately; take one coach and back down here, and the orders will be ready.'

" 'Good! The old gal can make the run in two hours, if she has a clean road and no bigger load than one coach. Glad to make the run—wanted to go to Memphis anyhow—sweetheart there—want to see her—was going to ask for leave anyway—ten minits we'll be off like a greased streak of lightnin'!'

"The greasy little man moved away as if he meant business.

" 'Number seven is in good order—Mr. Steelbrim anxious to make the run,' said the operator to the superintendent by wire.

" 'Start him at 8:50 with one coach. Let him make the run in 2:30 if he can. Order track to be cleared. Tell number four to take side track at Sardis. Number seven will only stop two minutes at Sardis for orders—two minutes at Hernando for same purpose—no other stop to be made.'

"As the operator repeated this order to me hope, which I thought had died within me, began to revive. A glimmering hope it was indeed, yet it was a live hope that I should once more gaze on those pretty blue eyes before death set his cold seal on them forever. I hurriedly wrote the following message, which the operator sent to Dr. Dodson:

" 'Will leave here by special train at 8:50, and arrive at depot at 11:20; have carriage at depot. Tell Lottie we are coming. For Heaven's sake keep her alive till we come! Answer this at Sardis. Don't fail nor lose time. Will send another telegram from Sardis.'

"By the time this dispatch had been forwarded, Mr. Steelbrim had moved his engine onto the main track, and began to back down to the depot.

" 'All right, cap; the old gal's a-pantin' to be off. Steam one-forty and a-risin'. What's the orders?'

"The operator read the orders carefully; then handed the paper to Mr. Steelbrim.

" 'Good! All aboard!' cried the greasy little man, as he leaped on the cab and seized the throttle-lever.

" 'Pile on the coal, Jim; keep her a-bilin'; time's up in three minits; old gal's a-champin' her bits; but I'm the chap that'll hold her on the rail and let her fly directly!'

"Harry and I stepped aboard and took seats opposite each other in silence. A dim lamp struggled for life in one corner of the coach, while a pale light cast a gloomy appearance over the seats.

" 'Time's up!' exclaimed Mr. Steelbrim, as he gave the lever a backward pull, and the engine dashed rapidly away."

CHAPTER XXVII.

MISS KATE DARLINGTON was the only daughter of Thaddeus Darlington, a real down-eastern Yankee, who had imbibed all those unreasonable prejudices prevailing in the New England States against all citizens of the South. He had been sent South by the government to look after some defaulting revenue collectors, and after discharging that duty, he concluded to locate in Jackson, Mississippi. His daughter, Kate, had received a polished education, but she had been petted and flattered until she was pretty well spoiled. Her disposition was gentle and kind when things went smoothly, but she had a temper which often got the upper hand, and then she usually made matters rather unpleasant.

After the maskers has dispersed Miss Darlington stole away from the crowd, and took a seat behind the ladies' cabin, in order to have what she called a day dream. A sentiment of a mysterious nature had of late been disturbing her mind —a strange feeling not altogether painful, and not entirely pleasant. A kind of joyful pain—a happy sorrow—a pleasant fear.

"What is the matter with me?" was the question she asked herself. "What sort of a pain is this that is mixed with delicious pleasure? How strange that such joy can be concealed under such misery!"

While she was thus soliloquizing the image of a man would every now and then pass across the path of her imagination. She could see the image plainer when her eyes were shut than with them open; and despite her efforts to drive it away, it would keep thrusting itself before her, sometimes in one shape, then in another, but always with the same look—the same form; that shape was the exact counterpart of the gallant sir knight of Ivanhoe.

"Yes, it is so; I am captured at last—it is love; heigh ho! there is no use to struggle any longer. What will dear papa say when he finds that I have fallen in love with a real double and twisted rebel—a man who fought through four years of bloody war against the union—a downright traitor, who brags of the part he played in the rebel army? Ah, me! how strange it is that I should fall in love with such a man! But didn't Juliet fall in love with a son of her father's bitterest enemy? Yes; but, alas! what a tragic ending did that love produce! Something tells me that this love will end in sorrow. But stop a moment; why should papa be Ralleigh's enemy? Why should I not love Captain Burk? He fought for his country—he fought in self-defense—he battled for his life—his liberty—his home—his mother and his sisters. He would have been less than a man if he had refused to fight—it would have been cowardly. No, he was right and I honor him for it; I love Captain Burk; papa will love him when he knows him better. I ought to be proud that such a man as Captain Burk has honored me with his love. I am proud of it. I will reciprocate his love; and, if papa is willing, I will be the wife of what my people have misnamed a *traitor*. Ah, me! there is the rub. Papa will raise a great row when he knows how I love a rebel."

Scottie then took out her handkerchief and wiped away the tears that were stealing down her cheeks.

"A gentleman is looking for you, miss," said a chambermaid who came through the back door and approached her.

"Who is it?"

"I believe they call him Divinghoe or Hivanhoe, or some such outlandish name."

"Where is he?"

"He is in the front part of the saloon; he sent me to hunt you."

"Very well; you may tell him where I am, if you wish."

But a moment elapsed before Ivanhoe was by Scottie's side.

"I have been looking all over the boat for you, Scottie. What induced you to hide from me?"

"I did not hide from you particularly, but I felt sad and wanted to be alone."

"I hope you will not be so cruel as to drive me away, when you know how it pleases me to be by your side!"

"Oh, no! I have had my little day dream, and am glad you came."

"Thank you; can we have a little chat here without being interrupted?"

"Yes, I guess so; take a seat."

"I have made another wonderful discovery."

"What is it?"

"We have got a counterfeit emperor aboard of this boat."

"What do you mean?"

"The real Napoleon has slipped out of his costume, and a counterfeit has slipped in. To be plain, a stranger got aboard somewhere, and is dressed in Napoleon's costume; and the real Napoleon has vamoosed the ranch—run away, disappeared, melted into thin air, fell overboard, become extinct, or something of the sort; anyway, the original emperor is not comeatible. Now, Scottie, I should like to know what you think of such doings?"

"I will tell you in short what I think: We are all struggling in a sea of nonsense; and I am heartily ashamed of my part of it. I wish I were at my father's house—that I do; and if things don't change pretty soon I shall set my sails in that direction. Napoleon is not the only one who has been playing tricks on this boat. Captain Quitman ought not to permit such doings."

"How did you get possession of the information?"

"I had had many conversations with the original Navarre; one subject in particular had been frequently discussed between us. A while ago I walked up and took Navarre's arm and began to talk about the special subject. He was startled when I took his arm; and I could feel his body trembling. After I had gone on talking for about five minutes he gave a grunt like a wild hog and abruptly walked away, leaving me thunderstruck with astonishment; I then discovered that he was not the real Navarre."

"Now, Scottie, if I had been present when that scamp had the impudence to grunt at you, I think I should have broken his head with my cane."

"I am very glad, then, you were not present, because I am on Grant's platform—Let us have peace."

"Peace is a very good thing in its proper place; but I feel very much inclined to get up a row here. I think I shall commit some sort of mischief if these things don't change very soon. The fact is, we may look out for squalls—some sort of deviltry is brewing aboard of this boat certain."

"I am of that opinion, myself; but I think we had better have nothing to do with it."

"That woman in the black domino keeps me on the rack all the time; and I would not be at all surprised if it should turn out that she is at the bottom of all this mysterious game."

"Suppose we change the subject and let the black domino and her co-conspirators work out their own schemes."

"Very good. What shall we talk about?"

"Oh, anything for a change."

"What book is that you hold in your hand?"

"Paradise Lost."

"I would rather see Paradise found; but how do you like Milton?"

"Too much imagination and not enough sentiment. Such extravagant ideas! Just think of his description of the war in Heaven. He says they plucked up great mountains by the roots and threw them at each other's heads. Now I think that is a little too extravagant."

"If you like sentiment, you admire Tom Moore."

"Ah! you are right as to that. Give me Moore and Burns above all others. I often steal away when at home and weep over the sweet sentimental songs of those favorite poets."

"Shakespeare is my poet. Speaking of sentiment, it gushes up on every page, and streams from every line. Rosalind, Imogene, Juliet, Romeo, Orlando and Hamlet—all are made to utter the most soul-stirring, heart-melting sentiment. But enough about poetry; take my arm and let us go on deck and enjoy the scenery."

As soon as they reached the upper deck, George III. came up with a look of mystery on his countenance.

"Good morning. I was wanting to speak a few words with you. Perhaps you have heard of my great mishap?"

"No! what is it?"

"My watch was stolen from my pocket within the last thirty minutes."

"Ah, ha!" exclaimed Scottie, "I told you so. The whirl-wind has started, and a tornado will wind up the scene."

"Have you any idea who was the thief?"

"Yes; but my suspicions may not be well founded."

"May I know whom you suspect?" inquired Ivanhoe.

"Yes, provided you will promise not to mention it to any one."

"Good! I promise, of course."

"So do I," said Scottie.

"My suspicions point to that man who appears in Napoleon's dress and mask; though he is a newcomer."

"Why not make the charge boldly, and demand the right to make a search for the watch?" said Ivanhoe.

"Let us wait and watch him, for he is bent on mischief, and we will catch him in the act of picking some man's pocket."

"I beg pardon, gentlemen," said an old man with long, white whiskers, as he bowed very low to Ivanhoe and George III. He was the same gentleman who had been so often seen with the lady in the black domino leaning on his arm. "I have a communication to make which I consider of some importance. The fact is, matters are becoming somewhat complicated on this boat; and if I might be so bold as to offer advice, I should say that it is high time for all these young people to lay aside their masks. Wolves have managed to get into the flock; and mischief will be done if matters go on in this way much longer. A lady aboard of this boat, whose name I am not at liberty to mention, has made a startling disclosure to me, which portends some dire mischief. The fact is, I am constrained to believe, from what she told, that murder is contemplated."

"May we know the particulars?"

"Of course, yes; that is the very matter I wish to communicate. If you will be so good as to request Ingomar to join us, I would be much obliged, as I think he ought to hear what I have to say."

Ivanhoe went after Ingomar, and soon returned accompanied by him.

"The young lady to whose sagacity I am indebted for the important information which I am about to communicate has a history—yes, a very strange history, full of queer incidents such as you see in novels. The young lady to whom I refer is the one in the black domino. You have often seen her leaning on my arm, gentlemen. She is a most elegant young lady, of remarkable beauty and superior intellect, whose protector I have the honor to be at this time. A combination of sad circumstances—unfortunate events, I might say—have clouded her young life. You may perhaps have noticed that she has not participated in any of the amusements in which the young people have been indulging on this boat. If I were at liberty to reveal the secrets of her unhappy life, I could unfold a most distressing story; but that is a sealed book, so far as we are concerned. You have probably noticed a disposition on the part of this young lady to wander about alone, seeking solitude, where she could give free vent to her grief, and let her tears flow unnoticed by the unsympathizing crowd. Well, I did not approve of this course, but was unable to prevent it; and perhaps, after all, it was fortunate that I did not stop it, for it was during one of these solitary rambles that the information which I am going to communicate was obtained. She had concealed herself on the larboard side of the boat just in front of the wheel-house, and behind a stack of furniture, where she could meditate alone, when two men came out and stood on the other side and held a consultation in very low tones. She could not hear every word that was said, but what she did hear was of a most startling character. As soon as the two men stepped into the saloon the young lady came and immediately imparted to me what she had heard. To say I was surprised would not convey the full meaning of what I felt. The fact is, I was shocked, startled, paralyzed with astonishment! Yes, gentlemen, it is most wonderful—I might say diabolical. I can repeat, word for word, all that the young lady heard, which I mean to do. It was unfortunate, however, that she did not see the two men—that is, she did not get a full view of them; but she saw the head and shoulders of one of the men as he passed through the door, and she thinks she knows who he is; but for fear that she might be mistaken as to that, she requested me not to mention the name of the man she suspects, which request I, of course, must respect. Now here is the conversation *verbatim,* as it was related to me by this unfortunate young lady:

" 'He is the man, beyond question,' said the first speaker.

" 'Yes, that's certain,' replied number two.

" 'He has lots of greenbacks,' says number one.

" 'We must have his money and his life, too. We must first
get his money, and then settle the other matter.'

" 'Do you know how much money he has?'

" 'No; but it is way up in the thousands—and I think I
may say tens of thousands.'

" 'Good; That's lucky; but have you matured any plan to
crib the game?'

" 'Yes.'

"Then they began to talk in a whisper, and the young
lady could not hear all that was said; but ever and anon she
could catch a word such as 'Throttle him—chuck him overboard—dead men keep secrets—revenge—old grudge—he
ruined me—money good—revenge better—could steal his
money—but rather have his life.' Then they whispered for a
long time in tones so low that the young lady could not hear
what was said. Now, gentlemen, I guess you will indorse me
when I say it is diabolical. Who is to be the victim? who is
to be chucked overboard? That is the question, gentlemen.
It may be you, or you, or you, or it may be me. What's to
be done? That's the question I put; shall we sit still and
wait for the catastrophe; or shall we go to work and prevent
it?"

"I can answer for one," said Scottie, in a tone of firmness,
as she rose from her seat: "I shall leave this boat as soon as
we reach Vicksburg, and make my way to my father's house
at Jackson, Mississippi; I wash my hands of this nonsense."

"If Scottie leaves the boat at Vicksburg," observed Ivanhoe, "I am inclined to the opinion that another passenger
will feel it his duty to fall back, too."

"I'll fight it out on this line if it takes all summer," said
George III. as he walked round, describing a circle of fifteen
feet. "The man who chucks me overboard shall go along
with me; and who robs me of my purse, only cheats himself,
and does not make me poor, indeed; because that has already
been done long, long ago."

"A man would be an expert pickpocket indeed who could
steal a purse from me," said Ivanhoe; "I have had no use for
an article of that sort for many years; Scottie can testify
truly."

"I don't suppose you have had any use for a purse since Confederate money went down," replied Scottie.

"I think we had better consult Captain Quitman about this matter," suggested Ingomar.

"Certainly, sir, I agree with you there," observed the old gentleman with the white whiskers, "and if you will wait a moment I will bring him here."

Captain Quitman soon appeared accompanied by the old gentleman.

"Well," said the captain, "what's the question to be discussed?"

The old man related, in a rambling manner, what the young lady in the black domino had heard. When he had finished the narrative, he began to stroke his long white whiskers with his left hand.

"What do you think of that, sir? Yes, yes, that's the question, Captain Quitman; what do you think of that, sir?"

"Gammon, sir! all gammon!" muttered the captain, as he lighted a fresh cigar and began to puff the smoke in clouds above the old gentleman's head.

"Gammon! gammon! zounds! sir, do you apply that epithet to the young lady who has the honor to be under my protection—I mean the young lady whom I have the honor to protect?" The old gentleman locked his hands under the tail of his coat, and began to prance around at a rapid rate. "Gammon! I think you said gammon, sir! What in the deuce do you mean by gammon, sir? Do you know the meaning of the word, sir? I ask you that, sir. Do you know, sir, that gammon and humbug mean the same thing? Why, didn't you say the young lady was a humbug, sir, in plain terms! Answer me that, sir. I'll have you understand, sir, that this young lady is no humbug; she is not gammon either, sir. If you call this unhappy young lady a humbug, sir, you shall answer for it; yes, answer for it. Is that plain enough for you, sir?"

"I beg pardon, sir," said Captain Quitman, politely; "you have entirely misunderstood me, my good friend; I had no allusion to the young lady when I made the remark, I assure you. I am convinced that the young lady heard just what she stated; but I was inclined to think that the conversation she heard was gammon, or humbug, if you please; I infer that the conversation alluded to something that had occurred, not to a plan for future execution."

"You did not mean to apply the word gammon to the young lady then?"

"Certainly not! certainly not! I had no thought of such a thing."

"Then, sir, there's my hand—I forgive you, sir, with all my heart. I am a peaceable man—fact is, sir, I never get excited. I am slow to anger; I love peace, but despise the word gammon. I don't think such an odious word should ever be used. I had an uncle once who committed suicide under circumstances of the most distressing character. My uncle was a very handsome young man—everybody said he resembled me. He was a very sensitive, melancholy man; had a fashion of looking on the dark side of everything; the fact is, my uncle was an unhappy young man. He fell in love with a beautiful young widow, and for a long time he tried to muster up courage to ask her to marry him; but it was postponed from month to month, until another man entered the lists to contend for the fair prize. At first the beautiful widow was rather favorably inclined toward my uncle. Time went on—my uncle went on, too; so did the beautiful widow. After so long a time, my uncle at last, in a fit of desperation, asked the beautiful widow to marry him. What do you think was her reply, sir? Why, sir, she looked him full in the face and sneeringly said, 'Gammon!' The next morning my uncle's remains were found in a briar patch with a bullet hole through his head; and on a sheet of paper, which he held clinched in his fist, appeared the odious word—gammon, in large letters made in red ink. Now, sir, you will readily understand why I was displeased when you used that word just now."

"Ah, sir, I again most humbly ask your pardon—I certainly did not mean to use the word as in any way applicable to you or the young lady."

"Again, sir, I offer you my hand; but I fear you do not attach as much importance to what the young lady heard as you should; in fact, sir, I think you are mistaken when you conclude that the conversation referred to something which had transpired at some previous time."

"I am inclined to agree with this gentleman's views," observed George III., "because part of the conversation evidently referred to some one on this boat who was to be the victim. By the by, had you heard that my watch was snatched from my pocket but an hour ago?"

"Ha! is that so?" exclaimed Captain Quitman, who for the first time began to look serious. "This, indeed, is news to me—it must be looked into; whom do you suspect?"

"The man wearing the mask and uniform of Napoleon. There are three men on this boat wearing costumes that were worn by other men when we left Memphis."

"I must confess that this information surprises me; this conduct looks suspicious; something must be done."

"I think all masks should at once be discarded," observed the old gentleman; "and I had advised that course before you came up."

"No! no!" said Captain Quitman, "that would prevent us from catching the thieves. I think I can suggest a better plan; in fact, I believe we can manage to capture the rascals, if my plan is adopted. We will employ some one to watch the three suspicious men; meantime don't mention this matter to any one; just let me manage the case. I'll place guards on all parts of the boat, both day and night, with instructions to keep an eye on those three men. Let the amusements proceed as if nothing had happened—mention the matter to no one, and I'll vouch for the result. I have a man on board who was in the detective service many years. I'll put him on their tracks. Your watch shall be found, if the matter is left to me; if not, you shall be paid for it."

"Your plan, sir, is evidently the best under the circumstances," said Ingomar, "because if we unmask now that would enable the thieves to evade detection. Let the young lady in the black domino understand that she is not to tell any one about what she heard."

"Do you remember the number of your watch?" inquired Captain Quitman, addressing George III.

"No."

"What is its value?"

"I don't know."

"Where did you purchase it?"

"I—I, that is, I ah, hem! I didn't buy it at all, sir."

"Ah! a present then, I suppose, from some dear friend?"

"No."

"You inherited it from deceased relations?"

"No."

"Then how in the deuce did you come by it?"

"I borrowed it from a friend."

"Ha! ha! ha!" laughed the jolly old captain, "that makes the loss a more serious one; but never mind, you shall have your watch again soon, or cash enough to satisfy your friend."

"But suppose those suspicious individuals should try to leave the boat," said the old gentleman with the white whiskers.

"I shall instruct the guards to arrest them, and compel them to unmask and submit to a search, whenever they attempt to leave the boat."

Ingomar and Captain Quitman then walked away, followed by the old gentleman with the white whiskers.

"Well, Scottie, I'll give you a nickel for your thoughts."

"Keep your nickel; and you had better not seek to know my thoughts just now, for they are not of a very pleasant nature. However, one idea has found its way into my scanty brain, which I have no objection to your knowing."

"Let me have it, pray; any little idea of yours would be acceptable to me."

"The black domino is a humbug, and her guardian is an old fool; there now, you have got at least one idea; do what you please with it."

"Yes, and a very bright little idea it is, too; something of the same sort has been knocking for admissioin at the back door of my brain-pan for some time."

"Ah, indeed! I hope it did not knock very hard."

"Scottie, dear, don't cut so deep, pray."

"Don't call me 'Scottie, dear,' if you please; I am tired of it. It is time for the queen's party to re-assemble, and I want Ingomar to hurry through with his story, because when that is done the masks must all be laid aside."

"Take my arm, Scottie."

"No, no, that's not the style now; you take mine."

"Good enough; anything to get you in a good humor."

"I smell tobacco, and something else; I believe it is gin."

"Ha, hem! I dare say you smell tobacco, but as to gin, I expect you are mistaken; it's brandy."

"Well, either is bad enough, and I despise both."

CHAPTER XXVIII.

A GREAT change was perceptible among the merry maskers when they had re-assembled in obedience to the orders of the queen. The different members of the party dropped in one at a time, taking their seats in silence. One circumstance happened which created some little excitement and no little curiosity. Henry of Navarre, who had kept away from the party up to this time, came forward and, bowing very low to the queen, asked permission to join the party to hear the story. As Navarre made his request she gave a sudden start, as if the sound of the voice had frightened her; and a perceptible tremor was discernible in her tone as she requested him to be seated. Napoleon, instead of taking his seat near the queen, took up his position by the corner of the pilot house, some distance from the spot occupied by the other maskers. One of the party called to him and requested him to take his place. He shook his head, but made no reply; and the queen commanded Ingomar to proceed.

"My good friends, I am now about to reach that part of my story which gives me more pain than pleasure to relate; in fact, I may venture to say that it will be all pain and no pleasure. I would gladly skip over a portion of the story, but that would leave a gap which would show an unfinished job. There is one circumstance, in this connection, which I consider it to be my duty to mention. During all my sufferings there was a sustaining influence that held me up—an invisible, indescribable presence all the time with me that kept me from dying with despair. That most potent influence was secured by humble, devout, sincere, secret prayer, coupled with an unswerving determination to discharge my whole

duty under all circumstances. This strange influence seemed
to surround me on all occasions; and it enabled me to keep
my head above the huge waves of trouble that were dashing
against me with great fury. To be plain, I put my trust in
God; and He did not forsake me. Some people would be disposed to sneer at sentiments of this character. In fact, I have
often heard such sentiments ridiculed; and I have as often
known men to change from the one extreme to the other. I
knew a young man in Memphis, a few years ago, who had occasion to change his views. The change was brought about in
a most singular manner. The young man was assisting
some workmen to cover a very tall house, situated on Shelby
street. A conversation had been going on for some time
among the laborers, on the questions connected with the
future state. The young man seemed to be the leader in
the conversation.

"'I don't believe that God answers prayers,' said he; 'I
don't believe He pays any attention to the concerns of men;
I never prayed in my life, and I am healthy and happy. I
think it is simple in a man to ask God for anything. He
knows what we want; and if He wishes us to have it He will
give it to us without our asking.'

"As he uttered the last word his feet slipped from under
him and he fell at full length on his back. The north side of
the roof was covered with a white frost, which caused the
young man's feet to slip. The building was three stories
high; and from the ground to the eaves was nearly forty feet.
The young man was standing near the top of the roof, and as
he uttered the sentence, he stepped over on the north side to
get a hammer that he had left there, when he fell flat on his
back; his body darted toward the edge of the roof like a lump
of ice gliding down the mountain side. At the very brink of
the roof, a nail caught in his clothes and stopped him. His
legs were hanging over the edge while his body lay back on
the shingles. The ground near the foundation of the house
was covered with innumerable large stones, with hundreds of
sharp corners and edges, which every one knew would cause
the young man's death, if he fell on them. There the man's
body swung forty feet above the ground—only held by a little
number four nail. The slightest movement might send his

soul across the dark river. I have heard many people pray, but such a prayer as that young man uttered then and there I have never heard before or since. The most solemn promises of reformation were made, the most earnest appeals to God for help. A ladder was quickly brought from an adjoining hook and ladder company's quarters, and the young man was saved. If any of my friends have a desire to know the name of this young man, go to all the churches in Memphis and hear all the Christians pray—then select the one that prays longest and loudest—that's he.

"But I crave your pardon, my friends, for this digression, and will return to my story. We left Grenada at 8.50 sharp. The night was unusually dark; heavy clouds overspread the horizon and a steady patter of rain-drops could be heard falling against the windows of the coach. Harry and myself were the only occupants, and the train consisted of the engine, tender, and a single car in which we rode. Occasionally I would hoist the sash of the window in order to let the cold damp atmosphere cool my burning cheeks—for I felt as if my blood were boiling hot. As the head-light of the engine cast its bright rays on the trees along the road, I could see that we were dashing on with lightning speed. I occupied a seat on the left side of the coach, while Harry sat on the right, and immediately opposite the one where I was. When the windows were all down, there was an overpowering feeling of suffocation that was unbearable; and when they were up, the wind came dashing in accompanied by streams of rain. I would close the window and endure the oppressive closeness as long as I could; then hoist the sash again, letting the wind and rain pour in until my face would be cooled. I had borrowed Harry's watch, and sat with it open in my hand, counting every second of time, which seemed to linger unusually long. A mental question kept presenting itself to my mind: Will I ever see Lottie again? Will she be dead before I get there? What is to be my fate in the future? Can I consent to drag out a long, miserable existence, after my darling has gone to Heaven? I made a solemn vow to God that I would not rebel against His will, but that I would humbly submit, to, and bear without complaint, such punishment as He, in His great wisdom, might send upon me. I earnestly begged for Lottie's life. No one ever prayed more humbly and sincerely than I did on that occasion; and I believe Harry did the same—though he sat silently in his seat, apparently buried in his own sad thoughts. Sometimes he would turn his face toward me and point to the watch which I held in my hand—this I understood to be an inquiry as to the time. The only answer I made was to hold the watch close to his eyes. He would glare at it, then lean back in his seat, without uttering a word.

"Every now and then the wind would dash in through the window, scattering the falling rain over my face, causing the lamp to flare up and spatter; then for an instant the feeble light would flicker and struggle as if in the last agonies of dissolution. After an unusual gust had dashed in, bringing with it a copious shower of rain, I was compelled to close the window to prevent the lamp from being totally extinguished. As soon as I had excluded the air, the same feeling of suffocation that had annoyed me so often came upon me with redoubled severity. I could not get enough air into my lungs notwithstanding I was struggling to do so. I felt as I suppose one feels when dying; in fact, I do not believe that the actual pains of dissolution could have increased my sufferings.

"Harry made a sign signifying a wish to know the time. I managed to hold the face of the watch so he could see it.

"'9.20,' he whispered, as he leaned back in his seat and closed his eyes. The lamp now began to sing and sputter, spitting the oil up through the chimney, making a dozen different sounds. It would dart a bright blaze nearly to the top of the chimney, then sink down so low that no light could be seen. It would whine like a young child, then sing; at times it would sputter—then pop, pop, pop, like the cracking of a small whip; anon it would whistle—and blaze up, casting a dazzling light all over the seats—then drop back to its usual dim dimensions. After it had performed a dozen such strange freaks, it gave one long shriek and suddenly expired. We were left in total darkness; a darkness as black as blindness itself. A ton's weight seemed to be pressing on my breast; I felt that my last moment had come. I sank down on the seat without the strength to hold up my head; I was in a swoon. The first sensation I experienced, after my reason returned, was that of the most delicious pleasure. The strangest, but most exquisite, feeling of happiness seemed to steal over me; the most mysterious influence appeared to surround me. The smothering sensation was gone, and a delightful absence of pain was in its stead, and at once the coach seemed to be filled with the most delicious perfume, such as I had so often enjoyed while with Lottie in her flower garden. 'What does it mean?' I asked myself. 'How could the coach be filled with such delightful odor when all the windows were closed?'

" 'Harry, what in Heaven's good name does this mean?' I at last managed to ask.

" 'Hush, Ed,' he whispered, 'some one is in this coach—it is a lady; I felt her skirts brush past my knees!'

" 'Lottie!' I exclaimed, as I sprang to my feet.

" 'What do you mean?' whispered Harry, as he caught me by the arm, while he was trembling like one in an ague fit.

" 'Lottie, darling, is it you?' I gasped, while Harry still held me by the arm.

" 'Are you mad?' he exclaimed, as he closed his fingers about my arm. 'Why do you call Lottie? Don't you know she is dying in Memphis?'

" 'She was here this very moment; I felt her skirt brush my knee, and I believe she called my name,' I replied.

" 'Nonsense! I think there's a lady in this coach—she passed me a moment ago. I distinctly felt her skirts brush against my knees as she went down the aisle.'

" 'Upon my honor, I thought I heard Lottie call my name.'

" 'Pshaw! Edward, of course that is all imagination, and I beg you not to talk so. I suspect that some one is trying to steal a ride; I am sure there is some one in this coach besides you and me. Try to calm yourself; what makes you tremble that way?'

" 'It is yourself who is trembling; let go my arm—you are hurting it! I declare, you are shaking as if you had an ague fit!'

" 'Yes, and your hand is as cold as ice.'

" 'Hark! what was that? did you hear anything?'

" 'No, but as I live I felt some one brush past me.'

" 'So did I; and it was a female, beyond all doubt, for I felt her skirts touch me as she passed, just as I did a moment ago.'

" 'Yes, and I distinctly felt something tickle my left cheek; it was the same feeling I had so often experienced when Lottie was near me, and a stray lock of hair would touch my face.'

" 'I declare, this is the strangest mystery that I ever heard of! Give me a match and let me relight the lamp, so we can see who it is.'

" 'I have not got a match—you will have to go and request the fireman to come and light it. Pray do so at once, for this darkness is distressing.'

"As soon as Harry went out to bring the fireman, I again felt something softly passing across my cheek. I threw out my arms, expecting to catch the living body of some person; but not so—I caught nothing. As I turned round I felt the same touch on my right cheek. It might have been imagination, but I thought I again heard Lottie calling my name. The truth is, I was so much overcome with excitement that I scarcely knew what was going on around me. Harry was out but a few moments, returning accompanied by the fireman, who immediately lighted the lamp. We procured a lantern and began to search for the mysterious passenger. We carefully examined every seat, looking under each bench, but could find nobody. We went out and examined the rear platform, thinking that probably some one might be stealing a ride, but nothing of the sort was to be seen. I became perfectly convinced that no one was concealed either in or outside of the coach. I was overwhelmed with astonishment at the singular mystery. When I told Harry what had occurred during the time he was gone after the fireman, informing him that I thought I heard Lottie's voice distinctly call my name, he fixed his eyes upon my face, and gazed steadily for a moment, as if to satisfy himself that I had not gone mad.

" 'Ed,' said he, 'your mind has been taxed too heavily of late; I think it is quite unsettled. I do not believe you ever were inclined to be superstitious.'

" 'No,' said I, 'superstition has never been classed among my many faults; but on this occasion I must confess that I am unable to tell exactly what I do think. It may be as you say, that sorrow has to some extent unsettled my mind; but nevertheless I am sure I heard some one call my name, with a voice I could recognize among ten thousand. My telegram will be answered; the answer will meet us at Sardis; it will bring news of Lottie's death; it will tell us that she died at 9:20; you will remember that was the exact time when the coach was filled with the delicious fragrance. That was the very moment when the lamp died, and then it was that we felt the skirts of a lady's dress brush past us. Harry, our darling is dead, and as sure as we live her sweet spirit was with us here in this coach.'

" 'Oh, Edward, don't talk that way, I beseech you! I declare, you frighten me. You are as pale as a ghost; sit down and try to be calm. You will regret this language when you get over the excitement.'

"I leaned back on the seat, closed my eyes, and endeavored to analyze the mysterious occurrences that had just happened; but the more I thought of the matter the more unsettled became my mind, and I began to try to fix my thoughts on other objects, but all seemed confusion and mystery. Harry settled himself down on the cushion and leaned his head on the back of the seat, closed his eyes and silently communed with his own thoughts. Not another word was uttered by either of us until the train drew up in front of the hotel at Sardis. A considerable crowd of people began to collect about the spot, having been somewhat surprised, no doubt, at the arrival of a train at that unusual time. Every now and then a man's head would be thrust in at the door— then suddenly withdrawn. It was but a few seconds after the train had halted when Mr. Steelbrim poked his head in at the door, and, holding an envelope in his hand, said:

" 'A telegram for Edward Demar.'

"My hands trembled so that I could scarcely open the envelope; but at length I did, and read as follows:

" 'MEMPHIS, 9.30 P. M.

" 'MY DEAR BOY—Trust in God. He will sustain you. All is over. Lottie died at 9.20. Her last words were love messages to you. She expired with your picture in her hand, while it was moist with her kisses. Don't let this awful blow crush you. Remember that you can go to her, if she cannot come to you. Rely on Him who alone can give you comfort now. Her last moments were free from pain, and she was not alarmed at the approach of death. Her mind was clear to the last. We know her pure soul is now in Heaven. God grant, my dear boy, that we may meet our darling there. The funeral will take place at 4 P. M. on to-morrow evening. A carriage will meet you at the depot.

"'DODSON.'

" 'It is just as I told you, Harry,' I said, as I handed him the dispatch and fell back on my seat. I did not faint; I did not even groan, because I was prepared for the awful blow. I felt as if some strong man held my throat in an iron grip, and that the breath was being choked out of me. I pushed the sash up and let the wind and rain pour in on my hot brow, while I was struggling to fill my lungs. As soon as Harry finished reading the dispatch he let it fall to the floor, and his body went down with it. I saw him fall, but I was unable to go to his assistance; in fact, I never thought of offering aid; I was thinking of my own grief.

CHAPTER XXIX.

"BEING so completely prostrated by the great mountain of grief that pressed heavily on my sad heart, I failed to notice the condition of Harry Wallingford, whose upturned face had put on a death-like expression. It was after several minutes had elapsed that I happened to look at him; I was considerably frightened when I beheld the ghost-like features. I ascertained, upon examination, that he had fainted; and also discovered a stream of blood flowing from his left temple, that came from an ugly wound caused by striking his head against the sharp corner of the seat as he fell. I dashed some cold water in his face, then lifted him from the floor and laid him on the seat, watching eagerly for signs of returning life, which I was gratified to see very soon. Fixing his eyes on me with a wild, restless expression, he said:

" 'Is is true that Lottie is dead? How can you gaze on me

with such a look of affection, Ed, when you know that by your kindness you are heaping coals of living fire on my unworthy head? If you would abuse me, curse me, spit on me, spurn me, or do anything to show that you despise me—I could bear it; but to receive disinterested kindness from one that I have so deeply wronged is a greater punishment than humanity can endure. You must remember that I have murdered Lottie, yes, I have closed those pretty blue eyes forever; I have pushed her fair body into the grave; I have invited the worms to banquet on her queenly form; I slapped you in the face, I drove Viola to desperation, and caused her to murder her little brother, and yet I am unhung, and you can look kindly on me! What kind of man are you? what sort of a heart is yours? why do you not plunge a dagger into my breast? Well, I suppose you think that you can kill me with kindness as well as any other way; and in that you are very correct. When I am dead, I want you to continue your kindness until you see my remains deposited by the side of my murdered sister. I know I don't deserve such honor, but I may rely on your goodness to have my last request complied with.'

"The strangeness of his conduct, the mystery of his language, had a tendency to add to the great waves of misery that were rolling over me, for I inferred that he was contemplating suicide. For full thirty minutes he continued to rave about innumerable blunders that he accused himself of having committed, and I positively assert that no prosecuting attorney could have given such an offensive coloring to willful and malicious murder as he gave to the cause of Lottie's death, all of which he declared had been produced by himself. I ventured to discuss the matter with him as soon as I regained sufficient self-command to enable me to do it, hoping to lead his mind away from the subject of Lottie's death; but it was like the blind trying to lead the blind. While I was endeavoring to console Harry Wallingford, I stood as much in need of it as he did; nevertheless, I put forth my utmost efforts to soothe him.

"I was somewhat surprised when the train came to a sudden halt in front of the Hernando Station. Mr. Steelbrim thrust his smutty head into the front door and said:

" 'By jing! we made the best time on record; the old gal
is in a splendid humor to-night—made a mile a minit from
Sardis here, and I bet she could distance a streak of greased
lightning from here to Memphis. If I had a track from here
to the moon, I could make the old gal climb the grade in time
to make the connection. We are now three minits ahead of
time, and according to orders, we must not move a peg
till time is up.' Then he turned round and addressed the
fireman :

" 'Feed the old gal a little, Mr. Smutty, and ile her j'ints
good, for I'm gwine to let her rip from here to Memphis;
she'll make it in twenty-five minits like a top. The old gal
knows me, and she allers makes up her mind for business
when this chap holds the throttle. Tom Scratchler undertook
to manage her t'other day, but she took the dumps and
wouldn't run worth a cent; but it takes me to hold her
down to work.'

" 'Wait a moment, Mr. Steelbrim,' said the telegraph operator, 'a dispatch is coming for Edward Demar.'

" ' 'All hunkadory,' replied the eccentric little engineer,
'plenty of time, and if necessary, I can persuade the old gal
to put in a few extra licks.'

"The rain had ceased, and the dark clouds began to move
rapidly northward; the moon, that had been obscured,
emerged from behind them, casting a bright, cheerful light
over the earth.

" 'Here we are, Demar,' exclaimed Mr. Steelbrim, as he
came in and handed me the telegram.

"I tossed it down on the seat, not caring to read any news
since Lottie was dead. In fact, I felt a peculiar hatred
against all telegraph lines, and more especially against the
one that had brought me the fatal news. Mr. Steelbrim
started his engine forward with such a sudden plunge that
it threw me to the third seat behind where I was standing,
pitching me head foremost against the stove-pipe, slightly
bruising my head. I think the effect of the shock was bene-
ficial, for it seemed to relieve the smothering sensation which
had afflicted me for some time. Seating myself where I
could watch Wallingford—for I was afraid he meditated self-
murder—I began to conjecture in regard to the contents of

aided, of course, by the jailer, who had orders to assist me.
the envelope that lay on the seat just in front of me, and as
is usual in such cases, never guessed anywhere near the truth.
I might have gone on conjecturing for a hundred years, and
I dare say I never would have made the right guess as to
the purport of the message. After taxing my mind in that
way for five minutes:

"'I have hit the mark at last,' I muttered to myself:
'The sheriff will let Miss Bramlett attend Lottie's funeral.'

"Having satisfied myself that I had at last made the proper
guess, I took the envelope, tore it open and held it carelessly
for some time before I commenced reading it. I have that
particular telegram here in my bosom; and I have no doubt
my friends would like to hear it read. I had often heard
men say that the danger of death being caused by good news
was equal to that produced by bad; but I never did credit
any such notions until after I received that dispatch. I am
now a full believer in the idea that death could be, and doubtless has often been, produced by the sudden shock occasioned
by the reception of unexpected good news; but let me read
you the telegram:

"'MEMPHIS, 10:10 P. M.

"'Bless God, my dear boy! A wonderful miracle has been
wrought! Medical science is all a humbug, a bauble, a farce,
nonsense, moonshine; the profession all bosh! I would not give
a nickel for any man's opinion; I never will give another opinion; don't ever ask me for an opinion; I won't give it. I telegraphed you, 40 minutes ago, that Lottie was dead! I thought
she was dead; we all thought so; medical science pronounced her
dead. If I had not the evidence of my own eyes to the contrary, I should continue to say she was dead; but when I see
those pretty eyes watching me, I am forced to halt. Lottie is
alive! and says she is not going to die! Plaxico says she will
not die; and if I had not vowed never to give another opinion, I
should say so, too. Plaxico says she was in a trance, sometimes
called an ecstasy—a sort of suspended animation. I say she was
dead; he says he has seen many such cases—I say gammon—
though, bear in mind, I venture no opinion. If the Mississippi
river were to commence running north it would not surprise me;
fact is, nothing could surprise me after what I have seen to-
night. Lottie talks very strangely; says she was with you on
the train to-night; what does it all mean? Plaxico contends that
the soul was temporarily released from the body; I say bosh.
Lottie is much better, mind clear, pulse regular, respiration good,

symptoms all favorable, no pain. Bless Gód, my boy! but **don't** construe this as an opïnion from me. Be cautious when you arrive; Lottie must be prepared to receive you. The slightest shock might prove fatal; will meet you at front gate, and advise you how to act. Get control of your feelings before you see Lottie.   DODSON.'

"Perhaps a man possessed of a vivid imagination might work his mind up to a point where he could make a pretty fair guess as to the joy that came to my crushed heart when I read that dispatch; but I know that no eloquent writer could set down anything approaching a correct description of it. It would not be an exaggeration to say that I was for a moment paralyzed with the excess of joy. I did not shout, scream, or move, but stood like one who had been stunned by a heavy blow, while I held my hand over my heart, pressing it very hard in order to still its violent throbbing. As soon as I recovered sufficiently to enable me to speak calmly I called to Wallingford, who was sitting there with his eyes closed, looking more like a block of white marble than a man.

" 'Are you asleep, Harry?' I inquired, as I laid my hand on his shoulder.

"He gave a sudden start, then gazed a moment at me.

" 'How can I sleep when the hot flames of torment are blazing in my bosom? Never shall I sleep any more; I have "murdered sleep," and my sweet sister, too. My career will soon be closed, and the world will be rid of the vilest wretch that ever dwelt in it!'

" 'Harry, do you believe that any man could be killed with good news?'

" 'No, of course not; but why do you ask me such a question?'

" 'Because it is in my power to impart to you some of the best news that ever was poured into the ears of mortal man!'

" 'Edward,' he groaned, 'you must not try to console me with false hopes; you had better leave me to endure my just punishment; it is the will of God that I should suffer, and I do not complain. You could not tell me anything in the shape of news that would relieve me, except it was to let me know that my darling sister lived, and the guilt of murder was not on my wicked soul.'

" 'That is the very thing I am prepared to assert.'

" 'What in Heaven's name do you mean?'

" 'Be perfectly quiet and I will explain. Could you calmly listen to the news of Lottie being alive?'

" 'Certainly I could, because it would not be true; and I must request you not to torture me in this manner.'

" 'Did you ever hear of a person being in a trance, when the friends thought it was death?'

" 'Yes, very often; Doctor Plaxico told me that such things frequently occurred; he mentioned two cases that had come under his observation.'

" 'Then why might we not hope that such was Lottie's condition when Doctor Dodson telegraphed us that she was dead?'

" 'Edward, pray tell me what you mean!'

" 'Exactly what I say. Now stop, Harry; don't lose control of yourself.'

" 'Edward, you must not trifle with my feelings.'

" 'I do not mean to trifle with your feelings, but I must request you to control them. Do you think you can do it?'

" 'Yes! yes! pray go on.'

" 'Well, in the first place, Lottie is not dead; and in the second place, she is much better; and in the third place, she is going to recover. Now, come, you promised to be calm; remember I hold you to your promise. I will read you the telegram if you will sit down and be perfectly quiet; if you do not, I shall not let you see or hear it.'

" 'What are you talking about? Am I not calm? You don't expect me not to tremble, do you?'

" 'There, now, just sit perfectly still and hear the good news.'

"He at last fell back on the seat and listened to the reading of the telegram, while his eyes were closed and his hands tightly clasped across his breast. When I had finished reading, I knelt down by his seat and whispered:

" 'Kneel down, Harry; now is the very time to offer thanks.'

"He fell on his knees in an instant, and remained there a long time; and when he got up there was a look of inexpressible joy on his countenance. I was satisfied that he was safe, and then I was happy, too.

" 'Eddie,' he said, after remaining silent for a few minutes, apparently soliloquizing, 'if God spares Lottie's life, I will love and worship Him as long as I live.'

" 'Indeed, we should feel very grateful to Him for such a great blessing,' I replied.

" 'What is the time?' he inquired, as he saw me looking at the watch.

" '11:10,' was the reply. 'We will soon see our darling, but we must remember Doctor Dodson's instructions. Do you think you will be able to command your feelings?'

" 'I believe I will, but it will cost a desperate effort.'

" 'We must remember what is at stake, and not forget ourselves when the critical moment arrives.'

" 'I think you may depend on me now. You know how much misery has resulted from my rashness, and I have had a severe, but I hope a useful, lesson.'

" 'Harry, I have always believed that experiential lessons were the only ones of much value.'

" 'I dare say you are correct in that belief; I have reasons to hope that the sad lessons taught me by experience will make a better man of me.'

"The shriek of the locomotive announced our arrival as the train dashed into the station at Memphis. We found the carriage waiting for us when we stepped on the platform.

" 'How is she?' I inquired eagerly as I grasped the hand of the old negro coachman.

" 'Better, much better, sir, thank God; we hope she will recover now.'

" 'Go as fast as you can,' I said, as we entered the carriage.

"The faithful old negro seemed to appreciate the situation, for he took us over the road at the rate of twenty miles an hour. The few pedestrians who were on the streets at that late hour stopped and stared at the carriage as it whirled past them as if they thought the horses were running away.

" 'Some one will be killed certain!' said a man who stood

gazing with wonder as we dashed by him. Many heads were thrust out of the windows; the owners of said heads seemed to have been startled from pleasant dreams by the rattling of the wheels on the pavement.

"Within two minutes from the time we started from the depot I was in the arms of Mrs. Dodson, my good mother. She had been watching at the front gate for our arrival. She kissed my lips, my cheeks, my brow, my temples, and did not slight my nose.

"'Ah, ha! Here we come, my boy!' exclaimed Doctor Dodson, as he snatched me from his wife's arms. 'Get out of my way, Dolly; ah, ha! don't smother the boy; don't you see how he is panting for breath? Stand back, old 'oman; don't you think I want to hug the boy, too? Ah, ha! here we come.' Then he made a grab at my body and jerked me against his breast and squeezed me as hard as a polar bear could have done. 'Ah, ha! my boy, "all's well that ends well," you know. Yes, we will all be happy yet; but don't construe this as an expression of my opinion, by any means. I don't express my opinion on any subject now.'

"While Doctor and Mrs. Dodson were paying their respects to me, Mrs. Rockland was weeping on Harry's breast, and Mr. Rockland, who rarely ever suffered anything to disturb his equanimity, was jumping around, trying to get hold of Harry.

"'How is my darling?' I inquired, as soon as I could release myself from Doctor Dodson's embrace.

"'Better, much better, my boy, thank Heaven!'

"'Let me see her instantly; I cannot wait a moment longer; I am dying to hold her in my arms!'

"We were at the front gate, some distance from the house.

"'Ah, ha! my boy, be calm; Lottie is asleep; can't let you see her now; crisis not passed yet—life hangs by brittle threads—patience, my boy, patience! Keep cool; ah, ha! keep cool, my boy. Give me another hug. There now; ah, ha! that's like old times. Plaxico is with Lottie; will consult with him; if he thinks there is no risk, you shall see her! ah, ha! that you shall, my boy! Let her sleep, though; she must not be disturbed until she awakes. Take your boots off

when you get to the house, my boy—Dolly will get you a
pair of slippers. Caution, my boy, caution, you see the necessity of it, don't you, my boy? Yes, of course you do. Ah,
ha! here we come!'

"In pursuance of instructions, I took off my boots and
thrust my feet into a pair of cloth slippers which Mrs. Dodson handed to me as we entered the front portico. Mrs.
Rockland furnished Harry with a pair of the same sort, and
the cat-like movements of all showed how they loved the angelic creature whose life was trembling in the balance. Doctor Dodson whispered a few words to me, then went into
Lottie's room, and soon returned, accompanied by Doctor
Plaxico.

" 'How is she now, doctor?' I inquired.

" 'Oh, she is all right now, sir; I think she will come round
handsomely. She is sleeping quite soundly—pulse greatly
improved—respiration regular.'

" 'Can we see her now?' I eagerly demanded.

" 'Yes, certainly, provided you obey instructions to the
very letter. Only one of you can go in at a time, and you
must not speak to or touch her; but if you have the slightest
doubt as to your ability to control your feelings, you had better
not go in.'

" 'You go in first,' said I to Harry.

" 'No, Edward, I yield to you—it is your privilege to see
her first. Go in and give me time to get my feelings under
control.'

"It was his generous heart that prompted him to give me
the preference.

" 'Come with me,' said Plaxico, as he took hold of my arm,
'I cannot trust you alone, when so much depends on your
actions.'

"As soon as I passed through the half open door I encountered the same sweet scent of flowers that had so strangely
come into the coach between Sardis and Grenada. I recognized it instantly; there was no mistaking the delicious fragrance; the carpet was covered with fresh flowers; the mantel was loaded with them. Two large bouquets lay on the
snow-white cover of the bed. There lay my darling, pale but
beautiful still. Her eyes and lips were closed, and the long,

pretty lashes fell over her eyes, concealing them from my view. I approached the bedside silently and fell on my knees near the beautiful patient. I could hear the gentle breathing, and see the regular rise and fall of her bosom, as her sweet breath fanned my cheeks, and it taxed my strength to its utmost capacity to keep from touching her. Doctor Plaxico, doubtless fearing that I might be unable to control myself, stood on the opposite side of the bed, so as to be in front of me, with his finger raised, by way of cautioning me to be quiet. The bed on which the pretty sleeper reposed was near the center of the room, a low French bedstead, and her arms were resting above the white counterpane that covered it. Occasionally a sweet smile would light up her pale, beautiful face, and I could hear her whispering my name.

" 'She is dreaming about you now, Demar,' whispered Plaxico, as he put his mouth close to my ear. 'She appears to be thinking of you all the time, both when asleep and awake; she holds your picture in her hand constantly, and I do not believe any one could steal it from her without awaking her.'

"Placing my ear close to her lips, in order to hear what she was saying, my long whiskers happened to touch her chin, when her body instantly began to tremble violently.

" 'Edward is coming home to-night, mother,' she whispered.

"Was it a sin to worship that charming girl, who dreamed of me while asleep, and loved and prayed for me when awake? If it was, then you may set me down as a very great sinner, for I did worship her with a devotion as fervent and sincere as that with which any heathen ever worshiped his god.

" 'You must retire now, Demar,' whispered the doctor, 'as I think there is danger of her being disturbed, for you do not seem to have control of your feelings. Refreshing sleep is what she needs most just now; it is the best restorative in cases of this sort, and it would be very unfortunate if you should happen to disturb her.'

"I reluctantly obeyed his command and withdrew to the parlor, accompanied by him.

" 'How is my dear sister now, doctor?' eagerly exclaimed Harry, as he met us at the door.

" 'Every symptom appears to be favorable,' the physician replied. 'She is sleeping quite soundly, and her fever is entirely gone; pulse greatly improved; but we must be extremely cautious not to give her a sudden shock when she awakes.'

" 'When can I see her?'

" 'I will let you go in any moment when you are sure that you can govern yourself completely, for you shall promise me not to touch or speak to your sister.'

" 'I make the promise now, and beg you to let me see her.'

"Plaxico took his arm and led him into Lottie's room; and at the end of five minutes he returned, and, sinking down on the sofa, buried his face in his mother's bosom and burst into tears.

" 'Weep, my dear son,' said Mrs. Rockland, as she pressed him to her heart, 'it will do you good; I often find relief in tears when sorrow weighs heavily upon me.'

" 'My dear, good mother,' he exclaimed, as he threw his arms around her neck, 'can you ever love me again after I have caused you so many hours of sorrow?'

" 'Love you, my son! Nothing could deprive you of my love; you have erred, but you were deceived by a combination of circumstances that would have misled any one.'

" 'Mother, can you forgive me?'

" 'There is nothing to pardon, my son; you thought your sister was betrayed, and that it was your duty to defend her; you acted upon what appeared to be proof, and not from an evil motive.'

"Doctor Plaxico took a seat near me, and requested Mrs. Rockland to go into Lottie's room and keep watch until the patient should wake. I then gave the doctor a detailed history of the strange events that happened on the train, and requested him to give me the benefit of his opinion on the subject.

" 'Ah! Demar,' said he, 'if you follow the profession as long as I have, you will encounter many curious things. This is the third case of the same sort that I have treated. I was not here when Dodson telegraphed you that she was dead; of course I should have prevented it. Dodson's heart is too large—it gets away with his judgment. Miss Wallingford was

merely in a short trance—a fortunate thing, too, by the by.
That was one of nature's scientific plans adopted to cure the
patient; and I think it has succeeded. The authorities differ
as to the causes of such a condition, and many different
theories have been advanced on the subject; but I am sorry
to say that nothing satisfactory has been developed. I am
decidedly inclined to the views of the minority, who think
that the soul for the time being is absolutely out of the body.
You say that Miss Wallingford was with you on the train at
exactly 9:20. I believe it, too, for that was the very moment
when she fell into the trance. Now if the soul was temporarily released from the body, where would it be most likely
to go? Of course to where her affections led—to the man of
whom she had been thinking all the time. If my theory is
not correct, your imagination was at fault, and you were mistaken in your belief. The fact is, Demar, the more we study
and theorize on this subject, the more complicated it seems.
I often rack my brain about the matter until it all ends in
confusion. God was the Artist who made the wonderful
machine called man, and he crammed him full of mystery,
eccentricities and unaccountable things. Well, Demar, the
best way to secure true happiness is to fear God and keep
His commandments; and let Him run the machine in his
own way. What is, is, and that's all we know about it. We
don't know the cause of things; and the less we puzzle our
brains about it the better for us. But let me tell you, Demar,
you ought to worship God day and night, as long as you live.
What have you ever done for Him, by way of compensation
for what He has done for you? He made Miss Wallingford;
she is the paragon of beauty and loveliness—an angel in disposition; and then He made her fall in love with you. That
is more than you deserve—more than any sinner deserves.'

" 'I know it, doctor, and I acknowledge my obligation, and
have resolved never to forget it.'

" 'Excuse me, Demar, I must now go and see my patient;
I will return presently.'

"After Lottie had slept three hours Doctor Plaxico consented for me to go into her room again.

" 'I think she will wake very soon,' said he, 'and you had
better be present then; you must be very cautious and not

exhibit any unusual emotion. Remember she is in a critical condition, and the slightest shock might prove fatal, and govern yourself accordingly. At first I thought that probably it would be better to let some one break the news of your arrival to her, before letting her see you; but upon second thought I have concluded to allow you to be present when she awakes. Place yourself near the bed, take hold of her hand, press it gently, and remain very quiet; be sure you do not make any demonstrations when you see her eyes open.'

"This was a hard command, but I made up my mind to obey it, believing, as I did, that it was wisely given. Kneeling down near the bed, I took her left hand in mine, pressing it gently to my lips, when she instantly commenced to roll her head from one side to the other.

" 'Let go her hand, quick!' the doctor whispered.

"I obeyed instantly, but was puzzled to know his reasons for giving such an order. Plaxico stood with his finger on his mouth, which I understood to be a command for me to maintain silence. Any one might have heard the throbbing of my heart across the room, while every nerve in my body was quivering violently.

" 'Now take hold of her hand again, and be careful to remain quiet.'

"The very instant my hand touched hers she again began to tremble; raising her other hand, she commenced to pass it round, as if searching for something, while her lips were continually moving; and every now and then I distinctly heard my name pronounced. I was informed by the doctor that she was under the influence of a very strong opiate, which I suppose accounted for the apparent uneasiness of her slumber. Five minutes, perhaps, had elapsed after I took hold of her hand the second time when she touched my cheek; then running her fingers among my whiskers, she began to pat me on the face. At length her eyes flew open; and after gazing at me for a moment in a bewildered way, she laid her right arm around my neck, drew my head down on the pillow, close to her cheek, and whispered in my ear many sweet expressions of affection. There were no evidences of violent emotion or extravagant outbursts of excitement, but her voice sounded like the cooing of a dove. My face was moistened with the tears that streamed from her eyes; but they were tears of unmixed joy.

" 'I thought they had killed my noble-hearted hero,' she whispered, as she drew her arm closer about my neck. 'I have been very unjust to my poor brother, but I thought he and Heartsell had murdered you; and you must bring him here, so I can ask him to pardon me. I was with you and brother on the train last night, and tried to speak to you, but could not make you hear me. Our mother was with me, and she says that she is our guardian angel, commissioned to watch over us—she was such a beautiful angel, too; I never beheld anything so pretty.'

" 'Miss Wallingford,' said Doctor Plaxico, 'I think it would be very imprudent for you to talk any more just now.'

" 'I would not venture to disobey a peremptory order of yours, doctor, but I believe that a conversation with Harry and Edward would do me more good now than any medicine you could give me. Let me see my dear brother immediately, and then you may demand silence.'

" 'I had better grant your request than to raise a row by refusing,' observed the doctor, as he went to bring Wallingford in.

"When Harry entered the room, I could see that he was making a vigorous effort to restrain his great emotions; sinking down on the opposite side of the bed, he allowed his sister to embrace him.

" 'Brother dear,' whispered Lottie, 'can you forgive the great wrong I have done by my unjust suspicions against you?'

" 'Ah! my darling sister, it is I who ought to sue for pardon; because if I had heeded your advice, all this sorrow might have been prevented. If you only will get well, and love me in the future as you have in the past, I shall yet be happy. Let us endeavor to eradicate from our memory the sad occurrences of the past; and I solemnly promise never again to set up my judgment against yours.'

" 'Oh, my good brother! how happy you have made me! I soon shall be well again. I thought at one time that I could leave this world without regret; but it is different with me now; I do not want to die, because I have something worth living for.'

" 'Now, Miss Wallingford,' said Plaxico, 'I must positively drive these two gentlemen out of the room, unless you will agree to be perfectly quiet.'

" 'I will make any promise, in the bounds of reason, if you will let them remain with me.'

" 'Very well; they may stay, if you will hush.'

"Harry held her right hand and I her left, while I drank deep draughts of love from the dear eyes that were gazing up into my own. Who can describe the inexpressible joy that one feels when he knows himself to be the exclusive owner of such a heart as the one that throbbed in the breast of Lottie Wallingford? It would be extreme folly on my part to attempt to convey to my audience a description of the great happiness I enjoyed then. My heart was almost drowned with the excess of delight.

CHAPTER XXX.

"For three days after Harry and I had arrived at home scarcely any change was perceptible in Lottie's condition, except an inclination to sleep all the time, which Plaxico contended was most favorable. This conjecture proved correct, for at the end of ten days her condition was so much improved that he pronounced her entirely out of danger.

" 'Good nursing is all she needs now,' said he.

"I never left the premises until I was satisfied that all danger was over, and I did not go then of my own accord; Lottie ordered me to go and see Viola, and to carry a hamper basket full of fresh flowers that she had caused to be gathered for her.

" 'Tell Viola that as soon as I am able to ride in the carriage I will come to see her. Ask her if she wants anything and tell her that she must be of good cheer, and we will defeat the enemy yet. Now do your best to encourage the poor thing, and assure her that I will soon be with her to stay all the time.'

" 'Lottie, you don't think of going back to stay in jail again, do you?'

" 'Certainly I do; why not?'

" 'People will talk, you know.'

" 'Let them talk as much as they please. God has spared my life in order that I might save my dear friend, and I mean to do it. Eddie, do you still doubt me? Can you trust me?'

"I did not make any answer, because I was bewildered and did not know what to say; hence I abruptly left the room to carry the flowers and message as directed.

"When I entered Viola's cell I was shocked at her appearance; there was a look of hopeless despair settled on her face, and her cheeks were bloodless and deadly pale. She was dressed in plain black silk without ornaments. Her pale face brightened up when I entered, and she rose to meet me, holding out her hand for me to take. When I delivered the flowers and Lottie's kind message, telling her that Lottie was out of all danger, she burst into tears and sank down on the sofa. After a while she brushed the tears away and said:

" 'Pardon me, Mr. Demar; this flow of tears has relieved my aching heart. God has answered my prayers, when I had lost all hope. Oh! sir, if you knew how I have prayed for dear Lottie's life, you would better understand my love for her. Take a seat, Mr. Demar, and tell me about your late troubles.'

"I complied with her request by giving her a detailed history of the unfortunate occurrences that had kept me away from home.

" 'You now know from experience, Mr. Demar, how hard it is to be punished for a crime you did not commit. You have not told me anything about your friends yet.'

"I knew that she wanted to hear from Harry, but I doubted the propriety of mentioning his name, because I did not know what he intended to do. I therefore confined my remarks to Doctor and Mrs. Dodson, and Mr. Rockland and his wife, studiously avoiding Harry's name. I saw that she was disappointed, and more anxious than ever to hear about him. I rose to depart, when she begged me to stay a while longer.

" 'You have not told me about all of your friends yet,' she said, as she blushed and looked down at the carpet.

"I noticed that she was trembling from head to foot, and her bosom rose and fell rapidly. I had arrived at the conclusion that it was best for me not to mention Harry's name. I thought that the best plan to bring about a reconciliation would be to say nothing on the subject, hoping that she would send an invitation to him to pay her a visit.

" 'Is there any one in particular whom you wish to inquire about, Miss Bramlett?'

" 'Yes—no—that is, no one in particular; but I was thinking that Lottie would be so happy to have her brother with her.' And as she said this, the crimson tinge on her cheeks became as red as blood could make it.

" 'Yes, she is very happy now, since her brother has returned.'

" 'Has he? Ah! never mind, Mr. Demar, I will not detain you any longer. Give my love to Lottie, and bring her to see me as soon as she is able to come.'

"I took her extended hand and felt it quiver; her eyes met mine for a second, and there was a meaning look in them which I understood. I could not leave her thus; my resolution vanished at once.

" 'What shall I tell him for you, Miss Bramlett?'

" 'Tell whom?'

" 'Have you no message for me to deliver to any one except Lottie?'

" 'Yes—no; I—I—good-by, Mr. Demar.'

"I passed out of the room and spoke a few words to the jailer, and when I went to leave I glanced a look into Viola's room. She was lying on the bed convulsed with grief, and weeping bitterly.

"I sought and obtained an interview with Mr. Rockland, in order to have a consultation about Miss Bramlett's case. The iron man shook his head ominously when I asked him to advise me what I should do about the case.

" 'The Supreme Court will reverse it,' said he, 'beyond question, but that will do no good. It will only serve to prolong our troubles. The lower court committed a very grave error in allowing the jury to disperse before the evidence closed; hence I say it is certain that a new trial will be granted; but again I ask where is the benefit to Miss Bramlett? Every one knows she is guilty—the proof established it beyond the possibility of a reasonable doubt. Poor girl! I pity her, for she was not responsible for the crime. She was crazy, beyond question, when she committed it. She shall not be punished, because I will secure executive clemency when the court shall have finally disposed of her case. Mr. Demar, I have just been informed that it is Lottie's intention to return to the jail, with a view of remaining with Miss Bramlett, as soon as she is able to go.'

" 'Yes, Mr. Rockland, I have heard Lottie say that such was her intention.'

" 'This must be prevented by all means, and no one can do it but you; I shall expect you to exert your influence in that direction. Her reputation has already suffered to some extent by her conduct, and it must be prevented in future.'

" 'Do you know, Mr. Rockland, that Lottie affirms that she knows Miss Bramlett is innocent?'

" 'Ah, Demar, that is one of her strange infatuations. She is a sensible girl, in whose judgment I have unbounded confidence, but her friendship for Miss Bramlett has caused her heart to get the upper hand of her brain. She thinks she knows that her friend is innocent, but what does she know about the rules of evidence? She thinks everything that she hears can be offered as proof.'

" 'I imagine, sir, that you will find Lottie better posted as to the rules of evidence than you think. She has been reading Mr. Greenleaf's treatise on evidence—also Mr. Starkie's and many others. She seems to comprehend and grasp the meaning as well as an experienced lawyer would. She says she will furnish evidence to clear Miss Bramlett, and to convict the real criminal.'

" 'Ah! Demar, that is the strangest mystery that has ever come under my observation. If she knew that Miss Bramlett was innocent, why should she let her remain in jail, when she could have got her out with a *habeas corpus?* No, Demar, if you build your hopes on that foundation, you will meet with nothing but defeat and disappointment.'

" 'The reasons which Lottie gives for witholding the proof

appear to me to be good. She says that she is waiting to collect evidence sufficient to convict the guilty one; and that
this is done at the request of Miss Bramlett.'

" 'Very well, Demar, I see that you are determined to pin
your faith to Lottie's skirts. The truth of it is, love has got
the upper hand of your judgment, while Lottie is carried
away by her affection for Miss Bramlett. I admire those
who stick to their friends, but we ought to be very cautious in
selecting them. Next week the Supreme Court will take up
the case, and then a new trial will be granted, certain, and
you and Lottie shall have a fair chance to establish the defendant's innocence if you can.'

"When I left the iron lawyer, I was chilled to the very
marrow of my bones by the coldness of his manner.

"About eight days after my arrival at home, I was called
from Lottie's side (where most of my time was being spent)
to assist Doctor Dodson in performing a difficult surgical
operation on one of his patients. In fact, I performed the
operation myself under Doctor Dodson's advice and assistance.

" 'Ah, ha! my boy,' said the old doctor, when the delicate
job was finished, 'you are an excellent surgeon, so you are.
I am proud of you—so I am. You will do to tie to; ah, ha!
that you will. Lottie need not be afraid to hitch on to you,
my boy; no indeed, you will make a living for her; yes, yes,
ah, ha! she won't starve by marrying you. You must remain
with this patient day and night until all danger is over. Ah,
ha! my boy, stick to it like a leech; I'll relieve you day after
to-morrow.'

"By this means I was kept away from Lottie two days and
nights, much against my wish; but I stood to my post until I
was relieved on the third morning by Doctor Dodson. I
hurried to Mr. Rockland's residence and met his wife at the
door.

" 'How is Lottie?' I hurriedly inquired, as I entered the
house.

" 'Improving rapidly, though I don't think she is quite as
prudent as she ought to be.'

" 'Can I see her now?'

" 'No, Edward, she is asleep, I believe; but come in to breakfast, and then you can see her.'

"I obeyed reluctantly, because I did not feel like eating. As soon as breakfast was over Mrs. Rockland went into Lottie's room to inform her that I was waiting to see her.

" 'She will receive you, Edward,' said the kind lady, as she came into the parlor where I was waiting. 'She bid me tell you to come in.'

"The door of Lottie's room was half open when I entered; and the bed, where I expected to see her, was made up and covered with a snow-white counterpane; every article of furniture was freshly dusted and properly arranged; two large vases of fresh 'flowers stood on the mantel, and the room contained no evidences of an occupant.

" 'Ah! she has moved to her old room up-stairs!' I exclaimed, as I turned to go out, when I felt some one pluck my hair behind. Imagine my amazement, if you can, when I hurriedly turned round and saw nothing but an empty room, where I had expected to see Lottie. I had not remained there, however, but a second or two, when I heard a suppressed laugh; and looking behind the door, I discovered my darling in full dress—beautiful, radiant, charming and lovely,—with a mischievous smile playing on her face. Never had I seen her looking so beautiful before; the color of the rose and lily were mingled on her fair cheeks, while evidences of restored health appeared. Her toilet had been arranged with great care and exquisite taste, evidently done to please me, for I had sent word that I was coming to see her that morning. She wore a most magnificent rose-pink brocade silk dress, with full train; the body and skirts were covered with point de Venice lace, while the bodice fitted the slender waist so neatly that her square shoulders and tall, queenly form exhibited their beauty to great advantage. My picture, incased in a heavy gold locket, was suspended by a costly chain around her neck, and my diamond ring sparkled on her finger. The great rolls of pretty golden curls had been half confined behind her head with a blue ribbon, while a fresh white rose, bordered on all sides with pink geraniums, adorned her throat. As soon as my eyes encountered the lovely creature before me I threw up my hands with an exclamation of surprise. When I left her, two days previous, she was in bed, where I had expected to find her still; but when I beheld her beautiful form standing before me, with all the loveliness and beauty of an angel, I was dazzled and overwhelmed with amazement. I was not able to understand how such a speedy recovery had been effected. The pretty blue eyes had regained all their charming brilliancy and the stately form its beauteous symmetry; in fact, my darling had never before appeared so lovely in my eyes as she did then.

"'Why, Eddie!' she exclaimed, as I took her in my arms, 'where have you been hiding all this time? I declare, if you play me another such a dodge, I will set the police on your track!'

"'Don't ask me any questions now, Lottie; I am too happy to talk. Let me look at you well; you are so pretty to-day; I never saw you looking so lovely!'

"'I never felt better in my life—am as strong as ever. I was up early this morning, dressed myself without assistance, made up my bed, re-arranged the furniture, and am now ready for breakfast. And such an appetite as I have—it is like that of a wolf! You were surprised to see me up and dressed; you admire my appearance; well, I am glad you do. You shall not see me eat breakfast; I should be ashamed to let you see how much I can devour. Go order the carriage while I am eating; I am going to see Viola this morning. Why don't you go along, Eddie? What are you waiting for?'

"'Don't you know?'

"'I have a very strong suspicion; very well, I suppose I must be kind to the old darling, since he has been so true to, and suffered so much for me. Take it quickly and go, for I am starving. There! there! Eddie, go along with you; don't you see how you have torn my hair down? I declare, you have almost smothered me; you are like a Russian bear.'

"She dodged under my arm, and went into the dining-room. I went out and ordered the coachman to get the carriage ready, then came back to the parlor and waited for Lottie.

"'Well, Eddie,' she said, as she entered the parlor and took a seat on the sofa by my side, 'I have devoured everything on the table, and, like Oliver Twist, I wanted more, but mother closed down on me, and even refused to let me eat the cold scraps that were left in the cupboard.'

" 'I fear you are imprudent, Lottie,' said I, 'but I am truly glad to know that you have an appetite.'

" 'Thank you, Eddie; but now I must ask you to talk business with me a while. We must lay aside all selfish thoughts, and go to work on Viola's case. You must not talk to me about love or marriage; I request you to promise me here and now that you will devote your whole attention to this business, and that you will not mention love to me until Viola's innocence shall be established. Will you or will you not do it?'

" 'I promise to obey you in all things, under all circumstances; but what is to be my fate if we fail to clear Viola? Would you then refuse to marry me?'

" 'Yes, I would, though it would break my heart to do it; but I love you too well to make you the husband of a miserable, unhappy woman, such as I would be if Viola is not cleared. But I tell you candidly that we shall all be happy yet, if you will trust me implicitly. I must have your entire confidence; there must be no doubting or hesitating in this business. Again I ask you, will you trust me in all things connected with this business?'

" 'So help me Heaven, I swear I will!'

" 'Enough; I ask no more. Read that letter carefully while I re-arrange my hair, and then I will tell you what you are to do.'

" 'Lottie, tell me where you got this letter.'

" 'Ask me no questions, but trust me implicitly. I will not submit to a cross-examination, mind you.'

" 'Very good; issue your orders, and I will obey. Nothing can astonish me after looking at this letter.'

" 'That is a mere mole-hill, by a mountain, when compared with other things that I know.'

" 'Lottie, this letter means death; it smells of blood; it is as black as the deepest hell!'

" 'Hush! don't become excited; coolness and courage will accomplish more than anger or excitement. The time has come to shake up the dry bones in the valley; God has spared me in order to make me His instrument in saving the innocent and punishing the guilty.'

" 'Lottie, I do believe you are aided in this business by inspiration directly sent to you from Heaven.'

" 'Perhaps so, and perhaps not; but Viola's day of deliverance is near at hand; and the day of retribution for the real murderer is drawing near. Society has condemned me for associating with Viola—the purest, best, most patient, suffering angel that ever lived. I will make society blush with shame for its cruelty in this case.'

, " 'Lottie, pardon me for using strong language; but I think the circumstances justify it; therefore, I say that the writer of that letter ought to be roasted in the hottest flames of——'

" 'Stop! stop! don't use such language as that; it does no good. We must move cautiously, as we have a wily foe to deal with. We must have a witness in court to prove that handwriting; and that is why I have shown you that letter. There is a woman in this city by whom we can make the proof—provided we can force her to swear the truth. She is a friend to the writer, and would suffer martyrdom before she would tell anything that would injure him if she knew it; but if you will execute a little plan which I have invented, I will answer for the result.'

" 'Explain the plan, and issue orders. I trust you now with more faith than an Arab would the author of the Koran. Consider me a machine made to do your bidding.'

" 'I like that kind of talk now, because everything depends on you and me.'

" 'More especially on you, Lottie. You are the pilot, and I am only the engine.'

" 'We will not dispute about that; but you must have an interview with a certain woman, with a view of proving the handwriting of that letter. You are acquainted with Miss Clattermouth, I believe?'

" 'To the best of my knowledge and belief, I should say I was; but I would not like to confess it in public.'

" 'I don't blame you for that, because there is not much honor in it; but it is a fortunate thing that you do know her, for it will aid you in this business. I want you to go and see her; take this letter with you; and I charge you under no circumstances to let her see the contents; but you will manage to show her the superscription, and by that means ascertain whether or not she knows who wrote it. Remember, she is a devoted friend of the writer, and if she suspects your object, your labor is lost. You must invent some plan to direct her attention to the letter, and she will probably ask you where you got it. Then you can ask her if she knows the handwriting; do you think you can manage the business so as to accomplish the purpose without rousing her suspicions?'

" 'Lottie, you have asked me to trust you, and I am going to do it. Now I ask you to trust me; will you do it?'

" 'That I will, with all the faith that is in me; and without intending to flatter you, I would risk my soul's future happiness on your judgment and integrity.'

" 'Thank you! thank you, darling! enough on that branch of the subject. Let us now discuss another. Shall we let Harry into our secrets and ask his assistance?'

" 'No, indeed, we must not, because his love for Viola would cause his heart to control his brain, and endanger our plans. He has quieted down since his late troubles, and it is better to let him alone. The breach between him and Viola will heal itself when she is cleared.'

" 'Be it so, then; you are the judge.'

" 'You must not lose sight of our Vicksburg witness; it would be advisable to write to him immediately. That evidence I consider the most important of all.'

" 'I must confess I cannot see its application to Viola's case; but you may depend on me for having the witness here when the trial comes on.'

" 'You shall be posted as to its application in due time. There are two individuals in this city who are mounted on very high horses, riding to their fate. They are enjoying the ride just now, unconscious of the precipice toward which they are hastening. They are reveling in their fancied security, little dreaming of the mine soon to be sprung under their feet.'

" 'One of them is the writer of this letter—the other the

one to whom it was directed. Am I not correct in that guess, Lottie?'

" 'You are correct.'

" 'Well, if anybody but my darling had told me this, I would not have believed a word of it. This business is going to cause some people's fine castles to come toppling topsy-turvey down; and great will be the fall thereof.'

" 'It won't be the first instance where a man was hung on the gallows he had built for another. You may have heard of a man who erected a gallows fifty cubits high, on which he intended to hang his neighbor; but the spectators were no doubt surprised, one morning, when they saw the body of the builder dangling from his own gallows.'

" 'Yes, that was a case in which God seems to have directly interfered.'

" 'Just so; and he has directly interfered in Viola's case, too.'

" 'Lottie, I am dying with curiosity to know how you got possession of that letter.'

" 'You shall know everything that I know; but not at present. I have a reason for withholding the information just now, which I cannot explain. Remember you have promised to trust me fully in this matter.'

" 'Yes, and I mean to do it; but the very sight of this letter freezes the warm blood in my veins. I feel cold rigors stealing over me now. It is horrible to contemplate. It surpasses my comprehension. It would make Satan blush to read this most diabolical composition. He would be inclined to abdicate in favor of the author of that letter, as the one best qualified to run the infernal government.'

" 'Hush! that is wicked language. Go see if the carriage is ready, while I get my hat and cloak. You will first go with me to the jail; leave me with Viola; go and see Miss Clattermouth about the proof as to the handwriting; then return to the jail, remain with us to dinner, and bring me home at night. There, now, you have the programme for the day, and remember, you must sharpen your wits before you tackle Miss Clattermouth. She is a clever little detective herself, and will get the best of you if you don't be careful.'

" 'If she gets the upper hand of me in this business, you nay take off both of my ears.'

" 'Come! I see the carriage is waiting for us. Don't take my arm—that is out of style now.'

CHAPTER XXXI.

"I ESCORTED Lottie to the jail, and when she and Miss Bramlett rushed into each other's arms, I was so deeply moved by the affecting meeting of those two devoted friends that I felt the tears begin to trickle down my cheeks. For full five minutes they remained silently clasped in each other's strong embrace.

" 'Heaven bless you, my precious, true, unselfish friend!' exclaimed Miss Bramlett, still holding Lottie to her heart; 'God has answered my prayers, for on my knees I have spent four hours every day in sending up my supplications in behalf of my darling Lottie. I am one of those who have unlimited confidence in the goodness and mercy of God, and believe He answers the prayers of those who ask in the spirit of true faith. Every time I knelt down to pray for the recovery of my darling friend, I thought of that precious promise which our dear Saviour made with His own lips, when He said: "Ask and it shall be given you; seek and ye shall find; knock and it shall be opened unto you. For every one that asketh, receiveth; and he that seeketh, findeth; and to him that knocketh, it shall be opened." Now, Lottie, when I prayed, I did honestly believe that our dear Jesus would remember His precious promise; and sure enough He has. Oh, dear God, receive my humble, but sincere, thanks for this great blessing!'

"Lottie then came to me, smiling through her tears and looking supremely happy.

" 'You may go to see Miss Clattermouth now, Edward; and you must not fail to return here punctually at four o'clock, for I am going to order another one of those cozy dinners, to be served in Viola's room; therefore you must not keep us waiting. Remember the instructions, and let no consideration or circumstance prevent the success of our enterprise, which you know to be of such great importance.'

"Pressing her hand to my lips, and promising to put in my appearance punctually at four o'clock, I jumped into the carriage and ordered the coachman to drive to the residence of Miss Clattermouth. As the vehicle went rumbling over the rough road, I began to reflect on the business before me, with a view of arranging my plans so as to be ready to act promptly at the proper time.

"The carriage halted in front of the house before any definite scheme was arranged in my mind. Walking up to the door, I gave the bell a vigorous pull, and a moment after I heard the slamming of innumerable doors, and then the front one flew open, and there appeared a living creature. It would be a misnomer to say it was a woman; yet it was not a man or monkey; and not being a believer in witches, I am at a loss to describe the horrible looking object that stood with glaring eyes riveted on me. Miss Cushman's representation of the Gypsy in 'Guy Mannering' would be a fairy when compared with the hideous object who darkened that door. I ran back eight or ten paces, while an involuntary shudder darted through my body. I did not smell brimstone, see fire, or hear thunder, but the same feelings of horror seized upon me that I had experienced once upon a time when I went to see the infernal regions in a museum. This she-demon (a name I think most proper to give her) held out her long bony arm toward me, and began to work her claw-like fingers as if she wanted to grab me.

" 'What do ye stand there for, staring at a body like an idiot?' she growled; 'are ye dumb? Can't ye tell what ye want?'

" 'I wish to see Miss Clattermouth,' I stammered with no little difficulty.

" 'Get along with ye to Tadpoddle's then!' and the door was closed with a slam, and I felt very much relieved. I was pleased to learn that I should find Miss Clattermouth and Miss Tadpoddle together, as I imagined that this circumstance would facilitate the important business which I was so anxious to transact. I lost no time, you may be sure, in leaping into the carriage, and as I did so, I gave the coachman instructions to hasten to the Tadpoddle mansion. I found the front hall door open when I arrived, and being well acquainted with the premises, I immediately and without ceremony passed through the hall, and made my appearance at the door of Miss Tadpoddle's boudoir, which I also found standing wide open. As I entered the house my ears were pierced with a succession of the most doleful and heart-rending cries that I had ever heard. Miss Tadpoddle was lying on the sofa in the middle of the room, and her mother was bathing her temples with some sort of liquid, while Miss Clattermouth was holding a smelling bottle to her nose.

"'Oh, mother! how can I live when my sweet, precious little darling is dead? Oh, ho! ho! ho! it will kill me, I know it will! Every time I shut my eyes I can see the pretty little darling in his tiny coffin, wrapped in his little ruffled shroud, with his sweet little eyes closed just as if he was asleep. Oh, ho! ho! ho! shall I never see him again in this world? Oh, mother, let me die! I do not want to live now, since my little angel is gone from me forever. He loved me so much, and was such a comfort to me—he was always crying after me when I was away from him.'

"My heart was deeply moved to hear the poor lady's sorrowful lamentations, and it was with some difficulty that I restrained my tears. I began to look round for a little coffin, but it was not there. I then cast a glance up and down the hall, expecting to see an empty baby carriage or tenantless crib, but I saw them not. No little baby shoes or baby frocks were in sight; no baby hats; no broken toys, or any article such as pleases little boys, were to be seen. That a boy baby was dead I concluded was certain, for I heard her speak of his little coffin, and his little shroud. Now what does it all mean? was a question which naturally presented itself to my mind. Who is the little angel that has been taken back to Heaven? Ah, I have it now! She has adopted some sweet little orphan child, and just as she began to love it dearly, the little darling has laid down and died.

"'I beg pardon, ladies,' said I, as I bowed to Miss Clattermouth, 'I did not know that death had entered this house, else I should not have intruded.'

"'Oh! doctor,' exclaimed Miss Tadpoddle, wringing her

hands and tossing her head from side to side, as if suffering untold anguish, 'I am so glad you have come; do pray put me to sleep as soon as you can, for my poor heart is forever crushed—I never shall survive this awful calamity. Ah! doctor, my poor little darling is taken from me, and no one will ever love me as he did; he was always crying to get in my lap; for Heaven's sake give me a sleeping drug; I don't care what it is; anything to make me forget this melancholy dispensation of Providence. Oh, me! it is more than I can bear —to think that I never shall see poor little Tottie any more; it will be the death of me; I know it will!'

"Now I was perfectly amazed when I heard Tottie's name mentioned, for the whole mystery was then cleared up. All this nonsense was produced by the death of an eight-ounce poodle dog; and I hastened to a pitcher of water, poured out a glass and pretended to get strangled, so I might have a chance to conceal the mirth that was about to precipitate me into a fit of laughter. I was compelled to walk out into the hall, in order to gain time to get control of myself, as I did not wish to appear rude. Miss Tadpoddle seemed to be growing worse all the time, and continued to implore me for a sleeping drug; and I concluded that it was best to make a show of compassion, which I did, but not without a considerable effort. I requested Miss Clattermouth to procure me a spoonful of flour, and while she went after it, I took out my medicines and scattered them about on the top of a bureau that stood in one corner of the room; and as I was thinking more about the proof which I wanted to make by Miss Clattermouth than anything else, I took out the letter and laid it down among the medicines, where I knew she could see it when she brought the flour. My mind was wrought up to a high pitch of anxiety; because I had been led by Lottie to believe that the fate of Miss Bramlett depended entirely on the success or failure of my enterprise. Consequently, an unusual degree of excitement seized upon me when I saw her eyes fixed on the letter as she handed me the flour. I felt my heart thumping violently in my breast, while I held my breath and tried to assume a careless air, as I began to finger my drugs. There was a large mirror swinging on the top of the bureau, which enabled me to watch Miss Clattermouth without letting her know what I was up to; and I could see that her little round eyes were intently fixed on the letter, while an expression of curiosity mantled her face. I felt my knees knocking against each other, and my whole frame began to shake from the intense anxiety that possessed me. When Banquo's ghost 'shook its gory locks' at Macbeth, at the banquet, he did not tremble more than I did on that important occasion.

" 'Oh, doctor!' exclaimed Miss Tadpoddle, 'are you going to let me die? Why don't you put me to sleep? Are you going to save my life or not?'

" 'My dear madame, I beg you to command a little patience —you shall soon be relieved; it is our duty to submit humbly to the decrees of Providence.'

" 'Yes! yes! I know it is, doctor, but those who never felt the heavy hand of affliction laid upon them, as it is now laid on poor me, cannot understand or appreciate the awful calamity.'

"I hastily prepared three wheat dough pills, and persuaded her to swallow them, assuring her that they would put her to sleep in a very short while; and in less than five minutes she declared that she felt a great deal better.

" 'Ah! doctor, you are such a good physician; you seem to comprehend the nature of one's complaint at a glance. Now you know I never exaggerate; there is nothing I despise more than I do exaggeration; still I do believe my nervous system is completely destroyed; but if anybody can restore my shattered system, you are the man to do it. I declare, I begin to feel drowsy now. Oh, what a relief! Just run your hand through my hair and over my throbbing temples. Oh, that is delicious! indeed it is! You do not know how much good it is doing me!'

"At the end of twenty minutes from the time I administered my pills Miss Tadpoddle was happy in the arms of Morpheus, probably dreaming sweetly about poodle dogs. Now, my friends, I wish to say that, as a practicing physician, I am able to recommend wheat dough pills as an infallible remedy for hysterics—especially when that dangerous disease is caused by the death of poodle dogs.

"As soon as I had succeeded in silencing Miss Tadpoddle,

I turned my attention to Miss Clattermouth and the important letter, on which I noticed she every now and then cast an inquiring look. I was waiting for her to propound the question, which I inferred from her restlessness she was on the eve of doing. After eying the letter for some time, she picked it up and, after scrutinizing it carefully, when she imagined I was not observing her movements (for I was watching her through the mirror by a side glance), she turned her back toward me, and began to slip the letter out of the envelope. I knew that it would not do to allow her to see the contents of the letter; therefore, as soon as I divined her object, I went to the bureau, pretending to be collecting my scattered medicines, where she could see that I was in a position to observe her actions.

" 'Did you drop this letter here, doctor?' she carelessly observed, as I came round so as to confront her.

" 'Yes, I believe I did; I must have dropped it when I took out my pocket case a while ago.'

" 'I should like to know what you are doing with that letter, Doctor Demar? I see that it was not addressed to you.'

"I was considerably puzzled by this question, because I did not know what sort of an answer I ought to make; but it occurred to my mind that it would be advisable to rouse her curiosity still higher if I could. Having made up my mind to act on that idea, I carelessly observed that there was a great secret connected with that letter, which I did not consider myself at liberty to reveal.

" 'Now I should like very much to know what great secret Ben Bowles could have to communicate to that woman?'

" 'Why do you mention Mr. Bowles' name in connection with that letter, Miss Clattermouth?'

" 'Oh, that is a great secret, which I do not consider myself at liberty to reveal,' she said in a tantalizing tone, which convinced me that she was piqued because I had mentioned a secret. 'It is a mystery to me,' she continued, 'why Mr. Bowles should constitute you as his messenger, to carry his letters to that woman!'

" 'What has Ben Bowles got to do with it?'

" 'I hope, Doctor Demar, that you do not consider me an idiot?'

" 'Indeed, madame, I do not; but on the contrary, I have set you down in my mind as one of the cleverest ladies in Memphis; but what has that to do with the question I propounded to you?'

" 'Do you imagine that I do not know who wrote that letter?'

" 'Why should I take the trouble to imagine anything about it?'

" 'You are a real Yankee; you answer my questions by propounding others. We will let the subject drop unless you can make a candid answer to a simple question.'

" 'I crave your pardon, madame, and promise to furnish a direct answer to all your questions, provided you will agree to do the same with my interrogatories.'

" 'Very good! I consent to the agreement. Where did you get that letter?'

"Now I was completely nonplussed by that question, and entirely thrown off my guard, and did not know what answer to make. I began to stammer and halt; and despite all my efforts to invent a suitable answer, I made an absolute failure; my confusion proved to be the very lever that enabled me to pry the secret out of its hiding-place. When Miss Clattermouth saw my great confusion, her curiosity went up to the highest pitch, and she exclaimed:

" 'Ah, ha! Doctor Demar, you are caught in your own trap. You have been a carrier of a clandestine correspondence between Ben Bowles and his "Dulcinia del Toboso," and I must say that I am surprised and mortified to make the startling discovery.'

" 'You may imagine that you know that handwriting, Miss Clattermouth, but I beg permission to inform you that you are very much mistaken.'

" 'I say, mistaken! indeed, I know that handwriting as well as I do my own; and if I were to find a line of Ben Bowles' writing in the great Sahara Desert, I would know it —yes, I would swear on a stack of Bibles as high as this house that that was written by Ben Bowles.'

" 'Thanks be to Heaven!' I mentally exclaimed; and it was all I could do to keep from shouting with joy. I seized the letter, and pretended that I had suddenly thought of an appointment down town; looking at my watch, I hurried from the house, leaving Miss Clattermouth angry and astonished at my conduct.

"Miss Tadpoddle recovered (thanks to my dough pills and a vigorous constitution); but she became misanthropic and sullen, resigning her office as vice-president of the Tramp Reform Association, which left that noble institution without her patronage, causing it to go into bankruptcy. The untimely death of an eight-ounce poodle dog caused many a forlorn tramp to seek a night's lodging in the station-house, who, but for the sad event, would have found comfortable entertainment at the headquarters of the Tramp Reform Association.

"As soon as I left Miss Clattermouth, I hastened to the jail, being anxious to acquaint Lottie with the success that had crowned my efforts as to the proof desired.

"'Eureka! Eureka!' I exclaimed, as I went hurriedly into the room where Lottie and Viola were. 'Our luck has changed at last; Miss Clattermouth says she will swear it is Bowles' handwriting and she will kiss a stack of Bibles on it as high as Tadpoddle's house, which you know is three stories high, not counting the cellar. She says she would recognize the writing if she were to find it in a desert, the name of which I do not just now remember, though it is situated somewhere on the other side of the globe.'

"'Sit down, Edward, and give me the letter; I declare, you are excited.'

"'Indeed I am excited; have I not good cause to be! Did you not tell me that Miss Bramlett's fate depended on the proof that I have procured?'

"'Yes, but sit down and tell us how you managed to succeed so well.'

"I then gave a graphic description of all that had occurred, dwelling eloquently on my splendid maneuvering; and the sweet smiles that were showered on me, and the numerous thanks tendered by those grateful girls, amply compensated me for all my trouble. The good-natured steward had an excellent dinner prepared, which was served in Miss Bramlett's room at four o'clock. It was very late in the evening when Lottie and I took our departure from the jail.

"About a week after those events occurred, I received a note from Mr. Rockland, requesting an interview with me at his office. When I read the note, it caused a pang of uneasiness to dart through my breast, because I always expected bad news when the iron lawyer had anything to communicate.

"I found the iron lawyer, as usual, busily at work with innumerable old papers piled high before him.

" 'Take a seat, Demar,' he said, without looking at me; 'I will be at leisure in a moment.'

"He then began to dash the papers about, as if he were angry with the inoffensive documents, while my mind was ill at ease, and full of curiosity. After the lapse of five minutes he wheeled his chair around so as to confront me.

" 'Demar, I have just received a telegram informing me that Miss Bramlett's case has been reversed and another trial granted. This is no news to me, for you remember I told you that the Supreme Court was bound to reverse the case. I must confess, however, that I cannot see wherein this is going to benefit that unfortunate girl, because (as you have often heard me say) there is no possible chance to secure an acquittal under the mountain of testimony that will be adduced against her. I want you to understand, however, Mr. Demar, that I mean to do all I can for Miss Bramlett; but I do not hesitate to say that during thirty years' practice at the bar I have never seen such a complete, unbroken chain of circumstantial evidence arrayed against a prisoner as was mustered on the trial against Miss Bramlett. If you will meet me at the criminal court-room in the morning at ten o'clock, we will arrange with Mr. Quillet to have a day set for the trial. Demar, you must watch Lottie, and not let her become entangled in this unfortunate affair. She may listen to you, but she outtalks me. The fact of the business is, I cannot have the heart to scold that dear girl; but she must be separated from Miss Bramlett, and I depend on you to do it.'

" 'Mr. Rockland, I think we had better let Lottie have her own way in this affair, for, if I am not very sadly mistaken, she will snap the strong chain of circumstantial evidence into a thousand pieces. You have always told me that you thought she possessed a high order of intellect; but, sir, when this case is tried you will have good cause to think she has a mind of a most extraordinary character.'

"'Demar, I think you and Lottie both are on the direct road to the lunatic asylum, and I hope you will take Miss Bramlett with you, and not leave her here on my hands. It is the height of folly to say Miss Bramlett did not murder her little brother; besides this, she has been guilty of other crimes so black that all the water in the Atlantic Ocean could not wash the stain from her character; though I believe she is insane, and intend to convince the Governor of it, and he will grant a pardon beyond question.'

"I felt a sensation of relief as soon as I stepped out of Mr. Rockland's office. I hastened to convey the good news of a new trial to Lottie, and the first thing she did was to offer up thanks to Providence for this evidence of His favors.

"'Have you heard from our Vicksburg witness lately, Edward?'

"'Yes,' I replied, 'and he will come at any time when he is notified that we want him.'

"'Very good, then; as soon as you ascertain the day the trial is to come off, you must send him a telegram immediately. We are ready for the grand battle, and victory will be ours!'

"'Lottie, don't be too sanguine of success; a good general always prepares for a retreat before he engages in battle, so that when the battle is lost, he can save his army.'

"'Edward, you must not talk of defeat in connection with this case. I have a magic wand, with which I can perform more wonders than could Aladdin with his magic lamp. There is a good genius serving me in this business, whose powers will surprise and startle you.'

"'Lottie, I do not think you are justifiable in keeping secrets from me in connection with this affair.'

"'I want to test your faith in me, to see whether you can trust me as I have trusted you. My brother told me you were untrue to me, and had eloped with another woman; I had faith in you, and refused to believe his information.'

"'Enough; keep your own secrets; I will serve you, and

believe in you, as faithfully as Orlando believed in his Rosalind.'

" 'Thank you, Edward; and I promise you I will perform more wonders for you than Rosalind did for her Orlando. She changed a shepherd boy to a beautiful maiden; but I will show an angel of purity, where everybody sees a she-demon.'

"Mr. Rockland and I met Mr. Quillet promptly at ten o'clock next morning at the court-room, and the attorney-general kindly consented that Mr. Rockland should fix any day for the trial that he chose; consequently it was set for Thursday—that being Tuesday. I repaired immediately to the telegraph office, and sent a dispatch to the Vicksburg witness, requesting his attendance and asking him to answer whether he could come or not. The reply came—he promised to come without fail.

" 'Now,' said Lottie, when I showed her the telegram, 'I have ordered the carriage, and want you to escort me to the court-house. Do not look at me as if you were angry; I must go to the court-room immediately.'

" 'Lottie, you know I could not be angry with you; but will you be so good as to inform me why you wish to go to the court-house to be stared at by a motley crowd of very rough people?'

" 'I certainly have no wish to conceal my motive from you. In the first place, I am going to examine all the papers connected with Viola's case, especially the evidence that was given in on the first trial.'

" 'I can get those papers and bring them to you, and you can have ample time to examine them.'

" 'Of course you could do that; but I have another reason for wishing to visit the court-house; I want you to introduce me to the judge, attorney-general and all the lawyers. I want to catch a few ideas in regard to the manner of proceeding in court, so that when Viola is put on trial I will not be very much embarrassed. I shall ask the judge to let me cross-examine some of the State's witnesses; and you know I ought to see how it is done; and that is exactly what I am going to find out to-day.'

" 'You are going to leap into the contest as an attorney, and plead your client's case?'

" 'No, I am not going to make any leap at all; but I have a trap set to catch certain birds, and I am going to arrange the bait myself, and at the proper time I shall spring the trigger and pen the game. It is my intention to spend the remainder of this day in the court-house; in fact, I think I shall make that place my headquarters until the trial is over.'

" 'Do you think you can stand the jokes and jeers and vulgar gaze of such a crowd as you must necessarily meet in a criminal court-room?'

" 'I can bear anything, endure anything, submit to anything, in order to save my dear, unfortunate friend!'

" 'Lottie, I do not believe this world ever contained another such a good-hearted, noble girl as you—so unselfish, so thoughtful of others, so generous and sympathetic!'

" 'Edward, reserve your compliments until Viola is clear, and then you may pile the flattery on as much as you please.'

" 'I suppose you will make an eloquent speech to the jury in defense of your client; I can in my imagination hear the sweet words echoing through the halls of justice.'

" 'Cease your levity, if you please; the occasion demands seriousness. You know very well I do not intend to make a speech; but I am in real downright earnest when I say that I am going to ask the judge to allow me to cross-examine some of the witnesses. You see I have been studying a great many commentaries on criminal evidence, and have learned that when a witness swears falsely to one material point, he is not to be believed in anything else. Now I am going to propound certain questions to some of the witnesses, and if they swear what they did on the former trial, why, then, they will be in my trap.'

" 'Lottie, don't you think it advisable to acquaint Mr. Rockland with all the new facts in your possession, so he could be prepared to handle them when the trial comes off?'

" 'No, I do not; and besides this, I cannot reveal to any one the secrets confided to me by another, without her consent.'

" 'Ah! it is a "her" ther who works the wires behind the curtains?'

" 'There are no wires to work nor any curtains to work behind; but enough of this; come, we will now go to the court-house.'

"As I entered the court-room with Lottie leaning on my arm, the eyes of the lawyers and spectators were at once fixed on her with a curious gaze, as she moved across the room like an empress, and advancing to the clerk's desk, asked for the papers in the Bramlett case. The little sleek-haired clerk, whose nose was very large, stood with his mouth wide open, his pen in his hand, gazing at the angelic beauty before him, as much astonished as if a ghost had suddenly risen out of the ground. Lottie again called for the papers, when the little clerk began to stammer:

" 'You had better—that is, we could not—I must ask you to see Mr. Quillet, madame—it is against the rules to let papers go out of the office, except to the attorneys.'

"I do not wish to take the papers out of the office, sir,' replied Lottie modestly, as she smiled sweetly, 'I can examine them here.'

"The little clerk was very much embarrassed, but refused to let her have the papers until he was ordered to do so by Mr. Quillet. Lottie took the great bundle of documents, and, scattering them about on the table, seated herself and began to read them, while the judge and Mr. Quillet eyed her closely. A group of lawyers assembled inside of the bar and began to whisper to each other, occasionally pointing at Lottie, who was too deeply engaged with the papers to notice them.

" 'She is the most beautiful woman I ever saw,' I heard Mr. Quillet whisper to a lawyer who sat near him.

" 'Who is she?' inquired the man to whom Quillet had addressed the remark.

" 'Miss Charlotte Wallingford, I believe—an adopted daughter of Mr. Rockland.'

" 'Well, Quillet, I indorse your judgment; I don't think I ever saw such a perfect model of beauty before. What is she up to there? She seems to work as if she meant business.'

" 'She is examining the evidence in the Bramlett case; she is a stanch friend to the defendant; you were not here when the case was tried, I believe?'

" 'No.'

" 'Well, it is an interesting case, full of strange, romantic mystery. It is to be tried again next Thursday; so you will hear the evidence.'

" 'Quillet, if I could marry such a woman as that, I think I should be willing to surrender my bachelor freedom, and put my neck under old Hymen's yoke.'

, " 'Yes, no doubt of it; and I dare say I could find a brigade of men in this city who would do likewise; but you need not lay siege to that castle—that article is already bespoke.'

" 'How is that?'

" 'She is going to marry that tall, awkward booby yonder, leaning against that column—the one with the long, shaggy whiskers.'

" 'Well! well! there is no accounting for a woman's taste. It is surpassingly strange that so glorious a beauty should take a fancy to such a bulk of humanity as that!'

" 'Hush! hush! he is listening to us.'

"Then they continued the conversation in lower tones, so I could not hear any more.

"The court took a thirty minutes' recess, which afforded me an opportunity to introduce Lottie; this I lost no time in doing.

" 'Miss Wallingford,' observed the judge, as he courtesied to her and dropped into a seat by her side, 'you seem to be deeply interested in those papers; may I inquire what they refer to?'

" 'Those papers refer to the evidence that was in the Bramlett case on the first trial,' said Lottie, as her pretty eyes rested on the handsome countenance of the judge.

" 'Oh, yes; that is the case that was set for Thursday; a very strange case it is, indeed! You are the young lady who has been staying in the jail with Miss Bramlett?'

" 'Yes, sir; and I am a true friend to that young girl.'

" 'Well, Miss Bramlett ought to be proud of the friendship of such a lady; and I promise you that your friend shall have a fair and impartial trial. I suppose you will be present to witness the proceedings?'

" 'Oh, yes, I certainly shall attend the trial; I should have been present at the first trial, but I was very ill at the time. I

have a little favor to ask of your Honor, which I hope you
will grant—provided it is not against the rules of practice.'

" 'I beg you to name it, Miss Wallingford; and I promise
in advance to grant it, if it is within my power, even if it
requires a change of our rules.'

" 'I thank you sincerely, sir; I should like very much to
have the privilege of cross-examining some of the State's
witnesses.'

" 'Oh, is that all? You shall cross-examine all of the
State's witnesses, if you like; and you may make a speech
in defense of your friend, if you wish.'

" 'I have no inclination to make a speech—I am not a lawyer, but I have been studying Miss Bramlett's case. There
are some very peculiar points in it, with which Mr. Rockland
is totally unacquainted; and I have other peculiar reasons for
wishing to cross-examine some of the witnesses.'

" 'Mr. Quillet,' said the judge, addressing that gentleman
with a bland smile, 'you had better look to your laurels, next
Thursday, for I think you are going to encounter heavier
mettle than usual.'

" 'A defeat caused by Miss Wallingford would be as good
as a victory over an ordinary adversary.'

" 'You are quite complimentary, Mr. Quillet; you seem to
understand the weakness of our sex; we all love flattery.'

" 'Candidly speaking, Miss Wallingford, I do most sincerely
wish you may be able to furnish evidence enough to justify a
jury in acquitting your friend.'

" 'Indeed, I thank you for your kind wish, and flatter
myself that I shall be able to put a different feature on the
case the next time from what it was on the first trial. On
next Thursday I am going to unravel one of the strangest
mysteries that ever was revealed in open court. I will make
you think I am a real magician. Lucio made a duke out of
a friar, and I will make a saint out of a murderess—that is,
I will show a saint where everybody sees a demon.'

" 'May God speed you, Miss Wallingford,' the judge replied; 'you deserve success, whether you achieve it or not.'

CHAPTER XXXII.

"The judge was so completely charmed by Lottie's brilliant conversation and sparkling wit that he forgot all about the business of his court, and consequently the thirty minute recess was prolonged to an hour, and probably would have gone on indefinitely, but Mr. Quillet reminded him of the McCay case, which had been set for trial that day.

" 'Ah, yes, Mr. Quillet,' said the judge, as he looked at his watch and rose from his seat, 'I crave your pardon; I was so much fascinated with Miss Wallingford's conversation that I had entirely lost sight of business. She is the most intellectual woman I ever met. Then her beauty is equal to her talent; the truth is, she is an animated library.'

" 'How could she be otherwise, after being tutored by old Rockland? I hope she is not as cold-hearted as that old iceberg.'

" 'No woman with such a face as hers ever possessed a cold heart, for I think she is the most beautiful woman I ever saw.'

"This conversation was carried on in an undertone, close to where I sat, and notwithstanding I had often heard extravagant encomiums passed on Lottie's beauty and intellect, I felt a sensation of pleasure at hearing her praised by a man possessing such a solid mind as Judge Flipout. I could scarcely realize the favors that fortune had showered on me, by enabling me to win the heart of a woman whose brilliant mind and dazzling beauty had won the admiration of all who beheld her.

" 'The State *vs.* McCay,' said the judge, as he resumed his seat and began to turn the leaves of the trial docket.

" 'Ready for the State,' replied Mr. Quillet.

" 'Bring in the prisoner, Mr. Sheriff,' observed the judge.

"That officer went into an antechamber and soon returned, followed by a pale-faced little man, whose emaciated appearance indicated the presence of severe illness. He was leaning on the arm of his wife, whose haggard features and sunken eyes exhibited unmistakable evidence of intense suffering. She held a sickly looking infant against her breast with one arm, while she supported her husband with the other. She was followed by two pale-faced little girls, about three years old, who clung to the tattered skirts of the faded calico dress worn by their mother. They were bright-eyed, pretty little timid twins, whose pinched features told a tale of want, misery and starvation as plain as print.

"'Who is your attorney, Mr. McCay?' inquired the judge, as he began to rub the left side of his nose with the forefinger of his left hand, which he always did when vexed about anything.

"'I have no attorney, sir,' replied the defendant meekly; 'I did not have any money to pay a lawyer to defend me.'

"Lottie instantly rose and whispered to Colonel Buff, a lawyer of considerable reputation:

"'Defend that unfortunate man, Colonel Buff, and I will compensate you liberally.'

"The attorney then stepped forward and announced himself as attorney for the defense.

"After the indictment was read, the prosecuting witness was ordered to take the stand. He was a large, red-faced man, with a hangdog look on his countenance, while an offensive scent of mean whisky and tobacco pervaded the atmosphere for ten feet in every direction from his filthy body. His evidence was in substance as follows:

"'I was passing along the street near defendant's residence with a wagon loaded with bacon, and when near his house, one of the wheels of the wagon broke down, causing one of the casks to roll out; falling against the curb-stone, it burst and scattered the meat on the ground. The defendant came and proposed to purchase a side of the bacon, stating that his wife and children were on the verge of starvation, caused by the sickness of himself and wife. I was at first disposed to make the trade with him, and perhaps would have done so, but I soon discovered that he did not have any money to pay for the meat. He begged me to sell it to him on a short credit, making at the same time a most solemn promise that he would pay me as soon as he got able to work. I of course declined to accept his proposition; he then offered to pawn his coat, hat and pocket-knife with me as a security that I should have the money. I rejected this nonsensical offer, and went away to get my wagon wheel mended at a shop hard by; when I returned I noticed that one of the sides of bacon had been cut, and a large piece of it was missing. I went immediately to the defendant's residence, where I found the stolen bacon in a pot which was boiling on the fire. I took it, and, replacing it in the spot where it had been cut away, found it exactly fitted—consequently I knew it was my meat.'

" 'We rest our case here, if the court please,' said Mr. Quillet, as the villainous looking witness retired from the stand.

" 'Have you any witnesses for the defense, Colonel Buff?' inquired the judge.

" 'We will introduce Mrs. McCay for the defense,' replied Buff.

"The poor woman staggered into the witness box, while the half-starved babe was vainly endeavoring to draw a little nourishment from her breast.

" 'Mrs. McCay,' said Colonel Buff, 'please tell the court and jury all you know about this case.'

"She wiped the fast falling tears from her pale cheeks with the sleeve of her tattered dress, and in a tremulous voice mingled with broken sobs, said:

" 'My husband is a railway engineer, and when he was able to work, we did not want for anything; but his health failed, and he was compelled to give up his situation; we did not suffer for food then until I fell ill. When we both lost our health, we were driven to the necessity of selling everything we had in order to buy provisions and medicines. Our condition continued to grow worse until we were driven to the very brink of starvation, when a beautiful angel visited our humble home, and furnished us everything necessary to make us comfortable. She continued to visit our house every day, supplying all our wants, and she engaged the services of a good, kind doctor, who came to see us often, and gave us his medicine and his kind attention. So long as that beautiful angel visited our home, my husband's health continued to improve, because she not only furnished all the provisions and medicine that we needed, but she was such a kind, gentle nurse, that we all improved while she was with us; but they put the beautiful angel in jail, and she never came to visit us any more.'

" 'Edward, that was Viola,' said Lottie, as she seized my arm and smiled through her tears; 'Heaven bless that dear girl, do you think now she ever committed murder?'

" 'Before the great Creator, I declare she is not guilty!'

"Mrs. McCay paused a moment to wipe the tears away; while Flipout put the friction heavy on his nose.

" 'My father died,' continued the witness, 'leaving an estate of ten thousand dollars, and I, being his only child, was entitled to all the money, which (had I received it) would have placed us beyond the reach of want; but the money was paid into the hands of Mr. Anterson, the public administrator, who kept it and refused to pay it to me.'

" 'If the court please,' said Mr. Quillet, 'while I deeply sympathize with this unfortunate woman, I must insist that her statement cannot be admitted as evidence in this case.'

" 'I concur with my learned friend,' said Colonel Buff, 'and shall not insist on her statement as testimony unless she can tell us something directly bearing on the case.'

"Then, addressing the witness, Colonel Buff propounded the following question:

" 'Mrs. McCay, do you know anything about the slice of bacon that is alleged to have been stolen?'

" 'My husband brought home a small piece of bacon, telling me——'

" 'Stop,' said Quillet, 'don't tell anything about what your husband said.'

" 'Then I have nothing more to tell, if you refuse to hear what my husband said, though I know he did not steal the bacon.'

" 'How do you know he did not steal it?'

" 'Because he told me so.'

" 'We ask your Honor to exclude what defendant said,' exclaimed Quillet.

" 'Certainly,' replied the judge, 'the statements of defendant will not go to the jury.'

" 'Any more witnesses, Colonel Buff?' inquired the court.

"After a hurried consultation with his client, the colonel rose and addressed the court:

" 'If your Honor please, I have advised the defendant to withdraw his plea of not guilty and throw himself on the mercy of the court, which he has consented to do. I have been induced to take this course because the jury could not, consistently with their oaths, acquit the prisoner in the face of the evidence. This is a case which appeals in the strongest terms to the mercy of the court, and I am sorry that your Honor does not possess the power to discharge the prisoner, because I do conscientiously believe the circumstances would justify your Honor in a course of that kind, and that you would not hesitate to do it if you had the legal authority.'

" 'Mr. McCay,' said the judge, 'have you any reason to urge against the sentence of the court?'

"The prisoner rose to his feet with trembling limbs, leaning against a table to steady himself, and said:

" 'The prosecuting witness has sworn falsely—I did not steal his bacon; he promised that if I would watch his property until he could go to the shop and get his wagon wheel mended he would give me enough of the meat for our dinner. I agreed to remain and watch the wagon until his return, and with this understanding he went away, leaving me with the property. Some time after he went away I cut off a few pounds of the bacon and carried it home, as I knew my little children were very hungry, intending to go immediately back to my post, but before I had time to return the witness came to my house in a great passion, and charged me with stealing the bacon.'

"As the unfortunate man resumed his seat, Flipout began to rub both sides of his nose furiously and said:

" 'The duty which the law imposes upon me in cases of this nature is a very painful one to perform. I cannot escape it, though much I wish I could. The court will take the liberty to say that the prosecuting witness in this case has shown himself to be a cruel, unfeeling wretch, and it is very sorry that it has not power to inflict upon him such punishment as his meanness so richly merits. The punishment in this case is about to fall on the wrong man, consequently the court will make it as light as possible. The sentence of the court is that the defendant be imprisoned in the penitentiary for two years.'

"Lottie now drew her chair near a table, seized a pen, and began to write very rapidly, and continued until she had covered two sheets of paper; then she directed me to hand it to the judge. He adjusted his spectacles and read the document.

" 'Mr. Quillet,' said Flipout, 'Miss Wallingford has prepared a truthful history of this case, with a petition asking the Governor to grant a pardon, and I shall sign it with a great deal of pleasure, and hope you will do likewise.'

" 'Indeed, sir, you could not ask me to do anything that would afford me more gratification.'

"The judge and Mr. Quillet placed their signatures to the paper, then every lawyer in the room promptly stepped forward and signed it.

" 'Now, Edward,' said Lottie, 'take this document to the telegraph office, have it sent by wire immediately at my expense, and tell them to send the answer to me without delay.'

"I gladly obeyed her instructions, and more than that, I hurried to Mr. Rockland's office and prevailed on him to send a private dispatch to the Governor, requesting a favorable consideration of the petition, knowing that the Governor would do anything reasonable to accommodate his friend Rockland.

"As soon as I had sent off the dispatches I again made my appearance in the court-room, supposing Lottie would be ready to return home; but in that respect I was very much disappointed.

" 'The next case on the docket, Mr. Quillet, is the State against Anterson,' said the judge.

" 'We are ready for the State,' replied Quillet.

" 'Is the defendant in court, Mr. Sheriff?'

" 'Yes,' replied a fat short man, whose skin appeared to be stretched to its utmost capacity in the effort to cover his ponderous body.

"Mr. Anterson then moved to the front with as much dignity as ever General Washington possessed, and announced himself ready for trial. He was exquisitely dressed in glossy black cloth, cut in the most approved style, while a large ring set with diamonds sparkled on one of his fingers, and a costly diamond pin glistened on his bosom. His boots were polished until they looked like the face of a mirror, and his hair was sleek, oily, and neatly combed; his little soft hands were as white as those of a delicate lady, and he was the most innocent, harmless looking little man I ever beheld. The indictment charged this innocent little man with embezzling the trifling sum of ninety thousand dollars of money belonging to sundry widows and orphans of the good city of Memphis, county of Shelby, State of Tennessee. Nineteen other bills of a similar character had been presented against that distinguished little gentleman, charging him with embezzlement. The fact is, he had made a clean sweep of something near three hundred thousand dollars of trust funds that had come into his hands as public administrator.

" 'Who are your attorneys in this case, Mr. Anterson?' inquired his Honor.

"With a dignified wave of his hand he pointed toward a dozen lawyers who had assembled near their distinguished client.

" 'You seem to be well supplied with attorneys, sir,' observed the judge, as he renewed the friction on his nose.

" 'My attorneys are not all present yet, sir,' said the handsome little man, 'but we can send for Mr. Rockland and Mr. Bullger, so as to have them here in a few minutes.'

" 'Are you ready to proceed with the case now, gentlemen?' inquired Flipout, addressing the brigade of lawyers.

" 'I believe we are ready,' replied Mr. Fullbrain, a red-faced lawyer, with large Roman nose, broad mouth and massive jaws. This distinguished lawyer was commonly called Hogjaw, which nickname had been suggested by the striking resemblance between his jaw and that of a fat Berkshire hog.

" 'We make a motion to quash the indictment in this case, if your Honor please,' said Hogjaw, as he held the bill up before the court.

" 'State the grounds of your motion, if you please, Mr. Fullbrain,' exclaimed the judge impatiently, as he began to warm up his nose with his finger, while his keen black eyes sparkled with anger.

"Mr. Quillet began to pace up and down the floor with his hands thrust deep in his pockets, while a defiant expression mantled his face. The clerks dropped their pens and moved

·to the front so as to witness the great brain-battle soon to be waged, while a motley crowd of idlers moved like an ocean wave toward the combatants, eager to view the interesting contest.

"Hogjaw surveyed the crowd for a moment, slowly running his eyes over the eager throng, as if inviting them to prepare for the intellectual banquet which he was about to dish out to them; then turning toward the court, he swelled out his brawny chest, as if taking in a supply of wind, which was to be converted into a terrific tornado, with which he expected to blow the attorney-general and his little bill of indictment out of the court-house.

"'If your Honor please,' began Hogjaw, 'we think there is a fatal defect in this bill of indictment, a patent incurable defect which must appear as clear as the sun at noontide to the mind of an intelligent court. It is a source of indescribable regret to me, sir, to find such a glaring defect in this bill, as we would have greatly preferred to try this case on its merits, because we are happy to be able to inform your Honor that we are prepared to vindicate the innocence of our client. His distinguished reputation for honor and unblemished integrity—his lacerated feelings—his wounded pride—all cry aloud for redress. We feel an abiding confidence in our ability to clear our distinguished client with the brilliant array of witnesses who are ready to testify to his innocence, but we find the bill of indictment so fatally defective that we are driven to the necessity of making the motion to quash. We would gladly have avoided this course but for the duty which we owe to the legal profession, which tells us that such mistakes should not be encouraged or countenanced by lawyers who profess to have such a feeling as self-respect. Who is the man intended to be indicted under this bill? yes, who is the man? that is the question I dare to ask of this honorable court. This innocent, much injured man has been seized and ruthlessly dragged away from the bosom of his family, and treated as a common malefactor, all of which unpardonable wrongs have been inflicted upon him by the officers of the law acting under a mistaken belief that the grand jury had presented a bill of indictment, into open court against him. Now, sir, I boldly assert in the presence of this honorable court and high Heaven that no such thing has ever been done. A thing, a scrap of worthless paper, is filed here, which ignorant people might be deceived into believing was a bill of indictment, but you cannot cram such nonsense into the brains of sensible men. My client's name is Anterson, which name I unhesitatingly assert cannot be spelled without a *t,* and if any man under the blue vault of Heaven will show *me* a *t* in connection with the name on this indictment, why, then, I promise to surrender the case. Doubtless the writer of this bill was endeavoring to make a *t* when that little deformed animal was made, but I have the temerity to assert that no gentleman with as much as a thimble full of brains in his head, or an ounce of self-respect in his heart, would undertake to call that animal a *t* in open court. So far as civilization extends, the English language is written and spoken, and that elegant language is composed of certain letters whose office it is to represent certain sounds. The twentieth letter in our alphabet is called *t,* which letter is made with a perpendicular stroke of the pen, then a horizontal stroke, making a cross near the top end of the upright line. Now we all know that the letter cannot be made without the cross. Your Honor is doubtless familiar with the wise and charming compositions of the celebrated poet Ramsquadlar, whose reputation is co-extensive with the world. That distinguished bard said:

> " " "When you can extract the salt from the sea,
> Then without a cross can you make a *t.*
> As sure as fog doth rise, the rain will fall,
> *T* without a cross is no *t* at all."

" 'Now, sir, if that eminent poet was correct in his beautiful composition, which I presume no one will be so bold as to doubt, I think it settles the hash (if I may be allowed the expression) with the motion now under consideration. If a *t* without a cross is no *t* at all, then it follows, as a matter of course, that no legal indictment has been filed against my client. If your Honor concedes that the *t* is not crossed—and that is too plain to admit of doubt—why then, of course, the motion to quash must prevail.'

"After haranguing the court for an hour, Hogjaw dropped,

overcome with exhaustion, into his seat, while the brother members crowded round him to offer their congratulations. One fanned his red face, another brought him a glass of whisky and water, a third brought a napkin, while all the rest appeared to be anxious to render some friendly aid.

"Mr. Quillet delivered an eloquent and learned argument against the motion, insisting that the defect was such as could be cured by amendment; but he was forced to confess that the *t* had not been crossed. It was very plain to be seen that the attorney-general was considerably embarrassed, and a lack of confidence appeared on his face, while his actions showed that he had an up-hill business.

"As soon as Mr. Quillet resumed his seat, Mr. Rockland, who had been silently watching the progress of the argument, stepped forward and began to address the court, favoring the motion to quash. He commenced by a learned dissertation on the laws of creation which prevailed anterior to the existence of Adam, then gave a graphic sketch of the rules which God laid down for the government of Eden, showing the awful consequences which had resulted from a disobedience of those holy laws. He then came down to the time of Moses, giving a brilliant history of the strict discipline which that great leader enforced in his magnificent army of exodusters, while marching out of the filthy land of Egypt; then taking up the laws of the Medes and Persians, he explained them to the satisfaction of the court; showing clearly wherein they applied particularly to the case under consideration. The renowned advocate then paid his respects to the Koran, citing many passages which he insisted had a direct bearing on the question now before the court; passing on thence to the birth of Christ, be descanted at large on the meekness and suffering of the great Saviour of mankind; and when he began to advert to the vulgar mob of Jews who clamored for the innocent blood of Christ, he compared them to the motley crowd of ill-bred wretches who were clamoring for the innocent blood of Mr. Anterson. When he plunged into the English law, he threw book after book behind him, while he hurled precedents and quotations at the head of the court so thick and rapidly that the judge became completely bewildered. After Mr. Rockland had exhausted the laws of England, he made a raid on the American decisions, pouring a mighty deluge of learning into the ears of the court; then wound up with such a burst of eloquence as to bring tears from the audience, and confusion to the mind of the court; he then sank back in his seat, and wiped the perspiration from his brow, and awaited the decision of the court.

"Flipout dropped his head on his hands and remained silent for several moments, evidently bewildered and confused by the vast waves of learning that had rolled over him. At length he rose up, rubbed both sides of his nose with his fingers, re-adjusted his spectacles, coughed two or three times, looked up at the ceiling as if he thought it were going to fall down on his head, then delivered the following learned opinion:

" 'The court has listened with exquisite pleasure to the lucid and learned argument made by the attorneys, and it feels profoundly thankful to those wise gentlemen for the valuable assistance which they have rendered in that respect. This case presents many strange and difficult features, such as we very seldom meet with in this country. The court is seriously impressed with the importance of this very peculiar case, because it involves the fortunes of many poor, destitute widows and starving orphans. The defendant is charged with the embezzlement of large sums of money belonging to a class of unfortunate people whose helpless condition cries aloud to the court for protection. The law is made to restrain the strong and to protect the helpless, and it is the duty of the court to enforce the law in such a manner as to attain the end which the makers had in view when the statutes were passed. Unscrupulous men who wantonly trample on the law should have the severest penalties pronounced against them; but we must not lose sight of the fact that no man can be compelled to answer for a felony except upon an indictment presented in open court by a grand jury. The law presumes every man to be innocent until such presumption is overthrown by competent proof; and we all remember the Scriptural maxim that declares it is better that ninety-and-nine guilty persons should escape than that one innocent man should suffer. This being the case, it behooves us to exercise great caution in the administration of the laws. It is contended by the able counsel for the defense that this indictment is fatally defective, because the letter *t* has no cross, and many learned decisions have been cited to sustain that view. The court had occasion, at a former term, to examine the authorities touching this identical question, and it considers that a very fortunate circumstance, as it will greatly aid the court in arriving at a correct conclusion in regard to the case now under consideration. In the celebrated case of Hikokolochuckle *vs.* Lokoklohichuckle, it was held that all the letters necessary to spell the defendant's name must appear plainly written, so that a man of ordinary understanding could easily determine what name was intended. Chief-justice Wangdoodle, in delivering the opinion in that case, said that it was a deplorable fact that men of learning very frequently fell into the despicable habit of neglecting to cross their *t*'s and dot their *i*'s. In the case of Changtookoo *vs.* Ronderbangtookoo, which was tried in the Celestial Empire, before the eminent Chief-justice Shooflytoto, it was held that the twelfth letter in the alphabet was entitled to ten tails and seven horns, and that it could not be considered complete if either of those tails or horns was left off. The points decided in that case appear to have a direct bearing on the one now before this court. The letter referred to in that famous case is not made with a pen, as it is in this country, but by drowning a large battle spider in black ink, and then carefully setting him down on white paper. The legs of the spider correspond exactly with the number of tails and horns necessary to constitute the letter. In the case referred to, it appeared that the spider which was used in making the letter had unfortunately lost a leg in a combat with a bumblebee, which was not discovered by the writer, consequently the letter had only six tails, when it should have had seven. Owing to that fatal defect, the plaintiff lost his case, which involved an immense fortune. Now, if the failure to make all the tails and horns rendered that letter defective, it would seem that a failure to cross the letter *t* in this case would be fatal. Spotted Tail, the renowned Indian chief, in his remarkable communications to the President of the United States, was very careful to cross his *t*'s and dot his *i*'s; therefore it is the opinion of this court that if an ignorant savage

can afford to dot his *i's* and cross his *t's* the attorney for the
State should be required to do likewise. Entertaining this
view of the case, the court feels conscientiously bound to sustain the motion. Let the indictment be quashed.'

" 'I suppose,' said Hogjaw, 'that all the other bills may be
considered as disposed of by this judgment, as they are all
in the same category?'

" 'Yes, let all the bills be considered quashed.'

"A grand rush was made toward Mr. Anterson by the lawyers and spectators, who showered congratulations thick and
rapid. Every one seemed to be eager to shake his hand, and
to offer obsequious congratulations. The little embezzler
was placed in a carriage and driven to a saloon, where champagne sparkled—corks flew in all directions—toasts were
drunk, and shouts of joy and hilarious laughter were wafted
on the breeze.

"The poor widow and helpless orphans went on starving
all the same. The world wags on, the sun continues to shine,
the moon blushes not, the rich robber revels in stolen wealth,
while Justice spreads her white wings and bids the world
farewell. The starving wretch who steals a slice of meat to
feed his starving children must expiate the crime in the penitentiary, while he who steals a million is champagned and
worshiped, lionized and petted.

"Lottie gave me the benefit of her opinion about courts,
lawyers and judges, with a vengeance, and that opinion was
anything but a compliment to that class. When court ad-
journed she beckoned me to follow her, and I knew from the
bright sparkle of her pretty eyes, and the manner in which
the corners of her mouth hung down, that she had something
of importance to communicate. I followed her into a small
antechamber adjoining the court-room, where I saw Mrs.
McCay weeping over her husband, while the two pretty little
twins were sound asleep on the floor.

" 'Oh! Charley,' said the unfortunate woman, as she threw
her arms around her husband's neck, 'if they take you to
prison now, it will kill you. You have been so ill, and you
are now so weak, that you cannot live if they start with you to
the penitentiary in your present condition.'

" 'Let me die, then; why should I care to live in a world

that is overflowed with injustice? I am unable to work any more, therefore it would be better for me to be out of the way!'

" 'Dear Charley, please do not talk that way, for my poor heart is breaking! If they take you to the penitentiary, they may take me to my grave, for it will kill me to lose you!'

" 'They are not going to take him to the penitentiary yet a while,' said Lottie, as she lifted Mrs. McCay's little babe in her arms; 'I have come to take you and your good husband home; so come along, for the carriage is waiting at the door.'

"Mrs. McCay wiped the tears from her eyes and began to stare at Lottie in a bewildered manner.

" 'We cannot go home now, because the sheriff was here a moment ago, and said he would be back soon to take my husband to jail. He told me he was going to take Charley to the penitentiary in the morning.'

" 'But I tell you, Mrs. McCay, that they shall not take your husband to prison; he is a free man—here is a dispatch from the Governor granting a full pardon, and your husband can go where he pleases; so come along and get in the carriage!'

"Mr. McCay fell on his knees at Lottie's feet, seized her hand and pressed it to his lips, while his wife knelt on the other side and took the other hand.

" 'You are a dear angel!' exclaimed the weeping woman as she pressed Lottie's hand to her lips. 'Heaven bless you, we will be your slaves as long as we live!'

" 'No, you will not be my slaves, either, but you shall be my good friends.'

"The whole family was crowded into the carriage, which forced me to take a seat by the driver. Lottie directed the coachman to stop at the nearest provision store, where she handed the salesman a bill of provisions, with orders to have them immediately sent to Mr. McCay's residence. Soon after we deposited the family at the front gate a dray stopped, and the driver began to place the provisions on the pavement in front of the house. A barrel of flour, a barrel of sugar, a sack of coffee and a cask of hams, with numerous other packages, were soon scattered about on the pavement.

" 'Edward,' said Lottie, as she cast one of her peculiarly

sweet smiles on me, 'did you ever read Dickens on the circumlocution office?'

" 'Yes,' I replied.

" 'Very well, then you will understand my meaning when I tell you I have started a circumlocution office of my own.'

" 'How is that?'

" 'Mr. Anterson steals ten thousand dollars from Mrs. McCay, and gives Mr. Rockland part of the money to keep him (Anterson) out of the penitentiary; Mr. Rockland gives me the money, I purchase provisions with it, and deliver them to Mrs. McCay.'

" 'That is circumlocution double and twisted!'

"We then took leave of the family who had been made happy by Lottie's bounty, and drove home. I attempted to embrace Lottie as I assisted her from the carriage.

" 'Stop, sir!' she said, 'remember the terms of our compact—no love demonstrations until Viola is clear!'

CHAPTER XXXIII.

"At length the long expected day arrived, the time to which I had been looking forward with a mind crowded with hope and anxiety; the day which was to settle the fate of Miss Bramlett, as well as my own, for Lottie had suffered herself to become so completely entangled with Viola's affairs that no power could separate them.

"I ate a light breakfast and hurried to Mr. Rockland's residence, in order to meet Lottie, according to previous arrangement, for the purpose of escorting her to the jail. As she met me at the front portico with both hands held out for me to shake, a smile of unusual brightness played on her beauteous face, while a hopeful confidence beamed from her pretty blue eyes. I noticed that her toilet was exquisitely arranged, displaying evidence of unusual care, skill, and taste. She was clad in a neat-fitting robe of dove-colored silk, the body cut so as to exhibit the symmetry of the waist without encumbering the movements of the arms, terminating close up round the throat, and crowned at the top with snow-white lace. A large golden chain encircled her neck, at the end of which was suspended a beautiful locket of the same kind of metal, containing a picture of my unworthy self, which was held against her bosom by a golden arrow running through a little ring, and fastened to her dress. The abundant wealth of golden hair was handsomely braided, and resting in beautiful coils at the back of her head, being pinned up with a Cupid dart, while an exquisite hat with two drooping plumes covered her well-shaped head.

" 'Edward, what is the matter with you this morning? I declare, you look as blue and solemn as if you were in a funeral procession, following a dear friend to the grave !'

" 'Lottie, have you no fears as to the result of the trial to-day ?'

" 'Now that is a real Yankee style of answering questions; nevertheless, I will give you a direct answer. I have no fears, but to the contrary, I am full of confidence and hope; this is to be a day of great triumph for us. But now I wish to know what makes you look so melancholy ?'

" 'While I am hopeful, I am full of doubts as to the result, and those doubts cling to me, despite my efforts to shake them off.'

" 'Well, all I can say is wait and see. But it is high time we were going, for I must have a private interview with Viola at the jail before she goes to the court-house; is the carriage ready ?'

" 'Yes, I saw it pass the window just a moment ago !'

"When we arrived at the jail, Miss Bramlett embraced Lottie enthusiastically, uttering many endearing words of affection and gratitude. Her toilet was in every respect exactly similar to Lottie's and save the color of the hair, they were very much alike. Lottie requested me to leave her alone with Miss Bramlett until the time arrived for her to go to the court-house, and I went out into the hall and began to pace up and down the floor, counting the moments, as they appeared to crawl at a snail's pace. When the two girls had been together about an hour, a gentle rap sounded on the door of Miss Bramlett's room, and when it was opened the sheriff said:

" 'I am ordered, Miss Bramlett, to accompany you to the court-house; you need not be in a hurry—I can wait until you are ready; take as much time as you wish.'

" 'I am ready, sir, as soon as I can put on my hat and cloak.'

" 'Doctor Demar,' said the sheriff as he came out, I will place my fair prisoner in your custody and request you to escort her to the court-house in the carriage, and I will walk.'

" 'Why not ride in the carriage with us?'

" 'I have too much respect for Miss Bramlett's feelings to do anything that would look like guarding a prisoner.'

"I seized the hand of the generous-hearted officer and thanked him for his kindness, promising to take the ladies as he requested, and he hurried away.

"When the carriage halted in front of the court-house, an immense crowd of curious idlers began to collect near the door, eager to get a look at the beautiful murderess (as they were pleased to designate Miss Bramlett), and it required the services of a couple of policemen to clear a road through the dense mass of humanity for the ladies to enter the door.

"Judge Flipout, who sat on the judicial bench reading the morning paper, laid it down and gazed intently at the fair prisoner for a moment, then descended, and taking Miss Bramlett's hand, inquired about her health. After a few minutes' conversation with her, he turned round and addressed Lottie:

" 'Miss Wallingford, have you concluded to deliver a speech in defense of your pretty client?'

" 'No, I have not, but if I were to make a speech, you would hear new ideas expressed, such as would not be complimentary to courts, lawyers and judges. I used to be simple enough to think that courts were the very fountains of justice, where the weak and helpless could procure redress for wrongs inflicted on them by the strong and powerful, but the scales of ignorance have lately been removed from my eyes.'

" 'Indeed! I am very sorry to learn that you have such an unfavorable opinion of us, but I trust you will alter it when you know more about us.'

" 'I am sure I should be delighted to see something that

might be considered an improvement on the farce I witnessed here the other day.'

" 'You must not set those two cases down as a sample of what we do all the time, because the court was forced by the law in those cases to render decisions the effect of which was to enable guilty parties to escape.'

"Then Judge Flipout again addressed Miss Bramlett, remaining by her side a moment.

" 'Open court, Mr. Sheriff,' he said as he looked at his watch. 'I wish you a speedy delivery, Miss Bramlett, as much for Miss Wallingford's sake as for your own. You have been quite fortunate in securing the friendly services of such an astute attorney.'

"Then his Honor resumed his seat and listened to the reading of the minutes, while the lawyers began to whisper to each other, and occasionally point toward Lottie and Viola. I was close enough to hear a whispered conversation carried on by Hogjaw and Quillet in regard to the two charming girls.

" 'Which one is the prisoner?' inquired Hogjaw, as he started toward the ladies.

" 'The one sitting nearest this way,' replied Quillet.

" 'There are no evidences of guilt in that face, certain. By Jupiter, she is pretty!'

" 'Yes, but I do not think her as beautiful as Miss Wallingford. I have never laid my eyes on such a model of perfection; there is an indescribable charm about the expression of her features that eclipses anything I ever beheld. Just look at that pretty golden hair—did you ever see anything like it? Look at those large blue eyes, and that saucy dimpled chin, the straight, symmetrical form, the exquisite neck, the rosy cheeks!'

" 'Stop, Quillet, I cry enough! you are done for, that is plain; that girl has captured you beyond question.'

" 'I would give a California gold mine if I could capture such a woman for a wife!'

" 'Do you think Miss Bramlett is guilty?'

" 'I am truly sorry to be compelled to say that I do, though I do not believe she was in her senses when she committed the murder.'

" 'Why do they not plead insanity then?'

" 'Ah, there is where the unaccountable mystery comes in; but I have lately been informed that Miss Wallingford is in possession of some very strange facts which she believes will secure the acquittal of her friend.'

" 'Is it true that Miss Wallingford has lived in the jail with the prisoner all the time?'

" 'She has been with her most of the time, despite the continued remonstrances of old Rockland and all of her friends. I tell you what it is, that girl understands law as well as a majority of young members of the bar, and we are going to have some rare fun here to-day.'

" 'How is that?'

" 'Miss Wallingford has secured permission of the court to cross-examine some of the witnesses for the State; and I think we shall see a regular duel between her and one of the female witnesses.'

" 'Well, Quillet, you must let Miss Wallingford have a fair chance.'

" 'Indeed I will! she shall have her own time, and shall be allowed the privileges of a regular member of the bar.'

" 'I guess Miss Wallingford picked up her legal knowledge from old Rockland's abundant store; he is a cold-hearted old cuss, but I regard him as the best lawyer in Tennessee.'

" 'Yes, and I believe he hates everybody in the world except his wife and Miss Wallingford, and they say he worships the very ground on which that girl walks; he has crammed her head full of solid information, and I do honestly believe she is the most intellectual woman I ever met.'

" 'There comes old Rockland now, looking as pale as a ghost.'

"The iron lawyer moved slowly across the room and dropped into a chair; resting his elbows on a table and placing his face between his hands, he stared vacantly at space without apparently noticing anybody in the house.

" 'Mr. Quillet,' said the judge, 'are you ready to proceed with the Bramlett case?'

" 'We are ready on the part of the State, if your Honor pleases.'

" 'What says the defense?'

"Mr. Rockland straightened himself up, gazed at the judge a moment, and ran his eyes slowly over the vast crowd of spectators, then fixed his gaze on Lottie as if he were waiting for her to answer the judge's question.

" 'Yes, papa,' she whispered, 'tell the judge we are ready.'

" 'I believe we are ready for the defense,' growled the old lawyer as he resumed his seat, and again rested his face in his hands.'

" 'Call the *venire*, Mr. Sheriff,' said Flipout, as a frown began to darken his brow, occasioned, no doubt, by the confusion produced by the restless crowd who had come in to witness the proceedings.

"The first juror who presented himself was Gabriel Mc-Cracken, a very little man, with large red nose of the Roman type.

" 'Have you formed or expressed any opinion as to the guilt or innocence of the prisoner at the bar?' inquired Mr. Quillet.

" 'I have.'

" 'Stand aside.'

"Thomas Tadler answered to the second call, who said he had formed and expressed an opinion, and was promptly ordered to stand aside.

"The forty-seventh man called was the first one who had not formed an opinion about the case, or anything else, because he did not have sense enough to shape an idea on any subject. He was a tall, hump-shouldered, slim man, with weak, watery eyes, a starvation look resting on his face, and a three-cornered head, covered with a profusion of long, tangled brown hair, and an idiotic expression of countenance.

" 'What is your name, sir?'

" 'Obadiah Crookwood!'

" 'What is your occupation?'

" 'I are a peanut peddler!'

" 'Have you formed or expressed any opinion as to the guilt or innocence of the prisoner at the bar?'

" 'No, I hain't; never hearn tell of the concern afore.'

" 'Where to you reside?'

" 'T'other side ov the bayou.'

" 'What is your age?'

" 'Don't 'zactly know—suppose summer about thirty, forty or fifty!'

" 'Are you a married man?'

" 'Not now—useta was.'

" 'Your wife is dead, then?'

" 'Bless your soul, her sort don't die!'

" 'Where is your wife?'

" 'She's livin' with another feller.'

" 'How does it happen that your wife is living with another man?'

" 'We swapped wives.'

" 'Then you have got his wife, and he has yours?'

" 'Not 'zactly, because hizen jumped the track and run off with Jim Stitcher.'

" 'Why did you not then take your wife back, when the other woman repudiated the trade.'

" 'Because I didn't want her.'

" 'If your Honor please, I think this a competent juror,' said Mr. Quillet.

" 'What say you for the defense, Mr. Rockland?'

"The iron lawyer waved his hand slowly toward the jury box, without looking up or uttering a word, and Mr. Crookwood took his seat.

"The next juror who answered was a coal-black negro, with large flat nose, flared nostrils, and a mouth extending from ear to ear, with a form measuring six feet three at least.

" 'What is your name?'

" 'Ebenezer, sah.'

" 'What is your Christian name?'

" 'Lord love your soul, boss, I iz no Christian nigger—I iz a stray sheep from de congregation!'

" 'Have you any other name besides Ebenezer?'

" 'Ah, you bet I has, boss—lots on 'em!'

" 'What are they?'

" 'Solomon, Absalom, Lazarus, Ebenezer, sah—dey calls me Laz for short.'

" 'Have you ever formed or expressed any opinion as to the guilt or innocence of the prisoner at the bar?'

" 'Lord love your soul, boss, I never goes in a bar, I iz a

temperance nigger; I iz an honorable member of de Murphy 'stution!'

" 'You do not understand my question: have you formed or expressed any opinion as to the guilt or innocence of Miss Viola Bramlett?'

" 'How could a nigger 'spress hisself about a lady 'cept he knowed her? I nebber seed dat ar gal afore in my born days!'

" 'Then you have never formed or expressed any opinion about her guilt or innocence?'

" 'Nebber 'spressed myself about white folks, nebber 'sociates wid white people—dis nigger 'fesses to be a ge'man!'

" 'I think this is a competent juror, if the court please.'

" 'What say you for the defense?'

"Another careless wave of Mr. Rockland's hand, and the juror was ordered by the court to take his seat in the box.

"It was very clear to my mind that Mr. Rockland was perfectly indifferent as to the material being collected on the jury, and it was also evident that he regarded the entire proceeding as a mere matter of form to be passed over in order to reach the inevitable verdict of guilty against the defendant.

"Out of a *venire* of three hundred men, they succeeded in securing a jury of brainless idiots, and if any man had been bound by contract to furnish a dozen fit subjects for a first-class lunatic asylum, he could have used that jury as a legal tender for the debt.

"While Mr. Quillet was reading the bill of indictment, Viola fixed her beautiful eyes on him, and listened attentively, and I could see the regular rise and fall of her bosom, while her breathing was as calm and gentle as that of a slumbering infant; not a muscle of her face moved, nor did any evidence of fear or excitement manifest itself on her features. Lottie's hands trembled slightly as she pulled the leaves from a rose, and let them fall at her feet; no other signs of emotion appeared.

"The spectators and lawyers were listening in breathless silence, anxious to hear what sort of a plea the defendant was going to put in. Absolute quiet reigned throughout the spacious room, only broken by the solemn tones of Mr. Quillet's deep bass voice, as he read the awful charge of willful and malicious murder against the beautiful prisoner. **When** he came to the last word in the bill he turned from the jury, and fixing his keen black eyes on Viola's face, paused for a moment, as the prisoner rose to her feet and looked firmly into the face of the attorney-general. It was not a bold, brazen-faced, defiant stare, but it was such a calm, dignified, charming look as I suppose the angels in Heaven are wont to cast on each other.

"'Miss Viola Bramlett,' said Quillet, as he bent forward, 'are you guilty or not guilty?'

"'Not guilty!' was answered in a firm but sweet tone.

"Then commenced a tremendous scramble among the spectators seeking to secure eligible seats, so as to hear the evidence. Flipout began to put the pressure on his nose, while the dark frown re-appeared on his brow.

"'Mr. Sheriff,' exclaimed the court, 'if you do not instantly put an end to this confusion the court will impose a heavy fine on you; order those people to sit down, and station a deputy at each end of the aisle with instructions to keep it clear, and report the names of persons who disturb the business of the court. Have your witnesses called, Mr. Quillet, and proceed with the case.'

"As the vast crowd of witnesses began to move to the front, I was reminded of Byron's 'Vision of Judgment,' wherein he gives such a sublime history of the trial of George III. When Saint Peter called on Satan for his witnesses, the King of darkness waved his hand down toward hell, when up rose a black cloud of lost souls, almost as numerous as the legions of locusts that infested the shores of Egypt. Now I do not by any means intend to assert that the crowd of witnesses who came forward to testify against Viola Bramlett were as numerous as the countless throng that come up to offer evidence against England's dead king, but I merely give it as my candid opinion that his Satanic Majesty would have scorned the idea of introducing into a decent court such a motley crowd of witnesses as those who appeared to swear against Miss Bramlett. I do not apply these remarks to all of them, however, for Doctors Dodson and Plaxico were of the number. I was horrified to see Mrs. Ragland step forward and array herself on the side of the State. Could it be possible that Viola's own aunt was to be a witness for the State. I looked at Lottie to. see if any evidences of alarm appeared in her face, but nothing of the sort was perceptible—all seemed calm as an unruffled lake, while the corners of her mouth were closely drawn down. Zip Dabbs appeared at the head of the long column of witnesses, and if he had held the sun in one pocket, the moon in the other, the world on his shoulder, with the final destiny of the entire human race in the palm of his hand, he could not have put on a more self-important air than he did on that occasion. Tadpoddle appeared with his little eye on duty, while he was making an ineffectual effort to imitate his illustrious leader. Miss Jemima Tadpoddle, with her tall, gaunt form looming high above ordinary women, moved deliberately toward the clerk's desk, and kissed the Bible with a smack as the oath was administered by the clerk. Miss Clattermouth stood by the side of. her tall friend, looking like a Lilliputian by the side of Gulliver, with her little mouth handsomely puckered as if she were afraid that the important facts known to her would escape before she got a chance to tell them to the jury.

"As soon as the clerk completed the task of swearing the vast number of State witnesses, the court ordered the defense to call and swear theirs.

" 'If your Honor please,' growled Mr. Rockland, as he deliberately rose up from his seat, 'I believe we have no witnesses on the part of the defense.'

" 'Yes, we have, papa,' said Lottie, in a whisper, as she plucked at Mr. Rockland's sleeve, 'we have some witnesses, but we do not wish to have them sworn just now.'

"Then the iron lawyer stated to the court that he had just learned the fact that the defense would probably have one or two witnesses, and asked permission to have them sworn at a later period, which was readily granted.

" 'We shall ask your Honor,' continued Mr. Rockland, 'to order the witnesses under the rule.'

"The court then instructed the sheriff to have all the witnesses conducted to a comfortable room adjacent to the courtroom, and. to station a reliable deputy with them, with orders to keep them together.

" 'Will you insist on the rule being enforced as to Doctors Dodson and Plaxico?' inquired Mr. Quillet.

" 'No,' said Mr. Rockland, 'we consent that they may remain here.'

"Doctor Plaxico was the first witness who took the stand on the part of the prosecution.

" 'Doctor Plaxico, you will please face the jury, and then proceed to relate all the facts and circumstances connected with the death of Harry W. Bramlett.'

"The doctor coughed two or three times, wiped his brow with his handkerchief, ran his fingers between his cravat and throat as if the supply of air in his lungs was about to be exhausted, then, in a voice tremulous with emotion, he began as follows:

" 'Harry W. Bramlett died on the night of the 10th of February; his death was caused by poison administered to him by some person to me unknown. Death was produced by strychnine, large quantities of it being found in the stomach of the deceased. I am a practicing physician, and have been actively engaged in that profession for ten years past; could have saved the boy's life if I had been called an hour sooner. Assisted at the autopsy, found considerable quantity of strychnine—more than sufficient to produce death.'

" 'If you found any strychnine concealed about the premises, please tell the jury all about it.'

" 'Immediately after the child expired I began to examine the premises with a view of securing any evidence which would tend to unravel the strange mystery that appeared to surround the affair; the circumstances having directed my suspicions to——'

" 'Stop, Doctor Plaxico,' said Mr. Rockland; 'don't say anything about your suspicions, if you please—just state the facts that are known to you.'

" 'Very well. I found a small phial of strychnine in a bureau drawer that stood in Miss Bramlett's sleeping room, which apartment adjoined the one in which young Bramlett died. The phial was concealed in a little secret niche on the inside of a large drawer, among a great quantity of fine jewelry, and upon very careful inspection I noticed that some of the strychnine had been dipped out of the phial with the blade of a knife, or some other smooth substance, which had left its imprint plainly to be seen on the surface of that remaining in the phial. When Doctor Dodson arrived, I gave him a detailed account of what had occurred, and requested him to grant me a private interview, which he immediately did. As soon as Doctor Dodson and I were alone, I proceeded to describe all the symptoms that had presented themselves in young Bramlett's case, at the same time informing him that the child had been poisoned.'

" 'Doctor Plaxico,' said Quillet, 'be so good as to describe the conduct of Miss Bramlett in every particular, from the moment of your arrival until the time you left the premises.'

" 'When I first arrived at the house, Miss Bramlett appeared to be in the deepest distress, wringing her hands and weeping bitterly; but when the boy expired, she ceased to weep and began to stare wildly about the room as if searching for something, while a strange, inquiring expression was perceptible on her features. I noticed that she frequently picked up the little blue papers that lay on the table, and examined each one attentively, then replacing them, she turned round and gazed at me with a mysterious look, as if she were waiting for me to say something. She would frequently glance at the door, as if she were expecting some one to enter, and any noise seemed to frighten her.'

" 'We now turn the witness over to the defense for cross-examination,' said Mr. Quillet.

" 'You may stand aside, doctor,' said the iron lawyer, 'we will not trouble you with any questions.'

" 'We will examine Doctor Dodson now, Mr. Sheriff, if you will call him in,' said Mr. Quillet.

" 'He is here, sir,' replied the officer as Doctor Dodson came forward and went on the stand.

" 'Tell the jury all you know about the death of Harry W. Bramlett, Doctor Dodson—the cause of his death and all the circumstances appertaining to it.'

"The old physician was greatly agitated, though making a vigorous effort to conceal his emotions, but with only partial success. A tear glistened in his eye, while his hands trembled, and his breathing was short and labored.

" 'I am a practicing physician; was called to see young Bramlett a few days before his death; ah, ha! and found him suffering with ordinary chills and fever, don't you see? ah, ha! Well, you see it was on the afternoon of February 10 that I prescribed quinine; making up five doses, I put them in blue papers and directed Miss Bramlett to administer one dose every two hours, commencing at four o'clock P. M., ah, ha! don't you see? I was again called to visit the patient late at night, and when I arrived was horrified to find the child dead, ah, ha! Plaxico then requested me to grant him a private interview, and when we were alone he informed me that the deceased had been poisoned with strychnine; then I was greatly frightened, thinking it possible that I might have made a terrible mistake, don't you see? I instantly went and examined the phial from which I had taken the medicine, which was left on the mantel, and found it was pure, unadulterated quinine, don't you see? I then carefully inspected the contents of the blue papers on the table, and found two of them containing quinine, just as I had prepared them, while the other three were empty. I felt greatly relieved, because I was convinced that I had made no mistake, don't you see how it is yourself, ah ha? Miss Bramlett said she had administered the medicine exactly according to my directions, commencing promptly at four, and when she gave the third dose at eight her brother soon thereafter became seriously ill. I assisted at the post-mortem examination, and found a large quantity of strychnine in the stomach, enough to produce death; am satisfied that deceased died from poison.'

" 'What was the nature of Miss Bramlett's conduct while you remained in the room?'

" 'The poor child appeared to be paralyzed, stunned, as you may say, with grief; the fact is, she seemed to be perfectly crazed by the sudden death, ah ha! yes, don't you see? She had a frightful, wild appearance difficult to describe!'

" 'Did you question Miss Bramlett about the phial of strychnine that Doctor Plaxico found in her bureau drawer?'

" 'Yes, I asked her for what purpose she had purchased the phial of strychnine? She hesitated a moment, and appeared to be greatly confused by the question; then she said that she would rather not tell, and I did not urge her any further. I asked her if any other person had been in the room after I had left the quinine and before her brother suddenly grew worse. She said that no one had entered the room, so far as she knew.'

" 'Did you examine the phial of strychnine? if so, how much had been taken out of it?'

" 'A small quantity had been dipped out with the blade of a knife, or some other smooth instrument, which had left its imprint on that which remained. The phial had the usual label on it, with the word *"poison"* in large printed letters, and a picture of a skull and crossbones just below.'

"Doctor Dodson was permitted to stand aside, Mr. Rockland declining to cross-examine him.

CHAPTER XXXIV.

"THE famous Philadelphia detective was then placed on the stand.

" 'Mr. Dabbs,' said Quillet, 'will you please face the jury and tell all you know about the facts and circumstances connected with the death of Harry W. Bramlett.'

"The renowned detective then unbuttoned his vest, leaned back in his seat, and thrusting his thumbs through the armholes, surveying the crowd for a moment, began as follows:

" 'I have for the last ten years practiced my profession in the city of Philadelphia, and was employed by Doctor Demar to work up the Bramlett· case. I had been led to believe that the case was going to be a difficult one to manage, and that impenetrable mysteries and dangerous plots would have to be encountered and mastered before a correct conclusion could be reached; but I do not hesitate to say that during all my successful career as a detective officer, I never have met with a case of murder by poison in which it was so easy to spot the perpetrator as it has proved in this one.'

" 'We do not want to hear your opinion as to the sufficiency

of your evidence, Mr. Dabbs,' growled Mr. Rockland. 'Tell
what you know about the case, and let the jury weigh the
proof.'

" 'That is exactly what I was coming to when you interrupted me. While searching the premises we succeeded in
making many wonderful discoveries, all tending to fix the
guilt on Miss——'

" 'Stop, sir!' exclaimed Mr. Rockland, as anger flashed
from his eyes. 'If your Honor please, we do most earnestly
protest against this manner of proceeding!'

" 'Tell what you know about the case, sir, and let us have
none of your opinions as to where it fixes the guilt.'

" 'Very well, your Honor,' said Dabbs, 'I was just going
to do that.'

" 'Proceed with your evidence,' said Quillet.

" 'Well, as I was telling you a moment ago, we made some
startling discoveries while going through the premises where
the murder was committed. In a large wardrobe that stood
in Miss Bramlett's bedroom we found a blue silk dress, which
proved to be the property of that person, and in the left-
hand pocket we discovered a dose of strychnine wrapped in a
blue paper, exactly similar in all respects to those containing
the quinine that had been prepared and left by Doctor Dodson. During our very satisfactory search, we discovered a
small quantity (say one dose) of quinine under the grate,
and upon chemical test we found that one of the blue papers
that had been left by the doctor contained traces of quinine
and strychnine both; the quinine was next to the surface of
the paper, and the strychnine on top of the quinine, showing
clearly that the quinine had been emptied out of the paper
and the poison put in its stead. In the right-hand pocket of
Miss Bramlett's blue silk dress we found a letter of a most
mysterious character, addressed to her by a man whom we
have been shadowing all this time—an accomplice, as we have
good reason to think, though the evidence against him is not
sufficient to warrant us in demanding his arrest. As soon as
I got possession of the letter and the strychnine, I began to
make my arrangements to take Miss Bramlett by surprise,
hoping thereby to precipitate her into a confession. I entered her room in the jail disguised as a bill collector, being

I began to approach the subject which had caused my visit. After beating round for some time, I threw off my disguise, and confronted her as the officer of the law, intending by my sudden change to surprise her, so she would not have time to invent a lie.

" ' "Miss Bramlett," said I, as I threw off my disguise, "you are caught at last, and the best thing for you to do is to confess and plead for pardon."

" 'I showed her the letter, and the strychnine that I had found in her dress pocket, at the same time demanding an explanation. Then, sir, commenced some of the most splendid acting that I ever witnessed in all my life. I have seen Charlotte Cushman in "Guy Mannering;" I have seen Julia Deen, Charlotte Thompson, Eliza Logan, and all of our favorite actresses on the stage, but never has it been my good fortune to witness such splendid acting as that performed by Miss Bramlett on that occasion. I am willing to state on my oath that she seemed to grow at least ten inches taller when I showed her that letter, and although I could not swear that real fire flashed from her pretty eyes, yet something of a strange light blazed from them that I considered a first-class imitation of living fire. The manner in which she pointed to the door, and the peculiar tone of voice she employed as she bid me go through it, were indescribably grand, such as if acted on the stage would create quite a sensation. The language used was of an emphatic nature, and the pose so sublime that it caused me to forget my position as an officer, and implanted in my mind a desire to be somewhere else. If, however, I did for a moment forget my position as an officer, I did not lose my self-respect as a gentleman; consequently, I at once made my way through the door at which she was pointing, extremely disgusted with my interview. The very impressive manner in which that young woman invited me out of her room had the effect, I confess, to produce a temporary confusion, causing me to withdraw rather hurriedly, and I did not discover the fact that I had left the letter in her possession until I was out of her presence. As soon as I could I returned to her room and requested her to deliver the important document to me; but, sir, you may imagine my astonishment, if you can, when she pointed down at her left heel, which was on the letter, grinding it against the floor. Yes, sir, she was, I will not say dancing a jig on the letter, but she was making a first-class imitation of that sort of sport. If you will take the trouble, Mr. Quillet, to examine this letter, sir, you will see the print of her boot-heel on it; the words "Dear V." you will observe have been almost obliterated by the print of her heel; but I can prove by Doctor Demar that "Dear V." was plainly written at the top of that paper.'

"Mr. Quillet now took the letter from Dabbs and read it to the jury.

" 'She is guilty beyond all doubt,' whispered Hogjaw to Quillet. 'Oh! it is horrible to think that such a beautiful creature could be so cruel! it will make me suspect everybody!'

" 'Mr. Dabbs, do you know the handwriting of that letter?'

" 'Being on my oath, and therefore bound to tell the truth, I regret to say that I do not, but I have a very strong suspicion.'

" 'We care nothing about your suspicions,' said Mr. Rockland; 'be so good as to confine your statements to what you know.'

" 'Very well, that is exactly what I meant to do, consequently, I say I do not know who wrote that letter. The handwriting has evidently been disguised, and the man I suspect is a shrewd rascal, who understands the art of deception and concealment of evidence. We found rather a singular contrivance at the back part of Mr. Ragland's vegetable garden—it would perhaps be a misnomer to call it a gate, but nevertheless, it had evidently served the purpose of one. We could see where persons had often passed through—the soft earth on the inside bore plainly the imprint of shoe tracks, one a number eight, the other a number three lady's shoe.'

" 'What size shoe does Miss Bramlett wear?'

" 'She wears a number three—I procured one of her shoes, and compared it with the track, and found that the fit was perfect! and I do not hesitate to swear that the track was made by the prisoner.'

"I cast a glance at Lottie, being curious to know what effect this startling evidence would have on her; but no signs of emotion were visible on her features. She sat with her pretty eyes fixed on Mr. Dabbs, as if endeavoring to read his thoughts, while the corners of her mouth were both drawn down, and her lips firmly pressed together.

"Mr. Dabbs was kept on the stand for more than an hour, and when he was ordered to stand aside every vestige of hope had fled from my bosom. The proof of Miss Bramlett's guilt appeared to me to be insurmountable and overwhelming.

"Mr. Tadpoddle was then put on the stand, and I noticed that he had the little eye on duty, while the large one calmly reposed in its hole. A roar of laughter greeted the arrival of that singular specimen of deformed humanity. Mr. Tadpoddle's evidence was nothing more nor less than a confirmation of that given by Dabbs; but it was all that the court and Mr. Rockland could do to prevent him from telling what his remarkable sister knew about the case.

" 'Call in your next witness,' exclaimed Flipout impatiently, as Tadpoddle left the stand.

" 'Bring Miss Tadpoddle now, Mr. Sheriff,' said Quillet as he turned round and addressed the officer.

"The eyes of two hundred men were riveted on the tall, straight form of the witness as she moved proudly down the aisle; a scornful curl on her thin, bloodless lips, and a haughty bend of her long, stringy neck, as she flashed a glance of defiance at the spectators, told plainly what contempt she felt for all of the human race, and that part of it in particular. Her costume was of the flashy style, the dress being crimson silk, with as much of the material in her train as had been used in the remainder of the garment; and as to cheap lace, and pinchbeck jewelry, she looked as if she had just been in a storm, where such articles had rained down on her from the clouds. She had as much paint on her face as a Comanche chief would have used in three months while on the war-path. Her hat contained all the colors of the rainbow, with the star-spangled banner thrown in, while three tall plumes of different colors waved high above her head, like those that I had seen on the hat of an old-fashioned militia captain at a regiment muster.

" 'Take a seat, Miss Tadpoddle,' said Quillet as he pointed toward the chair, 'and tell us all you know about the case now on trial.'

" 'La bless your soul, sir, if I were to tell everything I know about this case it would take me a week! Now I never exaggerate or get excited; I am different from other young girls—I despise exaggeration! You know there are a great many people who would not tell a lie under any circumstances, yet they have a despicable habit of exaggerating everything. Very well, I am not that sort of a girl—I always confine myself closely to the truth without exaggeration. There is my particular friend, Miss Clattermouth, Heaven bless her dear little soul! She is the sweetest creature in the world, though she has fallen into the detestable habit of exaggerating. You know her I presume, Mr. Quillet? Yes, I have heard her speak about you very often; the fact is, she is a stanch friend of yours, and so am I; but let that pass.'

" 'Please tell us what you know about the Bramlett murder?'

" 'Ah! yes, I beg your pardon, Mr. Quillet, that was the very thing I was doing when you interrupted me. Well, you see my sweet little friend Clattermouth came to see me one day—and, by the by, she visits me very often—and we were correcting the proof-sheets of her forthcoming lecture, which she was going to deliver at the next meeting of our Tramp Reform Association; the subject of the Bramlett murder came up, and Miss Clattermouth was thinking that it might be a good idea to mention the case in her lecture, when I said, says I :

" ' "Jerusha——" '

" 'Stop a moment, Miss Tadpoddle,' said the judge as he began to rub both sides of his nose with great vigor. 'Mr. Quillet,' he continued, 'you will have to propound direct questions to this witness—we cannot have the time wasted in listening to this rigmarole. Direct the mind of the witness to the facts you expect to prove by her, and put a stop to this nonsense.'

" 'Miss Tadpoddle,' said Quillet, as he moved closer to her, 'if you ever heard a conversation carried on between Miss

Bramlett and Benjamin Bowles, in which strychnine was mentioned, please tell all you heard.'

" 'La bless your soul, that is the very thing I was telling when the judge interrupted me! Yes, indeed, I did hear them talking about murder, poison and many other awful things—that is, I heard Miss Bramlett talking about them, but Mr. Bowles was a mere listener. I inferred from what I saw and heard that Mr. Bowles was greatly annoyed by her strange questions about the effect of strychnine as a poison; the fact is, I think he is a perfect gentleman—a little wild, I admit, but withal a man of honor; he has made many liberal donations to our Tramp Reform Association, and my friend Miss Clattermouth says that he promised to——'

" 'Miss Tadpoddle,' exclaimed the judge, 'can you not tell what you know about this case without giving a history of all creation?'

" 'La, bless your soul, yes!'

" 'Well, go on and do it then!'

" 'That is exactly what I was doing when you interrupted me. I was telling what my friend Miss Clattermouth said about Mr. Bowles.'

" 'Tell us what you know about Miss Bramlett's connection with her brother's death, and let Mr. Bowles and Miss Clattermouth alone.'

" 'Miss Tadpoddle,' said Quillet, 'if you will just answer my questions, I dare say we shall get along much better. What did Miss Bramlett say to Mr. Bowles about strychnine?'

" 'She asked him how much strychnine it would require to produce death, and if a doctor could tell when it had been caused by that sort of poison; I heard her say it with my own ears, and I would swear it on a stack of Bibles as high as this court-house; and I never exaggerate either—I despise people who do exaggerate! I told my friend Miss Clattermouth about it; I said, says I:

" ' "Jerusha," says I——'

" 'Stop, Miss Tadpoddle, don't tell what you said, but let us hear what Miss Bramlett said.'

" 'That is the very thing I have just told you; but if it will do you any good, I can tell it again.'

" 'When was it you heard the conversation which you have just mentioned?'

" 'About one week before she poisoned her poor little brother.'

" 'Where did it occur?'

" 'In the alley just in the rear of Mr. Bowles' apartments.'

" 'How did you happen to see Miss Bramlett and Bowles on that occasion?'

" 'Well, if you must know, I was playing the rôle of detective; I, had my suspicions aroused by a little circumstance that transpired previous to that time, and I resolved to unravel the little mystery—in other words, I made up my mind to get even with Miss Bramlett, for she insulted me when I asked her to join our Tramp Reform Association, and I determined to have my revenge. I told my friend Miss Clattermouth all about it, as soon as we met, and we then began to arrange our plans to expose that hussy. I told my dear friend, says I:

" ' "Jerusha," says I——'

" 'Never mind what you told your friend—confine your statements to what you heard Miss Bramlett say.'

" 'That is the very thing I was doing when you interrupted me.'

" 'If you ever saw Miss Bramlett go from Mr. Ragland's residence to the apartments of Mr. Bowles, tell all about it.'

" 'La, bless your soul, I was telling that very thing when you interrupted me; yes, I should say I did see her go to the apartments of Mr. Bowles! The night was quite dark, and the lamp-lights were very dim, but I was close enough to see her go through the slip-gap at the back of the garden. I was determined to stick to her until I could find out what she was up to. I never give up when I undertake anything—I despise people who always give up when they encounter difficulties! I followed her to Bowles' quarters, and it was after she came out of his apartments that I heard her asking about the strychnine.'

" 'If your Honor please,' said Mr. Rockland, 'I cannot imagine what object my friend has in view by the introduction of this rigmarole. It would seem that the attorney for the State had lost sight of the charges contained in his bill of indictment, and was seeking merely to destroy the young lady's character.'

" 'Let them go ahead, papa,' said Lottie, 'don't stop them—that is the very thing we want them to prove.'

" 'Pshaw! child, you don't know what you are talking about!' growled the iron lawyer.

" 'Yes I do, papa, let them walk into the trap—I'll spring the trigger directly.'

" 'If the court please,' said Mr. Quillet, 'we think the evidence is competent in all respects. We have proved by this witness that the defendant was planning the murder a week before it was perpetrated.'

" 'We withdraw the objections,' said Mr. Rockland, 'you may go on with the evidence.'

" 'We are through with the witness,' observed Mr. Quillet, 'and she may retire, unless you wish to cross-examine her.'

" 'Stand aside,' growled Mr. Rockland, as he waved his hand slowly.

" 'No, no, papa,' said Lottie, 'don't let her go yet—I have some questions to ask her.'

" 'Hold on a moment, if you please, Miss Tadpoddle,' exclaimed Mr. Rockland; 'if your Honor will permit Miss Wallingford to ask the witness a few questions, we will esteem it a favor. She has been with the defendant most of the time, and is very familiar with the points of the case.'

" 'Certainly, certainly!' said the judge, 'let Miss Wallingford ask as many questions as she pleases.'

"A great sensation was caused among the spectators at this new turn of things, and a scramble for front seat ensued. The crowd swayed back and forth, while all the lawyers moved close to Lottie, and gazed at her with open mouths.

" 'Now the fun begins,' whispered Quillet to Hogjaw.

" 'Miss Tadpoddle,' said Lottie, in a calm, firm tone, 'I believe you said the night you saw Miss Bramlett with Bowles was very dark?'

" 'Yes, of course I did; and I'll say it again, if it will do you any good.'

" 'Never mind, once will do. How did you know it was Miss Bramlett if the night was so dark?'

" 'How did I know it was she?'

" 'Yes, how could you know it was Miss Bramlett, when it was so dark that you could not see her face?'

" 'I never said I saw her face; the fact is, I did not see her face, because she had it concealed behind a heavy veil.'

" 'Then how did you know it was Miss Bramlett?'

" 'I knew her by the dress she had on—it was her blue silk and I knew it as well as I know my own silk, because I helped her alter it one day. It was too short in the skirt, and I let it out so as to make it the proper length.'

" 'How could you tell it was a blue silk dress when it was so dark?'

" 'I followed her down the street, and when she would pass near a lamp-post I could see the color of the dress distinctly.'

" 'Then the only reason you have for saying it was Miss Bramlett was because you knew the blue silk dress?'

" 'No, that is not the only reason, by a long jump, I'll let you know.'

" 'What other reasons have you besides the dress?'

" 'Didn't I see her come out of Mr. Ragland's house, and go to Bowles' quarters? Didn't I see her meet him in the garden at another time, when I was waiting to meet Mrs. Ragland?'

" 'Well, tell us about the first time you saw Bowles and the woman together in the garden.'

" 'Haven't I told it? What do you want me to tell it a dozen times for?'

" 'The witness will answer the questions promptly!' said the judge.

" 'Oh! very well, I can tell it over a thousand times if you want it. I saw Miss Bramlett meet Bowles in the garden one night, about a week before I saw her go to his quarters.'

" 'Did she have on the same blue silk dress the first time you saw her meet Bowles?'

" 'I don't know—I was not close enough to tell.'

" 'How did you know it was Miss Bramlett, then?'

" 'The servant told me that Mrs. Ragland had gone visiting, and while I was waiting for her return, I saw a woman meet Bowles in the garden, and knowing that Mrs. Ragland was not at home, I knew it must be Miss Bramlett—now you have it.'

" 'Then the only thing that caused you to think it was
Miss Bramlett was the fact that you saw a woman in the
garden, and having been informed that Mrs. Ragland was
not at home?'

" 'Yes, I suppose that is the way of it.'

" 'Did you go up to Miss Bramlett's room to ascertain
whether she was there or not?'

" 'Why should I go up to her room to look for her, when
I saw her in the garden?'

" 'You did not know it was Miss Bramlett you saw in the
garden; it might have been some one else.'

" 'It might have been somebody else, but it wasn't.'

" 'How can you swear that it was not somebody else?'

" 'How many times do you want me to tell it?'

" 'Only once.'

" 'Haven't I told you more than once?'

" 'Answer the question, madame,' said Flipout, while he
rubbed his nose unusually hard.

" 'What was the question?' inquired Miss Tadpoddle as
she looked daggers at Lottie.

" 'I asked you how you could swear it was not somebody
else you saw in the garden.'

" 'I never said I could swear it was not somebody else.'

" 'Very well; then can you swear that it was Miss Bramlett?'

" 'You can't make me swear a lie if you work on me till
Gabriel comes with his trumpet!'

" 'I do not want you to swear falsely; I would much rather
hear you swear the truth.'

" 'That is precisely what I mean to do; I never exaggerate;
I hate exaggeration—it is my nature to despise it!'

" 'Miss Tadpoddle, do you, or do you not, know who the
woman was that you saw in the garden?'

" 'I will not swear positively that I did know who she was,
but I thought it was Miss Bramlett.'

" 'When you were playing detective that other night, what
kind of a gown did you have on?'

" 'Now, I should like to know what on earth you ask such
a question as that for?'

" 'Answer the question,' thundered Flipout.

" 'Very well, if you must know, I did not have on any gown at all.'

" 'How did you happen to be parading the streets at night without a gown?'

" 'Did you never see any one clad without a gown?'

" 'How were you dressed on that occasion?'

" 'I had on a suit of my brother's clothes; now, then, what else do you want to know about it?'

" 'How far were you from Bowles when you heard the woman ask him about the strychnine?'

" 'I suppose I was twenty yards from him.'

" 'Did you recognize Miss Bramlett's voice?'

" 'I wouldn't swear that I did, because I wasn't close enough to do that; though I knew it was she by the dress.'

" 'What reply did Bowles make when she asked him how much strychnine it would take to kill?'

" 'I did not hear his reply distinctly.'

" 'Did Bowles accompany the woman to Mr. Ragland's house?'

" 'He parted with her in the garden, after kissing her a dozen times. I declare, it made me sick to see such carryings-on!'

" 'How did you get into the garden?'

" 'Why, I just put one foot on the railing and then set my other foot on the railing on the other side; then I jumped over, the same as a man does when he gets off a horse.'

" 'Did you see Mrs. Ragland on the first night you discovered Bowles and the woman in the garden?'

" 'No; I waited for her until I got tired, then I went home.'

" 'You may stand aside now,' said Lottie.

"Then Miss Tadpoddle gathered up her skirts and giving Lottie a scornful look, moved away with long and rapid strides.

" 'Quillet,' whispered Hogjaw, 'you have caught a tartar, I think.'

" 'How is that?'

" 'That Miss Wallingford has got a trap set for some of your witnesses, I infer from the shape of her questions. I tell you, she is a trump, as sure as you are born; and she will spring a mine under your case yet that will blow it skyward. I know by her looks and the manner of her questions that she means mischief; somebody is going to get scratched yet before this case is ended.'

" 'She lacks a great deal of being a fool, at any rate, and I should be very glad if she can develop any facts that would benefit her unfortunate friend.'

" 'Why did you not have Bowles arrested as an accomplice?'

" 'The proof against him is not sufficient to convict, though it looks very suspicious; and then I wanted to use him as a witness.'

" 'Which witness will you examine next?' said the judge.

" 'Bring in Benjamin Bowles, Mr. Sheriff,' said Mr. Quillet, without giving a direct answer to the judge's question.

"Mr. Bowles walked forward with a dignified step and serene countenance, and took his place in the witness box, as he cast a scornful glance on the jury. His dress was fashionable, faultless, and eminently exquisite, cut in the most approved style of dandyism. A large diamond pin flashed its bright rays from his bosom, and mingled with the sparkle of the gaudy rings on his fingers. His hair was very glossy, richly perfumed, and nicely parted in the middle, while his white cravat was tied in a most beautiful fashion. There was a look of bold impudence about the countenance that amounted to an insult, while you could see an indescribable something that convinced you that Satan had sealed him as his own property.

" 'Mr. Bowles,' said Mr. Quillet, 'are you acquainted with Miss Viola Bramlett?'

" 'Yes.'

" 'How long have you known her?'

" 'Five or six months.'

" 'If she ever asked you any questions about strychnine, please state what she said.'

" 'On several different occasions Miss Bramlett propounded questions to me of a very startling character, but I do not recall the exact words she used. I remember one night, about a week before her brother's death, she asked me if a

doctor could tell when any one had been killed with strychnine. She also wanted to know how much strychnine it
would take to produce death.'

" 'What reply did you make to such questions?'

" 'I evaded the questions by changing the conversation to
other topics, but she would whip round and get back to the
same subject. She persisted in pumping me on the subject,
until my suspicions were roused, and I avoided her after
that.'

" 'Where were you when you had the last conversation
with her about strychnine?'

" 'She commenced the conversation at my apartments, but
continued to talk on the same subject after we got into the
street.'

" 'She had been visiting you at your rooms, then?'

" 'Yes.'

" 'Did you ever meet Miss Bramlett in Mr. Ragland's garden?'

" 'Yes, very often.'

" 'If the court please,' said Mr. Rockland, 'I do most
earnestly protest against this sort of evidence.'

" 'Hush, papa!' whispered Lottie, as she kept plucking at
Mr. Rockland's sleeve, 'let him go on; he is already in my
trap, and is one of the main birds I have set the net to catch!'

" 'We withdraw all objections to the evidence,' said Mr.
Rockland as he resumed his seat and gazed inquiringly at
Lottie. 'What in the name of common sense do you mean,
daughter, by a trap set for the witnesses?'

" 'Bowles has sworn to an absolute falsehood, and I will
trap him before long.'

" 'Take the witness, Mr. Rockland,' said Mr. Quillet as
he leaned back in his seat, thrust his hands in his pockets,
while a smile of triumph played on his handsome features.

" 'I will cross-examine him,' whispered Lottie as she began
to turn the leaves of a memorandum book which she held in
her hand.

" 'Mr. Bowles, what is your occupation?'

" 'I am a sportsman.'

" 'Please explain what you mean by the word sportsman?'

" 'I mean that I am a turfman, and follow the business as an occupation.'

" 'Are you not the owner and proprietor of a gambling hell in this city?'

" 'I don't know that there is any hell about it.'

" 'You need not answer any question, Mr. Bowles, that would tend to criminate you,' said Mr. Quillet.

" 'Oh, I am perfectly willing to answer all questions.'

" 'Very good, then I will repeat the question. Are you not the keeper of a gambling house in this city?'

" 'No, I am not; but I keep a suite of rooms where my friends frequently assemble to engage in a harmless game of cards, merely for amusement.'

" 'Do you run a faro bank, and a roulette table at those rooms?'

" 'I am not a faro dealer myself, though such a machine is sometimes operated there.'

" 'Now, Mr. Bowles, do you swear that Miss Viola Bramlett ever was inside of your apartments?'

" 'Yes, certainly I do.'

" 'Did anybody else ever see her in your quarters, besides you?'

" 'I don't think they ever did.'

" 'Were you ever acquainted with a woman by the name of Victoria Totten?'

" 'If an adder had stung Mr. Bowles in a vital part, he could not have changed color as quickly as he did when the name of Victoria Totten was mentioned. His face, which was actually florid, turned as pale as death, and his white hands trembled as he put a glass of water to his lips. His agitation, however, was only temporary, for he was a bold villain, who could command himself under adverse circumstances.

" 'What name was it you asked me about, madame?'

" 'I asked you if you ever knew a woman named Victoria Totten?'

" 'I declare, I don't remember; the names, however, seem familiar to me, but I can't exactly call to mind any acquaintance of that name.'

" 'Perhaps I can assist your memory a little. Did you know the widow Totten, who resided three or four miles from Vicksburg, Mississippi, who had a daughter named Victoria ?'

" 'I don't think I did.'

"That answer was made by Bowles in a tremulous tone, while he showed signs of great uneasiness.

" 'Have you ever been married, Mr. Bowles?'

" 'No.'

" 'Did you ever live in New Orleans with a woman whom you represented to be your wife?'

" 'Yes.'

" 'If the court please,' said Mr. Quillet, as he sprang quickly to his feet, 'I must confess I cannot see wherein this kind of evidence can have any connection whatever with this case.'

"I heard Lottie whisper to Mr. Rockland, as I was sitting near her:

" 'Tell the court, papa,' said she, 'that we will connect it with the case very soon.'

"The iron lawyer then said to the court:

" 'We think we will be able to connect this testimony with this case, and if we fail, then your Honor can rule it out.'

" 'The court cannot see the applicability of the evidence to the case now on trial, but the defendant has a right to introduce evidence in the order chosen by her attorney. I will not give any opinion just now, but will decide upon it when all the testimony has been put before the court. Proceed with the examination.'

" 'What was the name of the woman whom you represented to be your wife?'

" 'I had rather not answer that question, as it might compromise a lady's character.'

" 'We object to the question,' said Quillet.

" 'We insist on an answer,' said Mr. Rockland; while Bowles changed from a deep red color to a deathly pallor.

" 'The court will not permit such questions to be propounded, unless the attorney for the defense can state some reasons for inquiring into the private history of a woman residing in New Orleans.'

" 'The woman alluded to,' said Mr. Rockland, 'does not

reside in New Orleans at this time; but she is here in the city of Memphis; and Miss Wallingford informs me that we will connect all this proof directly with the case now on trial.'

" 'In view of that statement, the court will permit the question to be asked.'

"Bowles moved uneasily backward and forward in his seat, wiped the big drops of perspiration from his brow and coughed several times. As he played with his watch chain I could see that his hands were trembling and his face became deathly in its pallor.

"Lottie repeated the question.

" 'Her name was Rose Elrod.'

" 'Where is she now?'

" 'I don't know.'

" 'Mr. Bowles, don't you know that you were living with Miss Victoria Totten, a young girl whom you had induced to elope with you?'

" 'No, I do not.'

" 'We have got him safe in the trap at last,' said Lottie, in a whisper, as she put her mouth close to my ear.

"I remembered the time when that identical scamp insulted her, when she was a helpless orphan child, and how he swore a lie against Harry. Then I thought of the old adages: 'Chickens will come home to roost,—'Every dog will have his day,' etc. Lottie was having her revenge now; though she was not actuated by any feeling of that sort—but she was working to save her friend.

"She took a letter from her satchel, and after carefully removing it from the envelope handed the latter to Mr. Bowles.

" 'Is that your handwriting, Mr. Bowles?'

"He first held the paper close to his eyes, then at arm's length; he next twisted himself round, as if he wanted some light, and wiped his brow hurriedly.

" 'I can't say—that is, I think—er—er—I was not certain —ahem! I was under the—well, the writing looks a little like mine, though I can't say I wrote it.'

" 'Can you swear that you did not write it?'

" 'I—I—I—that is, I don't know—I don't think I did!'

" 'Mr. Quillet,' said Lottie, 'please loan me the note about which Mr. Dabbs testified.'

"Mr. Quillet handed it to her.

" 'Mr. Bowles, did you write that note?'

" 'No, I did not.'

" 'Mr. Bowles, don't you know that that letter was intended for the woman whom you represented to be your wife, and not for Miss Viola Bramlett?'

" 'I know nothing whatever about that note.'

" 'Don't you know that the woman with whom you lived in New Orleans, the same one you represented to be your wife, is now living in the city of Memphis?'

" 'No, I do not.'

" 'The witness may stand aside,' said Lottie, as she turned round and whispered to me.

" 'Eddie, we have got the birds in the trap at last! I will spring the trigger when the next witness takes the stand.'

CHAPTER XXXV.

"THE next witness introduced was Mrs. Ragland, a very beautiful woman—a brunette of the Guluare type. She was elegantly attired in a gown of drab silk, with an abundant train, containing innumerable flounces trimmed with Valenciennes lace. Diamonds flashed from her bosom, neck and arms, and a massive gold chain encircled her neck two or three times, at the lower end of which was fastened an exquisite lady's watch, half concealed in a shallow pocket at her waist. Her large dark eyes rolled about wildly beneath very long, heavy lashes. There was a mysterious restlessness in the expression of her great black eyes which convinced me that she possessed a soul that was a stranger to happiness.

" 'Mrs. Ragland,' said Mr. Quillet, 'if you ever saw Miss Bramlett meet Mr. Bowles, please tell the jury when and where it was.'

" 'I have very often seen them meet in our garden; can't say exactly how often, though I can positively assert that they met as many as three times. The last time I saw them meet was but a very few days before Miss Bramlett's little brother died; don't know the exact date, but am sure it was less than a week before her brother's death.'

" 'If you ever heard any conversation between Miss Bramlett and Mr. Bowles, please, tell what was said by each of them?'

" 'I distinctly remember one occasion when I heard a conversation between them, but I think that most of the talking was done by Miss Bramlett. To the best of my recollection, it was about the 1st of February, at night; the weather was uncommonly warm and oppressive; I was suffering with a severe headache, and I concluded that probably a stroll in the garden would have the effect to ease my sufferings. After walking about in the garden for some time, I went into the summer-house and took a seat on one of the low wooden benches that stood near the wall, which was covered with honeysuckle vines, under which I was partially concealed. I had been there but a few minutes when I heard footsteps sounding on the ground, and was very much frightened when I discovered a man coming toward me from the extreme rear of the garden. He approached to a spot within five paces of the summer-house, and halting, instantly gave a low whistle which I suppose was a signal to notify Miss Bramlett of his arrival. As soon as he halted, I discovered that it was Mr. Bowles. I suppose he had been there somewhere about five minutes, when I saw Miss Bramlett coming from the house. She approached the spot where Mr. Bowles was and entered into a whispered conversation with him, all of which I could distinctly hear. She commenced the interview by urging him to fulfill a promise of marriage, which she alleged he had made, and which he did not deny. He made many protestations of love to her, which she returned in very earnest language, and after the conversation had run on the subject of love and marriage for some time, she asked him how strychnine was used to kill rats; then she brought the conversation round to the effect such a poison would have on the human system. After a while she put the question to him directly, by asking him how much of the poison it would require to kill a man; and then she asked how much it would take to kill a child under ten. She also asked him if a doctor could tell when a person had died from the effects of strychnine. Mr. Bowles endeavored to change the subject by asking questions about other things, but she invariably whipped round and came back to the subject and persisted in talking about it, until Mr. Bowles in an angry tone threatened to depart and leave her unless she would hush talking about poison.

" ' "Viola," said Mr. Bowles, "I do not like to have you talk that way—it makes me shiver to listen to it!"

" 'After they had conversed there about thirty minutes, he invited her to accompany him to his apartments, which she consented to do, and passed out through the garden and disappeared down the street.'

" 'You may take the witness, if you wish to cross-examine her,' said Mr. Quillet.

" 'Have you been friendly with Miss Bramlett all the time since she came to reside in your husband's house?'

" 'I cannot say that we were all the time friendly, for we did frequently have little disputes about matters of a trifling nature; but I never for a moment harbored any ill-will or malice toward Miss Bramlett. I, of course, did not approve of her conduct, and many times have remonstrated with her about the impropriety of it, but instead of thanking me for my good advice, she would fly into a passion; with that exception, our relations were undisturbed.'

" 'Mrs. Ragland, have you not often borrowed large sums of money from Miss Bramlett?'

" 'Well, I do not know what you would consider a large sum of money—people have different ideas on that subject, you know.'

" 'Very well, then; just tell us how much money you did borrow from her?'

" 'I remember borrowing five hundred dollars from her on one occasion.'

" 'What did you do with that five hundred dollars?'

" 'That is none of your business, Miss Wallingford; you have no right to be prying into my private affairs.'

" 'You must answer the question, madame,' said the judge.

" 'I could not tell now, to save my life, exactly what I did do with it.'

" 'Did you not borrow the money expressly for Benjamin Bowles?'

" 'No, I did not. Why should I be borrowing money for him?'

" 'That is the very thing we are endeavoring to find out. Did you not borrow as much as five hundred dollars from Miss Bramlett on two different occasions.'

" 'Perhaps I did.'

" 'Don't you know you did?'

" 'Well, yes, I believe I did.'

" 'Have you ever paid any of that money back?'

" 'No; I have not.'

" 'About one week before the death of Miss Bramlett's little brother, did you not borrow from her one thousand dollars?'

" 'I think I did.'

" 'Don't you know you did?'

" 'Yes.'

" 'What did you want with it?'

" 'I do not now remember exactly what I did want it for.'

" 'Did you not borrow it for Benjamin Bowles?'

" 'No, I did not; but I dare say I got it to pay for a set of diamonds, or something of the sort.'

" 'Were you acquainted with Mr. Bowles before you were married to Mr. Ragland?'

" 'No.'

" 'What was your maiden name?'

" 'Helen Herndon.'

" 'Are your parents living now?'

" 'No, they are both dead.'

" 'Where and when did they die?'

" 'In the State of Louisiana, ten years ago.'

" 'Were you ever acquainted with a woman named Victoria Totten?'

"At the mention of that name, Mrs. Ragland's face turned ghastly pale, and she gave a sudden start, as a person would when stung by a wasp, but she promptly answered:

" 'No.'

" 'Did you ever reside in the city of New Orleans?'

" 'No.'

" 'Have you ever been in that city?'

" 'Yes.'

" 'Now, Mrs. Ragland, will you state on your oath that you

never did reside in New Orleans as the reputed wife of Benjamin Bowles?'

" 'Yes, I will; and I do not thank you for asking me any such a question!'

" 'I do not wish or expect any thanks from you, madame, but I merely want to get at the truth. Mrs. Ragland, did you ever see a copy of Bolivar Bramlett's will?'

" 'Perhaps I have.'

" 'Don't you know you have?'

" 'Suppose I have: what does that signify?'

" 'Just answer the question, if you please.'

" 'Very well, then—I have seen a copy of the will.'

" 'Did you not send to New York for a copy of the will, and pay ten dollars for it?'

" 'Oh, yes, I declare, I had forgotten all about it!'

" 'Yes, I dare say you had forgotten all about such a trivial little circumstance; but I want you to tell the jury what object you had in view when you paid ten dollars for a copy of Mr. Bramlett's will.'

" 'I cannot remember precisely what I did want with the copy, but I suppose I was prompted by sheer curiosity.'

" 'Is this the copy of the will that you received from New York?'

"Lottie handed her a large bundle of papers, containing at least a dozen sheets of paper covered with writing, the last one being sealed with red wax, to which was attached a blue ribbon, just below the notary's signature.

" 'This looks very much like the copy I received, though I could not swear positively that it was the identical document. If it is the same paper, some thief has stolen it from my bureau drawer; and I should like very much to know how you got possession of it.'

" 'I dare say you would, and I promise that you shall know all about it very soon. Who, under Bolivar Bramlett, would inherit his immense wealth, if Miss Bramlett and her brother had both died childless?'

" 'I believe it would have come to my husband.'

" 'Don't you know it would?'

" 'Yes, I suppose I do.'

" 'Then your husband would have been the possessor of a very large fortune, if those two children had died childless?'

" 'Yes, I suppose that is the way of it.'

" 'But you did not want those two children to die, and leave your husband to be bothered with the management of such a large fortune?'

" 'I do not know that I ever gave a thought to that subject.'

" 'Well, were you not frequently in need of money?'

" 'I don't know that I was frequently in need of money, though I did sometimes borrow a little from my niece.'

" 'Why did you not get money from your husband when you stood in need of it, instead of borrowing it from Miss Bramlett?'

" 'My husband was not in a condition to let me have money.'

" 'Then how did you expect to pay the money back that you borrowed of Miss Bramlett?'

" 'I do not know that I ever gave a thought to that subject.'

" 'Were you ever in a gambling house on Canal street, New Orleans?'

" 'No, I was not; and I should like to know why you ask such absurd questions of me?'

" 'Be patient, madame, and it will all be very plain to you in a short time. What number shoe do you wear?'

" 'Number four.'

"Lottie then opened a little portmanteau which the coachman had brought in that morning, and placing it on the floor near her, took out a pretty little number three lady's boot, and handed it to Mrs. Ragland.

" 'Please examine that boot and tell me whether or not you ever saw it before?'

" 'La, yes, indeed, I have seen it before! it is mine—it was stolen from my boudoir, and I should like very much to know the thief.'

" 'You shall see the thief before you leave the stand; but tell us what is the number of that boot?'

" 'It is a number three, I believe; I know it is too small for me—I could not wear it, for that very reason.'

" 'Have you not very often worn this boot, along with its mate?'

" 'No, I don't think I have, because they hurt my feet so that I could not wear them.'

" 'Then will you be so good as to explain how this heel came to be so much whetted off?'

" 'I cannot tell, unless it was done by Miss Bramlett, as she very frequently wore them, because her foot is smaller than mine, and a number three exactly fits it.'

" 'Are you not wearing a number three shoe now?'

" 'Perhaps I am; in fact, I know I am, because I was pressed for time this morning, and during the confusion my maid put on a pair of number threes, which I did not notice until I got out of the carriage to come into the court-room, and then I found it out, because my feet were being pinched.'

" 'How does it happen that you have so many number three shoes about your house, when you say that you only wear number fours?'

" 'You know how foolish we ladies are about the looks of our feet, and you also know that we very often thrust them into shoes that are too small.'

" 'You admit, then, that you are now wearing number three shoes?'

" 'Yes.'

" 'I see that you have lost the set out of that beautiful ring on the third finger of your left hand; will you be so good as to let me examine it?'

" 'Now I should like to know what you want with one of my rings?'

" 'You must let Miss Wallingford examine the ring, madame,' said the judge as he leaned over his desk and watched Lottie with eager looks.

"Mrs. Ragland took the ring from her finger and handed it to Lottie, at the same time casting on her a gaze of intense hate.

" 'Where and when did you lose the set out of this ring, Mrs. Ragland?'

" 'I lost it somewhere about the 1st of last February, but I do not know where I lost it.'

" 'Would you recognize the set if you were to see it again?'

" 'I would, if I were to find it in an African desert, for it is a genuine diamond, for which I paid three hundred dollars.'

" 'Did you ever pass through a secret opening at the back part of your garden, and enter the street that leads near it?'

" 'Why should I pass through that way to get into the street, when we have two gates that open into the front street?'

" 'I did not ask you *why* you did it, but I asked you if you ever did do it?'

" 'Very well, miss, then I answer, No!'

" 'Did you not frequently visit Mr. Bowles at his apartments?'

" 'No, I did not; and I do not thank you for propounding such questions to me!'

" 'I am not seeking for thanks, but merely wish to get at the facts. Did you ever have an interview with Mr. Bowles in the summer-house in your garden?'

" 'No, I did not; what business could I have with Mr. Bowles?'

" 'That is the very thing we are trying to find out. Is this the set that belongs to your ring?'

"Lottie handed Mrs. Ragland a large diamond set, the same that had been found by the detectives.

" 'La, yes, that is the very identical set that I lost; but I dare say that the same thief who stole my shoes took the set out of my ring!'

" 'Look at this picture, madame, and tell me if you recognize it?'

" 'Oh, yes; that is a picture of Mr. Bowles.'

" 'Will you be so good as to tell the jury how it happened to be hidden away in your bedroom bureau?'

" 'I do not know why you should choose to employ the word *hidden* unless you take pleasure in making insulting insinuations. I dare say the thief who stole that picture might have taken many others from the same place if she had tried, for I am sure there were many others there!'

" 'Did not Mr. Bowles give you this picture in exchange for yours, which was found in his possession?'

" 'In the first place, I did not know he had my picture in his possession, for I am sure I never gave it to him.'

" 'Now, Mrs. Ragland, don't you remember that you had your picture put in a costly gold locket for the express purpose of presenting it to Mr. Bowles?'

" 'I do not remember anything of the sort: Mr. Bowles may have purchased a gold locket, and he may have bought one of my pictures, but I know he never received one from me.'

" 'Please examine this locket, Mrs. Ragland, and then tell me whether or not you gave it to Benjamin Bowles.'

" 'I never saw it until this moment.'

" 'You see that the words, "From Victoria to Benjamin" are engraved on the back of this locket; now, can you explain why the name of Victoria should appear on this locket, when you swear that your name is Helen?'

" 'Why should you expect me to be able to explain it any more than you could, when you have just heard me say that I never saw that locket until this moment? Mr. Bowles could very easily put my picture in any sort of a case he pleased, and if he chooses to put it into a locket containing another person's name, it does not in any manner disturb me.'

" 'Mrs. Ragland, do you not know that you had that locket made to order, about two years ago, at the house of F. H. Clark?'

" 'If I ever ordered such a job, I do not now remember it.'

" 'Mrs. Ragland, don't you know that your maiden name was Victoria Totten, and that you lived in New Orleans as the reputed wife of Benjamin Bowles?'

" 'No, I do not know any such thing! It is my opinion that no lady would ask a witness any such insulting question; but I suppose you are anxious to play smart.'

"A sweet smile played for a moment over Lottie's beautiful face, and then resuming her usual calm, composed demeanor, she proceeded with the examination, without evincing any signs of annoyance at the ill-natured remarks.

" 'Mrs. Ragland, were you ever acquainted with a widow lady residing a few miles east of the city of Vicksburg, Mississippi?'

" 'No.'

" 'Please examine this letter, and tell the jury whether you ever saw it before or not.'

"The letter which Lottie handed to the witness was the one that Mr. Dabbs said he had found in the pocket of Miss Bramlett's silk dress, in which the loan of five hundred dollars was mentioned, and the same that was signed with the letter 'B.' and directed to 'Dear V.' As Mrs. Ragland gazed at the mysterious letter, her hands trembled violently, while a deathly pallor spread over her face.

" 'This is the first time I ever laid my eyes on this letter. I suppose it was intended for Miss Bramlett, as I see that it was directed to her, and I understand that it was found in her dress pocket.'

" 'Do you recognize the handwriting?'

" 'No.'

" 'Don't you know that it is the handwriting of Mr. Bowles?'

" 'I don't think it is, though it somewhat resembles his writing.'

" 'Here is another letter which I want you to examine, and then tell me if you ever saw it before.'

"Mrs. Ragland's agitation now increased until her body was shaking like one in an ague fit, while her face lost all signs of blood, and the letter fairly rattled in her hand as she attempted to read it.

" 'I never saw that paper until this very minute.'

" 'Now, Mrs. Ragland, if you never saw that letter before to-day, will you be so good as to explain how it came to be concealed in the pocket of one of your silk dresses?'

" 'How should I be expected to explain how it came there, when I did not know it was there, and when I did not have anything to do with it? I dare say Miss Bramlett could give you the information you seek, for if it was found in the pocket of my dress, you may be sure she placed it there, in order to avert suspicion from herself, and to fix it on me. You see that the letter was directed to her, and as she was in the habit of wearing my dresses very frequently, it may be possible that she left it there by mistake.'

"Lottie then, in a low whisper, requested Mr. Rockland to read the letter to the jury.

" 'If the court please,' said the iron lawyer, as he rose from his seat, 'we now offer the letter as evidence in this case, and ask permission to read it to the jury.'

" 'Let me examine it first, if you please,' said Mr. Quillet, as he began to exhibit signs of agitation.

"The letter was handed to him, and after reading it carefully, he said:

" 'We object to the reading of this letter as evidence, unless it can be clearly shown who wrote it, and wherein it can in any manner be made to apply to the case now on trial.'

" 'We promise the court,' replied Mr. Rockland, 'that we will, at the proper time, show who wrote it, and also make it clear that it applies most forcibly to this case.'

" 'You may read the letter,' said the judge, 'and if you can make the proof which you mentioned, it may be considered as competent evidence; if you fail, then the court will direct it to be excluded.'

"Mr. Rockland then read the letter in his deep, solemn tone of voice, which caused a shudder to shake my body from head to foot. Here is the mysterious letter:

" 'DEAR V.—Strychnine, as I have often told you, is the best medicine to rid you of rats. You may depend on me to settle the hash with the old rat, and I shall expect you to do the job for the two young ones. Exercise caution, and success is certain; be sure to remember that the stakes for which we play are of immense value. Love and fortune will be ours when the task is finished. You will be the richest lady in the land, and shall reign as the queen of fashion, as well as queen of hearts. A gilded palace in the sunny land of Italy shall be the dwelling place of my beauteous wife. Burn this letter as soon as you read it; be brave, act promptly, and we will reap a rich reward. I am dying with impatience to clasp your dear form to my heart. Yours, and yours only, B.'

"If Mrs. Ragland had been chained in a lake of liquid fire the evidence of torture could not have been greater than that which she exhibited while Mr. Rockland was reading that letter. Her eyeballs seemed to have grown much larger, while a wild, frightened expression shot forth from them, and every little jostle made by the spectators caused her to start suddenly as if she were badly frightened. She insisted that the letter had been placed in her dress pocket by Miss Bramlett, in order to divert suspicion from herself.

" 'If,' said she, 'Miss Bramlett could have the heart to murder her poor little brother, it is not at all strange that she should try to fix the crime on some one else, in order to save her own neck.'

" 'Mrs. Ragland,' said Lottie, in a tone full of gentleness, 'did you ever know a young man named Charles Everson?'

" 'No.'

" 'Why, then, did you give such a sudden start when I mentioned his name?'

" 'I don't know that I did any such thing; but what if I did: is it strange that I should be nervous and restless under the circumstances by which I am surrounded?'

" 'Mrs. Ragland, did you at any time wear a blue silk dress that belonged to Miss Bramlett?'

" 'No, I did not; why should I borrow any of her silk dresses when I had plenty of my own?'

" 'That, madame, is the very strange mystery which we are endeavoring to solve. Are you willing to state on your oath that you never at any time wore a blue silk gown of Miss Bramlett's?'

" 'Have I not just now stated it under oath? How many times do you wish me to say it?'

" 'Mrs. Ragland, where did you first make the acquaintance of Mr. Bowles?'

" 'In Memphis!'

" 'Did you ever live in Mississippi?'

" 'No!'

" 'Did you ever meet Mr. Bowles at Vicksburg, Mississippi?'

" 'No!'

" 'Did you ever meet him in New Orleans?'

" 'No!'

" 'Have you ever met Mr. Bowles outside of Memphis?'

" 'No!'

" 'Were you ever engaged to be married to any other man than your present husband?'

" 'No!'

" 'Were you ever in love with any other man than Mr. Ragland ?'

" 'No !'

"Lottie then whispered to me, and requested me to hurry to the library room and call Mr. Everson, who had been waiting there until he should be wanted. I met with no little difficulty in forcing my way back to where Lottie was, but by dint of vigorous pushing and squeezing among the densely packed masses of humanity, I at length shoved my man suddenly in front of Mrs. Ragland.

"As soon as she saw Mr. Everson, she sprang up from her seat, stared wildly at him for a moment, then throwing both hands up above her head, uttered a loud, piercing scream, fell back on her seat, and buried her face in her hands. After holding her hands over her face a moment, she let them drop on her lap, and I noticed that her lower jaw had dropped down, as do those of dead persons.

" 'Catch that lady there, quick !' exclaimed the judge, 'she is going to faint !'

"Mr. Quillet hastened forward, but he was too late, for the helpless body of Mrs. Ragland fell on the floor before he got to her. The excitement among the members of the bar, as well as the spectators, continued to increase, until the limp body of Mrs. Ragland was removed to an adjoining room.

"I never had seen Mr. Rockland lose his self-possession until that moment, but he managed to let his heart have its way then. He seized Lottie and pressed her to his breast:

" 'God bless you, my daughter ! No lawyer ever displayed such skill and shrewdness as you have, and no lawyer ever received such a fee as you shall have in this case. My entire fortune shall be your fee !'

"Then he seized Miss Bramlett and pressed a kiss on her brow.

" 'Poor child, how deeply you have been wronged ! how you have suffered for the sins of another person !'

" 'Sit down, papa,' said Lottie, as she caught him by the arm ; 'don't you see how all the lawyers are laughing at you ?'

" 'Let them laugh, Lottie—I hope it will do them good ; I wish it could make them as happy as you have made me.'

"I thought while the excitement was up to fever heat that I would slip through the crowd and drop a kiss on my darling's brow, in order to show the high appreciation I had for her great talent; but she evidently divined my object, for she pushed me back abruptly and exclaimed:

" 'Do, pray, Edward, take a seat—don't you see papa has gone crazy? and I do believe you are trying to follow his example!'

"I felt quite sheepish, because I considered the rebuke well deserved; but I took my seat, and with great difficulty managed to regain my equanimity. Colonel Buff, who was near enough to hear what Lottie said to me, gave me a punch under the arm with his thumb, at the same time making a noise as a frog does when he jumps into his pond.

" 'Eh! Demar, your boat struck a snag, I see; well, never mind, old fellow, I saw from her looks that she was not offended.'

" 'Do you wish to introduce any more witnesses, Rockland?' inquired the judge.

" 'My daughter informs me that she wishes to introduce her brother, Harry Wallingford, as a witness, who is now waiting in the clerk's office.'

" 'Go after brother Harry, Edward,' Lottie whispered as she caught hold of my arm, 'and be sure to caution him about the control of his temper. Much depends upon the manner in which he shall conduct himself on the stand.'

"When I entered the clerk's office, I found Wallingford seated near a table, with his face buried in his hands; and when I spoke to him, he started up suddenly and endeavored to conceal the tears that he had been shedding.

" 'She is saved, Ed,' he said in tones husky with emotion, 'but she is lost to me forever! I have played such a contemptible part in this affair as to justify her in despising me, and to make me hate myself. I have deeply wronged her, and I must make up my mind to lose her.'

" 'Nonsense, Harry,' said I; 'she loves you as well as ever, and will be yours if you will only ask her; but come, Lottie sent me to bring you in, and she told me to caution you in regard to that unfortunate temper of yours.'

" 'I shall get along all right, unless Quillet offers me an

insult; that, you know, I will not submit to, either in or out of court.'

" 'You and your case are both gone up the spout, Quillet,' whispered Hogjaw as I entered the room, accompanied by Wallingford. 'You are defeated, vanquished, quashed, conquered, overthrown, trampled under, ground up, and chopped into hash, all by a woman.'

" 'If that girl would agree to marry me,' replied Quillet, 'I think I could forgive her, and bear my defeat with becoming fortitude; but I tell you what it is, I mean to fight till the death, and die bravely in the last ditch, if die I must; and

" ' "Though I hope not hence unscathed to go,
   Who conquers me shall find a stubborn foe." '

" 'Proceed with the case, Mr. Rockland,' said the judge, who began to show signs of impatience.

" 'Let Mr. Wallingford be sworn and placed under the rule until we examine Mr. Everson,' said Mr. Rockland.

"That young man then took the stand. He was a sad-faced young man, whose features contained unmistakable evidence of untold sufferings endured.

" 'Mr. Everson,' said Lottie, 'were you ever acquainted with a young lady by the name of Victoria Totten?'

" 'Yes.'

" 'Where did you know her?'

" 'At Vicksburg, Mississippi.'

" 'Were you acquainted with Benjamin Bowles at Vicksburg?'

" 'Yes.'

" 'When did you last see Victoria Totten?'

" 'I saw her a few minutes ago—she is the woman who fainted when I came in.'

" 'Was she ever married to Mr. Bowles?'

" 'No.'

" 'If Miss Victoria Totten left Vicksburg in company with any one, please tell who it was, and under what circumstances she left.'

" 'She eloped with Benjamin Bowles, and they went to New Orleans, where they lived as husband and wife, though they never were married.'

" 'Were you acquainted with Victoria Totten's mother?'

" 'Yes.'

" 'Where did she reside?'

" 'Near Vicksburg; and she is now living there.'

" 'Can it be possible that you are mistaken when you say that the woman who fainted on the stand is the same person you knew as Victoria Totten?'

" 'No, for I have been well acquainted with her for twenty years.'

"Mr. Quillet suffered Mr. Everson to stand aside without cross-examination.

"Harry Wallingford was then ordered to take the stand, which he did with a dignified and rather haughty mien, while his eyes glanced over the crowd with a careless look of indifference; I noticed that he was careful to avoid the gaze of Miss Bramlett, who had her eyes eagerly fixed on him. After gazing intently at him for a moment, her head sank down on the table that stood in front of her, and I saw tears begin to drop from her chin.

" 'Brother Harry,' said Lottie, 'if you are in possession of facts that would tend to throw any light on the case now on trial, please tell them in your own way.'

" 'I employed what I thought was an experienced detective, and set him to work on this case; he either would not, or could not, see or believe anything that pointed to any one else as the guilty party but Miss Bramlett. It is with feelings of the deepest shame and mortification that I am compelled to confess that he at one time managed to shake my confidence in the innocence of Miss Bramlett. After becoming convinced that it was folly to depend any longer on Mr. Dabbs, I concluded to take the matter into my own hands. In order to enable me to accomplish my purpose, I secured the services of a first-class locksmith, who undertook to manufacture for me such keys as I might require. About ten days ago I managed to enter the premises of Benjamin Bowles, disguised as a farmer, and after letting him win a small sum of money from me, I feigned intoxication, and was permitted by him to take a nap on a sofa in an adjoining room; but while he thought I was sound asleep, I was busy taking wax impressions of all the locks and keys of the apartments, as well as all trunks, bureaus, wardrobes, etc. Having accomplished the object of my visit, I hurried to my locksmith, and ordered him to make the keys necessary to enable me to open the locks, which he proceeded to do immediately. The next day I paid a visit to the residence of Mrs. Ragland, disguised as a gardener, and was so fortunate as to secure a job of work in her flower garden, which I managed to accomplish to her satisfaction. She went down town shopping, taking her maid with her, leaving no one on the premises except the cook and myself; I managed to enter the house through a back door, which was left unlocked. I proceeded to take wax impressions of every lock and key I could find on the premises, and gave them to my locksmith, and soon I was prepared with keys to fit them. Being armed with my false keys, I managed to enter the apartments of Mr. Bowles at a time when I knew he was away from home. I succeeded in making a thorough search of all his rooms, trunks, bureaus, dressing cases, wardrobes, etc., and carefully examined all of his papers. I spent three consecutive days and nights in Mr. Bowles' establishment. In a bureau drawer that stood in his sleeping room I found a large gold locket containing the picture of Mrs. Ragland; on the back of the locket the words, "From Victoria to Benjamin" were plainly engraved. After I had finished my inspection of the apartments of Mr. Bowles, I turned my attention to the residence of Mrs. Ragland, where I found many curious things, among which were several letters from Benjamin Bowles. One of these letters mentioned strychnine as a good poison for rats.'

" 'Is this the letter to which you refer?' said Lottie as she handed a paper to her brother.

" 'Yes, I found that letter in the pocket of a silk dress which belonged to Mrs. Ragland.'

" 'If you ever saw this boot before,' said Lottie, as she handed it to him, 'please tell when and where you saw it !'

"About five days ago I brought that boot from Mrs. Ragland's sleeping room. While searching a trunk in Mrs. Ragland's bedroom, I found several pictures of Benjamin Bowles, one of which was incased in a golden shell handsomely inlaid with pearls. I brought the picture away, and have it here now. This picture was wrapped up in a letter, which I have here.'

" 'Read it,' said Mr. Rockland.

" 'DEAR V.—I herewith send you my picture, according to promise, which I had taken when you were so good as to give me the pretty image of your dear self. I tried to make the present more acceptable by putting it in a costly case, and if you knew how highly I prize the dear image of your sweet self which you condescended to give me, you would no doubt value my ugly picture more than you do. I am sorry indeed to be compelled to tell you that I am just now in a terrible strait for the want of funds. Luck has been giving me the cold shoulder for the last fortnight, and you must by all means try to wheedle Miss Bramlett out of another thousand for me, and I shall soon be able to make a rise with it. The little scheme that I have so often mentioned to you is a feasible one, which will insure us a great fortune, and richly reward us for any risk; though there can be no risk, if we exercise caution. When rats annoy us, why not destroy them?'

" 'Have you any other facts to communicate' said Lottie; 'if you have, please proceed.'

" 'One night, while I was concealed in a bathroom in the apartments of Mr. Bowles, he was visited by a woman whose face I did not see, but whose voice I readily recognized as that of Mrs. Ragland. She arrived there about nine o'clock, and remained until after the clock struck twelve, when she went away accompanied by Bowles. While they remained in the room adjacent to the one in which I was concealed, I could distinctly hear everything they said. When Mrs. Ragland first entered the house, she threw herself into the arms of Bowles, exclaiming:

" ' "Oh, Ben, let us fly before it is too late; for Suspicion has already begun to point her finger at me! What a fortunate thing it was that I happened to wear Miss Bramlett's blue silk dress that night when Miss Tadpoddle was watching me! She thinks it was Miss Bramlett, and will swear in open court that it was she."

" ' "Yes," replied Bowles; "and that makes it necessary for us to swear the same thing."

" ' "For Heaven's sake, Ben," replied Mrs. Ragland, "do not, I beseech you, ask me to add the awful sin of perjury to the long list of crimes that I have committed!"

" ' "Pshaw! Vick, we have crossed the dead line long ago, and it is too late to talk about retreating now; never will I move an inch toward the rear; I will win by boldness and audacity. If we were to attempt to fly now, it would insure our destruction, for we could not escape. Do as I tell you, dear Vick, and I will vouch for a favorable termination."

" ' "Ah, Ben, you know too well how I love you; and you also know how much I would suffer and endure to serve and please you; but there is a mysterious influence, which I cannot describe, that constantly whispers strange words into my mind, telling me that my days are numbered, and that I shall soon be called to render an account of my sinful deeds."

" ' "Come, Vick, don't be so silly! I declare, you are continually talking about retribution and repentance!"

" ' "If all the wealth of the world belonged to me, I would willingly give it for a clear conscience! Oh, Ben, let us quit our wicked ways, ere it is forever too late, for I believe that I shall not live much longer—a sort of presentiment whispers of death to me continually!"

" ' "Stop, stop! Vick, I swear I will not listen another moment to this sentimental nonsense. Come, let us go in and take some champagne, and then you will feel better."

" 'They then went into another room and remained until midnight, when Mrs. Ragland went home, accompanied by Bowles.'

"Wallingford was then turned over to Mr. Quillet for cross-examination.

"The usual smooth temper of the attorney-general had been considerably ruffled by the taunts and jeers that had been thrown at him by the other members of the bar, and notwithstanding he had lost all hopes of sustaining the prosecution, he had resolved to have his revenge, which he thought he could best secure by handling Harry Wallingford with gloveless hands. As soon as he commenced the cross-examination I could tell from his manner and the tone of his voice that he meant to cut deep; and I also knew that he was treading on very dangerous ground when he undertook the job.

" 'Mr. Wallingford,' he said, in an imperative tone, 'I should like you to tell us by what authority you ventured to enter the apartments of Mrs. Ragland, and, without her knowledge or consent, carry off private property belonging to her?'

" 'I did it, sir, by the authority which God gives to all men in order to enable them to protect innocence and expose guilt.'

" 'Are we to understand, sir, that you had a commission direct from God, empowering you to enter a lady's private chamber by false keys, and, without her consent, carry off her private property?'

" 'The shape of your question, sir, carries with it an insult, and I think it would be advisable for you to modify it.'

" 'I ask your pardon,' said Quillet, smiling sarcastically. 'I assure you, sir, I did not think of insulting you; but really, I had a curiosity to know what prompted you to take the law into your own hands in such a presumptuous manner. As the shape of the question seems to displease you, and as I should dislike very much to incur your displeasure, I will take your advice, and change the shape of the question: What induced you to interest yourself in Miss Bramlett's affairs, and why did you choose to spend so much money for her?'

" 'Because I loved her, sir, and because I believed she was innocent!'

"As Wallingford uttered those words his voice trembled slightly, while his proud soul seemed to be standing in his eyes.

" 'Was not Miss Bramlett at one time betrothed to you?'
" 'Yes!'
" 'Is she now betrothed to you?'
" 'No!'
" 'Did you cancel the engagement?'
" 'No!'
" 'Did she do it?'
" 'Yes!'
" 'Why did she do it?'
" 'Because she found me to be unworthy of her love and respect.'

"Miss Bramlett started as if she were going to rise from her seat, then dropped her head back on the table.

" 'Did you concur with her views in that respect?'
" 'Yes!'

" 'Why did you continue to work in her interest after she had discarded you?'

" 'To gratify my sister and win the approval of my conscience.'

" 'Is your conscience easy now?'

" 'No!'

" 'Why not?'

" 'Because I wronged an innocent lady by my unjust suspicions.'

"The excitement by this time had been wrought up to fever heat, and I could plainly see that an explosion was imminent, unless something was done to prevent it.

" 'Stand aside, Mr. Wallingford!' exclaimed Flipout in a tone that convinced Quillet that no further trifling would be allowed.

CHAPTER XXXVI.

"HARRY passed out of the witness box and left the court-room without looking toward Viola, which it was plain to see was a great disappointment to her, for she followed him with her eyes until he disappeared, and then gave vent to her feelings in tears.

" 'Who is your next witness?'

" 'We have sent for Mrs. Ragland's maid, as we have just been informed by Mr. Wallingford that she is in possession of some important facts connected with the case.'

"Zuleka Zenobia was half French and half Spanish.

" 'How long have you been serving Mrs. Ragland?' said Lottie.

" 'Six years.'

" 'Where did you first become acquainted with her?'

" 'At New Orleans.'

" 'Who was she living with then?'

" 'She was living with Mr. Bowles.'

" 'Were they living together as husband and wife?'

" 'Yes.'

" 'Were you at Mr. Ragland's house on ·the night that Harry Bramlett died?'

" 'Yes.'

" 'If you saw Mrs. Ragland in Harry Bramlett's room that night, tell all you know about it.'

" 'About eight o'clock Miss Bramlett came into the kitchen to get some tea for her little brother, and requested me to go after a cup and saucer that were in young Master Bramlett's room. When I got to the head of the stairs I saw Mrs. Ragland in the room; she had one of the blue papers of medicine in her hand; she laid it down among the other papers and went out through Miss Bramlett's room.'

" 'Did she see you on that occasion?'

" 'I don't think she did.'

" 'Did you ever see Mrs. Ragland dressed in one of Miss Bramlett's gowns?'

" 'Yes, very often; I assisted her to put on a blue silk dress which belonged to Miss Bramlett.'

" 'Where did your mistress go when she had on Miss Bramlett's blue silk dress?'

" 'She went to meet Mr. Bowles at the summer-house and then accompanied him to his apartments.'

" 'What was Mrs. Ragland's maiden name?'

" 'Victoria Totten.'

"The loud report of half a dozen pistol shots in rapid succession now came ringing through the court-room, causing a stampede among the spectators, who made a rush for the door.

" 'Go quick, Eddie!' said Lottie, as she seized my arm, while her whole body trembled. 'Run quick—it is Bowles and Harry fighting.'

"Policemen came running in from all directions, shouting:

" 'Stop the thief! Catch the murderer! Shoot the villain! Where is he?'

" 'What has happened, Mr. Quillet?' demanded Flipout, who had rubbed his nose until it was as red as fire.

" 'Ben Bowles made an attempt to assassinate Harry Wallingford; but I am happy to inform your Honor that no serious harm has been done, though the scoundrel, Bowles, has succeeded in effecting his escape. He met Wallingford at the door, as he went out, and slapped him on the mouth; then both parties began to shoot at each other, and Wallingford received a slight flesh wound in the left arm, and Bowles fled. He knocked a man down in the streets, and took the horse that the man was holding, mounted and went north at full speed.'

" 'If your Honor please,' said the prosecuting officer, 'I think it is my duty (to perform which will afford me great pleasure) to enter a *nolle prosequi* in this case, being convinced that this young lady is innocent. She has suffered too much already, and I am unwilling to allow her to spend another night in prison.'

" 'I am much obliged,' replied Mr. Rockland, 'to my honorable friend for his kind offer, but we would prefer to have a verdict from the jury.'

" 'Very well, then,' replied Mr. Quillet, 'let Miss Bramlett accompany her friends home, and she can return in the morning to hear the verdict—I consent to any plan that will be agreeable to her and her friends.'

"As soon as Mrs. Ragland recovered from the swoon into which she had fallen, the judge ordered the sheriff to remove her to her home, at the same time instructing that officer to have the premises securely guarded until her condition should be such as to justify her imprisonment.

" 'Edward,' said Lottie, as she smiled through her tears, 'I want you to assist Viola into the carriage—and you had better escort her home; and when you have done so you will return here as speedily as possible, in order to help me get Harry home. Let mother understand that Harry is not severely hurt, and that there is no cause whatever for alarm; go now and attend to these things as quickly as you can.'

"After escorting Miss Bramlett home, I hurried back to help bring Harry. We had to carry him to the carriage, as he was not able to walk without assistance. His face was as white as it could have been if he had been dead.

" 'Are you suffering very much, brother Harry?' Lottie inquired as she drew his head down so as to let it rest on her bosom.

" 'Oh, no, not at all.'

" 'I want you to tell me why you did not look at, or speak to, Viola this evening, when you came in the court-room; did you not notice how your conduct distressed her?'

" 'My dear sister, don't you know that I could not look in that dear girl's face, if death was to be the penalty of the refusal? You certainly must know how deep is the feeling of contempt that she has for me.'

" 'I am convinced that you have entirely misjudged Miss Bramlett's feelings toward you, for I happen to know that she is anxious for a reconciliation; and she would not hesitate to make the first advances, if she were not afraid of being repulsed.'

" 'Sister, you seem to have lost sight of the fact that I am a pauper, though I trust you do not expect me to be a beggar. Miss Bramlett's great fortune has rendered any thought of a marriage between us impossible; beside this, I do not believe I could ever be to her such a husband as she deserves. I have lately received a letter from my attorney at San Francisco, informing me that he has discovered evidence which leads him to think that my Uncle Stanley made a later will, and that, after all, there is a probability that the property was left to me. He advises me to come there immediately, and it is my intention to do so as soon as I am able to endure the fatigues of the journey. If it should be my fortune to inherit my uncle's estate, I will then be in a condition to sue for Miss Bramlett's hand.'

"The carriage now drew up to the front gate, and Mrs. Rockland, who had been watching for us, seized Harry in her arms and burst into tears.

"Harry had been supported from the front gate to the house by Lottie and me, as we thought he was too weak to walk alone; but as soon as he came to the steps at the front portico, he suddenly disengaged himself from us, and briskly ran up into the hall. The exertion proved too heavy a tax on his strength, for I noticed that he began to reel.

"Miss Bramlett, who was watching him from the parlor door, sprang quickly forward and caught him in time to check the force of the fall, but her strength was not sufficient to entirely prevent it. When I got to him I discovered that he had fainted, but Miss Bramlett was sitting on the carpet holding his head on her bosom. By this time Lottie came running in, and snatching a bottle of hartshorn from the mantel, she directed Miss Bramlett to hold it to his nostrils;

then she moistened her brother's pale face with eau de Cologne, and in a few moments I saw signs of returning life appear. I was about to lift Wallingford in my arms, with a view of placing him on a bed, when Lottie suddenly seized me by the arm and pulled me into the nearest room.

" 'Come away, Edward,' she whispered, as she hurried me along; 'let them alone—don't you see how tenderly she is nursing him?'

"We took up a position in the adjacent room, where we could observe them through an open window.

"Wallingford opened his eyes, and as they met those of Miss Bramlett, a convulsive shudder shook his body for a moment, then he closed them, and remained silent a long time. When he again opened his eyes I noticed that they were filled with tears.

" 'He is weeping,' whispered Lottie, as she gave my arm a vigorous pinch; 'thank Heaven,' she continued, 'all is safe.'

CHAPTER XXXVII.

"Soon after the court opened next morning I was considerably surprised to see Zuleka Zenobia come hurriedly into the room and deliver a large yellow envelope to Mr. Rockland.

" 'My mistress requested me to deliver this paper to you immediately after the court met this morning,' said Zuleka, as she put the envelope in Mr. Rockland's hand.

"The iron lawyer deliberately commenced reading the contents of the letter. I imagined that his hands began to tremble slightly, and I thought I could see a perceptible deepening of the color on his face.

" 'If the court please,' said he, 'I hold in my hand a most extraordinary paper, which has just been handed to me by Mrs. Ragland's maid. This document makes a most startling disclosure. I do not think the contents of this letter ought to be made public, until an officer shall have been sent to inquire about Mrs. Ragland.'

" 'Perhaps her maid can enlighten you as to the condition of her mistress's health,' observed Flipout.

"Mr. Rockland then asked the maid if she had seen her mistress that morning.

" 'No,' said the maid, 'I have not seen her since eleven o'clock last night. She rang for me at eleven, and gave me the envelope, and told me to deliver it to Mr. Rockland at ten o'clock this morning.'

" 'Mr. Sheriff,' said Flipout, 'send a deputy to Mrs. Ragland's residence immediately and instruct him to report her condition to the court without delay.'

"At last a short, dumpy little deputy with ponderous nose and bushy hair came dashing into the room, with a face very pale, and excited manner.

" 'If your Honor please, Mrs. Ragland is dead, sir. She has killed herself. The door was locked on the inside, and we had to break it open before we could get in. We found her lying on the bed cold and stiff!'

" 'With your Honor's permission,' said Mr. Rockland, 'I will now read this letter, which will explain everything.'

" 'Read it,' said the judge.

" 'MR. ROCKLAND:

" 'DEAR SIR—When you read these lines, the hand that wrote them will be cold in death, and my soul will have appeared before its Creator. Perhaps God will have mercy on my sinful soul; for He alone knows how I was tempted and betrayed; and He, I hope, will have pity on a poor, unfortunate wretch like me. There was a time when I was an innocent, artless, confiding girl, the petted child of doting parents. I was the only daughter of Alexander Totten, who died when I was thirteen, leaving a small fortune, though ample for the support of myself and my mother. It is useless to warn other giddy girls to avoid a fate like mine, because until men change their natures unsuspecting girls will continue to listen to the honeyed words of the libertine and the villain. My great fault—the one that led me to destruction— was a love of display, and a fondness for theatres, balls and all kinds of frivolous amusements. Mr. Bowles drove fast horses, and spent money freely—dressed in style, and took me with him to all the balls and other places of amusement within reach. It would be folly to undertake to describe the manner in which I went, step by step, from the temple of honor to the gulf of in- famy. It would merely be a reiteration of the old story. I did not leap from the high temple of honor to the bottom of the in- famous pit at a single bound, but I went down by slow degrees, until I was at the very bottom.

" 'I have committed a most cruel, cold-blooded murder. Oh!

that I had died when I was an innocent babe! Oh, God, have mercy on my sinful soul. My only hope is based on the boundless mercy of Him who knows how I was tempted. Miss Viola Bramlett is as pure as an angel, and has suffered innocently for a crime committed by me. When she and her little brother came to live at our house, Mr. Bowles began to speak of the large fortune that had been left them by their father. He told me that if the two children should happen to die I would be the richest lady in the land. At first he spoke of the matter cautiously, but in such a manner as to create a hope in my mind that such a thing might happen. He informed me that my husband's habits of dissipation would soon put him out of the way, and that if the children were to die all the property would be mine.

"This matter formed the topic of his conversation every time we met, and it was a long time before he developed his murderous designs. While we lived in New Orleans Mr. Bowles kept a gambling hell, and often he induced me to entice men into it to be drugged and robbed. Step by step he led me down—down— down—until all conscience, all virtue, all honor was gone. I was frightened when he first began to persuade me to ensnare his unsuspecting victims, but I soon became familiar with crime, and embraced vice with pleasure. How truly did Mr. Pope describe things when he said:

"'"Vice is a monster of so frightful mien,
As to be hated, needs but to be seen;
Yet seen too oft, familiar with her face,
We first endure, then pity, then embrace."

"'Oh, how accurately those four lines describe the circumstances in my case! I never loved Mr. Ragland, and would not have married him, but I thought Mr. Bowles was dead at the time I became his wife. My love for Bowles had by no means diminished since my marriage with Mr. Ragland; and we met very often, sometimes in the summer-house, and frequently I went to his quarters. Miss Tadpoddle was mistaken when she said she saw Miss Bramlett go to Mr. Bowles' apartments. It was I, dressed in Viola's blue silk, which I had ordered my maid to steal for me. The paper of strychnine found in the pocket of the blue silk dress was placed there by me. The understanding between Bowles and me was that I was to put the children out of the way, so that my husband would inherit the great fortune; then he (Bowles) was to dispatch Mr. Ragland, and we were to be married, and reside in Italy. I stole into the room when I knew Miss Bramlett was in the kitchen preparing some tea for her little brother, and finding the child sound asleep, I hurriedly emptied the quinine out of one of the blue papers, and put the strychnine in it, and replaced it on the table. That was the fatal dose that killed the boy. I do not ask or expect forgiveness from the citizens of Memphis, because it will require a

higher power to absolve me. I think I can muster courage to
die, unloved and unmourned by any; but I have not enough to
enable me to live in the face of the tornado of indignation which
I know would confront me in this community.

" 'But for the awful load of guilt that presses like a great
mountain on my soul, I would quit this cruel world without regret. I suppose that one who has committed so many cruel
crimes as I have would not be considered a proper person to give
advice to others. But the rich man who lifted his voice up in
hell was anxious that his brothers should not come where he
was; and I, who am about to appear before my God with the
stain of murder on my soul, would gladly persuade others to
shun a fate like mine. When you hear that I have inflicted on
myself the same kind of murder that I did on Harry Bramlett.
using the same deadly drug, you will doubtless conclude that I
have gone mad; but no—the hand that directs this pen is as
steady as it ever was, and the mind that manufactures these
thoughts is as clear. I would prefer to live and repent of the
awful crimes I have committed, but I know that the law would
cry aloud for my blood.

" 'The letter that was found in Miss Bramlett's dress pocket
was placed there by me; or, rather, it was left there by mistake
when I returned the dress. It was written by Mr. Bowles, and
addressed to me, instead of Miss Bramlett, as was believed by the
detectives.

" 'I shall instruct my maid to deliver this communication into
your hands when court opens in the morning, and I most humbly ask you to read it to the court and jury, in order that all
suspicion of Miss Bramlett's guilt may be removed. I am sorry
that this is all the reparation I can make for the great wrongs I
have done to that innocent girl.

" 'With a full knowledge of the fact that I shall soon stand before my great Creator, I declare the foregoing statement to be
true.   Victoria Ragland.'

" 'Take the jury to a room, Mr. Sheriff, and let them
make up their verdict and return it into court as soon as possible.'

"At last the jury came in, with Crookwood leading the van,
while he held the papers in his hand.

" 'Have you agreed on a verdict, gentlemen?'

" 'We have, if yer Honor please,' said Crookwood, as he
wiped the water from his eyes with the tail of his coat.

" 'Read the verdict, Mr. Clerk.'

" 'I don't think I am able to read it, sir,' said the clerk.

" 'Let me see it,' said Mr. Quillet.

" 'Read it then!' said Flipout.

" 'I'll try, but I do not agree to accomplish the task accurately.'

" 'We thee juree do agree thatt Misstress Victoree Ragg-linn didd pizenn thee pour child, annd we woosh we hadd a chans to hangg her, butt wee kant bekase shee iz ded. Wee finde Benn Boals giltee ov merder, and sentns himm to be hungg thee furst Fridee atter he is kotch. Wee cleer Mis Brammlitt, annd the shurref shal paa the kost.'

"That is the identical verdict, each word spelled just as you see it, but here is a correct copy which the clerk was kind enough to transcribe for me, after the orthography had been properly corrected.

" 'We the jury do agree that Mistress Victoria Ragland did poison the poor child, and we wish we had a chance to hang her, but we can't, because she is dead. We find Ben Bowles guilty of murder, and sentence him to be hung on the first Friday after he is caught. We clear Miss Bramlett, and the sheriff shall pay the cost.'

"It was agreed between the attorney-general and Mr. Rockland that the verdict might be so changed as to comply with the usual legal form; consequently, the record merely shows a verdict in the following words: *'We the jury find the defendant not guilty.'*

CHAPTER XXXVIII.

" 'LOTTIE,' said Mr. Rockland, one bright morning as he rose from the breakfast table, 'I am going to bring half a dozen friends to dinner this evening, and want you to have everything arranged in splendid order. The Governor will be among the distinguished guests. May I depend on you?'

" 'Give me a check for three hundred dollars, and six kisses, and then I will discuss the matter with you.'

" 'There is the check, and you may take the kisses—there, there, don't smother me! What are you going to do with that money?'

" 'I am going to give it to Mrs. McCay.'

" 'I inferred as much; but you had better not let her have

.t all at once; give it to her in small sums, as she needs it—
)ut what about the dinner?'

" 'You may trust that matter entirely to me.'

" 'Very good. I shall expect a first-class dinner, to be
served at six o'clock.'

" 'It shall be done.'

" 'Give me back one of those kisses, then I will go.'

" 'Take it, dear papa, and as many more as you wish.'

"The iron lawyer drew her fondly to his heart, stamped a
kiss on her lips, and went to his office.

" 'Now, Eddie,' said Lottie, as she took my arm, 'take this
money and spend it for Mrs. McCay, in such a manner, and
in such sums, as in your judgment will best promote her wel-
fare. You may consider yourself invited to dinner.'

" 'What hour shall I come?'

" 'You are a privileged guest, and may come when you
please. Go along now, and attend to Mrs. McCay, and I
will arrange my plans for the dinner.'

"I made my appearance at Mr. Rockland's residence by
five and met Lottie at the front portico.

" 'What induced you to come so early, Edward?'

" 'I wanted to be with you—that is all; but how does it
happen that you are dressed so exquisitely this evening? . I
declare, you have made a complete success of it! You look
like an empress prepared to receive a dozen kings as her
guests. I never saw you looking so pretty as you do now.
What does it mean?'

" 'Read that note, and it will tell you.'

" 'DEAR LOTTIE—Prepare dinner for a dozen distinguished
guests. Two senators and their wives are with the Governor,
and will dine with us. The Honorable Cyrus Bramlett, a cousin
to Viola, has just arrived, and will sojourn with us two weeks.
" 'YOUR PAPA.'

" 'Who is Cyrus Bramlett? I never heard of him before.'

" 'He is a member of Congress from New York, and said
to be an orator of wonderful powers. He will object to a
marriage between Harry and his cousin.'

" 'Why so?'

" 'Because he will want her himself.'

" 'I hope he will leap into the arena at once, and contend for the prize.'

"The guests had all arrived by six, and a feeling of delight thrilled me when I saw Lottie receiving her distinguished guests with so much dignity and self-possession.

"When dinner was announced, the Governor offered his arm to Lottie, Mr. Rockland took charge of one of the senators' wives, while Flipout escorted the other, and Mr. Bramlett gave his arm to his fair cousin; and as the guests marched into the dining-room, I could see Wallingford eying Mr. Bramlett in a manner which plainly showed that he was greatly annoyed at the attentions bestowed on Miss Bramlett by her distinguished cousin. I imagined that I could perceive signs indicative of an approaching storm, and the thought gave rise to serious apprehensions in my mind. The young member of Congress from New York had scarcely taken his seat at the table when he commenced an animated conversation with Lottie.

" 'Bramlett,' said the Governor as he promenaded the veranda with that gentleman, a few moments after dinner, 'that Miss Wallingford is a most extraordinary girl—she surpasses any one I have ever met, both as respects beauty of person, and mind. They say she outwitted all the lawyers on the trial of your cousin's case, and set a trap which caught two of the State's witnesses.'

" 'Yes, it is true, and my pretty cousin is much indebted to Miss Wallingford for her deliverance in that unfortunate affair. I intended to be present at the trial myself, but was prevented by severe illness. I have come to take my fair cousin home with me.'

" 'Yes, and to make her your wife, I suppose.'

" 'My aspirations have not dared to soar quite so high as that, though to win such a rich gem would be a triumph worth contending for; but I vaguely suspect that the heart of my fair cousin has already been captured. Did you notice how she appeared to drink inspiration from Wallingford's eyes across the table?'

" 'No, I did not, but what of that? you must remember the old threadbare motto, "Faint heart never won fair lady." Go in and cry.'

" ' "Since the struggle must enlarge,
    Thy motto be—Charge, Chester, charge!"

" 'Your excellency offers good advice, but I believe I will
lay siege to the other castle.'

" 'Ah! Bramlett, you will lose your labor there, for Demar
has been commander of that fair castle so long that the memory of man runneth not to the contrary.'

" 'Yes, but Harry Wallingford shall not marry my fair
cousin, unless he gives his beauteous sister to me.'

"As the dinner progressed, the flow of wit increased until
every guest began to participate in it. Politics and religion
—finance and agriculture—science and art—music and history, were all largely discussed.

" 'Come,' said Harry as he laid his hand on my arm, 'let
us go out on the corridor and smoke a cigar.'

"I took his arm and we began to pace up and down the
floor. The weather was quite warm, and not a breath of air
could be felt.

" 'Come, let us go into the garden; I could not control
myself if I remained here. Let us sit under these vines, on
this little bench—I feel the oppressive heat more than usual.'

"We had not been there more than twenty minutes when
Quillet and Bullger came walking slowly toward us. The
night was not a very dark one, though there was no moon,
but the stars appeared to shine unusually bright. We were
completely hidden by the overhanging vines, and as we preferred to be alone, we remained silent, hoping that the two
lawyers would pass on; but they went into the summer-house,
which was not more than twenty feet from where we sat.
They were conversing in very low tones, but we could hear
every word they said. I started to rise from my seat, as I
was unwilling to play the part of an eavesdropper; but Harry
caught my sleeve and pulled me back to the seat, and in a
whisper requested me to be still and listen.

" 'What do you think of Miss Bramlett now, Bullger?'
inquired Quillet.

" 'The more I see of her the better I like her; but it is no
use for a fellow to fall in love with her, for they say she is
going to marry Harry Wallingford.'

" 'Yes, and I must confess that I am astonished to hear it.'

" 'Why?'

" 'Because he was engaged to her before she got into her late trouble; but as soon as she was put in jail, he told her to her face that he thought she was guilty. She ordered him to leave her presence, and commanded him never to speak to her again. He deserted her, while she was under the cloud, and left her to paddle her own canoe; but as soon as it appeared that she was innocent, what does he do but beg pardon and make matters smooth again.'

" 'I suppose he loves her money better than he does the girl. I always did despise a fortune-hunter.'

" 'Yes, and so does every honest man; but I cannot understand how such a sensible girl could be so ready to give her hand to such a man.'

" 'Pshaw! don't you know that where a woman once loves a man, she never forsakes him, no matter what he does?'

" 'Well, I suppose there is something in that, but Harry Wallingford is a very brilliant young man, and I used to think he was the very soul of honor; I did not think he would ever justly win the name of fortune-hunter.'

" 'Neither did I, but human nature is very weak, you know, and the prize in this case is a very tempting one, because Miss Bramlett is very beautiful, and possessed of an amiable disposition, as well as a great fortune.'

" 'By Jove, the bait is enough to trap anybody!'

" 'Ah! you are right there; but Lottie Wallingford is the apple of my eye. I had rather have her for my wife than to be king of England.'

" 'Yes, no doubt you would; but there is no likelihood of your ever being king of England or the husband of Lottie Wallingford, either, because she belongs to Ed Demar.'

" 'Well, he is a lucky dog, anyway.'

" 'Come, let us walk back to the house; it is no use to covet our neighbors' property—those two girls are not for us.'

"While that conversation was going on, Harry had his hand on my arm, and it was all I could do to keep from crying out, for his finger nails sank down into my flesh so as to bring blood.

" 'Let go my arm, Harry; you are hurting me.'

" 'I ask pardon—I did not think what I was doing; does it not surprise you to see me sitting quietly by your side?'

" 'No, why should I be surprised?'

" 'Do you think I would let any man talk that way about me, unless he was telling the truth? Have I not been guilty of every charge they made against me? Of course I have; but thank Heaven it is not too late to make the proper atonement. Edward, it is all over with Viola and me. I do now solemnly swear, by everything that I hold sacred, that I never will marry her until my fortune is equal to hers; so help me Heaven!'

" 'Harry, I do believe you are a real coward.'

" 'Yes, that is certain, but there is no use to scold me about it. If Viola will agree to wait till my fortune is made, all right; if she refuses, let her marry her cousin, and be done with it.'

" 'As to that, you need have no fears whatever, for she worships you, and if you forsake her, it will kill her; yes, I mean exactly what I say—it will certainly kill her.'

" 'In the first place, I do not intend to forsake her, for I love her as no man ever loved a woman before, and if she will wait for me, I will make a fortune as sure as my name is Harry Wallingford.'

" 'By the by, Harry, I have a little secret to tell you.'

" 'What is it, pray?'

" 'You know that Viola bought a little bottle of strychnine, and refused to tell why she purchased it?'

" 'I certainly do, and her refusal to tell why she bought it was the strongest evidence against her.'

" 'True enough; well, I can tell you all about it; she got it when you were very ill, and everybody thought you were going to die. She was preparing to commit suicide; and if you had died, she would not have survived you an hour.'

" 'Great Heavens! is that so?'

" 'It is; for Lottie pumped the secret out of her. Now you must be very cautious when you inform her of your intention to go to California.'

" 'If she will only trust me, and agree to wait for me, I

will never forsake her; but let us walk back to the house, else we will be missed.'

"Time glided on, and Harry lingered by Viola's side, strolling about the flower garden with her arm locked in his, and dreading to make his intentions known to her. Love was urging him to marry the girl of his choice, and be happy, while pride was making a desperate effort to separate him from his love.

"Miss Bramlett and Lottie were seated on a low wooden bench in the summer-house engaged in an earnest conversation. Harry Wallingford made his appearance at the door.

" 'Come in, brother,' said Lottie. 'I am glad you happened here, because I want you to join me in persuading Viola to abandon the idea of going with her cousin to New York.'

" 'If Miss Bramlett will not yield to your solicitations, I am sure she would not to mine. It would be unjust to her distinguished relative to deprive him of the company of his fair cousin. The fact is, we ought not to expect Miss Bramlett to remain among such dull people as ours, when such brilliant members of Congress claim her company.'

"Miss Bramlett bent her eyes toward the ground, while her cheeks were red with anger; but she bit her lips to smother her feelings. Lottie turned pale, and gazed at her brother with a look of astonishment, while a painful sensation darted through her heart. She was convinced that her brother had become jealous of Cyrus Bramlett, and she well knew that it was without cause.

" 'Take a seat here, brother,' said Lottie, 'and arrange that bouquet for me, while I go and gather more flowers.'

"This was a ruse on Lottie's part to leave Harry and Viola alone, as she thought it the best plan to insure a reconciliation between them.

" 'Miss Bramlett, I suppose if you go with your distinguished cousin, you will spend the winter in Washington?'

" 'No; I shall remain in New York.'

" 'We shall be very far apart when you go to New York and I to San Francisco.'

" 'What do you mean, Mr. Wallingford?'

" 'Viola, I am going to start for California in the morning, and it may be a long time before we meet again; I wish to ask you a serious question, and I want you to give me a serious answer.'

"All color now instantly fled from her cheeks, and her body trembled violently.

" 'I am going to seek my fortune in the far West, and I wish to know if you will promise to be mine when I return?'

" 'If you go to California, it is my opinion that we never shall meet again.'

" 'Why do you think that?'

" 'There are many reasons I might mention that cause me to think it; but if you will excuse me, I had rather not talk about such a painful subject.'

" 'Miss Bramlett, have I been mistaken in believing that you loved me?'

" 'If we ever meet again, ask the question and you shall have a candid answer.'

" 'Would you have me go so far away without knowing my fate?'

" 'I would not have you go at all; but it appears that your resolve is made, and I suppose you know best what you ought to do.'

" 'I know that I am an idiot, and that I have succeeded in convincing you of that interesting fact, and that you will rejoice to be rid of me.'

" 'This is not the first time you have unjustly suspected me, but I hope it will be the last.'

" 'Why, then, did you so suddenly conclude to leave us and that, too, before you knew of my intention to go to California?'

" 'Because I have no home here; in fact, I have no home anywhere, but I have friends and relatives in New York who will give me a home.'

" 'Yes, indeed, you have one distinguished kinsman who, I dare say, will offer you a home, and a heart to boot, and I could not blame you for accepting such a brilliant offer.'

" 'Mr. Wallingford, your language does not afford me any pleasure, and unless you have something else to talk about, I guess we had better separate.'

"'I crave your pardon—I assure you I did not **mean to** annoy you.'

"Then, in a fit of anger, he abruptly walked away.

"Harry started to California next morning, without having any other interview with Miss Bramlett, thus letting his pride again master his heart.

"Ragland's body was found floating in the river, at the head of President's Island, without any marks of violence on it, showing clearly that he had committed suicide. Poor man! perhaps he deserved a better fate, though he had not led the sort of a life that produces happiness. An appetite for strong drink, and a love for the gambling table, had ruined him before the discovery of his wife's infidelity was made.

"Mr. Rockland received a letter from one of the trustees at New York stating that the death of Mr. Ragland created a necessity for Miss Bramlett to come there immediately. Within ten days after Harry had started for California, Viola was on her way to New York, accompanied by her cousin Cyrus.

"Over a month had elapsed after Viola's departure, when Mr. Rockland received a letter from a lawyer in New York, of a most startling nature, the perusal of which plunged us all into the deepest gulf of distress. Here is the letter—let it speak for itself:

" 'NATHANIEL ROCKLAND, ESQ.:

" 'DEAR SIR—I know you will be surprised and deeply pained to learn that the trustees appointed by Bolivar Bramlett's will have converted the entire estate into cash and fled to parts unknown. Every possible effort has been made to capture them, but without success, and it is pretty well ascertained that they have crossed the ocean, and are safe in some foreign land. But, my dear sir, I have not told you the serious part of the story yet—and you will think so when I do. Miss Viola Bramlett has mysteriously disappeared from her boarding house, and despite the efforts of the police to discover her whereabouts, the mystery remains unsolved. A week ago she left her boarding house on Fifth avenue, telling her friends that she was going to A. T. Stewart's store on Broadway. Nothing was thought about it until night, when her friends began to make inquiries about her. She had been to the Stewart store, and made some trifling purchases, but instead of ordering the articles to be sent to her boarding house, as was her usual custom, she took them with her. Three experienced detectives were employed immediately, and up to this writing, they have failed to make any discoveries, except that she was seen standing on the wharf near the water's edge just before dark on the day she left her boarding house. If she was alive, it seems to me that the detectives could not fail to find her; therefore I fear we may expect the very worst. Ever since her arrival in this city she has appeared to be very unhappy, and was often found weeping. She avoided company, rarely speaking to any one, and the only conclusion we can arrive at is that the poor girl has committed suicide. Every possible effort will be made to find her, and if we succeed, I will immediately inform you by wire.

" 'Very respectfully,

" 'Albert Dalmaxim.'

"I shall not trouble you with a history of our misery, produced by this awful news, but drive on to the end of this unpleasant part of my story. In obedience to Lottie's request I set out immediately to New York to do all in my power to unravel the strange mystery; promising if Viola was found to bring her home with me. I wrote a short letter to Harry, inclosing Mr. Dalmaxim's letter, and urged him to come home without delay.

"When I arrived at New York I learned that no clew to the missing girl had been discovered, and that the police and detectives had given up the contest. I went to work in earnest, determined to exhaust every plan I could think of to find Viola. But at the end of ten days hope died in my breast, and I was compelled to conclude that Viola had drowned herself. I remained in New York a month, and it was with a sad heart I started home, when I thought of the distressing news that I would be compelled to communicate to Lottie. I had not been back home but a short time when Harry returned from California looking more like a ghost than a man.

" 'Is she found?' he gasped, as he staggered into my office and dropped into a chair.

" 'No, but we still have hopes. You are ill, Harry; let me go home with you—Lottie is looking for you.'

" 'No, I will not go home—I cannot bear to look into dear Lottie's face now. I am going immediately on to New York, to spend the remnant of my life in searching for poor Viola; though I have but little hope of ever seeing her dear face again.'

" 'What about your uncle's will?'

" 'Oh! don't let us talk about that now; money has been my ruin. I am a rich man now, but it comes too late. Fortune still continues to hurl her deadly missiles with unerring aim at me. Everything goes wrong with me; my uncle did make another will, and placed it in the hands of a trusted friend, who happened to be traveling in Europe when my uncle died. If that friend had been at home all would have been well, but my luck would not have it so. The man with whom the will had been left fell ill and died in Scotland, and when his administrator took charge of his effects in San Francisco, my uncle's will came to the surface, giving his property to Lottie and myself. Curse the will—curse the money—curses on my luck—a double curse on my foolish pride! Why did I not take Viola with me as my wife? Because I never was known to do anything that ought to be done. Viola told me that if I went to California we never would meet again. I did not understand her meaning then, but it is plain to me now. She was contemplating suicide then, and she has since carried out her intention. Here, Eddie, take this envelope, and when you know I am dead you may open it. Don't stare at me that way, please—it is nothing but my will, giving all my property to Lottie. She has the good sense to make the proper use of it. Give my love to my darling sister, and tell her when I find Viola she shall see me, but never until I do. Comfort my darling sister, and don't let her grieve about her unfortunate brother. She will make you happy, as you deserve. I would give all the world if I had your happy disposition; but alas, it cannot be so! Good-by, old fellow; we may meet again, but never until I find Viola.'

"Before I could muster courage to answer, he was gone.

*   *   *   *   *   *

CHAPTER XXXIX.

"NEARLY a year has elapsed since I last parted with Harry Wallingford under very peculiar circumstances. It was at the cemetery in the city of New York, where I took my painful leave of him, and I never have seen him since, though we have received several letters from him. I believe it was on the next Monday after Wallingford set out on his journey to New York, that Mr. Rockland received a letter from Mr. Dalmaxim, which furnished a solution of the mystery connected with Miss Bramlett's sad fate. In order to enlighten my audience as much as possible in connection with that distressing affair, I will read you the letter:

" 'NATHANIEL ROCKLAND:

" 'DEAR SIR—It is with feelings of the deepest sorrow that I perform the sad duty of conveying to you the news of Miss Bramlett's death. The body of that unfortunate young lady was discovered on yesterday floating in East river, where it had evidently remained a considerable length of time, for it was in an advanced stage of decomposition. The features were very much disfigured, probably occasioned by being eaten by the fish, but her friends here readily recognized the drab silk dress as the one worn by Miss Bramlett on the day of her disappearance. A large gold ring with a diamond set was found on one of her fingers, which was also identified by her friends as the property of Miss Bramlett. On the inside of the ring the letters "From Harry to Viola," appeared, plainly engraved, which settles the question of identity beyond the possibility of a doubt. The body was found under the wharf, where it had been held by a large iron spike that projected from one of the piles, which had caught in the skirt of the silk dress, thus preventing the corpse from floating out. A white handkerchief of very costly fabric, bordered with lace, was found in the left-hand pocket of her dress, which was found to be marked in one corner with the letters "V. B.," plainly wrought with green silk thread. The handkerchief was also identified as the property of Miss Bramlett. That, the poor girl committed suicide there seems to be no room for doubt, as upon critical examination, made by experienced surgeons, no marks of violence could be discovered. A large number of witnesses were examined before the jury of inquest, including many friends and relatives of Miss Bramlett; all of them recognized the dress, ring, and handkerchief as her property. Notwithstanding the vigorous efforts made by Miss Bramlett's friends to ascertain the cause that induced her to destroy herself, nothing definite has been developed; though I hear it suggested that it was a disappointment in a love affair with Mr. Wallingford. I am thoroughly convinced that it was not the loss of her fortune that caused it, for all concur in the idea that she despised money, and was often heard to say that she regretted being a rich heiress. With many wishes for your health and success, I am, sir, yours very respectfully,

" 'ALBERT DALMAXIM.'

"Before Harry Wallingford arrived at New York, the remains of the drowned girl had been deposited in the grave.

"I was induced by Lottie to make a second trip to New York to bring Harry home. Upon my arrival at the city, I was not a little surprised to learn that Wallingford had caused a costly monument to be erected at the head of the grave, with a suitable inscription made in plain Italian letters.

"When I inquired for Harry at his hotel, I was told by the clerk that I would probably find him at the cemetery, as he had been in the habit of making diurnal visits there. I encountered many difficulties in threading my way through the city of the dead. But after making several mistakes, and traveling many hundreds of yards unnecessarily, I at length succeeded in finding the spot I sought.

"Harry was busily engaged with a florist in arranging some pinks and geraniums at the foot of the grave, and consequently did not observe me until I had stood leaning against the palings gazing at him for several minutes. When he looked up and saw me he dropped the trowel with which he had been transplanting the flowers, and walked briskly toward me, saying as he held out his hand:

" 'Ah, Edward, I have killed her at last! Here lies my poor victim—driven into the grave by an unworthy wretch who is himself unfit to live, and not prepared to die. You told me I would kill her, and alas! how true it has come to pass.'

" 'I am sent by Lottie to bring you home,' I at length managed to say. 'Your sister is almost driven to despair by this distressing occurrence, and it is your duty to go to her as speedily as possible.'

" 'No, Edward, it would only serve to increase my darling sister's sorrow for me to be with her. Tell my beloved sister that it is my wish to remain in New York, where I can water the grave of my victim with my tears, and commune with her gentle spirit.'

"Now, my good friends, here I am at the end of my awkward story, and if I have bored you with the telling of it, I am truly sorry for it; but if I knew I had been so fortunate as to interest you, I should be very much gratified. To all of my good friends who have been so kind as to honor me with their attention, I beg permission to express my grateful thanks; and by way of winding up the entertainment, I suggest the idea that we now adjourn to the saloon and engage in a quadrille."

"Wait a moment, sir, if you please," said Ivanhoe, as he threw himself in front of Ingomar, as if he was determined to force him to halt; "you have not yet finished your story, and we do not intend to permit you to retire until you have told us what has become of Lottie Wallingford."

"Yes, yes, yes!" exclaimed a dozen voices at once. "Let us know what has become of Lottie Wallingford."

"My friends," replied Ingomar, "I pledge you my word that there is no such person as Lottie Wallingford now living, so far as I know or believe; but if her Majesty will remove her mask, I will be very glad to introduce to you Mrs. Lottie Demar, my beloved wife, of whom I am exceedingly proud."

By the time Ingomar concluded the sentence, the mask was removed, and Lottie stood, radiant, beautiful, and blushing before the admiring multitude.

For a moment the spectators gazed in breathless wonder at the angelic loveliness of the beautiful creature who stood before them; then the audience began to press around the charming object, eager to offer their congratulations. Captain Quitman, in whose eyes tears of joy trembled, leaped on a box, and brandishing his cane in the air, called out, "Three cheers for the Barbarian Chief and his beautiful Parthenia!" Then rose such a joyous shout as to drown the great noise caused by the machinery of the boat. A proposition was made by Ingomar, and indorsed unanimously by the crowd, that all disguises should instantly be laid aside. When Don Quixote removed his mask, Lottie sprang forward, and seizing both of his hands, exclaimed:

"Oh, bless us! it is Doctor Plaxico, and I am so much delighted to meet my valued friend! And here is Captain Burk, too! I am really ashamed to acknowledge that I did not recognize either of you."

When Scottie removed her mask, Captain Burk threw up his hands with surprise, as he moved rapidly to her side, while his handsome features lighted up with a delightful smile.

"Miss Darlington," he ejaculated, "two years ago I considered you very pretty, but now I am ready to swear on the Bible and the Koran that you are the most beautiful girl on the globe!"

"Captain Burk," replied Miss Darlington, as she smiled sweetly on him, "I beg to remind you that, notwithstanding all women are fond of flattery, they do not like to be praised in public."

All of the maskers promptly complied with the agreement by immediately dispensing with their disguises, except Napoleon, Navarre, and the lady in the black domino, all three of whom abruptly retired from the deck as soon as the proposition was made.

Ingomar conducted Lottie down to the saloon, where they were immediately followed by all the passengers.

"Ladies and gentlemen," said the captain, "I have a communication to make to you, which I am happy to believe will be heartily indorsed by my young friends. We are now approaching a landing where we expect to take on a large lot of cotton bales, which will detain us at least six hours; and I have ordered the steward to prepare a picnic dinner to be served on shore, where you will find charming scenery, cool shade, and green turf. I have also ordered the band to be ready to make music for those who may wish to enjoy a rustic dance."

The spot selected for the picnic was about two hundred yards from the river-bank, where the soft velvet turf was shaded by the thick green leaves of innumerable tall beech-trees, whose branches were covered with verdant vines.

The band struck up a lively waltz, and then a dozen couples went skipping over the greensward.

After the amusements had been progressing about an hour, a colored woman appeared on the grounds with a large hamper basket of flowers, which she offered for sale. Among the flowers there was a magnificent bouquet, containing every variety known to the South, which Demar immediately purchased and presented to Lottie. The young people began to crowd around Lottie, eager to behold the beautiful present, and each one, of course, was permitted to examine it. Napoleon, although still wearing his mask and refusing to participate in any of the amusements, condescended to handle and admire the beautiful bouquet. It was noticed that he retained it for a long time, apparently interested in the delicate workmanship and ingenuity of its construction, occasionally pulling the flowers apart, as if he wanted to see how it was held together. After he had inspected it for five minutes he handed it back to Lottie, who immediately held it close to her face and began to inhale the rich perfume afforded by the rare flowers.

"Oh! Edward," she exclaimed as she let the bouquet fall to the ground, "the scent of those flowers has made me sick, and I must request you to take me aboard the boat as soon as you can."

"Darling, are you very ill! Your cheeks have suddenly turned deadly pale! What is the matter?"

"I do not know, Edward. I never experienced such a strange feeling before. My throat and lungs feel as if they were full of burning fire, and my head is as light as air! You will have to carry me to my room immediately, for I do not believe I could walk a step unsupported."

"Mrs. Demar," said Doctor Plaxico, as he held his fingers on her pulse, "have you ever been subject to any sudden attacks of illness before?"

"I have never been ill at all but one time during the last ten years."

"If you feel able to talk, I would be glad if you would give me a minute description of the first symptoms of the attack."

"I was in perfect health when we went on shore—never felt better in my life. Edward purchased a large, handsome bouquet and gave it to me, and I buried my face among the fragrant flowers, inhaling the sweet odor until I was seized with a sudden faintness, and would have fallen to the ground, but Edward caught me in time to prevent it. Then my throat and lungs began to burn with an intolerable heat, and have been growing worse every moment. Oh! Edward, can you not give me something to quench this blazing fire in my lungs? You know I am not childish, or in the habit of complaining at trifles, but I cannot endure this intolerable suffering!"

"Plaxico, for Heaven's sake give her something to stop her sufferings!" exclaimed Demar, as he knelt down by the bedside, wringing his hands in despair.

Plaxico made no reply to Demar's request—in fact, he seemed to be perplexed, and full of hesitation, which was an unusual thing with him, for he generally acted promptly, and with energy.

"Doctor Plaxico," said Demar, "do you know what is the matter with my wife?"

"No."

"Have you no means by which you can ascertain the nature of her disease?"

"No."

"Have you no suspicions as to the cause of her sudden illness?"

"Yes."

"Tell me then what you suspect."

"I shall not do it without further investigation."

"Oh, Edward," exclaimed Lottie, as she tore the lace collar from her neck, "do, pray, give me something to cool my throat—I cannot endure this horrible torture much longer!"

She tore away the fastenings that confined the dress about her throat, and began to tear the skin with her finger nails, until the blood commenced to gush out.

"Plaxico," exclaimed Demar indignantly, "I am sorry to say that your conduct on this awful occasion is to me inexplicable, and, I might say, inexcusable. Are you going to sit here with folded hands and see my darling die, without making an effort to save her?"

"By Heaven! I would gladly give my life to save her!"

"Why not give her an opiate?"

"Because I am afraid."

"What do you mean?"

"Exactly what I say."

"Doctor Plaxico, for Heaven's sake have pity on me, and quit speaking in riddles!"

"I am not dealing in riddles—I do not know what is the matter with your wife."

"Can you not suggest some harmless drug that would afford temporary relief?"

"Demar, why do you stare at me that way?"

"I am full of astonishment to witness such a lack of self-confidence in one possessing such unlimited knowledge of medical science as I know you do."

It did not require the eye of science to see that death would soon step in to relieve the sufferer, unless she could be speedily relieved by other means. This fact was now patent to Edward Demar, who was so completely crazed with grief that he sank down by Lottie, and gave way to despair.

"Oh! Edward!" cried Lottie as she threw out both arms as if she were feeling for him, "where are you? I do believe I am going blind, for I cannot see you."

Lottie was then seized with a frightful spasm that lasted five or six minutes, which, when it passed off, left her in a state of exhaustion. Her hands and feet became icy cold, while her throat and lungs were burning up with unnatural heat.

Captain Quitman, who had just heard of Lottie's dangerous illness, came hurriedly into the room to make inquiries.

"How is she?"

"Bad enough. She will die inside of two hours unless a radical change sets in very soon."

"Great Providence forbid!" exclaimed the kind-hearted man. "What is the matter with her?"

"Don't know."

"Have you never seen any one afflicted as she is?"

"Yes."

"Why not try the same remedies now that you did then?"

"Because that other patient died."

"What was the matter with the patient whose symptoms resembled these?"

"Poison."

The old captain leaped over two chairs, dashing them to the other side of the room, and seizing Plaxico by both shoulders, fairly lifted him off of the floor, letting him down with a slam; then in a thundering tone exclaimed:

"Plaxico, by the great Jupiter, tell me what you mean!"

"I mean what I say."

"See here, doctor, do you intend to insinuate that one of my passengers has been poisoned?"

"No, I insinuate nothing, for I know nothing."

The old captain then rushed out of the room and hurried toward the cook house to have an interview with the steward, knocking over a dozen chairs as he went, and jostling a group of ladies who attempted to intercept him with a view of inquiring about Lottie.

"Dying, I believe," he muttered, as he elbowed his way among the anxious crowd.

Lottie's mind began to wander, and she would converse about occurrences that had transpired in the days of her childhood.

She suddenly regained her reason, and began to call for her husband.

"Here I am, darling; what can I do to relieve you?"

"Nothing, Edward; oh! I do not want to die now, because I have so much to live for. I am not afraid to die, but I was so happy with my darling that I wanted to remain with him; but if it is God's will that I shall be taken away from him, I must not rebel."

The lady in the black domino now came dashing into the room, and fell on her knees by the bedside and burst into a violent fit of weeping. Her conduct was so violent and mysterious that it filled the minds of all with wonder, and caused Doctor Plaxico to whisper a request to Demar to have her removed.

Captain Burk now made his appearance at the door, and requested an interview with Plaxico.

The doctor passed through the door and taking the captain's arm, went with him out on the guards.

"Doctor Plaxico," said Burk, "do you know what is the matter with Mrs. Demar?"

"No."

"Have you no suspicions?"

"Yes."

"Have you any objections to telling me what you suspect?"

"Yes."

"Why?"

"Because it would do no good, and might do much harm."

"Would you be surprised if I were to guess exactly ¡what you suspect?"

"Indeed, I would."

"I have a suspicion myself, and I propose that we both write down what we suspect and then compare notes, with the distinct understanding that this transaction is to remain a profound secret between us."

"Agreed."

The two men turned their backs together and with pencils hurriedly wrote something on their memorandum books; then facing each other, Captain Burk handed his book to Plaxico.

"Poison!" exclaimed Plaxico.

"Poison!" cried Burk.

Then both men stared wildly at each other.

"What caused you to suspect that she was poisoned?" inquired Captain Burk.

"The peculiar symptoms," was the prompt reply. "What aroused your suspicions?"

"My poor Newfoundland dog has just died from the effects of poison; or at least such is my belief."

"What led you to such a conclusion?"

"When Mrs. Demar was so suddenly taken ill, we were dancing on the green turf, but we all immediately ceased dancing and returned to the boat; before I had reached the shore some one of the ladies called my attention to the beautiful bouquet which Mrs. Demar had dropped, and requested me to bring it aboard. I was then about thirty yards from the spot where the bouquet had been dropped, and pointing at it, I commanded Don to fetch it to me. He started instantly, running swiftly to the spot, seized the bouquet in his mouth and soon deposited it at my feet. It was but a moment after he had deposited the flowers at my feet, when he began to whine and reel, and in three minutes he was dead."

"Merciful God! Captain Burk, some treacherous, double-damned villain has intentionally murdered that poor lady. Where is the bouquet?"

"In my state-room."

"Go bring it here—quick!"

Burk returned instantly with the flowers.

"Now get me a dog, cat or any live animal that you can find, so we may make a test."

A deck hand was found who had a worthless dog that he had been trying to hire some one to kill. The dog's nose was forced deep into the body of the bouquet and held there three minutes, and three minutes afterward he was dead. Then such a panic spread among the passengers as to beggar all powers of description. Several ladies were precipitated into hysterical fits, while brave men, who had often faced death on the battle field unmoved by fear, now trembled like pale-faced cowards. What motive could any one have for murdering the most beautiful, the most charming woman aboard the boat? Suspicion soon began to point her finger at the lady in the black domino, while the matter was discussed in low whispers by the passengers. Meantime Lottie's condition was growing worse rapidly, and the doctor declared that there were no grounds for hope. Despair and horror were visible on every face, while tears began to stream from the eyes of many strong men who did not often weep.

"Who is the abandoned wretch?" inquired George, as he elbowed his way through the crowd near the door; "I handled that bouquet, I buried my face among the flowers, and for at least twenty seconds enjoyed the fragrance, yet it did not poison me, which proves beyond doubt that the fatal drug was placed in it after I handled it."

"Who was the last one to handle it before it was returned to Lottie?" exclaimed Captain Burk.

"The lady in the black domino," replied Scottie.

"You are mistaken there, I think, Miss Darlington," said George, "for it is my recollection that Napoleon was the one who returned the bouquet to Lottie. I remember distinctly that he held it in his hand a long while, and that he kept pulling the flowers apart as if desirous to see how it was held together."

"It is a settled fact," said Captain Quitman, "that the one who returned that bouquet to Mrs. Demar is the one that deposited the poison on it; and if that person can be pointed out, we may be able to detect the poisoner."

When the fact that Mrs. Demar was poisoned was first

announced by Doctor Plaxico, the lady in the black domino (who had been expelled from Lottie's room a short time before) uttered a loud, piercing scream, and ran rapidly toward her own state-room.

"What on earth does that mean?" exclaimed Captain Burk as the woman came dashing past him.

"I would risk my life on her being the poisoner," said Scottie. "She has just now heard Doctor Plaxico say that Lottie would be dead in less than two hours. I was present when the announcement was made, and as soon as that woman heard it she uttered the scream and dashed away. It was not a scream of distress, but it was a shout of joy. She is the very wretch who deposited the poison in that bouquet, and it is my opinion that she is in love with Demar, and that she has murdered Lottie to get her out of the way."

"That is the most plausible theory I have heard mentioned in connection with this horrible affair," said Captain Burk, "for I cannot believe that such a charming woman as Mrs. Demar could have an enemy except such as are made by the green-eyed monster."

Doctor Plaxico now came out of Lottie's room looking unusually serious, and when a dozen anxious friends inquired all at once about the condition of the patient, he shook his head and in a voice choked with deep emotion, said:

"Dying!" and passed on.

As the doctor passed out the lady in the black domino was seen running as fast as she could from her own to Lottie's room, holding a large phial of liquid in each hand.

"Stop, madame!" exclaimed Doctor Plaxico as he placed his back against the door of Lottie's room; "you must not go in there."

"By what authority do you forbid it?"

"I am the attending physician, which confers the authority on me to protect my patient from intruders."

"I heard you say just now that you had abandoned all hopes of saving your patient's life."

"I do not deny it."

"Then I will save her."

"You!"

"I."

"Madame, did you know that suspicion was pointing at you as the murderess?"

"No; nor do I care where suspicion may choose to point. This is no time to discuss suspicions, when the purest, the best and noblest lady on earth is in great peril. Stand aside, sir, and let me go in!"

"What stuff is contained in those two bottles? More poison, I dare say."

"That which I hold in my left hand, sir, is an antidote for vegetable poison, and this is a certain cure for the most deadly mineral poison. Now let me go in, and since you have given your patient up, you cannot deny me a chance to save her."

"Demar, this woman is crazy beyond all question; and if you let her administer any drug to your wife, I want you to distinctly understand that you do it against my advice or consent."

Demar, whose mind was overflowed with sorrow, gazed wildly at the mysterious woman before him.

"Madame," he groaned, "why do you wish to murder such a sweet angel as Lottie?"

"You are all murderers who stand here caviling about nonsense, while your victim is dying! I can and will save Lottie's life, if you will only let me do it."

"Did you place the poison in the bouquet?"

"No, but I know who did; and if you will let me, I will save Lottie's life and then show you the poisoner."

"How am I to know that the drug you propose to give my wife is not poison?"

"Give me a spoon and see me drink the same quantity that I shall offer to your wife."

"Your request is reasonable, and I will take the risk."

A spoon was brought, when the strange woman took the phial and with a steady hand measured out exactly ten drops of the liquid and instantly swallowed it. Then pouring out ten more drops, she said:

"Shall I administer it to your wife, or will you do it?"

Demar hesitated a moment while he stared with a look of perplexity toward Plaxico, who was watching the proceedings with silent contempt.

"Demar," said he, "I want you to remember that all this nonsense is being enacted contrary to my advice, and in the face of the fair warning I have given you."

"And I warn you," said the lady in the black domino firmly, "that if you stand here halting and caviling about trifles much longer Mrs. Demar will die, and you will be to blame for it."

"Who are you, madame?" inquired Demar, in a hesitating tone.

"It matters not who I am; let me be judged by what I shall do; and if I do not save the life of that poor lady, you may plunge me into the river, or roast me in the furnace."

"Why did you shout with joy a moment ago when you heard Doctor Plaxico say that Lottie was poisoned, and that she would surely die?"

"Because when he said she was poisoned I knew I could save her life. This antidote was given to me by a learned German surgeon who had served in the British army for many years in India. It was my good fortune to nurse him, in Cincinnati, through a long, lingering spell of typhus fever, and as a reward for my services he gave me these two phials with their contents."

"Enough!" exclaimed Demar eagerly, "I believe and will trust you, and may God grant you success! Approach and administer the medicine yourself."

Lottie's eyes were rolling wildly, while her breathing was difficult, and all evidences of reason had disappeared. All who saw her were convinced that she had commenced the struggle with the dreadful destroyer. The lady in the black domino lifted Lottie's head from the pillow and emptied the medicine into her mouth, holding her still until she saw the patient swallow it, then laid her down gently, and waited for the result. Plaxico stood by with one hand on the patient's pulse, and his watch in the other, and although he had disapproved of the experiment, he earnestly prayed in silence that it might be attended with success. Fifteen minutes after the antidote was administered, Lottie closed her eyes and appeared to be asleep, while the breathing grew less labored. The pale face of Doctor Plaxico began to brighten.

"How is she now?" Demar whispered as he seized Plaxico's arm.

"Better!"

"She is saved, thank Heaven!" exclaimed the lady in the black domino as she fell on her knees by the bed and burst into tears.

"Be still, Demar!" said Plaxico, "and let go my arm—you are hurting me!"

A purse of fifteen hundred dollars in money was made up among the passengers, and a committee appointed with instructions to present it to the lady who had saved Lottie's life; but the astonishment was boundless when the committee reported the fact that the lady in the black domino had politely, but firmly refused to accept the money.

The next morning Lottie was able to rise from her bed, and when she appeared in the saloon leaning on her husband's arm, the enthusiasm was indescribable. Congratulations were showered on the lovely favorite, and everybody appeared to be happy.

CHAPTER XL.

As soon as breakfast was over, the next morning after Lottie had been so miraculously cured, Captain Quitman arose from the head of the table and began to address his passengers as follows:

"My young friends, when I purchased the 'White Rose of Memphis' and placed her on this line, the height of my ambition was to make her the headquarters of pleasure-seekers. It was my aim to make it to the interest of travelers to patronize my boat, and to furnish excursion parties with facilities for enjoyment. I had always adhered to the idea that it was the duty of a steam-boat commander to protect his passengers against ruffians and thieves, and I mean to do so to the utmost of my capacity. It is with emotions of the deepest regret that I am compelled to inform my friends that, by some means unknown to me, shrewd pickpockets and robbers have managed to get aboard of my boat. One of my passengers has been robbed of a large sum of money, amounting, I believe, to something near ten thousand dollars; another has lost a splendid gold watch; and others have been deprived of jewels and other valuable articles. I therefore request every passenger to consent to be searched and to permit the state-rooms to be thoroughly examined; and, in order to prevent any attempt to conceal the stolen property, I ask all the passengers to fall into line now. Let the ladies form on my left and the gentlemen on my right."

The captain had scarcely concluded his request before the two lines were formed, the ladies promptly arranging themselves to the left and the gentlemen on his right. A few of the passengers had retired to their state-rooms, but as soon as the wishes of the captain were transmitted to them they immediately appeared and took their places in the line. Napoleon and Navarre arranged themselves side by side at the head of the gentlemen's line.

"That woman is the thief," whispered one of the passengers, addressing the man on his left.

"That is exactly the conclusion that has possessed my mind," was the reply.

"Let no one leave the line without permission until the search is ended; and I request Mrs. Demar and Miss Darlington to take their places in state-room number seven, and let the ladies go there, one at a time, and submit to a thorough search."

The lady in the black domino left her place in the line, and, with a slow, measured tread, moved round and paused in front of Captain Quitman. This movement, being a plain violation of the explicit instructions of the captain, produced no small amount of curiosity, and led to innumerable exclamations of surprise.

"I would most respectfully ask you, sir, to wait a moment," said she, in a voice which slightly trembled, but had a sweet, melancholy sound. "I have something to communicate, which, I doubt not, will have a tendency to change the programme which you have been pleased to mention. I must ask you to let me see the gentleman who had the misfortune to lose his watch."

George Woodburry (a young man who had been personating
George III.) then promptly stepped out from the line and
confronted the black domino.

"Are you the gentleman whose watch was stolen?"

Mr. Woodburry merely answered by a slight inclination of
the head, without opening his lips. She then drew from her
pocket a large, double-cased gold watch to which was attached
a massive chain. Holding it out toward him, she said:

"Is this your property, sir?"

"Yes."

Then addressing the captain again, she requested him to
produce the gentleman whose money had been stolen. Henry
of Navarre stepped from his place in the line and confronted
the black domino.

"I am the one who has been so unlucky as to lose a large
sum of money."

"Take a seat, sir," replied the woman, "near that table
there, and do me the favor to count the contents of this pocket-
book carefully, and when you have finished inform me whose
it is, and the amount of money in it."

Navarre, taking the pocket-book, drew a chair to the table
and began to count the money.

"Poor woman," observed Captain Burk, "she has stolen
the money, and now when she sees all chances of escape destroyed, she is going to confess and beg for mercy."

"For my part," replied Woodburry, "I am inclined to think
she is crazy. I have noticed her singular conduct ever since
we left Memphis, and I am unable to account for her actions
upon any other theory."

Nearly all the passengers felt a sentiment of compassion
for the unfortunate woman, and several suggested the propriety of requesting Captain Quitman to let her off without
exposure, inasmuch as she had restored the stolen property.

"I make a motion," said Demar, "that we jointly petition
the captain not to expose the poor unfortunate creature."

The motion was unanimously adopted and Demar selected
as commissioner to lay the petition before Captain Quitman.
Meantime Navarre finished counting the money.

"This is my pocket-book, madame," said he as he rose from
the table, "and I find all my money in it, just as it was when

it was stolen." Then, handing Captain Quitman a little paper box, she said:

"In this box, sir, you will find all the other stolen articles, which you will oblige me by returning to the owners."

The captain received the articles and instantly delivered them to the parties from whom they had been filched; then, addressing the mysterious woman, he said:

"Madame, the circumstances just developed force me to the performance of a very painful duty which I would gladly shun, but I must place you under arrest."

"Captain Quitman," said Demar, as he advanced to the spot where he stood, "I am requested by a large number of your passengers to inform you that it is their wish that this unfortunate woman should be forgiven and dismissed without exposure. We must remember that the most prominent trait in our great Saviour's character was His boundless mercy toward malefactors. When He was bleeding on the cross, suffering the agonies of death for the sins of fallen man, He spoke the words of pardon to the poor thief who was dying by His side. Now, in humble imitation of the merciful example set us by our great Redeemer, let us pardon this poor unfortunate woman, and bid her go and sin no more."

"Doctor Demar," said Captain Quitman, "nothing would gratify me more than to comply with the wishes of you and your friends; but the duty which I was performing is one not to be avoided by me unless the request shall be endorsed by the parties whose property was stolen."

"We indorse the request most willingly," said Navarre.

"I most heartily join in that request," said George Woodburry.

"Madame," said the captain, "you have heard the noble expressions of compassion which have just been made in your behalf, and I am happy to be permitted to speak the words of pardon to you. You will be permitted to remain in mask, and no further effort will be made to expose you, but you must leave this boat when we arrive at Vicksburg."

"Captain Quitman," began the strange woman, "for the manifestations of mercy and forgiveness so generously expressed by these kind ladies and gentlemen, I am profoundly grateful; but I must be pardoned for saying that while I appreciate the generosity that prompts the offer, I do not ask or wish any mercy from these good ladies and noble men. When I want mercy, I will dispatch my supplication to a higher tribunal, where the secrets of all hearts are known, and where good and bad deeds are correctly recorded. I am by no means ignorant of the old legal maxim th'at holds the possessor of stolen goods responsible for the theft, until such possession is explained by competent evidence. I do not deny the fact that a *prima facie* case has been made out in this instance against me; nevertheless, I am not the thief. You were correct, indeed, when you concluded that you had a shrewd thief aboard of this boat. I can assert of my own knowledge, that a demon is among you, whose black soul is steeped in crime, an inhuman monster, who neither fears God, man nor Satan.

> " 'Earth gapes, Hell burns, fiends roar, saints pray,
> To have him suddenly carried away;
> Cancel his bond of life, dear God; I pray
> That I may live to say the dog is dead.'

"I trust that my good friends will pardon me for using such strong language—I have borrowed it from Shakespeare's 'Richard III.' It was suggested to my mind by the striking resemblance between the bloody King and this diabolical monster—this lapper up of innocent blood—this destroyer of confiding virtue—this cruel fiend whose hands are red with blood—whose soul is stained with perjury. This false, bloody villain is named Benjamin Bowles, and here he stands."

As quick as thought she sprang forward before the sentence had been half uttered and tearing away Napoleon's mask, there stood Ben Bowles, pale but defiant as ever, while anger and hate blazed from his eyes. Half a dozen ladies fainted, others fled to their state-rooms, while the men stood still, perfectly stupefied with astonishment. Henry of Navarre then slowly moved round and confronting Bowles, while his arms were folded across his breast.

"Mr. Bowles! you and I have met before to-day. A duty which I owe to society and the laws of my country compels me to take a step which will somewhat interfere with your pleasure excursion. The grand jury at Memphis have decided that you committed a cruel murder upon a little boy named Bramlett. Now you will have to abandon your little pleasure trip and go with me back to Memphis. If they do not hang you for the murder of young Framlett, you can then stand your trial for your cowardly attempt to assassinate Mrs. Demar. You know we can take the train at Vicksburg, and return to Memphis."

"I know you very well, Harry Wallingford, and am always glad to meet you. You would be glad to create the impression that you are a man of courage, but I happen to know that that you are a coward. I despise and defy you, and·am sorry I cannot employ words sufficiently insulting to induce you to fight."

"I have too much self-respect, Mr. Bowles, to resent an insult offered by men of your sort. The fact is, I pity you, for the awful situation in which you are placed, and so far as I am individually concerned, I mean to place you in the hands of the law, and leave you to deal with God and your own conscience."

"Indeed, sir, that is exceedingly kind in you; but I must be permitted to make some disposition of you, since you have been so mindful of my comfort. You say you are going to place me in the hands of God—the law—my conscience, and the grand jury, and how many other distinguished individuals have you chosen to act as my guardian. I flatter myself that I shall be able to make a better disposition of you, than you have promised to make of me; because I have concluded to make hell a present of your cowardly soul, so you will not be annoyed with so many masters. I think I shall be able to make a better job this time than I did when I clipped your left wing at Memphis."

As Bowles uttered the last sentence, he snatched a large navy revolver from under his coat, and cocking it as he brought it round, leveled it at Wallingford's breast; but the lady in the black domino, who was standing near, seized his arm and instantly jerked it round; a short scuffle ensued—the loud report of the pistol rang out through the saloon—a cloud of blue smoke gushed up—a column of red flame blazed out—a loud scream escaped the mysterious woman's lips, and she fell bleeding into Navarre's arms. As the body of the lady dropped forward against Navarre's breast, he saw a crimson stream gush out from her left side and trickle over his vest. As her head fell back across his arm her mask fell off, and her dark brown hair dropped unconfined about his shoulders.

"Merciful God!" exclaimed Wallingford, "it is Viola, and the cruel villain has killed her!"

As soon as Bowles fired the pistol he darted quickly through a side door, and ran rapidly toward the front end of the boat, evidently intending to leap into the river and effect his escape by swimming to the shore.

When Wallingford made the startling discovery that it was Miss Bramlett's blood that spurted against his breast, thoughts of revenge instantly filled his mind. Gently laying the bleeding girl on a sofa, he dashed through the saloon, reaching the head of the stairs that led from the middle to the lower deck, just as Bowles arrived on the lower floor. Making a tremendous spring, he leaped down in season to catch the fugitive before he had time to leap overboard.

As soon as Wallingford leaped on the lower deck, he seized hold of the sleeve of Bowles' coat, and called the deck hands to assist in arresting the murderer. A stalwart Irishman hurried forward intending to render the aid, but Bowles, who still held the pistol in his hand, leveled it at the man's head and fired. The bullet grazed the man's temple, knocking him down, which induced the other deck hands to believe that their comrade was killed; consequently they all beat a precipitate retreat, leaving Wallingford to fight it out alone.

Bowles knew that his only chance to effect his escape was to disable his adversary and leap into the river before assistance could come from the saloon; hence he attempted to shoot Wallingford, which he would have succeeded in doing but his hand was knocked up just as his finger touched the trigger, which caused the ball to fly harmless overhead.

The instant Bowles succeeded in disengaging himself from Wallingford's grasp, and just as Demar reached the floor, the fugitive leaped into the river and began to swim toward the shore, leaving the pistol on the floor. Wallingford seized the pistol and commenced firing at Bowles, who kept diving under the water in order to dodge the bullets which were whistling in close proximity to his head.

"The White Rose" at that time was running close to the shore. Bowles was an expert swimmer, and it was very plain that, unless prevented, he would easily effect his escape. He had reached a point at least thirty yards from the boat before Wallingford became convinced that all of his shot had missed his man. Throwing off his coat and boots, still holding the pistol in his hand, Wallingford plunged into the water, and set out in pursuit of the escaping outlaw.

"Turn her head in toward the shore, Mr. Haliman, as quick as you can!" cried Captain Quitman, who stood on the hurricane deck; "don't lose a moment; that foolish boy will be drowned if he attacks that huge villain in the water."

"It is somewhat dangerous, captain, to attempt to land her there," replied Mr. Haliman; "we might get her aground."

"Let her get aground, Mr. Haliman; I had rather sink her than to see that boy drowned by such a monster as Bowles. Go ahead on the starboard, and hold steady on the larboard; point her head toward that tall tree yonder, and stick her nozzle in that sand-bank—quick, quick, Mr. Haliman!"

After Demar had done all he could to dissuade the rash young man from venturing to tackle such a giant while in the water, and being unable to recall him, he threw off his coat and plunged into the river, determined to save the life of his kinsman, or perish with him.

The passengers crowded the hurricane deck and watched the approaching struggle with breathless anxiety.

Wallingford continued to gain on his hated foe, while thoughts of revenge crowded all prudence or fear from his breast. He was thinking of the blood that had spouted against his breast from Viola's side.

Mr. Haliman, owing to the treachery of the current, was encountering some difficulty in bringing his boat round to the shore, and, despite his vigorous efforts to drive her nozzle on the sand-bank, she swung round and began to drift further down.

Demar soon became convinced that he would not be able to overtake Harry in time to render any assistance. Con-

sequently he began to call to Wallingford, begging him to
wait until he could get to him; but the imprudent boy dashed
forward without heeding the call. He might as readily have
checked a tornado with a lady's fan as Harry Wallingford,
by reminding him of the danger into which he was rushing.

When Bowles became convinced that he would be overtaken before he could reach the shore, he slackened his efforts, and merely exerted sufficient motion to keep himself on
the surface, being, no doubt, conscious of the great advantage which his superior strength would give him over his
adversary in a duel fought in the water.

When Wallingford had arrived within twenty feet of his
enemy, he began to move obliquely to the left, so as to come
up where he would have the advantage of the current. Bowles
turned round and leisurely floated on the surface of the
water, eying his pursuer as if he were anxious to get hold of
him; but Wallingford began to swim round the desperado.
When he came up within six feet of him, he made a sudden
dash forward and attempted to strike him on the head with
the pistol which he still held in his hand, but at that instant
the bright blade of a long dagger gleamed in the rays of the
setting sun, as the arm of the outlaw descended toward Wallingford's body.

A suppressed scream escaped the lips of a dozen ladies
who witnessed the strange duel from the hurricane deck of
the "White Rose," as they saw the glittering steel being driven
into Wallingford's body.

Then commenced a hand-to-hand struggle, one using the
pistol as a club, the other striking rapidly with the dagger;
every now and then both parties would for a moment disappear under the water, then rise to the surface, grappling each
other in a deadly embrace. Stains of blood began to appear
on Wallingford's shirt, and blood was streaming over his
face.

Demar, finding that his efforts to render aid by swimming
were fruitless, turned his course and went toward the yawl.
Leaping into it, he urged the four men to pull for dear life,
promising a handsome reward to the oarsmen if they could
get to the combatants in time to save Wallingford's life. After
the combat had been continued for two or three minutes the

parties separated for a moment, as if by mutual consent, in
order to get a little breath, and to maneuver for advantage.
Only a few seconds elapsed, however, before Bowles began to
advance toward his antagonist, being anxious, no doubt, to
end the combat before the yawl could come to Wallingford's
assistance, which was now not very far away. The two men
now began to swim round each other, each seeking to get the
benefit of the current. A scuffle then ensued, but here Wallingford's activity stood him in good stead, for he managed
to give a sudden twist, disappearing under the water, while
Bowles swam round, watching the spot where Harry had gone
under. But no little amount of astonishment was that which
Bowles felt when he saw his wily foe rise up at least twenty
feet away. Wallingford was up the stream, which circumstance would enable him to make a successful plunge, as he
would be coming with, instead of against, the strong current.

The pilot had by this time succeeded in driving the nozzle
of his boat against the bank, but in consequence of the
treachery of the current, he had been compelled to strike the
shore nearly a hundred yards below the point first designated
by the commander.

The spectators were horrified to see that Wallingford's face
was covered with blood, and when he raised his body above
the water they could see the blood spouting from a dozen
wounds on his neck, face and shoulders. For several seconds
he paused, as if endeavoring to take a little breath; then,
giving his head a sudden shake as if to dash the bloody hair
back from his face, he raised his body high up out of the
water, and, quick as lightning, darted on his adversary, dealing him a tremendous blow on the back of the head with the
butt end of the pistol. The sharp point of the hammer went
crashing like a bullet through the villain's skull, and the
body of Ben Bowles sank, never to rise again until it and his
soul were separated. The lifeless body of the desperate outlaw was found ten days afterward, floating in the water thirty
miles from the spot where it and the soul parted. Wallingford, being completely overcome with fatigue and the loss of
blood, was incapable of making any further exertion. He
fell off of the piece of timber and disappeared under the water,
but as he came up a few seconds afterward, Demar seized him

by the wrist, as he was sinking the second time, and lifted him into the yawl, when he fell insensible on the floor. The lifeless body of the rash young man was hurriedly conveyed to a state-room on the "White Rose," where Doctor Plaxico was instantly summoned to take charge of the case.

"There is where the danger lies," said Plaxico. "The dagger that inflicted that wound penetrated the cavity of the lungs, and internal hemorrhage has resulted."

"Lottie, who had at all times been famous for her courage and self-possession under adverse circumstances, was now completely mastered by her grief. As soon as she recovered her self-possession, she implored the doctor to tell her the very worst.

"You need not be afraid to tell me the truth, doctor. Tell me candidly, is my brother mortally wounded or not?"

"Mrs. Demar, it is impossible for me to give anything like a reliable opinion just now, but, to be frank with you, I fear we may expect a fatal result." Then, addressing Demar, he said, "Go to Miss Bramlett without delay and examine her wound, and see if anything can be done for her."

"What a pity it is that such a pretty girl should be murdered by such a fiend as Ben Bowles!" observed George Woodburry, in a whisper to Captain Burk.

"Yes," replied the captain; "she has lost her life in the attempt to save Wallingford."

"Were they not engaged to be married?"

"Yes, though it was thought by Miss Bramlett's friends that she had committed suicide in New York nearly a year ago. There appears to be some strange mystery connected with this business."

"I wonder if she knew that Navarre was Harry Wallingford in disguise?"

"I am inclined to think she did; but I am of the opinion that he did not know that the lady of the black domino was Miss Bramlett."

"What a strange and fatal coincidence it is that they should have met here, to die at the same time and place, both murdered by the same desperate villain!"

"Indeed it is!"

"Is Miss Bramlett dead?" inquired Captain Quitman, who was watching attentively near the door.

"No," replied Demar, "and I am exceedingly glad to be able to inform you that she is not going to die from any cause now existing. Her wound is not at all of a serious character, though she has received a very severe shock; she has entirely recovered from its effect, and is now soundly sleeping, under the influence of an opiate, and I think it is safe to predict that she will be as well as ever in less than a week. The ball struck a rib, glancing round and making its exit just to the left of the spine, inflicting merely a slight flesh wound."

"Heaven bless you, Demar, for this good news!" exclaimed Captain Quitman, as he seized the surgeon's hand.

"Go in and see Wallingford immediately, and I pray to God to enable you to bring us such good news from him!"

As soon as Demar went into the room he inquired of Plaxico the condition of the patient.

"Bad enough, Heaven knows!" was the answer. "He is totally unconscious—fever rising—respiration difficult—left lung gorged with blood, and every symptom most unfavorable. That stab under the shoulder-blade is the dangerous one. Demar, you must get some reliable nurse to remain with Miss Bramlett all the time, and let it be distinctly understood that she is to be closely watched—if your wife would undertake the task, I should be very glad."

"What do you mean, Plaxico? have I not just told you that Miss Bramlett is scarcely hurt at all—she will be able to get up by to-morrow morning. Where is the necessity of such vigilant nursing."

"That poor girl will commit suicide if Wallingford dies. I think the chances are about a thousand in favor of a fatal result, to one of recovery. You must not lose sight of the fact that Miss Bramlett did on a former occasion contemplate suicide, when she thought Wallingford was hopelessly ill; and you may be assured she will again make the attempt if he dies, which I honestly believe he will do inside of forty hours! It would be advisable to keep her in ignorance of his condition until we know exactly what is to be the result; and I shall depend on you and your wife to do it."

"I think you will find that rather a difficult task, for the very first word she uttered after she recovered from the swoon was an inquiry about Wallingford; and she will be sure to ask about him as soon as she awakes."

"We must resort to strategy; and a little deception, under the circumstances, would be perfectly justifiable—you may tell her that I say Wallingford is not dangerously hurt; and if the recording angel has no worse crimes set down against me in the great Day of Judgment, I shall not fear the result."

Demar and Lottie watched by Miss Bramlett's bedside during the night, while Plaxico, at his own earnest request, was left alone with Harry, where he sat during the whole night, watching with an anxious eye every movement of his patient.

CHAPTER XLI.

SOON after breakfast Miss Bramlett announced her determination to see Wallingford, and no amount of remonstrance which Doctor Plaxico and Demar could bring to bear against the step could prevent it.

"Lottie, help me down on my knees, and I will pray for strength and courage to sustain me under this trying ordeal."

Lottie gladly rendered the assistance requested, and both girls knelt and prayed in silence for a long time; and when they rose up, an expression of calmness was visible on the pale, beautiful face of Miss Bramlett.

"Lottie dear, you can trust me now, and I fear you will think me superstitious when I tell you that our prayers have been answered; he will not die, and we shall all be happy again. You may let me see him now, without any fears as to my actions; if you will let me lean on your shoulder, I can walk very well."

The door of Wallingford's room was thrown open, and a chair placed near his bed. As Miss Bramlett was led to it the pallor of her cheeks increased, but no other signs of emotion were to be seen. The wounded man was muttering continually in a rambling way, and every now and then thrusting his arms out as if striking at an imaginary enemy; and it was plain to be seen that his mind was still on the combat he had had with Bowles.

"He is exhausting his strength very rapidly," said Plaxico, "and I have been as yet unable to quiet him; I believe if I could keep him still that the internal hemorrhage would cease."

Just at that moment Harry made a sudden spring, and would have leaped out of the bed, but Miss Bramlett caught and gently laid him down and began to rub his brow with her hand, when he instantly became quiet, and in three minutes was sound asleep.

"Did you see that, Demar?" said Plaxico, in a low whisper.

"See what?"

"How quick he became quiet when she put her hand on his brow?"

"Yes; I suppose it is mesmerism, magnetism, or something of the sort."

"If we were to live a thousand years, we might learn something new every day; this is a most wonderful occurrence! See, he is sleeping soundly; the respiration is less labored, and his pulse much better. Now, I imagine this strange phenomenon would furnish material for an article in the *Lancet,* and I think I shall undertake to write it."

The very instant Miss Bramlett removed her hand from the wounded man's brow, he awoke and began to move restlessly from side to side; but she immediately replaced it and he was again quiet.

"Well!" observed Demar, "I must say that this is the strangest occurrence that I ever saw. I believe their souls are communing intelligently with each other, and that, notwithstanding Wallingford's reason is dethroned, he is in some way made to know that Miss Bramlett is near him."

"I have often read about two souls melting into one," replied Plaxico, "but this is the first occular demonstration of the process that has ever been witnessed by me. There is more mystery in the anatomy of the human body than is generally believed to exist, anyway."

"Yes," rejoined Demar; "especially does that remark apply to the human heart. I speak from experience, to some extent, and I dare say that the hearts of Miss Bramlett and Wallingford are at this very moment conversing intelligently with each other. A sort of telegraph which love has erected is now conducting sweet messages from one heart to the other."

Wallingford continued to slumber undisturbed for four hours, except when Miss Bramlett would remove her hand from his brow, and then he would begin to show signs of restlessness, which never failed to disappear as soon as she would replace it. The burning fever that had been raging began to subside, and the hemorrhage ceased, curiously, while all the symptoms took a favorable turn.

"Demar," whispered Plaxico, after he had held his finger on the patient's pulse for a long while; "I think Miss Bramlett's treatment has saved our friend's life; the fact is, she has performed a most wonderful miracle."

It was late in the evening when Wallingford opened his eyes and began to stare in a bewildered way at the beautiful face that hovered near him, while evidences of restored reason unmistakably appeared in his movements. For two or three minutes he gazed earnestly at Miss Bramlett, then placing his hand on her head, he gently stroked her hair, and then ran his hand over her face, and then took hold of her arm.

"Yes," he whispered; "it is her, and it was all a dream; and such a horrible one, too; I thought she was dead, and I dreamed that Bowles had killed her, and then drowned me in the river. Why do you not speak to me, Viola? Am I mistaken in thinking I see you?"

As he uttered the last words, he placed his arm round her neck and drew her head down until her cheek touched against his.

"Come away, Demar," said Plaxico, as he plucked him by the sleeve; "I shall shout with joy if I remain here another moment. That scene is enough to make the angels weep with delight."

It was on the morning of the fourth day after Wallingford received his wounds, that he made his appearance in the saloon supported by Miss Bramlett and Lottie, each one with a shoulder under his arm, fairly lifting him along by main strength.

Harry Wallingford was lazily reclining in a large cushioned armchair on the hurricane-deck, listening to Lottie, who was reading Mazeppa to him, while Miss Bramlett sat near him, gazing vacantly at the rolling waves that dashed up behind the boat. A long pause ensued when Lottie laid the book down and began to fondle her brother's dark-brown hair.

"Viola," said Harry, "I want you to tell me what induced you to give your friends in New York the dodge, leaving them to conclude that you had committed suicide; in fact, I want you to tell me all about everything connected with your history from the time we parted, until the present moment."

"There is but very little to tell, I assure you, and as I have nothing better to do, and being anxious to amuse you, I suppose I must undertake the task; but before I begin, you must allow me to express my thanks for the beautiful monument you caused to be erected over my grave in New York. Your generosity in that instance, indeed deserves my profound gratitude, and it has convinced me that you did really care something for me.

"But let me leave that subject for future discussion while I proceed with my little history. When I was, by the dishonesty of the trustees who had control of my money, reduced to a pauper, I felt that it was my duty to seek some means of earning an honest living. That there were many friends and relatives of mine ready and anxious to offer me a home, I very well knew, but I could not for a moment bear the idea of being dependent on relatives for support. Above all things I abhor anything like gilded bondage or idle dependence; consequently, I resolved to seek employment. I knew very well that this step would be bitterly opposed by my aristocratic relations, especially if I should dare to seek employment in New York; therefore, I concluded to give them the slip and hunt a distant home. Disguising myself completely, I went to Cincinnati and had the good fortune to secure a position as governess in the family of Mr. Gaterine, the kind-hearted old gentleman who is accompanying me on this trip.

"One evening I was passing along one of the principal streets of Cincinnati, when I was overwhelmed with astonishment to meet Benjamin Bowles. He was disguised, but notwithstanding that I recognized him, and I knew in an instant, from his manner, that he was aware of the fact that I had penetrated his deception. I hurried to the Chief of Police and imparted the information, hoping to have him arrested; but he must have immediately fled, as the officers could not find him. I hired a detective to look for him, but after working a month nothing was accomplished. But when I tell you to whom I am indebted for the discovery of Bowles' hiding-place I know you will be greatly astonished. Do you see that little, pale-faced, sickly-looking boy yonder, leaning over the bannisters?"

"Yes."

"Very well, it is to that little hero that I owe the great obligation. His name is Robert Spratt, son of a widow woman residing in Memphis; you doubtless remember him, though he has changed very much in his personal appearance since he left Memphis. They used to call him haunch-back Bob, for his spine was diseased, causing an ugly hump to appear between his shoulders, and seriously affecting his general health, and as I think, greatly retarded his growth. You will notice that he is quite a child in stature, but I can tell you he has the heart, brain and soul of a man. He is a real gallant hero, and you could not find another such a good detective anywhere. He is much older, though, than his little body would indicate.

"I prevailed on him to let me send him to an infirmary at Cincinnati, where he was effectually cured, for which I paid one thousand dollars; and as good luck would have it, I met my little protege on the streets not more than ten minutes after I had met Bowles. I was delighted to see that the ugly hump had disappeared and that my little friend was effectually cured. I hurriedly gave him a description of Bowles, and told him in which direction the murderer had gone, requesting him to follow and try to find him. I did not see Robert any more, or hear a word from him for two months, and I concluded that he had returned to his home in Memphis; but not so, the noble little hero was tracking the great outlaw.

"I cannot command language to describe the surprise as well as joy I felt when I received a telegram from my little hero, informing me that Bowles was on his way to Mexico, and would probably stop a few days at New Orleans, and advising me to come down there as soon as I could. He also requested me to inquire for a dispatch that he would send to Memphis, which would meet me there on my way to New Orleans. He was at Friar's Point, Mississippi, where Bowles had stopped to wait for one of his pals who had agreed to meet him there.

"Mr. Gaterine kindly consented to go with me to New Orleans, and when I arrived at Memphis I found the promised telegram, which informed me that Bowles was still at Friar's Point. The 'White Rose' being the first boat that would start for New Orleans, we concluded to take passage on her, but learning that Lottie and Edward had been married on the day before I reached Memphis, and that they were going on a bridal tour to the Crescent City, I at once procured a black domino and mask to wear in order to keep them from knowing me. I am sure that I could not have sufficiently disguised my voice to have enabled me to deceive Lottie, had it not been for a severe cold, which, although quite painful, I was glad to endure as long as it would aid me in the accomplishment of my purpose. It was my intention to leave the boat at Friar's Point, but soon after the 'White Rose' landed I was delighted to see my little detective come aboard. He informed me that Bowles had just come aboard, and was going to New Orleans on the 'White Rose.' I was overjoyed at this information. You doubtless remember that we landed at Friar's Point in the night; if I remember correctly, it was about three o'clock in the morning, and you must know how bitter was my disappointment next morning, when, after a diligent search, we failed to find Bowles. I soon ascertained from inquiries made, that the 'White Rose' had not landed since we left Friar's Point, which led me to believe that our man was concealed somewhere on the boat. My little detective was of the same opinion, and I knew that if it was as we suspected, that he would soon discover where the murderer was hidden. I do not know what it was that caused Robert to suspect Napoleon, but nevertheless I soon learned from him that he did suspect him of being the man we were after. It was some time before he succeeded in convincing himself that his suspicions were well founded. By some means which I did not care to know, he succeeded in effecting an entrance to the state-room occupied by Napoleon, when, sure enough, he discovered that it was Bowles. All the stolen money and other property was found hidden in an old boot under the bed, and when I found out that it was stolen property, I instructed my little friend to bring it to me, which he did."

"Yes," exclaimed Wallingford, "and I promise you now, Viola, that your brave little friend shall never know what it is to want for anything as long as he lives."

"Thank you, Harry, a thousand times I thank you," replied Miss Bramlett, as fresh tears began to trickle down her cheeks, "but you must let me finish my story. Well, my little friend ascertained that Bowles had paid fifty dollars to the gentleman who originally personated the Emperor Napoleon, for his uniform and mask, and you must not blame that gentleman for selling his costume to Bowles, because he did not know he was aiding a cruel murderer to escape, but he was tired of the nonsense, as he was pleased to call it, and finding a chance to get his money back, he at once closed the trade, believing that the purchaser merely wished to enjoy a little innocent sport by deceiving the ladies. As soon as I ascertained the fact that the money, and other valuable things had been stolen, I resolved to restore them to their owners, but before I could carry out my intentions in that respect, Captain Quitman inaugurated his plans to make a search, the result of which you already know."

"Yes," said Harry, "that is all very well explained, but how did the dead woman happen to have my ring?"

"I think I can explain that also," replied Miss Bramlett. "Soon after I arrived in New York, I engaged a young Irish woman to serve me as waiting maid, and soon after she entered my service, I began to miss little articles, which I at first supposed were accidentally lost or mislaid, but it was not long before I became convinced that they were stolen. One of my dresses, a drab silk, mysteriously disappeared, then my ring, and various other valuable articles were missing, and when I became convinced that my maid was a thief I discharged her. It is clear to my mind that the unfortunate woman was wearing my dress and ring when she was drowned."

"Viola!" said Wallingford in a voice choking with deep emotion, "did you recognize me in my Navarre costume?"

"Yes, indeed I did."

"How could you remain near me so long without speaking to me? Do you not know that I would have swum through lakes of fire to have found you?"

Viola's voice now for the first time refused to obey her will, and she was unable to make any reply. Her eyes were bent on the ground, while the violent throbbings of her heart could be distinctly heard by Lottie, who sat near her.

"Viola," continued Wallingford, "will you not try to love me a little?"

"No!" she replied in a trembling tone which seemed to be uttered with an effort.

"Why?"

"Because I do not think it would be good for me to love any one more than I have loved you for the last ten years."

"Now stop that, Harry," exclaimed Demar, as he approached the group. "You may embrace Miss Bramlett if you wish, but to have two women in your arms at once is a little too much. I think you are very selfish; you may embrace Miss Bramlett as often as she will allow it, but you must not be quite so familiar with my wife."

"Leave me alone with Viola immediately, I beseech you, Ed," Wallingford whispered as he placed his mouth close to his ear. "Pray, go quick and take Lottie with you. I think Viola is now in the notion to pardon the past errors, and I hope and believe she will promise to marry me."

"Come, Lottie!" said Demar, endeavoring to assume an indifferent tone, "let us take a little stroll together, as I have a little secret to tell you. I suppose Miss Bramlett can take care of your brother while we are away."

As soon as Demar and his wife were gone, an embarrassing pause ensued while Harry and Miss Bramlett silently inspected the floor. Each one could distinctly hear the violent throbbings of the other's heart.

"Viola!" Harry said, after a full five minutes had been spent in silence, "dare I ask you to forgive the great wrong that I have done to you?"

No answer. "I know that I do not deserve, nor have I

the right to expect your pardon, yet I am very unhappy in thinking that you must entertain a very unfavorable opinion of the contemptible part I played in that unfortunate affair at Memphis."

"Harry, how could you ask me to forgive you, when you must know that my heart is overflowing with gratitude to you for the valuable assistance you rendered in that affair? You must indeed have a poor opinion of me, if you could for a moment suppose that I could ever forget your noble, generous exertions in my behalf. If I were to live a hundred years I would remember you and your sweet sister with sentiments of the deepest gratitude. It is I who should seek forgiveness, and I do here, now, most sincerely declare that no act that I have ever committed has caused me half the pain, shame, and mortification that my hateful temper caused me to feel by inducing me to insult you that day in jail. If you can forget and forgive me for that despicable conduct, you are indeed the most generous, noble-hearted man living."

"Viola, you and I have had many trials and much trouble, and suffered much sorrow since we first met, and we have no doubt learned some valuable lessons, which I have reason to believe will prove a blessing in the end. The hand of a kind Providence seems to have guided our destinies. He first used me as His instrument in saving your life many years ago, and then enabled you to save mine, the other day. Therefore let us agree to let by-gones be forgotten, while we endeavor to profit by the sad lessons taught us by experience."

"I say amen to that with all my heart."

"Now, darling, knowing as you do the numerous faults and imperfections that unfortunately belong to my nature, are you willing to trust your happiness to me? Will you confirm my hopes of happiness by promising to be mine?"

"Are you willing to marry a pauper?"

"Don't mention the money question, I implore you."

"Yes, but I must mention it, because I owe at least ten thousand dollars, and have no money to pay with."

"I wish it was five times ten thousand, then I would have the more pleasure in paying it."

"Are you willing to take such a pauper, with all her faults and debts together?"

"I am willing to take the best, the noblest, the prettiest, and the most charming girl in America, if she is not afraid to trust her fate to my humble self."

"Harry, there is my hand, and you have been the sole owner of my heart ever since we rolled down the embankment together, when you broke your leg to save my life. One promise I shall require you to make, and then I am yours forever. When you were so badly wounded a few days ago, I most solemnly promised God that if He would spare your dear life, that I would love and serve Him all the days of my life, and that I would endeavor to induce you to do the same. Now I promise to be your wife, if you will promise to make good the vow I made to God."

"I do most willingly make the promise, and may the great Creator help me to fulfill it."

"Did you not hear the gong sounding the summons to supper?" shouted Lottie, as she surprised her brother in the act of embracing Miss Bramlett. "Come along, and let us go down to supper; everybody is anxious to have the table cleared away so the dance can begin."

CHAPTER XLII.

THREE years after the "White Rose of Memphis" had accomplished her memorable pleasure trip, two elegantly dressed ladies were leisurely strolling along the graveled walks in Court Square, Memphis, Tennessee, engaged in an earnest conversation; while two mulatto girls were pushing a couple of silver-mounted baby carriages along just behind the two ladies. Each one of the handsome vehicles contained a very small specimen of sleeping humanity, richly attired in expensive and stylish clothes.

One of the children, a bright, blue-eyed boy, about two years old, with bright, brown curly hair, woke up, and when he saw a large number of pretty pet squirrels hopping about near his carriage, he became greatly excited. Hurriedly clambering out, he hastened to where the little girl lay soundly sleeping, and tried to wake her.

"Dit up, Ottie," said he, as he began to tug at her gown; "see petty pet."

The little girl did not respond, for she was sleeping very soundly; but he was determined to make her get up. When he found that he could not accomplish his object by gentle means, he resorted to those of a more vigorous nature. Seizing her left ear between his finger and thumb, he gave it a violent twist that caused the little sleeper to start up with a loud scream.

"You, Harry!" exclaimed one of the ladies, as she hurried toward the carriage; "what on earth have you been doing to Lottie?"

She then lifted the little girl out of the vehicle and placed her on the ground.

The little boy made no answer, but went dashing after one of the squirrels, and the little girl soon joined in the chase, while their joyful shouts rang out on the air.

"Ah, ha! here we come," exclaimed Doctor Dodson, as he came rapidly across the park, and seizing the little boy he tossed him up and down a dozen times. "Ah, ha! Lottie, this boy is the very image of his mother, don't you see? yes, that is Viola's nose to a T."

"Where did you leave Harry and Eddie, Doctor?" said Mrs. Viola Wallingford.

"Ah, ha! yes; they went by the post office and made me wait for them here—yonder they come now. Ah, ha! Eddie, old boy, it took you a long time to go to the post office."

"We were detained at Mr. Rockland's office," replied Demar.

"Yes," said Harry, "that is true, Doctor, and here is a packet of letters for you; and here, Lottie, is one for you."

"O! Viola, this is from Scottie; I know her hand."

"Read it," said Viola; "I am anxious to hear what she has to say."

Lottie tore off the envelope hurriedly, and read as follows:

"'JACKSON. MISS., May 4th.

" 'DEAR LOTTIE—I received your dear letter yesterday, and hasten to reply. I am too happy to write a long letter. Papa has at last become reconciled with Raileigh, and has given his consent to our marriage, which is to be solemnized next Thursday.

Raleigh is such a dear, good old fellow, and I do believe he loves me with all his heart. My dear, good old papa did not like Raleigh at first, but he has gotten over his prejudice, and they are now the best of friends. Raleigh has quit politics, and is doing well at the law; and, oh! Lottie, how I do love him. I know we shall be very happy, for I have got my temper completely subdued, and I mean to make him a good, devoted wife. Raleigh told me that your daughter was the prettiest little darling in the world. I am glad you named it Lottie, because you know how I adore that sweet name. Raleigh says that Viola's boy is the very image of his mother; he also tells me that Viola and Harry were the happiest couple he had ever seen, except you and Eddie. Well, I am delighted to hear it. If ever people deserved to be happy you and Viola do; because you have suffered more than your share. I think your husband is one of the noblest specimens of humanity I ever saw. This is saying a great deal, but I mean it, and Raleigh agrees with me.

"'I must tell you what a pretty joke was put upon me by the Rev. C. K. Marshall, a celebrated minister of Vicksburg. He had been holding a series of meetings here, and was a frequent visitor at our house. He is an eloquent orator, and much admired and beloved by all who know him. My darling old papa is a member of his church, and would swim a river any time to hear him preach. When Mr. Marshall was about to start to his home in Vicksburg, he invited me to accompany him. "If you will go with me," he said, "I will insure you to hear one of the most eloquent sermons that you ever listened to, from a mere boy, who has lately been licensed to preach." Of course I went, as my curiosity was aroused; and Mr. Marshall took me to church the same night we arrived at Vicksburg. Now, I had neglected to ask the name of the boy preacher, so intent was I engaged in drawing his picture in my mind. The church was a very large one, and when Mr. Marshall led me in, the house was crowded, but he succeeded in securing me a seat in one corner, some distance from the pulpit. The music was splendid; the choir sang with deep feeling. Then a pause, and I riveted my eyes on the pulpit, intently watching for the appearance of this wonderful boy. After gazing until I was tired and impatient, I picked up a hymn book, and began to turn the leaves over, when the sweet, solemn tones of a familiar voice fell on my ears. Looking up at the pulpit, there I saw Harry Wallingford reading his text. If a whizzing cannonball had come crashing through the house I would have been less startled. I had never heard an intimation that Mr. Wallingford was a preacher. I remembered him as a proud, passionate man of ungovernable temper and rather wickedly inclined. I was shedding tears like rain, and it cost me a great struggle to keep from shouting aloud. Now, I mean exactly what I say when I assert that it was the most charming, eloquent sermon that I ever heard. His voice fell on my ears like sweet music, a feeling of delicious joy stole over me, and I was overcome with happy emotions. He closed his sermon with an invitation to sinners to come forward and seek salvation, and I was one among many who accepted the invitation, and oh! my darling friend, I do believe that God, in His great mercy, has pardoned my sins. Mr. Wallingford delivered five sermons here, and the result was one hundred new members to the church.

"'Mr. Marshall thinks the world and all of Mr. Wallingford. He says that Viola is entitled to the credit of making a preacher of her husband, for she made him promise to serve God before she married him. Well, how could anybody fail to go to Heaven with such an angel to guide as Viola? Do you know that I think she is the best woman on the earth, except one? And you know who that is, of course. If you do not, just look into a mirror, and you will see the one I allude to.

"I have given my hand and heart to a (so-called) rebel, and I mean to show him that a Yankee heart can and will love him; and I wish all the people of the North and South loved each other as well as I love Ralleigh; what a great and glorious nation would ours be! Now good-by, Lottie dear, until we meet, which will be immediately after my marriage. To visit you will be bridal tour enough for me. Yours lovingly,

"'KATE DARLINGTON.'"

Doctor Dodson died in 1879. He was one of the heroic victims who sacrificed his life while battling in the ranks of the noble Howards, during the yellow fever epidemic.

Mrs. Dodson expired thirty minutes before death won the victory over her husband. She died in a room adjoining the one in which the doctor lay, and they endeavored to conceal her death from him. His mind was as clear as a cloudless sky, and when death began to lay his cold, icy finger on his body, he took hold of Lottie's hand with his right, and Viola's with his left.

"Ah, ha! my darlings, God says I must leave you for a while—yes, I go on before you, and I shall meet you all again, ah, ha! don't you see? Eddie, my boy, good-by; you are sure to come to Heaven—Lottie would fetch you, anyway—Viola, she has put Harry on the right road. You are all safe, ah, ha!—yes, you are all safe now."

Then he became quiet for a few moments, and they thought he was dead, but he began to mutter strange words.

"Ah, ha! here we come, Dolly; wait for me a moment— we will go to Heaven together, don't you see, ah, ha! Dollary, I am coming. There she is, Lottie, don't you see her;

she is beckoning for me to come. Yes, Dollary, I am coming
—ah, ha! Dolly, here we come—here we come!"

Then the noble soul stepped out and went with Dolly to
Heaven.

The day that Dodson and his wife died, was to have been
their golden wedding; but God had prepared for them a
wedding feast of a different sort. They were buried in one
grave, over which fragrant flowers bloom every spring, where
friendly tears bedew the soil.

If any one should be disposed to think that this world is
full of cold-hearted, selfish people, let him go and investigate
the inward history of the great epidemics of 1878 and 1879,
and he will soon see his great error. Look at the long list of
those heroic physicians who fell in the fore-front of the battle,
fighting to protect suffering humanity. Remember the large
number of Protestant clergymen and Catholic priests who
walked day after day, in the very jaws of death, comforting
the sick; wrestling with the dreadful foe; and yielding up
their lives, that others might live. Historians have written,
and poets sung, about Leonidas, and his heroic band; but if
I were a poet, I would find a band of heroes at Memphis,
whose brave deeds should be the theme of my song. It is a
slander to say that the world is full of selfish men; and any
one who will investigate the history of those awful times, will
admit it.

Harry Wallingford purchased a handsome residence, situated in the midst of a beautiful grove of native poplars, just
east of Mr. Rockland's, and not more than two hundred yards
from it. Viola had her flower garden laid off, so as to adjoin
Lottie's, and they were only separated by a clean gravel walk.
Those two devoted friends would often seat themselves on a
rustic bench in the garden, spending long hours watching the
two little children as they frolicked like young lambs on the
green turf of the lawn.

"Viola," said Lottie, "I think your boy has a disposition
very much like brother Harry's used to be."

"Well, you ought to pity his mother," replied Viola, "for
that boy is never satisfied unless he is doing something
where there is danger of being hurt."

"By the by, Viola, yonder comes Harry and Edward; I wonder what brought them home so early?"

"Ah! Lottie," replied Viola, "they wanted to be with us; don't you think we have got the best husbands in the world?"

"Indeed, I do; and we ought never to forget our obligations to God for His goodness to us."

"I shall never do that as long as life lasts."

Doctor Demar lifted his pretty little daughter from the ground as she came running to meet him, and seated her on his shoulder and began to dance round with her, while Harry began to romp with his boy, who was galloping about astraddle of a stick which he was lashing with a whip.

"Edward," said Lottie, as she ran her hand under his arm, "how did you manage to get here so soon? We did not expect you for two hours yet."

"Because we were both in love with our pretty wives, and wanted to be with them; and because we knew that our wives were in love with their ugly old husbands. Now, darling, I demand toll for coming so early; give me a kiss."

"Take it, old Barbarian Chief, and hand Lottie to me."

Mr. Rockland, whose hair had grown very white, was sitting on an easy chair on the front portico, watching the happy group on the green lawn.

"I thank God," he muttered, "because He was so good as to send Lottie Wallingford to direct my steps toward Heaven. and to be my guardian angel on earth."

www.ingramcontent.com/pod-product-compliance
Lightning Source LLC
Chambersburg PA
CBHW051933020726
47501CB00001B/98